THE HANGING VALLEY
&
INNOCENT GRAVES

Peter Robinson grew up in Yorkshire, and now lives in Canada.

His critically acclaimed Inspector Banks series has won numerous awards in Britain, the United States, Canada and Europe.

PETER
ROBINSON

THE HANGING VALLEY

&

INNOCENT GRAVES

INSPECTOR BANKS MYSTERIES

PAN BOOKS

The Hanging Valley first published 1989 by Penguin Books Canada.
First published in Great Britain 1989 by Viking.
First published by Pan Books 2002
Innocent Graves first published 1997 by Constable.
First published by Pan Books 2003

This omnibus edition published 2005 by Pan Books
an imprint of Pan Macmillan Ltd
Pan Macmillan, 20 New Wharf Road, London N1 9RR
Basingstoke and Oxford
Associated companies throughout the world
www.panmacmillan.com

ISBN 0 330 44098 5

A CIP catalogue record for this book is available from
the British Library.

Typeset by SX Composing DTP, Rayleigh, Essex
Printed and bound in Great Britain by
Mackays of Chatham plc, Chatham, Kent

THE HANGING VALLEY

For Jan

PART ONE:

MOTION IN CORRUPTION

1

ONE

It was the most exhilarating feeling in the world. His thighs ached, his calves throbbed and his breath came in short sharp gasps. But he had made it. Neil Fellowes, humble wages clerk from Pontefract, stood at the summit of Swainshead Fell.

Not that it was an achievement comparable to Sir Edmund Hillary's; after all, the fell was only 1,631 feet high. But Neil was not getting any younger, and the crowd at Baxwell's Machine Tools, where he worked, had taken the mickey something cruel when he told them he was going on a fell-walking holiday in the Yorkshire Dales.

'Fell?' taunted Dick Blatchley, one of the mail-room wags. 'Tha'll a fell before tha's got started, Neil.' And they had all laughed.

But now, as he stood there in the thin air, his heart beating deep in his chest like the steam-driven pistons in the factory, he was the one to laugh. He pushed his wire-rimmed glasses back up to the bridge of his nose and wiped off the sweat over which they had slid. Next he adjusted the straps of his rucksack, which were biting into his shoulders.

He had been climbing for well over an hour: nothing too dangerous – no sheer heights, nothing that required special equipment. Fell-walking was a democratic recreation, just plain hard work. And it was an ideal day for walking. The sun danced in and out between plump white clouds and a cool breeze kept the temperature down. Perfect late May weather.

He stood in the rough grass and heather with nothing but a few sheep for company – and they had already turned their backs on him and scuttled a safe distance away. Lord of the whole scene, he sat on a weathered limestone boulder to savour the feeling.

Back down the fell he could just make out the northern tip of Swainshead village, from where he had come. He could easily pick out the whitewashed front of the White Rose across the beck, and the lichen-covered flagstone roof of the Greenock Guest House, where he had spent a comfortable night after the previous day's walking in Wharfedale. He had also enjoyed there a breakfast of sausage, bacon, black pudding, fried bread, grilled mushrooms, tomato, two fried eggs, tea, toast and marmalade before setting off that morning.

He stood up to take in the panorama, starting with the west, where the fells descended and rolled like frozen waves to the sea. To the north-west ranged the old rounded hills of the Lake District. Neil fancied he could see the Striding Edge along Helvellyn and the occasional glint of sun on Windermere or Ullswater. Next he looked south, where the landscape hardened into the Pennines, the backbone of England. The rock was darker there, with outcrops of millstone grit ousting the glinting white limestone. Miles of wild forbidding moorland stretched down as far as Derbyshire. South-east lay Swainsdale itself, its valley bottom hidden from view.

But what astonished Neil most of all was a small wooded valley down the eastern slope just below where

4

he stood. The guidebooks hadn't mentioned anything of particular interest on the route he had chosen; indeed, one of his reasons for taking it was that nobody was likely to spoil his solitude. Most people, it seemed to Neil, would be off in search of stone circles, old lead mines and historic buildings.

In addition to its location and seclusion, the dale also had unusual foliage. It must have been a trick of the light, Neil thought, but whereas the trees everywhere else were fresh and green with spring, the ash, alders and sycamores below him seemed tinged with russet, orange and earth-brown. It seemed to him like a valley out of Tolkien's *Lord of the Rings*.

It would mean an extra mile or two and an unplanned climb back out again, but the sides didn't appear too steep, and Neil thought he might find some interesting wild flowers along the shaded banks of the beck. Balancing his pack, he struck out for the enchanted valley.

Soon, the rough tussocks underfoot gave way to springier grass. When Neil entered the woods, the leaves seemed much greener now the sunlight filtered through them. The smell of wild garlic filled his nostrils and made him feel light-headed. Bluebells swayed in the breeze.

He heard the beck before he saw it between the trees; it made a light bubbling sound, joyful and carefree. From the inside too, the valley clearly had a magical quality. It was more luxuriant than the surrounding area, its ferns and shrubs more lush and abundant as if, Neil thought, God had blessed it with a special grace.

He eased off his rucksack and laid it down on the thick grass by the waterside. Taking off his glasses, he thought he would stay a while and relax, perhaps drink some coffee from his flask before carrying on. He rested his head on the pack and closed his eyes. His mind emptied of everything but the heady scent of the garlic, the song of the beck, the cool fingers of the wind that rustled through wild roses and honeysuckle and the warbling of skylarks as they aimed themselves up at the sun and floated down like feathers, singing.

Refreshed – indeed feeling as if he had been born anew – Neil wiped his eyes and put on his glasses again. Looking around, he noticed a wild flower in the woods across the water. It seemed, from where he was, to be about a foot high, with red-brown sepals and pale yellow petals. Thinking it might be a rare lady's slipper orchis, he decided to cross over and have a closer look. The beck wasn't very wide, and there were plenty of fortuitously placed stepping stones.

As he neared the flower, he became aware of another smell, much more harsh and cloying than the garlic or loam. It clogged his nose and stuck to his bronchial passages. Wondering what it could be, he looked around, but could see nothing unusual. Near the flower, which was definitely a lady's slipper, some branches fallen from a tree lay on the ground and blocked his way. He started to pull them aside to get a better view.

But he didn't get very far. There, under a makeshift cover, lay the source of the smell: a human body. In the instant before he turned to vomit into the shrubs, Neil noticed two things: that it had no face, and that it seemed to be moving – its flesh was literally crawling.

Pausing only to wash his face and rinse out his mouth in the beck, Neil left his rucksack where it was and hurried as fast as he could back to Swainshead.

TWO

Disgusting, thought Katie Greenock, turning up her nose as she emptied the waste bin of room three. You'd think people would be ashamed to leave such things lying around for anyone to see. Thank God they'd left that morning. There always had seemed something unwholesome about them anyway: the way they kissed and canoodled at the breakfast table, how it was always so long before they set off for the day and so early when they returned to their room. She didn't even believe they were married.

Sighing, Katie brushed back a strand of ash-blonde hair and emptied the bin into the black plastic bag she carried with her on her rounds. Already she was tired out. Her day began at six o'clock, and there were no easy rustic mornings of birdsong and dew for her, just sheer hard work.

First she had to cook the breakfasts and coordinate everything so that the eggs weren't cold when the bacon was ready and the tea was fresh for the guests as soon as they decided to come down. They could help themselves to juice and cereal, which she had put out earlier – though not too early, for the milk had to be chilled. The toast could get as cold as it liked – cold toast seemed to be a part of the tradition of an English breakfast – but Katie was pleased when, as sometimes happened, she succeeded in serving it warm at exactly the right time. Not that anyone ever said thank you.

Then, of course, she had to serve the meals and manage a smile for all the guests, whatever their comments about the quality of the food and no matter what their sweet little children saw fit to drop on the floor or throw at the walls. She was also often asked for advice about where to go for the day, but sometimes Sam would help with that part, breaking off from his usual morning monologue on current events with which he entertained the visitors daily whether they liked it or not.

Next, she had to clear the tables and wash the dishes. The machine Sam had finally bought her helped a lot. Indeed, it saved her so much time that she could hurry down to Thetford's Grocery on the Helmthorpe Road and take her pick of the morning's fresh produce. Sam used to do that before he had installed the machine, but now he had more time for the sundry business matters that always seemed to be pressing.

When Katie had planned the menu for the evening meal and bought all the ingredients, it was time to change the sheets and clean the rooms. It was hardly surprising then that by noon she was almost always tired. If she was lucky, she could sometimes find a little time for gardening around mid afternoon.

Putting off the moment when she would have to move on to the next room, Katie walked over to the window and rested her elbows on the sill. It was a fine day in a beautiful part of the world but to her the landscape felt like an enormous trap; the fells were boulders that shut her in, the stretches of moorland like deserts impossible to cross. A chance of freedom had offered itself recently, but there was nothing she could do about it yet. She could only wait patiently and see what developed.

She looked down on the grassy banks at each side of the fledgling River Swain, at the children sitting patiently with their home-made fishing nets, a visiting couple having a picnic, the old men gossiping as usual on the small stone bridge. She could see it all, but not feel the beauty of any of it.

And there, almost dead opposite, was the White Rose, founded in 1605, as its sign proudly proclaimed, where Sam would no doubt be hobnobbing with his upper-class chums. The fool, Katie thought. He thinks he's well in, but they'll never really accept him, ever after all these years and all he's done for them. Their kind never does. She was sure they laughed at him behind his back. And had he noticed the way Nicholas Collier kept looking at her? Did Sam know about the times Nicholas had tried to touch her?

Katie shuddered at the thought. Outside, a sudden movement caught her eye and she saw the old men part like the Red Sea and stare open-mouthed as a slight figure hurried across the bridge.

It was that man who'd set off just a few hours ago, Katie realized, the mild-mannered clerk from Castleford or Featherstone or somewhere like that. Surely he'd said he was heading for the Pennine Way? And he was as white as the pub front. He turned left at the end of the bridge, hurried the last few yards and went running into the White Rose.

Katie felt her chest tighten. What was it that had brought him back in such a state? What was wrong? Surely nothing terrible had happened in Swainshead? Not again.

THREE

'Well,' Sam Greenock was saying about the racial mix in England, 'they have their ways, I suppose, but—'

Then Neil Fellowes burst through the door and looked desperately around the pub for a familiar face.

Seeing Sam at his usual table with the Collier brothers and John Fletcher, Neil hurried over and pulled up a chair.

'We must do something,' he said, gasping for breath and pointing outside. 'There's a body up on the fell. Dead.'

'Calm down, mate,' Sam said. 'Get your breath, then tell us what's happened.' He called over to the barman. 'A brandy for Mr Fellowes, Freddie, if you please. A large one.' Seeing Freddie hesitate, he added, 'Don't worry, you bloody old skinflint, I'll pay. And get a move on.'

Conversation at the table stopped while Freddie Metcalfe carried the drink over. Neil gulped the brandy and it brought on a coughing fit.

'At least that's put a bit of colour back in your cheeks,' Sam said, slapping Neil on the back.

'It was terrible,' Neil said, wiping off the brandy where it had dribbled down his chin. He wasn't used to strong drink, but he did approve of it in emergencies such as this.

'His face was all gone, all eaten away, and the whole thing was moving, like waves.' He put his glass to his thin lips again and drained it. 'We must do something. The police.' He got up and strode over to Freddie Metcalfe. 'Where's the police station in Swainshead?'

Metcalfe scratched his shiny red scalp and answered slowly. 'Let me see. . . There aren't no bobbies in T' Head itself. Nearest's Helmthorpe, I reckon. Sergeant Mullins and young Weaver. That's nigh on ten miles off.'

Neil bought himself another double brandy while Metcalfe screwed up his weather-beaten face and thought.

'They'll be no bloody use, Freddie,' Sam called over. 'Not for something like this. It's CID business, this is.'

'Aye,' Metcalfe agreed, 'I reckon tha's right, Sam. In that case, young feller mi' lad,' he said to Neil, 'it'll be that chap in Eastvale tha'll be after. T' one who were out 'ere last time we 'ad a bit o' bother. Gristhorpe, Chief Inspector Gristhorpe. Years back it was though. Probably dead now. Come on, lad, you can use this phone, seeing as it's an emergency.'

FOUR

'Chief Inspector' Gristhorpe, now Superintendent, was far from dead. When the call came through, he was on another line talking to Redshaw's Quarries about a delivery for the drystone wall he was building. Despite all the care he had put into the endeavour, a section had collapsed during an April frost, and rebuilding seemed a suitable spring project.

The telephone call found its way instead to the office of Detective Chief Inspector Alan Banks, who sat browsing through the *Guardian* arts pages, counting his blessings that crime had been so slack in Eastvale recently. After all, he had been transferred from London almost two years ago for a bit of peace and quiet. He liked detective work and couldn't imagine doing anything else, but the sheer pressure of the job – unpleasant, most of it – and the growing sense of confrontation between police and citizens in the capital had got him down. For his own and his family's sake, he had made the move. Eastvale hadn't been quite as peaceful as he'd expected, but at the moment all he had to deal with were a couple of minor break-ins and the aftermath of a tremendous punch-up in the Oak. It had started when five soldiers from Catterick camp had taunted a group of unemployed miners from Durham. Three people ended up in hospital with injuries ranging from bruised and swollen testicles to a bitten-off earlobe, and the others were cooling off in the cells waiting to appear before the magistrate.

'Someone asking for the super, sir,' said Sergeant Rowe, when Banks picked up the phone. 'His line's busy.'

'It's all right,' Banks said. 'I'll take it.'

A breathless, slightly slurred voice came on the line. 'Hello, is that Inspector Gristhorpe?'

Banks introduced himself and encouraged the caller, who gave his name as Neil Fellowes, to continue.

'There's a body,' Fellowes said. 'Up on the fells. I found it.'

'Where are you now?'

'A pub. The White Rose.'

'Whereabouts?'

'What? Oh, I see. In Swainshead.'

Banks wrote the details down on his scrap pad.

'Are you sure it's a human body?' he asked. There had been mistakes made in the past, and the police had more than once been dragged out to examine piles of old sacks, dead sheep or rotten tree trunks.

'Yes. Yes, I'm sure.'

'Male or female?'

'I . . . I didn't look. It was—'

The next few words were muffled.

'All right, Mr Fellowes,' Banks said. 'Just stay where you are and we'll be along as soon as possible.'

Gristhorpe had finished his call when Banks tapped on the door and entered his office. With its overflowing bookcases and dim lighting, it looked more like a study than part of a police station.

'Ah, Alan,' Gristhorpe said, rubbing his hands together. 'They said they'll deliver before the weekend, so we can make a start on the repairs on Sunday, if you'd care to come?'

Working on the drystone wall, which fenced in nothing and was going nowhere, had become something of a ritual for the superintendent and his chief inspector. Banks had come to look forward to those Sunday afternoons on the north daleside above Lyndgarth, where Gristhorpe lived alone in his farmhouse. Mostly they worked in silence, and the job created a bond between them, a bond that Banks, still an incomer to the Yorkshire Dales, valued greatly.

'Yes,' he answered. 'Very much. Look, I've just had a rather garbled phone call from a chap by the name of Neil Fellowes. Says he's found a body on the fell near Swainshead.'

Gristhorpe leaned back in his chair, linked his hands behind his head and frowned. 'Any details?'

'No. He's still a bit shook up, by the sound of it. Shall I go?'

'We'll both go.' Gristhorpe stood up decisively. 'It's not the first time a body has turned up in The Head.'

'The Head?'

'That's what the locals call it, the whole area around Swainshead village. It's the source of the River Swain, the head of the dale.' He looked at his watch. 'It's about twenty-five miles, but I'm sure we'll make it before closing time if I remember Freddie Metcalfe.'

Banks was puzzled. It was unusual for Gristhorpe to involve himself so much in an actual field investigation. As head of Eastvale CID, the superintendent could use his discretion as regards his role in a case. Theoretically, he could, if he wanted to, take part in searches and house-to-house enquiries, but of course he never did. In part, his job was administrative. He tended to delegate casework and monitor developments from his office. This was not due to laziness, Banks realized, but because his talent was for thinking and planning, not for action or interrogation. He trusted his subordinates and allowed them far greater leeway with their cases than many superintendents did. But this time he wanted to come along.

They made an incongruous couple as they walked to the car park at the back: the tall bulky Gristhorpe with his unruly thatch of grey hair, bristly moustache, pockmarked face and bushy eyebrows; and Banks, lean, slight, with angular features and short almost cropped black hair.

'I can't see why you keep on using your own car, Alan,' Gristhorpe said as he eased into the passenger seat of the white Cortina and grappled with the seat belt. 'You could save a lot of wear and tear if you took a department vehicle.'

'Have they got radio-cassettes?' Banks asked.

'You know damn well they haven't.'

'Well, then.'

'Well, what?'

'I like to listen to music while I'm driving. You know I do. It helps me think.'

'I suppose you're going to inflict some on me, too?'

It had always surprised Banks that so well read and cultured a person as Gristhorpe had absolutely no ear for music at all. The superintendent was tone-deaf, and even the most ethereal Mozart aria was painful to his ears.

'Not if you don't want,' Banks said, smiling to himself. He knew he wouldn't be able to smoke on the way, either. Gristhorpe was a non-smoker of the most rabid kind – reformed after a twenty-year, twenty-a-day habit.

Banks pulled into the cobbled market square, turned

left on to North Market Street, and headed for the main Swainsdale road, which ran by the river along the valley bottom.

Gristhorpe grunted and tapped the apparatus next to the dashboard. 'At least you've had a police radio fitted.'

'What was it you said before?' Banks asked. 'About this not being the first body in Swainshead.'

'It was before your time.'

'Most things were.' Banks made the sharp westward turn, and soon they were out of the town, driving by the river meadows.

Gristhorpe opened his window and gulped in the fresh air. 'A man had his skull fractured,' he said. 'It was murder, no doubt about that. And we never solved it.'

'What happened?'

'Some Boy Scouts found the body dumped in an old mineshaft on the fell side a couple of miles north of the village. The doctor said it had been there about a week.'

'When?'

'Just over five years ago.'

'Was it a local?'

'No. The victim was a private detective from London.'

'A private investigator?'

'That's right. Name of Raymond Addison. A solo operator. One of the last of the breed, I should imagine.'

'Did you find out what he was doing up here?'

'No. We had his office searched, of course, but none of his files had any connection with Swainsdale. The Yard asked around among his friends and acquaintances – not that he had very many – but they turned up nothing. We thought he might have been on holiday, but why choose Yorkshire in February?'

'How long had he been in the village?'

'He'd arrived fairly late in the day and managed to get a room in a guest house run by a chap named Sam Greenock, who told us that Addison said nothing except for some remarks about the cold. He wrapped up well and went out for a walk after the evening meal, and that was the last anyone saw of him. We made enquiries, but nobody had seen or heard him. It was dark when he went out, of course, and even the old men who usually hang about chatting on the bridge come rain or shine had gone in by then.'

'And as far as you could find out he had no connection with the area at all?'

'None. And, believe me, we dug and dug. Either nobody knew or, more likely, someone wasn't talking. He was an ex-serviceman, so we checked up on old army pals, that kind of thing. We ended up doing a house-to-house of the entire village. Nothing. It's still unsolved.'

Banks slowed down as he drove through Helmthorpe, one of the dale's largest villages. Beyond there, the landscape was unfamiliar to him. Though still broader than most of the dales, thanks to a glacier of particularly titanic proportions, the valley seemed to narrow slightly as they got closer to The Head, and the commons sloped more steeply up the fell sides. There were none of the long limestone scars that characterized the eastern part of Swainsdale, but the hills rose to high rounded summits of moorland.

'And that's not all,' Gristhorpe added after a few moments of silence. 'A week before Addison's body was found – the day after he was killed, as far as the doctors could make out – a local woman disappeared. Name of Anne Ralston. Never been seen since.'

'And you think there must have been a connection?'

'Not necessarily. At the time she went, of course, the body hadn't been discovered. The whole thing could have been a coincidence. And the doctor admitted he could have been wrong about the exact day of death, too. It's hard to be accurate after a body's been buried that long. But we've no idea what happened to her. And you've got to admit it's damned odd to get a missing person and a murder in the same village within a week of each other. She could have been killed and buried, or maybe she simply ran off with a fellow somewhere. We'd hardly cause to block all the ports and airports. Besides, she could have been anywhere in the world by the time the body was found. At best we'd have liked her to answer a few questions, just to put our minds at rest. As it was, we did a bit more poking around the landscape but found no traces of another body.'

'Do you think she might have murdered Addison and run off?'

'It's possible. But it didn't look like a woman's job to me. Too much muscle work involved, and Anne Ralston wasn't one of those female bodybuilders. We questioned her boyfriend pretty closely. He's Stephen Collier, managing director of the company she worked for. Comes from a very prominent local family.'

'Yes,' Banks said. 'I've heard of the Colliers. Did he cause any problems?'

'No. He was cooperative. Said they hadn't been getting on all that well lately, but he'd no idea where she'd gone, or why. In the end we'd no reason to think anything had happened to her so we had to assume she'd just left. People do sometimes. And Anne Ralston seemed to be a particularly flighty lass, by all accounts.'

'Still . . .'

'Yes, I know.' Gristhorpe sighed. 'It's not at all satisfactory, is it? We reached nothing but dead ends whichever direction we turned.'

Banks drove on in silence. Obviously failure was hard for Gristhorpe to swallow, as it was for most detectives. But this murder, if that's what it really turned out to be, was a different case, five years old. He wasn't going to let the past clutter up his thinking if he could help it. Still, it would be well to keep Raymond Addison and Anne Ralston in mind.

'This is it,' Gristhorpe said a few minutes later, pointing to the row of houses ahead. 'This is Lower Head, as the locals call it.'

'It hardly seems a big enough place to be split into two parts,' Banks observed.

'It's not a matter of size, Alan. Lower Head is the newest part of the village, the part that's grown since the road's become more widely used. People just stop off here to admire the view over a quick cup of tea or a pint and a pub lunch. Upper Head's older and quieter. A bit more genteel. It's a little north–south dale in itself, wedged between two fells. There's a road goes north up there too, but when it gets past the village and the school it gets pretty bad. You can get to the Lake District if you're willing to ride it out, but most people go from the Lancashire side. Turn right here.'

Banks turned. The base of a triangular village green ran beside the main road, allowing easy access to Swainshead from both directions. The first buildings he passed were a small stone church and a village hall.

Following the minor road north beside the narrow River Swain, Banks could see what Gristhorpe meant. There were two rows of cottages facing each other, set back quite a bit from the river and its grassy banks. Most of them were either semis or terraced, and some had been converted into shops. They were plain sturdy houses built mostly of limestone, discoloured here and there with moss and lichen. Many had individualizing touches, such as mullions or white borders painted around doors and windows. Behind the houses on both sides, the commons sloped up, criss-crossed here and there by drystone walls, and gave way to steep moorland fells.

Banks parked the car outside the whitewashed pub and Gristhorpe pointed to a large house farther up the road.

'That's the Collier place,' he said. 'The old man was one of the richest farmers and landowners around these parts. He also had the sense to invest his money in a food-processing plant just west of here. He's dead now, but young Stephen runs the factory and he shares the house with his brother. They've split it into two halves. Ugly pile of stone, isn't it?'

Banks didn't say so, but he rather admired the Victorian extravagance of the place, so at odds with the utilitarian austerity of most Dales architecture. Certainly it was ugly: oriels and turrets cluttered the upper half, making the whole building look top-heavy, and there was a stone porch at each front entrance. They probably had a gazebo and a folly in the back garden too, he thought.

'And that's where Raymond Addison stayed,' Gristhorpe said, pointing across the beck. The house, made of two knocked-together semis, was separated from the smaller terraced houses on either side by only a few feet. A sign, GREENOCK GUEST HOUSE, hung in the colourful well-tended garden.

''Ey up, lads,' Freddie Metcalfe said as they entered, 't' Sweeney's 'ere.'

'Hello again, Freddie,' Gristhorpe said, leading Banks over to the bar. 'Still serving drinks after hours?'

'Only to the select few, Mr Gristhorpe,' Metcalfe replied proudly. 'What'll you gents be 'aving?' He looked at Banks suspiciously. 'Is 'e over eighteen?'

'Just,' Gristhorpe answered.

Freddie burst into a rasping smoker's laugh.

'What's this about a body?' Gristhorpe asked.

Metcalfe pursed his fleshy lips and nodded towards the only occupied table. 'Bloke there says he found one on t' fell. 'E's not going anywhere, so I might as well pull you gents a pint before you get down to business.'

The superintendent asked for a pint of bitter and Banks, having noticed that the White Rose was a Marston's house, asked for a pint of Pedigree.

''E's got good taste, I'll say that for 'im,' Metcalfe said. 'Is 'e 'ouse-trained an' all?'

Banks observed a prudent silence throughout the exchange and took stock of his surroundings. The walls of the lounge bar were panelled in dark wood up to waist height and above that papered an inoffensive dun colour. Most of the tables were the old round kind with cast-iron knee-capper legs, but a few modern square ones stood in the corner near the dartboard and the silent jukebox.

Banks lit a Silk Cut and sipped his pint. He'd refrained from smoking in the car in deference to Gristhorpe's feelings, but now that he was in a public place he was going to take advantage of it and puff away to his heart's and lungs' content.

Carrying their drinks, they walked over to the table.

'Someone reported a death?' Gristhorpe asked, his innocent baby-blue eyes ranging over the five men who sat there.

Fellowes hiccuped and put his hand in the air. 'I did,' he said, and slid off his chair on to the stone floor.

'Christ, he's pissed as a newt,' Banks said, glaring at Sam Greenock. 'Couldn't you have kept him sober till we got here?'

'Don't blame me,' Sam said. 'He's only had enough to put some colour back in his cheeks. It's not my fault he can't take his drink.'

Two of the others helped Fellowes back into his chair and Freddie Metcalfe rushed over with some smelling salts he kept behind the bar for this and similar exigencies.

Fellowes moaned and waved away the salts, then slumped back and squinted at Gristhorpe. He was clearly in no condition to guide them to the scene of the crime.

'It's all right, Inshpector,' he said. 'Bit of a shock to the syshtem, thass all.'

'Can you tell us where you found this body?' Gristhorpe spoke slowly, as if to a child.

'Over Shwainshead Fell, there's a beautiful valley. All autumn colours. Can't mish it, just down from where the footpath reaches the top. Go shtraight down till you get to the beck, then cross it . . . Easy. Near the lady's slipper.'

'Lady's slipper?'

'Yes. The orchish, not the bird's-foot trefoil. Very rare. Body's near the lady's shlipper.'

Then he half twisted in his chair and stretched his arm up his back.

'I left my rucksack,' he said. 'Thought I did. Just over from my rucksack, then. Ruckshack marks the spot.' Then he hiccuped again and his eyes closed.

'Does anyone know where he's staying?' Banks asked the group.

'He was staying at my guest house,' Sam said. 'But he left this morning.'

'Better get him back there, if there's room. He's in no condition to go anywhere and we'll want to talk to him again later.'

Sam nodded. 'I think we've still got number five empty, unless someone's arrived while I've been out. Stephen?' He looked over to the man next to him, who helped him get Fellowes to his feet.

'It's Stephen Collier, isn't it?' Gristhorpe asked, then turned to the person opposite Greenock. 'And you're Nicholas. Remember, I talked to you both a few years ago about Anne Ralston and that mysterious death?'

'We remember,' Nicholas answered. 'You knew Father too, if I recall rightly?'

'Not well, but yes, we bent elbows together once or twice. Quite a man.'

'He was indeed,' Nicholas said.

Outside, Banks and Gristhorpe watched Sam and Stephen help Neil Fellowes over the bridge. The old men stood by and stared in silence.

Gristhorpe looked up at the fell side. 'We've got a problem,' he said.

'Yes?'

'It's a long climb up there. How the bloody hell are we going to get Glendenning and the scene-of-crime team up if we need them? Come to that, how am I going to get up? I'm not as young as I used to be. And you smoke like a bloody chimney. You'll never get ten yards.'

Banks followed Gristhorpe's gaze and scratched his head. 'Well,' he said, 'I suppose we could give it a try.'

Gristhorpe pulled a face. 'Aye,' he said. 'I was afraid you'd say that.'

2

ONE

'**Problem, gentlemen?**' Nicholas Collier asked when he walked out of the White Rose and saw Banks and Gristhorpe staring up dejectedly at Swainshead Fell.

'Not at all,' Gristhorpe replied. 'Simply admiring the view.'

'Might I suggest a way you can save yourselves some shoe leather?'

'Certainly.'

'Do you see that narrow line that crosses the fell diagonally?' Nicholas pointed towards the slope and traced the direction of the line with a long finger.

'Yes,' said Gristhorpe. 'It looks like an old track of some kind.'

'That's exactly what it is. There used to be a farmhouse way up on the fell side there. It belonged to Father, but he used to let it to Archie Allen. The place has fallen to ruin now but the road that leads up is still there. It's not in good repair, of course, and you might find it a bit overgrown, but you should be able to get a car well above halfway up, if that's any help.'

'Thank you very much, Mr Collier,' Gristhorpe said. 'For a man of my shape any effort saved is a blessing.'

'You'll have to drive two miles up the road here to the next bridge to get on the track, but you'll see your way easily enough,' said Nicholas, and with a smile he set off for home.

'Odd-looking sort of fellow, isn't he?' Banks remarked. 'Not a bit like his brother.'

Whereas Stephen had the elegant, world-weary look of a *fin de siècle* decadent, Nicholas's sallow complexion, long nose and prominent front teeth made him appear a bit horsy. The only resemblance was in their unusually bright blue eyes.

'Takes after his father, does Nicholas,' Gristhorpe said. 'And Stephen takes after his mother, as handsome a woman as I've seen around these parts. There's many a man drowned his sorrows in drink when Ella Dinsdale married Walter Collier. Didn't last long though, poor lass.'

'What happened?'

'Polio. Before inoculations came in. Come on, let's go and have a look at this body before it gets up and walks away.'

Banks found the bridge and track easily enough, and though the old road was bumpy, they managed to get as far as the ruined farmhouse without any serious damage to the car.

A little to the left, they saw the footpath Neil Fellowes had taken and began to follow it up the fell side. Even though they had been able to drive most of the way, the path was steep and Banks soon found himself gasping for air and wishing he didn't smoke. Gristhorpe, for all his weight, seemed to stride up much more easily, though his face turned scarlet with the effort. Banks guessed he was more used to the landscape. After all, his own cottage was halfway up a daleside, too.

Finally, they stood at the top, where Fellowes had surveyed the scene a few hours earlier. Both were puffing and sweating by then, and after they'd got their breath back Gristhorpe pointed out the autumnal valley below.

'It looks enchanted, doesn't it,' he said as they walked down the slope towards the woods. 'Look, there's the rucksack.'

They crossed the beck as directed and headed for the lady's slipper orchis by the fallen branches. When they smelled the corpse, they exchanged glances. Both had known that stench before; it was unmistakable.

'No wonder Fellowes was in such a state,' Banks said. He took out a handkerchief and held it to his nose. Cautiously, Gristhorpe pulled more branches aside.

'By Christ, Glendenning's going to love this one,' he said, then stood back. 'By the look of that mess below the ribs there, we've got a murder case on our hands. Probably a knife wound. Male, I'd say.'

Banks agreed. Though small animals had been at parts of the body and maggots had made it their breeding ground, the dark stain just below the left ribcage stood out clearly enough against the white shirt the man was wearing. Fellowes had been right about the movement. The way the maggots were wriggling under his clothes made it look as if the body were rippling like water in the breeze.

'"Motion in corruption",' Gristhorpe muttered under his breath. 'I wonder where the rest of his gear is. By the look of those boots he was a walker sure enough.'

Banks peered as closely as he could at the cleated rubber Vibram treads. 'They look new as well,' he said. 'Hardly worn at all.'

'He must have had more stuff,' Gristhorpe said, rubbing his whiskery chin. 'Most walkers carry at least a rucksack with a few dried dates, compass, maps, torch, changes of clothing and what have you. Somebody must have taken it.'

'Or buried it.'

'Aye.'

'He's not wearing waterproofs, either,' Banks observed.

'That could mean he knew what he was doing. Only amateurs wear waterproofs all the time. Experienced walkers put their clothes on and off in layers according to the weather. If this is all he was wearing when he was killed, we might be able to get some idea of the date of death by checking weather records.'

'It's been fairly constant these past few weeks,' Banks pointed out. 'We had a late spring, but now it looks like an early summer.'

'True enough. Still, forensic might be able to come up with something. Better get the team up, Alan.'

'The way we came? It's not going to be easy.'

Gristhorpe thought for a moment. 'There might be a better way,' he said at last. 'If my geography's correct.'

'Yes?'

'Well, if I'm right, this'll be the beck that ends in Rawley Force on the Helmthorpe road about a mile east of Swainshead village. It's a hanging valley.'

'Come again?'

'A hanging valley,' Gristhorpe repeated. 'It's a tributary valley running into Swainsdale at a right angle. The glacier here was too small to deepen it as much as the larger one that carved out the dale itself, so it's left hanging above the main valley floor like a cross-section. The water usually reaches the main river over a waterfall, like Rawley Force. I thought you'd been reading up on local geology, Alan.'

'Haven't got that far yet,' Banks mumbled. In fact, he'd put aside the geology book after reading only two chapters in favour of a new history of Yorkshire that his daughter, Tracy, had recommended. The trouble was that he wanted to know so much but had so little time for learning that he tended to skitter from one subject to another without fully absorbing anything.

'Anyway,' Gristhorpe went on, 'Rawley Force is only about ninety feet high. If we can get in touch with the Mountain Rescue post at Helmthorpe and they're willing to rig up a winch, we'll be able to get the team up and down without much trouble. I can hardly see Glendenning, for one, walking the way we did. There'll be a lot of coming and going. And we'll have to get the body down somehow, too. A winch just might be the answer. It should be easy enough. The Craven and Bradford pothole clubs put one up at Gaping Gill for a few days each year to give the tourists a look, and that's a hell of a lot deeper.'

'It sounds good,' Banks said dubiously. He remembered swinging the three hundred feet down Gaping Gill, which opened into a cavern as huge as the inside of York Minster. It was an experience he had no wish to repeat. 'We'd better get cracking though, or it'll be dark before they all get here. Should we get Sergeant Hatchley in on this, too?'

Gristhorpe nodded.

'DC Richmond?'

'Not just yet. Let's see exactly what we've got on our hands before we bring in all our manpower. Richmond can hold the fort back at the station. I'll stay here while you go back to the car and radio in. You'd better let the doctor know what state the body's in. He might need some special equipment.'

Banks glanced towards the corpse, then back at Gristhorpe.

'Are you sure you want to stay here?'

'It's not a matter of wanting,' Gristhorpe said. 'Somebody should stay.'

'It's been here alone long enough. I doubt that another half-hour will make any difference.'

'Somebody should stay,' Gristhorpe repeated.

Banks knew when to give up. Leaving the superintendent sitting like Buddha under an ash tree by the beck, he set off back through the woods to the car.

TWO

'What's wrong?' Katie Greenock asked as Sam and Stephen staggered in with Fellowes between them.

'He's had a bit too much to drink, that's all,' Sam said. 'Out of the way, woman. Is number five still vacant?'

'Yes, but—'

'Don't worry, he's not going to puke on your precious sheets. He just needs sleep.'

'All right,' Katie said, biting her lip. 'Better take him up.'

Stephen smiled apologetically at her as they passed and struggled up the stairs. Finally, they dumped their burden on the bedspread and left Katie in the room with him. At first she didn't move. She just stood by the window looking at Fellowes in horror. Surely Sam knew how much she hated and feared drunks, how much they disgusted her. And Mr Fellowes had seemed such a nice sober man.

She couldn't really picture her father clearly, for he had died along with her mother in a fire when Katie was only four, but he had certainly been a drunk, and she was sure that he was at the root of her feelings. The only vague image she retained was of a big vulgar man who frightened her with his loud voice, his whiskers and his roughness.

Once, when they hadn't known she was watching, she saw him hurting her mother in the bedroom, making her groan and squirm in a way that sent shivers up Katie's spine. Of course, when she got older, she realized what they must have been doing, but the early memory was as firmly established and as deeply rooted as cancer. She also remembered once when her father fell down and she was afraid that he'd hurt himself. When she went to help him though, he knocked her over and cursed her. She was terrified that he would do the same thing to her as he had done to her mother, but she couldn't remember any more about the incident, no matter how hard she tried.

The fire was a memory she had blocked out too, though strange tongue-like flames sometimes roared and crackled in her nightmares. According to her grandmother, Katie had been in the house at the time, but the firemen had arrived before the blaze reached her room. Katie had been saved by the grace of God, so her granny said, whereas her parents, the sinners, had been consumed by the flames of hell.

The fire had been caused by smoking in bed, and her grandmother had seemed especially satisfied by that, as if the irony somehow marked it as God's special work, an answer to her prayers. It had all been God's will, His justice, and Katie was obliged to spend her life in gratitude and devoted service.

Katie took a deep breath, rolled Fellowes over carefully and pulled back the sheets – they could be washed easily, but not the quilted spread. Then she unlaced his walking boots and put them on some newspaper by the bed. They weren't muddy, but fragments of earth had lodged in the ribbed treads.

'Cleanliness is next to godliness,' her grandmother had

drilled into her. And a lot easier to achieve, Katie might have added if she had dared. Apart from an unusually long list of its attributes – mostly 'thou shalt nots', which seemed to include everything most normal people enjoyed – godliness was an elusive quality as far as Katie was concerned. Lately, she had found herself thinking about it a lot, recalling her grandmother's harsh words and 'necessary' punishments: her mouth washed out with soap for lying; a spell in the coal hole for 'swaying wantonly' to a fragment of music that had drifted in from next door's radio. These had all been preceded by the words, 'This is going to hurt me more than it will hurt you.'

Fellowes stirred and snapped Katie out of her reverie. For a second, his grey eyes opened wide and he grasped her hand. She could feel the fear and confusion flow from his bony fingers through her wrist.

'Moving,' he mumbled, falling back into a drunken sleep again. 'Moving . . .'

Spittle gathered at the edges of his lips and dribbled down his chin. Katie shuddered. Leaving him, she hurried back downstairs. There was still the evening meal to prepare, and the garden needed weeding.

THREE

Banks leaned over the edge of Rawley Force and watched Glendenning coming up in the winch. It was an amusing sight. The tall white-haired doctor sat erect, trying to retain as much dignity as he could. A cigarette dangled from the left corner of his mouth, as usual, and he clutched his brown bag tightly against his stomach.

Luckily there had been hardly any rain over the past

two weeks, so the waterfall to the doctor's right was reduced to a trickle. The staff at the Mountain Rescue post had been only too willing to help and had come out and set up the winch in no time. Now the police team were ready to come up slowly, one at a time, and Glendenning, as befitted his status, was first in line.

Puffing, as he struggled out of the harness, the doctor nodded curtly at Banks and straightened the crease in his suit trousers. Banks led him half a mile along the wooded valley to the scene, where Gristhorpe still sat alone.

'Thanks for coming so quickly,' the superintendent said to Glendenning, getting up and dusting off his seat. Everyone in Eastvale Regional Police Headquarters found it paid to be polite, even deferential, to the doctor. Although he was a crusty old bugger, he was one of the best pathologists in the country and they were lucky he had chosen Eastvale as his home.

Glendenning lit another cigarette from the stub of his old one and asked, 'Where is it, then?'

Gristhorpe pointed towards the pile of branches. The doctor cursed under his breath as he tackled the stepping stones, and Gristhorpe turned to Banks and winked. 'Everyone here, Alan?'

'Looks like it.'

Next the young photographer, Peter Darby, came hurrying towards them, trying to head off Glendenning before the doctor could get to work. To Banks he always looked far too fresh-faced and innocent for his line of work, but he had never been known to bat an eyelid, no matter what they asked him to photograph.

After him came Sergeant Hatchley, red-faced after his short walk from Rawley Force along the hanging valley. The fair-haired sergeant was a big man, like Gristhorpe, and although he was twenty years younger, his muscle was turning quickly to fat. He resembled a rugby prop forward, a position he had indeed played on the local team until cigarettes and beer took their toll on his stamina.

Banks filled him in on the details while Gristhorpe busied himself with the scene-of-crime team.

Glendenning, kneeling by the corpse, kept shooing the others away like flies. At last, he packed his bag and struggled back over the beck, stretching out his arms for balance like a tightrope walker. With one hand he clung on to his brown bag, and in the other he held a test tube.

'Bloody awkward place to go finding a corpse,' he grumbled, as if the superintendent were personally responsible.

'Aye, well,' Gristhorpe replied, 'we don't get to pick and choose in our business. I don't suppose you can tell us much till after the post-mortem?'

Glendenning screwed up his face against the smoke that rose from his cigarette. 'Not much,' he said. 'Looks like a stab wound to me. Probably pierced the heart from under the ribcage.'

'Then someone got very close to him indeed,' Gristhorpe said. 'It must have been someone he knew and trusted.'

Glendenning sniffed. 'I'll leave that kind of speculation to you boys, if you don't mind. There are lacerations and blows to the face, too. Can't say what did it at the moment, or when it was done. Been dead about ten days. Not more than twelve.'

'How can you be certain?' Banks asked, startled by the information.

'I can't be certain, laddie,' Glendenning said, 'that's the problem. Between ten and twelve days doesn't count as accurate with me. I might be able to be more precise after the PM, but no promises. Those chappies over there have got a bag to put him in. He'll need to soak in a Lysol bath for a day or two.' Glendenning smiled and held up his test tube. 'Maggots,' he said. '*Calliphora erythrocephalus*, if I'm not mistaken.'

The three detectives looked at the white, slow-moving blobs and exchanged puzzled glances.

Glendenning sighed and spoke as he would to a group of backward children. 'Simple really. Bluebottle larvae. The bluebottle lays its eggs in daylight, usually when the sun's shining. If the weather's warm, as it has been lately, they hatch on the first day. Then you get what's called the "first instar" maggot. That wee beauty sheds its skin like a snake after eight to fourteen hours, and then the second instar, the one you use for fishing' – and here he glanced at Gristhorpe, a keen angler – 'that one eats like a pig for five or six days before going into its pupa case. Look at these, gentlemen.' He held up the test tube again. 'These, as you can see, are fat maggots. Lazy. Mature. And they're not in their pupa cases yet. Therefore, they must have been laid nine or ten days ago. Add on a day or so for the bluebottles to find the body and lay, and you've got twelve days at the outside.'

It was the most eloquent and lengthy speech Banks had ever heard Glendenning deliver. There was obviously a potential teacher in the brusque chain-smoking Scot with the trail of ash like the Milky Way down his waistcoat.

The doctor smiled at his audience. 'Simpson,' he said.

'Pardon?' Banks asked.

'Simpson. Keith Simpson. I studied under him. Our equivalent of Sherlock Holmes, only Simpson's real.'

'I see,' said Banks, who had learned to tease after so

long in Yorkshire. 'A kind of real-life Quincy, you mean?'
He felt Gristhorpe nudge him in the ribs.

Glendenning scowled and a half-inch of ash fell off the
end of his cigarette. 'Quite,' he said, and put the test tube
in his bag. 'I hope that glorified truss over there can get me
back down safely.'

'Don't worry,' Gristhorpe assured him. 'It will. And
thank you very much.'

'Aye. Now I have first-hand knowledge of what it feels
like to have my arse in a sling,' Glendenning said as he
walked away.

Banks laughed and turned back to watch the experts at
work. The photographs had been taken, and the team
were busy searching the ground around the body.

'We'll need a more thorough search of the area,'
Gristhorpe said to Hatchley. 'Can you get that organized,
Sergeant?'

'Yes, sir.' Hatchley took out his notebook and pen. 'I'll
get some men in from Helmthorpe and Eastvale.'

'Tell them to look particularly for evidence of anything
recently buried or burned. He must have been carrying a
rucksack. We're also looking for the weapon, a knife of
some kind. And I think, Sergeant,' Gristhorpe went on,
'we'd better bring DC Richmond in on this after all. Get
him to check on missing persons with the Police National
Computer.'

Vic Manson, the fingerprint expert, approached them,
shaking his head. 'It'll not be easy,' he complained. 'There
might be prints left on three or four fingers but I can't
promise anything. I'll try wax injections to unwrinkle the
skin, and if they don't work, it'll have to be formaldehyde
and alum.'

'It'll be a devil of a job finding out who he was,'

Banks said. 'Even if we can get prints, there's no guaranteeing they'll be on record. And someone's gone to great lengths to make sure we can't recognize him by his face.'

'There's always the clothes,' Gristhorpe said. 'Or teeth. Though I can't say I've ever had much luck with them myself.'

'Me neither,' Banks agreed. He always thought it amusing when he watched television detectives identify bodies from dental charts. If they really knew how long it would take every dentist in the country to search through every chart in his files . . . Only if the police already had some idea who the body was could dental charts confirm or deny the identity.

'He might even be German,' Hatchley added. 'Or an American. You get a lot of foreigners walking the fells these days.'

Across the beck, two men wearing face masks slid the body into the large zip-up bag they had brought. Banks grimaced as he watched them brush off the maggots, shed in all directions, before they were finally able to secure the zip. They then started to carry their burden along the valley towards the winch.

'Let's go,' Gristhorpe said. 'It's getting late. There's nothing more to be done here till we can start a search. We'd better post a couple of men here for the night though. If the killer knows we've discovered the body and he's buried important evidence nearby, he might come back after dark.'

Hatchley nodded.

'We'll arrange to send someone up,' Gristhorpe went on. 'You'd better stick around till they get here, Sergeant. See if you can persuade the rescue people to wait for them

with the winch. If not, they'll just have to come the long
way, like we did.'

Banks saw Hatchley glance towards where the corpse
had lain and shiver. He didn't envy anyone stuck with the
job of staying in this enchanted valley after dark.

FOUR

Sam took Katie as roughly as usual in bed that night. And
as usual she lay there and gave the illusion of enjoying
herself. At least it didn't hurt any more like it had at first.
There were some things you had to do, some sins you had
to commit because men were just made that way and you
needed a man to take care of you in the world. The
important thing, Katie had learned from her grandmother,
was that you must not enjoy it. Grit your teeth and give
them what they want, yes, even cheat a little and make
them think you like it – especially if they treat you badly
when you don't seem enthusiastic – but under no circumstances should you find pleasure in it.

It never lasted long. That was one consolation. Soon
Sam started breathing quickly, and she clung to him
tighter and mouthed the sounds he liked to hear, told him
the things he liked to know. At last he grunted and made
her all wet. Then he rolled over on his side and quickly
began snoring.

But sleep didn't come so easily for Katie that night. She
thought about the body on the fell and pulled the sheets
up tighter around her chin. Last time it had been awful: all
those questions, all the trouble there'd been – especially
when the police tried to connect the dead man with the
missing girl, Anne Ralston. They'd acted as if Stephen or

one of his friends might have killed both of them. And what had they found out? Nothing. Raymond Addison seemed to have come from nowhere.

Katie had hardly known Anne, for she and Sam hadn't been in Swainshead long when all the trouble started five years ago. The only reason they had met her at all was because Sam wanted to seek out the 'best people' in the village. He latched on to the Colliers, and Anne Ralston had been going out with Stephen at the time.

She hadn't been Katie's type though, and they'd never have become good friends. Anne, she remembered, had seemed far too footloose and fancy-free for her taste. She had probably just run off with another man; it would have been typical of her to go off without a word and leave everyone to worry about her.

Katie turned on her side to reach for some Kleenex from the bedside table, dragging the sheets with her. Sam stirred and yanked back his half. Gently, she wiped herself. She hated that warm wetness between her legs. More and more every time she hated it, just as she had come to loathe her life with Sam in Swainshead.

And things had been getting worse lately. She had been under a black depression for a month or more. She knew it was a woman's place to obey her husband, to stay with him for better, for worse, to submit to his demands in bed and slave for him all day in the house. But surely, she thought, life shouldn't be so bleak. If there was any chance of escape from the drudgery that her life had become and from the beatings, would it really be such a sin to take it?

Things hadn't always been so bad. When they had met, Katie had been working as a chambermaid at Queen's Hotel in Leeds, and Sam, an apprentice electrician, had turned up one day to check the wiring. It had hardly been love at first sight; for Katie, love was what happened in the romantic paperbacks she read, the ones that made her blush and look over her shoulder in case her granny could see her reading them. But Sam had been presentable enough – a cocky young bantam with curly chestnut hair and a warm boyish smile. A real charmer.

He had asked her out for a drink three times, and three times she had said no. She had never set foot in a pub. Her granny had taught her that they were all dens of iniquity, and Katie herself held alcohol responsible for her father's wickedness and for the misery of her mother's life. Katie didn't realize at the time that her refusal of a drink was taken as a rejection of Sam himself. If only he would ask her to go for a walk, she had thought, or perhaps to the Kardomah for a coffee and a bite to eat after work.

Finally, in exasperation, he had suggested a Saturday afternoon trip to Otley. Even though Katie was over eighteen, she still had a difficult time persuading her grandmother to let her go, especially as she was to ride pillion on Sam's motorbike. But in the end the old woman had given in, muttering warnings about the Serpent in Eden and wolves in sheep's clothing.

In Otley they had, inevitably, gone for a drink. Sam had practically dragged her into the Red Lion, where she had finally broken down and blurted out why she had refused to go for a drink before. He laughed and touched her shoulder gently. She drank bitter lemon and nothing terrible happened to either of them. After that she went to pubs with him more often, though she always refused alcohol and never felt entirely comfortable.

But now, she thought, turning over again, life had become unbearable. The early days, just after their marriage, had been full of hope after Katie had learned how to tolerate Sam's sexual demands. They had lived with his parents in a little back-to-back in Armley and saved every penny they earned. Sam had a dream, a guest house in the Dales, and together they had brought it about. Those had been happy times, despite the hours of overtime, the cramped living quarters and the lack of privacy, for they had had something to aim towards. Now it was theirs, Katie hated it. Sam had changed; he had become snobbish, callous and cruel.

Like every other night for the past few months, she cried quietly to herself as she tried to shut out Sam's snoring and listen to the breeze hiss through the willows by the nameless stream out at the back. She would wait and keep silent. If nothing happened, if nothing came of her only hope of escape, then one night she would sneak out of the house as quiet as a thief and never come back.

FIVE

In room five, Neil Fellowes knelt by the side of the bed and said his prayers.

He had woken from his drunken stupor in time to be sick in the washbasin, and after that he had felt much better. So much so, in fact, that he had gone down and eaten the lamb chops with mint sauce that Mrs Greenock had cooked so well. Then he spent the rest of the evening in his room reading.

And now, as he tried to match the words to his thoughts and feelings, as he always did in prayer, he found he couldn't. The picture of the body kept coming back, tearing aside the image of God that he had retained from childhood: an old man with a long white beard sitting on a cloud with a ledger on his lap. Suddenly, the smell was in his nostrils again; it was like trying to breathe at the bottom of a warm sewer. And he saw again the bloody maggot-infested pulp that had once been a face, the white shirt rippling with corruption, the whole thing rising and falling in an obscene parody of breathing.

He tried to force his mind back to the prayer but couldn't. Hoping the Lord would understand and give him the comfort he needed, he gave up, put his glasses on the table and got into bed.

On the edge of sleep, he was able to reconstruct the sequence of events in his mind. At the time, he had been too distraught, too confused to notice anything. And very soon his head had been spinning with the drink. But he remembered bursting into the pub and asking for help. He remembered how Sam Greenock and the others at the table had calmed him down and suggested what he should do. But there was something else, something wrong. It was just a vague feeling. He couldn't quite bring it to consciousness before sleep took him.

3

ONE

'**What is it?**' Banks asked, examining the faded slip of paper that Sergeant Hatchley had dropped on the desk in front of him.

'Forensic said it's some kind of receipt from a till,' Hatchley explained. 'You know, one of those bits of paper they give you when you buy something. People usually just drop them on the floor or shove them in their pockets and forget about them. They found it in his right trouser pocket. It'd been there long enough to go through the washer once or twice, but you know what bloody wizards they are in the lab.'

Banks knew. He had little faith in forensic work as a means of catching criminals, but the boffins knew their stuff when it came to identification and gathering evidence. Their lab was just outside Wetherby, and Gristhorpe must have put a 'rush' on this job to get the results back to Eastvale so quickly. The body had been discovered only the previous afternoon, and it was still soaking in a Lysol bath.

Banks looked closely again at the slip, then turned to its accompanying transcription. The original had been too faint to read, but forensic had treated it with chemicals and copied out the message exactly:

CHOOSE FRESH
CHOOSE WENDY'S
Store 006308

SNGL / CHZ	
WITH . . .	
TOMATO	
BACON	2.69
FRIES	.89
SMALL COKE	.85
Tax	.35
Inside	4.78
	05.26PM 04/25

'Wendy's,' Banks said. 'That's a burger chain. There's a few branches in London. Look at those prices, though.'

Hatchley shrugged. 'If it was in London . . .'

'Come on! Even in London you don't pay two pounds sixty-nine just for a bloody hamburger. At least not at Wendy's you don't. You don't pay eighty-five pence for a Coke, either. What does that tax work out at?'

Hatchley took out his pocket calculator and struggled with the figures. 'Eight per cent,' he announced finally.

'Hmm. That's an odd amount. You don't pay eight per cent VAT on food in England.'

'I suppose it's an American company,' Hatchley suggested, 'if they sell hamburgers?'

'You mean our man's an American?'

'Or he could have just come back from a trip there.'

'He could have. But that'd make it a bit soon for another holiday, wouldn't it? Unless he was a businessman. What about the labels on his clothes?'

'Torn off,' Hatchley said. 'Trousers and underpants seem to be ordinary Marks and Sparks cotton and polyester. Same with the shirt. The boots were Army and Navy.

They could have been bought at any of their branches.'

Banks tapped his ballpoint on the edge of the desk. 'Why is it that somebody doesn't want us to know who he is or where he's from?'

'Maybe because if we knew that we'd have a good idea who the killer was.'

'So the quicker we identify the body, the better our chances. Whoever did it was obviously counting on no one finding it for months, then being unable to identify it.' Banks sipped some lukewarm coffee and pulled a face. 'But we've got a lead.' He tapped the receipt. 'I want to know where this Wendy's is located. It shouldn't take you long. There's a store code to go on.'

'Where do I go for that kind of information?' Hatchley asked.

'Bloody hell!' Banks said. 'You're a detective. At least I hope you are. Start detecting. First, I'd suggest you call Wendy's UK office. It's going to be a couple of days before we get anything from Glendenning and Vic Manson, so let's use every break we get. Did Richmond come up with anything from missing persons?'

'No, sir.'

'I suppose our corpse is still supposed to be on holiday then, if no one's reported him missing. And if he's not English it could be ages before he gets into the files. Check the hotels and guest houses in the area and see if any Americans have registered there lately. If they have, try and track them down.'

Dismissed, Hatchley went to find Richmond, to whom, Banks knew, he would pass on as much of the load as possible. Still, he reasoned, the sergeant's work was solid enough once he built up a bit of momentum, and the pressure would serve as a test of Richmond's mettle.

Since passing his computer course with flying colours, the young detective constable looked all set for promotion. That would cause problems with Hatchley though. There was no way, Banks reflected, that the sergeant could be expected to work with Richmond at equal rank. Things had been bad enough when Banks came from the Metropolitan force to fill the position Hatchley had set his own sights on. And Hatchley was destined to stay a sergeant; he didn't have the extra edge needed to make inspector, as Richmond did.

Grateful that promotion was not his decision, Banks glanced at his watch and headed for the car. Neil Fellowes was waiting in Swainshead, and the poor sod had already had to arrange for one extra day off work.

TWO

As he drove along the dale, Banks marvelled at how familiar some of its landmarks had become: the small drumlin with its four sick elms all leaning to the right like an image in one of those Chinese watercolours that Sandra, his wife, liked so much; the quiet village of Fortford with the foundations of a Roman fort laid bare on a hillock by the green; the busy main street of Helmthorpe, Swainsdale's largest village; and above Helmthorpe, the long limestone edge of Crow Scar gleaming in the sun.

The Kinks sang 'Lola', and Banks tapped his fingers on the steering wheel in time with the music as he drove. Though he swore to Sandra that he still loved opera, much to her delight he hadn't played any lately. She had approved of his recent flirtation with the blues, and now he seemed to be going through a nostalgic phase for the

He walked up the thick-pile burgundy carpet, found the room and knocked.

Fellowes answered immediately, as if he had been holding the doorknob on the other side. He looked much better than the previous day. His few remaining strands of colourless hair were combed sideways across his bald head, and thick-lensed wire-rimmed glasses perched on the bump near the bridge of his nose.

'Come in, please er . . .'

Banks introduced himself.

'Yes, come in, Chief Inspector.'

Fellowes was obviously a man who respected rank and title. Most people automatically called Banks 'Inspector', some preferred plain 'Mister', and others called him a lot worse.

Banks glanced out of the window at the wide strips of grass on both sides of the Swain. Beyond the cottages and pub rose the overbearing bulk of a fell. It looked like a sleeping elephant, he thought, remembering a passage from Wainwright, the fell-walking expert. Or was it whale? 'Nice view,' he said, sitting down in the wicker chair by the window.

'Yes,' Fellowes agreed. 'It doesn't really matter which side of the house you stay in. At the back you can see Swainshead Fell, and over there it's Adam's Fell, of course.'

'Adam's Fell?'

Fellowes adjusted his glasses and cleared his throat. 'Yes. After Adam and Eve. The locals do have a sense of humour – of a sort.'

'Do you visit the area often, Mr Fellowes?'

'No, not at all. I just like to research the terrain, so to speak, before I embark. By the way, Chief Inspector, I do apologize sincerely about yesterday. Finding that . . . that corpse was a great shock, and I never take liquor as a rule – or tobacco, I might add. I wouldn't have thought of it myself, but Mr Greenock was kind enough . . .' He slowed and stopped like an old gramophone winding down.

Banks, who had taken note of Fellowes' declaration of abstemiousness and let go of the cigarette packet he'd been toying with in his pocket, smiled and offered a cliché of consolation. Inwardly, he sighed. The world was becoming too full of non-smokers for his comfort, and he hadn't yet succeeded in swelling their ranks. Perhaps it was time to switch brands again. He was getting tired of Silk Cut, anyway. He took out his notebook and went on.

'What made you visit that spot in the first place?' he asked.

'It just looked so inviting,' Fellowes answered. 'So different.'

'Had you ever been there before?'

'No.'

'Did you know of its existence?'

'No. It's certainly not mentioned in my guidebook. Locals would know it, I suppose. I really can't say. Anyone could wander into it. It's on the maps, of course, but it doesn't show up as anything special.'

'But you do have to make quite a diversion from the footpath to get there.'

'Well, yes. Though I'd hardly say it's that much of a haul.'

'Depends on how fit you are,' Banks said, smiling. 'But you reckoned it would be worthwhile?'

'I'm interested in wild flowers, Chief Inspector. I thought I might discover something interesting.'

'When did you arrive in Swainshead?'

'Three days ago. It was only a short break. I'm saving most of my holidays for a bicycle tour of Provence in autumn.'

'I hope you have a less grim time of it there,' Banks said. 'Is there anything else you can remember about the scene, about what happened?'

'It was all such a blur. First there was the orchis, then that awful smell, and . . . No. I turned away and headed back as soon as I'd . . . as soon as I refreshed myself in the beck.'

'There was nobody else in the valley?'

'Not that I was aware of.'

'You didn't get a feeling of being followed, observed?'

'No.'

'And you didn't find anything close to the body? Something you might have thought insignificant, picked up and forgotten about?'

'Nothing, Chief Inspector. Believe me, the feeling of revulsion was sudden and quite overwhelming.'

'Of course. Had you noticed anything else before you found the body?'

'What do you mean?'

'The victim's rucksack was missing. We think he must have been carrying his belongings with him but we can't find them. Did you notice any signs of something being buried, burned, destroyed?'

'I'm sorry, Chief Inspector, but no, I didn't.'

'Any idea who the victim was?'

Fellowes opened his eyes wide. 'How could I have? You must have seen for yourself how . . . how . . .'

'I know what state he was in. I was simply wondering if you'd heard anything about someone missing in the area.'

Fellowes shook his head.

Banks closed his notebook and put it back in the inside pocket of his pale blue sports jacket.

'There is one thing,' Fellowes said hesitantly.

'Yes?'

'I don't like to cast aspersions. It's only a very vague impression.'

'Go on.'

'And I wasn't in full control of my faculties. It was just a feeling.'

'Policemen have feelings like that, too, Mr Fellowes. We call them hunches and they're often very valuable. What was this feeling you had?'

Fellowes leaned forward from the edge of the bed and lowered his voice. 'Well, Chief Inspector, I only really thought about it in bed last night, and it was just a kind of niggling sensation, an itch. It was in the pub, just after I arrived and, you know, told them what I'd seen. I sat at the table, quite out of breath and emotionally distraught . . .'

'And what happened?'

'Nothing happened. It was just a feeling, as I said. I wasn't even looking, but I got the impression that someone there wasn't really surprised.'

'That you'd found a body?'

'Yes.'

'Was that all?'

Fellowes took off his glasses and rubbed the bridge of his nose. Banks noticed how small his eyes looked without the magnifying lenses. 'More than that,' Fellowes went on. 'I was looking away at the time, but I felt an odd sort of silence, the kind of silence in which glances are exchanged. It was very uncomfortable for a moment, though I was too preoccupied to really notice it at the time. I've thought about it a lot since last night, and that's the only way I can put it, as if a kind of understanding look passed between some of the people at the table.'

'Who was there?'

'The same people as when you arrived. There was the landlord over at the bar, then Sam Greenock, Stephen and Nicholas Collier and John Fletcher. I'd met them the previous day when I was enquiring about the best places to search for wild flowers.'

'Did it seem to you as if they were all in on some kind of conspiracy?'

'I'm not paranoid, if that's what you're getting at, Chief Inspector.'

'But you were upset. Sometimes our senses can overreact.'

'Believe what you wish. I simply thought you ought to know. And in answer to your question, no, I didn't sense any gigantic conspiracy, just that someone at the table knew something.'

'But you said you thought a glance was exchanged.'

'That's what it felt like.'

'So more than one person knew?'

'I suppose so. I can't say how many or how I received the impression. It just happened.'

Banks took his notebook out again and wrote down the names.

'I don't want to get anybody into trouble,' Fellowes said. 'I could be wrong. It could have happened just as you said, an overreaction.'

'Let *us* worry about that, Mr Fellowes. We don't usually ask people to stand up in a court of law and swear to their feelings. Is that all you can tell me?'

'Yes. Will I be able to go home now? There'll be trouble at work if I'm not back tomorrow.'

'Better give me your address and phone number in case we need to talk to you again,' Banks said.

Banks made a note of Fellowes' address and left, thinking what a celebrity the man would be at work for a while. He went out of the open door without seeing Katie Greenock and breathed in the fresh air by the beck. A young man dangled his legs over the bank, eating a sandwich from greaseproof paper and reading a thick paperback; the old men still huddled around the eastern end of the stone bridge; and there were three cars parked outside the White Rose. Banks looked at his watch: twenty past one. With a bit of luck the same crowd as yesterday would be there. He read over the names Fellowes had given him again and decided to make a start.

THREE

First things first, Banks thought, and headed for the bar. He ordered Cumberland sausage, beans and chips, then paid, took his numbered receipt, and waited while Freddie Metcalfe poured him a pint of Pedigree.

'Is tha getting anywhere?' Metcalfe asked, his biceps bulging as he pulled down on the pump.

'Early days yet,' Banks answered.

'Aye, an' it got to late days an' all last time, and still tha didn't find owt.'

'That's how it goes sometimes. I wasn't here then.'

'Thinks tha's better than old Gristhorpe, does tha, eh?'

'That's not what I meant.'

'From down sahth, aren't tha?'

'Yes. London.'

'London.' Metcalfe placed the foaming brew on the cloth in front of Banks and scratched his hairy ear. 'Bin there once. Full o' foreigners, London. All them A-rabs.'

'It's a busy place,' Banks said, picking up his beer.

'Don't get many o' them arahnd 'ere. Foreigners, that is. That why tha came up 'ere, to get shut on t' A-rabs, eh? Tha'll find plenty o' Pakis in Bradford, like, but I don't reckon as I've ever seed a darkie in Swainshead. Saw one in Eastvale, once.'

Banks, growing quickly tired of Metcalfe's racist inanities, made to turn away, but the landlord grabbed his elbow.

'Don't tha want to ask me any questions then, lad?' he said, his eyes glittering.

Holding back his temper, Banks lit a cigarette and propped himself up against the bar. He had noticed that the three men he recognized from the previous day were only into the upper thirds of their pints, so he had enough time to banter with Metcalfe. He might just pick up some interesting titbit.

'What do you want me to ask you?' he opened.

'Nay, tha's t' bobby. Tha should know.'

'Do you get many walkers in here?'

'Aye. We don't fuss 'em abaht rucksacks and boo-its and whatnot like that stuck-up pillock on t' main road.'

'But I understand this is the "select" part of town?'

'Aye.' Metcalfe laughed. 'Tha could say that. It's t' oldest, anyroads. And t' Colliers drink 'ere, as did their father before them. Select, if tha likes, but dahn to earth, not stuck up.' He shook his head slowly. 'A right lad, were Walter Collier.' Then he leaned forward and whispered, 'Not like 'is sons, if tha knows what I mean. Wouldn't know a cratch from a gripe, neither on 'em. And they was brought up by a farmer, too.'

Banks, who didn't know a cratch from a gripe either, asked why.

'Eddication,' Metcalfe said, intoning the word as if it were responsible for most of the world's ills. 'Fancy bloody Oxford eddication. Wanted 'em to 'ave a better chance than 'e'd 'ad, did old Walter. Farming don't pay much, tha knows, an' Walter were sharp enough to get out 'imself.' Metcalfe turned up his nose. 'Well, tha can see what eddication does.'

'What are they like, Stephen and Nicholas?' Banks asked.

Metcalfe sniffed and lowered his voice. He was clearly enjoying his role as dispenser of local opinion. 'Right bloody useless pair, if y'ask me. At least yon Nicholas is. Mr Stephen's not so bad. Teks after old Walter, 'e does. Bit of a ladies' man. Not that t' other's queer, or owt.' Metcalfe laughed. 'There were a bit o' trouble wi' a servant lass a few years back, when 'e were still a young lad, living at 'ome, like. Got 'er up t' spout, Master Nicholas did. Old Walter 'ad to see 'er right, o' course, and I've no doubt 'e gave t' lad a right good thrashing. But it's Mr Stephen that's t' ladies man. One after t' other.'

'What's the difference in their ages?'

'Nobbut a couple o' years. Stephen's t' eldest.'

'What happened to the farm land?'

'Old Walter sold some on it,' Metcalfe said, 'and leased t' rest. T' Colliers are still t' biggest landowners in t' dale, mind thee. John Fletcher over there bought a goodly chunk on it.' He wagged his chin in the direction of the table. The drinkers were now into the last thirds of their drinks, and Banks decided it would be a good time to approach them.

'Tha still an't asked me no real questions,' Metcalfe protested.

'Later,' Banks said, turning. 'I'd like to talk to these gentlemen here before they leave.' Of the gentlemen in question, he recognized Nicholas Collier and Sam Greenock from the previous day; therefore, the third had to be John Fletcher.

'Wait on a minute,' Metcalfe said. 'Dun't tha want tha sausage and chips?'

And as if on cue, a freckled little girl in a red dress, her hair in pigtails, appeared from the kitchens and called out, 'Number seventy-five! Sausage, beans and chips.'

Banks gave her his receipt and took the plate, then helped himself to the condiments from the bar.

When he walked over to the table, the three men shifted around, scraping their chair legs on the flagged floor, and made room for him.

'Do you mind if I eat at your table?' he asked.

'Not at all. Freddie been giving you a rough time, Inspector?' Nicholas Collier asked. His smile showed his prominent teeth to great disadvantage; they were dis- coloured with nicotine and crooked as a badly built drystone wall. His speech, Banks noticed, bore traces of the local accent under its veneer of public school English.

'No,' he said, returning the smile. 'Just entertaining me. Quite a fellow.'

'You can say that again. He's been behind the bar as long as I can remember.' Nicholas leaned forward and lowered his voice. 'Between you and me, I don't think he quite approves of Stephen and myself. Anyway, have you met John, here?'

The squat man with the five o'clock shadow was indeed John Fletcher, gentleman farmer. Stephen Collier, his brother said, was away dealing with some factory business.

'Is this just a social visit or do you have some questions for us?' Sam asked.

'Just one, really,' Banks said, spearing a mouthful of sausage. 'Have you any idea who it was we found up there?'

After a short silence Nicholas said, 'We get quite a lot of visitors in the area, Inspector. Especially when we're blessed with such a fine start to the year. There's nobody local missing, as far as I know, so it must be a stranger. Can't you check?'

'Yes,' Banks said. 'Of course we can. We can go through every name in every hotel and guest house registration book and make sure everyone's accounted for. But, like you I'm sure, we're all for anything that saves extra effort.'

Collier laughed. 'Naturally. But no, I can't think of anyone it might be.'

'Your victim hadn't necessarily come through Swainshead, you know,' Sam pointed out. 'He could have been heading south from Swaledale or beyond. Even from the Lake District. He could have set off from Helmthorpe too, or any number of other villages in the dale. Most of them have at least one or two bed and breakfast places these days.'

'I know,' Banks said. 'Believe me, we're checking.' He turned to Fletcher. 'I hear that you own quite a bit of land?'

'Yes,' Fletcher said, his dark eyes narrowing suspiciously. 'Walter sold it to me when he gave up farming and went into the food business.' He glanced at Nicholas, who nodded. 'Neither Nick here nor his brother Stephen wanted to take over – in fact Walter hadn't wanted them to, he'd been preparing to sell for quite a while – so I thought I'd give it a go.'

'How is it working out?'

'Well enough. I don't know if you understand much about Dales farming, Mr Banks, but it's a hard life. Old Walter himself had had enough, and he was one of those men – rare around these parts – with enough vision to get out and put what he'd got to better use. I'd never blame a farmer for wanting a different life for his sons. I've got no family myself,' he said, and a hard look came into his eyes. 'I'm not complaining, though. I make a living – the EEC and the National Parks Commission notwithstanding.'

Banks turned to Nicholas. 'What do you do?'

'I teach English at Braughtmore, just up the road here. It's only a small public school of course, but it's a start.'

'But you don't actually live there?'

'No. Hardly necessary, really. The house is so close. The pupils live in. They have to; it's so damn far from civilization. And we have housemasters. Some of the teachers live in the grounds, but a couple of others have chosen to settle here in the village. The school's only five miles north, quite isolated. It's a good school, though I say so myself. Do you have any children, Inspector?'

'Yes. A boy and a girl.'

'What school do they attend?'

'Eastvale Comprehensive.'

'Hmm.' The corner of Collier's lip twitched, giving just a fleeting hint of a sneer.

Banks shifted uneasily in his chair. 'Your brother runs the family business, I gather.'

'Yes. Managing director of Collier Food Enterprises. It's over the Lancashire border, about ten miles west, just off the main road. The arrangement suits us both perfectly.

Stephen never had a great deal of academic ambition, despite the excellent education he received, but he's bright and he's put his mind to good enough use – making money. It was one of father's wisest moves, buying up that old mill and setting up the food-processing operation. And as for me, I'm happy with my books and a few pliant young minds to work on.' Again he bared his teeth in a smile.

They had all finished their drinks and Banks was wondering how to edge them gently towards the murder again, when Fletcher stood up and excused himself. Immediately, the others looked at their watches and decided they ought to leave and take care of various tasks.

'There's nothing else, is there, Inspector?' Nicholas asked.

'No,' Banks said. 'Not yet.'

Freddie Metcalfe ambled over to the table to pick up the plate and the empty glasses as Banks was stubbing out his cigarette.

'Find owt aht yet?' he asked.

'No,' Banks said, standing up. 'Nothing.'

'Early days, eh?'

And the deep chortling laughter followed Banks out into the street.

FOUR

Back at Eastvale police station things were quiet. Grabbing a cup of coffee from the filter machine on the way, Banks walked upstairs to his office, a plain room furnished with nothing but filing cabinets, metal desk and a calendar of local scenes. The illustration for May showed the River Wharfe as it flowed among the limestone boulders of

Langstrothdale. More recently Banks had added, next to it, one more decoration: a broken pipe, which he had just rediscovered at the back of his drawer. It represented a vain attempt to project a rural image and wean himself from cigarettes at the same time, but he had cursed it constantly and finally thrown it at that very same wall in frustration over the Steadman case almost a year ago. It hung there like a piece of conceptual art to remind him of the folly of trying to be what one is not.

There were quite a few cars parked in the cobbled market square outside, and visitors walked in and out of the small Norman church and the shops that seemed almost built into its frontage. The gold hands of the clock stood at three thirty against its blue face. Banks looked down on the scene, as he often did, smoking a cigarette and sipping his coffee. The police station itself was a Tudor-fronted building on narrow Market Street across from the Queen's Arms, which curved around the corner so that one of its entrances stood on the side of the square opposite the church. Looking to his right, Banks could see along the street, with its coffee houses, boutiques and tourist shops, and in front was the busy square itself, with the NatWest bank, the El Toro coffee bar and Joplin's newsagent's on the opposite side.

A knock at the door interrupted him. Sergeant Hatchley came in looking very pleased with himself. When he was excited about something he moved much faster than usual and seemed unable to stand still. Banks had come to recognize the signs.

'I've tracked it down, sir,' Hatchley said. 'That bit of paper he had in his pocket.'

The two of them sat down and Banks told the sergeant to carry on.

'Like you said, I tried the London office. They said they'd check and get back to me. Anyway, they found out that that particular branch is in Canada.'

'So our man's a Canadian?'

'Looks that way, sir. Unless, like I said before, he'd just been on holiday there. Anyway, at least we know there's a close connection.'

'Anything else?'

'Yes. Once he'd discovered the outlet was in Canada, the bloke from Wendy's became very helpful.'

Such helpfulness was a common enough occurrence, Banks knew from experience. He'd even invented a term for it: the amateur sleuth syndrome.

'That particular branch is in Toronto, on Yonge Street near Dundas Street, if that means anything.'

Banks shook his head. 'Never been over the Atlantic. You?'

Hatchley grunted. 'Me? I've never been further west than Blackpool. Anyway, that narrows things down quite a bit, I'd say.'

'It does,' Banks agreed. 'But it still doesn't tell us who he was.'

'I got on to the Canadian High Commission and asked a bloke there to check if anyone from Toronto had been reported missing over here lately, but nobody has.'

'Too early yet, I suppose. If he *is* from Toronto, obviously everyone back there still thinks he's on holiday.'

'Aye, but that won't last for ever.'

'We haven't got for ever. Who knows, he might have been a student and come over for the whole bloody summer. How's Richmond doing?'

'He's covered quite a few places already – Lyndgarth, Relton, Helmthorpe, Gratly.'

'Well, his task ought to be a bit easier now we know it's a Canadian we're after.'

'There's been quite a few Canadians staying locally,' Hatchley said. 'It's easy enough to call the B and Bs and make a list from their records, but it's damned hard to trace people's movements after they've left. They don't usually leave forwarding addresses, and it's only once in a while a landlady is able to tell us where they said they were going next.'

'There can't be that many men from Toronto travelling alone,' Banks said. 'I'm sure if he was a member of a group or a family somebody would have reported him missing by now. Better stick at it. At least you've narrowed the field considerably. Heard anything from Dr Glendenning?'

'The super called him a while ago. Still killing off those bloody maggots in disinfectant. Says he won't be able to make a start till tomorrow morning at the earliest.'

Banks sighed. 'All right. You'd better go and help Richmond now. And thanks, Sergeant; you did a good job.'

Hatchley nodded and left the office. They'd been working together for almost two years now, Banks realized, and he still couldn't bring himself to call the sergeant Jim. Maybe one day he would, when it came naturally to his lips. He lit another cigarette and went back to the window, where he watched the people wander about in the square, and drummed a tattoo on the sill.

FIVE

'Sam's not in,' Katie said that evening when she opened the back door to find Stephen Collier standing there. 'He's having a night out with his old mates in Leeds.'

'Can't I come in, anyway?' Stephen asked. 'Just for a cup of tea?'

'All right,' Katie said, and led him through to the spotless kitchen. 'Just five minutes, mind you. I've work to be doing.' She turned away from him and busied herself with the kettle and teapot. She felt her face burning. It wasn't right being alone in the house with a man other than her husband, even if it was someone as pleasant as Stephen. He had a reputation as a womanizer. Everybody knew that. Someone might even have seen him coming in.

'Nick tells me the police were around today,' Stephen said.

Katie glanced at him over her shoulder. 'It's to be expected, isn't it? One of our guests did find a dead body.'

'He still here?'

'No. He left this afternoon.'

'Well,' Stephen said. 'I just thought I'd drop by to see if you were all right. I mean, it can be a bit of a shock to the system, something like that happening right on your door-step, so to speak. Did the police ask a lot of questions?'

'Not to me, no. Why should they?'

'Just wondering,' Stephen said. 'How are things, anyway?'

'All right, I suppose,' Katie answered. Though she had known him for over five years and certainly preferred him to his brother, Katie hadn't really spent much time alone with Stephen Collier before. Mostly, they had met socially at summer garden parties the Colliers liked to throw, in the pub and at occasional dinners. She liked Stephen. He seemed kind and thoughtful. Often at social functions she had caught him looking at her in an odd way. Not *that* way, not like Nicholas. It was a look she didn't quite understand, and she had never been able to return his gaze for long without lowering her eyes. Now she was alone with him she felt shy and awkward; she didn't really know how to behave. She brought the tea to the table and opened a packet of Fox's Custard Creams.

'Come on, Katie,' Stephen said. 'You're not very convincing. You don't sound all right to me.'

'I don't know what you mean.'

'Yes, you do. I can tell. I've felt some sort of bond with you right from the start. I've been worried about you these past few months.'

'Worried? Why?'

'Because you're not happy.'

'Of course I'm happy. That's silly.'

Stephen sighed. 'I can't make you open up, can I? But you *can* talk to me if you want, if you need to. Everybody needs somebody to talk to now and then.'

Katie bit her lower lip and said nothing. She couldn't talk to him. She couldn't tell anyone the things that went on in her mind, the sins she dreamed of, the desperation she felt. She couldn't tell him about her one chance of escaping from her miserable life, and what it had already cost her.

'Anyway,' Stephen went on, taking a biscuit, 'I might not be around here for much longer.'

'What do you mean?'

'I've had enough of it, Katie. The plant, the house, the village. Lord, I'm nearly thirty. It's about time I got out and about, saw a bit of the world before I get too old.'

'B-but you can't,' Katie said, shocked. 'Surely you can't just up and go like that? What about—'

Stephen slapped the table. 'Oh, responsibilities be hanged,' he said. 'There's plenty of others willing and able to run Collier Foods. I'll take a long holiday, then maybe try something else.'

'Why are you telling me all this?' Katie asked.

Stephen looked at her, and she noticed that he suddenly looked old, much older than his twenty-eight years.

He ran his hand through his short brown hair. 'I don't know,' he said. 'I told you, we're kindred spirits. You're the only person I've told. There's nobody else, really.'

'But your brother . . .'

'Nicky? He wouldn't understand. He's too wrapped up in his own world. And don't think I haven't noticed the way he looks at you, Katie, even if Sam hasn't. I'd stay away from him if I were you.'

'Of course I will,' Katie said, blushing. 'Why shouldn't I?'

'Oh, he can be very persuasive, Nicky can.'

'What about John?' Katie asked. 'Or Sam? Can't you talk to them?'

Stephen laughed. 'Look, Katie,' he said, 'Nicky, Sam and the rest, they're all good drinking friends, but there are things I can't talk to them about.'

'But why me?'

'Because I think it's the same for you. I think you're unhappy with your life and you've nobody to talk to about it. Why are you so afraid of talking to me? You've got all your problems bottled up inside you. Don't you like me?'

Katie traced rings on the table with her forefinger. 'It's not that,' she said. 'I'm fine, really I am.'

Stephen leaned forward. 'Why don't you open up, show some feeling?' he urged her.

'I do.'

'Not for me.'

'It's not right.'

'Oh, Katie, you're such a moralist.' Stephen stood up to leave. 'Would that I had your moral fibre. No, it's all right, there's no need to show me out.'

Katie wanted to call after him, but she couldn't. Deep inside, she felt a thick darkness swirling and building in power, trying to force its way out. But it was evil and she had to keep it locked in. She had to accept her lot, her place in life. She was Sam's wife. That was her duty. There was no point talking about problems. What could she say to Stephen Collier? Or he to her? Why had he come? What did he want from her? 'The thing that all men want,' said a strong harsh voice inside her. 'The same thing his brother wants. Don't be fooled by talk of companionship. Satan has a sweet tongue.'

'But he was reaching out to you,' another, quieter voice said, 'reaching out in friendship, and you turned him away.'

Katie's chest tightened and her hands shook as she tried to bring the teacup to her mouth. 'I'm lost,' she thought. 'I don't know what to do. I don't know what's right any more. Help me, someone, please help me!' And the cup rolled to the floor and smashed as Katie laid her head on the table and wept.

4

ONE

Two days later, on 31 May, forensic information started trickling in. During that time, Richmond and Hatchley had tracked down all but two wandering Canadians who had left local hotels or guest houses between ten and thirteen days ago.

Events were moving too slowly for Banks. Most leads appear during the first twenty-four hours after a murder has taken place, but this body was about two hundred and forty hours old by the time it was found. Still they had very little to go on.

Therefore, when the first report from the forensic lab landed on his desk at ten thirty that morning, Banks drank in the information like a man stranded in a desert without water for three days.

Dr Glendenning had established that death was due to a stab wound from a single-edged blade, probably a sheath knife about six inches long. One upward thrust had penetrated the heart from beneath the ribs. After that, the face had been slashed and then beaten with a rock until it was unrecognizable. The victim was white, in his early thirties, five feet eleven inches tall, ten and a half stone in weight, and in good physical condition. That last part always irritated Banks: how could a corpse ever be in good physical condition? This one, certainly, had been about as far from it as one could get.

Vic Manson had finally managed, through peeling the skin off and treating it with glycerine, to get three clear prints. He had already checked these against the Police National Computer and discovered that they weren't on record. So far no good, Banks thought. The forensic odontologist, a note said, was still working on his reconstruction of the dental chart.

Calling for Sergeant Hatchley on his way out, Banks decided it was time for a discussion over elevenses in the Golden Grill. The two men weaved their way through the local shoppers and parties of tourists that straggled along both pavements and the narrow street, and found a table near the window. Banks gave the order for coffee and toasted teacakes to Peggy, a plump girl with a bright smile, and looked across at the whitewashed front of the police station with its black timber beams. Black and white, he thought. If only life was as simple as that.

As they drank their coffee, Banks and Hatchley tried to add up what they had got so far. It wasn't much: a ten-day-old corpse of a white male, probably Canadian, found stabbed in an isolated hanging valley. At least cause of death had been established, and the coroner's inquest would order a thorough investigation.

'Perhaps he wasn't travelling alone,' Banks said. 'Maybe he was with someone who killed him. That would explain the need to disfigure him – to give the killer plenty of time to get back home.'

'If that's the case,' Hatchley said, 'it'll be for the Canadian police to handle, won't it?'

'The murder happened on our turf. It's still our problem till the man at the top says different.'

'Maybe he stumbled into a coven of witches,' Hatchley suggested.

Banks laughed. 'They're mostly bored accountants and

housewives in it for the orgies. I doubt they'd go as far as to kill someone who walked in on them. And Glendenning didn't mention anything about ritual slaughter. How's the search for the elusive Canadians going?'

Hatchley reached slyly for another cigarette to prolong the break. 'I'm beginning to feel like that bloke who had to roll a rock up a hill over and over again.'

'Sisyphus? Sometimes I feel more like the poor sod who had his liver pecked out day after day.'

Hatchley lit his cigarette.

'Come on then,' Banks said, standing up to leave. 'Better get back.'

Hatchley cursed under his breath and followed Banks across the street.

'Chief Inspector Banks!' Sergeant Rowe called out as they passed the front desk. 'Telephone message. You're to call a Dr Passmore at the lab. He's the odonto . . . the odotol . . . Oh, the bloody tooth fairy, or whatever they call themselves.'

Banks smiled and thanked him. Back in his office, he picked up the phone and dialled.

'Ah, Chief Inspector Banks,' said Passmore. 'We've never met, but Dr Glendenning brought me in on this one. Interesting.'

'You've got something for us?' Banks asked eagerly.

'It's a bit complicated. Would it be a great inconvenience for you to drop into the lab?'

'No, not at all.' Banks looked at his watch. 'If I leave now I can be there in about an hour. Can you give me some idea over the phone?'

'I think we'll be able to trace the identity of your corpse before too long, if I'm not mistaken. I don't think his dentist is too far away.'

'With all due respect, I don't see how that can be, Doctor. We're pretty sure he was a Canadian.'

'That's as may be,' Passmore replied. 'But his dental work's as English as yours or mine.'

'I'm on my way.'

Still puzzled, Banks slipped a cassette into the machine and eased the Cortina out of the car park at the back of the station. At least something was happening. He drove slowly, dodging the tourists and shoppers who seemed to think Market Street was for pedestrians only. The breathy opening of Donovan's 'Hurdy Gurdy Man' started on the tape.

He passed the new estate under construction on the town's southern edge, then he put his foot down once he got out of the built-up area. Leaving the Dales for the plain, he drove through a patchwork landscape of green pasture and fields of bright yellow rape, divided by hawthorn hedgerows. Bluebells and buttercups, about the only wild flowers Banks could put a name to, were in bloom among the long grass by the roadside. A frightened whitethroat darted out in front of the car and almost ended up, like so many unfortunate rabbits and hedgehogs, splattered all over the tarmac.

The forensic lab was a square three-storey red-brick building just north of Wetherby. Banks identified himself at reception and climbed up to Passmore's second-floor office.

Dr Passmore gave new meaning to the term 'egghead'. The Lilliputians and the Blefuscudians could have had a fine war indeed over which end to open his egg-shaped skull. His bare shiny dome, combined with circumflex eyebrows, a putty nose and a tiny rosebud of a mouth, made him look more like an android than a human being. His mouth was so small that Banks wondered how there could be room for teeth in it. Perhaps he had chosen his profession out of tooth-envy.

Banks sat down as directed. The office was cluttered with professional journals and its one glassed-in bookcase was full to overflowing. The filing cabinets also bulged too much to close properly. On Passmore's desk, among the papers and pencil stubs, stood a toothless skull and several sets of dentures.

'Glad you could make it, Chief Inspector,' Passmore said, his voice surprisingly rich and deep coming from such a tiny mouth. 'I'm sorry to drag you all the way down here, but it might save time in the long run, and I think you'll find it worth the journey.'

Banks nodded and crossed his legs. He looked around for an ashtray, but couldn't see one; nor could he smell any traces of smoke when he surreptitiously sniffed the air. Bloody hell, another non-smoker, he cursed to himself.

'The victim's teeth were very badly damaged,' Passmore went on. 'Dr Glendenning said that he was hit about the face with a rock of some kind, and I concur.'

'He was found close to a stream,' Banks said. 'There were plenty of rocks in the area.'

'Hmm.' Passmore nodded sagely and made a steeple of his fingers on the desk. 'Anyway, I've managed to make a rudimentary reconstruction for you.' He pushed a brown envelope towards Banks. 'Not that it'll do you much good. You can hardly have every dentist in the country check this against every chart he or she has, can you?'

Banks was beginning to wonder why he'd come when Passmore stood up with surprising energy and walked over to a cabinet by the door. 'But,' he said, pausing dramatically to remove something and bring it back to the table, 'I think I might be able to help you with that.' And he dropped what looked like a fragment of tooth and pink plastic on the desk in front of Banks. 'A denture,' he announced. 'Upper right bicuspid, to be exact.'

Banks stared at the object. 'You got this from the body?'

Passmore nodded. 'It was badly shattered, of course, but I've managed to reassemble most of it. Rather like putting together a broken teacup, really.'

'How does this help us?'

'Well, in the first place,' Passmore said, 'it tells us that the deceased was more likely to be British than Canadian.'

'How?'

Passmore frowned, as if Banks was being purposely obtuse. 'Contrary to what some people believe,' he began, 'British dentists aren't very far behind their North American cousins. Oh, they might instigate new procedures over there before we do, but that's mostly because they have more money. Dentistry's private over there, you know, and it can be very expensive for the patient. But there are differences. Now, if your victim had come from Russia, for example, I could have told you immediately. They use stainless steel for fillings there. But in this case, it's merely an educated guess, or would be if it weren't for something else, which I'll get to in a moment.'

Come on, Banks thought, fidgeting with the cigarette packet in his jacket pocket, get to the bloody point. Putting up with rambling explanations – full of pauses for dramatic effect – seemed to be the price he so often had to pay for information from specialists like Passmore.

'The mere fact that your corpse has denture work leads me to conclude that he's European rather than North American,' the doctor continued. 'The Americans go in for saving teeth rather than replacing them. In fact, they hardly do denture work at all.'

'Very impressive,' Banks said. 'You mentioned something else – something important.'

Passmore nodded. 'This,' he went on, holding up the false tooth, 'is no ordinary denture. Well, it is, but there's one big difference. This is a coded denture.'

'What do you mean?'

'A number of dentists and technicians have taken to signing their work, so to speak, like painters and sculptors. Look here.'

Passmore prodded the denture with a pointed dental instrument, the one that always gave Banks the willies when he was in the chair. He looked closely at the pink plastic and saw a number of dark letters, which he couldn't quite make out.

'The code,' Passmore said. 'It's formed by typing the letters in a small print face on a piece of nylon, which you put between the mould and the plastic. During the manufacturing process, the nylon becomes incorporated into the denture and the numbers are clearly visible, as you can see.'

'Why do they go to such trouble?' Banks asked.

Passmore shrugged. 'For identification purposes in case of loss, or fire.'

'And what does the code tell us?'

Passmore puckered his mouth into a self-satisfied smile. 'Everything we need to know, Chief Inspector. Everything we need to know. Have a closer look.'

Banks used a pair of tweezers to pick up the denture and looked at the code: 5493BKJLS.

'The last two letters give us the city code, the ones before that are the dentist's initials, and the rest is for identification of the owner.'

'Amazing.' Banks put the false tooth down. 'So this will lead us to the identity of the victim?'

'Eventually. First, it'll lead us to his dentist.'

'How can I find out?'

'You'd consult the directory in the library. But, luckily, I have a copy here and I've done it for you.'

'And?'

Passmore smiled smugly again and held up a school-teacherly finger. 'Patience, Chief Inspector Banks, patience. First, the city. Do you recognize that postcode?'

'Yes. LS is Leeds.'

'Right. So the first thing we discover is that our man's dentist practises in Leeds. Next we look up the initials: BKJ. I found two possibilities there: Brian K. Jarrett and B. K. James.'

'We'll have to check them both,' Banks said. 'Can I use your phone?'

Passmore rubbed his upper lip. 'I, er, I already took the liberty. B. K. James doesn't do denture codes, according to his assistant, so I called Brian K. Jarrett.'

'And?'

Passmore grinned. 'The patient's name is Bernard Allen.'

'Certain?'

'He's the one who was fitted with the denture. It was about four years ago. I'll be sending down the charts for official confirmation, of course, but from what we were able to compare over the phone, I'd say you can be certain, yes.'

'Did you get an address?'

Passmore shook his head. 'Apparently Allen didn't live in Leeds. Mr Jarrett did give me the sister's address, though. Her name's Esther Haines. Is that of any use?'

'It certainly is.' Banks made a note of the first real lead so far. 'You've done a great job, Dr Passmore.' He stood up and shook hands.

Passmore inclined his head modestly. 'If ever you need my help again . . .'

TWO

Katie walked down to the shops in Lower Head later than usual that day. There was no road on her side of the beck, just a narrow path between the houses and the grassy bank. At the junction with the main Helmthorpe road, where the River Swain veered left into the dale proper, a small wooden bridge, painted white, led over to the village green with its trees and benches, and the path continued to the row of shops around the corner from the church.

As she neared the road, a grey Jaguar passed by with Stephen Collier behind the wheel. He slowed down at the intersection, and Katie became flustered. She half raised her hand to wave, but dropped it quickly. Stephen didn't acknowledge her presence at all; he seemed to be looking right through her. At first she told herself he hadn't seen her, but she knew he had. Perhaps he was thinking of something else and hadn't noticed his surroundings. She often walked around in a daze like that herself. The blood ran to her face as she crossed the road and hurried on to the shops.

'Afternoon, Katie love,' Mrs Thetford greeted her. 'A bit late today, aren't you? Still, I've saved you some nice Brussels sprouts.'

Katie thanked her and paid, her mind still on Stephen Collier. Why had he called last night when he knew Sam was out? Katie couldn't understand his desire to talk to her about his problems, or his apparent concern for her.

'Your change, dearie!' Mrs Thetford called after her.

Katie walked back to the counter and held out her hand, smiling. 'I'd forget my head if it was loose.'

She called at the butcher's and bought some pork loin chops, the best he had left, then turned back towards home. Stephen really had sounded as if he needed a friend. He had been tired, burdened. Katie regretted letting him down, but what else could she have done? She couldn't be his friend; she didn't know how. Besides, it wasn't right.

She noticed the speeding Mini just in time to dodge it and crossed the green again. A few people, mostly old women, sat on the benches nattering, and a light breeze rustled the new pale green leaves on the trees. What Stephen had said about her being unhappy was true. Was it so obvious to everyone, or did he really sense a bond between them? Surely with all his money and success he couldn't be unhappy too.

Katie tried to remember when she had last been happy, and thought of the first weeks in Swainshead. It had been hard work, fixing up the house, but they had done it. And what's more, they had done it together. After that though, when everything was ready, Sam left the running of it all to her. It was as if he'd finished his life's work and settled into early retirement.

'Ideas above his station,' her granny had always said of Sam. And sure enough, no sooner were they in residence than he was off to the White Rose ingratiating himself with the locals. As soon as he found out that the Colliers, who owned the big house over the road, were the dale's wealthiest and most powerful family, there was no stopping him. But give him his due, Katie thought, he never fawned or lowered himself; he just seemed to act as if he'd found his natural place in the order at last. Why they accepted him, if indeed they did, she had no idea.

When she wasn't busy running the guest house, Katie became an adornment, something for Sam to hang on his arm at the summer garden parties. She was a kind of Cinderella for whom the ball was always ending. But unlike the fairy-tale character, Katie hated both her roles. She had no love for gowns and glass slippers. Finery, however stylish and expensive, made her feel cheap and sinful. Once, a workmate fortunate enough to go on holiday to Paris had brought her back a pretty green silk scarf. Her granny had snipped it into pieces and scattered them like spring leaves into the fire.

Perhaps, though Katie hated to admit it, she had last been truly happy when her grandmother died. She and Sam hadn't seen much of the old woman after they went to live with his parents in Armley. They visited her in hospital though, where she lay dying of cancer of the colon, bearing all the pain and humiliation with the same hard courage as she had suffered life. She lay there, silver head against the white pillow, and would accept no comfort for what 'God's Will' was gracing her with. It was almost, Katie thought, as if she had found true joy in the final mutiny of the flesh, of its very cells, as if dying was proof to her that life on earth really was nothing but a vale of tears. But that couldn't be true, Katie realized, for her granny had never taken pleasure in anything in her life.

Katie fainted at her funeral and then gagged on the brandy the minister gave her to bring her round. Now all she had left of Granny was the heavy wooden cross on the living-room mantelpiece. A bare dark cross, with no representation of the crucified Christ (for such things smelled too much of popish idolatry for Granny), it symbolized perfectly the harsh arid life the old woman had chosen for herself and her granddaughter. Katie hated the thing, but she hadn't been able to pluck up the courage to throw it out. Outbreaks of boils and plagues of locusts would surely follow such a blasphemous act.

So Stephen Collier was right – she was unhappy. There was nothing anyone could do about it though, except perhaps . . . But no. She had a terrible feeling of apprehension about the future, certain that her only possible escape route was cut off now. Why she should feel that way she didn't know, but everyone was behaving oddly again – Stephen, Sam, John Fletcher. Could it really be a coincidence that Anne Ralston's name had been mentioned to her again so recently? And that so soon after it had come up, there had been another murder in the village?

Shuddering as if someone had just stepped over her grave, Katie walked back up the path and into the house to get on with cleaning the rooms.

THREE

After leaving the lab, Banks first drove into Wetherby and bought an *A to Z* street atlas of Leeds. He knew the city reasonably well, but had never been to Armley, where Allen's sister lived. He studied the area and planned a route over lunch in a small pub off the main street, where he ate a rather soupy lasagne and drank an excellent pint of Samuel Smith's Old Brewery Bitter.

He listened to the Donovan tape as he drove. Those old songs certainly brought back memories. Why did the past always seem so much brighter than the present? Because he had been more innocent then? Surely every childhood summer couldn't have been as sunny as he recalled. There must have been long periods of rain, just as there always seemed to be these days. What the hell, he thought, humming along with 'Teen Angel' as he drove – today's beautiful, enjoy the sun while it's here. Most of all, he wanted to put out of his mind for as long as possible what he would soon have to tell Bernard Allen's sister.

He lit a cigarette and turned on to the Leeds Inner Ring Road, which skirted the city centre by a system of yellow-lit tunnels affording occasional flashes into the open and glimpses of church spires, tower blocks and rows of dark terraced houses. It still felt warm, but the sun was now only a blurred pearl behind a thin grey gauze of cloud.

He came out on to Wellington Road, by the *Yorkshire Post* building, then crossed the River Aire and, immediately afterwards, the Leeds and Liverpool Canal.

There had been a great deal of development in the area, and one or two very colourful red-and-gold barges stood moored by the quay. But the river and canal banks were still very much of a wasteland: overgrown with weeds, littered with the tyres and old prams people had dumped there.

Many of the huge Victorian warehouses still hung on, crumbling and broken-windowed, their red brick blackened by the industrial smoke of a hundred years or more. It was a little like the Thames, Banks thought, where old wharfs and warehouses, like the warrens where Fagin had run his band of child-thieves, were daily being converted into luxury apartment complexes, artists' studios and office space. Because Leeds was in the depressed and abandoned North though, the process of regeneration would probably take quite a bit longer, if indeed it ever happened at all.

Skilfully navigating the lanes of traffic and a huge roundabout, Banks managed to get on Armley Road. Soon he was at the bottom of Town Street, where the road swung right, past the park, to Bramley and Stanningley. He turned left up Crab Lane, a narrow winding one-way street by a small housing estate built on a hill, and parked on the street near the library.

Banks soon found Esther Haines's house. It had a blue door, freshly painted by the look of it. In the garden was an overturned plastic tricycle, green with thick yellow wheels.

Banks pressed the bell and a thin-faced woman answered. She was perhaps in her late twenties, but she seemed haggard and tired. Judging from the noise inside the house, Banks guessed that the cares of motherhood had worn her down. She frowned at him and he showed her his identification card. Immediately, she turned pale and invited him in. For people on estates like this, Banks realized, a visit from the police always means bad news. He felt his stomach muscles tighten as he walked inside.

In the living room, cluttered with children's toys, Mrs Haines had already sat down. Hands clasped in her lap, she perched on the edge of her seat on the sofa. A dark-haired man came through from the kitchen, and she introduced him as her husband, Les. He was wearing only vest and trousers. His shoulders and chest were matted with thick black hair, and he had a tattoo of a butterfly on his right bicep.

'We were just having our tea,' Esther Haines said. 'Les is on the night shift at the yeast factory.'

'Aye,' her husband said, pulling up a chair and facing Banks aggressively. 'What's all this about?'

A child with jam smeared all over his pale grinning face crawled through the open kitchen door and busied himself trying to tear apart a fluffy toy dog.

'I'm sorry,' Banks said, 'but I've got some bad news for you.'

And the rest followed as it always did: disbelief, denial, shock, tears and finally a kind of numb acceptance. Banks was relieved to see that the first thing Mr Haines did was light a cigarette. He followed suit. Esther clutched a handkerchief to her nose. Her husband went to make tea and took the child with him.

After Mr Haines had brought in the teapot and cups, leaving the child to play in the kitchen, Banks leaned forward in his seat and said to Esther, 'There are some questions I've got to ask.'

She nodded. 'Are you sure?' she said. 'Are you sure it's our Bernie?'

'As sure as we can be at this point,' Banks told her. He didn't want to have to tell her what state her brother's corpse had been in. 'Your answers will help us a lot. When did you last see him?'

'It was a couple of weeks ago, now,' she said. 'He stayed with us a week.'

'Can you find out the exact date he left here, Mrs Haines? It's important.'

Her husband walked over to a calendar of Canadian scenes and ran a stubby finger along the squares. 'It was the thirteenth,' he said, then looked over at Esther. 'Remember, love, that morning he went to the dentist's for that filling he needed?'

Mrs Haines nodded.

'Did he leave immediately after his visit to Mr Jarrett's?'

'Yes,' said Les Haines. 'He was heading for the Dales, so he had to be off about eleven. He was after taking one of them trains on the Settle–Carlisle route.'

'And that was the last time either of you saw him, at eleven o'clock on May the thirteenth?'

They both nodded.

'Do you know where he was going?'

'Of course,' Esther said. 'He were off back to Swainshead.'

'Going back? I don't understand. Is that where he was before he came to stay with you?'

'No, it's where he grew up; it's where we used to live.'

Now Banks remembered where he'd heard the name before. Allen. Nicholas Collier had directed Gristhorpe and himself to the ruins of Archie Allen's old farmhouse high on the side of Swainshead Fell.

'Is your father Archie Allen?' he asked.

'Yes, that's right.'

'And you lived on the fell side, worked a farm?'

'Until it went belly up,' Mr Haines cut in.

'Did you live there too?' Banks asked him.

'Me? No. Leeds born and bred. But the missus grew up there.'

'How long ago was this, Mrs Haines?' Banks asked Esther, who had started weeping quietly again.

'It's ten years since we moved, now.'

'And you came straight here?'

'Not until Les and I got married. We lived in an old back-to-back off Tong Road. It's not far away. Dad got a job at Blakey's Castings. It were all he could get. Then they went to Melbourne – Australia, like – to go and live with our Denny after they retired. Oh God, somebody'll have to tell Mum and Dad.' She looked beseechingly at her husband, who patted her arm. 'Don't worry about that, love,' he said. 'It'll keep a while.'

'As far as I can gather,' Banks said when Mrs Haines had regained her composure, 'your brother had some connection with Toronto in Canada. Is that right?'

She nodded. 'He couldn't get a job over here. He was a

bright lad, our Bernie. Got a degree. But there was no jobs. He emigrated eight years ago.'

'What did he do in Toronto?'

'He's a teacher in a college. Teaching English. It's a good job. We was off out to see him next year.'

Banks lit another cigarette as she wiped away the tears and blew her nose.

'Can you give me his address?'

She nodded and said, 'Be a love, Les.' Her husband went to the sideboard and brought out a tattered Woolworth's address book.

'How often did Bernard come home?' Banks asked, writing down the Toronto address.

'Well, he came as often as he could. This was his third trip, but he hadn't been for four years. Proper homesick he was.'

'Why did he stay in Canada, then?'

She shrugged. 'Money. No work for him here, is there? Not with Thatcher running the country.'

'What did he talk about while he was with you?'

'Nothing really. Just family things.'

'Did he say anything odd to you, Mr Haines? Anything that struck you as unusual?'

'No. We didn't talk a lot. We'd not much in common really. I'm not a great reader, never did well at school. And he liked his books, did Bernie. We talked about ale a bit. About what the boozers are like over there. He told me he'd found a nice pub in Toronto where he could get John Smith's and Tartan on draught.'

'Is that all?'

Haines shrugged. 'Like I said, we didn't have much in common.'

Banks turned to Mrs Haines again. 'What state of mind

was he in? Was he upset about anything, depressed?'

'He'd just got divorced about a year ago,' she said, 'and he were a bit upset about that. I think that's what made him homesick. But I wouldn't say he were really depressed, no. He seemed to think he might be able to come back and live here again before too long.'

'Did he say anything about a job?'

'No.'

'How could he manage to move back here then?'

Esther Haines shook her head. 'I don't know. He didn't say. He just hinted. Maybe it were wishful thinking, like, now he didn't have Barbara any more.'

'That was his wife?'

'Yes.'

'What happened between them?'

'She ran off wi' another man.'

'Where had Bernie been before he visited you?'

Esther took a deep breath and dabbed at her red eyes. 'He'd come to England for a month, all told,' she said. 'First off, he spent a week seeing friends in London and Bristol, then he came up here. He'd be due to go back about now, wouldn't he, Les?'

'Do you know how to get in touch with these friends?' Banks asked.

She shook her head. 'Sorry. They were friends of Bernie's from university.'

'Which university?'

'York.'

'And you didn't know them?'

'No. They'd be in his notebook. He always carried a notebook full of names and stuff.'

'We didn't find it. Never mind, we'll find them somehow.' If necessary, Banks knew he could check with the university authorities and track down Bernard Allen's contemporaries. 'Do you know where he was heading after Swainshead?'

'He were going to see another friend in Edinburgh, then fly back from Prestwick. You can do that with Wardair, he said, fly to London and go back from somewhere else.' She put her handkerchief to her nose again and sniffed.

'I don't suppose you have this person's address in Edinburgh?'

She shook her head.

'So,' Banks said, stubbing out his cigarette and reaching for the tea, 'he left here on May the thirteenth to do some fell-walking in the Dales, and then—'

Mrs Haines cut in. 'No, that's not right. That's not the reason he went.'

'Why did he go, then? Sentimental reasons?'

'Partly, I suppose. But he went to stay with friends.'

'What friends?'

'Sam and Katie. They run a guest house – Greenock's. Bernie was going to stay with Sam and Katie.'

Struggling to keep his excitement and surprise to himself, Banks asked how Bernard had got to know Sam and Katie. At first, Mrs Haines seemed unable to concentrate for weeping, but Banks encouraged her gently, and soon she was telling him the whole story, pulling at the handkerchief on her lap as she spoke.

'They knew each other from Armley, from after we came to Leeds. Sam lived there, too. We were neighbours. Bernie was always going on about Swainshead and how wonderful it was, and I think it were him as put the idea into Sam's head. Anyways, Sam and Katie scrimped and saved and that's where they ended up.'

'Did Bernie have any other close friends in Swainshead?'

'Not really,' Esther said. 'Most of his childhood mates had moved away. There weren't any jobs for them up there.'

'How did he get on with the Colliers?'

'A bit above our station,' Esther said. 'Oh, they'd say hello, but they weren't friends of his, not as far as I know. You can't be, can you, not with the sons of the fellow what owns your land?'

'I suppose not,' Banks said. 'Was there any bitterness over losing the farm?'

'I wouldn't say that, no. Sadness, yes, but bitterness? No. It were us own fault. There wasn't much land fit for anything but sheep, and when the flock took sick . . .'

'What was Mr Collier's attitude?'

'Mr Walter?'

'Yes.'

'He were right sorry for us. He helped out as much as he could, but it were no use. He were preparing to sell off to John Fletcher anyway. Getting out of farming, he were.'

'How would that have affected you?'

'What do you mean?'

'The sale.'

'Oh. Mr Walter said he'd write it into the terms that we could stay. John Fletcher didn't mind. He and Dad got on quite well.'

'So there was no ill feeling between your family and John Fletcher or the Colliers?'

'No. Not to speak of. But I didn't think much of them.'

'Oh?'

She pulled harder at the handkerchief on her lap, and it began to tear along one edge. 'I always thought they were a pair of right toffee-nosed gits, but I never said nowt.

Stephen thinks he's God's gift to women, and that Nicholas is a bit doolally, if you ask me.'

'In what way?'

'Have you met him?'

'Yes.'

'He's like a little kid, gets all overexcited. Especially when he's had a drink or two. Practically slavers all over a person, he does. Especially women. He even tried it on with me once, but I sent him away with his tail between his legs.' She shuddered. 'I don't know how they put up with him at that there school, unless they're all a bit that way.'

'What about Stephen?'

Esther shrugged. 'Seems a pleasant enough gent on the outside. Bit of a smoothie, really. Got a lot more class than his brother. Bit two-faced, though.'

'In what way?'

'You know. All friendly one minute, then cuts you dead next time he sees you. But they can afford to do that, can't they?'

'Who can?'

'Rich folks. Don't have to live like ordinary people, like you and me, do they?'

'I don't imagine they have the same priorities, no,' Banks said, unsure whether he approved of being called an ordinary person. 'Did he try it on too?'

'Mr Stephen? No. Oh, he liked the girls, all right, but he was too much of a gentleman, for all his faults.'

Mrs Haines seemed to have forgotten her grief for a few moments, so absorbed had she been in the past, but as soon as silence fell, her tears began to flow again and her husband put his arm around her. In the kitchen, something smashed, and the child ran wailing into the room and buried his jammy face in Esther Haines's lap.

Banks stood up. 'You've been very helpful,' he said. 'I'm sorry to have been the bearer of such bad news.'

Esther nodded, handkerchief pressed to her mouth, and Mr Haines showed him to the door. 'What are we to do about . . . you know . . .'

'The remains?'

'Aye.'

'We'll be in touch soon,' Banks said. 'Don't worry.'

Upstairs, a baby started crying.

The first thing Banks did was look for a phone box to call Sandra and tell her when he'd be back. That didn't prove as easy as it sounded. The first three he came across had been vandalized, and he had to drive almost two miles before he found one that worked.

It was a pleasant drive back to Eastvale through Harrogate and Ripon. In a quiet mood, he slipped in Delius's *North Country Sketches* instead of the 1960s pop he'd been listening to. As he drove, he tried to piece together all the information he'd got that day. Whichever way he looked at it, the trail led back to Swainshead, the Greenocks, the Colliers and John Fletcher.

5

ONE

Only the cry of a distant curlew and the sound of water gurgling over rocks in the stream at the back broke the silence.

Then Sam Greenock echoed the news: 'Bernie? Dead? I can't believe it.'

'I'm afraid so,' Banks said. It was the second time in two days that he had been the bearer of bad news, but this time it was easier. The investigation proper had begun, and he had more on his mind than Sam Greenock's disbelief, real or feigned.

They sat in the living room at the back of the house: the Greenocks, Banks, and Sergeant Hatchley taking notes. Katie gazed out of the window, or sometimes she stared at the huge ugly wooden cross on the mantelpiece. She had said nothing, given no reaction at all.

'It's true he was staying with you then, is it?' Banks asked.

Sam nodded.

'Why didn't his name show up on the register? We went to a lot of trouble checking every place in Swainsdale.'

'It's not my fault,' Sam said. 'He was staying with us as a friend. Besides, you know as well as I do that those guest books aren't legal requirements; they're only for people to write comments in if they want, show they've been here.'

'When our man called and asked if you'd had any Canadians staying recently, why didn't you mention Bernard Allen?'

'He didn't ask me anything. He just looked at the register. Besides, I never thought of Bernie as a Canadian. Oh, I know he lived there, but that's not everything, is it? I've known people who lived in Saudi Arabia for a year working on the oil fields but I don't think of them as Saudis.'

'Come off it, Sam. Bernard Allen had been in Canada for eight years, and you hadn't seen him for four. This was only his third trip back,' said Banks.

'Still . . .'

'Did you have any reason to lie about Bernie being here?'

'No. I told you—'

'Because if you did, we can charge you with concealing information. That's serious, Sam. You could get two years.'

Sam leaned forward. 'Look, I never thought. That policeman who came, he didn't tell us what he was looking for.'

'We can check, you know.'

'Bloody check then. It's true.'

Sam couldn't remember the officer's name, so Banks asked Hatchley to make a note of the time and date. It would be easy enough to find out who had made the visit and what approach he had taken. He still wasn't sure about Sam Greenock, though.

Banks sighed. 'All right. We'll leave that for now. Which room did he stay in?'

Sam looked at Katie. She was staring out on the fell side, so he had to nudge her and repeat the question.

'Five,' she said, as if speaking from a great distance. 'Room five.'

'We'll need to have a look,' Banks told her.

'It was two weeks ago,' Sam said. 'There's been other people in since then. That's where we took Fellowes after he'd found the body.'

'We'll still need to look.'

'Do you think he's hidden some secret message there, Inspector? Taped it to the bottom of the dresser drawer, maybe?'

'You've been reading too many espionage novels. And if I were you, I'd cut the bloody sarcasm. You might start me thinking that there's some reason you don't want me to look in Bernie Allen's room. And while we're at it, he's not the first person to get killed after leaving this guest house, is he, Sam?'

'Now wait a minute,' said Sam. 'If you're trying to imply—'

Banks held his hand up. 'I'm not trying to imply anything. What was it the man said: once is happenstance, twice is coincidence? Let's just hope there's not a third time.'

Sam put his head in his hands and rubbed his eyes. 'I'm sorry,' he said. 'Really, I am. It's the shock. And now all these questions.'

'Look at it from my point of view, Sam. Bernard Allen was killed after he left your guest house. That's given his killer about two whole weeks to cover his tracks, leave the country, arrange for an alibi, whatever. I need everything I can get, and I need it quickly. And the last thing I need is some clever bugger who just might have been withholding information to start playing the comic.'

'Look, I've said I'm sorry. What more do you want?'

'First of all, you can tell us when he left.'

'About two weeks ago.'

'Can you be more specific?'

'Katie?'

Again, with great difficulty, Katie turned her attention to the people in the room. Banks repeated his question.

'It was a Friday,' she said.

Hatchley checked the dates against his diary. 'That'd be the seventeenth, sir,' he said. 'Friday. May the seventeenth.'

'What time?'

'Just after breakfast. About nine thirty. He said he wanted to get an early start,' Sam said.

'Where was he going?'

'He was heading for the Pennine Way, then up to Swaledale.'

'Do you know where he was intending to stay?'

Sam shook his head. 'No. He just said he'd find somewhere on the way. There are plenty of places; it's a very popular route.'

'Did he say anything to you about visiting the hanging valley on his way?'

'No. I wouldn't have been surprised, though. He used to play there when he was a kid, or so he said.'

'What did you do after he'd gone?'

'I drove to Eastvale to do some shopping. I always do on a Friday morning.'

'What shops did you go to?'

'What is this? Are you trying to tell me I'm a suspect in the murder of my friend?'

'Just answer the bloody question.'

'All right, Inspector, there's no—'

'It's Chief Inspector.' Banks didn't usually pull his rank,

but Sam Greenock had rubbed him up the wrong way.

'Chief Inspector, then. Where did I go? I went to Carter's for some seeds, peat moss and fertilizer. Katie's trying to get a vegetable patch going in the back garden. It'll save us a bit of money in the long run.'

'Is that all?'

'No. But they'll remember me there. I called in at a newsagent's for some magazines – that one on King Street opposite the school road.'

'I know it.'

'I'm a regular there, too.'

'Thanks, that'll do fine for a start. What kind of car do you drive?'

'A Land Rover. It's in the garage.'

'And you, Mrs Greenock, what did you do after Bernard Allen left?'

'Me? Housework. What else?'

Banks turned back to Sam. 'You met Allen in Leeds about ten years ago, is that right?'

'Yes. In Armley. We lived just off Tong Road and the Allens came to live next door after they gave up the farm. Bernie and I were about the same age, so we palled up.'

'What was he doing then?'

'Just finishing at university. It was only York, so he was home most weekends and holidays. We used to go for a jar or two every Saturday night.'

'How did the family take the move?'

Sam shrugged. 'They adapted. At first Mr Allen, Bernie's dad, went around as if he'd been kicked out of paradise. It must have been very hard for him though, swapping farm work for a crummy factory job. Hard on the pride.'

'Is that what he said?'

'Never in so many words, no. You could just tell. He's a tough old bird anyway, so they survived.'

'And Bernard?'

'He tried to fit in. But you know what it's like. He got his degree and all, but he couldn't get the kind of work he wanted. He lived at home and did all kinds of odd jobs – mushroom picking at Greenhill Nurseries, sweeping factory yards, production line . . . all dull routine work.'

'Is that when he decided to go to Canada?'

'After a year or so of it, yes. He'd had enough. Someone he knew from university had already gone over and said it wasn't too hard to get teaching jobs in the colleges. He said they paid well, too.'

'Who was this?'

'His name was Bob Morgan. I think he and Bernie taught at the same place, Toronto Community College.'

'Was Bernie homesick?'

'I suppose so. I mean, you don't forget your roots, do you? But he stayed. One thing leads to another. He made friends over there, got married, divorced.'

'What was his state of mind while he was staying here?'

'He was fine. Cheerful. Happy to be back.'

'Did he talk about coming home to stay?'

Sam shook his head. 'He knew better than that. There aren't any jobs for him.'

'So he didn't seem unusually homesick or depressed, and he didn't say he was planning to come back.'

'No.'

Banks lit a cigarette and studied Katie's profile. She was a blank; he had no idea what she was thinking.

'How long have you been in Swainshead?' he asked Sam.

'Six years.'

'And it's going well?'

Sam nodded. 'Can't complain. We're hardly million-aires, but we like the life.'

'And you, Mrs Greenock?'

Katie turned and focused on him. 'Yes. It's better than cleaning rooms at the Queen's Hotel.'

'Did Bernie have any other friends in the village apart from you?'

'Not really,' Sam answered. 'See, most of the kids he grew up with had moved away. A lot do these days. They see the good life on telly and soon as they're old enough there's no stopping them. Like Denny, Bernie's older brother. Off to Australia like a shot, he was.'

'Was Bernie friendly with the Colliers?' Esther Haines had said not, but Banks thought she might have been prejudiced by her own opinions of Nicholas and Stephen.

'Well, I'd hardly say they were friends. Acquaintances, more like. But we had an evening or two in the White Rose together. I think Bernie was always a bit uncomfortable around Stephen and Nick though, them having been his landlords so to speak, the local gentry and all.'

Banks nodded. 'Can you think of anyone in the village who might have wanted him out of the way?'

'Bernie? Good Lord, no.'

'He had no enemies?'

'None that I know of. Not here.'

'What about in Leeds?'

'Not there either, as far as I know. Maybe somebody followed him over from Canada, an enemy he'd made there?'

'Mrs Greenock,' Banks said, turning to Katie again, 'do you know of anyone with a reason for getting rid of Bernard Allen?'

Katie hesitated before answering. 'No. He was harmless. Just a friendly sort of person. Nobody would want to hurt him.'

'One more thing: what was he carrying when he left here?'

'Carrying?' Sam said. 'Oh, I see. His belongings. A big blue rucksack with his clothes, passport, money, a few books.'

'And what was he wearing?'

'I don't really remember. Do you, Katie?'

Katie shook her head. 'It was a warm day, though,' she said. 'That I do remember. I think he was just wearing an open-necked shirt. White. And trousers, not jeans. It's only the amateurs wear jeans for walking.'

'They're too heavy, you see,' Sam explained. 'Especially if they get wet. We try to give a bit of advice to our guests sometimes, and we always make sure we know where they're going if they're due back in the evening. That way, if they don't return, we can let the Mountain Rescue post know where they were heading.'

Banks nodded. 'Very sensible. Have you any vacancies at the moment?'

'I think so,' Sam said.

'Six and eight,' Katie added.

'Good, we'll take them.'

'You're staying here?'

'There'll be quite a lot of questions to ask in Swainshead,' Banks said, 'and it's fifty miles to Eastvale and back. We'll be staying here tonight at least.'

'One's a single,' Katie said. 'The other's a double.'

Banks smiled at her. 'Fine. Sergeant Hatchley will take the single.' It was patently unfair, Banks knew. He was much more slightly built than the well padded Hatchley, and a good four or five inches shorter. But rank, he reflected, did have its privileges.

'Don't sulk, Sergeant,' he said as they walked over to the car to pick up their overnight bags. 'My room might be bigger, but it's probably right next to the plumbing. What did you think of Mrs Greenock?'

'Not bad if you like those wand-like figures,' Hatchley said. 'Prefer 'em with a bit of meat on their bones, myself.'

'I wasn't asking you to rate her out of ten on looks. What about her attitude?'

'Didn't say much, did she? Seemed in a bit of a daze to me. Think there might be more to her than meets the eye?'

'I think there might indeed,' said Banks. 'In fact, I got the distinct impression that she was holding something back.'

TWO

The Greenocks ate their lunch in silence, then Sam dashed out. Katie, who had lost her appetite and merely played with her food, piled the dishes in the washer, set the controls and turned it on. There was still shopping to do and the evening meal to prepare, but she felt she could afford to relax for a few minutes.

As she lay down on the sofa and looked out on the slopes of Swainshead Fell beyond the back garden, she thought of Bernie helping her clear the dishes, talking about Toronto, watching cricket on the telly. She remembered the little presents he had brought each time – no doubt picked up at the airport at the last minute, for Bernie was like that – jars of pure maple syrup, a box of cigars or a bottle of malt Scotch for Sam, Opium perfume or Chanel

No. 5 for Katie. She'd never had the heart to tell him that she didn't wear perfume, that the one time she had tried she had felt like a tramp, even though it had been White Linen, and had scrubbed it off straight away. Now the three little bottles lay in the dark inside her dresser drawer, untouched.

Bernie had even helped her with the garden sometimes; he might not have had green fingers, but he could wield a trowel or a hoe well enough. Bernie: so considerate, so kind. But the dark images began to crowd out her thoughts. Frowning, she pushed them away. Instead she saw endless prairies of golden wheat swaying in the breeze, heard the sea beating against a rough coastline where redwood forests reared as tall as the sky. Bernie had told her all about Canada, all the places he'd been. She'd never get to see them now, she realized, because Bernie was dead.

Fellowes' words came back to her, what he'd said in his drunken stupor when he grasped her hand by the bed: 'Moving,' he'd said. 'Moving.' And she hadn't understood at the time. Now she did. If Bernie had been lying up there for two weeks he would have been like that dead lamb she had seen on Adam's Fell last year. It didn't bear thinking about.

She'd given a bad impression to the police, she knew that, but at the time she had been unable to help herself. The lean dark one, the one who seemed too short to be a policeman, would want to talk to her again, that was for sure. How could she keep her secret? She pictured her grandmother standing over her, lined face stern and hard, eyes like black pinheads boring into her. 'Secrets, girl, secrets are the devil's doing. God loves a pure and open heart.' But she had to keep this secret.

There were so many things, it seemed, one had to do in

life that went against God's commandments. How could a person live without sinning? She was no longer even sure that she knew what was right or wrong. Sometimes she thought it was a sin to breathe, to be alive. It seemed you had to sin to survive in today's world. It was wrong to keep secrets and tell lies; but was it wrong to keep your word, your promise? And if you had broken it once for a special reason, was it all right to break it again?

Wearily, Katie got up and prepared to go to the shops down in Lower Head. Work and duty, they were the only constants in life. Everything else was a trap, a trick, a temptation to betrayal. The only way to survive was to shun pleasure. She picked up her purse and shopping basket and pulled a face at the nasty soap taste in her mouth as she left the house.

THREE

After Banks and Hatchley had carried their bags to their rooms, they walked over to the White Rose for lunch. The place was busy with Saturday tourists who had let their curiosity lead them to the northern part of Swainshead, but none of the regulars was present. Luckily, Freddie Metcalfe was too busy to chat. They both ordered gammon and chips and carried their pints over to a corner table.

'I want you to get on to Richmond after lunch,' Banks said, 'and have him check to see if anyone in Swainshead has connections with Canada, specifically with Toronto. I know it sounds like a big job, but tell him to start with the people we already know: the Greenocks, Fletcher, the Colliers. You might also add,' he said, lowering his voice, 'Freddie Metcalfe over there, and Neil Fellowes too.'

'The bloke who found the body? But he's from Pontefract.'

'No matter. Remember, we thought Allen was from Canada at first, then from Leeds. And while we're on the subject, have him check on the brother-in-law, Les Haines. I want to know if he's made any trips to this area in the past few weeks. Ask him to get as much background as he can on all of them. I'm sure the superintendent will be able to get him some help from downstairs. And get someone to go to Carter's and that newsagent's to check Greenock's alibi. Tell them to make sure they get the times as exact as possible.'

'Don't you believe him?'

Banks shrugged. 'He could be telling the truth. He could also have driven to a convenient spot along the main road and approached the valley from the other side.'

The little waitress brought over their food and they ate in silence. At the bar they could hear Freddie Metcalfe enthralling visitors with examples of Yorkshire humour filched from *The Dalesman*, and at the next table two middle-aged women from Lancashire were talking about lager louts: 'They get right confident after a few drinks, young 'uns do.'

When they had finished eating, Banks sent Hatchley to radio in to Richmond, then he stood outside the pub for a moment and took a deep breath of fresh air. It was June 1, another fine day. Nobody knew what the Dales had done to deserve such a long stretch of good weather, but according to a radio Banks overheard, it certainly wasn't any thanks to Yorkshire County Cricket Club, currently 74 for 6 at Somerset.

Banks wanted to talk to the Colliers, but first he returned to his room to change his shirt. On his way back down, he spotted Mrs Greenock in the hall, but she seemed to see or hear him coming and scuttled off into the back before he could catch her. Smiling, he walked back out into the street. He knew he could have followed her and confronted her with his suspicions there and then, but decided instead to let her play mouse to his cat until she tired of it.

There were plenty of people on the grassy banks of the River Swain that afternoon. Three children fished for tiddlers with nets at the end of cane rods while their parents sat and watched from deckchairs, dad with a knotted handkerchief over his head reading the *Daily Mail* and mum knitting, glancing up occasionally to make sure the offspring were still in sight.

The Dales were getting as crowded and noisy as the coast, Banks thought as he crossed the bridge. There was even a small group of teenagers farther down, towards Lower Head, wearing cut-off denim jackets with the names of rock bands inked on the back. Two of them, a boy and a girl, Banks assumed, were rolling on the grass in an overtly sexual embrace while tinny music rattled out of a portable stereo placed close to one prostrate youth's ear.

Many of his colleagues, Banks knew, would have gone over and told them to move on, accused them of disturbing the peace and searched them for drugs. But despite his personal distaste for some gangs of youngsters and their music, Banks made it a rule never to use his power as a policeman to force his own will on the general public. After all, they were young, they were enjoying life, and apart from the noise, they were really doing no one any harm.

Banks passed the old men on the bridge and made a

mental note to have a chat with them at some point. They seemed to be permanent fixtures; maybe they had seen something.

He met Sergeant Hatchley at the car and they headed for the Collier house.

'Have you noticed,' Banks said, 'how Allen seemed to have a different story for everyone he talked to? He was upset; he was cheerful. He was coming home; he wasn't.'

'Maybe,' said Hatchley, 'it's just that all the people he talked to have a different story for us.'

Banks gave the sergeant an appreciative glance. Thinking things out wasn't Hatchley's strong point, but there were times when he could be quite surprising.

'Good point,' Banks said. 'Let's see what the Colliers have to add.'

Gristhorpe was right; the Collier house was a Victorian monstrosity. But it had its own grotesque charm, Banks thought as he walked up the crazy paving with Hatchley. Most Dales architecture was practical in nature and plain in style, but this place was for show. It must have been the great-grandfather who had it built, and he must have thought highly indeed of the Collier status.

Banks rang the bell on the panelled door and Stephen Collier answered, a frown on his face. He led them through a high-ceilinged hall into a sitting room at the back of the house. French windows opened on to a patio. In the centre of the large lawn stood an elaborate stone fountain. White dolphins and cherubim curled about the lip of the bowl.

The room itself contrasted sharply with the exterior of the house. Off-white walls created a sense of light and space on which the ultra-modern Swedish pine and chrome and glass furnishings made hardly any encroachment at all. Abstract paintings hung over a blue-tiled mantelpiece:

bold and violent splashes of colour reminiscent, in their effect on Banks's eyes, of the Jackson Pollocks Sandra had insisted he look at in a London gallery years ago.

The three of them sat in white wicker chairs around a table on the patio. Banks half-expected a servant to arrive with a tray of margaritas or martinis, but Collier himself offered them drinks. It was warm, so both men eagerly accepted a cold bottle of Beck's lager.

Before he went to fetch the drinks, Stephen Collier rapped on the French windows of the next room and beckoned to Nicholas. Banks had wanted to talk to them separately, but it wasn't important at this point. Stretching, he got up and walked over as Nicholas emerged on to his half of the patio. He was just in time to catch a glimpse of a much darker room, all oak panelling, leather-bound books and oil paintings of ancestors gleaming on the walls.

Nicholas smiled his horsy yellow smile and held out his hand.

'It's an interesting set-up you've got here,' Banks said.

'Yes. We couldn't bear to get rid of the house, however ugly it might seem from the outside. It's been in the family for years. Lord knows what prompted my great-great-grandfather to build such a folly – ostentatious display of wealth and position, I suppose. And it's so inappropriate for the area.' Despite the deprecating tone, Banks could tell that Nicholas was proud of the house and the status of his family.

'Do you share the place?' Banks asked Nicholas after they had sat down at the table.

'Sort of. It's divided into two halves. We thought at first that one of us could take the upstairs and the other the downstairs, but it's better like this. We've got the equivalent of two completely separate houses. Stephen and I have very different tastes, so the two halves make quite a contrast. You must let me show you round my half one day.'

Stephen returned with the drinks. Dressed all in white, he looked like a cricketer breaking for tea. Nicholas, however, with his slight stoop, pale complexion and comma of black hair over his forehead, looked more like an ageing umpire. It was hard to believe these two were brothers; even harder to accept that Stephen was the elder.

After giving both of them time to register surprise and shock at the news of Bernard Allen's death, of which he was certain they knew already, Banks lit a cigarette and asked, 'Did you see much of him while he was here?'

'Not a lot,' Stephen answered. 'He was in the pub a couple of times with Sam, so naturally we talked, but that's about all.'

'What did you talk about?'

'Oh, just small talk, really. This and that. About Canada, places we'd both been to.'

'You've visited Canada?'

'I travel quite a bit,' Stephen said. 'You might think a small food-freezing plant in the Dales isn't much, but there are other businesses connected. Import, export, that kind of thing. Yes, I've been to Canada a few times.'

'Toronto?'

'No. Montreal, as a matter of fact.'

'Did you ever see Bernard Allen over there?'

'It's a big country, Chief Inspector.'

'Did you get the impression that anything was bothering Allen while he was over here?'

'No.'

'What about you?' he asked Nicholas.

'No, I can't say I did. I've always found it a bit awkward

talking to Bernard, to tell you the truth. One always feels he has a bit of a chip on his shoulder.'

'What do you mean?'

'Oh, come on,' Nicholas said, grinning. 'Surely you know what I mean. His father spent his life working on land rented from my father. They were poor. From where they lived they had a fine enough view of this place, and you can't tell me that Bernard never thought it unfair that we had so much and he had so little. Especially when his father failed.'

'I didn't know Bernard Allen or his father,' Banks said, peeling the foil from the neck of the Beck's, which he preferred to drink straight from the bottle. 'Tell me about him.'

'I'm not saying I knew him well myself, only that he became a bit of a lefty, a socialist. Up the workers and all that.' Nicholas grinned again, showing his stained teeth. His eyes were especially bright.

'Are you saying that Bernard Allen was a communist?'

'I don't know about that. I don't know if he was a party member. All I know is he used to spout his leftist rot in the pub.'

'Is this true?' Banks asked Stephen.

'Partly. My brother exaggerates a bit, Chief Inspector. It's a tendency he has. We sometimes had arguments about politics, yes, and Bernard Allen had left-wing views. But that's as far as it goes. I'd hardly say he was a proselytizer or that he toed some party line.'

'His political opinions weren't particularly strong, then?'

'I wouldn't say so, no. He said he left the country partly because Margaret Thatcher came into office. Well, we all know about unemployment, don't we? Bernard couldn't find work in England, so he left. You could hardly say he was running from country to country to escape political tyranny, could you?'

'He just used to whine about it, that's all,' Nicholas cut in. 'Expected the government to do everything for him without him having to lift a finger. Typical socialist.'

'As you can gather, Chief Inspector,' Stephen said with a strained smile, 'my brother's something of a young fogey. That hardly gave either of us reason to do away with Bernard, though.'

'Of course not,' Banks said. 'And I was never suggesting it did. I just want to know as much about the victim as possible. Would you say that there was any real animosity between you – political arguments aside – over the farm?'

'Do you mean did he blame us?' Stephen asked.

'Yes.'

'He blamed everyone but himself,' Nicholas cut in.

Stephen turned on him. 'Oh, shut up, Nicky. You're being bloody awkward, you know.'

'Did he?' Banks asked Stephen again.

'Not that I ever knew of. It was nothing to do with us, really. As you know, Father was preparing to give up farming anyway, and he certainly hadn't groomed us to take over. Nobody kicked Archie Allen off the land. He could have stayed there as long as he wanted to. It just wasn't financially viable any more. Ask any farmer; they'll tell you how things have changed over the past twenty years or so. If Bernard was holding a grudge, then it was a very unreasonable one. He didn't strike me as an unreasonable person. Does that answer your question?'

'Yes, thank you,' Banks said. He turned to Nicholas again. 'I understand you knew Mr Allen's sister, Esther.'

Nicholas reddened with anger. 'Who said that?'

'Never mind who said it. Is it true?'

'We all knew her,' Stephen said. 'I mean, we knew who she was.'

'More than that,' Banks said, looking at Nicholas, whose eyes were flashing. 'Nicholas knows what I mean, don't you?'

'Don't be ridiculous,' Nicholas said. 'Are you trying to suggest that there was anything more to it than a landlord–tenant relationship?'

'Was there?'

'Of course not.'

'Didn't you find her attractive?'

'She was hardly my type.'

'Do you mean she was of a lower class?'

Nicholas bared his teeth in a particularly unpleasant smile. 'If you want to put it that way, yes.'

'And what about the servant girl? The one who used to work here.'

'I insist you stop this at once, Chief Inspector,' Stephen said. 'I can't see how it's relevant. And I'm sure I don't have to remind you that the deputy chief constable is a good friend of the family.'

'I'm sure he is,' Banks said. He wasn't at all put out; in fact, he was enjoying their discomfort tremendously. 'Just a couple of minor points, then we'll be on our way. When was the last time you saw Bernard?'

Nicholas said nothing; he appeared to be sulking. Stephen paused for a moment and answered in a business-like manner, 'I'd say it was in the White Rose the evening before he left. Thursday. I remember talking to him about Tan Hill in Swaledale.'

'Is that where he was heading?'

'Not specifically, no, but it's on the Pennine Way.'

'Did he talk about the hanging valley at all, the place where his body was found?'

'No, not that I remember.'

'Did either of you see him set off from Swainshead?'

Both the Colliers shook their heads. 'I'm usually at the office before nine,' Stephen said. 'And my brother would have been at Braughtmore.'

'So you saw nothing of him after that Thursday evening in the White Rose?'

'Nothing.'

'Just one more thing: could you tell us where John Fletcher lives?'

'John? He's a couple of miles north of the village. It's a big farmhouse on the eastern fell side. You can't miss it; it's the only one in sight.'

'Fine, then.' Banks nodded to Hatchley and they stood up to leave. Stephen Collier led them out and Nicholas followed, still sulking. As soon as the door closed, Banks could hear them start arguing.

Hatchley turned up his nose in disgust. 'What a pair of wankers,' he said.

'Aptly put,' said Banks. 'But we did learn a few things.'

'Like what?'

'I never told them what time Allen left Swainshead, so why should Stephen Collier make a point of mentioning nine o'clock?'

'Hmm,' said Hatchley. 'I suppose he could have just been assuming that Allen would leave after breakfast. Or maybe it had been mentioned the night before?'

'It's possible,' Banks said. 'Come to that, Sam Greenock could have told them. Nicholas Collier seemed much more annoyed by my reference to Esther Haines than I thought he'd be. There could be much more to that than even she let on.'

'I thought you were pushing it a bit there,' Hatchley said. 'I mean, the super did say to take it easy on them. They're important.'

Banks sniffed. 'The problem is, Sergeant, that it's all arse backwards, isn't it?'

'What do you mean?'

'Let's say Nicholas Collier might have been messing around with Allen's little sister, or Allen might have been bitter over losing the farm and eventually having to leave England. That gives him a motive for murder, but he's the one who ends up dead. Odd that, don't you think?'

'Aye, when you put it like that,' Hatchley said.

'Get on the radio and see if Richmond has turned up anything yet, will you? I want a word with these blokes here.'

Hatchley carried on to the car. Banks neared the bridge and steeled himself for the encounter with the old men. Three of them stood there silently, two leaning on walking sticks. No flicker of interest or concern showed on their weather-beaten faces when Banks approached them. He leaned against the warm stone and introduced himself, then asked if they had been out as early as nine o'clock a couple of weeks ago.

No one said a word at first, then one of them, a gnarled, misshapen man, turned to face Banks. With his flat cap and dark brown clothing, he looked like some strange plant with the power to uproot itself and walk among people.

He spat in the beck and said, ''Appen.'

'Do you know Bernard Allen?'

'Archie Allen's lad? Aye, o' course.'

'Did you see him that morning?'

The man was silent for a moment; he screwed up his eyes and contemplated Adam's Fell. Banks took out his cigarettes and offered them around. Only one of them, a man with a huge red nose, took one. He grinned toothlessly at Banks, carefully nipped off the filter and put the other end in his mouth.

'Aye,' the spokesman said finally.

'Where did he come from?'

The man pointed towards the Greenock Guest House.

'Did he stop anywhere on his way?'

The man shook his head.

'Where did he go?'

'Up there.' The man pointed with his stick to the footpath up Swainshead Fell.

'And that was the last you saw of him?'

'Aye.'

'What was he wearing?'

'Nay, lad, I don't remember that. 'E was carrying one o' them there 'aversacks on 'is back, that's all I recollect. P'raps 'e was wearing a shirt. I don't remember no jacket.'

'Did you notice anyone go after him?'

The man shook his head.

'Could someone have followed him without you seeing?'

''Appen. There's plenty o' ways to get up t' fell.'

'We know he went to the hanging valley over the fell top,' Banks said. 'Are there many other ways to get there?'

'A few. Tha can go from t' main road, 'bout a mile past Rawley Force, and from further up t' valley.'

'How could anyone know where he was heading?'

'That's tha job, bobby, in't it?'

He was right. Someone could easily have watched Allen

set off up the side of Swainshead Fell and then gone up by another route to head him off somewhere out of sight. And Sam Greenock had said he wouldn't have been surprised if Bernard had visited the hanging valley. Anyone else could have known that too, and gone up earlier to wait for him there.

Typically, as more information came to light the case was becoming more and more frustrating. Clearly it would be necessary to do a house-to-house in the village and ask the people with an eastern view if they had noticed anything that morning. It would also be useful to know if anyone had seen a car parked off the Helmthorpe road near the other access point. The trouble was that 17 May was so long ago most people would have forgotten.

And those were only the most obvious ways in. Someone could surely have approached the hanging valley from almost any direction and lain in wait overnight if necessary, especially if he knew Bernard Allen was bound to pass that way. The break, if it came, didn't look likely to come from establishing opportunity – just about everyone who had no alibi seemed to have had that – but from discovering a motive.

Banks thanked the old men and walked off to find Sergeant Hatchley.

6

ONE

Hatchley started the next day in a bad mood. He grumbled to Banks that not only was his bed too small but the noise of the plumbing had kept him awake.

'I swear there was some bugger in there for a piss every five minutes. Flushed it every time, too. The bloody thing took at least ten minutes to quieten down again.'

Banks, who had slept the sleep of the truly virtuous, overlooked the sergeant's spurious arithmetic. 'Never mind,' he said. 'With a bit of luck you'll be snug and warm in your own bed tonight.'

'Not if I can help it.'

'Carol Ellis?'

'Aye.'

'How long's it been now?'

'Over eighteen months.'

'It'll be wedding bells next, then?'

Hatchley blushed and Banks guessed he wasn't far from the truth.

'Anyway,' Banks went on. 'I'm sorry to keep you away from your love life, but I think we'll be finished here today unless Richmond comes up with anything else.'

Hatchley had been on to the detective constable back in Eastvale, but Richmond had discovered nothing of importance except that Sam Greenock's alibi seemed to hold. There remained, however, some doubt about the exact times he had called at Carter's and the newsagent's, so he wasn't entirely out of the running.

Also, Richmond had spoken to PC Weaver, who had called at the Greenocks' to ask about Canadian visitors. Weaver said that in all cases he had both checked the register and made enquiries. It looked like Sam Greenock was lying. Weaver could have been covering himself, but he was a good officer and Banks tended to believe him.

The previous evening, Banks and Hatchley had gone to interview John Fletcher, but he had been out. On the way back, they called in at the White Rose for a nightcap and had an early night. Mrs Greenock had still been skilfully managing to avoid them.

Breakfast seemed to cheer Hatchley up. Delivered by Katie, who blushed and ran as soon as she put, or almost dropped, the plates in front of them, the main course consisted of two fried eggs, two thick rashers of Yorkshire bacon, Cumberland sausage, grilled mushrooms and tomato, with two slices of fried bread to mop it all up. Before that they had drunk grapefruit juice and eaten cereal, and afterwards came the toast and marmalade. By some oversight, the toast was actually hot, and Hatchley, his equilibrium much restored, recoiled in mock horror.

'What's on after we've talked to Fletcher?' he asked.

'We've got to put it all together, write up the interviews, see what we've got. I'm due for lunch with the super, so as far as I'm concerned you can take the rest of the day off and make an early start in the morning.'

Sergeant Hatchley beamed.

'I'll drop you off at home,' Banks said. 'I've got to go back to Eastvale to pick up Sandra and the kids, anyway.'

They finished their tea and left the room to the quiet

Belgian couple by the window and the young married in the corner who hadn't noticed anyone except each other. The Greenocks themselves were nowhere in sight.

Outside, the three men Banks had spoken to the previous day were on the bridge as usual. The one who had acted as spokesman gave him a curt grudging nod of acknowledgement as he passed.

Hatchley nudged him as they got in the car. 'It usually takes an incomer two generations to get any sign of recognition from those characters. What did you do, slip 'em a tenner each?'

'Southern charm, Sergeant,' Banks said, grinning. 'Sheer charm. That and a lot of luck.'

About two miles up the valley, they crossed the low bridge and took a narrow dirt road up the fell side. Fletcher's farmhouse was a solid dark-stone construction that looked as if it had been extruded from the earth like an outcrop of rock. Around the back were a number of pens and ditches for dipping and shearing. This time, he was at home.

'I'm sorry I wasn't in,' he said when Banks mentioned their previous visit. 'I was doing a bit of business over in Hawes. Anyway, come in, make yourselves comfortable.'

They followed him into the living room, a spartan kind of place with bare plastered walls, stiff-backed chairs and a solid table on which rested an old wireless and precious little else. Whatever money Fletcher had in the bank, he certainly didn't waste any on luxurious living. The small window looked out across the valley. With a view like that, Banks thought, you'd hardly need paintings or television.

One thing in particular caught Banks's eye immediately, partly because it just didn't seem to fit in this overtly masculine environment. Propped on the mantel-piece was a gilt-framed photograph of a woman. On closer inspec-tion, which Banks made while Fletcher went to brew tea, the photo proved doubly incongruous. The woman, with her finely plucked eyebrows, gay smile and long wavy chestnut hair, certainly didn't look as if she belonged in Fletcher's world. Banks could imagine her cutting a fine figure at society cocktail parties, sporting the latest hat at Ascot or posing elegantly at fashion openings, but not living in this godforsaken part of the world with a dark, squat, rough-cheeked sheep farmer.

When Fletcher came back, Banks pointed to the photo-graph and asked who she was.

'My wife,' he said. 'She's been gone two years now.' There was a distinct chill in his tone that harmonized with the lonely brooding atmosphere Banks sensed in the house.

He didn't like to ask, but curiosity, as it often did, got the better of him. 'I'm sorry,' he said. 'Is she dead?'

Fletcher looked sharply at him. 'Not dead, no. If you must know, she left me.'

And you're still in love with her, Banks thought. At least that explained something of the heaviness that Fletcher seemed to carry around inside himself.

'We've come about Bernard Allen,' Banks said, accept-ing a cup of tea and changing tack quickly.

'Aye, I heard,' Fletcher said. 'Poor sod.'

'Did you know him well?'

'Not really, no. Just used to pass an evening or two in the White Rose when he dropped in for a visit.'

'Did you know him before he went to Canada?'

'I met him a few times. Hard not to when I was dealing with Walter Collier. Archie Allen worked some of his land.'

'So I heard. What were you going to do about that?'

Fletcher shrugged. 'I wasn't going to evict them, if that's what you're getting at. They were quite welcome to stay as far as I was concerned.'

'But they couldn't make a go of it?'

'That's right. It's tough, sheep farming, like I said before. I felt sorry for them, but there was nothing I could do.'

'So you only knew Bernard through his father at first?'

'Aye. He was off at university around then, too. And his brother had emigrated to Australia. There was only the young lass left.'

'Esther?'

'Aye. How is she? Have you seen her?'

'Yes,' Banks said. 'She's well. Married. Lives in Leeds. Did you ever hear anything about her and Nicholas Collier?'

Fletcher frowned. 'No, I can't say as I did. Though I wouldn't put it past him. She were a nice lass, young Esther. I've often thought things might've worked out different if the others had stuck around, kept the family together, like.'

'You mean Bernard and Denny going away might have caused their father's problems?'

'Some of them, perhaps. Not all, mind you. But it costs money to hire men. If you've got a family, there might be more mouths to feed, but there's more hands to help, too.'

'Did you have any connection with Bernard other than his father? There can't have been much of an age difference between you.'

'Nay, I'm older than I look,' Fletcher said, and grinned. 'Like I said, we'd pass the time of day in the White Rose now and then. Him and his girlfriend were in there often enough.'

'Girlfriend? Who was that, Mr Fletcher?'

'The one who disappeared. Anne Ralston, her name was.'

Banks felt a tremor of excitement. 'She was Bernard Allen's girlfriend?'

'Aye. Childhood sweethearts. They grew up together. I don't think it was owt serious later, like, or he wouldn't have gone off to Canada and left her. But they were thick as thieves, them two – more like brother and sister, maybe, as they got older.'

'And after he'd gone, she took up with Stephen Collier?'

'Aye. Got a job at Collier Foods and, well . . . Stephen's got a way with the women.'

'Did Bernard Allen ever say anything about this?'

'Not in my hearing he didn't. You're thinking maybe he was jealous?'

'Could be.'

'Then the wrong one got himself killed, didn't he?'

Banks sighed. 'It always seems to look that way in this case. But if Allen thought Stephen Collier had harmed her, he might have been out for revenge.'

'Waited long enough, didn't he?' Fletcher said.

'I'll be frank with you, Mr Fletcher,' Banks said. 'We've no idea why Bernard Allen was murdered, none at all. At the moment I'm gathering as much information as I can. Most of it will probably turn out to be useless. It usually does. But right now there's no way of telling what's of value and what isn't. Can you think of any reason why someone in Swainshead would want him out of the way?'

Fletcher paused to think for a few moments, his dark eyebrows knitting together. 'No,' he said finally. 'It's nothing to do with the farming business, I'm sure of that. There's not enough money in it to make murder worthwhile. And there was no animosity between myself and the Allens. Like I said, I don't think there was bad feeling between Bernard and the Colliers, but I couldn't swear to it. I know he bated them a bit about being capitalist oppressors, but I don't think anyone took that seriously enough to kill for.'

'What was your impression of Bernard Allen?'

'I liked him. As I said, I didn't know him well, and I can't say I agreed with his politics – with him on one side and Nicholas on the other, it was hardly my idea of a peaceful evening's drinking. But he was bright, thoughtful, and he loved the land. He knew he wasn't cut out to be a farmer – few are – but he loved The Head.'

'When was the last time you saw him?'

'The evening before he left. We were all in the White Rose. He was getting quite maudlin about coming home. Said if only he could get a job, however little it paid, or maybe a private income, then he'd be back like a shot. Of course, Nicholas jumped on that one – a socialist wanting a private income!'

'Were there any serious arguments?'

'No. It was all playful. The only serious bit was Bernard's sentimentality. He really seemed to convince himself that he was coming back here to live. But he'd had a few too many, of course. Sam had to help him back to the house. I'm sorry I can't be more useful, Mr Banks. I'd like to, but I don't know anything. I had no reason to harm Bernard and, as far as I know, nor did any of the others. If there are motives, they're hidden from me.'

'Did he mention his divorce at all?'

'Oh aye,' Fletcher said grimly. 'I could sympathize with him over that.'

'Did he seem upset about it?'

'Of course. His wife had run off with another man. Wouldn't you be upset? I think that's what set him thinking about coming back home to stay. You get like that when you lose whatever it is that keeps you away.'

'Did Mr Allen know your wife?'

Fletcher's face hardened. 'What do you mean "know"? "Know" in the biblical sense? Are you suggesting there was something between them and I killed him in a fit of jealousy?'

'No,' said Banks, 'I'm simply trying to get a grasp on the web of relationships.'

Fletcher continued to eye him suspiciously. 'She didn't know him,' he said. 'Oh, I'm not saying their paths never crossed, that they wouldn't say hello if they passed one another in the street, but that's all.'

'Where is your wife?'

Fletcher looked at the picture. 'In Paris,' he said, his voice shaking with grief and anger. 'In Paris with that bastard she ran off with.'

The silence that followed weighed on them all. Finally, Banks gestured to Hatchley and they stood up to leave. 'I'm sorry if I upset you,' he said. 'It wasn't intentional, believe me, but sometimes in a murder investigation . . .'

Fletcher sighed. 'Aye, I know. You've got to ask. It's your job. No offence taken.' And he held out his square callused hand.

Driving down the fell side, Banks and Hatchley said very little. Banks had been impressed by Fletcher's solidity; he seemed a man with great integrity and strong foundations. But such a man, he knew, could kill when pushed too far. It was easier to push an earnest man too far than it was a more frivolous one. Although he was inclined to believe Fletcher, he nonetheless made a mental note of his reservations.

'Ideal place, isn't it?' Hatchley said, looking back at Fletcher's farm as they crossed the bridge.

'In a way,' Banks answered. 'A bit dour and spartan for my tastes, though.'

'I didn't mean that, sir.' Hatchley looked puzzled. 'I meant it's an ideal location for approaching the hanging valley unseen.'

Banks slowed down on the narrow road as Sam Greenock's Land Rover passed them going in the other direction. Sam waved half-heartedly as he drove by.

'Yes,' Banks said absently. 'Yes, I suppose it is. I'd just like to stop off at the Greenocks' before we go back to Eastvale. There's something I'd like to do. You use the radio and get on to Richmond. See if anything's come up.'

TWO

Katie flinched and backed towards the wall when she saw Banks appear in the doorway of the room she was cleaning.

'It's all right, Katie,' he said. 'I'm not going to hurt you. We've got to have a little talk, that's all.'

'Sam's out,' Katie said, clutching the yellow duster tightly over her breast.

'I know he is. I saw him drive off. It's you I want to talk to. Come on, Katie, stop playing games. You've been trying to avoid us ever since we got here. What is it? What are you afraid of?'

'I don't know what you're talking about.'

Banks sighed. 'Yes, you do.' He sat down on the corner of the bed. 'And I'm prepared to wait until you tell me.'

Now, as she stood cringing by the window, Banks

realized who she reminded him of: Hardy's Tess Durbeyfield. Physically, she resembled Nastassja Kinski, who had played Tess in the film version, but the similarity went deeper than that. Banks had a sense of Tess as a child in a woman's body, not fully aware of her own beauty and sexuality, or of the effect she might have on men. It wasn't entirely innocence, but it was close – a kind of innocent sensuality. He made a note to look up the description of Tess in the book when he got home.

'Look,' he went on, 'we can either talk here, or we can go to police headquarters in Eastvale. It's up to you. I don't really mind at all.'

'You can't do that,' Katie said, thrusting out her bottom lip. 'You can't just take a person away like that. I haven't done anything. I've got my work to finish.'

'So have I. You're withholding evidence, Katie. It's a crime.'

'I'm not withholding anything.'

'If you say so.' Banks stood up with exaggerated slowness. 'Let's go, then.'

Katie stepped back until she was flat against the wall. 'No! If you take me away Sam . . . Sam'll . . .'

'Come on, Katie,' Banks said, more gently, 'don't be silly.' He pointed to the chair. 'Sit down. Tell me about it.'

Katie flopped into the chair by the window and looked down at the floor. 'There's nothing to tell,' she muttered.

'Let me try and make it a bit easier for you,' Banks said. 'Judging by the way you behaved when we talked to you and Sam yesterday, I'd guess that something happened between you and Bernard Allen while he was staying here. Maybe it was personal. You might think it's your business and it has nothing to do with his death, but I'm the one to be the judge of that. Do you understand?'

Katie just stared at him.

'You'd known him a long time, hadn't you?'

'Since he came to Leeds. We lived next door.'

'You and Sam?'

'With his parents.'

'What happened to your own parents?'

'They died when I was a little girl. My grandmother brought me up.' Katie lowered her gaze down to her lap, wringing the yellow duster in her hands.

'Did you ever go out with Bernie Allen?'

She looked up sharply, and the blood ran to her cheeks. 'What do you mean? I'm married.'

'Well, something happened between you, that's clear enough. Why won't you tell me what it was?'

'I've told you,' Katie said. 'Nothing happened. We were friends, that's all.' She went back to twisting the duster on her lap. 'I'm thirsty.'

Banks brought her a glass of water from the washbasin.

'Were you lovers, Katie?' he asked. 'Did you sleep with Bernard Allen while he was staying here?'

'No!' Tears blurred Katie's clear brown eyes.

'All right.' Banks held up his hand. 'It's not important. I believe you.' He didn't, but he often found it useful to pretend he believed a lie. It was always clear from the teller's obvious relief that it had been a lie. Afterwards it was easier to get at the information that really mattered. And he had a feeling she was hiding something else.

'But you spent some time together, didn't you? Time alone, like friends do?'

Katie nodded.

'And you must have talked. What did you talk about?'

Katie shrugged. 'I don't know, just things. Life.'

'That's a broad subject. Anything in particular?'

She was chewing on her bottom lip now, and Banks could sense that she was on the verge of talking. He would have to tread carefully to avoid scaring her off again.

'It might be important,' he said. 'If he was a friend of yours, surely you want his killer caught?'

Katie looked at him as if the idea was completely new to her. 'Yes,' she said. 'Yes, of course I do.'

'Will you help me, then?'

'He talked about Canada, his life in Toronto. What it was like there.'

'What about it?'

'How wonderful and exciting it was.'

It was like drawing a confession out of a naughty child. 'Come on,' Banks prompted her. 'There was something special, wasn't there? You'd have no reason to hide any of this from me, and I know you're hiding something.'

'He told me in confidence,' she said. 'I wasn't to tell anyone. Sam'll kill me if he finds out.'

'Why?'

'He doesn't like me talking to people behind his back.'

'Look, Katie. Bernard is dead. Somebody murdered him. You can't keep a secret for a dead man, can you?'

'Life doesn't end with death.'

'Maybe not. But what he said might be important.'

There was a long pause while Katie seemed to struggle with her conscience; each phase of the skirmish flashed across her flawless complexion. Finally, she said, 'Annie was there. That's what he told me. Annie was in Toronto.'

'Annie?'

'Yes. Anne Ralston. She was a friend of Bernie's from years ago. She disappeared when we had all that trouble here five years back.'

'I've heard of her. What exactly did Bernard say?'

'Just that she was living in Toronto now. He'd heard from her about three years ago. She was in Vancouver then. They'd kept in touch, and now she'd moved.'

'Did he say anything else about her?'

Katie looked at him blankly. 'No. She just asked him not to go telling everyone in Swainshead that he'd seen her.'

'This is what Bernard told you?'

'Yes.'

'Why did he tell you, do you think, when Anne had told him not to tell anyone?'

'I . . . I . . . don't know,' Katie stammered. 'He trusted me. He was just talking about people leaving, finding a new life. He said she was happy there.'

'Were you talking about wanting a new life for yourself?'

'I don't know what you mean.'

Her words lacked conviction. Banks knew he was right. Katie had probably been telling Bernard Allen that she wanted to get away from Swainshead. Why she should want to leave he didn't know, but from what he'd seen and heard of Sam so far, she might have one good reason.

'Never mind,' Banks said. 'Did he say anything about coming home to stay?'

Katie seemed surprised. 'No. Why should he? He had a wonderful new life out there.'

'Did he tell you this on the morning he left or before?'

'Before. Just after he arrived.'

'And you were the only one he told?'

'Yes.'

'You're hesitating, Katie. Why?'

'I . . . I don't know. You're confusing me. You're making me nervous.'

'Were you the only one he told?'

'As far as I know, yes.'

'And who did you tell?'

'I didn't tell anyone.'

'You're lying, Katie.'

'I'm not. I—'

'Who did you tell? Sam?'

Katie pulled at the duster so hard it tore. 'All right, yes! I told Sam. He's my husband. Wives aren't supposed to keep secrets from their husbands, are they?'

'What did Sam say?'

'Nothing. He just seemed surprised, that's all.'

'Did he know Anne Ralston?'

'Not well. It was only about a year after we arrived that she disappeared. We met her with Bernie, and she was going out with Stephen, but Sam didn't know the Colliers as well then.'

'Are you sure you told no one else?'

'No one,' Katie whispered. 'I swear it.'

Banks believed her.

Sam Greenock, he reflected, was quite a one for passing on news, especially to his cronies in the White Rose, with whom he seemed intent on ingratiating himself. Socially, he was beneath them all. The Colliers were cocks of The Head, and Fletcher owned quite a bit of land. Stephen Collier, as Katie said, had been going out with Anne Ralston around the time she disappeared, which had also been coincidental with the murder of Raymond Addison, the London private detective. Somewhere, somehow, Sam Greenock was involved in it all.

What if Sam had told Stephen that Bernard Allen had been in touch with Anne? And what if she was in a position to tell Allen something incriminating about

Collier, something to do with the Addison murder? That would certainly give Stephen a motive. And if that was what had happened, to what extent was Sam Greenock an accessory? For the first time, there seemed to be the strong possibility of a link between the murders of Raymond Addison and Bernard Allen. This would certainly interest Superintendent Gristhorpe, who had withdrawn into his usual role because the two cases hadn't seemed connected.

'Thank you, Katie,' Banks said, walking to the door. 'You'd better keep our rooms for us. I think we'll be back this evening.'

Katie nodded wearily. Pale, slumped in the chair, she looked used and abused like a discarded mistress.

THREE

'Anne Ralston?' Gristhorpe repeated in disbelief. 'After all these years?'

He and Banks knelt beside the pile of stones. Usually when they worked on the wall together they hardly spoke, but today there was pressing police business to deal with. Sandra had taken Brian and Tracy down into Lyndgarth after lunch to see a local craft exhibition, so they were alone with the twittering larks and the cheeky wagtails on the valley side above the village.

'You can see how it changes things,' Banks said.

'I can indeed – if it had anything to do with Bernard Allen's murder.'

'It must have.'

'We don't even know that Anne Ralston's disappearance was connected with Addison's killing, for a start.'

'It's too much of a coincidence, surely?' Banks said. 'A private detective is killed and a local woman disappears on practically the same day. If it happened in London, or even in Eastvale, I'd be inclined to think there was no link, but in a small village like Swainshead . . .?'

'Aye,' said Gristhorpe. 'Put like that . . . But we need a lot more to go on. No, not that one; it's too flat.' Gristhorpe brushed aside the stone Banks had picked up.

'Sorry.' Banks searched the pile for something better. 'I'm working on the assumption that Anne Ralston knew something about Addison's murder, right?'

'Right. I'll go along with that just for the sake of argument.'

'If she did know something and disappeared without telling us, it means one of two things: either she was paid off, or she was scared for her own life.'

Gristhorpe nodded. 'Or she might have been protecting someone,' he added.

'But then there'd be no need to run.'

'Maybe she didn't trust herself to bear up under pressure. Who knows? Go on.'

'For five years nobody hears any more of her, then suddenly Bernard Allen turns up and tells Katie Greenock he's been seeing the Ralston woman in Toronto. The next thing we know, Allen's dead before he can get back there. Now, Katie said that Bernard had been told not to spread it around about him knowing Anne. Was she protecting him, or herself? Or both? We don't know. What we do know, though, is that she didn't want her whereabouts known. Allen tells Katie, anyway, and she tells her husband. I think we can safely assume that Sam Greenock told everyone else. Allen must have become a threat to someone because he'd met up with Anne Ralston, who might have known something about Addison's murder. Stephen Collier was closely associated with her so he looks like a good suspect, but there's no reason to concentrate on him alone. It could have been any of them – Fletcher, Nicholas, Sam Greenock, even Katie – they were all in Swainshead at the time both Addison and Allen were killed, and we've no idea what or who that private detective was after five years ago.'

'What about opportunity?'

'Same thing. Everybody knew the route Allen was taking out of Swainshead. He'd talked all about it in the White Rose the night before. And most of them also knew how attached he was to that valley. The killer could easily have hidden among the trees up there and watched for him.'

'All right,' Gristhorpe said, placing a through-stone. 'But what about their alibis?'

'We've only got Fletcher's word that he was at home. He could have got to the valley from the north without anyone knowing. He lives alone on the fell side and there are no other houses nearby. As for the Colliers, Stephen says he was at the office and Nicholas was at school. We haven't checked yet, but if Nicholas wasn't actually teaching a class and Stephen wasn't in a meeting, either of them could have slipped out for a while, or turned up later. It would have been easy for Nicholas, again approaching from the north, and Stephen could have got up from half a mile past Rawley Force. It's not much of a climb, and there's plenty of cover to hide the car off the Helmthorpe road. I had a look on my way over here.'

'The Greenocks?'

'Sam could have got there from the road too. He went to Eastvale for supplies, but the shopkeepers can't say exactly what time he got there. Carter's doesn't open till nine, anyway, and the chap in the newsagent's says Sam usually drops in at about eleven. That gives him plenty of time. He might have had another motive, too.'

Gristhorpe raised his bushy eyebrows.

'The woman denies it, but I got a strong impression that something went on between Katie Greenock and Bernard Allen.'

'And you think if Sam got wind of it . . .?'

'Yes.'

'What about Mrs Greenock?'

'She says she was at home cleaning, but all the guests would have gone out by then. Nobody could confirm that she stayed in.'

'Have you checked the Colliers' stories?'

'Sergeant Hatchley's doing it tomorrow morning. There's no one at the factory on a Sunday.'

'Well, maybe we'll be a bit clearer when we get all that sorted out.'

'I'm going back to Swainshead for another night. I'll want to talk to Stephen Collier again, for one.'

Gristhorpe nodded. 'Take it easy though, Alan. I've already had an earful from the DCC about your last visit.'

'He didn't waste any time, did he? Anyway, I could do with a bit of information on the Addison case and the Ralston woman's disappearance. How did the alibis check out?'

Gristhorpe put down the stone he was weighing in his hand and frowned. Banks lit a cigarette – at least smoking was allowed in the open, if not in the house. He looked at the sky and noticed it had clouded over very quickly. He could sniff rain in the air.

'Everyone said they were at home. We couldn't prove

otherwise. It was a cold dark February evening. We pushed Stephen Collier as hard as we dared, but he had a perfect alibi for the day of the girl's disappearance: he was in Carlisle at a business meeting.'

'Was Walter Collier around in those days?'

'No. He was dead by then.'

'What was he like?'

'He was quite an impressive man. Complex. He had a lot of power and influence in the dale, some of which has carried over to the sons, as you've already found out. Now, you know how I feel about privilege and such, but you had to respect Walter; he never really abused his position. He was proud, especially of the family and its achievements, but he managed to be kind and considerate without being condescending. He was also a regular churchgoer, a religious man, but he liked the ladies and he could drink most villagers under the table. Don't ask me how he managed to square that with himself. It's rare for a Dales farmer, especially one from a family as long-established as the Colliers, to sell up. But Walter was a man of vision. He saw what things were coming to, so he shifted his interests to food processing and encouraged his sons to get good educations rather than strong muscles.'

'What was he like as a father?'

'I'd imagine he was a bit of a tyrant,' Gristhorpe answered, 'though I can't say for certain. Used to being obeyed, getting his own way. They probably felt the back of his hand more than once.'

Banks held out his palm and felt the first, hesitant drops of rain. 'When Anne Ralston disappeared,' he asked, 'were there no signs at all of what might have happened to her?'

'Nothing. There were a few clothes missing, that's all.'

'What about money, bank accounts?'

'She didn't have one. She got a wage packet every two weeks from Collier Foods. What she did with the cash, I've no idea. Maybe she hid it under the mattress.'

'But you didn't find any in the cottage?'

'Not a brass farthing.'

'So she could have packed a few things, a bit of money, and simply run off?'

'Yes. We never found out what happened to her, until now.' Gristhorpe stood up and scowled at the grey sky. A flock of rooks wheeled above the valley side. 'Better go inside.'

As they walked round to the side door, they saw Sandra and the children come hurrying up the drive with their coats thrown over their heads. Banks waved to them.

'It would be very interesting to have a chat with Anne Ralston, wouldn't it?' he said.

Gristhorpe looked at him and narrowed his eyes. 'Aye, it would. But I'm not sure the department would be able to justify the expense.'

'Still . . .'

'I'll see what I can do,' Gristhorpe said. Then Sandra, Brian and Tracy came racing into the house.

7

ONE

Katie finished her cleaning in a daze when Banks had gone, and she was so distracted she almost forgot to put the roast in on time. The Greenock Guest House always served a traditional Yorkshire Sunday dinner, both for guests and non-residents, at two o'clock. It was Sam's idea. Thank God he was in the pub, his usual Sunday lunch-time haunt, Katie thought. He'd be bending elbows with the wonderful Colliers.

Perhaps Sam needn't know what the policeman had made her tell. But the inspector would be sure to question him, she knew, and he would find out; he was bound to accuse her of betraying him.

With a start, she realized she was in room five, where the talk had taken place on the second morning of Bernie's stay. But it wasn't his words she thought of now. The rush of images almost overwhelmed her at first, but she forced herself to re-examine what had happened. Perhaps it hadn't been such a sin, after all? Of course it was, she told herself; it was a double sin, for she was a married woman. But it had happened, she couldn't deny that. The first time in all her married life.

That morning she had been cleaning the rooms as usual, when Bernie had come back to put on his walking boots. The sky had brightened, he said, and he had

decided to go for a good long walk after all. They'd talked
for as much time as she dared take off from her chores,
then he had sat on the bed while she washed the windows. All the time she had been aware of him watching
her. Finally, when she felt his arms around her waist, she
told him no. She had her back to him and he bent to kiss
her neck where the wisps of blonde hair were swept up
and tied while she worked. She struggled, but he held her
tightly and his hands found her breasts. She dropped the
chamois and it fell in the bucket and splashed water on
the carpet.

Why did she let him? She had always liked him, but
why this? Why let him do what she hated most? She
thought perhaps it was because he offered her a chance to
escape, and that this was the price she would have to pay.
He was gentler than Sam. His mouth moved over her
shoulder and his hands slid down along her stomach and
over her thighs. She didn't have the heart or the courage
to put up a fight; men were so strong. Surely, she thought,
it could do no harm as long as she didn't feel pleasure. She
couldn't tell Sam. That would mean she'd have to lie, too.
She would have to wash her mouth out with soap.

Then he said he loved her, that he'd always wanted her,
as his hands unfastened her skirt. She struggled again,
but less violently this time, and he backed her towards
the bed. There, he finished undressing her. She was
trembling, but so was he; even body language speaks
ambiguously at times. She held on to the bedposts tightly
as he bore down on her, and she knew he thought her
groans were sounds of pleasure. Why did men want
her like this? Why did they want to do these things to her?

He kissed her breasts and said he would take her back
to Canada with him, and suddenly that seemed like the

answer. She wanted to get away, she needed to. Swainshead and Sam were stifling her.

So she didn't struggle any more. Bernard talked of the vast prairie skies and of lakes as boundless as oceans as his hands caressed her still body. Yes, he would take her with him, he said; he had always wanted her. Urgently, he drew himself along the length of her body and entered her. She bit her tongue in loathing and self-disgust, and he looked into her eyes and smiled as she made little strangled cries that must have sounded like pleasure.

After, as they dressed, Katie had tried to hide the shame of her nakedness from his gaze. He had laughed and told her he found her modesty very appealing. She said he'd better go, that Sam would be back, and he reminded her about Canada.

'I'll send for you when I get back,' he promised. 'I'll find a place for us and I'll send for you. Anne's there, too. She wanted to get away, just like you. She's happy now.'

'Yes,' she had said, anxious to get rid of him. 'I'll come with you.' Then he had kissed her and left the room.

After that morning, they had hardly spoken to one another – mostly because Sam had been around or Katie had contrived to avoid Bernie – but he kept giving her meaningful glances whenever nobody was looking. She believed him. He would send for her.

Not any more. All for nothing. All gone. All she had left was the guilt. 'As ye sow, so shall ye reap,' her granny had always said. She had behaved wantonly, like that time she had swayed to the distant music. It didn't matter that she hadn't enjoyed it; now everything was a mess, Bernie was dead, and the police were all over the place. She was reaping what she had sown.

TWO

Stephen Collier was sitting in his spacious living room reading a thick leather-bound report when Banks and Hatchley called that evening. The French windows were open on to the patio and lawn, and the fountain played against a backdrop of drystone-walled fell side. A brief heavy shower had cleansed the landscape and in the gentle evening light the grass was lush and green, the limestone outcrops bright as marble.

Stephen seemed surprised and annoyed at a second visit from the police so close on the heels of the first, but he quickly regained his composure and offered drinks.

'I'll have a Scotch, please,' Banks said.

'Sergeant Hatchley?'

'Don't mind if I do, sir.' Hatchley glanced towards Banks, who nodded his permission. After all, he had spoiled the sergeant's weekend. Hatchley took out his notebook and settled in a corner with his drink.

'What can I do for you this time?' Stephen asked. 'Do you want to see my brother, too?'

'Not at the moment,' Banks said. 'I want to talk to you about Anne Ralston.'

Collier frowned. 'Anne Ralston? What about her? That was years ago.'

'I'd like to know what happened.'

'Aren't I entitled to know why?'

'Will you just bear with me for a while?'

'Very well.'

'As far as I know,' Banks began, 'she disappeared the day after the private detective, Raymond Addison, was killed. Am I right?'

'I wouldn't know when he was killed,' Stephen said. 'Though I do remember Superintendent Gristhorpe saying something about a post-mortem report.'

'But it was around that time she disappeared?'

'Yes.'

'And she was an employee of Collier Foods?'

'Yes. Your superintendent already knows all this. Please get to the point, Chief Inspector.' He tapped the book on his lap. 'I have an important report to study for a meeting in the morning.'

'I won't keep you long, sir,' Banks said, 'if you'll just answer my questions. Were you going out with Anne Ralston at the time of her disappearance?'

'Yes. You know I was. But I don't see—'

Banks held up his hand. 'Let me finish, please. Can you think of any reason why she should disappear?'

'None.'

'What do you think happened to her?'

Collier walked over to the cocktail cabinet and refilled his glass. He offered Banks and Hatchley cigarettes from a box on the glass-topped coffee table.

'I thought she might have gone off to see the world,' he answered. 'It was something she'd often talked about.'

'Didn't it worry you?'

'Didn't what worry me?'

'Her disappearance.'

'I must admit, in some of my darker moments I thought something might have happened to her – a wandering psychopath or something – especially with the Addison business. But I decided it wasn't so out of character for Anne to just up and go.'

'Weren't you bothered that she never got in touch with you? Or did she?'

Collier smiled. 'No, Chief Inspector, she didn't. And, yes, it was a bit of a blow to the ego at first. But I got used to it. It wasn't as if we were engaged or living together.'

'I noticed you mentioned a moment ago that you linked her disappearance with the Addison killing – a wandering psychopath. Did it occur to you to link the two events in any other way?'

'What do you mean?'

'Could Anne Ralston have had something to do with Addison's visit to Swainshead? He was a private detective, after all.'

'Yes, I know. But nobody here had any idea why he was in the area. If it was anything to do with Anne, she certainly kept quiet about it. Maybe he was just on holiday. I'm sure private eyes have holidays too.'

'Would she have been likely to tell you?'

'I don't know. I don't imagine she told me everything about her life. Ours was a casual relationship. I'd never have expected her to bare her soul.'

'Are you sure it wasn't more serious on her part?'

'Not at all. She'd been around.'

'And you?'

Stephen smiled. 'I wasn't new to the wily ways of the fair sex, no. Another drink?'

Hatchley passed his empty glass and Banks nodded. He lit a Silk Cut and looked out on to the lawn. Two sparrows were taking a bath in the fountain. There was plenty of room, but each defended its territory with an angry flapping of wings, splashing water all over the place. A shadow fell over the patio and Nicholas Collier popped his head round the French windows.

'Hello,' he said, stepping into the room. 'I thought I heard voices.'

'If you don't mind, sir . . .' Sergeant Hatchley stood up and blocked the entrance, a task for which he might have been specially designed.

Nicholas tilted his head back and looked down his long nose at Hatchley. 'What's going on?'

'I'm just having a little chat with your brother,' Banks said. 'You're perfectly at liberty to stay, but I'd be obliged if you'd refrain from interrupting.'

Nicholas raised his black eyebrows. He seemed to have forgotten his sulking, but he clearly wasn't used to being told what to do. For a moment, anger flashed in his eyes, then he simply nodded and sat by the windows.

'Look,' Stephen said, frowning at his brother and coming back with the drinks. 'Where on earth is all this leading? Anne Ralston is history now. I haven't seen or heard from her in five years. Quite frankly, it was embarrassing enough at the time having our relationship, such as it was, plastered all over the local papers. I wouldn't like to relive that.'

'You mean you didn't know?' Banks said, sipping his Scotch.

'Didn't know what?'

'About Anne Ralston.'

'Look here. If this is some kind of a game . . .'

Did he or didn't he? Banks couldn't be sure. Sam Greenock would know the answer to that – when he got home, and if he could be persuaded to talk.

'Anne's turned up again.'

'But . . . where?'

'Bernard Allen knew where she was. He told the Greenocks. Surely Sam told you?'

'No. No, I'd no idea. How is she? What happened?'

'I don't know all the details,' Banks said. 'Just that

she's alive and well and living in Canada. Are you sure nobody told you?'

'I've already said so, haven't I? This is a complete surprise to me. Though I was sure she'd turn up somewhere, some day.' He went over and poured himself another drink; his hand was shaking. Banks glanced sideways at Nicholas, who sat impassively in his chair. There was no way of telling what he knew or didn't know.

Banks and Hatchley finished their drinks and stood up.

'I'm sorry it came as such a shock, Mr Collier,' Banks said. 'I just thought you ought to know.'

'Yes, of course,' Stephen said. 'I'm very grateful to you. If you do hear anything else . . .'

'We'll let you know.'

'There is just one thing,' Stephen said, standing in the doorway. 'What has this to do with Bernard Allen's death? Do you see any connection?'

'I don't know, Mr Collier,' Banks said. 'I really don't know. It does seem like a bit of a coincidence though – Anne disappearing the day after Addison's killing, then turning up again, so to speak, around the time of Allen's murder. It makes you wonder, doesn't it?'

And they walked back over the bridge, where the three men stood like shadows in the soft light. On impulse, Banks sent Hatchley on ahead and stopped.

'Do you remember Anne Ralston?' he asked the gnarled spokesman.

As was his custom, the man spat in the fledgling River Swain before answering. 'Aye. Allus in and out o' there.' He nodded over at the Collier house.

'Have you seen her at all over the last few years?'

'Nay. She flitted.'

'And she hasn't been back?'

He shook his head.

'Have you seen either Mr or Mrs Greenock go over to the Collier house this afternoon?'

'Aye,' the man said. 'Sam Greenock went over about three o'clock.'

'To see Stephen or Nicholas?'

'It were Mr Stephen's door he knocked on.'

'And did Stephen Collier answer it?'

The man scowled. 'Aye, course he did.'

'How long was Mr Greenock in there?'

'Baht ten minutes.'

'Thank you,' Banks said, heading for the guest house. 'Thank you very much.'

He heard his reluctant informant hack into the beck again, then the murmur of their voices rose up behind him.

THREE

Katie Greenock hurried away when she saw Banks coming, but he couldn't help noticing that she moved with some difficulty.

'Katie!' he called, hurrying down the hall after her and grasping her elbow.

She spun round and faced him, one hand over her stomach. Her face was white and tense with suppressed pain. 'What do you want?' she asked angrily. 'Haven't you caused enough trouble?'

'There'll be a lot more before this business is over, Katie. I'm sorry, but there it is. You'll just have to learn to face the world. Anyway, that's not why I called you. What's wrong? You look ill.'

'Nothing's wrong.'

'You're white as a ghost. And what's wrong with your stomach? Does it ache?'

'What do you care?' she asked, breaking away.

'Is it Sam? Has he hurt you?'

'I don't know what you mean. I've got a tummy ache, that's all.'

'Did you tell Sam you'd told me about Anne?'

'I had to, didn't I? He knew there was something wrong. I'm not good at hiding things.'

'And what did he do, beat it out of you?'

'I told you, I've just got a tummy ache. Leave me alone, I feel sick.'

'Where is he?'

She gestured with her head. 'In back.'

'Will you stay out here for a few minutes, Katie, while I talk to him?'

Katie nodded and edged into the dining room.

Banks walked down the hall and knocked on the door that separated the Greenocks' part of the house from the rest. Sam let him in.

'Chief Inspector Banks,' he said. 'What a surprise. I hope nothing's wrong?'

'Has your wife told you we had a little talk earlier today?'

Greenock sat down. 'Well, yes. She did right, too. I'm her husband.'

'Why didn't you tell me about the Ralston woman earlier, as soon as we found out it was Bernard Allen feeding the maggots up in the hanging valley? This is the second time you've obstructed our investigation, and I'm having serious thoughts about taking you in.'

'Now hold on a minute.' Sam stood up again and puffed

out his chest. 'You can't come round here making accusations like that.'

'She said she told you that Bernard had met up with Anne Ralston in Canada.'

'So?'

'So you should have told me.'

'You never asked.'

Banks glared at him.

'I didn't think it was relevant. Dammit, Chief Inspector, the woman's been gone for five years.'

'You know bloody well how important she is. She's important enough for you to dash out and tell Stephen Collier that Katie had told me what Bernie said. What's going on, Greenock? Just what is your involvement in all this?'

'Nothing,' Sam said. 'There's nothing going on. I don't know what you're talking about.'

'But you did go over to Stephen Collier's this afternoon?'

'So what? We're friends. I dropped in for a drink.'

'Did you also dash over a few weeks ago and tell him what Bernie said about Anne Ralston turning up?'

'I didn't tell anyone.'

'I think you did. I also think you told him this afternoon that your wife had let the cat out of the bag to me about Anne Ralston. Didn't you?'

'I did no such thing. And you can't prove it either.'

'I will prove it,' Banks said. 'Believe me, I will. And when I do, your feet won't touch the ground.'

'You don't scare me,' Sam said.

Banks drew closer and Greenock backed towards the wall. They were both about the same size, though Sam was heavier.

'I don't?' Banks said. 'Well, I bloody well should. Where I come from, we don't always do things by the book. Do you know what I mean?' It was Hatchley's line, Banks knew, but it wasn't as if he was intimidating some scared kid. Sam was a villain, and Banks knew it. His dark eyes glittered with pent-up energy and Sam flinched as he felt his shoulder blades make contact with the wall.

'Leave me alone!' Sam shouted. 'I'll bloody report you, I will.'

Banks sneered. 'That's a laugh.' Then he backed away. 'Keep out of my sight, Greenock,' he said. 'If I want you, I'll know which rock to look under. And when I do, I'll have proof. And if I see or hear any more evidence – even the merest hint – that you've been hurting your wife again, I'll make you bloody sorry you were ever born.'

FOUR

'Will there be anything else?' the waitress asked, clearing away the empty plate.

'What? Oh, yes. Yes. Another cup of tea, please.' Katie Greenock had to pull herself back from a very long way. It would be her third cup but why not? Let it simply be another part of her little rebellion.

She sat at a table with a red-checked cloth – very clean, she noticed – by the window of the Golden Grill in Eastvale. The narrow street outside was busy with pedestrians, even in the thin drizzle, and almost directly opposite her was the whitewashed building with the black beams and the incongruous white-on-blue sign over the entrance: POLICE.

It was early Monday afternoon, and she didn't know

what she was doing in Eastvale. Already she was beginning to feel guilty. It was simply a minor gesture, she tried to convince herself, but her conscience invested it with the magnitude of Satan's revolt.

That morning, at about eleven o'clock, she had felt so claustrophobic cleaning the rooms that she just had to get out – not only out of the house, but out of Swainshead itself for a while. Walking aimlessly down the street, she had met Beryl Vickers, a neighbour she occasionally talked gardening with, and accepted her offer of a lift into Eastvale for a morning's shopping. Beryl was visiting her sister there, so Katie was left free to wander by herself for a few hours. After buying some lamb chops and broccoli at the indoor market for that evening's dinner, she had found the Golden Grill and decided to rest her feet.

She had only been sitting there for fifteen minutes when she saw three men come out of the pub next door and hurry through the rain back into the police station. Two of them she recognized – the lean dark inspector and his fair heavy sergeant – but the young athletic-looking one with the droopy moustache and the curious loping walk was new to her. For a moment, she thought they were sure to glance over their shoulders and see her through the window, so she covered the side of her face with her hand. They didn't even look.

As soon as she saw the inspector, she felt again the bruises that Sam had inflicted on her the previous afternoon. She knew it wasn't the policeman's fault – in fact, he seemed like a kind man – but she couldn't help the association any more than she could help feeling one between room five and what she had let Bernie do to her.

'What's wrong with you?' Sam had asked when he came home.

Katie had tried to hide her red-rimmed eyes from him, but he grasped her chin between his thumb and forefinger and asked her again. That was when she told him the police had been back and the inspector had interrogated her so hard she couldn't hide it from him any more.

Sam had hit the roof.

'But it's not that important,' Katie protested. 'It can't be!'

'That's not for you to say,' Sam argued. He threw up his hands. 'You stupid bloody bitch, have you any idea what trouble you might have caused?'

Though she was scared, Katie still felt defiant. 'What do you mean, trouble?' she asked, her lower lip trembling. 'Trouble for who?'

'For everyone, that's for who.'

'For your precious Colliers, I'll bet.' As she said it, her image was of Nicholas, not Stephen.

And that was when Sam hit her the first time, a short sharp blow to the stomach. She doubled up in pain, and when she was able to stand again he thumped her left breast. That hurt even more. She collapsed on the sofa and Sam stood over her. His face was red and he was breathing oddly, in short gasps that seemed to catch in his throat. 'If we make something of ourselves in this place,' he said, 'it won't be any thanks to you.'

He didn't hit her any more. He knew when enough was enough. But later that night, in bed, the same cruel hands grasped the same wounded breast. He pulled her roughly to him, and there was nothing she could do about it. Katie shuddered, trying to shake off the memory.

'Will that be all?' the waitress asked, standing over her again.

'Oh, yes. Yes, thank you,' Katie said, paying the bill.

Awkwardly, aware of the ache in her breast and the Black Forest gateau sitting uneasily in her sore stomach, she made her way out into the street. She had one more hour of freedom to wander in the rain before meeting Beryl near the bus station at two thirty. Then she would have to go home and face the music.

FIVE

After a pub lunch in the Queen's Arms and a chat with Hatchley and Richmond about the case, Banks was no further ahead. Back in his office, he sat down, sent for some coffee and put his feet up on the desk to think things out. When PC Craig arrived with the coffee – looking very put out, no doubt because Susan Gay had coerced him into carrying it up – Banks lit a Silk Cut and went over what he'd got.

Richmond had discovered that Les Haines, Bernie Allen's brother-in-law, had done a brief stretch in Armley Prison for receiving stolen goods (i.e. two boxes of Sony E-120 video cassette tapes). It was his second offence, hot on the heels of an assault charge against a man in an alley outside a Leeds bar. But Haines had been at work on the day of Allen's murder, so he would have had no opportunity to get to Swainshead and back, even if there had been some obscure family motive. Besides, as Banks well knew, just because a man has a record as a petty thief, it doesn't make him a murderer. Esther had been at home with the kids, as usual, and Banks could hardly visualize her trailing them up to the hanging valley and knocking off her brother.

Most interesting of all were the Colliers' alibis, or lack

PETER ROBINSON

of them. Nicholas never taught classes on Friday mornings, but he usually went in anyway and used the time for
paperwork. On the Friday in question, however, the head-
master's administrative assistant remembered seeing him
arrive late, at around eleven o'clock. This was nothing
unusual – it had happened often enough before – but it did
leave him without a valid alibi.

Stephen Collier, it turned out, had no meetings
scheduled for that day, again quite normal in itself, and
nobody could remember whether he had been in or not.
Work days, the world-weary secretary explained to
Sergeant Hatchley, are so much the same that most office
workers have difficulty remembering one from another. Mr
Collier was often off the premises anyway, and the people
who actually ran the business never saw much of him.

PC Weaver from Helmthorpe, who had been questioning people in Swainshead that morning, reported that
nobody remembered seeing Bernard Allen out there on the
morning in question, let alone noticed anyone follow him.

At about two o'clock, Richmond popped his head round
the door. He'd been using the computer to check with
various business agencies and immigration offices, but so
far he'd found no one in Swainshead with Canadian
connections. Except for Stephen Collier, who dealt with a
Montreal-based food products corporation.

'What's a food product, do you think?' Banks asked
Richmond.

'I wouldn't know, sir. Something that's not real food,
I'd imagine.'

'And I thought he was trading Wensleydale cheese for
maple syrup. That reminds me: what time is it in Toronto?'

Richmond looked at his watch. 'It'll be about nine in
the morning.'

'I'd better phone the Mounties.'

'Er . . . they won't be Mounties, sir. Not in Toronto.' Richmond stroked his moustache.

'Oh? What will they be?'

'The Toronto Metropolitan Police, sir. The RCMP's federal. These days they mostly do undercover work and police the more remote areas.'

Banks grinned. 'Well, you learn something new every day.'

When Richmond had left, he lit a cigarette and picked up the phone. There was a lot of messing about with the switchboard, but after a few minutes of clicks and whirrs, the phone started ringing at the other end. It wasn't the harsh and insistent sound of an English telephone though; the rings were longer, as were the pauses between them.

When someone finally answered, it took Banks a while to explain who he was and what he wanted. After a few more clicks, he finally got through to the right man.

'Chief Inspector Banks? Staff Sergeant Gregson here. And how's the old country?'

'Fine,' said Banks, a little perplexed by the question.

'My father was a Brit,' Gregson went on. 'Came from Derbyshire.' He pronounced the e as in clergy, and shire came out as sheer. 'Do you know it?' he asked.

'Oh, yes. It's just down the road.'

'Small country.'

'Right.'

Gregson cleared his throat and Banks could hear papers rustling three thousand miles away. 'I can't say we've got any good news for you,' the Canadian said. 'We've had a look around Allen's apartment, but we didn't find anything unusual.'

'Was there an address book?'

'Address book . . . let me see . . .' More paper rustled. 'No. No address book. No diary.'

'Damn. He must have taken them with him.'

'Makes sense, doesn't it? If he was going on vacation he'd be sure to want to send pretty postcards to all his buddies back home.'

'What about his friends? Have you seen any of them?'

'We talked to his colleagues at work. There's not many of them around. College finishes in early May, so teachers are pretty thin on the ground at this time of year. Nice work if you can get it, eh? Now they're all off swimming in the lake and sunning themselves on the deck up at their fancy summer cottages in Muskoka.'

'Is that like a villa in Majorca?'

'Huh?'

'Never mind. What did they have to say?'

'Said he was a bit aloof, stand-offish. Course, a lot of Brits over here are like that. They think Canada's still part of the Empire, so they come on like someone out of *The Jewel in the Crown*.'

'Did you find his ex-wife?'

'Yup. She's been in Calgary for the past six months, so you can count her out.'

'Apparently, there was a lover,' Banks told him. 'Someone at the college. That's why they got divorced.'

'Have you got a name?'

'Sorry.'

Gregson sighed. 'I'd like to help you, Chief Inspector, I really would,' he said, 'but we can't spare the men to go tracking down some guy who ran off with Allen's wife. We just don't have the manpower.'

'No, of course not.'

'Besides, people don't usually steal a man's wife and then kill him.'

'They might if he was causing them problems. But you're right, it's not likely. Did he have any girlfriends?'

'As I said, his colleagues thought he was a bit stuck-up. One of them even thought he was gay, but I wouldn't pay much mind to that. Sometimes, with their accents and mannerisms and all, Brits do seem a bit that way to us North Americans.'

'Yes,' Banks said, gritting his teeth. 'I think that just about covers it all. I can see now why they say you always get your man.' And he hung up. Nothing. Still nothing. He obviously couldn't expect any help from across the Atlantic.

Still feeling a residue of irrational anger at Gregson's sarcasm, he walked over to the window and lit a cigarette. The drizzle had turned into steady rain now and the square below was bright with open umbrellas. As he gazed down on the scene, one woman caught his eye. She walked in a daze, as if she wasn't sure where she was heading. She looked soaked to the skin, too; her hair was plastered to her head and the thin white blouse she wore was moulded to her form so that the outline of her brassiere stood out in clear relief. It took Banks a few moments to recognize Katie Greenock.

He grabbed his raincoat and made a move to go down and make sure she was all right, but when he looked out for her one last time, she was nowhere in sight. She had disappeared like a phantom. There was no sense in searching the town for her just because she was walking in the rain without an umbrella. Still, he was strangely disturbed by the vision. It worried him. For the rest of the wet afternoon he felt haunted by that slight and sensuous figure staring into an inner distance, walking in the rain.

PART TWO

THE THOUSAND-DOLLAR CURE

8

ONE

The powerful jet engines roared and Banks felt himself pushed back in his seat. It was his first time in a jumbo. The plane lumbered along the runway at Manchester International Airport, fixtures and fittings shaking and rattling, as if defying anyone to believe that a machine of such bulk could fly. But it did. Soon, Lancashire was a chequerboard of wet fields, then it was lost completely under the clouds. The NO SMOKING sign went off and Banks lit up.

In a few moments, the blue-uniformed stewardess with her shocking pink lipstick and impossibly white teeth – the same one who had managed to put such drama into the routine demonstration of the use of the life jacket – came around with more boiled sweets and personal headphones in plastic bags. Banks took a set, as he knew there would be a film later on, but he gave the designer music a miss and took out his own Walkman. Soon the plane was over Ireland, an occasional flash of green between the clouds, the Beatles were singing 'Dear Prudence', and all was well with the world.

Banks ordered Scotch on the rocks when the trolley came around and relaxed with his miniature Johnnie Walker Red.

Closing his eyes, he settled back to reconsider the events that had led to his present unnatural position – about 35,000 feet above the Atlantic Ocean, hurtling at a speed of roughly 600 miles an hour towards a strange continent.

It was Saturday, 3 July, almost a month since the Bernard Allen case had stalled. Banks had visited Swainshead once or twice and found things relatively quiet. Stephen and Nicholas Collier had remained polite in their arrogant way; Sam Greenock had been surly, as usual; Katie Greenock still seemed troubled and distracted; and John Fletcher had expressed passing interest in the progress of the case.

The problem was that there really wasn't a case any more. Enquiries had turned up neither new witnesses nor motives. A number of people had had the opportunity to kill Bernard Allen, but no one had a clear reason. As long as the suspects stuck to their stories, it didn't matter whether they were lying or telling the truth; there was no solid evidence to break the case. That was why it was vital for Banks to find Anne Ralston – she was the link between the Addison and Allen murders – and he had convinced Gristhorpe he could do it in a week.

'How?' the superintendent had asked. 'Toronto's a strange city to you. A big one, too.'

'Where would you head if you were an Englishman living abroad?'

Gristhorpe rubbed his chin. 'I'd seek out the expatriate community, I suppose. The club. I'd want to be among my own.'

'Right. So, given we're not dealing with the gentry, I'd expect Allen to hang around the English-style pubs. Every big city has them. His brother-in-law, Les Haines, told me Allen liked his ale and had found a pub where he could get imported British beer. There can't be all that many of them in Toronto.'

'But it's Anne Ralston we're looking for, remember that.'

'I know. I'm just assuming that if Allen was a bit stand-offish with his mates at work, he had a crowd of fellow émigrés he hung around with in his spare time. The odds are they'd meet up in a pub and stand at the bar quaffing pints. They might know the Ralston woman.'

'So you want to go on a pub crawl of Toronto?'

'Looks like it, doesn't it?'

'Better not tell Jim Hatchley or you'll get nowt out of him for a month or more. Why can't you get the Toronto police to find her?'

'For a start, I got the impression on the phone that they didn't have time or didn't give a damn, or both. And anyway, they wouldn't know how to question her, what to ask. Someone would have to brief them on two murder investigations, the sociology of the Yorkshire village, the history of—'

Gristhorpe held up his hand. 'All right, all right, I get the point.'

'And I think they'd scare her off, too,' Banks added. 'She was nervous enough about what she knew to warn Allen not to spread it around, so if she thinks the police are after her, the odds are she'll scarper.'

'Have you considered that she might not be using her own name?'

'Yes. But I've got her photograph from our missing persons files – it's a bit old, but it's all we've got – and I think I know where to look. Being English myself gives me an advantage in that kind of environment, too. Do you think it makes sense?'

'It's all a bit iffy, but yes, yes I do, on the whole. If you can track down Allen's drinking companions, there's a good chance he'll have told them about Anne Ralston. She might even drop in at his local herself from time to time, if she's the kind that likes to be among her own.'

'So you'll see what you can do about getting me over there?'

Gristhorpe nodded. 'Aye. I'll see what I can do.'

About a week later, on a Thursday morning, the superintendent had asked Banks to come to his office. Banks stubbed out his cigarette and carried his full coffee mug carefully along the corridor. As usual, Gristhorpe's door was slightly ajar. Banks nudged it open with his shoulder and entered the cosy book-lined room. He took his usual seat and put his coffee on the desk in front of him.

Gristhorpe pushed a long envelope over the blotter.

'You've done it?'

'Open it.'

Inside was a return ticket on a charter flight from Manchester to Toronto.

'There's an important international conference on policing the inner city in London, Ontario. I thought you ought to go.'

'But this ticket's for Toronto.'

'Aye, well, there isn't an international airport in London.'

'And Eastvale doesn't have an inner city.'

Gristhorpe scratched his hooked nose. 'We might have, one day. We did have a riot a few months ago, didn't we? It pays to be prepared.'

'Will you be expecting a report?'

'Oh, a brief verbal account will do.'

Banks grinned.

'There's one catch, though.'

'Oh?'

'Money. All I could scrounge was the ticket and a bit of loose change for meals. You'll have to supply most of your own pocket money.'

'That's all right. I'm not likely to be spending a fortune. What about accommodation, though?'

'You'll be staying with my nephew – at least, you can stay in his apartment. He's off to Banff or some such place for the summer. Anyway, I've been in touch and he says he'll be happy to meet you at the airport. I described you to him, so just stand around and look lost. He's rather a lanky lad, as I remember. His hair's a bit too long and he wears those silly little glasses – granny glasses, I think they're called. He's a nice enough lad – graduate student, organic chemistry or some such thing. He says he lives downtown, whatever that means. You told me a week, Alan. I'm depending on you.'

'I'll do my best,' Banks said, pocketing the ticket.

'Find Anne Ralston and discover what she knows. I don't care how you do it, outside torture. And for Christ's sake, keep away from the local police. They wouldn't appreciate your trespassing on their patch. You're a tourist, remember that.'

'I've been wondering why you're sending me,' Banks said. 'You're very much concerned with this case yourself, especially the connection with the Addison murder. Why don't you go?'

'I would,' Gristhorpe said slowly. 'Believe me, I would.' He looked sideways towards the open window. 'I did my National Service in the RAF. I'd always hero-worshipped fighter pilots in the war and I suppose, in my folly, I wanted to be just like them. First time up one of the engines caught fire. If the pilot hadn't been so damn good we'd have both been dead. Even so . . . I've never fancied the idea since.'

'I can't say I blame you,' Banks said. 'I'll find her, don't worry. At least I've an idea where to look.'

And that was that. Sandra and the children were excited and, of course, disappointed that they couldn't go with him. Sergeant Hatchley acted as if Banks had been given a free holiday in an exotic place. And now here he was, high above the Atlantic Ocean, the pink lips and white teeth leaning over him with a tray of food.

Banks took off his headphones and arranged the tray in front of him. The main course appeared to be a small shrivelled chicken leg with pale wrinkled skin, accompanied by tiny potatoes and carrots covered in gravy. On further inspection, Banks discovered that one half of the meal was piping hot and the other still frozen solid. He called the attendant, who apologized profusely and took it away. When she delivered it again, the frozen side was warm and the other overcooked. Banks took a few mouthfuls and gave up in disgust. He also felt no inclination to investigate the mound of jelly-like substance with a swirl of cream on its top, or the limp lettuce leaves that passed for a salad. Instead, he turned to his cheese and biscuits which, being wrapped in cellophane, were at least fresh, and washed them down with a small plastic bottle of harsh red wine.

Feeling the onset of heartburn, Banks declined the offer of coffee and lit a cigarette. After the trays had been cleared, more drinks came. They really were very generous, Banks thought, and wondered what havoc a plane full of drunks might wreak – especially if the booze ran out. But it didn't. He was kept well supplied with Johnnie Walker Red – a kind of sedation, he supposed, insurance against restless and troublesome passengers – and soon people were asked to pull down their blinds against the blazing sunlight in preparation for the movie. This turned out to be a dreadful cops-and-robbers affair full of car chases and shoot-outs in shopping precincts. After about ten minutes, Banks put his headset aside, closed his eyes and went over in his mind the questions he wanted to ask Anne Ralston. The jet engines were humming, the Scotch warmed his veins, and soon he fell into a deep sleep. The last thing he remembered was the crackly voice of the pilot saying they were soon going to reach the tip of Newfoundland and would then fly along the St Lawrence River.

TWO

While Banks was asleep somewhere over Quebec City, Detective Superintendent Gristhorpe sat hunched over a pint of Theakston's bitter and a veal and egg pie in the Queen's Arms, waiting for Sergeant Hatchley.

Frowning, he looked at his watch. He'd told Hatchley to arrive no later than seven thirty. He glanced out of the window at the market square, but saw no sign of the sergeant. It was still raining. That very morning the clouds had closed in again, draining the valley sides of their lush greens and flattening the majestic perspective of fells and moors.

At last Hatchley burst in and looked anxiously around for the superintendent. His hair was slicked down by the rain, emphasizing the bullet shape of his head, and the shoulders of his beige trench coat were splotched dark with wet patches.

'Sorry, sir,' he apologized, sitting opposite Gristhorpe. 'The damn weather's slowing down traffic all along the dale.'

Gristhorpe could smell the beer on his breath and guessed that he'd probably stopped for a quick one in Helmthorpe on his way, or maybe he had even made a minor diversion to the Black Sheep in Relton, where the landlord brewed his own prize-winning beer on the premises. He said nothing though. Without Banks around, Hatchley and Richmond were all he had, and he had no wish to alienate the sergeant before putting his plan into action.

Gristhorpe accepted Hatchley's offer of another pint and leaned back in his seat to avoid the drift of smoke when the sergeant lit a cigarette.

'Did you tell them?' Gristhorpe asked.

'Aye, sir. Found them all in the White Rose.'

'I hope you weren't too obvious.'

Hatchley looked offended. 'No, sir. I did it just like you said. When Freddie Metcalfe started probing and prodding about why I was there, I just told him it was a few loose ends I had to tie up, that's all.'

'And then?'

'Ah, well. Then, sir, I got myself invited over to the table. It was all very casual, like, chatting about the cricket and the local markets as if we was old mates. Then Sam Greenock asked me where my boss was.'

'What did you say?'

'Just what you told me, sir. I said he'd gone off to Toronto to talk to Anne Ralston.'

'And?'

'And what, sir?'

'What happened next, man? How did they react?'

Hatchley took a long pull at his beer and wiped his lips with the back of his hairy hand. 'Oh, they just looked at one another and raised their eyebrows a bit.'

'Can you be a bit more specific, Sergeant? What did Sam Greenock say?'

'He didn't really say anything. Seemed excited to hear the news. I got the impression it made him a bit angry. And Stephen Collier went distinctly pale. That poncy brother of his just looked down his nose like I was something the cat dragged in.'

'Who else was there?'

'Only John Fletcher.'

'Did he react in any way?'

Hatchley scratched his ear. 'I'd say he got a bit tight-lipped. You wouldn't really say he reacted, but it was as if it rang a bell somewhere and sent him off in his own world. More puzzled and worried than anything else.'

Gristhorpe thought over the information and filed it away in his mind. 'Good work, Sergeant,' he said finally. 'You did well.'

Hatchley nodded and started casually rocking his empty pint glass on the table. 'What now, sir?' he asked.

'We keep an eye on them. Tomorrow I'm going to send DC Richmond to stay at the Greenock Guest House for a few days. I don't think his face is well known in Swainshead.' Gristhorpe turned up his nose and leaned forward to grind out Hatchley's cigarette butt, which still smouldered in the ashtray. 'We keep an eye on them,' he repeated. 'And we watch very carefully for one of them to make a slip or try and make a run for it. All right, Sergeant. You don't have to break the bloody glass on the table. I know it's my round. Same again?'

THREE

Somewhere, with maddening metronomic regularity, a bell was ringing. Banks rubbed his eyes and saw the seat-belt sign was lit up. The NO SMOKING sign was still out, so he lit a cigarette immediately to clear his head. Looking out of the window, he saw a vast urban area below. It was too far down to distinguish details, but he could make out the grid system of roads and fancied he could see cars flash in the sun.

The attendant said something over the PA system about a final descent, and passengers were then asked to extinguish their cigarettes. Banks's ears felt funny. He swallowed and yawned to clear them, and the noise of the plane roared in again. All the way down he had to keep repeating the process every few seconds.

The plane banked to the left and now individual buildings and moving vehicles stood out quite clearly. After a long turn, a great expanse of water came into sight on the right and a cluster of tall buildings appeared on the waterside. The plane was dropping quickly now, and within moments it touched the runway smoothly. The loud retro-jets kicked in. They felt like ropes tied to the back of the plane, dragging it to a halt. Several nervous passengers applauded.

After some delay, the doors slid open and the slow line of people left the aircraft, running a gauntlet of fixed smiles from the attendants. Banks negotiated the stairs and corridors, then found himself in a long queue at Immigration. After that, there was another wait until the baggage came round on the carousel. Clutching his small suitcase, duty-free Scotch and cigarettes, he walked past the customs officers, who paid him no attention, and out into the throng of people waiting to welcome friends and relatives. As Gristhorpe suggested, he stood to one side and looked lost. It was easy.

Soon he noticed an Adam's apple the size of a tennis ball stuck in a long skinny neck below a head covered with long brown hair making its way through the crowd. As the head also wore a pair of ridiculously old-fashioned granny glasses, Banks risked a wave of recognition.

'Gerry Webb,' the man said, shaking hands. 'Are you Chief Inspector Banks?'

'Yes. Just call me Alan. I'm not here officially.'

'I'll bet,' Gerry said. 'Come on, let's get out of here.'

They pushed their way through the crowds of relatives embracing long-lost children or parents, and took a lift to the multi-storey car park.

'This is it,' Gerry said, pointing proudly to a saffron Volkswagen bug. 'I call her Sneezy because she's a bit of a dwarf compared to most of the cars here, and she makes a funny noise when I try to start her in the mornings, especially during winter. Still, she gets me around.' He patted Sneezy on the bonnet and opened the boot at the front. Case and duty-free securely stored, Banks got in the passenger door after a false start on the left.

'It always happens when people visit from England,' Gerry said, laughing. 'Without fail. Just wait until you try and cross the road.'

The first thing Banks noticed as Gerry drove out on to the expressway were the huge cars and the stifling heat. It was like trying to breathe at the bottom of a warm bath. In no time, his shirt was stuck to his skin. He took off his jacket and tossed it on the back seat. Even the draught through the open window was hot and wet.

'You've come in the middle of a heatwave, I'm afraid,' Gerry explained. 'It's been between thirty-three and thirty-six degrees for the past three days now. Above ninety per cent humidity, too.'

'What's a hundred like?'

'Funny, that,' Gerry said. 'We never get a hundred. Not even during a thunderstorm. Summer can be a real bitch here. Toronto's a city of extremes as far as climate is concerned. In winter it's bloody cold, real brass monkey weather, and in summer it's so hot and humid it's unbearable, as you can tell. Pollution count goes way up, too.'

'What about spring?'

'We don't have one. Just a lot of rain and then the sun. Fall's the best. September. October. Warmish days, cool evenings. Beautiful.' He glanced sideways at Banks. 'I suppose you were expecting icicles and snowmen?'

'Not exactly. But I didn't expect the heat to be this bad.'

'You should see the Americans,' Gerry said. 'I lived in Windsor for a while when I was doing my M.Sc., and I worked for customs during summer. They'd come over the border from the Detroit suburbs in the middle of July with skis on top of their cars and fur coats on the back seats. What a laugh that was. Americans know bugger all about Canada.'

'I can't say I know much, myself,' Banks admitted.

'Worry not. Keep your eyes and ears open and all will be revealed.' Gerry had an odd accent, part Yorkshire and part North American, with a mixed vocabulary to match.

They swung eastwards around a bay. For a moment, Banks thought they were on the wrong side of the road. He tensed and the adrenalin prickled in his veins. Then, again, he realized he was in Canada.

On the right was Lake Ontario, a ruffled blue sheet with millions of diamonds dancing on it. The white triangular sails of yachts leaned at sharp angles. There seemed to be at least a cooler breeze coming from the water and Banks envied the idle rich who could spend their days sailing like that.

'Those are the Islands over there,' Gerry said, pointing towards a low hazy blur of green. 'They're just a long sandbar really, but everyone calls them islands. People live on the far ones, Ward's and Algonquin, but the politicians want to chuck them off and make a heliport or a mini golf course.'

'That sounds typical,' Banks said, recalling the various schemes for developing adventure playgrounds and safari parks in the Dales.

'A lot of trouble over it,' Gerry said. 'At first, the islanders even got themselves a home guard organized – hard hats, the lot. They were prepared to fight off an invasion.'

'What happened?'

'It's still going on really. Oh, various bright sparks come up with ideas for long-term leases and whatnot, but there's always trouble brewing. It's jealousy, I think. Most of the people who live there now are academics or artists and a lot of people stuck in the city envy them their lives. They think only the filthy rich ought to be able to afford such a pleasant environment.'

'What about you?'

'I don't envy anyone who survives winter after winter out there in not much more than a wooden shack. Look.' He pointed ahead.

In front of them a cluster of tall buildings shimmered in the heat like a dot matrix block graph. A few were black, others white, and some even reflected the deep gold of the sun. Close to the lake, dominating them all, was a tapering tower with a bulbous head just below its long needle-point summit. It was a phallic symbol of such Olympian proportions that it made the London Post Office Tower look like it had a serious sexual dysfunction.

'The CN Tower,' Gerry said. 'Toronto's pride and joy. Tallest free-standing structure in the world – or at least it will be until the Japanese build a bigger one. See those elevators going up the outside?'

Banks did. The mere thought of being in one made him feel dizzy. He wasn't afraid of heights up to a certain point, but he'd never felt like risking a meal in a revolving restaurant at the top of a tower.

'What's it for?' he asked.

'Well you may ask. For show really.'

'What's at the top?'

'A restaurant, what else? And a disco, of course. This is the height of Western civilization. A feat on a par with the Great Pyramids and Chartres cathedral.'

'A disco?'

'Yes. Honest. Oh, I suppose I'm being flippant. They do use the place as a radio and TV transmitter, but it's basically just one of man's muscle-flexing exercises. This is downtown.'

The expressway, on a kind of elevated ramp, rolled past the backs of warehouses and billboards. Because the buildings were so close, the speed the car was travelling at was exaggerated and Banks felt as if he was on a roller coaster.

Finally, Gerry branched off, drove through an industrial wasteland of dirty old factories with external plumbing, then turned on to a busy street. Most of the buildings seemed quite old and run-down, and Banks soon noticed that nearly all the shop signs were in Chinese. Roast ducks hung by their feet in shop windows and teeming stalls of colourful fruit and vegetables blocked the pavements in front of grocery stores. One shop displayed a handwritten sign offering a mysterious combination of LIVE CRABS & VIDEOS. The street was bustling with people, mostly Chinese, pushing and shoving to get to the best deals, picking up and examining wares. The rich smell of food gone bad in the heat, mingled with the aroma of exotic spices, drifted into the car along with the suffocating air. A red and cream tram rattled along its track beside them.

'Chinatown East,' Gerry said. 'Not far to go now.'

He continued up the street past a prison and a hospital. To the left was a broad green valley. Beside the road, it sloped like a huge lawn down to the broad bottom, where a busy expressway ran beside the brown river. Above the trees on the far side, the downtown towers shimmered, greyish blurs in the heat haze. Gerry turned right into a tree-lined street and pulled up in the driveway of a small brick house with a green and white porch.

'Home,' he announced. 'I've got the bottom floor and there's a young couple upstairs. They're generally pretty quiet, so I wouldn't worry too much about noise.' He put his key in the lock and opened the door. 'Come on in. I'm dying for a cold beer.'

The place was small and sparsely furnished – apparently with cast-offs bought from second-hand shops – but it was clean and comfortable. Books stuffed every possible shelf and cavity. The Gristhorpe clan certainly seemed to be great readers, Banks thought.

Gerry led him into the small kitchen and took two cans of Budweiser from the fridge. Banks pulled the tab and poured the iced, slightly malty beer down his throat. When Gerry tipped back his can to drink, his Adam's apple bobbed wildly.

'That's better,' he said, wiping his lips. 'I'm sorry it's so hot in here too, but I can't afford an air-conditioner. Actually, I've lived in worse places. There's a good through-draught, and it does cool down a bit at night.'

'What's this area of town called?' Banks asked.

'Riverdale. It's gone very yuppie in the past few years. Property values have shot up like crazy. You'll see the main drag, the Danforth, if you walk or take a streetcar up to the corner. It used to be all Greek cafés, restaurants and twenty-four-hour fruit and vegetable stores. Now it's all health foods, late-night bookshops, and bistros with long-stemmed wineglasses and coral-pink tablecloths. All right if you like that kind of thing, I suppose.'

'And if you don't?'

'There's a few unpretentious places left. You get some good blues at the Black Swan on Saturday afternoons. And then there's Quinn's, not a bad pub. Some of the old Greek places are still around, but I can't say I've ever been fond of Greek food myself – it's all greasy lamb, eggplant and sticky desserts as far as I'm concerned.'

They sat down on the sofa, an overstuffed maroon 1950s monstrosity with arms like wings, and finished their beers.

'Your uncle said you had to go to a conference somewhere,' Banks said. 'I hope I'm not driving you out?'

'Not at all. Actually, the conference isn't so important, but Banff is a great place – right on the edge of the Rockies – so I'll get a bit of hiking and partying done too.'

'How are you getting there?'

'Sneezy.'

'How far is it?'

'A couple of thousand miles. But you get used to distances like that here. Sneezy's done it before. She quite likes long journeys. I'll take my tent and camp out on the way. If you need a car . . .'

Banks shook his head. 'No. No, I wouldn't dare drive on the wrong side of the road. What's the public transport like?'

'Very good. There's a subway, buses and the streetcars you've seen. We don't call them trams here.'

'I was surprised,' Banks said. 'I haven't been on one of them since I was a kid.'

'Well, now's your chance to make up for lost time. I use them a lot myself to get around the city. Often it's not worth the bother of parking in town, and the cops can be pretty sticky about drinking and driving. Oops, sorry.'

Banks laughed.

'Anyway,' Gerry went on, delving into a drawer and bringing out a couple of maps, 'this is the city – easy to find your way about as it's mostly an east–west, north–south grid system. And here's the transit map. It's not as complicated as the London Underground, so you shouldn't have much trouble.'

And Gerry went on giving information about subway tokens and free transfers from one mode of transport to another. But after the journey and in the sweltering heat, Banks felt his eyes closing. He could do nothing about it.

'Here,' Gerry said, 'I'm boring you to death. I don't suppose you're taking any of this in.'

'Not much.'

'Do you want to go to bed?'

'I wouldn't mind a nap.'

Gerry showed him the bedroom.

'Isn't this your room?' Banks asked.

'It's OK. I'll bed down on the couch tonight.'

'I can do that.'

'Not necessary. I'm off early in the morning anyway. This'll be your room for the next week.'

Too tired to argue more and, frankly, grateful for a bed, Banks undressed, sank on to the mattress and fell asleep within seconds.

When he woke he was disoriented at finding himself in an unfamiliar bed. It took him a few moments to remember where he was. It was hot and dark, and the sheets felt moist with sweat. Hearing sounds in the front room, Banks rubbed his eyes, pulled on his trousers and walked through. He found Gerry stuffing clothes into a huge backpack. For a moment, it made him think of Bernard Allen.

'Hi,' Gerry said. 'I thought you were out for the count.'

'What time is it?'

'Ten o'clock. Three in the morning, your time.'

'I just woke up suddenly. I don't know why.'

'Jet lag does funny things like that. It's much worse going the other way.'

'Wonderful.'

Gerry grinned. 'Beer?'

'Any chance of a cup of tea?'

'Sure. We're not all coffee-drinking barbarians out here, you know.'

Gerry switched on the television and went into the kitchen. Banks sank into the sofa and put his feet up on a battered pouffe. A pretty woman was talking very intensely about a debate in the House of Commons. Again Banks felt the shock of being in a foreign land. The TV newscaster spoke with an odd accent – less overbearing than the Americans he had heard – and he knew none of the politicians' names.

Gerry brought the tea and sat beside him.

'There might be a couple of things you can help me with,' Banks said.

'Shoot.'

'Where can I find Toronto Community College?'

'Easy. The subway's the quickest.' And Gerry told him how to get to Broadview station by streetcar or on foot, where to change trains, and where to get off.

'There's another thing. Do you know anything about the English-style pubs in town? Somewhere that sells imported beer.'

Gerry laughed. 'You've certainly got your work cut out. There's dozens of them: the Madison, the Sticky Wicket, Paupers, the Hop and Grape, the Artful Dodger, the Jack Russell, the Spotted Dick, the Feathers, Quigley's, not to mention a whole dynasty of Dukes. I'll try and make a list for you. What's it all about, by the way, if that's not top secret?'

'I'm looking for a woman. Her name's Anne Ralston.'

'What's she done?'

'Nothing, as far as I know.'

'How very secretive. You're as bad as Uncle Eb, you are.'

'Who?'

'Uncle Eb. You mean you don't know . . .?'

Banks shook his head. Gristhorpe had never mentioned his first name, and his signature was an indecipherable scrawl.

'Well, maybe I shouldn't tell you. He won't thank me for it, if I know him.'

'I won't tell him I know. Scout's honour. Come on.'

'It's short for Ebenezer, of course.'

Banks whistled through his teeth. 'No wonder he never lets on.'

'Ah, but that's not all. His father was a grand champion of the labouring man, especially the farm workers, so he called his oldest son Ebenezer Elliott – after the "Corn Law Rhymer".'

Banks had never heard of Ebenezer Elliott but made a mental note to look him up. He was always interested in new things to read, look at or listen to.

'Ebenezer Elliott Gristhorpe,' he repeated to himself. 'Bloody hell.'

'Thought you'd like that,' Gerry said, grinning. 'It does have a certain ring to it, doesn't it? My poor mum got lumbered with Mary Wollstonecraft. Very progressive, Grandad was, respected the rights of women, too. But my dad was plain old George Webb, and thank the Lord he'd no hobby horse to tie his kids to.'

On the news, a gang of street kids in Belfast threw stones and tossed Molotov cocktails at police in riot gear. It was night, and orange flames blossomed all along the street. Black smoke rose from burning tyres. The world really was a global village, Banks thought, feeling his attention start to slip. Consciousness was fading away again. He yawned and put down his teacup on the low table.

'You can tell me something now,' Gerry said. 'Where did you get that scar?'

Banks fingered the white scar by his right eye. 'This? I passed out from lack of sleep and hit my head on the corner of a table.'

Gerry laughed. 'I get the point. I'm keeping you up.'

Banks smiled. 'I'm definitely falling asleep again. See you in the morning?'

'Probably not,' Gerry said. 'I've got a long way to go and I'm setting off at the crack of dawn. There's coffee and sugar in the cupboard above the sink. Milk and stuff's in the fridge. Here's a spare door-key. Make yourself at home.'

Banks shook his bony hand. 'Thanks,' he said. 'I will. And if you're ever in England . . .'

'I'll be sure to visit Uncle Ebenezer. I always do. And we'll have a jar or two in the Queen's Arms. Goodnight.'

Banks went back into the bedroom. A light breeze had sprung up to ease the suffocating heat a little, but it was still far from comfortable. He flopped down on the damp sheets. Outside, a short distance away, he heard a street-car rattle by and remembered exciting childhood trips to big cities when the trams were still running. He thought of the Queen's Arms on the edge of sleep, and pictured the pub on the corner of Market Street and the cobbled square. He felt very far from home. The Queen's Arms was a long, long way away, and there was a lot to do if he was to track down Anne Ralston before the week was over.

9

ONE

They were going to church: the women smiling in their wide-brimmed hats and cotton print dresses, the men ill at ease in tight ties and pinching waistcoats.

Every Sunday morning Katie watched them as she cleaned the rooms, and every week she knew she should be with them, dragging Sam along with the promise of an hour in the pub for him later while she cooked dinner. But he went to the pub anyway, and she cooked dinner anyway. The only thing missing was the hour in church. And that she couldn't face.

All through her childhood, Katie had been forced to go to the Gospel with her grandmother, and the icy devotion of the congregation had scared her half to death. Though they were praising God, they hardly dared sing so loud for fear He would think they were taking pleasure in the hymns. Katie could never understand the readings or the lessons, but she understood the passionate menace in the tones of those who spoke; she understood the meanings of the spittle that sometimes dribbled over their lips and the way their eyes glazed over. As she grew older, all her fear affixed itself to the sights, sounds and smells of the church: the chill mustiness rising from worn stone flags; the pews creaking as a bored child shifts position; the unearthly echo of the minister's voice; the wooden board announcing the hymn numbers; the stained glass fragmenting colour like broken souls. Just thirty seconds in a church meant panic for Katie; she couldn't breathe, she started trembling, and her blood turned to stone.

But she knew she should go. It was, after all, God's Mansion on Earth, and she would never escape this vale of tears if she didn't give herself to Him completely. Instead, she watched the rest of the village go off in their finery and listened to the hymns on the radio as she dusted, tidied and swept, humming along very quietly under her breath. Surely, surely, He would approve? She was working, doing her duty. It was the sabbath, of course, but there were still guests to take care of, and she suspected deep in her heart that the sabbath was only meant for men anyway. Surely He would approve. Her work would count in her favour. But it was a sin, she remembered vaguely, to court His favour, to say, 'Look what I've done, Lord.' It was the sin of pride. At least some said it was. She couldn't remember who, or whether she had been told to believe or disbelieve them – there were so many heresies, traps awaiting those impure in body and mind – but words such as faith, works and elect circled one another in her thoughts.

Well, Katie concluded dismally, working on Sundays could only add to the weight of sin she carried already. She picked up the black plastic bag. There were still three more rooms to do, then there was dinner to see to. When, she wondered, was it all going to end?

She went downstairs to put the roast in and immediately recognized the new guest standing over the registration book in the hall. He signed himself in as Philip Richmond, from Bolton, Lancashire, and he told Sam, who was dealing with the details, that he was simply after a few relaxing days in the country. But Katie remembered the moustache and the athletic spring in his step; it was the man she had seen with Chief Inspector Banks and Sergeant Hatchley the day she had run away to Eastvale.

Seeing him there brought back the whole day. Nothing had come of it really, except that she had caught a minor cold. The housework got done. Not on time, but it got done. Sam never even found out, so there was no retribution at his hands. Nor were there any outbreaks of boils, thunderbolts from heaven, plagues of locusts or other such horrors her grandmother had assured her would happen if she strayed from the path.

She felt as if she had lost sight of the path completely now. That was all she really knew about what was happening to her. The conflicting voices in her mind seemed to have merged into one incomprehensible rumble, and much of the time she felt as if she had no control over her thoughts or deeds.

There were clear moments though. Like now. Outside, the landscape was fresh after the previous few days' rain, which was now rising in sun-charmed wraiths of mist from the lower fell sides and the valley bottom. And here, in their hall, stood a man she recognized as having a close association with the police.

She hadn't seen what all the fuss was about the previous evening, when Sam had stumbled home from the White Rose in a very bad mood.

'He's gone to find her,' he had said, scowling. 'All the way to bloody Canada. Just to find her.'

'Who?' Katie had asked quietly, confused and frightened of him. In moods like this he was likely to lash out, and she could still feel the pain in her breast from the last time.

'Anne Ralston, you silly bitch. That copper's taken off to Toronto after her.'

'Well, what does it matter?' Katie had argued cautiously. 'If she killed that man all those years ago, they'll put her in jail, won't they?'

'You don't know nothing, woman, do you? Nothing at all.' Sam hit out at her and knocked the wooden cross off the mantelpiece.

'Leave it,' he snarled, grabbing Katie by the arm as she bent to pick it up. 'Can't you think of anything but bloody cleaning up?'

'But I thought you wanted me—'

'Oh, shut up. You don't know nothing.'

'Well, tell me. What is it? Why does it matter so much that he's gone chasing after Anne Ralston in Canada? You hardly knew her. Why does it matter to us?'

'It doesn't,' Sam said. 'But it might to Stephen. She might make things difficult for him.'

'But Stephen hasn't done anything, has he? How could she harm him?'

'She was his fancy woman, wasn't she? Then she ran off and left him. She could tell lies about his business, about . . . hell, I don't know! All I know is that it's all your bloody fault.'

Katie said nothing. Sam's initial rage was spent, she could tell, and she knew she would remain fairly safe if she kept quiet. It was tricky though, because he might get angry again if she didn't give the proper response to his ranting.

Sam sat heavily on the sofa and turned on the television. There was an old black and white film about gangsters on. James Cagney shot Humphrey Bogart and ran for it.

'Get me a beer,' Sam said.

Katie got him a can of Long Life from the fridge. She knew it was no good telling him he'd had enough already. Besides, on nights like this, when he'd had a bit more than usual, he tended to fall asleep as soon as he got to bed.

'And don't forget the Colliers' party next week,' he added, ripping open the can. 'I want you looking your best.'

Katie had forgotten about the garden party. The Colliers had two or three every summer. She hated them.

In the morning, Sam had a thick head and remembered very little about the night before. He sulked until after breakfast, then managed a welcome for the new guest before disappearing somewhere in the Land Rover. Katie showed Richmond his room, then went to get on with her work.

So there was a policeman in the house. She wondered why he was there. Perhaps he was on holiday. Policemen must have holidays too. But if he was from Eastvale, he was hardly likely to travel only twenty-five miles to Swainshead. Not these days. He'd be off to Torquay, or even the Costa del Sol. Katie didn't know how much policemen got paid, so she couldn't really say. But he wouldn't come to Swainshead, that was for sure. He was a spy, then. He thought nobody would recognize him, so he could keep an eye on their comings and goings while the little one with the scar was in Toronto and the big one was God knows where.

And Katie knew who he was. The problem now was what to do with her knowledge. Should she tell Sam, put him on his guard? He'd spread the word then, like he always did, and maybe he'd be grateful to her. But she couldn't remember anything about Sam's gratitude. It just didn't stand out in her memory like the other things. Did she need it? On the other hand, if Sam had done something wrong – and she didn't know whether he had or not – then the policeman, Richmond, if that was his real name, might find out and take him away. She'd be free then. It was an evil thought, and it made her heart race, but . . .

Katie paused and looked out of the back window at the gauze of mist rising like breath from the bright green slopes of Swainshead Fell. It would take a bit of thinking about, this dilemma of hers. She knew she mustn't make a hasty decision.

TWO

'I'm afraid there's hardly anybody here to talk to, Mr . . . er . . .?'

'Banks. Alan Banks. I was a friend of Bernard Allen's.'

'Yes, well, the only person I can think of who might be able to help you is Marilyn Rosenberg.' Tom Jordan, head of the Communications Department at Toronto Community College, looked at his watch. 'She's got a class right now, but she should be free in about twenty minutes, if you'd like to wait?'

'Certainly.'

Jordan led him out of the office into a staff lounge just big enough to hold a few chairs and a low coffee table littered with papers and teaching journals. At one end stood a fridge and, on a desk beside it, a microwave oven. The coffee machine stood on a table below a connecting window to the secretary's office, beside a rack of pigeon-holes for staff messages. Banks poured himself a coffee and Jordan edged away slowly, mumbling about work to do.

The coffee was strong and bitter, hardly the thing to drink in the thirty-three-degree heat. What he really needed was a cold beer or a gin and tonic. And he'd gone and bought Scotch at the duty-free shop. Still, he could leave it as a gift for Gerry Webb. It would surely come in handy in winter.

It was Monday morning. On Sunday, Banks had slept in and then gone for a walk along the Danforth. He had noticed the signs of yuppification that Gerry had mentioned, but he had found a pleasant little Greek restaurant which had served him a hearty moussaka for lunch. Unlike Gerry, Banks enjoyed Greek food.

After that, he had wandered as far as Quinn's. Over a pint, he had asked around about Bernie Allen and shown Anne Ralston's photograph to the bar staff and waitresses. No luck. One down, two dozen to go. He had wandered back along the residential streets south of Danforth Avenue and noticed that the small brick house with the green and white porch fence and columns was a sort of Toronto trademark.

Too tired to go out again, he had stayed in and watched television that evening. Oddly enough, the non-commercial channel was showing an old BBC historical serial he'd found boring enough the first time around, and – much better – one of the Jeremy Brett *Sherlock Holmes* episodes. The only alternatives were the same American cop shows that plagued British TV.

He had woken at about nine o'clock that Monday morning. Still groggy from travel and culture shock, he had taken a shower and had had orange juice and toast for breakfast. Then it was time to set off. He slipped a 1960s anthology tape of Cream, Traffic and Rolling Stones hits in the Walkman and put it in the right-hand pocket of his light cotton jacket. In the left, he placed cigarettes and Hardy's *Tess of the D'Urbervilles*, the only book he'd brought with him.

Jacket slung over shoulder, he set off, following Gerry's directions. A rolling rattling streetcar ride took him by the valley side, rife with joggers. The downtown towers were hazy in the morning heat. Finding the westbound platform at Broadview subway station was every bit as straightforward as Gerry had said, but changing trains at Yonge and getting out to the street at St Clair proved confusing. All exits seemed to lead to a warren of underground shopping malls – air-conditioned, of course – and finding the right way out wasn't easy.

Still, he'd found St Clair Avenue after only a momentary diversion into a supermarket called Ziggy's, and the college was only a short walk from the station.

Now, from the sixth floor, he looked out for a while on the office buildings opposite and the cream tops of the streetcars passing to and fro below him, then turned to the pile of journals on the table.

Halfway through an article on the teaching of 'critical thinking' he heard muffled voices in the corridor, and a young woman with a puzzled expression on her face popped around the door. Masses of curly brown hair framed her round head. She had a small mouth and her teeth, when she smiled, were tiny, straight and pearly white. The greyish gum she was chewing oozed between them like gum disease. She carried a worn overstuffed leather briefcase under her arm, and wore grey cords and a checked shirt.

She stretched out her hand. 'Marilyn Rosenberg. Tom tells me you wanted to talk to me.'

Banks introduced himself and offered to pour her a cup of coffee.

'No thanks,' she said, grabbing a Diet Coke from the fridge. 'Far too hot for that stuff. You'd think they'd do something about the air-conditioning in this place, wouldn't you?' She pulled the tab and the Diet Coke fizzed. 'What do you want with me?'

'I want to talk about Bernard Allen.'

'I've been through all that with the police. There wasn't really much to say.'

'What did they ask you?'

'Just if I thought anyone had a reason to kill him, where my colleagues were over the last few weeks, that kind of thing.'

'Did they ask you anything about his life here?'

'Only what kind of person he was.'

'And?'

'And I told them he was a bit of a loner, that's all. I wasn't the only one they talked to.'

'You're the only one here now.'

'Yeah, I guess.' She grinned again, flashing her beautiful teeth.

'If Bernard didn't have much to do with his colleagues here, did he have a group of friends somewhere else, away from college?'

'I wouldn't really know. Look, I didn't know Bernie that well . . .' She hesitated. 'Maybe it's none of your business, but I wanted to. We were getting closer. Slowly. He was a hard person to get to know. All that stiff-upper-lip Brit stuff. Me, I'm a simple Irish-Jewish girl from Montreal.' She shrugged. 'I liked him. We did lunch up here a couple of times. I was hoping maybe he'd ask me out sometime but . . .'

'It never happened?'

'No. He was too damn slow. I didn't know how much

clearer I could make it without ripping off my clothes and jumping on him. But now it's too late, even for that.'

'How did he seem emotionally before he went to England?'

Marilyn frowned and bit her bottom lip as she thought. 'He hadn't quite got over his divorce,' she said finally. 'So I guess he might have been off women for a while.'

'Did you know his ex-wife?'

'No, not really.'

'What about her lover?'

'Yeah, I knew him. He used to work here. He's a louse.'

'In what way?'

'Every way. Strutting macho peacock. And she fell for it. I don't blame Bernie for feeling bad, but he'd have been well rid of her anyway. He'd have got over it.'

'But he was still upset?'

'Yeah. Withdrawn, sort of.'

'How did he get on with his students?'

'Well enough, considering.'

'Considering what?'

'He cared about literature, but most of the students don't give a damn about James Joyce or George Orwell. They're here to learn about business or computers or electrical engineering – you know, useful stuff – and then they think they'll walk into top high-paying jobs. They don't like it when they find they all have to do English, so it makes our job a bit tough. Some teachers find it harder than others to adjust and lower their expectations.'

'And Bernie was one?'

'Yeah. He complained a lot about how ignorant they were, how half of them didn't even know when the Second World War was fought or who Hitler was. And, even worse, they didn't care anyway. Bernie couldn't understand that. He had one guy who thought Shakespeare was a small town in Saskatchewan. That really got to him.'

'I don't understand,' Banks said. 'How could someone like that get accepted into a college?'

'We have an open-door policy,' Marilyn said. 'It's a democratic education. None of that elitist bullshit you get in England. We don't send our kids away to boarding schools to learn Latin and take a lot of cold showers. All that Jane Eyre stuff.'

Banks, who had not attended a public school himself, along with the majority of English children, was confused. 'But don't a lot of them fail?' he asked. 'Doesn't it waste time and money?'

'We don't like to fail people,' Marilyn said. 'It gives them a poor self-image.'

'So they don't need to know much to get in, and they aren't expected to know much more when they leave, is that it?'

Marilyn smiled like a nurse with a particularly difficult patient.

'What did Bernie think about that?' Banks hurried on.

She laughed. 'Bernie loved youth, young people, but he didn't have much respect for their intelligence.'

'It doesn't sound like they had much.'

'There, you see. That's exactly the kind of thing he'd say. You're so sarcastic, you Brits.'

'But you liked him?'

'Yeah, I liked him. We might have disagreed on a few things, but he was cute and I'm a sucker for an English accent. What can I say? He was a nice guy, at least as far as I could tell. I mean, he might not have thought much of his students, but he treated them well and did his damnedest to arouse some curiosity in them. He was a good teacher. What are you getting at, anyway? Do you think one of his students might have killed him over a poor grade?'

'It sounds unlikely, doesn't it?'

'Not as much as you think,' Marilyn said. 'We once had a guy come after his English teacher here with a shotgun. Luckily, security stopped him before he got very far. Still,' she went on, 'I shouldn't think an irate student would go to all the trouble of following him over to England and killing him there.'

'What did Bernie do when he went home after work? Did he ever mention any particular place he went to?'

Marilyn shook her head and the curls danced. 'No. He did once say he'd had a few pints too many in the pub the night before.'

'The pub?'

'Yeah.'

'He didn't say which pub?'

'No. He just said he'd had six pints when five was his limit these days. Look, what is all this? What are you after? You're not one of those private eyes, are you?'

Banks laughed. 'No. I told you, I'm a friend of Bernie's from England. Swainsdale, where he grew up. I want to piece together as much of his life as I can. A lot of people over there are hurt and puzzled by what happened.'

'Yeah, well . . . me too. He wasn't the kind of guy who gets himself killed. Know what I mean?'

Banks nodded.

'Swainsdale, you said?' she went on. 'Bernie was always going on about that place. At least the couple of times we talked he was. Like it was some paradise on earth or something. Especially since the divorce, he started to get homesick. He was beginning to feel a bit lost and out of place here. It can happen, you know. So he took the thousand-dollar cure.'

'The what?'

'The thousand-dollar cure. I guess it's gone up now with inflation, but it's when Brits take a trip back home to renew their roots. Used to call it the thousand-dollar cure. For homesickness.'

'Did he ever talk of going back to Swainsdale to stay?'

'Yeah. He said he'd be off like a shot if he had a job, or a private income. He said there was nothing for him here after he split up with Barbara. Poor guy. Like I said, he got withdrawn, dwelled on things too much.'

Banks nodded. 'There's nothing else you can tell me? You're sure he didn't name any specific pub or place he used to hang out?'

'Sorry.' Marilyn grinned. 'I'd remember if he had because I'd have probably dropped in there one evening. Just by chance, you know.'

Banks smiled. 'Yes. I know. Thanks anyway. I won't waste any more of your time.'

'No problem.' Marilyn tossed her empty can into the waste-paper basket. 'Hey!' she called, as Banks left the staff lounge. 'I think your accent's cute, too.'

But Banks didn't have time to appreciate the compliment. Coming along the corridor towards him were two very large police officers.

'Mr Banks?' the taller one asked.

'Yes.'

'We'd like you to come with us, if you don't mind.'

'What for?'

'Just a few questions. This way, please.'

There was hardly room for them to walk three abreast

down the hallway, but they managed it somehow. Banks felt a bit like a sardine in a tin. As they turned the corner, he noticed from the corner of his eye Tom Jordan wringing his hands outside his office.

Banks tried to get more out of the officers in the lift, but they clammed up on him. He felt a wave of irrational fear at the situation. Here he was, in a foreign country, being taken into custody by two enormous uniformed policemen who refused to answer his questions. And the feeling of fear intensified as he was bundled into the back of the yellow car. The air smelled of hot vinyl upholstery; a strong wire mesh separated him from the men in the front; and the back doors had no inside handles.

THREE

'What does tha write, then?' Freddie Metcalfe asked, expertly refilling the empty pint glass with Marston's Pedigree Bitter.

'Science fiction,' said Detective Constable Philip Richmond. In his checked Viyella shirt and light brown cords, he thought he looked the part. Posing as a writer would make him less suspicious, too. He would be expected to spend some time alone in his room writing and a lot of time in the pub, with perhaps the occasional constitutional just to keep the juices flowing.

'I knew a chap used to write books once,' Freddie went on. 'Books about t' Dales, wi' pictures in 'em. Lived down Lower 'Ead.' He placed the foaming pint in front of Richmond, who paid and drained a good half of it in one gulp. 'I reckon one of them there detective writers would 'ave a better time of it round 'ere these days.'

'Why's that?'

Freddie leaned forward and lowered his voice. 'Murder, that's why,' he said, then laughed and picked up a glass to dry. 'Right baffled, t' police are. It's got that southron – little chap wi' a scar by 'is eye – it's got 'im running around like a blue-arsed fly, it has. And t' old man, Gristhorpe – well, we all know he durst hardly show his face around 'ere since t' last one, don't we?'

'Last what?'

'Murder, lad! What's tha think I'm talking about? Sheep-shagging?'

'Sorry.'

'Think nowt on it. I'm forgetting tha's a foreigner. Tha sounds Yorkshire to me. Bit posh, mind you, but Yorkshire.'

'Lancashire, actually,' Richmond lied. 'Bolton.'

'Aye, well, nobody's perfect. Anyroads, as I were saying – blue-arsed flies, t' lot of 'em.'

An impatient customer interrupted Freddie's monologue, and Richmond took the opportunity to sip more beer. It was eight thirty on Monday evening, and the White Rose was about half full.

'Keep your eyes skinned, lad,' Sergeant Hatchley had instructed him. 'Watch out for anybody who looks like doing a bolt.' The orders couldn't have been more vague. What on earth, Richmond wondered, did someone about to do a bolt look like? Would he have to sit up all night and watch for the culprit stealing down by the Swain with his belongings tied in a bag on the end of a stick slung over his shoulder, faithful cat at his heels, like Dick Whittington? Richmond had no idea. All he knew was that all the suspects had been told Banks had gone to Toronto.

Richmond also had strict instructions not to identify

himself and not to push himself forward in any way that might make the locals suspicious. In other words, he wasn't to question anyone, no matter how casually. He could keep his ears open then, he was relieved to hear, especially for anything Sam Greenock might let slip over breakfast, or some titbit he might overhear in the White Rose. At least he'd pack away a few pints of Marston's tonight. Maybe even smoke a panatella.

'Where was I?' Freddie asked, leaning on the bar again.

'Murder.'

'Aye, murder.' He nodded in the direction of the table in the far corner and whispered again. 'And them there's all t' suspects.'

'What makes them suspects?' Richmond asked, hoping he was not exceeding his brief by asking the question.

''Ow would I know? All I know is that t' police 'ave spent a lot of time wi' 'em. An' since yesterday they've all been on hot coals. Look at 'em now. You wouldn't think they 'ad a big party coming up, would you?'

It was true that the group hardly seemed jolly. John Fletcher chewed the stem of his stubby pipe; his dark brows met in a frown. Sam Greenock was staring into space and rocking his glass on the table. Stephen Collier was talking earnestly to Nicholas, who was trying very hard not to listen. Nicholas, in fact, seemed the only unconcerned one among them. He smiled and nodded at customers who came and went, whereas the other three hardly seemed to notice them.

Richmond wished he could get closer and overhear what they were saying, but all the nearby tables were full. It would look too suspicious if he went and stood behind them.

He ordered another pint. 'And I'll have a panatella too,

please,' he said. He felt like indulging in a rare treat: a cigar with his beer. 'What party's this?' he asked.

'A Collier do. Reg'lar as clockwork in summer.'

'Can anyone go?'

'Tha must be joking, lad.'

Richmond shrugged and smiled to show he was, indeed, jesting. 'What's wrong with them all, then?' he asked. 'You're right. They don't look like they're contemplating a booze-up to me.'

Metcalfe scratched his mutton chops. 'I can't be certain, tha knows, but it's summat to do wi' that London copper taking off for Canada. Talk about pale! Ashen, they went. But I'll tell tha summat, it were good for business. Double brandies all round!' Freddie nudged Richmond and laughed. 'Aye, there's nobody drinks like a murder suspect.'

Richmond drew on his cigar and looked over at the table. Outside some enemy back in Toronto, it came down to these four. Come on, he thought to himself, make a bolt. Run for it, you bugger, just try it!

FOUR

'I don't know what people do where you come from, but over here we like a bit of advance warning if some foreigner's come to invade our territory.'

Banks listened. There was nothing he could say; he had been caught fair and square. Fortunately, Staff Sergeant Gregson of the Toronto Homicide Squad was nearing the end of what had been a relatively mild bollocking, and even more fortunately, smoking was allowed – nay, encouraged – in his office.

It was an odd feeling, being on the carpet. Not that this was the first time for Banks. There had been many occasions at school, and even one or two in his early days on the Metropolitan force, and they always brought back those feelings of terror and helplessness in the face of authority he had known as a working-class kid in Peterborough. Perhaps, he thought, that fear of authority might have motivated him to become a policeman in the first place. He knew he didn't join in order to inflict such feelings on others, but it was possible that he did it to surmount them, to conquer them in himself.

And now here he was, tongue-tied, unable to say a word in his own defence, yet inwardly seething with resentment at Gregson for putting him in such a position.

'You've got no power here, you know,' Gregson went on.

Finally, Banks found his voice. Holding his anger in check, he said, 'I wasn't aware that I needed any special power to talk to people – either in England or in Canada.'

'You won't get anywhere being sarcastic with me,' Gregson said, a smile tugging at the corners of his tightly clamped mouth.

He was a round man with a square head. His grey hair was closely cropped, and a brush-like wedge of matching moustache, nicotine-yellow around the ends of the bristles, sprouted under his squashed nose. As he spoke, he had a habit of running his fingers under the collar of his white shirt as if it was too tight. His skin had a pinkish plastic sheen, like a balloon blown up too much. Banks wondered what would happen if he pricked him. Would he explode, or would the air hiss out slowly as his features folded in on themselves?

'What have you got against irony, Sergeant?' Banks

asked. That felt odd, too: being hauled up before a mere sergeant.

'You know what they say about sarcasm being the lowest form of wit, don't you?' Gregson responded.

'Yes. But at least it is a form of wit, which is better than none at all.'

'I didn't bring you here to bandy words.'

'Obviously.'

Banks lit another cigarette and looked at the concrete and glass office blocks out of the window. His shirt was stuck with sweat to the back of the orange plastic chair. He felt his anger ebb into boredom. They were somewhere downtown in a futuristic air-conditioned building, but the office smelt of burning rubber and old cigar smoke. That was all he knew.

'What are you going to do, then?' Banks asked. 'Arrest me?'

Gregson shrugged. 'For what? You haven't done anything wrong.'

Banks leaned forward. 'Then why the bloody hell did you get Laurel and Hardy out there to bundle me in the back of a car and bring me here against my will?'

'Don't be like that,' Gregson said. 'When Jordan phoned me and said there was a suspicious Englishman asking questions about Bernard Allen, what the fuck else could I do? What would you have done? Then it turned out to be you, a goddamn police inspector from England. And I hadn't even been advised of your visit. I considered that an insult, which it is. And I didn't find your remark on the phone about getting my man particularly funny, either. I'm not a Mountie.'

'Well, I'm sorry for any inconvenience I've caused you, Sergeant,' Banks said, standing up, 'but I'd like to enjoy the rest of my holiday in peace, if you don't mind.'

'I don't mind,' Gregson said, making no move to stop him walking over to the door. 'I don't mind at all. But I think you ought to bear a few things in mind before you go storming off.'

'What things?' Banks asked, his palm slippery on the doorknob.

'First of all, that what I said to you on the phone before is true: we don't have the resources to work on this case. Secondly, yes, you can talk to as many people as you wish, providing they want to talk to you. And thirdly, you should have damn well asked for permission before jumping on that fucking jet and flying here half-cocked. What if you find your killer? What are you going to do then? Have you thought about that? Smuggle him out of the country? You could be getting yourself into a damn tricky legal situation if you're not very careful.' Gregson rubbed his moustache with the back of his hand. 'All I'm saying is that there are things you can't do acting alone, without authority.'

'And you don't have the resources. I know. You told me. Look, this is where I came in, so if you don't mind—'

'Wait!' Gregson jumped to his feet and reached for his jacket.

'Wait for what?'

Gregson pushed past him through the door. 'Come on,' he said, half turning. 'Just come with me.'

'Where?'

'You'll see.'

'What for?'

'I'm going to save you from yourself.'

Banks sighed and followed the sergeant down the corridor and down in the lift to the car park.

There was enough room for a football team on the front seat of Gregson's car. With the open windows sucking in what hot wet air they could, the staff sergeant drove up Yonge Street and turned right at the Hudson's Bay building. On the crowded street corner, vendors sold ice-cream, T-shirts and jewellery; one man, surrounded by quite a crowd, was drawing large portraits in coloured chalk on the pavement.

Farther along, Banks recognized the stretch of the Danforth he'd walked the previous day: the Carrot Common shopping centre; the little Greek restaurant where he'd eaten lunch; Quinn's pub. They came to an intersection called Coxwell, and Gregson turned left. A few blocks up, he pulled to a halt outside a small apartment building. Sprinklers hissed on the well kept lawn. Banks was tempted to run under one for a cold shower.

They walked up to the third floor, and Banks followed Gregson along the carpeted corridor to apartment 312.

'Allen's place,' the staff sergeant announced.

'Why are you helping me?' Banks asked, as Gregson fitted the key in the door. 'Why are you bringing me here? You said your department didn't have the resources.'

'That's true. We've got a hunt on for a guy who sodomized a twelve-year-old girl, then cut her throat and dumped her in High Park. Been looking for leads for two months now. Twenty men on the case. But this is personal time. I don't like it that a local guy got killed any more than you do. So I show you where he lived. It's no big deal. Besides, like I said, I'm saving you from yourself. You'd probably have broken in, and then I'd have had to arrest you. Embarrassing all round.'

'Thanks anyway,' Banks said.

They walked into the apartment.

'Building owner's been bugging us to let him rent it out again, but we've been stalling. He knows he's sitting on a gold mine. We've got a zero vacancy rate in Toronto these days. Still, Allen paid first and last month when he moved in, so I figure he's got a bit of time left. To tell you the truth, we don't know who's gonna take care of the guy's stuff.'

There wasn't much: just a lot of books, Swedish assemble-it-yourself furniture, pots and pans, a few withered house plants and a desk and typewriter by the window. Bernard Allen had lived simply.

The room was hot and stuffy. There was no sign of an air-conditioner, so Banks went over and opened a window. It didn't make much difference.

'What kind of search did your men do?' Banks asked.

'Routine. We didn't open up every book or read every letter, if that's what you mean. The guy didn't keep much personal stuff around, anyway. It was all in that desk drawer.'

Banks extracted a messy pile of bills and letters from the drawer. First, he put aside the bills then examined the sheaf of personal mail. They were all dated within the last six months or so, which meant that he threw his letters out periodically instead of hoarding them like some people. There were letters from his parents in Australia and one brief note from his sister acknowledging the dates of his proposed visit. Banks read these carefully, but found nothing of significance.

It was a postcard from Vancouver dated about two weeks before Allen set off for England that proved the most revealing, but even that wasn't enough. It read:

Dear Bernie,

Wrapping things up nicely out here. Weather great,
so taking some time for sunbathing on Kitsilano Beach.
It'll be a couple more weeks before I get back, so I'll
miss you. Have a great trip and give my love to the folks
in Swineshead! (Only joking – best not tell anyone you
know me!) See you in the pub when you get back.

Love,
Julie

It was perfectly innocent on the surface – just a postcard from a friend – so there was no reason why Gregson
or his men should have been suspicious about it. But it
was definitely from Anne Ralston, and it told Banks that
she was going under the name of Julie now.

'Looks like you've found something,' Gregson said,
looking over Banks's shoulder.

'It's from the woman I'm looking for. I think she knows
something about Allen's murder.'

'Look,' Gregson said, 'are we talking about a criminal
here? Are there charges involved?'

Banks shook his head. He wasn't sure. Anne Ralston
could certainly have murdered Raymond Addison and run
for it, but he didn't want to tell Gregson that and risk the
local police scaring her off.

'No,' he said. 'They used to know each other in
Swainshead, that's all.'

'And now they've met up over here?'

'Yes.'

'So?'

Banks told him about Ralston's disappearance and the
Addison murder, stressing that she wasn't seriously
implicated in any way.

'But she might have known something?' Gregson said.

'And told Allen. You think that's what might have got him killed?'

'It's possible. We know that she asked him to keep quiet about meeting her over here, and we know he didn't.'

'Who did he talk to?'

'That's the problem. Someone who makes it his business to make sure that everyone who counts knows.'

'It won't be easy.'

'What?'

Gregson tapped the postcard. 'Finding her. No address. No phone number. Nothing.'

Banks sighed. 'Believe me, I know. And all we've got is her first name. I'm just hoping I can dig out some of the spots she might turn up. She mentioned the pub, so at least I was right about her drinking with him there.'

'Know how many pubs there are in Toronto?'

'Don't bother to tell me. I'd only get discouraged. It's the kind of job I should have sent my sergeant on.' Banks explained about Hatchley's drinking habits and Gregson laughed.

'Can I have a good look around?' Banks asked.

'Go ahead. I'll be down in the car. Lock up behind you.'

After the staff sergeant left, Banks puzzled over him for a moment. He was beginning to warm to Gregson and get some understanding of Canadians, especially those of distant British origin. They behaved with a strange mixture of patronage and respect towards the English. Perhaps they'd had British history rammed down their throats at school and needed to reject it in order to discover themselves. Or perhaps the English had simply become passé as far as immigrants went, and had been superseded by newer waves of Koreans, East Indians and Vietnamese.

The next item of interest Banks found was an old photograph album dating back to Allen's university days. There were pictures of his parents, his sister, and of the Greenocks standing outside a typical Armley back-to-back. But the most interesting was a picture dated ten years ago, in which Allen stood outside the White Rose with a woman named as Anne in the careful white print under the photo on the black page. The snap was a little blurred, an amateur effort with a Brownie by the look of it, but it was better than the one he'd got from Missing Persons. Anne looked very attractive in a low-cut T-shirt and a full, flowing Paisley skirt. She had long light brown hair, a high forehead and smiling eyes. Her face was heart-shaped and her lips curved up slightly at the corners. That was ten years ago, Banks thought, carefully taking the photo from its silver corners and pocketing it. Would she look like that now?

He went on to make a careful search of the rest of the apartment, and he did take out every book and flip through the leaves, but he came up with nothing else. The postcard signed 'Julie' and the old photograph were all he had to go on. By the time he'd finished, his shirt was stuck to his back.

Outside, Gregson seemed quite at ease smoking in his hot car.

'Find anything?' he asked.

'Only an old photograph. Probably useless. What time is it?'

'Ten after four.'

'I suppose I'd better make my way home.'

'Where are you staying?'

'Riverdale.'

'That's not far. How about a beer first?'

'All right.' It was impossible to resist the thought of an ice-cold beer.

Gregson drove back downtown and pulled into a car park behind a grimy cinder-block building with a satellite dish on the roof.

Despite the warm gold sunlight outside, the bar was dark and it took a while for Banks' eyes to adjust. He did notice though, that it was cold, gloriously cold. There wasn't any sawdust on the floor, but he got the feeling there ought to be. It was a high-ceilinged room as big as a barn, peppered with black plastic tables and chairs. At one end was the bar itself, a feeble glimmer of light in the distance, and at the other was a stage littered with amps and speakers. At the moment a rather flat-chested young girl was dancing half-naked in a spotlight to the Rolling Stones' 'Jumpin' Jack Flash'. The volume was much too high. Against a third wall was a huge TV screen on which a game of baseball was in progress.

A waitress sashayed over, shirt-ends tied in a knot under her ample breasts, and took their orders with a weary smile. Shortly, she returned with the drinks on a tray. As Banks looked around, other figures detached themselves from the gloom and he saw that the place was reasonably full. Smoke swirled and danced in the spot beam. Whatever this bar was, it wasn't one of the English-style pubs where Bernard Allen went for his pint. The four glasses of draught beer in front of them were tiny and tapered to thick heavy stems.

'Cheers.' Gregson clinked glasses and practically downed his in one.

'If you have to order two each at a time,' Banks asked, leaning over and shouting against the music, 'why don't they switch to using bigger glasses?'

Gregson shrugged and licked foam off his moustache. 'Tradition, I guess. It's always been like this as long as I can remember.' He offered Banks a cigarette. It was stronger than the ones he usually smoked.

The music ended and the girl left the stage to a smattering of polite applause.

Gregson nodded towards the TV screen. 'Get baseball back home?'

Banks nodded. 'We do now. My son likes it, but I'm a cricket man myself.'

'Can't figure that game at all.'

'Can't say I know much about baseball, either.' Banks caught the waitress's attention and put in another order, changing his to a bottle of Carlsberg this time. She smiled sweetly at him and made him repeat himself.

'Likes your accent,' Gregson said afterwards. 'She heard you the first time. You'll be all right there, if you're interested.'

'Married man.'

'Ah. Still, while the cat's away . . . And you are in a foreign country, a long way from home.'

Banks laughed. 'The problem is, I have to take myself with me wherever I go.'

Gregson nodded slowly. 'I know what you mean.' He tapped the side of his square head. 'There's a few pictures stuck in here I wish I could throw out, believe me.' He looked back at the screen. 'Baseball. Greatest game in the world.'

'I'll take your word for it.'

'Listen, if you've got a bit of time, how about taking in a game next Saturday? I've got tickets. Jays at home to the Yankees.'

'I'd like that,' Banks said. 'Look, don't get me wrong,

but I got the impression you were distinctly pissed off with me a few hours ago. Now you're inviting me to a baseball game. Any reason?'

'Sure. You were out of line and I did my duty. Now I'm off duty and someone's got to show you there's more to Canada than snow, Mounties, beavers and maple trees.'

'Fair enough. Don't forget the Eskimos.'

'Inuit, we call them now.'

Banks finished his beer and Gregson ordered more. The spot came on again and an attractive young woman with long wavy black hair and brown skin came on to the stage.

Gregson noticed Banks staring. 'Beautiful, eh? She's a full-blooded Indian. Name's Wanda Morningstar.'

She certainly was beautiful, in such an innocent natural way that Banks found himself wondering what the girl was doing taking her clothes off for a bunch of dirty old men in the middle of a summer's afternoon. And, come to think of it, what the hell was he doing among them? Well, blame Gregson for that.

More drinks came, and more strippers walked on and off the stage, but none could hold a candle to Wanda Morningstar. It was after ten when they finally left, and by then Banks felt unusually merry. Because the beer was ice-cold it had very little taste and therefore, he had assumed, little strength. Wrong. It was stronger than what he was used to, and he felt light-headed as he followed Gregson to the car.

Gregson paused as he bent to put his key in the door. 'No,' he said to himself. 'Time to take a cab. You've been leading me astray, Alan. It'd be damned embarrassing if I got done for drunken driving in my own city, wouldn't it?'

They walked out on to the street. It was still busy, and many of the shops were open – all-night groceries and the ubiquitous Mac's Milk. Or was this one Mo's, Mc's or Mick's? You'd never get anything but an off-licence open past five thirty in Eastvale, Banks reflected.

Gregson waved and a cab pulled up. They piled in the back. The driver, an uncommunicative West Indian, nodded when he heard the directions. He dropped Banks off first outside Gerry's house, then drove on with Gregson waving from the back.

Banks walked into the hot room and slumped in front of the TV. A rerun of *Perry Mason* came on. Finally, a little dizzy and unable to keep his eyes open any longer, he went into the bedroom and lay down. The events of the day spun round chaotically in his mind for a while, but the last image, the one that lulled his consciousness to sleep, was of Wanda Morningstar dancing naked, not on a stage in a seedy bar but in a clearing somewhere in the wilderness, her dark skin gleaming in firelight.

But the scene shifted, as it does in dreams, and it was no longer Wanda Morningstar dancing but Anne Ralston running ahead of him in her long Paisley skirt. It was a typical policeman's dream too, for try as he might, he just couldn't run fast enough. His feet felt as if they were glued to the earth. Every so often, she would pause and beckon him, smiling indulgently when she saw him try to drag himself along. He woke at six, covered with sweat. Outside, the birds were singing and an early-morning streetcar clattered by. He got up and took a couple of Gerry's aspirins with a pint of water, then drifted off to sleep again.

10

ONE

The sun had just gone down behind Adam's Fell, silhouetting the steep hillside against its deep crimson glow. The guests milled around in the Colliers' large garden. Doors to both parts of the house were open, allowing access to drinks and a huge table of cheeses, pâtés, smoked salmon and fresh fruit. Music drifted out from Stephen's stereo. Now it was Mozart, but earlier there had been Motown and some ersatz modern pop. The crowd was mostly early to mid thirties, apart from one or two older landowners and friends of the family. There were a couple of bright young teachers from Braughtmore, several members of Stephen's management staff, and a great assortment of entrepreneurs, some with political ambitions, from all over the dale. The parties were a fairly regular affair; they helped maintain the social status of the Colliers and introduce those who had something to those who might be willing and able to pay for it.

Katie stood alone by the fountain, with a glass of white wine in her hand. She had been holding it so long it was warm. Occasionally a well dressed young man would approach her and begin a conversation, but after a few minutes of her averted looks, blushes and monosyllabic answers, he would make an excuse to get away.

As usual, Sam had insisted she come.

'I didn't buy you those bloody expensive dresses for nothing, you know,' he had railed when she told him at the last minute that she didn't want to go.

'I didn't ask you to buy them,' Katie said quietly. 'I don't even want them.' And it was true. She felt uncomfortable in finery, full of pride and vanity.

'You'll damn well do as I say. There'll be some important people there and I want you to make a good impression.'

'Oh, Sam,' she pleaded, 'you know I never do. I can't talk to people at parties. I get all tongue-tied.'

'Have a few drinks like everyone else, for a change. That'll loosen you up. For Christ's sake, can't you let your hair down for once?'

Katie turned away.

Sam grasped her arm. 'Look,' he said, 'you're coming with me and that's that. If you're so worried about talking to people, then just stand around and look decorative. At least you can do that. But you are coming. Got it?'

Katie nodded and Sam let go of her. Rubbing her arm, she went up to her room and picked out a cotton print dress just right for the occasion, gathered at the waist and cut low down the back. It looked particularly good if she tied her hair up. She decided to take a fringed woollen shawl, too; sometimes, even in July, the evenings got chilly. After Sam had approved of her appearance and suggested a bit more eye make-up, they left.

She could see Sam in his white suit talking and laughing with a couple of local businessmen. He had a glass of wine too, though she knew he hated the stuff. He only drank it because that was the thing to do at the Colliers' parties.

Katie looked around for John Fletcher, but she couldn't

see him. John was always kind and, of all of them, she found him the easiest to talk to, or even to be silent with. She liked Stephen Collier, but felt more comfortable with John Fletcher. He was a sad and haunted man since his wife ran off, but at least she hadn't gone because he mistreated her. Maureen Fletcher, Katie remembered, had been beautiful, vain, haughty and foolhardy. The small community of Swainshead couldn't hold her. Katie thought John ought to be glad to be rid of her, but she never said anything to him. They never discussed anything personal, but he seemed, beyond the depths of his sadness, a good man.

Katie shivered. The sunset had faded, leaving the sky above Adam's Fell a deep dark violet colour. Even over the clinking glasses and the Motown music, which had started up again because some people wanted to dance, she could hear the eerie mournful call of a curlew high on the fell. She began to make her way into Nicholas's part of the house to pick up her shawl where Sam had left it, then decided she wanted to go to the bathroom too. Pausing on the way, she admired the oak panelling and the old-fashioned style of his living room, with its watercolours of Nelson and Wellington on the walls, and its rows of leather-bound books. She wondered if he ever read them. On a small teak table by the Adam fireplace stood a bronze bust. Looking closer, Katie saw the name Oscar Wilde scratched into the base. She'd heard the name before somewhere, but it didn't mean very much to her. What a beautiful place for a monster like Nicholas Collier to live. It would be difficult to clean though, she thought, taking in all the nooks and crannies with a professional eye.

Finally, she found the toilet, which was more modern than the rest of the house. There, she poured her drink down the bowl and hid for a while, idly glancing at one of the copies of *Yorkshire Life* so thoughtfully set out by the bath. Then she got worried that Sam might be looking for her.

On her way back down the hall, she met Nicholas coming up. He was walking unsteadily, and his bright eyes were glassy. A stubborn lock of hair near his crown stood straight up. He looked like a naughty schoolboy.

'Ah, Katie my dear,' he said, reaching out and holding her shoulders. His voice was slurred and his cheeks were flushed with drink. 'Come to me, for thy love is better than wine.'

Katie blushed and tried to wriggle free, but Nicholas only tightened his grip. He looked behind him.

'Nobody around,' he whispered. 'Time for a little kiss, my rose of Sharon, my lily of the valley.'

Katie struggled, but he was too strong. He held her head still, brought his mouth closer to hers and seemed to suffocate her with a long wet kiss. His breath tasted rank with wine, garlicky pâté and Stilton cheese. When he stopped, she gulped in the air. But he didn't let her go. One hand was on her bare back now and the other was feeling her breasts.

'Ah, thy breasts are like two young roes that are twins,' he said, breathing hard. 'Come on, Katie. In here. In the bedroom.'

'No!' Katie shouted. 'If you don't let me go I'm going to scream.'

Nicholas laughed. 'I like a girl with a bit of spirit. Come on, I'll make you scream, sure enough. But not yet.' He put one hand over her mouth and started dragging her along the hall. Suddenly, she heard a familiar voice behind them and Nicholas's grip loosened. She shook herself free and turned to hear John Fletcher tell Nicholas to take his hands off her.

'You go to hell!' Nicholas said, clearly too far gone in temper to pull back. 'Who are you to tell me what to do? You're nothing but a jumped-up farm boy.'

And suddenly, John hit him. It was a quick sharp blow to the mouth, and it stopped Nicholas in his tracks. He glared at John as the blood welled to his lips and a thin line trickled down his chin. Out in the garden, a glass smashed and somebody giggled loudly above Mary Wells' 'My Guy'. Nicholas bared his teeth at John, put his hand over his mouth and stalked off to the bathroom.

Fletcher rubbed his knuckles. 'Are you all right, Katie?' he asked.

'Yes, yes, thank you.' Katie stared down at the patterned carpet as she spoke. 'I-I'm sorry . . . I'm so embarrassed. It's not the first time he's tried to touch me, but he's never been that rough before.'

'He's drunk,' Fletcher said, then smiled. 'Don't worry. I've been wanting to do that for a long time.'

'But what will he do? He looked so angry.'

'He'll cool off. Come on, let's get back to the others.'

Katie picked up her shawl, and they walked back into the garden, which was lit now by strategically placed antique lanterns. Katie excused herself, thanking John again, and sneaked around the side of the house into the street. She felt she needed to be out of there for a while, at least until her heart stopped beating so wildly and she could catch her breath again. Her flesh felt numb where Nicholas's hands had touched her. She shuddered.

There was no one in the street. Even the old men had gone from the bridge. The lights were on in the White Rose though, and Katie heard the sound of laughter and talk from inside. She thought the young policeman would be in there, the one nobody knew about but her. He hadn't been invited to the party, of course, so he wouldn't get the chance to spy on them that night. She wondered why he was really in the village. He hadn't asked any searching questions of anyone; he just seemed to be there, somehow, always in sight.

Sighing, Katie crept back into the garden. A slow song was playing and some of the couples held each other close. Suddenly, she felt a hand on her back and flinched.

'It's only me. Dance?'

'B-but I . . . can't . . .'

'Nonsense,' Stephen Collier said. 'It's easy. Just follow what I do.'

Katie had no choice. She saw Sam looking on and smiling with approval from Stephen's doorway. She felt like she had two left feet, and somehow her body just wouldn't respond to the music at all. It felt like wood. Soon, she began to feel dizzy and everything went dark. At the centre of the darkness was a biting, sooty smell. She stumbled.

'Hey, I'm not as bad as all that.' Stephen supported her with one arm and led her to the fountain.

Katie regained her balance. 'I'm sorry,' she said. 'I told you I was no good.'

'If I didn't know better,' Stephen said, 'I'd say you'd had too much to drink.'

Katie smiled. 'About one sip of white wine. It's too much for me.'

'Katie?' Stephen suddenly seemed earnest.

'Yes?'

'I enjoyed our little chat in your kitchen that time. It's good to have someone . . . someone outside to talk to.'

'Outside what?'

'Oh, business, family . . .'

The occasion seemed so long ago that Katie could hardly remember. And Stephen had ignored her ever since. She certainly hadn't imagined it as an enjoyable occasion for either of them. But there was something so little-boyish about Stephen, especially now when he seemed so nervous and serious. The muscle in the corner of his left eye had developed a tic.

'Remember what we talked about?' he went on.

Katie didn't, but she nodded.

He looked around and lowered his voice. 'I think I've made my mind up. I think I'm going to leave Swainshead.'

'But why?'

Stephen noticed a couple of his senior executives heading in their direction. 'We can't talk here, Katie. Not now. Can I see you on Friday?'

'Sam goes to—'

'Yes, I know Sam goes to Eastvale on Fridays. I don't want to see Sam, I want to see you. We'll go for a walk.'

'I-I don't know.'

His tone was urgent and his eyes were pleading with her. The two men had almost reached them. 'All right,' she said. 'A walk. A little one.'

Stephen relaxed. Even the tic in his eye seemed to disappear.

'Ah, Stephen, here you are,' one of the executives, a plump florid man called Teaghe, said. 'Trust you to corner the prettiest filly at the party, eh?' He cast a lecherous glance at Katie, who smiled politely and made an excuse to leave.

She poured herself another glass of wine for appearance's sake and leaned by the side of the French windows, watching the lantern-lit dancers in relief against the huge black mass of Adam's Fell. The garden was a tangled web of shadows, crossing and knotting like an enormous cat's cradle. As the warm light caught their features at certain angles, some of the dancers looked positively satanic.

So, although she had never thought of herself as a sympathetic listener – so bound up in her own shyness and discomfort was she – Stephen had asked her to be his confidante and she had agreed to go for a walk with him, to listen to his problems. It was more than Sam ever asked her to do. There were only two things he wanted from her: work and sex.

She trusted Stephen as far as she could trust any man. He hadn't tried anything last time, when he could have, and he'd been distinctly cool towards her since. But why did he want to leave Swainshead? Why did he seem so on edge? Was he running away from something? Still, she thought, if he was going away, and he really liked her, then there was just a chance he might take her with him.

She suspected that it might be a sin to desert her husband, but she had thought so much about it that she decided it was worth the risk. Surely God would forgive her for leaving a man with such vile and lascivious appetites as Sam Greenock? She could make amends, do good works. She might have to give Stephen her body too, she knew that. If not on Friday, then later, if he took her away with him. But that was one sin nobody could catch her out on. She had learned how to comply with all the things men wanted, but she got no pleasure from them herself. She thought it was just because of Sam, her only lover for years, but when Bernie had forced himself on her and she hadn't had the energy or the power to fight him off, she knew that she could never enjoy the act with any man. Bernie had at least been kind and gentle when he got her where he wanted her, but it made no difference to the way she felt about what he was doing.

She looked at the lantern-lit guests again. Sam was dancing with an attractive brunette, probably from Collier Foods, and Nicholas was back in circulation, talking and laughing by the fountain with a group of commuters who lived in Swainsdale and made their money elsewhere. His lower lip was swollen as if he'd been stung by a bee. When he caught her glance, he glared at her with such lust and hatred that she shivered and pulled her shawl up more tightly around her shoulders.

TWO

In Toronto, Banks combined sightseeing with his search for Anne Ralston in the English-style pubs. The weather remained uncomfortably hot and humid, and a window-rattling thunderstorm one night only seemed to make things worse the next day.

Banks gave the CN Tower a miss, but he walked around the Eaton Centre, a huge shopping mall with a glass roof and a flock of sculptured Canada geese flying in to land at one end, and he visited Yonge and Dundas after dark to watch the hookers and street kids on the neon strip. He took a ferry to Ward's Island and admired the Toronto skyline before walking along the boardwalk on the south side. Lake Ontario glittered in the sun, as vast as an ocean. He went to Harbourfront, where he sipped Carlsberg on a waterfront patio and watched the white sails of the yachts cut slow as knives through treacle in the haze.

One morning he took a bus to Kleinburg to see the

McMichael collection. Sandra, he thought, would love the Lawren Harris mountain-scapes and the native art. Also in the collection was a painting by Emily Carr that he associated with Jenny Fuller, a psychologist friend who sometimes helped with cases in Eastvale. She had a print of it on her living-room wall, and it was at her suggestion that he had made the visit.

Nor could he bear to miss Niagara Falls. If anything, it was even more magnificent than he had expected. He went out on the *Maid of the Mist*, wrapped up in oilskins, and the boat tossed like a cork when it reached the bottom of the falls. From a certain angle, he could see a rainbow cut diagonally across the water. When the boat got closer, the spray filled his eyes like a mist and he could see nothing; he could hear only the primeval roar of the water.

The rest of the time, he visited pubs. Allowing an hour or so in each, he would sit at the bar, show the photographs and ask after Bernard Allen and Anne Ralston of bar staff and customers.

This part of the job was hard on his liver and kidneys, so he tried to slow down his intake and pace himself. To make the task more interesting – for solo pub-crawling is hardly the most exciting pastime in the world – he sampled different kinds of draught beer, both imported and domestic. Most of the Canadian beers tasted the same, and they were uniformly gassy. The English beers, he found, didn't travel well. Double Diamond and Watney's he determinedly ignored, just as he did back home. By far the best were the few local brews that Gerry Webb had told him about: Arkell Bitter, Wellington County Ale, Creemore Springs Lager and Conner Bitter. Smooth and tasty, they had body and, when required, boasted fine heads.

Despite good beer, he was heartily sick of pubs. He was smoking too much, drinking too much and eating too much fried food. On Tuesday, after getting back from Kleinburg, he had tried the Sticky Wicket, the Madison and the Duke of York, all close to the university. No luck. On Wednesday, after his return from Niagara Falls, he had started out at the Spotted Dick, then made his way down busy Yonge Street among the shoppers and pleasure-seekers to the Hop and Grape, via the Artful Dodger and the Jack Russell. He had sat in the Hop and Grape, on the ground floor of an office block near Yonge and College, and watched long-haired heavy metal fans in the street flock towards a rock concert at Maple Leaf Gardens. His clothes were soaked with sweat and his feet hurt. The pub was quiet at that time, as the office workers had gone home and the evening crowds hadn't yet turned up. There were only two days left, and he was very much conscious of time's winged chariot at his rear. Fed up, he had gone back to the house for an early night.

He knew he had to be right though; Bernard Allen had frequented an English-style pub, and he must have had drinking companions who would be mourning his loss.

On Thursday at about three fifteen, Banks got off a streetcar outside the Feathers, in the east end of the city. The inside door opened opposite a small darts area: two boards against a green baize backing, pockmarked with misses. To his left was the pub itself, all darkly gleaming wood, polished brass and deep red velvet upholstery. And it was cool.

The wall opposite the bar was covered with framed photographs, mostly of English and Scottish scenes. Banks recognized a pub he knew in York, Theakston's brewery in Masham, a road sign he'd often passed on the way to

Ripon and, most surprising of all, a photo of the Queen's Arms in Eastvale's cobbled market square. It was an odd sensation, seeing that. He was in a pub over three thousand miles from home looking at a photo of the Queen's Arms. Eerie.

The place was almost empty. Near the door sat a group of four or five people listening to a silver-haired man with a lived-in face and a Lancashire accent complain about income tax.

Banks stood at the bar close to a very tall man with short neat hair. He was smoking a pipe and staring abstractedly into space as if musing about the follies of mankind. Behind the bar, above the till, was a small Union Jack.

'I'll have a pint of Creemore, please,' Banks said, noticing the logo on one of the pumps.

The barmaid smiled. She had curly auburn hair and brown eyes full of humour and mischief. When she walked over to the end of the bar to fill a waitress's order, Banks noticed she was wearing a very short skirt. It did more than justice to a fine pair of legs.

'Quiet,' Banks commented, when she placed the ice-cold pint in front of him.

'It usually is at this time,' she said. 'We get busy around five when people drop in after work.'

Banks took a deep breath and reached for the photographs in his jacket pocket. They were getting dog-eared. He was so used to disappointment that he put hardly any enthusiasm into his question: 'I don't suppose you had a regular here by the name of Bernard Allen, did you?'

'Bernie?' she said. 'Bernie who got killed over in England?'

Banks could hardly believe his ears. 'Yes,' he said. 'Did you know him?'

The barmaid's eyes turned serious as she spoke. 'He was a regular here,' she said. 'I wouldn't say I really knew him, but I talked to him now and then. You know, like you do when you're waitressing. He was a nice guy. Never made any trouble. It was terrible what happened.'

'Did he drink alone?'

'No. There was a group of them – Bernie, Glen, Barry and Ian. They always sat on that corner over there.' She pointed to a round table opposite the far end of the bar.

'Was there ever a woman with them?'

'Sometimes. But I never talked to her. Why do you want to know all this? Are you a cop or something?'

Banks decided on honesty. 'Yes,' he said. 'But I'm here unofficially. We think Bernie met an old friend over here who might have some information for us. It could help us find out who killed him.'

The barmaid rested her elbows on the bar and leaned forward.

Banks showed her the photographs. 'Is this her?'

She looked closely and frowned. 'It could be. The shape of the face is the same, but everything else is different. These must be old photos.'

'They are,' Banks said. 'But it could be her?'

'Yes. Look, I'm sorry, I can't stand here talking. I honestly don't know much more. Jack over there used to talk to Bernie sometimes. He might be able to help.'

She pointed to a man on the periphery of the group near the entrance. He was a solidly built man with a moustache and a fine head of greyish hair, in his mid to late thirties, Banks guessed. At the moment he seemed to be poring over a crossword puzzle.

'Thank you.' Banks picked up his half-finished pint and

walked over to the table. He introduced himself and Jack told him to pull up a chair. The Lancastrian at the next table lit a cigarette and said, 'I'll just have another gin and tonic, then I'll go.'

'We weren't really close friends,' Jack said when Banks had asked about Bernie, 'but we had some decent conversations.' He had a Canadian accent, which surprised Banks. He'd assumed that apart from the bar staff all the regulars were British.

'What did you talk about?'

'Books, mostly. Literature. Bernie was about the only other guy I knew who'd read Proust.'

'Proust?'

Jack gave him a challenging look. 'Greatest writer who ever lived. He wrote *Remembrance of Things Past*.'

'Maybe I'll give him a try,' Banks answered, not sure what he was letting himself in for. He tended to follow through on most of his self-made promises to read or listen to things other people recommended, though time constraints always ensured he had a huge backlog.

'Do that,' said Jack. 'Then I'll have someone to talk to again. Excuse me.' He got up and went to the washroom.

The Lancastrian belched and said to the waitress, 'Gin and tonic please, love. No fruit.'

Banks observed the other people at the table: a small slim youth with an earring and a diamond stud in his left ear; a taller thin-faced man with a crewcut and glasses; a soft-spoken man with a hint of an Irish accent. They were all listening to a Welshman telling jokes.

Jack sat down again and ordered another pint of Black Label. The waitress, a nicely tanned blonde with a beautiful smile, took Banks' order for another Creemore too, and delivered both drinks in no time. Banks paid, leaving her a good tip – one thing he'd soon learned to do on his pub crawl of Toronto.

'Did you know any of Bernie's friends?' he asked.

Jack shook his head. 'Self-important Brits, for the most part. They tend to pontificate a bit too much for my liking. But Bernie seemed to have transcended the parochial barriers of most English teachers.'

Marilyn Rosenberg, at Toronto Community College, had said much the same thing in a different way. Whether it was a plus or a minus in her eyes, Banks hadn't been sure.

'When do they usually come in?'

'About five, most days.'

Banks looked at his watch; it was just after four.

'Thanks a lot,' he said. 'By the way, six across is sculls. "Rows – of heads, we hear!" Head . . . skull. To row . . . to scull.' Jack raised his eyebrows and filled in the answer.

They worked at the crossword together for the next hour as the place filled up. At quarter past five, they were puzzling over 'Take away notoriety and attack someone (6)' when two men in white shirts and business suits walked in.

'That's them over there,' Jack said. 'Excuse me if I don't join you.'

Banks smiled. 'Thanks for your help, anyway.'

'Nice meeting you,' Jack said, and they shook hands. 'Defame. Of course!' he exclaimed just before Banks moved away. '"Take away notoriety and attack someone." Defame. Amazing how you get so much more done when there are two minds working at it.'

Banks agreed. It was the same with police work. He could certainly have done with some help on this trip. Not Sergeant Hatchley – he hadn't the self-control to separate work from a pub crawl – but DC Richmond would have been fine.

When he got to their table, the two men had already taken the opportunity to loosen their ties, take off their suit jackets and roll up their sleeves. One was tall and skinny with a bony face and fine blond hair plastered flat against his skull to cover the receding hairline; the other, who only came up to his friend's shoulders, was pudgy and also balding. What little hair he had stood out like a kind of mist or halo around his head. He wore a fixed smile on his lips, and his dark eyes darted everywhere.

Banks walked over to them and told them why he was in Toronto.

'I'm Ian Grainger,' said the tall blond one. 'Sit down.'

'Barry Clark,' the other said, still smiling and looking everywhere but at Banks.

'Glen should be along in a while,' Ian said. 'How can we help you?'

'I'm not sure if you can. I'm looking for Anne Ralston.'

For a moment, both men frowned and looked puzzled.

'You might know her as Julie.'

'Oh, Julie. Yes, of course,' Barry said. 'You lost me there for a second. Sure we know Julie. But what could she have to do with Bernie's murder?' His accent was English, as was Ian's, but Banks couldn't place either of them exactly.

'I don't honestly know if she had anything to do with it,' Banks said, 'but she's the only real lead we've got.' He explained about her disappearance just after the Addison murder.

The drinks arrived just before Glen Tadworth, a dark-bearded, well padded young man with a pronounced academic stoop and a well developed beer belly, walked over to join them. His red shirt seemed glued to his skin, and there were wet patches under the arms and across the chest. He carried a battered black briefcase stuffed with papers, which he plonked on the floor as he sat down and sighed.

'Bloody students,' he said, running his hand through his greasy black hair. '"Dover Beach" – a simple enough poem, you'd say, wouldn't you?' He looked at Banks as he talked, even though they hadn't been introduced. 'One bright spark came up with the theory that it was about Matthew Arnold's hangover. Quite elaborate, it was too. The "grating roar" was the poet being sick. And as for the "long line of spray" . . . Well, I suppose one should be grateful for their inventiveness, but really . . .' He threw his hands up, then reached over and took a long swig from Ian's pint.

'Don't mind him,' Barry said, managing to keep his eyes on Banks for a split second as he spoke. 'He's always like this. Always complaining.' And he introduced them.

'From Swainsdale, eh?' Glen said. 'A breath of fresh air from the old country. Lord, what I'd give to be able to live back there again. Not Swainsdale in particular, though it'd do. I'm from the West Country myself – Exeter. The accent's flattened out a bit over the years here, I'm afraid.'

'Why can't you go back if you want to?' Banks asked, reaching for another cigarette. 'Surely you weren't sent into permanent exile?'

'Metaphorically, my dear Chief Inspector, metaphorically. You know, some people have got hold of the idea that we expatriates, scattered around the ex-colonies and various watering holes of Europe and Asia, are all pipe-puffing Tories enjoying life without income tax.'

'And aren't you?'

'Far from it. Where is that waitress? Ah, Stella, my dear, a pint of Smithwick's please. Where was I? Exile. Yes. If the government really did seek our proxy votes in the next election, I think they'd bloody well regret it. Most of us feel like exiles. We have skills that no one back home seems to value any more. It's hard enough getting jobs here, but at least it's possible. And they pay well. But I, for one, would be perfectly happy to do the same work back home for less money. There's hardly a day goes by when I don't think about going back.'

'What about Bernie?'

'He was as bad as Glen, if not worse,' Barry said. 'At least recently he was. Full of nostalgia. It's time-travel they're after really, you know, not just a flight across the Atlantic. All of us baby boomers are nostalgic when it comes down to it. That's why we prefer the Beatles to Duran Duran.'

Banks also liked the Beatles better than Duran Duran, a group that his son, Brian, had inflicted on him once or twice before moving on to something new. He thought it was because of the quality of the music, but maybe Barry Clark was right and it was more a matter of nostalgia than anything else. His own father had been just the same, he remembered, going on about Glenn Miller, Nat Gonella and Harry Roy when Banks had wanted to listen to Elvis Presley, The Shadows and Billy Fury.

'The longer you're away, the more you idealize the image of home,' Barry went on, eyes roving the room. The place was packed and noisy now. People stood three deep at the bar. Jack, Banks noticed, had been joined by a small pretty woman with short dark hair laid flat against her skull. The Lancastrian and his friends had left. 'Of course, what people don't realize is that the country's changed beyond all recognition,' Barry continued. 'We'd be foreigners there now, but to us home is still the Queen's Christmas message, the last night of the Proms, Derby Day, a Test Match at Lords, the FA Cup Final – without blood-shed! – leafy lanes, a green and pleasant land. Ordered and changeless. Bloody hell, even the dark Satanic mills have some sort of olde worlde charm for homesick expatriates.'

'Damn right,' Glen said. 'I'd work in a bloody woollen mill in Bingley if it meant being back home. Well, maybe . . . It's the wistfulness of the exile, you see, Chief Inspector. You get it a lot in poetry. Especially the Irish.'

Banks was beginning to see what Jack had meant.

'Bernie was just the same,' Ian said. 'You should have heard him going on about Yorkshire. It was bloody Dales this and bloody Dales that. You'd think he was talking about paradise. You'll never catch me going back to live over there. Canada's a great place as far as I'm concerned.'

'That's because you're in real estate,' Glen said. 'You're making a bloody fortune. Is that all you care about – the material things? What about your soul, your roots?'

'Oh, shut up, Glen. You're getting tiresome.'

'If he could have got a job over there,' Banks asked, 'do you think he would have gone back?'

'Like a shot,' Ian answered. The others agreed.

'Did he ever mention anything about a job?'

'He did say there was a chance of getting back to stay,' Glen said. 'Lucky bastard. But I didn't know whether to believe him or not.'

'What was this chance?'

'He didn't say. Very hush-hush, apparently.'

'Why?'

Glen scratched his shoulder and tried to unstick the shirt from his armpit. 'Dunno. It was just one of those nights when you've had a few too many, if you know what I mean. Bernie said something about a plan he had to get himself back home.'

'But he gave you no details?'

'No. Said he'd let us know after he got back.'

'Was it a job he mentioned?'

'Not specifically, no. Just a chance to get back. I assumed it must have been some possible job offer. How else would he be able to live?'

'How attached was he to teaching?'

'He liked it up to a point,' Glen answered. 'It was something he was good at. He should have been teaching at university. He was good enough, but there aren't any jobs. Like most of us though, he hated the conditions he had to work in and he despised the students' wilful ignorance. They don't know anything and they don't want to know – unless it's in a ballpark or on video. They expect you to spoon-feed them knowledge, then ask them to regurgitate it in a test. For that they expect to be given an A-plus, no matter how bad their writing or how inaccurate their answers. I could go on—'

'You usually do, Glen,' Barry cut in, 'but I don't think Mr Banks wants to hear it.'

Banks smiled. 'Actually, I am running out of time,' he said. 'I need to find Julie as quickly as possible. Do you know where she lives?'

'No,' said Ian. 'She just comes in on a Friday after work for a couple of drinks.'

'It's somewhere near here, I think,' Barry added. 'She mentioned sunbathing in Kew Gardens once.'

'Have you any idea what surname she's using?'

'It's Culver, isn't it?' Barry said. 'Or Cleaver, Carver, something like that.'

None of the others could improve on Barry's contribution.

'Do you know where she works?'

'In one of those towers near King and Bay,' Ian answered. 'The TD Centre or First Canadian Place. She complained that the elevators made her ears go funny.'

'That's a lot of help,' Glen said. 'Do you know how many businesses operate from those places?'

Ian shrugged. 'Well, that's all I know. What about you?'

Glen and Barry both shook their heads.

'She should be in here at about six tomorrow though,' Barry said. 'She hasn't missed a week yet.'

'Fine. Look, would you do me a favour? If she turns up early or if I'm late, please don't tell her I want to see her. It might scare her off. You know how some people react to the police.'

'Are you sure you're not after her for something?' Glen asked suspiciously.

'Information. That's all.'

'All right,' Glen agreed. 'If it's going to help catch Bernie's killer, we'll do whatever you want.' He paused to pick up his pint glass and raise it for a toast. 'There is one good thing in all this, you know. At least Bernie died in the place he wanted to live.'

'Yes,' Banks said. 'There is that.'

And they all drank to dying where they wanted to live.

11

ONE

'**John told** me about Nick's behaviour at the party the other night,' Stephen Collier said. 'I'm sorry. I warned you to stay away from him.'

Katie looked down at the stony path and blushed. 'I didn't go seeking him,' she said. 'He's an animal, a filthy animal.'

'But he is my brother, Katie. He's the only family I've got left. I know he acts outrageously sometimes, but . . . I promise it won't happen again.'

Katie remembered a phrase from the Bible: 'Am I my brother's keeper?' Could Stephen keep Nicholas like an animal in a zoo? He looked strained, she thought. He poked at the stones and sods with his ashplant stick as they walked; his face was pale and the tic in his eye was getting worse.

It was fine walking weather: warm but not hot, with a few high white clouds and no sign of rain. Sam was in Eastvale for the day – not that Katie's walking out with Stephen would have mattered to him, she thought; he practically threw her at the Colliers as if she were his membership ticket to some exclusive club.

They took the diagonal path up the side of Swainshead Fell, heading for the source of the river. The air was clear, and after a few minutes' walking even Stephen's pallid cheeks began to glow like embers.

At last they reached their destination. The source of the River Swain was an unspectacular wet patch on the side of Swainshead Fell. All around it, the grass was greener and grew more abundantly than anywhere else. Only yards away was the source of another river, the Gaiel, which, when it reached the valley below, perversely turned north towards Cumbria.

Stephen had brought a flask of coffee and some dark chocolate. They sat down to eat on the dry grass above the source and looked back on Swainshead. A lapwing went into his extended 'pee-wit' song as he wove through the air, plummeted and levelled out just before hitting the ground. His wings beat like sheets flapping in a gale.

'He must be trying to attract a mate,' Stephen said.

'Or scare us away.'

'Perhaps. Coffee? Chocolate?'

Katie accepted the plastic cup of black coffee. She usually liked hers with plenty of milk and a spoonful of sugar, but she took it as it came without complaint. The dark bitter chocolate puckered her taste buds.

'I shouldn't be here, you know,' she said, pushing back a stray wisp of fair hair behind her ear.

'Relax,' Stephen said. 'Sam's in Eastvale.'

'I know. But that's not the point. People will talk.'

'Why should they? There's nothing to talk about. Everybody knows we're all friends. You're so old-fashioned, Katie.'

Katie flushed. 'I can't help it. I wish I could,' she added in a whisper.

'Look,' Stephen went on in a soothing voice, 'we've just gone for a short walk up the fell side, as many people do.

Where's the harm in that? We're not hiding from anyone, we're not sneaking off. You act as if we're guilty of something terrible.'

'It just feels wrong,' Katie said, managing a brief smile. 'Oh, don't mind me. I'm trying, I really am. I'm just not very good with people.'

'Don't you feel comfortable with me?'

Katie fidgeted with the silver paper from the chocolate wrapper, folding it into a neat shiny square. 'I don't know,' she said. 'I don't feel afraid.'

Stephen laughed. 'At least that's a start. But seriously, Katie, sometimes it's necessary to talk. I told you the other night I've got nobody. Nick's hardly the type to make a good listener, and the people at work are just that: employees, colleagues, not friends.'

'What about all those guests at the party?'

'Nick's people, most of them. Or from work, business acquaintances. Don't you ever need to talk to someone real, Katie? Don't you ever have problems you want to let out and share?'

Katie frowned and stared at him. 'Yes,' she said. 'Yes, of course I do. But I'm no good at it. I don't know where to start.'

'Start with your life, Katie. Are you happy?'

'I don't know. Am I supposed to be?'

'That's what life's for, isn't it, to be enjoyed?'

'Or suffered.'

'Are you suffering?'

'I don't think I'm happy, if that's what you mean.'

'Why don't you do something about it?'

'There's nothing I can do.'

'But there must be. You must be able to change things if you want.'

'I don't see how. What would I do? Without the guest house I've got nothing. Where would I go? I don't know anywhere outside Leeds and Swainsdale.' She toyed with a stray tress of hair. 'I could just see me down in London or somewhere like that. I wouldn't last five minutes.'

'Cities aren't quite as bad as you think they are. You only see the worst on television. Many people live happy lives there.'

'Still,' Katie said, 'I'd be lost.' She finished the coffee and wiped her lips with the back of her hand.

'Perhaps by yourself you would be.'

'What do you mean?'

Suddenly Stephen seemed closer, and somehow he seemed to be holding her hand. Katie tensed. She didn't want to upset him. If he wanted to touch her she would have to let him, but her stomach clenched and the wind roared in her ears. His touch was oddly chaste though; it didn't seem to threaten her at all.

'I don't know, Katie,' he said. 'I'm not sure what I'm saying. But I've got to go away. I can't stay around here any longer.'

'But why not?'

She felt him trembling as he moved even closer and his grip tightened on her hand. 'There are things you don't know anything about, Katie,' he said. 'Dear, sweet Katie.' And he brushed his fingers down her cheek. They felt cold.

Katie wanted to move away, but she didn't dare struggle. 'I don't know what you mean,' she burst out. 'Sam's always telling me I know nothing, too. What is it? Am I so blind or so stupid?' There were tears in her eyes now, blurring her vision of the valley below and the water that bubbled relentlessly from the source.

'No,' Stephen said. 'No, you're not blind or stupid. But

things aren't always what they seem; people aren't what they pretend to be. Listen, let me tell you . . .'

TWO

The woman who sat opposite Banks in the dining section of the Feathers had changed considerably from the one in Bernard Allen's photograph, but it was definitely the same person. She wore her hair cut short and tinted blonde now, and was dressed in a cream business suit. When she sat down and fished in her bag for a cigarette, Banks also noticed that the carefree laughter in her eyes had hardened into a wary, suspicious look. Her long cigarette had a white filter which soon became blotched with lipstick; she had a habit of tapping it on the edge of the ashtray even when there was no ash, and she held it straight out between the V of her first two fingers like an actress in an old movie, pursing her lips to inhale. Her nails were long and painted red.

She had turned up at six, as Glen had said, and she and Banks had left the others to go and talk privately over dinner. There wasn't much separation between the two areas of the pub except for the way the seating was arranged, and they could still hear the conversations at the bar and the tables.

The waitress, a petite brunette with a twinkle in her eye and a cheeky smile, came up and gave them menus. 'Something to drink?' she asked.

Julie ordered a White Russian and Banks a glass of red wine, just for a change.

'I need to know why you left Swainshead in such a hurry,' he said, when the waitress had gone for the drinks.

'Can't a woman do as she pleases? It's not a police state, you know. Or it wasn't when I was last there.'

'Nor is it now. It was your timing that interested us.'

'Oh? Why?'

'We tend to be suspicious of someone who disappears without a trace the day after a murder.'

'That was nothing to do with me.'

'Don't play the innocent. What did you expect us to think? You could have been in danger yourself, or you could have been the killer. For all we knew you could have been buried down a disused mineshaft. You didn't stop to let anyone know what had happened to you.'

'Well, I'm telling you now. That killing had nothing to do with me.'

'How do you know about it? You don't seem at all surprised at my mentioning it, but the body wasn't discovered until after you'd left.'

Julie ground her cigarette into the ashtray. 'Don't try your tricks on me,' she said. 'I read the papers. I know what happened.'

The waitress arrived with the drinks and asked if they were ready to order. Banks asked for a few more minutes and she smiled and went away. Julie turned to her menu.

'What would you recommend?' Banks asked.

She shrugged. 'The food's always good here. It depends what you fancy. The prime-rib roast and Yorkshire pudding on special is excellent, if you don't mind being reminded too much of home.'

Banks looked around at the decor and the photos on the walls. 'Not at all,' he said, smiling.

This time a different waitress came for their orders, an attractive woman with reddish blonde hair and a warm manner. Banks hoped he hadn't offended the other.

'Where did you go?' he asked Julie, as soon as they'd ordered their meals.

'None of your damn business.' She sipped her White Russian.

'A week after you left,' Banks pressed on, 'the body of a London private detective called Raymond Addison was discovered in Swainshead. He'd been murdered. Did you know anything about that?'

'No.'

'We've got good reason to think you did. Listen, if you want to make things difficult, Miss Ralston—'

'It's Culver, Mrs. Mrs Julie Culver. And it's quite legal. Julie's my middle name and Culver is my husband's. Ex-husband's, I should say.'

'Why change your name if you've nothing to hide?'

She shrugged. 'It was a new start. Why not a new name?'

'Not very convincing. But Mrs Culver it is. We're on good terms with the Canadian government. We have extradition arrangements and a mutual help policy. If I wanted to, I could make enough fuss to have you sent back to England to answer my questions. This is the easy way.'

Julie lit another cigarette. 'I don't believe you. I'm a Canadian citizen now. You can't touch me at all.'

'That doesn't matter,' Banks said. 'You're connected to a murder in England. Don't expect your government to protect you from that.'

'But you can't prove I had anything to do with it. It's just a coincidence I went away then.'

'Is it? What about your involvement with Stephen Collier?'

Julie paled. 'What about it? What's he been telling you?'

'Nothing. What does he know?'

'How should I know?'

Banks sighed. 'A few weeks ago a friend of yours, Bernard Allen, was murdered in the hanging valley just over Swainshead Fell.'

'I know the place,' Julie said sadly. 'I've been there with him. It always looked like autumn. But what makes you think his death had anything to do with me? I wasn't even in the country. I was here. It could have been a thief or a psycho . . . or a . . .'

There was something in her tone that let Banks know she was interested now, no longer so hostile. 'In the first place,' he said, 'we know that you told him not to let anyone know he'd met you here, which is suspicious enough in itself. And in the second place, he did tell someone: a woman called Katie Greenock. Her heart seems to be in the right place, but she told her husband, Sam, who soon broadcasted it to the whole White Rose crowd. In the third place, Bernard had been talking about going home to stay, and there's no evidence he had a job lined up. Then Bernard got killed before he had a chance to leave the dale. What does all that indicate to you?'

'You're the sleuth. You tell me.' Julie blew cigarette smoke down her nose.

Banks leaned forward. 'The way I read it,' he said, 'is that you knew something about Raymond Addison's murder. Something incriminating. I'm not sure who else was involved, or why, but it had to be someone with money. I'd guess that Stephen Collier played a large part. I think you told Bernard what you knew and he intended to use that knowledge to blackmail his way to what he wanted most – his return to Swainshead.'

'My God! I . . . Are you trying to say I'm responsible for Bernie's death?'

'I'm not placing any blame, Mrs Culver. I simply want to know what happened. I want to nail Bernie's killer.'

Julie seemed to be thinking fast. Conflicting emotions flashed across her face. 'I'm not guilty of anything,' she said finally. 'I've nothing to be afraid of. And I don't believe you. Bernie could never have been a blackmailer.'

The waitress brought their food. Before she left, they ordered another round of drinks, then Banks tucked into his roast while Julie picked at a Caesar salad. They remained silent while they ate. It wasn't until they both pushed their plates aside and reached for their cigarettes that Julie started to talk again.

'It's been such a long time, you know,' she began. 'A lot's happened. There've been long stretches when I haven't thought about Swainshead at all.'

'Not homesick?'

'Me? I'm at home anywhere. Almost anywhere. Though I can't say I cared for the Middle East much.'

'Bernie was homesick.'

'He was the type though, wasn't he? If you'd known him you'd have understood. The place was in his blood. He couldn't even really settle down in Leeds. Yes, Bernie wanted to go back. Which was a shame. I'd kind of been hoping . . .'

'You and Bernie? Again?'

She raised a thin dark-pencilled eyebrow. 'You know about that?'

'It was hardly a state secret.'

'True. Anyway, why not? We were both free agents again.'

'Tell me what happened five years ago that sent you running off around the world.'

The waitress came to pick up their plates. Banks

ordered a pint of Creemore this time and Julie asked for a coffee and a double cognac. All the spaces were occupied now. Next to them, a group of eight people had pulled two tables together.

'It seems more like a million years ago,' Julie said when she got her drink. 'I suppose I was a naive young thing back then. My education really began after I left.'

She was stalling for time, Banks thought, telling the story her own way. Perhaps she wasn't sure yet whether she was going to tell him the truth or not. The best thing for now, he decided, was to let her go with it and subtly steer her in the right direction. 'Where did you go?' he asked.

'First I went to Europe. I'd been saving up for quite a long time – kept my money under the mattress, believe it or not – just waiting for the day when I knew I would take off and never come back. I took a boat over to Holland and ended up in Amsterdam for a while. Then I bummed around France, Italy, Germany. To cut a long story short, I met a man. A Canadian. This'd be about a year later. He took me back to Vancouver with him and we got married.' Julie blew out a steady stream of smoke. 'Life was fine for a while . . . then he decided I wasn't enough for him. Two can play at that game, I thought . . . Anyway, it ended.'

'When did you first get in touch with Bernie?'

'About eighteen months ago. That was after I split up with Charles. Bernie was having marriage problems of his own, I soon found out, and he seemed happy enough to hear from me. I might have got in touch with him earlier, but I'd been wary about doing so. I knew he was here, of course. He left Swainshead before I did. But I felt that I'd burned all my bridges.'

'What made you contact him, then?'

'Circumstances, really. I'm a freelance publicity agent. I started the business in Vancouver because I liked the idea and it gave me something to do while my husband was . . . not around.' She tapped her cigarette against the glass ashtray. 'It turned out I had a knack, a flair, so I decided to open an office in Toronto as well. I don't know how much you understand about Canada, but Toronto is pretty much the centre of the universe here. I knew Bernie lived in the city, so I thought what the hell. Any trouble I might have caused would have blown over by now anyway.'

'Trouble?'

She narrowed her eyes and looked at him closely. 'I had thought Bernie might not want to see me.'

'I don't understand.'

'I went out with Stephen Collier.'

'But Bernard was over here by then. What was that to him?'

'It's not that. Bernie and I were never much more than childhood sweethearts anyway. But we were close friends, like brother and sister. I was hoping that might change here . . .' She sighed. 'Anyway, it's just that Stephen . . . well . . . he's a Collier.'

'And Bernie was very class conscious?'

'Yes.'

'So he'd feel betrayed.'

'Something like that.'

'And did he?'

'He wrote me some pretty nasty letters at the time. Then, when I went away, we lost touch for a while. But when we met up again here it had all blown over. Bernie was compassionate. He understood. That's why I can't believe he was a blackmailer.'

'He might not have been. I can't be sure. He might just have opened his mouth out of turn.'

Julie smiled. 'That sounds more like him.'

'What about Nicholas Collier?' Banks asked. 'Were you ever involved with him?'

Julie raised her eyebrows. 'What on earth do you think I am?' she asked, smiling. 'I didn't get around that much. And credit me with some taste. Nicky really did nothing for me, though I caught him giving me the eye once or twice.'

'Sorry,' Banks said. 'I'm not trying to insinuate you're a—'

'Tart? Slut? Harlot? Jezebel? Loose woman? Believe me, I've been called much worse.' The old laughter lit up Julie's eyes for a moment. 'Do you know the difference between a slut and a bitch?'

Banks shook his head.

'A slut is a woman who sleeps with anyone; a bitch is a woman who sleeps with anyone but you.'

Banks laughed. 'That's from the man's point of view, of course.'

'Of course.'

'So what happened?' he asked. 'What made you leave when you did?'

'You're a persistent man, Mr Banks,' Julie said, lighting another long white cigarette. 'Even my tasteless jokes don't seem to deflect you for very long. But I'm still not sure I ought to tell you.'

Banks caught her eyes and held them. 'Mrs Culver,' he said quietly, 'Bernard Allen – your childhood sweetheart, as you called him – was murdered. All murders are cruel and vicious, but this one was worse than many. First he was stabbed, and then his face was slashed and beaten in with a rock so nobody could recognize him. When we found him he'd been hidden away in the hanging valley for nearly two weeks and there were maggots crawling out of his eye sockets.'

Julie turned pale and gripped her cognac glass so tightly Banks thought she was going to shatter it. Her jaw was clenched and a muscle just below her ear twitched. 'Bastard,' she whispered.

The silent tension between them seemed to last for hours. Banks could hear the aimless chatter around him as if it were from a distant movie soundtrack: snippets of conversation about marathon running, beer, cricket and teaching native children up north, all in a medley of Canadian, Yorkshire, London and Scottish accents. Julie didn't even seem to realize he was there any more. She was staring at the wall just to the left of him. He half turned and saw a photograph of a wooded valley. The leaves were russet, yellow and orange.

He lit a cigarette. Julie finished her cognac and a little colour returned to her cheeks. The waitress came and they ordered another round.

When they had their drinks, Julie shook her head and regarded Banks with something close to hatred. 'For Bernie, then,' she said, and began: 'The night before I left I was supposed to see Stephen. We'd arranged to go to dinner at the Box Tree in Ilkley. He picked me up about half an hour late and he seemed unusually agitated – so much so that he pulled into a lay-by after we'd not gone more than four or five miles. And then he told me. He said there'd been some trouble and someone had got hurt. He didn't say killed at that time, just hurt. He was in a terrible state. Then he said something about the past catching up, that it was connected with something that had happened in Oxford.'

'When he was at university there?'

'I suppose so. He did go to Oxford. Anyway, this man, a private investigator, had turned up out of the blue and was intent on causing trouble. Stephen told me that Sam Greenock called and said there was someone looking for a Mr Collier. Sam was a bit suspicious about the newcomer asking questions and didn't give anything away. The man said he was going for a short evening walk up the valley. Stephen said he went after him and they talked and the man was going to blackmail the family.'

'About this event that had occurred in Oxford?'

'Yes. According to Stephen, tempers were raised, they fought and the man was hurt, badly hurt. I told Stephen he should call an ambulance.

'He got angry then and told me I didn't understand. That was when he said the man was dead. He went on to say there was nothing to connect them. Sam would keep quiet if they humoured him and let him play the local squire. Stephen just had to tell someone, to unburden himself, and he didn't really have anyone else he felt he could talk to but me.'

'What was your reaction?'

Julie lit a fresh cigarette from the stub of her old one. 'You have to understand Stephen,' she said. 'In many ways he's a kind, considerate, gentle man. But he's also a businessman and he can be ruthless when he feels the need. But more than all that, he's a Collier. There are few things more important to him than the good name of his family and its history. I wouldn't say I was in love with him, but I thought a lot of him and I didn't want to see him suffer. Needless to say, we didn't have dinner that night. We stopped at the nearest pub and had a bit too much to drink, then we—' Julie stopped. 'The rest is of no interest. I never saw him again after that night.'

'Why did you leave the next day? Did he suggest it to you?'

'No. I think he trusted me. He knew I was on his side.'

'So why did you go?'

'For my own reasons. First, and perhaps least, I'd been thinking about making a break for a while. I've no family. My parents died ten years ago and I just kept on the cottage. I had no real ambitions, no plans for my life. I was getting bored with my job and I was realistic enough not to see myself as the future Mrs Stephen Collier. Stephen wasn't going to propose, and I'd had hints from him that Nicholas didn't consider me to be of the right class, as if I wasn't aware of that already. These new events just hurried me along a bit. Secondly, I didn't trust myself. I thought if the police came around and started asking me questions, they'd know something was wrong and they'd keep pressuring me until I gave Stephen away. I didn't want to let that happen. I'm not a good liar, Mr Banks, as you can see.'

'And third?'

'Fear.'

'Of Stephen?'

'Yes. As I said, he's a complex man. There's a dark side to him. He's vulnerable in some ways, but very practical in others. Sentimental and pragmatic. It can sometimes make for a frightening combination. Didn't someone once say that Mafia dons are very sentimental people? Don't they send flowers to the widow when they've killed some-one? And weren't the Nazis sentimental too? Anyway, he'd done it before, confided in me one day then cut me dead the next – no pun intended – just pretended we'd never been intimate at all. Basically, Stephen couldn't get close to anyone. He'd try, and one of the ways he did it was by confiding. But then he'd regret it the next day and turn cold. What worried me was the importance of this confidence. It was the kind of thing he might not be able to live with, someone as weak as me knowing his secret.'

'In other words, you were worried you might become his next victim.'

'I know it sounds a horrible thing to say about someone you basically like and respect – even loved, perhaps, once – but yes, it did cross my mind. Much easier to disappear, as I'd been thinking of it anyway. And there was no one to make a fuss about my going.'

'What kind of things did he confide in you about before?'

'Oh, nothing much. Perhaps a slightly shady business deal; he was pleased if he'd put one over on somebody. Or an income tax fiddle. He hated the Inland Revenue.'

'Nothing more?'

'No. Not until that time.'

They sipped their drinks and let the conversations flow around them. Julie seemed more relaxed now she had told her story, and Banks could see no traces of that hateful look left in her eyes.

'Did he say anything else about this incident in Oxford?' he asked.

Julie shook her head. 'Nothing.'

'So you don't know what happened there, or who else might have been involved?'

'No. I'm sorry. At the time I never even thought to ask. It was all hard enough to take in as it was.'

Banks sighed. Still, even if he hadn't uncovered the whole story yet, he'd done well. The trip had been worthwhile. Julie rejoined the others. Banks said his farewells and left. It was about nine o'clock, a hot humid evening. Instead of taking the bus, he crossed Kingston Road and started walking towards the lake. The road sloped steeply at one point, crossed another main street with tram rails, then a hundred yards or so farther on ended at a beach.

Couples walked hand in hand along the boardwalk or sat on benches and stared out at the water. Some people jogged by, sweating, and others ambled along with dogs on leashes. Banks made his way over the soft sand to where a group of rocks stuck out into the lake. He clambered as far forward as he could and sat down on the warm stone. Water slopped around just below his feet. The horizon was a broad mauve band; above it, the sky's pink was tinged with misty grey. Banks lit a cigarette and wondered if it was the United States he could see in the distance or just a low narrow layer of mist.

He'd got what he came for, though he still couldn't put everything together. At least when he got back he would be able to question Stephen Collier more thoroughly, no matter what the man's influence with the deputy chief constable. Collier had killed Raymond Addison, and he might even have killed Bernard Allen too. There was no proof as yet, but Banks would find some if it took him a lifetime. Collier wasn't going to escape justice because of influence or social position, of that Banks would make sure.

By the time he had finished his cigarette, the sun had gone down much lower and the sky had changed. The horizon was now grey and the mauve band much higher in the sky. The lake seemed scattered with pink, as if the colour had transformed itself into raindrops and shattered the ice-blue surface of the water. Carefully, Banks got to his feet on the angled rock and made his way back towards a streetcar stop.

THREE

Earlier that day, back in Swainsdale, Detective Constable Philip Richmond had sat on a knoll high on Adam's Fell and unwrapped his cheese and pickle sandwiches. He flicked away the flies that gathered and poured some coffee from his flask. Up there, the air was pure and sharp; below, the sun glinted on the steel kegs in the back yard of the White Rose and flashed in the fountain playing in the Colliers' huge garden behind the ugly Gothic mansion. The old men stood on the bridge, and the Greenocks' front door was closed.

Sam had driven off on one of his regular jaunts to Leeds or Eastvale, and Katie had gone for a walk with Stephen Collier up Swainshead Fell. He thought he could see them across in the north-east, near a patch of grass that was greener than that around it, but it could have been some-one else.

Sipping the bitter black coffee, Richmond had reminded himself that tomorrow was his last day in Swainshead. He was expected back at the station with a report on Sunday morning. Not that he hadn't enjoyed himself – it had been very much like a week's holiday – but he longed to get back to his Eastvale mates. Tomorrow the rugby team was playing Skipton, a game he would have to miss. There was always a good booze-up and sing-song after the match, and it would be a shame to miss that too. Jim Hatchley was usually there for the booze, of course. An honorary member they called him now he wasn't fit enough to play any more. But even the sergeant's presence didn't spoil Richmond's fun: a few jars, a good sing-song, then, with a bit of luck, a kiss and a cuddle with Doreen on the way home. He prided himself on being a man of simple tastes, yet he also liked to think that nothing else about him was simple.

Finishing his sandwich, he unwrapped a Kit-Kat and picked up *The Three Stigmata of Palmer Eldritch*, the last of the four Philip K. Dick books he'd brought along. But he couldn't concentrate. He began to wonder why nothing had happened during Banks' absence. Was the killer certain that the chief inspector would find out nothing in Toronto? Or was there, perhaps, no connection at all between the Addison and Allen murders?

Certainly there had been a bit of a fuss or flap, as Freddie Metcalfe had said, earlier in the week. But it had soon died down and everyone carried on as normal. Was it a false sense of security? The lull before the storm. Perhaps they knew who Richmond was and were being especially careful? He certainly couldn't keep an eye on all of them.

He stroked his moustache and turned back to his book. Not ours to reason why . . . But still, he thought, an arrest would have helped his career. A thrilling car chase, perhaps, or a cross-country marathon. He pictured himself bringing in the killer, arm twisted up his back, and throwing him in Eastvale nick under Banks' approving smile. Then he laughed at himself, brushed a persistent wasp away and went back to Philip K. Dick.

FOUR

That Saturday, the afternoon of his last day in Toronto, Banks went to his first baseball game. The retractable roof was open and a breeze from the lake relieved some of the humidity at the SkyDome, where the Toronto Blue Jays were playing the New York Yankees, but the temperature was still almost thirty degrees. In England, people would have been fainting from the heat.

Banks and Gregson sat in the stands, ate hot dogs and drank beer out of flimsy plastic cups.

'Lucky to be drinking it at all,' Gregson said when Banks complained. 'It took a lot of doing, getting drinking allowed at ball games.'

A fat boy of about twelve sitting next to Banks stopped shovelling barbecue-flavoured potato crisps into his maw to stand up and hurl obscene death threats at the Yankees' pitcher. His equally obese mother looked embarrassed but made no attempt to control him.

Banks wished his son, Brian, could be there. Unlike Banks, he had watched enough baseball on Channel 4 to be able to understand the game. When Banks first took his seat, the only baseball term he knew was home run, but by the end of the third innings, Gregson had explained all about RBIs, the tops and bottoms of the innings, designated hitters, knuckle balls, the bullpen, bunting, the balk rule, pinch hitters and at least three different kinds of pitches.

The game mounted to an exciting conclusion, and the boy next to him spilled his crisps all over the floor.

Finally, the home crowd went wild. Down five–four at the bottom of the ninth, with two out, the sixth Blue Jay up drove one home with all the bases loaded – a grand slam, Gregson called it. That made the score eight–five, and that was how the game ended.

They pushed their way out of the stadium, and Gregson negotiated the heavy traffic up Spadina to Bloor, where they stopped in at the Madison for a farewell drink.

'Are you planning to do anything about the Culver woman?' Gregson asked.

Banks sipped his pint of Conner bitter. They were out on the patio, and the late afternoon sun beat down on his shoulders.

'No,' he answered. 'What did she do, after all?'

'From the sound of it, she withheld evidence. She was a material witness. If she'd spoken up, this new homicide might never have happened.'

Banks shook his head. 'She didn't have much choice really. I know what you mean, but you've got to understand what things are like around Swainshead. It's not like Toronto. She couldn't tell what she knew. There was loyalty, yes, but there was also fear. The Colliers are a powerful family. If she'd stayed we might have got something out of her, but on the other hand something might have happened to her first.'

'So she left under threat?'

'That's the way I'd put it, yes.'

'And you think this Collier guy killed Allen because he knew too much?'

'I think it was more to do with what Allen intended to do with his knowledge. I can't prove it, but I think he was going to blackmail Stephen Collier. Julie Culver disagrees, but from what one of Allen's boozing buddies told me, he had some plan to get back home to England. I think he asked Collier for the money to come home and live in Swainshead again, or maybe to fix him up with a job. Collier's brother teaches at a small public school, and Allen was a teacher. Maybe he suggested that Stephen tell Nicholas to get him a job there. Instead, Stephen decided to get rid of Allen the same way he did with Addison.'

'Shit,' said Gregson. 'I'd no idea Toronto was so bad

that people would stoop to blackmail to get out of here.'

Banks laughed. 'Maybe it's just that Swainsdale is so beautiful people would do anything to get there. I don't know. Allen was seriously disturbed, I think. A number of things took their toll on him: the divorce, the distance from home, the disappointment of not getting the kind of job that would really challenge his mind. Someone told me that he had gone beyond the parochial barriers of most English teachers, but he found himself in a system that placed no value on the exceptional, a system that almost imposed such barriers. The teaching he was doing was dreary, the students were ignorant and uninterested, and I think he tended to blame it on the local educational system. He thought things would be better in England. He probably remembered his own grammar school days when even poor kids got to learn Latin, and he thought things were still like that. Perhaps he didn't even think he was doing anything really bad when he approached Collier. Or maybe he did. He had plenty of cause to resent him.'

'That old British class system again?'

'Partly. It's hard to figure Allen out. Mostly, he seems like a decent person gone wrong, but he also had a big chip on his shoulder all along. I don't suppose we'll ever know what really motivated him.'

'But you do have your killer.'

'Yes – if he hasn't done a bunk. But we've no proof yet.'

'He knows you're here, on to the girl?'

'The whole village knows. We've got a man there.'

'Well, then . . . What time's your flight?'

'Nine o'clock.' He looked at his watch. 'Christ, it's six now. I'd better get back and pick up my stuff.'

'I'll drive you,' Gregson said. 'I'm off duty all day, and it can be a real hassle getting to the airport.'

'Would you? That's great.'

At the house, Banks packed his meagre belongings and the presents he had bought for his family, then left a thank-you note with the bottle of Scotch for Gerry. In a way, he felt sad to leave the house and neighbourhood that had become familiar to him over the past week: the sound of streetcars rattling by; the valley with its expressway and green slopes; the downtown skyline; the busy overflowing Chinese shops at Broadview and Gerrard.

The traffic along Lakeshore Boulevard to the airport turn-off wasn't too heavy, and they made it with plenty of time to spare. The two policemen swapped addresses and invitations outside the departures area, then Gregson drove straight off home. Banks didn't blame him. He'd always hated hanging around airports himself if he didn't have a plane to catch.

After the queue at the check-in desk, the trip to the duty-free shop and the passage through security and immigration, it was almost time to board the plane. As they took off, Banks looked out of the window and saw the city lit up in the twilight below him: grids and figure eights of light as far as he could see in every direction except south, where he could pick out the curve of the bay and the matt silver-grey of Lake Ontario.

Once in the air, it was on with the Walkman – Kiri te Kanawa's soaring arias seemed most appropriate this time – down the hatch with the Johnnie Walker and away with the food. A seasoned traveller already. This time even the movie was tolerable. A suspense thriller without the car chases and special effects that so often marred that type of film for Banks, it concentrated on the psychology of police-man and victim.

He slept for a while, managed to choke down the coffee

and roll that came for breakfast, and looked out of the window to see the sun shining over Ireland.

It was nearly ten o'clock in the morning, local time, when he cleared customs and reclaimed his baggage. Among the crowd of people waiting to welcome friends and relatives stood Sandra, who threw her arms around him and gave him a long kiss.

'I told Brian and Tracy they should come, too,' she said, breaking away and picking up the duty-free bag, 'but you know what they're like about sleeping in on Sunday mornings.'

'So it's not that they don't love me any more?'

'Don't be silly. They've missed you as much as I have. Almost.'

She kissed him again, and they set off for the car.

'It's a bloody maze, this place,' Sandra complained, 'and they really fleece you for parking. Then there's road-works everywhere on the way. They're still working on Barton bridge, you know. It was misty too, high up in the Pennines. Oh, I am going on, aren't I? I'm just so glad to see you. You must be tired.'

Banks stifled a yawn. 'It's five in the morning where I am. Where I was, rather. And I can't sleep on planes. Anything interesting happen while I was away?'

Sandra frowned and hesitated. 'I wasn't going to tell you,' she said, loading the small case and the duty-free bag into the boot of the white Cortina, 'at least not until we got home. Superintendent Gristhorpe called this morning just before I set off.'

'On a Sunday morning? What about?'

'He said he wants to see you as soon as you get back. I told him what state you'd be in. Oh, he apologized and all that, but you've still got to go in.'

'What is it?' Banks lit cigarettes for both Sandra and himself as she drove down the spiral ramp from the fourth floor of the multi-storey car park out into the sunlit day.

'Bad news,' she said. 'There's been another death in Swainshead.'

PART THREE:

THE DREAMING SPIRES

Part Three

THE DREAMING SPIRES

12

ONE

'**Accidental death!** Don't you think that's just a bit too bloody convenient?'

Sergeant Hatchley shrugged as if to imply that perhaps if Banks didn't go gallivanting off to the New World such things might not happen. 'Doctor says it could have been suicide,' he said.

Banks ran his hand through his close-cropped black hair. It was twelve thirty. He was back in his office only an hour after arriving home, jet-lagged and disoriented. So far, he hadn't even had a chance to admire his favourite view of the cobbled market square. The office was smoky and a cup of black coffee steamed on the desk. Superintendent Gristhorpe was keeping an appointment with the deputy chief constable, whose personal interest in events was a measure of the Colliers' influence in the dale.

'And where the hell was Richmond?' Banks went on. 'Wasn't he supposed to be baby-sitting the lot of them while I was away?'

'Yes, sir.'

'Where was he then?'

'Asleep at the Greenocks', I suppose. He could hardly invite himself to spend the night with the Colliers, could he?'

'That's not the point. He should have known something was wrong. Send him in.'

'He's just gone off duty, sir.'

'Well, bloody well bring him back again!'

'Yes, sir.'

Hatchley stalked out of the office. Banks sighed, stubbed out his cigarette and walked over to the window. The cobbled market square was still there, a bit rain drenched, but still there. Tourists posed for photographs on the worn plinth of the ancient market cross. The church door stood open and Banks could hear the distant sound of the congregation singing 'Jerusalem'.

So he was home. He'd just had time to say hello to Brian and Tracy, then he'd had to hurry down to the station. He hadn't even given them their presents yet: a Blue Jays sweatshirt for Brian, the *Illustrated History of Canada* for his budding historian daughter, Tracy, and a study of the Group of Seven, with plenty of fine repro-ductions, for Sandra. They were still packed in his suitcase, which stood next to the duty-free cigarettes and Scotch in the hall.

Already Toronto was a memory with the quality of a dream – baseball, the community college, Kleinburg, Niagara Falls, the CN Tower, and the tall downtown buildings in black and white and gold. But Staff Sergeant Gregson, the Feathers crowd and Anne Ralston/Julie Culver weren't a dream. They were what he had gone for. And now he'd come back to find Stephen Collier dead.

There was no suicide note; at least nobody had found one so far. According to Nicholas Collier, John Fletcher and Sam Greenock, who had all been with Stephen on his last night at the White Rose, Stephen, always highly strung and restless, had seemed excessively nervous. He had got much more drunk than usual. Finally, long beyond closing time, they had had to help him home. They had deposited Stephen fully clothed on his bed, then adjourned to Nicholas's half of the house, where they had a nightcap. John and Sam then left, and Nicholas went to bed.

In the morning, when he went to see how his brother was, Nicholas had discovered him dead. The initial findings of Dr Glendenning indicated that he had died of suffocation. It appeared that Stephen Collier had vomited while under the influence of barbiturates and been unable to wake up. Such things often happened when pills and booze were mixed, Glendenning had said. All that had to be determined now was the amount of barbiturate in Stephen's system, and that would have to wait until the post-mortem. He had suffered from insomnia for a long time and had a prescription for Nembutal.

So what had happened? According to Hatchley, Stephen must have got up after the others left and taken his sleeping pills as usual, then gone downstairs and played a record – Mozart's *Jupiter Symphony* was still spinning on the turntable – had another drink or two of Scotch from a tumbler, which was still half full, gone back upstairs, taken some more sleeping pills and passed out. By that time, given how much he'd had to drink, he probably wouldn't have remembered taking the first lot of pills. The only question was, did he do it deliberately or not? And the only person who could answer that was Stephen himself.

It was damned unsatisfactory, Banks thought, but it looked like an end to both the Addison and Allen cases. Stephen Collier had certainly confessed to Anne Ralston. He knew that Banks would find her and that when she heard Bernie had been killed, she would pass on the information. He must have gone through a week of torment trying to decide what to do – make a run for it or stay and brazen it out. After all, it was only her word against his. The strain had finally proved too much for him, and either accidentally or on purpose – or accidentally on purpose – he had put an end to things, perhaps to save himself and the family name the ignominy of a trial and all the publicity it would bring down on them.

Feeling calmer, Banks lit another cigarette. He finished his coffee and determined not to haul Richmond over the coals. After all, as Hatchley had said, the constable couldn't be everywhere at once. He still felt restless though; his nerves were jangling and his eyes ached. He had that strange and disturbing sensation of wanting to sleep but knowing he couldn't even if he tried. When he rubbed his chin, he could feel the bristles. He hadn't even had time for a shave.

When Richmond arrived, they walked over to the Queen's Arms. After the morning sunshine, it had turned cool and rainy; a wonderful relief after the hellish steam bath of Toronto, Banks thought as he looked up and let the rain fall on his face. Cyril, the landlord, rustled them up a couple of ham and tomato sandwiches. They found an empty table in a corner, and Banks got the drinks in.

'Look, I'm sorry for dragging you back, Phil,' he said, 'but I want to hear your version of what happened.'

'In the White Rose, sir?'

'The whole week. Just tell me what you saw and thought.'

'There's not very much to tell, really,' Richmond said, and he gave Banks his version of the week's events in as much detail as he could.

'Katie Greenock went off with Stephen Collier on Friday afternoon, is that right?'

'Yes, sir. They went for a walk up Swainshead Fell. I took a walk up Adam's Fell and I could see them across the dale.'

'Did they go towards the hanging valley?'

'No, sir, they didn't go over the top – just diagonal, as far as the river's source. It's about halfway up and a bit to the north.'

Banks wondered if anything had gone on between Katie and Stephen Collier. It seemed unlikely, given the kind of woman she seemed to be, but he was sure that she had surrendered to Bernard Allen. And in her case, the old-fashioned term 'surrendered' was the right word to use. Banks recalled the image of Katie standing in the market square, soaked to the skin, just before he'd left, and he remembered the eerie feeling he'd had that she was coming apart at the seams. It would certainly be worth talking to her again; at the very least she would be able to tell him something more about Collier's state of mind on the day before he died.

'What about Saturday night in the White Rose? How long were you there?'

'From about nine till closing time, sir. I tried to pace myself, not drink too much.'

Banks grinned, remembering his own nights in the Toronto pubs. 'A tough job, eh? Never mind. Notice anything?'

'Like I told the super and Sergeant Hatchley, sir, it seemed pretty much of a normal night to me.'

'You didn't think Stephen Collier was drinking more than usual?'

'I don't know how much he usually drank, sir. I'd say from the other three nights I saw him in the White Rose during my stay, he did drink more on Saturday. But it was

Saturday night. People do overdo it a bit then, don't they? No work in the morning.'

'Unless you're a copper.'

Cyril called last orders and Banks hurried to the bar for another two pints.

'What was the mood like at the table?' he asked when he got back.

'A bit festive, really.'

'No arguments, no sullen silences?'

'No. Everyone seemed to be enjoying themselves. There was one thing . . .'

'Yes?'

'Well, I couldn't hear anything because Sam and Stephen were talking quite loudly, but I got the impression that at one point John Fletcher and Nicholas Collier were having a bit of a barney.'

'What do you mean?'

'I'm just going by the expressions on their faces, sir. It looked like Nicholas was angry with Fletcher for some reason and Fletcher just brushed him aside.'

'Did the others appear to notice?'

'No. Like I said, sir, they were talking, arguing about politics or something.'

'And this was Nicholas Collier and John Fletcher, not Stephen?'

'Yes, sir.'

'Odd. How did Stephen seem?'

'I'd say he was a fairly happy drunk. Happier than he ever seemed sober.'

'What was he drinking?'

'They were all drinking beer.'

'How many pints would you say Stephen had?'

Richmond flushed and fiddled with his moustache. 'I

wasn't really counting, sir. Perhaps I should have been, but . . .'

'You weren't to know he'd be dead in the morning. Don't worry. It's the bane of our lives. If we all had twenty-twenty hindsight our job'd be a lot easier. Just try and remember. Picture it as clearly as you can.'

Richmond closed his eyes. 'At a guess, I'd say about five or six, sir.'

'Five or six. Not a lot, really, is it? Not for a Yorkshireman, anyway. And he was practically legless?'

'Yes, sir. Maybe he was drinking the vodka as well.'

'What vodka?'

'I'm not clear on it, but I remember Freddie Metcalfe, the landlord, muttering something about having to change the bottle after one of them had been up and bought a round. It was busy and he said he needed eight hands to do his job.'

'But you never saw Stephen put a shorts glass to his lips?'

'No, sir.'

'Did anyone?'

'Not that I remember.'

'Odd, that, isn't it? What happened to the vodka, then?'

'Perhaps whoever bought it just drank it down at the bar.'

'Hmm. It's possible. But why? Let's leave it for the moment, anyway. Did you hear any mention at all of Oxford during the week?'

'You mean the university, sir?'

'Any mention at all. The name: Oxford.'

Richmond shook his head.

'All right, that'll do for now.' Banks rubbed his eyes.

They drifted out into the street with the others as Cyril

prepared to lock up for the afternoon. There was a lot more to think about now. Nothing that Banks had heard since he got back had been at all convincing. Something was wrong, he felt, and the case was far from over. Sending Richmond back home, he decided on a short walk in the rain to freshen himself up before returning to the station.

TWO

Katie watched the rain swell the becks that rushed down Swainshead Fell as it got dark that night. The rhythmic gurgle of water through the half-open window calmed her. All day she had been agitated. Now it was after ten; Sam was still at the pub, and Katie was brooding over the day's events.

If only she had told Sam that their guest was a policeman, probably sent to spy on them. Then he'd have informed all and sundry, and maybe things would have been different. But now Stephen had to die, too; another escape route cut off. Had the policeman noticed anything? Katie didn't think so. There had been nothing really to notice.

Ever since morning, when Stephen's body had been discovered, Upper Head had been stunned. Women gathered in the street after church and lowered their voices, looking over at the Gothic house and shaking their heads. The Colliers were, when all was said and done, still regarded as lords of the manor.

All the curtains of their spooky Victorian mansion across the river had been drawn since morning, when the police and doctors had finished and taken Stephen's body

away. One or two people had dropped in to offer condolences, including John Fletcher, who'd have got a rude
reception from Nicholas, Katie thought, under any other
circumstances. Sam, of course, had been one of the first,
keen to establish himself with the new squire now that
the more approachable Stephen was gone. Now Sam and
John were no doubt getting maudlin drunk in the White
Rose. Katie hadn't gone across to the house; she couldn't
face Nicholas Collier alone again after the incident at the
party.

Rain spilled in over the window sill. Katie dipped a
finger in it and made patterns on the white paintwork. The
water beaded on the paint no matter what she tried to
make it do. A breeze had sprung up and it brought the
scent of summer rain indoors; shivering, she pulled her
grey lambswool cardigan around her shoulders.

'Be sure your sins will find you out,' another of her
grandmother's favourite maxims, sprang into her mind.
With it came the dim and painful memory of a telltale
boy's hair on her collar when she had come home from her
one and only visit to the church-run youth club. It must
have got there in the cloakroom, somehow, but her grandmother had thrust it forward as irrefutable evidence of
Katie's lewd and lascivious nature before making her
stand 'naked in her shame' in the corner of the cold stone-
flagged kitchen all evening. She had been supposed to
repeat 'Be sure your sins will find you out' under her
breath all the time she stood there, but she hadn't. That
was another sin: disobedience. The vicar had got an earful, too, about running a house of ill repute and corrupting
local youth. That had pleased Katie; she didn't like him
anyway because his breath smelled like the toilet when he
came close, which he always did. Taking pleasure in the

misfortune of others was another sin she had been guilty of that day.

Katie closed the window and turned to get into bed. It was after ten thirty. Sam would probably be back soon. There was a chance that if she pretended to be asleep . . .

But sleep didn't come easily. She thought of Stephen again, of his chaste touch. Life might not have been so bad if he had taken her away with him. She knew he would want to have her eventually – it would be part of the price – but he seemed a gentle person, like Bernard had been, and perhaps he wouldn't be too demanding. The images blurred in her mind as sleep came closer: her grandmother brandishing the hair, black eyes flashing, Bernard breathing hard as he pulled at her clothes . . . She heard the back door open and close noisily. Sam. Quickly, she turned over and pulled the covers up to her ears. Her feet were cold.

THREE

'What do you think, then, Alan?'

Banks and Gristhorpe sat at the dining-room table later that night and sipped duty-free Bell's. The children were in bed and Sandra was leafing through the book Banks had brought her from Toronto. Banks felt better after the short nap he had taken late in the afternoon.

'It stinks. I track down Anne Ralston in Toronto and she tells me Stephen Collier practically confessed to killing Addison because of some scandal he was involved in at Oxford. Then, when I get back, I find Collier's conveniently dead – accidental death. It's too pat.'

'Hmm.' Gristhorpe sipped his Scotch. 'It could be true. But let's suppose it's not. What else could have happened?

I'm sorry, I know you're still tired, Alan. Maybe tomorrow would be better?'

Banks lit a cigarette. 'No, it's all right. What do I think happened? I don't know. I thought I'd got it all worked out but now everything's gone haywire. I know it makes sense that Collier killed himself rather than face the trouble he knew he'd be in when I got back. Maybe the pressure built in him over the week. On the other hand, what if he didn't kill Allen? What if he knew who did, and whoever it was was afraid he'd crack under pressure and give it away. That would have given someone enough motive to get rid of him, wouldn't it? We still don't have a clear connection between Addison and Allen, though.'

'Except the Ralston girl.'

'What if there's something else? An angle we haven't really considered.'

'Such as?'

'That's the trouble. I've no idea.'

Gristhorpe swirled the Bell's in his glass. 'Then it has to be connected with Addison and Ralston.'

'I'd like to go down to Oxford as soon as possible and dig around. Ted Folley's in the local CID there. We were at training school together.'

Gristhorpe nodded. 'That's no problem.'

'Maybe Addison found something out and was going to blackmail Collier.'

'He had a clean record.'

'True. But you know as well as I do what private investigators are like, especially solo operators. We can also assume that Bernard Allen had the same information, or part of it, and that he too was blackmailing Collier.'

Gristhorpe rubbed his whiskery chin. 'Aye. But if Collier did kill Allen for that reason, who killed Collier, and why?'

'That's what we have to find out.'

'So we're still looking at the lot of them?'

'It seems that way. Any one of them could have gone back to the house – the French windows at the back weren't locked – and given him another drink with the barbiturates. Or someone could have mixed a few nembies with his drinks earlier. He was so far gone he probably wouldn't have noticed.'

'Risky, though.'

'Yes. But what murder isn't?'

'Aye.'

'And then there's the matter of the vodka. I want to talk to Freddie Metcalfe about that.'

'What vodka?'

'Someone in the party was buying vodka that night, but Richmond never actually saw anyone drink it.'

'So you think someone was spiking Collier's drinks with vodka, making sure he got really drunk?'

'It's a strong possibility, yes. Vodka's pretty much tasteless in a pint.'

'Aye, in more ways than one,' Gristhorpe said.

'The trouble is,' Banks went on, 'it was such a busy night that I can't rely on anyone remembering. It could have been Sam Greenock, John Fletcher or Nicholas Collier – any one of them. I'm assuming they all bought rounds.'

'What about the Greenock woman?'

Banks saw again in his mind's eye the image of Katie standing soaked to the skin in the market square. 'Katie? I suppose she could play some part in all this. As far as I can tell though, she's in a world of her own. There's something not quite right about her. I thought it was just her marriage. Sam's a real bastard – thrashes her every now and then – but I think there's more to it than that. According to Richmond though, she wasn't in the White Rose that night.'

Gristhorpe looked at his watch and stood up. 'Good Lord, is that the time? I'd better be off. Don't worry about being in early tomorrow.'

'I probably will be,' Banks said. 'I want to go to Swainshead and see a few people. Then I'll go to Oxford. Mind if I take Sergeant Hatchley? There might be a bit of legwork, and I'd rather have Richmond up here taking care of business.'

'Aye, take him. He'll feel like a fish out of water in Oxford. Do him good though. Broaden his horizons.'

Banks laughed. 'I'm afraid Sergeant Hatchley's horizons are firmly fixed on beer, idleness, sport and sex – in that order. But I'll try.'

Gristhorpe drained his glass and left. Banks sat beside Sandra and looked at some of the pictures with her, but his eyes began to feel suddenly prickly and heavy. He'd been wondering whether to let the superintendent know that Gerry Webb had revealed his full name, but decided against it. Names were, after all, a kind of power. He would tell no one at the station, but it was too good to keep to himself.

'Do you know,' he said, slipping his arm around Sandra's shoulders, 'I found out a very interesting thing about Superintendent Gristhorpe in Toronto.'

'It sounds like you discovered a lot of interesting things there,' Sandra said, raising an arched black eyebrow. Her eyebrows contrasted sharply with her natural blonde hair, and that was one of the features Banks found sexy about her. 'Go on,' she urged him. 'Tell me.'

'I've missed you,' Banks said, moving closer. 'I'll tell you in bed, later.'

'I thought you were tired.'

'Only my eyes.'

'Is it worth knowing?'

'It's worth it.'

'Right, then.' Sandra turned towards him. 'Let's not waste time and energy climbing upstairs. It has been a whole week, after all.'

FOUR

It was good to be home, Banks thought, as he drove the white Cortina along the dale. The sun was out, the water glittered silver, the valley sides shone vibrant green, and the Beatles were singing 'And Your Bird Can Sing' on the cassette. He lit a cigarette and slowed down to pass a colourful group of hikers. They clustered together in the deep grass by the drystone wall and waved as he drove by.

Who to visit first? That was the question. It was still only ten thirty, so perhaps he'd best leave Freddie Metcalfe till the White Rose opened at eleven and call on Nicholas Collier – the interview he was least looking forward to.

Accordingly, he carried on past the pub and pulled up on the verge outside the Collier house. Nicholas opened the door at the first ring of the bell.

'Chief Inspector Banks,' he said. 'Long time, no see. Come in.' He looked tired; his usually bright eyes had lost their sparkle and there were dark pouches under them. 'Please, sit down.' He pointed towards a leather upholstered armchair by the open French windows. 'I'm not in a mood to sit in the sun today, but I feel I must remind myself of its presence.'

'I'm sorry about what happened,' Banks said. 'I'd been hoping to talk to Stephen when I got back.'

Nicholas turned to look at the fountain outside and said nothing. Banks thought he could see a fading bruise at the side of his mouth.

'I hope you're not going to ask me to go through it all again,' Nicholas said at last, taking a cigarette from the porcelain box on the low table beside him. 'Policemen always seem to be asking people to repeat their stories.'

'There's a good reason for that,' Banks said. 'Sometimes people remember things. Little things they thought insignificant at the time.'

'All the same, I very much doubt that I can help you.'

'I was wondering if you had any knowledge of your brother's problems?'

'Stephen's problems? No, I can't say I did. Though he seemed a bit edgy this past week or two, as if he had something on his mind.'

'Did you ask him what it was?'

'No. Does that surprise you? Well, it shouldn't. Stephen wasn't the most forthcoming of people. If he wanted to talk, he would, to whoever struck his fancy at the moment. But if you asked him, you got nowhere. Certainly I never did.'

'I see. So you've no idea what he was worried about?'

'Not at all. I take no interest in the business, so I wouldn't know about that side of things. Did he have business problems? Trouble at t' mill?'

'Not that I know of, no, Mr Collier. His problem was that we think he may have killed a man over five years ago because of something that happened at Oxford. We also think he might have been responsible for the murder of Bernard Allen more recently.'

'Stephen! You're joking, Chief Inspector, surely?'

Banks shook his head. 'When was Stephen at Oxford?'

'He went there nine years ago. But nothing untoward happened to him in Oxford as far as I know.' He paused and his eyes turned hard. 'You're not joking, are you?'

'I'm afraid not.'

'Well, what can I say? Your wording would seem to indicate that this is mere supposition, that you have no proof.'

'Only the testimony of Anne Ralston.'

'That woman Stephen was seeing all those years ago?'

'Yes. I found her in Toronto.'

'And you'd take a slut's word that Stephen was a murderer?'

'She'd no reason to lie. And I don't believe she's a slut.'

Nicholas shrugged dismissively. 'As you like. She certainly wasn't the type of woman I'd want for a sister-in-law. But haven't you considered that she might have been the guilty party? As I remember, she disappeared the morning after the man was killed.'

'Yes, she did.'

'So she'd have everything to gain by trying to put the blame on Stephen.'

'It's possible, yes. But there's Bernard Allen's murder to take into account, too. She wasn't in Swainshead at the time. She was in Toronto.'

'So?'

'So she couldn't have killed Allen.'

'I'm sorry but I don't see the connection. You admit she could have killed the other man, but not Bernard Allen. What I don't see is why you should even think the same person killed both of them. What had Allen and that private detective chappie got in common?'

'Nothing, as far as we can tell. Except that they were both killed in Swainshead.' Banks lit a cigarette. 'There are too many coincidences, Mr Collier. One of the most interesting ones is that Bernard Allen was friendly with Anne Ralston in Toronto. That would make him the only person from Swainshead to see her since she disappeared. And the whole village was aware of that, thanks to Sam Greenock. It's also a coincidence that Stephen was going out with Anne Ralston at the time she left Swainshead, and that she told me he confessed to her about killing Addison. It's another coincidence that Stephen is dead when I return.'

'I can't argue with your logic, Chief Inspector. There certainly are a lot of coincidences. But they *are* coincidences, aren't they? I mean, you've no real evidence to link them or to back up your suppositions, have you?'

'Are you sure you knew nothing about your brother's problems?' Banks asked.

'I've told you.' Collier sighed. 'We just weren't that close. You can see for yourself how we split the house – into two very different halves, I might add. All we had in common was family. Even if he had been a murderer, which I don't believe for a moment, Stephen would hardly have told me.'

'But he told Anne Ralston.'

'So you say. I can only repeat that the woman must be lying to save her own skin.' He leaned forward to stub out his cigarette but didn't slouch back in the chair again. 'Chief Inspector,' he said, folding his hands on his lap, 'I hope you're not going to spread these accusations about my brother around the dale. After all, you admit you've no proof. You could do untold damage to the family name, not to mention my career.'

'Rest assured, Mr Collier. I'm not in the habit of spreading unfounded accusations.'

'And might I suggest,' Nicholas added, 'that even if Stephen had been guilty, he's certainly suffered adequate penalty for his sin, and no useful purpose would be served by going poking around in his past affairs.'

'Ah, that's where we differ,' Banks said. 'I'm not judge or jury, Mr Collier. I just try to dig out the truth. And until there are answers to a number of questions, Stephen's file remains open – wherever Stephen himself may be.' Nicholas opened his mouth to protest but Banks ignored him and went on. 'I don't care who you are, Mr Collier. You can threaten, you can pull strings, you can do what you bloody well want. But I'm going to get to the bottom of this.' He stood up and walked over to the door. Nicholas sat where he was and stared coldly at him.

'One more question,' Banks said. 'Which one of you was drinking vodka in the White Rose on Saturday night?'

'Vodka?' Nicholas grunted. 'None of us, I shouldn't think. Can't stand the stuff, myself.'

'Did you see your brother drink any?'

Nicholas walked over to the door and grasped the handle. 'No, I didn't. Stephen never drank vodka.' He opened the door. 'Now would you mind leaving? And you can be damn sure you haven't heard the last of this.'

Was he lying? Banks found it hard to tell. People of Nicholas Collier's class had so much self-confidence bred into them that they could carry most things off.

'What was your argument with John Fletcher about?' he asked, leaning against the open door.

'What argument?'

'You didn't have words?'

Nicholas flicked his wrist. 'We may have done, but I can't remember why. A trifle, I should imagine. Now . . .' He nodded towards the path.

Banks set off.

It hadn't been satisfactory at all. Banks swore under his breath as he headed down the path. He should have pushed Nicholas even harder. Still, there would be time later. Plenty of time. There was still Oxford. And Katie Greenock and Freddie Metcalfe. He looked at his watch and walked into the White Rose.

'I understand tha's been globetrotting,' Freddie Metcalfe said, pouring out a pint of Marston's Pedigree.

'That's right,' Banks answered. 'Been to visit the New World.' He counted out the money and put it on the damp bar towel.

'I don't 'old wi' Americans,' Freddie said, screwing up his face. 'Get plenty on 'em in 'ere, tha knows. Allus asking for fancy drinks – bourbon and branch water and t' like. Can't understand none on 'em. And Perrier. Bloody Perrier wi' a twist o' lemon them purple-haired old women want. Mutton dressed up as lamb, if y'ask me.' He sniffed and carried the money to the till.

Banks thought of pointing out that Canada was not the same as the USA, but he didn't want to miss a good opening. 'Not get a lot of fancy drinks orders in here, then? Not many drink shorts?' he asked.

'Nah,' said Freddie, ambling back. 'Most tourists we get's fell-walkers, and they like a good pint, I'll say that for 'em. T' lasses sometimes ask for a brandy and Babycham, like, or a Pony or Cherry B. But mostly it's ale.'

'What about vodka?'

'What about it?'

'Get through much?'

'Nah. Bloody Russkie muck, that is. Can't taste it. We get through a good bit o' single malt Scotch, but vodka . . . nah.'

'I understand you had a vodka drinker on Saturday night?'

'What makes tha think that? Tha weren't 'ere then.'

'Never mind that. Did you?'

Freddie scratched his mutton chop whiskers. 'Aye, come to think on it, I do remember 'aving to change t' bottle, so somebody must've been at it.'

'Who, Freddie, who?'

'I can't rightly say. It might not've been me who served 'im. I don't recollect as I did. Lot o' strangers in last weekend 'cos t' weather brightened up, like. It were a busy night, Sat'day, and that gormless lass from Gratly never showed up. S'posed to give me an 'and behind t' bar. No, I'm sorry, lad. It's no good. I know I changed t' bottle, but I were allus serving four orders at once. Need eight bloody arms on this job, specially on Sat'day night. And I only 'ad young Betty to 'elp me.'

'Were there any arguments in the pub that night?'

Freddie laughed. 'Well, it'd 'ardly be a Sat'day night wi'out a few 'eated words, would it?'

'I suppose not. What about at the Collier table?'

'I don't recollect owt. Billy Black and Les Stott were barneying about whippets, and Wally Grimes – Wally's a local farmer, like – 'ad a little disagreement wi' some walkers about National Trust footpaths. But that's all I can remember.'

'You don't remember anything between Nicholas Collier and John Fletcher?'

'Nah. But that wouldn't be nowt new. Now John and Mr Stephen, they understood each other. But John

270

Fletcher never did 'ave time for young Nicholas, even when 'e were a lad.'

'But you heard nothing on Saturday?'

'Nay. Too much bloody noise. I only 'eard t' others because they were standing at t' bar right a-front o' me.'

'Did you clear the tables later?'

'Nay, Betty did that.' He pointed towards a buxom rosy-cheeked girl washing glasses.

'Can I talk to her?'

'Aye. Betty, lass, come over 'ere. T' inspector wants a word wi' thee.'

The roses quickly spread over Betty's entire complexion, and down as much of her throat and chest as was exposed. She lowered her big brown eyes and stood in front of Banks like a schoolgirl before the head.

'It's all right, Betty,' Banks said, 'I just want to ask you a couple of questions about Saturday night when you worked here.'

She nodded but still didn't look up.

'Do you remember serving Mr Collier's group at all?'

'Aye,' she said. 'Well . . . no . . . I mean, I did serve them, but it were that busy I don't remember nothing about it.'

'And you collected all the glasses later?'

'Aye.'

'Do you remember picking up any shorts glasses from Mr Collier's table?'

Betty thought for a moment – a process Banks fancied he could almost hear – and then shook her head. 'I remember picking up some shorts glasses off t' bar,' she said, 'but I can't say who drank 'em.'

'Is this the part of the bar the Collier group came to for their orders?'

'Aye, it would've been,' Freddie said.

'But neither of you can say which member of the Collier group was ordering vodka?'

They both shook their heads glumly.

Banks sighed, then finished his pint philosophically and lit a cigarette.

'What's it all about, then?' Freddie asked.

'Eh? Oh, never mind for now,' Banks said. 'Probably nothing.'

'They were all a bit merry, like.'

'The Collier group?'

'Aye. All on 'em. But Mr Stephen were t' worst.'

'Did he drink more than the rest?'

Freddie shook his head. 'I can't say. Shouldn't think so, though. They was drinking rounds. Unless . . .' Then comprehension dawned on his round red face. 'Unless 'e were drinking vodka as well as pints.'

'And was he?'

Again, Freddie shook his head. 'I can't say.'

Suddenly Betty, who had remained standing there as if she were waiting to be dismissed, raised her head. Brown curls bobbed around her chubby cheeks. 'I can tell yer!' she said excitedly. 'I can tell yer!'

'What?' Banks asked.

'It can't've been Mr Stephen buying vodka.'

'Why on earth not, lass?' Freddie said.

'Well, yer know,' Betty spluttered, ' 'e allus used to say 'ello, like, Mr Stephen. Proper gentleman. And 'e'd ask me 'ow I was. Well, once on Sat'day night 'e were on 'is way to t' loo and 'e nearly bumped into me, and me carrying a trayful o'—'

'Get on wi' it, lass!' Freddie bellowed. 'T' inspector dun't want to know what tha et for breakfast an' all, tha knows.'

Betty cast him a dark glance and announced, ''E'd forgotten 'is wallet.'

''E'd what?'

''E sometimes slips me a quid – a tip, like,' she added proudly. 'But on Sat'day 'e patted 'is pockets and said 'e was sorry 'e 'ad no change and 'e'd left 'is wallet at 'ome. 'E was 'aving to depend on t' generosity of 'is friends.' She turned to Banks. 'Those were 'is very words, "the generosity of my friends". 'E'd 'ad a few, like, when 'e said it . . .'

'Thank you, Betty,' Banks said. 'I don't suppose you overheard Nicholas Collier and John Fletcher having an argument?'

Betty's face dropped. 'No. Not while I were picking t' glasses up. Is it important?'

'It might be. But it's not as important as what you've just told me.'

It wasn't a great help, but if Stephen Collier hadn't been up to the bar to buy rounds, and if Freddie had found empty shorts glasses at the spot where the orders had been placed, then one of the party might have been spiking Stephen's beer with vodka. Of course, he realized, anyone could have left the glasses there, and any member of the group could have tipped back a quick shot while waiting for Freddie to pull the pints. But it was a start.

Betty beamed as if she'd solved the case. Freddie sent her back to her glass cleaning and turned to face Banks.

'There,' he said. 'Any 'elp?'

'I hope so.'

'Well, so do I. Tha's taking tha bloody time, I'll say that about thee. Does tha know, t' last Yankee we 'ad in 'ere . . .'

Banks left Freddie mid-sentence and almost bumped into Katie Greenock as he was leaving the pub.

'Ah,' he said, holding the door for her, 'just the person I want to see.'

But she turned and started to hurry away.

'What is it?' Banks called after her. He could sense her fear; it was more than just the adrenalin produced by a shock.

'It's nothing,' she said, half turning. 'I was just looking for Sam, that's all.' He could see a tear streaking down her flushed cheek.

'Katie, have you got something to tell me?' Banks asked, approaching her.

She carried on walking away. Banks put his hand gently on her shoulder. 'Katie?'

'No!' She recoiled and started running down the empty street. Banks dashed after her and soon she slowed, dazed, to a halt.

'Come on, Katie,' he said. 'Let's talk.' He offered his hand, but she wouldn't take it. Instead, she walked obediently beside him back to the car. She was shaking.

'A drink?' Banks suggested.

She shook her head. Her fair hair was tied back, but a few strands freed themselves and stuck to her damp cheeks.

'Let's go for a ride, then.'

She got in the Cortina beside him and he drove north out of Swainshead. Thinking it might help her relax, he took out the Beatles cassette and put on Vivaldi's *Four Seasons*, turning the volume low.

'I was lying,' Katie blurted out as they passed the bridge to John Fletcher's farmhouse. Then she said something else that Banks didn't quite catch. It sounded like 'wash my mouth out with soap'.

274

'What about?' he asked.

'I wasn't looking for Sam. I saw you go in there. I saw you leave Nicholas Collier's, too. I was trying to get my courage up.'

'For what? Are you sure a drink wouldn't help?'

'No, I don't take alcohol.'

'What is it, Katie?'

'You've got to help me,' Katie said, staring down into her lap and twisting her hands. 'I did it . . . I killed them . . . I killed them all.'

13

ONE

Looking at the ornate limestone building, Banks realized he had never seen Braughtmore school before. Built in the mid-nineteenth century after the previous building had burned down, it had oriels projecting from the first floor, then two floors of tall sash windows topped by dormers and a red pantile roof. It stood at the mouth of a small valley which a tributary had carved on its way down to the Gaiel, and enough flat ground had been cleared around it for rugby and cricket fields.

Banks pulled into a lay-by across the road, lit a cigarette and turned to Katie.

'Tell me about it,' he said.

'I did it,' Katie repeated. 'I killed them.'

'Who did you kill?'

'Bernie and Stephen.'

'Why?'

'Because I . . . because they . . . It was God's judgement.'

'God's judgement for what, Katie?'

'My sins.'

'Because you made love to them?'

Katie turned and glared at him through her tears. 'Not love,' she said. 'They were going to take me away, take me away from here, from my husband.'

'But you made love with Bernard Allen. Did you sleep with Stephen, too?'

'Bernie took me in his room. It was the price. I found no pleasure in it. He said he'd send for me when he got back.'

Banks didn't have the heart to tell her that Bernie had been bent on returning to Swainshead, not staying in Canada.

'And Stephen?' he asked.

'He . . . he kissed me. I knew I would have to pay, but later. And now . . .'

'Did you kill him so that you wouldn't have to pay?'

Katie shook her head. 'He was going to take me away, like Bernard. He had to die.'

'How did you kill him?'

'Everyone who wants to help me dies.'

'But how did you kill him?'

'I don't know, don't remember.'

'Katie, you didn't kill Stephen Collier or Bernard Allen, did you?'

'They died because of me. The Lord's vengeance. Nicholas was the Lord's vengeance, too. Against me. To show me my vile nature.'

'Nicholas? What happened with Nicholas?'

'He put his hands on me. His filthy hands. The hands of the beast.'

'When was this? Where?'

'At his house. The party Sam made me go to. I didn't want to go, I told him. I knew it would be bad.'

'What happened?'

'John came and they fought.'

'John and Nicholas?'

'Yes.'

At least that explained their argument in the White Rose, Banks thought. 'Did Sam know? Did you tell Sam?'

Katie shook her head. 'Sam doesn't care anyway. Not where his precious Colliers are concerned.'

'But you didn't kill anyone, did you?'

She put her head in her hands and wept. Banks moved to put his arm around her, but she stiffened and jerked away towards the door. She rested her cheek against the window and stared ahead at the dale.

'Are you protecting Sam, Katie? Is that what you're doing? Do you think Sam killed them because they were going to take you away?'

'I killed them. I told you.'

'Maybe you think you're responsible, Katie, but you didn't kill anyone. There's a big difference between feeling guilty and taking someone's life, you know. You haven't done anything wrong.'

'I wanted to escape my husband, didn't I?'

'He beats you. He's not a good man.'

'But he's my husband.' She started to sob again. 'I must serve him. What else can I do? I can't leave him and go away by myself. I don't know how to live.'

Banks wound down his window and tossed out his cigarette end.

'Do you want to walk a while?' he asked.

Katie nodded and opened her door.

There was a pathway worn in the hillside opposite the school, and they set off slowly up towards the ridge. About halfway, they sat on warm grass among limestone boulders and gazed down at the scene. The building glowed like mother-of-pearl, and the red S-shaped tiles shone bright in the sun. Some pupils dressed in whites were practising in the cricket nets by one of the mowed fields, and a group in shorts and vests were running around the cinder track. Plenty of exercise and cold showers, Banks thought. Cross-country runs and Latin unseens to keep their minds off sex – and perhaps a bit of masturbation in the dorms, a little buggery in the bushes, sodomy in the cycle sheds. It was every outsider's version of public-school life. Probably the reality was much more innocent. After all, these people were being groomed to run the country, the government. Still, look how many of them ended up on the front pages of the tabloid press. Perhaps the outsider's version wasn't so far from the truth.

Katie plucked blades of grass and scattered them on the light breeze.

'Tell me what happened with Stephen,' Banks said.

'We walked up to the source. He said he was going away. I thought he would take me with him if I let him kiss me. That's all.'

'What else did he say? You must have talked about things.'

'Oh, yes.' Katie's voice sounded like it was coming from a great distance.

'Why was he going away?'

'He said he'd had enough, he couldn't stand being here any longer. He said something about getting away from the past and from who he was.'

'What did he want to get away from?'

For the first time, Katie looked directly at him. Her eyes were red-rimmed with crying but still shone warm brown in the sunlight. Banks could feel her attraction. The desire to protect her merged with the impulse to touch her. She made him want to reach out and brush the blonde hairs away from her cheeks, then kiss her white throat and explore the gentle curves and mounds of her body. And he also knew that she was largely unaware of the effect she had; it was as if she couldn't understand the natural sexual instinct that draws people to one another. She knew what men wanted, yes, but she didn't know why or what it was all about. She was innocent, a unique and vulnerable wild flower growing here at the edge of the moorland.

'What did he want to get away from?' she echoed, shattering his illusion. 'What we all want to get away from. The traps we make for ourselves. The traps God makes for us.'

'It's not such a terrible thing to want to escape a bad marriage, Katie,' Banks said. But he felt he couldn't get the tone right, couldn't find the way to talk to this woman. What he said came out as patronizing when he didn't intend it to.

'It's a woman's duty,' Katie answered. 'Her cross to bear.'

'What was Stephen running away from? Was it me? Did he mention me?'

Katie seemed surprised. 'No,' she said. 'Not you. His past, the life he led.'

'Did he mention anything in particular?'

'He said he'd been bad.'

'How?'

'I don't know. He just talked. I didn't understand it all. I was thinking about something else. The river bubbling up from the grass, how green and shiny the grass was where the water always flowed over it and in it.'

'Can you remember anything? Anything at all?'

'He talked about Oxford. Something bad happened at Oxford.'

'Did he say what it was?'

'A girl. A girl died.'

'Is that all he said?'

'Yes. That's how it started, he said. The nightmare.'

'With a girl dying at Oxford?'

'Yes.'

'How was he involved with this girl?'

'I don't know. Just that she died and it was bad.'

'And now he'd had enough and he was going away to escape the past, the consequences?'

Katie nodded, then she stared at him sharply. 'But you can't escape consequences, can you? Bernie couldn't. Stephen couldn't. I can't.'

'Was Stephen unhappy?'

'Unhappy? I don't think so. He was worried, but not unhappy.'

'Do you think he would have harmed himself?'

'No. Stephen wouldn't have done that. He had plans for the future. He was going to take me with him. But his future killed him.'

'I thought it was his past?'

'It was me,' she said calmly. 'Whatever you say, I know it was me who killed him.'

'That's not true, Katie. I wish I could get you to believe it.' Banks took out his cigarettes and offered her one. She said no and carried on plucking blades of grass and rubbing them between her fingers.

'Why didn't he go away before?' Banks asked. 'He had plenty of time, plenty of opportunity.'

'I don't know. He said it was hard for him – the family name, the house, the business. He seemed to be trying to find the courage to make a break, like me. I didn't tell him, if that's what you're thinking.'

'Didn't tell him what?'

'About the policeman you sent to spy on everyone. I saw him with you one day in Eastvale, but I didn't tell Stephen.'

'Did you tell Sam?'

Katie shook her head slowly. 'No,' she said. 'Not this time.'

So Stephen had been struggling with himself over whether to run or whether to stay and brazen it out. After all, he probably knew that the police could have no real proof of his guilt, just hearsay. Anne Ralston's word against his.

'If he'd gone,' Katie said, as if she'd been reading Banks' mind, 'it would have been like admitting his guilt, wouldn't it?'

'Perhaps.' Banks stood up and brushed the grass from his trousers. 'Come on.' He held out his hand and Katie took it. As soon as she'd stood up, though, she let go and followed him back to the car in silence.

TWO

'What else did she say?' Sergeant Hatchley asked, as the white Cortina with Banks at the wheel, hurtled down the M1.

'Nothing,' Banks answered. 'I told her to get in touch with us if she remembered anything else at all, then I drove her home. She went in without a word. To tell you the truth, I'm worried about her. She's so bloody fragile and she's close to breaking point. The woman needs help.'

Hatchley shrugged. 'If she doesn't like her nest she can always change it.'

'It's not as easy as that for some people. They get stuck; they don't know where to turn, how to take care of themselves. Katie Greenock's like that.'

They passed Sheffield's cooling towers, shaped like

giant whalebone corsets by the motorway. Even with the windows and many of the factories closed, the sulphurous smells of steelworks seeped into the car.

'What exactly will we be doing in Oxford?' Hatchley asked.

'We'll be trying to track down an incident involving the death of a girl about nine years ago, maybe two or three years later. Undergraduate courses are usually three years long, so that's a welcome limit.'

'Unless Collier wasn't actually a student when it happened.'

'That's bloody helpful,' Banks said. 'We'll deal with that if we draw a blank on the other.'

'What kind of incident?'

'It strikes me we're looking for an unsolved crime, or a freak accident. Could have been hit and run, drug over-dose, anything.'

'Then what? Whoever this lass was, she won't be doing much talking now.'

'I don't know,' Banks admitted. 'We try and link her to Stephen Collier.'

'And what if we come up blank?'

Banks sighed and reached for a cigarette. He swerved quickly to avoid a Dutch juggernaut meandering into the centre lane. 'You're being bloody negative today, Sergeant,' he said. 'What's the matter, did you have some-thing planned for tonight? A date with Carol, maybe?'

'No. Carol understands my job. And I like a nice ride out. I'm just trying to cover all the angles, that's all. I find the whole damn thing confusing. I'm not even sure we've got a case. After all, Collier is dead, whether he died accidentally or killed himself.'

'It is confusing,' Banks agreed. 'That's why I don't

believe we're at the bottom of it yet. That's why we're off to Oxford, to try and make it simpler.'

'Oh, I see.' Hatchley wound down his window a couple of inches. With the two of them smoking, the fug in the car was making his eyes water. 'I suppose it's full of silly-looking buggers in caps and gowns, Oxford?'

'Maybe so,' Banks said. 'Never been there, myself. They say it's a working town, though.'

'Aye. It might have been at one time. But there's not many left making cars these days. Some nice buildings there, though. I saw those on telly as well. Christopher Wren, Nicholas Hawksworth.'

'Bloody hell, Jim, have you been watching BBC2 again? We'll not have much time for sightseeing. Except for what you can take in on the job. Anyway, it's Hawksmoor. Nicholas Hawksmoor.'

He realized with a shock that it was the first time he had called Sergeant Hatchley by his first name. It felt strange, but Hatchley said nothing.

Banks drove on in silence and concentrated on the road. It was after five o'clock and the stretches of motorway that passed close to urban areas were busy with rush-hour traffic. By the time they got to Oxford they wouldn't have time to do much but check in at the police station, say hello to Ted Folley and maybe discuss the case over a pint – which would certainly appeal to Hatchley – before bed. Banks had booked them in at a small hotel recommended by Ted on the phone. In the morning the real work would begin.

Holding the wheel with one hand, Banks sorted through the cassettes. 'Do you like music?' he asked. It was odd; he knew Gristhorpe was tone-deaf – he couldn't tell Bach from the Beatles – but he had no idea what

Hatchley's tastes ran to. Not that it would affect his choice. He knew what he wanted to hear and soon found it – the Small Faces' greatest hits.

'I like a good brass band,' Hatchley mused. 'A bit of country and western now and then.'

Banks smiled. He hated country and western and brass bands. He lit another cigarette and edged up the volume. The swirling chords of 'All or Nothing' filled the car as he turned off near Northampton on to the road for Oxford. The music took him right back to the summer of 1966, just before he started in the sixth form at school. Nostalgia. A sure sign he was pushing forty. He caught Hatchley looking at him as if he were mad.

THREE

There weren't many caps and gowns in evidence on High Street in Oxford the following morning. Most of the people seemed to be ambling along in that lost but purposeful way tourists have. Banks and Hatchley were looking for somewhere to eat a quick breakfast before getting down to work at the station.

Hatchley pointed across the street. 'There's a McDonald's. They do quite nice breakfasts. Maybe . . .' He looked at Banks apprehensively, as if worried that the chief inspector might turn out to be a gourmet as well as a southerner and a lover of 1960s music. Despite all the times they'd enjoyed toasted teacakes and steak pies together, maybe Banks would insist on frogs' legs with anchovy sauce for breakfast.

Banks glanced at his watch and scowled. 'At least they're fast. Come on then. Egg McMuffin it is.'

Astonished, Hatchley followed him through the golden arches. Most of the places Banks had eaten in on his trip to Toronto had provided quick friendly service – so much so that it had been one of the things that had impressed him – but it seemed that even McDonald's could do nothing to alter the innate sloth and surliness of the English catering industry. The look they got from the uniformed girl behind the counter immediately communicated that they were being a bloody nuisance in placing an order, and, of course, they had to wait. Even when she slung the food at them, she didn't say, 'Thank you, please come again.'

Finally, they sat by the window and watched people walk in and out of W. H. Smith's for the morning papers. Hatchley ate heartily, but Banks picked at his food, then abandoned it and settled for black coffee and a cigarette.

'Nice bloke, that Ted Folley,' Hatchley said with his mouth half full of sausage. 'Not what I expected.'

'What did you expect?'

'Oh, some toffee-nosed git, I suppose. He's real down-to-earth, though. Dresses like a toff, mind you. They'd have a bit of a giggle over him in the Oak.'

'Probably in the Queen's Arms, too,' Banks added.

'Aye.'

They had found time for a few drinks with Folley before returning to their hotel for a good night's sleep, and Banks wondered whether it was Ted's generosity that had won Hatchley over, or his store of anecdotes. Either way, the sergeant had managed to down a copious amount of local ale (which he pronounced to be of 'passable' quality) in a very short time.

They had stood at the bar of a noisy Broad Street pub, and Ted – a dapper man with Brylcreemed hair and a penchant for three-piece pinstripe suits and garish bow ties – had regaled them with stories of Oxford's privileged student classes. Hatchley had been particularly amused by the description of a recent raid on an end-of-term party: 'And there she was,' Folley had said, 'deb of the year with her knickers round her ankles and white powder all over her stiff upper lip.' The sergeant had laughed so much he had got hiccups, which kept returning to haunt him for the rest of the evening.

'Come on,' Banks said. 'Hurry up. It can't be so bloody delicious you need to savour every mouthful.'

Reluctantly, Hatchley ate up his food and slurped his coffee. Ten minutes later they were in Ted Folley's office in St Aldates.

'I've got the files out already,' Ted said. 'If you can't find what you're after there, come and see me. I think you will, though. They cover all unsolved crimes, including hit-and-runs, involving women during the three-year period you mentioned.'

'Thank God there aren't many,' Banks said, picking up the slim pile.

'No,' Folley said. 'We're lucky. The students keep us busy enough but we don't get all that many mysterious deaths. They're usually drug-related.'

'These?'

'Some of them. Use that office over there.' Folley pointed across to a small glass-partitioned area. 'Doug's on holiday, so you won't be disturbed.'

Most of the cases were easily dealt with. Banks or Hatchley would phone friends or parents of the deceased, whenever phone numbers appeared in the files, and simply ask if the name Stephen Collier meant anything. On the off chance, they also asked if anyone had hired a private investigator named Raymond Addison to look into the unsolved crime. In the cases where no numbers were given or where people had moved, they made notes to follow up on later. In some of those cases, the phone directory told them what they needed to know, and Ted also proved as helpful as ever.

By mid-afternoon, after a short lunch break, they had only three possibilities left. Folley was able to rule one of those out – the girl's parents had died tragically in a plane crash less than a year after their daughter's death – which left one each for Banks and Hatchley. They tossed for it, and Banks drew the phoneless family in Jericho, Hatchley the paraplegic father in Woodstock.

Wedged between Walton Street and the canal, Jericho is a maze of small nineteenth-century terraced houses, originally built for the foundry workers and navvies of the city. Most of the streets are named after Victorian battles or military heroes. It is as far away in spirit and appearance from the magnificent architectural beauty of the old university city as is Eastvale's East End Estate from its cobbled market square and Norman church.

Banks drove slowly down Great Clarendon Street until he found the turning he wanted. His car attracted the attention of two scruffy children playing jacks on the pavement, and he was manoeuvred into paying them fifty pence to 'protect' it for him.

At first no one answered the cracked blue door, but eventually Banks heard someone move inside and when the door opened an old haggard face stared out. He couldn't tell whether it was male or female until a deep man's voice asked him roughly what he wanted.

'It's about your daughter, Cheryl,' he said. 'May I come in?'

The man blinked and opened the door a bit wider. Banks could smell boiled turnip and stale pipe smoke.

'Our Cheryl's been dead six years or more,' the man said. 'Nobody did anything then; why should they bother now?'

'If I could just come in . . .?'

The man said nothing, but he opened the door wider to admit Banks. There was no hall; the door opened directly into a small living room. The curtains were half closed, cutting out most of the light, and the air felt hot and cloying. From what Banks could see, the place wasn't dirty but it wasn't exactly clean either. A grey-haired old woman with a blanket over her knees sat in a wheelchair by the empty grate. She looked round as he came in and gave him a blank smile.

'It's about our Cheryl,' the man said, reaching for his pipe.

'I heard.'

'Look, Mrs Duggan,' Banks said, perching on the arm of the settee, 'I know it's a long time ago, but something might have come up.'

'You've found out who killed her?'

'It's possible. But I still don't know that she was killed. You'll have to help me.'

The file was still fresh in his mind. Cheryl Duggan had been fished out of the River Cherwell not too far from Magdalen Bridge and St Hilda's College on a foggy November Sunday morning over six years ago. The coroner's inquest said that death was due to drowning, or so it appeared. Several odd bruises indicated that her head may have been held under the water until she drowned. She had had sexual intercourse shortly before death, and the stomach contents indicated that she had been drinking heavily the previous evening. In view of all this, an open verdict was recorded and a police investigation was ordered.

To complicate matters, Cheryl Duggan, according to Folley, had been a well known local prostitute since the age of fifteen. She had been only seventeen when she died. The investigation, Folley admitted, had been cursory. This was due to other pressures, in particular the drug-related death of a peer's daughter in which the heir to a brewery fortune was implicated as a pusher.

'It could have been an accident,' Banks said.

'It warn't no accident, Mr Banks,' Mrs Duggan insisted.

'There was water in the lungs,' Banks countered weakly.

Mr Duggan snorted. 'You'd think she were a mermaid, our Cheryl, the way she took to water.'

'She'd been drinking.'

'Yes, well, nobody's saying she was perfect.'

'Did you ever hear her mention a man by the name of Stephen Collier?'

Mr Duggan shook his head slowly.

There was a sense of defeat about the Duggans that weighed heavily in the dim and stuffy room and made Banks feel sick. Their voices were flat, as if they had repeated their stories a hundred times and nobody had listened; their faces were parchment-dry and drawn, the eyes wide and blank, with plenty of white showing between the lower lashes and the pupils. Dante's words came into Banks' mind: 'Abandon all hope, ye who enter here.' This was a house of defeat, a place without hope.

Banks lit a cigarette, which would at least give him a more concrete reason to feel sick and dizzy, and went on. 'The other thing I'd like to know,' he asked, 'is if you hired anyone to look into Cheryl's death. I know you didn't think much of the police investigation.'

Mr Duggan spat into the grate. His wife frowned at him. 'Why does it matter?' she asked.

'It could be important.'

'We did hire someone,' she said. 'A private investigator from London. We looked him up in the phone book at the library. We were desperate. The police hadn't done anything for more than a year, and they were saying such terrible things about Cheryl. We took out all our savings.'

'What happened?'

'He came from London, this man, and he asked us about Cheryl – who her friends were, where she liked to go out and everything – then he said he'd try and find out what happened.'

'He never came back,' Mr Duggan cut in.

'You mean he ran off with your money?'

'Not all of it, Alf,' Mrs Duggan said. 'Only a retainer, that's all he'd take.'

'He took off with the money, Jessie, let's face it. We were had. He never meant to do anything about our Cheryl; he just took us for what he could get. And we let him.'

'What was his name?'

'Don't remember.'

'Yes you do, Alf,' said Mrs Duggan. 'It was Raymond Addison. I haven't forgotten.'

'So what did you do?'

'What could we do?' she said. 'He'd got most of our money, so we couldn't hire anyone else. The police weren't interested. We just tried to forget, that's all.' She pulled the tartan blanket up higher around her hips.

'Mr Addison didn't report back to you at all then, after the first time you saw him?'

'No,' Mr Duggan said. 'We only saw him the once.'

'Can you remember the date?'

The old man shook his head.

'I can't remember the exact day,' his wife said, 'but it was in February, about fifteen months after Cheryl was killed. The police seemed to have given up and we didn't know where to turn. We found him, and he let us down.'

'If it's any consolation, Mrs Duggan, I don't think Mr Addison did let you down.'

'What?'

'He was found killed himself, probably no more than a day or so after you saw him, up in Yorkshire. That's why you never heard from him again, not because he'd run off with your money.'

'In Yorkshire? What was he doing there?'

'I think he did find out something about Cheryl's death. Something the police had missed. You've got to under-stand that we don't have enough time or men to devote ourselves full time to every single case, Mrs Duggan. I don't know the circumstances, but maybe the police here weren't as active as you think they should have been. It's only in books that policemen find the killer every time. But Mr Addison had only the one case. He must have visited every possible place Cheryl might have been that night, talked to everyone who knew her, and what he found out led him to a village in Yorkshire, and to his death.'

Mrs Duggan bit her knuckles and began to cry silently. Her husband moved forward to comfort her.

'It never does any good raking up the past,' he snapped at Banks. 'Look how you've upset her.'

'I can understand that you're angry, Mr Duggan,' Banks said, 'but if I'm right, then we know who killed your daughter.'

Duggan looked away. 'What's it matter now?'

'Maybe it doesn't, at least not to you. But I think it ought to mean something that Addison didn't let you down, didn't run off with your money. He found a lead, and instead of reporting in he set off while the trail was hot. I think you owe his memory some kind of apology if you've been blaming him and thinking ill of him all these years.'

'Maybe so,' Duggan admitted. 'But what use is it now? Two people dead. What use?'

'More than two,' Banks said. 'He had to kill again to cover his tracks. First Addison, then someone else.'

'All over our Cheryl?' Mrs Duggan said, wiping her eyes.

Banks nodded. 'It looks like that's where it started. Is there anything else you can tell me? Did Cheryl ever talk about anyone at all she knew from Yorkshire? A student she was seeing, perhaps?'

They both shook their heads, then Mrs Duggan laughed bitterly. 'She said she was going to marry a student one day, a lord's son, or a prime minister's. She was very determined, our Cheryl. But she'd too much imagination. She was too flighty. If only she'd done as I said and stuck to her station.'

'Did she hang around with students much?'

'She went to the same pubs as they did,' Mr Duggan said. 'The police said she was a prostitute, Mr Banks, that she sold herself to men. We didn't know nothing about that. I still can't believe it. I know she liked to tart herself up a bit when she went out, but what girl doesn't? And she wasn't really old enough to drink, but what can you do . . .? You can't keep them prisoners, can you? She was always talking about what fun the students were, how she was sure to meet a nice young man soon. What were we to do? We believed her. Our Cheryl could make you believe she could do anything if she set her mind to it. Every day she woke up with a smile on her face, and that's no lie. Happiest soul I've ever known. What did we do wrong?'

Banks had no answer. He dropped his cigarette in the grate and walked to the door. 'If you think of anything, let the local police know,' he said.

'Wait a minute.' Mrs Duggan turned to him. 'Aren't you going to tell us?'

'Tell you what?'

'Who did it. Who killed our Cheryl?'

'It doesn't matter now,' Banks said. 'It looks like he's dead himself.' And he closed the door on their hopelessness and emptiness.

FOUR

'I'm sorry, Alan,' Ted Folley said when he'd heard the story. 'I told you it wasn't much of an investigation. We looked into it, but we got nowhere. We were sure the girl drowned. She'd been drinking and there was water in her lungs. The bruises could have been caused by a customer; it's a rough trade she was in. She didn't have a ponce, so we'd no one we could jump on right from the start.'

Banks nodded and blew smoke rings. 'We got nowhere with the Addison case, either,' he said. 'There was nothing to link him with Oxford, and we couldn't find out why he was in Swainshead. Not until now, anyway. What on earth could he have found out?'

'Anything,' Folley said. 'Maybe he found the last pub

she'd been in, tracked down a pusher who'd run a mile if he even smelled police.'

'Was she on drugs?'

'Not when she died, no. But there had been trouble. Nothing serious, just pills mostly. If Addison trailed around all her haunts and talked to everyone who knew her, showed a photo, flashed a bit of money . . . You know as well as I do, Alan, these blokes who operate outside the law have a better chance. He must have picked up your man's name somewhere and set off to question him.'

'Yes. It's just a damn shame he wasn't more efficient.'

'What do you mean?'

'If he'd gone back and told the Duggans what he'd found out before rushing off to Yorkshire. If he'd just filed some kind of report . . .'

'He must have been keen,' Folley said. 'Some of them are, you know.'

At that moment, Sergeant Hatchley came in from Woodstock. 'Bloody waste of time,' he grumbled, slouching in a chair and fumbling for a cigarette.

'Nothing?' Banks asked.

'Nowt. But judging by the expression on your face, you're that cat that got the cream. Am I right?'

'You are.' He told Hatchley about his interview with the Duggans.

'So that's it, then?'

'Looks like it. Stephen Collier must've met up with this young girl, Cheryl Duggan, gone drinking with her then taken her to the meadows by the river for sex. It was unusually warm for that time of year. He got a bit rough, they fought, and he drowned her. Or she fell in and he tried to save her. It could have been an accident, but it was a situation he couldn't afford to be associated with. Maybe he was on drugs; we'll never know. He might not even have been responsible for the bruising and the rough sexual treatment she'd received; that could have been a previous customer. Collier might even have been comforting her, trying to persuade her back on to the straight and narrow. I suppose the version will vary according to what kind of person you think Stephen was. One mistake – one terrible mistake – and three deaths have to follow. Christ, it could even have been some silly student prank.'

'Do you think he killed himself?'

Banks shook his head. 'I don't know. In his state of mind, if he'd been carrying the guilt all this time and feeling the pressure build, suicide and accidental death might have been much the same thing. It didn't matter any more, so he just got careless. Katie Greenock said he was planning to leave Swainshead, and I suppose he didn't much mind how he went.'

'What do we do now?' Hatchley asked.

Banks looked at his watch. 'It's three thirty,' he said. 'I suggest we pay Stephen's old tutor a visit and see if we can find out whether he was in the habit of taking up with young prostitutes. We might find some clue as to what really happened, who was responsible for what. Then we'll head back home. We should be able to make it before nine if we're on the road soon.' He turned to Folley and held out his hand. 'Thanks again, Ted. We appreciate all you've done. If I can ever return the favour . . .'

Folley laughed. 'In Swainsdale? You must be joking. But you're welcome. And do pay us a social call sometime. A few days boating in the Thames Valley would be just the ticket for the wife and kids.'

'I will,' Banks said. 'Come on, Jim lad, time to hit the road again.'

Hatchley dragged himself to his feet, said goodbye to Folley and followed Banks out on to St Aldates.

'There you are,' Banks said, near Blackwell's on Broad Street. 'Caps and gowns.'

True enough, students were all over the place: walking, cycling, standing to chat outside the bookshops.

'Bloody poofters,' Hatchley said.

They got past the porter, crossed the quadrangle, and found Dr Barber in his office at Stephen's old college.

'Sherry, gentlemen?' he asked, after they had introduced themselves.

Banks accepted because he liked dry sherry; Hatchley took one because he had never been known to refuse a free drink.

Barber's study was cluttered with books, journals and papers. A student essay entitled 'The Dissolution of the Monasteries: Evidence of Contemporary Accounts' lay on the desk but didn't quite obscure an old green-covered Penguin crime paperback. Banks tilted his head and glanced sideways at the title: *The Moving Toyshop*, by Edmund Crispin. He had never heard of it, but it wasn't quite the reading material he'd have expected to find in the office of an Oxford don.

While Dr Barber poured, Banks stood by the window and looked over the neat clipped quadrangle at the light stone façades of the college.

Barber passed them their drinks and lit his pipe. Its smoke sweetened the air. In deference to his guests, he opened the window a little, and a draught of fresh air sucked the smoke out. In appearance, Barber had the air of an aged cleric, and he smelled of Pears soap. He reminded Banks of the actor Wilfrid Hyde-White.

'It was a long time ago,' Barber said, when Banks had

asked him about Collier. 'Let me check my files. I've got records going back over twenty years, you know. It pays to know whom one has had pass through these hallowed halls. As a historian myself, I place great value on documentation. Now, let me see . . . Stephen Collier, yes. Braughtmore School, Yorkshire. Is that the one? Yes? I remember him. Not terribly distinguished academically, but a pleasant enough fellow. What's he been up to?'

'That's what we're trying to find out,' Banks said. 'He died a few days ago and we want to know why.'

Barber sat down and picked up his sherry. 'Good Lord! He wasn't murdered, was he?'

'Why would you think that?'

Barber shrugged. 'One doesn't usually get a visit from the Yorkshire police over nothing. One doesn't usually get visits from the police at all.'

'We don't know,' Banks said. 'It could have been accidental, or it could have been suicide.'

'Suicide? Oh dear. Collier was a rather serious young man – a bit too much so, if I remember him clearly. But suicide?'

'Possibly.'

'A lot can change in a few years,' Barber said. He frowned and relit his pipe. Banks remembered his own struggles with the infernal engines, and the broken pipe that now hung on his wall in Eastvale Police Headquarters. 'As I said,' Barber went on, 'Collier seemed a sober sensible kind of fellow. Still, who can fathom the mysteries of the human heart? *Fronti nulla fides*.'

'There's no real type for suicide,' Banks said. 'Anyone, pushed far enough—'

'I suppose you're the kind of policeman who thinks anyone can become a murderer too, given the circumstances.'

Banks nodded.

'I'm afraid I can't go along with that,' Barber said. 'I'm no psychologist, but I'd say it takes a special type. Take me, for example, I could never conceive of doing such a thing. The thought of jail, for a start, would deter me. And I should think that everyone would notice my guilt. As a child, I once stole a lemon tart from the school tuck shop while Mrs Wiggins was in the back, and I felt myself turn red from head to toe. No, Chief Inspector, I'd never make a murderer.'

'I'm thankful for that,' Banks said. 'I don't need to ask you for an alibi now, I suppose.'

Barber looked at him for a moment, unsure what to do, then laughed.

'Stephen Collier,' Banks said.

'Yes, yes. Forgive me. I'm getting old; I tend to ramble. But it's coming back. He was the kind who really did have to work hard to do well. So many others have a natural ability – they can dash off a good essay the night before – but you'd always find Collier in the library all week before a major piece of work was due. Conscientious.'

'How did he get on with the other students?'

'Well enough, as far as I know. Collier was a bit of a loner though. Kept himself to himself. I hardly need to tell you, Chief Inspector, that quite a number of young lads around these parts go in for high jinks. It's always been like that, ever since students started coming here in the thirteenth century. And there's always been a bit of a running battle between the university authorities and the people of the city: town and gown, as we say. The students aren't vindictive, you realize, just high-spirited. Sometimes they cause more damage than they intend.'

'And Collier?'

'I'm sure he didn't go in for that kind of thing. If there had been any incidents of an unsavoury nature, they would have appeared in my assessment file.'

'Did he drink much?'

'Never had any trouble with him.'

'Drugs?'

'Chief Inspector Banks,' Barber said slowly, 'I do realize that the university has been getting a bad reputation lately for drugs and the like, and no doubt such things do happen, but if you take the word of the media, you'd be seriously misled. I don't think Stephen Collier was involved in drugs at all. I remember that we did have some trouble with one student selling cannabis around that time – most distressing – but there was a full investigation, and at no point was Stephen Collier implicated.'

'So, as far as you can say, Collier was a model student, if not quite as brilliant as some of his fellows?'

'I know it sounds hard to believe, but yes, he was. Most of the time you'd hardly have known he was here. I'm having great difficulty trying to guess what you're after. You say that Stephen Collier's death might have been suicide or it might have been an accident, but if you don't mind my saying so, the questions you're asking seem preoccupied with unearthing evidence that Collier himself was some kind of hell-raiser.'

Banks frowned and looked out of the window again. The shadow of a cloud passed over the quadrangle. He drained his sherry and lit a cigarette. Sergeant Hatchley, quietly smoking in a chair in the corner, had emptied his glass a while ago and sat fidgeting with it as if he hoped Barber would notice and offer a refill. He did, and both policemen accepted. Banks liked the way the dry liquid puckered his taste buds.

'He's a suspect,' Banks said. 'And I'm afraid that's all I can tell you. We have no proof that Collier was guilty of anything, but there's a strong possibility.'

'Does it matter,' Barber asked, 'now that he's dead?'

'Yes, it does. If he was guilty, then the case is closed. If not, we still have a criminal to catch.'

'Yes. I see. Well, I'm afraid I can't offer you any evidence at all. Seemed a thoroughly pleasant hard-working nondescript fellow to me as far as I can remember.'

'What about six years ago? It would have been his third year, his last. Did anything unusual happen then, around early November?'

Barber frowned and pursed his lips. 'I can't recall anything . . . Wait a minute . . .' He walked back over to his ancient filing cabinet and riffled through the papers. 'Yes, yes, I thought so,' he announced finally. 'Stephen Collier didn't finish his degree.'

'What?'

'He didn't finish. Decided history wasn't for him and left after two years. Went to run a business, as far as I know. I can confirm with the registrar's office, of course, but my own records are quite thorough.'

'Are you saying that Stephen Collier wasn't here, that he wasn't in Oxford in November six years ago?'

'That's right. Could it be you've got him mixed up with his brother, Nicholas? He would have just been starting his second year then, you know, and I certainly remember him, now I cast my mind back. Nicholas Collier was a different kettle of fish, a different kettle of fish entirely.'

ONE

Katie stared at her reflection in the dark kitchen window as she washed the crystal glasses she couldn't put in the machine. The radio on the table played soothing classical music, quiet enough that she could even hear the beck at the bottom of the back garden rippling over its stones.

Now that Stephen was dead and she had unburdened herself to Banks, she felt empty. None of her grand-mother's maxims floated around her mind, as they had been doing lately, and that tightness in her chest that had seemed to squeeze at her very heart itself had relaxed. She even noticed a half-smile on her face, a very odd one she'd not seen before. Nothing hurt now; she felt numb, just like her mouth always did after an injection at the dentist's.

Chief Inspector Banks had told her that if she remem-bered anything else, she should get in touch with him. Try as she might though, she couldn't remember a thing. Looking back over the years in Swainshead, she had noticed hints that all wasn't well, that some things were going on about which she knew nothing. But there was no coherent narrative, just a series of unlinked events. She thought of Sam's behaviour when Raymond Addison first appeared. She hadn't heard their conversation, but Sam had immediately left everything to her and gone running off across the street to the Collier house. Later, Addison had gone for a walk and never returned. When they found out the man had been murdered, Sam had been unusually pale and quiet for some days.

She remembered watching Bernie pause and glance towards the Collier house before going on his way the morning he left. She had also seen him call there one evening shortly after he'd arrived and thought it odd because of the way he usually went on about them being so rich and privileged.

None of it had meant very much at the time. Katie wasn't the kind of woman to look for bad in anyone but herself. She had had far more pressing matters to deal with and soon forgot the suspicious little things she'd noticed. Even now, she couldn't put it all together. When she told Banks that she had killed Bernie and Stephen, she meant it. She hadn't physically murdered them, but she knew she was responsible.

The things she remembered often seemed as if they had happened to someone else. She could view again, dispassionately, Bernard Allen sating himself on her impassive body, as if she were watching a silent film from the ceiling. And Stephen's chaste kiss left no trace of ice or fire on her lips. Sam had taken her roughly the previous evening, but instead of fear and loathing she had felt a kind of power in her subservience. It wasn't pleasure; it was something new, and she felt that if she could only be patient enough it would make itself known to her eventually. It was as if he had possessed her body, but not her soul. She had kept her soul pure and untainted, and now it was revealing itself to her. Somehow, these new feelings were all connected with her sense of responsibility for the deaths of

Bernie and Stephen. She had blood on her hands; she had grown up.

The future was still very uncertain. Life would go on, she supposed, much as it had done. She would clean the rooms, cook the meals, submit to Sam in bed, do what she was told, and try to avoid making him angry. Everything would continue just as it had done, except for the new feelings that were growing in her. If she stayed patient, change would come in its own time. She wouldn't have to do anything until she knew exactly *what* to do.

For the moment, nothing touched her; nothing ruffled the calm and glassy surface of her mind. Caught up in her dark reflection, she dropped one of a set of six expensive crystal glasses. It shattered on the linoleum. But even that didn't matter. Katie looked down at the shards with an indulgent pitying expression on her face and went to fetch the brush and dustpan.

As she moved, she heard a sound out at the back. Hurrying to the window, she peered through her own reflection and glimpsed a shadow slipping past her gate. A moment later – before she could get to the unlocked door – she heard a cursory tap. The door opened and Nicholas Collier popped his head round and smiled. 'Hello, Katie. I've come to visit.'

TWO

The sun was a swollen red ball low on the western horizon. It oozed its eerie light over the South Yorkshire landscape, silhouetted motionless pit wheels and made the slag heaps glow. On the cassette, Nick Drake was singing the haunting 'Northern Sky'.

Much of the way, the two had sat in silence, thinking things out and deciding what to do. Finally, Hatchley could stand it no longer. 'How can we nail the bastard?' he asked.

'I don't know,' Banks answered. 'We don't have much of a case.'

Hatchley grunted. 'We might if we hauled him in and you and me had a go at him.'

'He's clever, Jim,' Banks said. The sergeant's first name didn't feel so strange to his lips after the first few times. 'Look how he's kept out of it so long. He's not going to break down just because you and I play good-cop-bad-cop with him. That'll be a sign of our weakness to him. He'll know we need a confession to make anything stick, so it will only strengthen his position. No, Nicholas Collier's a cool one. And don't forget he's got pull around Swainsdale. We'd no sooner get started than some fancy lawyer would waltz in and gum up the works.'

'What I'd give for a bloody good try, though!' Hatchley thumped the dashboard. 'Sorry. No damage done. It just makes me angry, a stuck-up bastard like Nicholas Collier getting away with it. How many people has he killed?'

'Three, maybe four if we count Stephen. And he hasn't got away with it yet. The trouble is, we don't know if he killed anyone apart from the girl, Cheryl Duggan. We can't even prove that he killed her. Just because Dr Barber told us he had a reputation for pestering the town's working girls doesn't make him guilty. It certainly doesn't give us grounds for a conviction.'

'But it was Cheryl Duggan's death that sent Addison up to Swainshead.'

'Yes. But even that's circumstantial.'

'Who do you think killed Addison and Allen?'

'At a guess, I'd say Stephen. He'd do it to protect his little brother and his family's reputation. But we don't know, and we never will if Nicholas doesn't talk. I'll bet, for all his cleverness, Nicholas is weak. I doubt he has the stomach for cold-blooded murder. They might both have been at the scene – certainly neither had a good alibi – but I'd say Stephen did the killing.'

'What do you think happened with the Duggan girl?'

Banks shifted lanes to overtake a lorry. 'I think he picked her up in a pub and took her down by the river. She was just a prostitute, a working-class kid, and he was from a prominent family, so what the hell did it matter to him what he did? I think he got overexcited, hurt her perhaps, and she started to protest, threatened to scream or tell the police. So he panicked and drowned her. Either that or he did it because he enjoyed it.'

The tape finished. Banks lit a cigarette and felt around in the dark for another cassette. Without looking at the title, he slipped in the first one he got hold of. It was the 1960s anthology tape he'd taken to Toronto with him. Traffic came on singing 'No Face, No Name and No Number'.

'I think Addison was a conscientious investigator,' Banks went on. 'He more than earned his money, poor sod. He did all the legwork the police didn't do and found a connection between Cheryl Duggan and Nicholas Collier. Maybe they'd been seen leaving a pub together, or perhaps her friends told him Collier had been with her before. Anyway, Addison prised the name out of someone, or bought the information, and instead of reporting in he set off for Swainshead. That was his first mistake.

'His second was to ask Sam Greenock about Nicholas Collier. Greenock was anxious to get in with the local gentry and he was a bit suspicious of this stranger asking questions, so he stalled Addison and took the first opportunity to run over the bridge and tell Collier about it. There must have been real panic in the Collier house that evening. Remember, it was about fifteen months after the girl's death and the Colliers must've thought all was well. I don't know the details. Maybe Sam arranged for Addison to go over to the house when the village was quiet, or maybe he even arranged for the Colliers to go up to Addison's room and kill him there. I don't know how it happened, but I think it was Stephen who struck the blow. That would explain the state he was in when he met Anne Ralston later that night.'

'What about Bernard Allen?' Hatchley asked.

'At first I thought he was just unlucky,' Banks said. 'He told Katie Greenock that he knew Anne Ralston in Toronto. She told Sam, who did his usual town crier routine. Not that it mattered this time, if Allen was intent on blackmail. Stephen Collier was an odd kind of bloke from what I can make out – a real combination of opposites. When he'd killed Addison, he had to unburden himself to his girlfriend, but I'm sure he soon regretted it. He must have had a few sleepless nights after Anne first disappeared. Anyway, Bernard Allen knew that Stephen was involved in Addison's murder and that it was something to do with an incident back in Oxford. He obviously assumed that if the police knew that they could put the whole thing together. Which we did, rather too late.'

'You said you thought Allen was unlucky at first,' Hatchley said. 'What about now?'

'I think he was going to blackmail the Colliers. I've not had time to tell you much about Toronto, but I met a few people there who said that Bernard Allen really wanted to come home to Swainshead. His sister mentioned it too, but the others all played it down. He'd even let on to Katie Greenock that he'd send for her when he got back to Canada. That was because she wanted to escape Swainsdale and he wanted to get into her pants.

'I wondered why I was getting so many conflicting pictures of Allen's state of mind, so many contradictions. But that was his motive. He was blackmailing the Colliers to get himself home. A job at the school, money in the bank . . . I don't know what he'd asked for, but I'm certain that was his reason. And it got him killed. I don't doubt that whoever said "You can't go home again" meant it as literally as that. Anyway, the Colliers decided they couldn't live with the threat, so one or both of them waited for him in the hanging valley that morning. They knew he'd be there because he'd often talked about it and he was heading that way.'

'And what happened to Stephen? Why would Nicholas kill him, if he did?'

'Stephen was getting too jittery. Nicholas knew it was just a matter of time before his brother broke down completely, and he couldn't allow him to remain alive when I got back from Toronto after talking to Anne Ralston. Stephen must have told his brother that he didn't give anything away to Anne about the Oxford business, but that he'd made a serious mistake in hinting at his own involvement in Addison's killing. Nicholas knew that what Anne had to tell me would give me enough grounds to bring Stephen in, and he couldn't trust his brother to stand up under questioning. If we could discover the motive behind Addison's murder, then we'd know everything. Nicholas couldn't allow that.

'What he did was risky, but there was a lot at stake: not

just the family name now, but Nicholas's own freedom, his home, his career. He had to kill his own brother to survive. And if he succeeded, it would look like the accidental death of a disturbed man or the suicide of a guilty one.'

It was dark when Banks negotiated the tricky connections on to the A1 east of Leeds. Cream were singing 'Strange Brew' on the tape and Hatchley had fallen silent.

Banks still didn't understand it all. Stephen had killed to preserve what was important to him, but Nicholas Collier remained something of an enigma. In all likelihood he had drowned Cheryl Duggan, but what bothered Banks was why. Had he done it from pleasure, accident or desperation? And was he also responsible for the bruising and marks of sexual abuse found on her body? Dr Barber had said that Nicholas had been in trouble once or twice over consorting with prostitutes and offering Oxford factory girls money for sex. Banks wondered why. Nicholas had all the advantages. Why hadn't he hung around with his own set, girls of his own social class?

'Let's call in at the station first,' Banks said. 'Something might have turned up.' They were approaching the turn-off on to a minor road that would take them over the moors to Helmthorpe and the main valley road. 'We can always drive to Swainshead later if there's nothing new.' He looked at his watch. 'It's not late, only nineish.'

Hatchley nodded and Banks drove past the exit ramp and on to the Eastvale road.

The station was quiet. There had been no serious crimes while Banks and Hatchley had been gone. There was, however, a message from John Fletcher timed at five o'clock that evening asking if they would call and see him as soon as possible. He said it was important – something to do with Stephen Collier's death – and he would be at home all evening.

There was also a copy of Dr Glendenning's preliminary post-mortem report on Stephen Collier. The doctor had found the equivalent of about five capsules of Nembutal in Collier's system – not enough in itself to cause death but potentially lethal when mixed with alcohol. And his alcohol level had been far higher than the amount five or six pints would account for. It looked as if Banks was right and Collier had been slipped vodka in the pub and more drinks back at the house.

'Should we go to see Fletcher tonight?' Banks asked Hatchley. 'Or leave it until tomorrow?'

Under normal circumstances he would have expected Hatchley to take any opportunity to get off work for a pint or a session on the sofa with Carol Ellis, but this time the sergeant was angry.

'Let's go,' he said. 'Maybe Fletcher's got the answer. I wouldn't want to leave it till he went and got himself killed, too. And I wouldn't mind paying a call on Nicholas bloody Collier either.'

THREE

'Go away!' Katie said, rushing forward and trying to close the door.

But Nicholas had his foot wedged in. 'Let me in, Katie,' he said. 'I want to talk to you about Stephen. He was very fond of you, you know.'

'He's dead,' Katie said, still pushing at the door with her shoulder. But Nicholas was too strong for her and the door knocked her backwards against the kitchen table as he entered. He shut the door behind him and walked towards her.

'I won't hurt you,' he said. 'I know you were talking to Stephen the day before he died. I just wondered if he'd been saying anything silly. He wasn't well, you know.' He reached out and grabbed Katie's arm as she tried to slip away. 'There's no need to be afraid of me,' he said, relaxing his grip a little. 'No need to run away. I won't hurt you. I just want to talk to you.'

'I don't know what you mean,' Katie said. 'There was nothing wrong with Stephen.'

'He was upset. He might have said things he didn't mean.'

'What things?'

'I don't know. That's what I'm asking you, you stupid bitch,' Nicholas shouted, then lowered his voice again. 'Just tell me what you talked about. Aren't you going to offer me a drink?'

'I don't have anything.'

'Liar.' Nicholas opened Sam's drinks cabinet and poured himself a large gin. 'I've been here before, remember? With Sam.' He held out the glass. 'Go on, have some. You like gin, don't you?'

Katie shook her head. Nicholas hooked the back of her neck with one hand, put the glass to her closed lips and tipped it forward. The vile-smelling spirit spilled down Katie's chin and on to the front of her dress. It burned her throat and made her gag.

'Stop it!' she cried, spluttering and pushing him away.

Nicholas laughed, showing his yellowed teeth, and put the glass down. He went back to the cabinet and poured himself some Scotch.

'What did Stephen tell you?' he asked.

'Nothing.' Katie coughed and rubbed at her lips with the back of her hand.

'He must have said something. He was quite a one for confiding in the wrong people, Stephen was, especially women. And I saw you talking to that policeman. Where is he now? What's he doing?'

'I don't know. I haven't seen him since yesterday.'

'What did he ask you? What did you say to him?'

'Nothing. He doesn't know anything.'

'Stop lying, Katie. Did you do it with him too, just like you do with all the others?'

Katie turned pale. 'What do you mean?'

Nicholas grinned. The dark comma of hair had flopped over his brow and his cheeks were flushed. 'You know what I mean. Just like you did with Stephen and everyone else. Did you let him do it to you, Katie, that policeman?'

'No!'

'Oh, don't be shy. You do it with everyone, don't you? You know you're nothing but a slut. A filthy whore. Tell me you're a filthy whore, Katie, say it.'

'I'm not.'

Katie rushed desperately for the connecting door, but Nicholas got there before her.

'There's no way out,' he said. 'All your guests are in the White Rose; I saw them. And Sam's off with his fancy women as usual.'

'He's what?'

'Didn't you know? Oh, don't tell me you didn't know. All those times he goes off to see his friends in Leeds or Eastvale. It's women, Katie. Loose women. Can't you smell them on his skin when he comes home? Or do you like it when he comes straight from another woman and takes you? Do you like to smell other women on your husband's skin?'

Katie put her hands to her ears. 'Stop it! Stop it!' she screamed. 'You're evil!'

Nicholas applauded quietly. 'Oh, Katie, what an act.'

Katie dropped her hands to her sides. 'What are you going to do?'

'Do? Why, I'm going to take you away from here. I don't trust you, Katie. There's no telling what you know and what you might say.'

'I don't know anything.'

'I think you do. Stephen told you, didn't he?'

'Told me what?'

'About Oxford.'

Katie could think of nothing to say.

'Look at you blushing,' Nicholas said, pointing at her. 'You know, don't you? I can tell. Be sure your sins will find you out.'

Suddenly, Katie realized what he meant and a terrible thought dawned on her.

'You killed him,' she said quietly. 'You killed Stephen.'

Nicholas shrugged and spoke in a cold passionless voice. 'I couldn't trust him any more. He was falling apart on me.'

Katie stiffened. She felt like a trapped animal. 'What are you going to do?'

'I'm going to take you away, far away. What did he tell you about Oxford?'

'Nothing.'

'Did he tell you about that girl, that stupid slut?'

Katie shook her head.

'He did, didn't he?'

'No! He told me nothing.'

Nicholas leaned against the table. His bright eyes glittered and his breath came in short sharp gasps. He looked like a madman to Katie. A wild, terrifying madman.

'She was nothing but a prostitute, Katie,' he said. 'A fallen woman. She sold herself to men. And when I . . . when I took her, she didn't . . . She told me I was too rough and she tried to make me stop. Me! Nicholas Collier. But I didn't. I couldn't. I knew that was the way she really wanted it. A common tart like her. Like you.'

'No!' Katie said. 'I'm not.'

'Yes, you are. I've had my eye on you. You do it with everyone. Do they pay you, Katie, or do you do it for nothing? I know you like to struggle. I'll pay you if you want.'

'I don't know what you're talking about.'

'I want you to say it for me. Say you're a filthy whore.'

'I'm not.'

'What's wrong? Why won't you say it? I bet you even let that policeman do it. I'm better than the lot of them, Katie. Say it.'

'No! I won't.'

He spoke very softly, so quiet she could hardly hear. 'I want you to go down on your knees, Katie, and tell me you're a filthy whore and you want me to do it to you like an animal. Like a dog. I want you to lift your dress up and crawl, Katie.'

He was moving towards her now, and his eyes held hers with a power that seemed to sap what little strength she had. She felt her shoulders hit the wall by the mantelpiece. There was nowhere else to go. But Nicholas kept coming closer, and when he was near enough he reached out and grabbed the front of her dress.

FOUR

Banks drove fast along the dark dale by the River Swain, passed through Helmthorpe and into the darker fell-shadowed landscape beyond. He turned sharp right at Swainshead, tyres squealing, and carried on up the valley to Upper Head. He slowed down as they passed the Collier house, but the lights were out.

'I hope the bastard hasn't done a bunk,' Hatchley said.

'No, he's too cool for that. We'll get him, don't worry.'

The glimmer of light high on the fell side about two miles north of the village came from Fletcher's isolated cottage. It was a difficult track to manage in the dark, but they finally pulled up outside the squat solid house with its three-foot-thick walls. Fletcher had heard them coming and stood in the doorway. Again they were ushered into the plain whitewashed room with its oak table and the photograph of Fletcher's glamorous ex-wife.

Fletcher was ill at ease. He avoided looking at them directly and fussed around with glasses of beer. Hatchley stood by the window looking into the darkness. Banks sat at the table.

'What is it?' he asked, when Fletcher had sat down opposite him.

'It's about Stephen's death,' Fletcher began hesitantly. 'He was my friend. It's gone too far now. Too far.'

Banks nodded. 'I know. I understood there was no love lost between you and Nicholas.'

'You've heard about that? Well, it's true enough. I never had much time for him. But old Mr Walter was like a father to me, and I always felt like an older brother to Stephen.'

Banks passed around the cigarettes.

'Saturday night,' Fletcher burst out suddenly. 'I thought nothing of it at the time – it was just the kind of silly trick Nicholas would play – but when he went to buy a round I saw him pour a glass of clear spirits into Stephen's drink. As I said, I thought nothing of it. I knew Stephen was upset about something – what it was, I don't know – and he seemed to want to get drunk and forget his problems anyway. No point causing trouble, I thought, so I kept quiet.

'That family has a secret, Mr Banks, a dark secret. Stephen's hinted at it more than once, and I reckon it's something to do with Nicholas and the ladies, though ladies is too dignified a term. Did you know he once forced himself on Molly Stark from over Relton way?'

'No, I didn't.'

'Aye. Well, it was hushed up, like most things Nicholas got up to. All neat and businesslike.'

'Wasn't there also some trouble with a girl when his father was alive?' Banks asked.

'Aye,' said Fletcher. 'Got her in the family way. But money changed hands and shut mouths. It was all arranged, no expense spared, and she did away with it. He had a lust for lasses below his station, as they used to say. Working-class girls, servants, factory girls, milkmaids . . . I even caught him mauling Katie Greenock at Stephen's party last week.'

At last it made sense to Banks. Nicholas Collier couldn't keep away from women of a lower social class: Cheryl Duggan, Esther Haines, Katie Greenock, Anne Ralston, the servant girl, Molly Stark – they were all beneath him socially. Although the term had lost a lot of its meaning over the past few years, they might still be called working-class women. Obviously it didn't matter who they were as individuals; that didn't interest Collier. He probably had some Victorian image of the working class as a seething, gin-drinking, fornicating, procreating mass. He thrust himself on them and became violent when they objected. No doubt like most perverse sexual practices, his compulsion had a lot to do with power and humiliation.

'I knew something serious was up when we had those two murders here,' Fletcher went on, refilling their beer glasses. 'That detective and young Bernard Allen. I knew it, but I didn't know what. Whenever I asked, Stephen clammed up, told me to leave it be and I'd be better off not knowing.' He took a sip of beer. 'Maybe I should've pushed a bit harder. Maybe Stephen would still be alive . . . But I don't think he killed himself. That's what I wanted to tell you. As I said, I saw Nicholas putting something into his drink, and he was in a hell of a state at closing time, worse than if he'd just had a few jars. And the next thing I hear, he's dead. An overdose, they said. I knew he took sleeping tablets, but an overdose . . .?'

'Yes, barbiturates,' Banks said. 'Usually fatal, mixed with as much alcohol as Stephen Collier had in his system.'

'So it's murder, isn't it? That bastard brother of his murdered him.'

'It looks like it, Mr Fletcher, but we've got to tread carefully. We've got no evidence, no proof.'

'I'll testify to what I saw. I'll help put him away, as God's my witness.'

Banks shook his head. 'It'll help, but it's not enough. What if Nicholas was putting vodka in his brother's beer? As you said, it could have been a simple prank, and that's exactly what he'll say. It's all circumstantial and theoretical. We need more solid evidence or a confession.'

'Then I'll bloody well beat it out of him,' Fletcher said, grasping the table and rising to his feet.

'Sit down,' said Banks. 'That's not going to help at all.'

'Then what are you going to do?'

'I honestly don't know yet,' Banks said. 'We might just be able to put together a case, especially if we bring in Anne Ralston, but I don't want to risk it. Even if we could convince the court it's worth a risk, I don't want to take the chance of him getting off, which he might well do on what we've got so far.'

'I know I should've spoken up earlier,' Fletcher said. 'I knew there was something wrong. If I'd told you before you went to Toronto, you might have had something to push at Stephen with, and he just might have told you the truth. He was on the edge, Mr Banks. That's why Nicholas had to get rid of him, I suppose.'

'I think you're right,' Banks said. 'But we still can't prove it. You shouldn't blame yourself though. You might have thought you were going to get Stephen in trouble. I imagine you were protecting him?'

Fletcher nodded. 'I suppose I was. Him and his father's memory.'

'To get Nicholas, you'd have had to betray Stephen. He was protecting his brother, or his father, like you were.'

'What'll happen to me? Will you prosecute?'

'For what?'

'Withholding evidence? Accessory after the fact?'

Banks laughed. 'You have a very thin grasp of the law, Mr Fletcher. Sure, you could have spoken earlier, as could a number of other people around Stephen Collier. But he kept everyone just enough in the dark so there was nothing, really, to say – nothing but vague fears and

318

suspicions. Believe me, few people come to us with those; they don't want to look silly.'

'So nothing's going to happen to me?'

Banks stood up and gestured to Hatchley that it was time to leave. 'No. You've helped us. It's up to us now to put a case together, or set a trap.'

'I'll do anything to help,' Fletcher said. 'Tell the bastard I know something and let him come and try to bump me off.'

'I hope it doesn't come to that,' Banks said, 'but thanks for the offer.'

They sat in the car for a few minutes and lit cigarettes. It was pitch-black, and far down in the valley below the lights of Swainshead glittered like an alley of stars.

'How hard should we push Collier?' Hatchley asked.

'We don't push,' Banks said. 'At least not the first time. I told you, he's clever. He'll see we're desperate.'

'So what do we do?'

'We confront him with what we've got and try to trip him up. If he's too clever to fall for that, and I suspect he is, then we try again and keep trying.' He started the engine and broke the silence.

'You can't help admiring the bastard's nerve though, can you,' Hatchley said. 'What if Freddie Metcalfe and Richmond had remembered seeing him order vodka and pour it in Stephen's pints?'

'Then all he'd have had to say was that he played a practical joke, like Fletcher said. There's nothing illegal about chasers. As things stand, it's only Fletcher's word against his, and a good defence lawyer would soon prove that John Fletcher had more than just cause to want to incriminate Collier. They'd bring up the incident at the party, for a start. Could you imagine Katie Greenock on the stand?'

Hatchley shook his head. 'That lass never seems to know whether she's coming or going.'

For some reason, Banks began to feel uneasy at the thought of Katie. What if she really did know more than she was telling? And what if Nicholas Collier suspected she knew? He might easily have seen her talking to Stephen. And Katie was exactly the kind of woman to set off his violent sexual behaviour.

He turned on to the road and headed south for Swainshead. There was still no light on in Collier's house. Hatchley hammered at the door but got no answer.

'Let's try the pub,' Banks suggested.

Hatchley brightened up at that. He hadn't completely forgotten his priorities in a burst of professional zeal.

'Well, if it isn't Chief Inspector Banks,' Freddie Metcalfe greeted them. 'And Sergeant Hatchley, isn't it? What can I do for you?'

Banks ordered two pints of Pedigree and lit a Silk Cut. Maybe a pint would calm down his jangling nerves. The hairs at the back of his neck were bristling.

'Seen Nicholas Collier tonight?' he asked.

'No, he's not been in,' Freddie said. 'Has tha got any further wi' t' murder?'

'We're getting there, we're getting there,' Banks said.

'Aye, and pigs can fly,' Freddie said, passing their drinks.

'None of the usual lot been in tonight?'

'Nope. It's been as quiet as this since opening time,' Freddie answered miserably, and loped off to serve a youth in hiking boots.

'You know,' Banks said, 'I've been thinking about what to do next, and there's someone else we might profit from leaning on in this case.'

'Sam Greenock?' Hatchley said.

'Yes. Threaten him with arrest as an accessory, and we might just get him to open up. He's cocky, but I don't think he's as cool as Nicholas. Stephen Collier's dead now. If we can convince Sam that Nicholas will fall from grace with or without his help, we might be able to strike a bargain. After all, without gentry to suck up to, what's Sam going to get out of it? Nicholas might well have sawn off the branch he was sitting on by killing Stephen.'

'It's an idea,' Hatchley said.

'And Greenock's a bully,' Banks said. 'Bullies are the easiest of the lot to lean on, especially men who beat up their wives.'

'I think I might be able to work up a bit of enthusiasm,' Hatchley said, grinning.

'Good. Let's go.'

'What? Now? But we haven't finished our drinks.'

'I've just got a feeling, that's all. We can come back to them. Let's see if Sam's in.'

They left the White Rose and crossed the bridge. There were no lights on in the front lower or upper rooms of the Greenock Guest House.

'He's not in,' Hatchley said. 'Let's go back to the pub and call again later.'

'It looks like there's nobody in at all,' Banks said. 'That's odd.' He couldn't explain why he felt disturbed by the dark silent house, but he couldn't ignore the feeling. 'No,' he said. 'I'm going in.'

Hatchley sighed and followed. 'I'll bet the bloody door's locked.'

Before they could close the gate behind them, they heard a car coming. It was Sam's Land Rover. He parked near the pub across the narrow Swain, as there was no road on the Greenocks' side, and came bounding over the bridge.

'Evening, gents,' he called out. 'And what can I do . . . Oh, it's you.'

'Don't sound so disappointed,' Banks said. 'We might be able to do something for you.'

'Oh?' Sam's boyish face looked puzzled. He patted his curly hair. 'All right. Never turn down a favour from a copper, that's me.'

'Can we go in?'

'Of course. I'll get the missus to brew a pot of tea.' He dug in his pocket for his keys, finally found the right one and stuck it in the lock, where he poked and twisted it for a while, then turned to Banks and frowned. 'That's odd. It was already open. Katie usually locks up at ten sharp and the guests let themselves in with their own keys. And it's not usually as dark as this. She puts the hall light on for the guests. They're probably still in the pub, but I can't imagine where she is.'

Banks and Hatchley followed him through the front door into the dark hall. Sam turned the light on. The guest book lay open on its varnished table by a stack of tourist guides, maps and brochures advertising local businesses and leisure pursuits. Automatically, Sam looked at himself in the mirror over the phone and patted his curly hair again.

'Katie!' Sam called.

No answer.

He went into the dining room and flicked the light switch on. 'Bloody hell!'

Banks followed him inside. 'What is it?' All he could see was the room where he and Hatchley had eaten breakfast. The varnished tables gleamed darkly in the shaded light.

'She's not set the tables for the morning. She's not even

put the bloody cloths on,' Sam said. He sounded more angry than worried about why or where Katie might have gone.

They paused at the foot of the stairs, where Sam called again and got no answer. 'It doesn't look like she's at home,' he said, puzzled. 'I can't imagine where she'd be at this time.'

'Maybe she's left you,' Banks suggested.

'Don't be daft. Where would she go? Why would she do a thing like that anyway?'

They carried on to the door that separated the Greenocks' living quarters from the rest of the house.

'Katie!' Sam called once more, hand on the knob.

Still no reply. The absolute silence in the house made Banks' hackles rise.

Sam opened the door and walked along the short narrow corridor that linked the two parts of the house. Banks and Hatchley followed close behind. Coats on hooks on either side brushed against them as they walked in single file behind Sam. The only faint illumination was at the end of the passage.

'At least she's left this light on,' Sam said.

The light came from the pane of frosted glass on the door that led into the Greenocks' living room. Sam called his wife's name again but got no answer. He walked into the room and stopped dead in his tracks.

'Jesus Christ,' he gasped, then stumbled backwards into Banks and started to slide slowly down the wall, hands over his eyes.

Banks regained his balance, pushed past Sam and went in, Hatchley close behind. They stopped in the doorway, awed and horrified by the scene before them. Banks heard Hatchley mutter a prayer or a curse.

There was blood all over the room: on the carpet, the sofa, the hearth, and even splashed like obscene hiero-glyphs over the wall above the mantelpiece. Nothing moved. Nicholas Collier lay awkwardly, half on the sofa and half on the carpet, his head bashed in, his face a bloody pulp. He wouldn't even have been recognizable if it hadn't been for the prominent yellowish teeth splintered and bared in agony and shock.

Katie sat on the arm of the settee still holding the heavy wooden cross of her granny's that had stood on the mantelpiece. Her beautiful brown eyes were looking at things nobody else could see. The front of her dress was ripped open at one side and a few drops of blood glistened against the pale skin of her blue-veined breast.

INNOCENT GRAVES

For Sheila

ACKNOWLEDGEMENTS

I would first like to thank several people for reading and commenting upon the manuscript through its several drafts: my agent, Dominick Abel; Cynthia Good, from Penguin Books Canada; Natalee Rosenstein, from Berkley; and my copy editor, Mary Adachi.

I would also like to acknowledge expert help from a variety of sources. Thanks, as ever, to Detective Sergeant Keith Wright, of Nottingham CID, who answered my frequently silly questions with his characteristic patience and humour. Thanks also to Pamela Newall, from the Centre for Forensic Sciences, for saving me from sounding like a complete idiot on DNA, to Paul Bennett for reading and commenting on the trial scenes, to John Halladay for further information on legal procedure and to Dr Marta Townsend for the displacement.

In addition, I would like to offer special thanks to Elly Pacey and Nancy Galic for the Croation insults and to Emily Langran for the Yorkshire schoolgirl slang. And, last but not least, I must thank John Irvine for keeping my computer going through thick and thin, and for the occasional wicked line.

As usual, any mistakes are entirely my own and are made in the interests of the story.

1

ONE

The night it all began, a thick fog rolled down the dale and enfolded the town of Eastvale in its shroud. Fog in the market square, creeping in the cracks between the cobbles; fog muffling the sound of laughter from the Queen's Arms and muting the light through its red and amber panes; fog rubbing and licking against cool glass in curtained windows and insinuating its way through tiny gaps under doors.

And the fog seemed at its thickest in the graveyard of St Mary's Church, where a beautiful woman with long auburn hair wandered barefoot and drunk, a wineglass full of Pinot Noir held precariously in her hand.

She weaved her way between the squat, gnarled yews and lichen-stained stones. Sometimes she thought she saw ghosts, grey, translucent shapes flitting among the tombs ahead, but they didn't frighten her.

And she came to the Inchcliffe Mausoleum.

It loomed ahead out of the fog, massive and magnificent: classical lines formed in marble, steps overgrown with weeds leading down to the heavy oak door.

But it was the angel she had come to see. She liked the angel. Its eyes were fixed on heaven, as if nothing earthly mattered, and its hands were clasped together in prayer. Though it was solid marble, she often fancied it was so insubstantial she could pass her hand right through it.

She swayed slightly, raised her glass to the angel and drained half the wine at one gulp. She could feel the cold, damp earth and grass under her feet.

'Hello, Gabriel,' she said, voice a little slurred. 'I'm sorry but I've sinned again.' She hiccupped and put her hand to her mouth. ''Scuse me, but I just can't seem to—'

Then she saw something, a black-and-white shape, sticking out from behind the mausoleum. Curious, she squinted and stumbled towards it. Only when she was about a yard away did she realize it was a black shoe and a white sock. With a foot still in it.

She tottered back, hand to her mouth, then circled around the back of the tomb. All she could make out were the pale legs, the fair hair, the open satchel and the maroon uniform of St Mary's School for Girls.

She screamed and dropped her glass. It shattered on a stone.

Then Rebecca Charters, wife of the vicar of St Mary's, fell to her knees on the broken glass and started to vomit.

TWO

The fog tasted of ashes, thought Detective Chief Inspector Alan Banks, as he pulled up his raincoat collar and hurried down the tarmac path towards the faint, gauzy light. Or perhaps he was being fanciful. Even though he hadn't seen the body yet, he felt that familiar clenching in his stomach that murder always brought.

When he reached the scene, just off a narrow gravel path past the shrubbery, he saw the blurred silhouette of Dr Glendenning through the canvas screen, bent over a vague shape lying on the ground, like a dumb-show in a Jacobean drama.

Fog had played havoc with the usual order of arrival. Banks himself had been at a senior officers' meeting in Northallerton when he got the call, and he was consequently almost the last person to arrive. Peter Darby, crime-scene photographer, was there already, and so was Detective Inspector Barry Stott, who, for reasons clear to anyone who saw him, was more commonly known as 'Jug-ears.' Stott, who had recently been transferred from Salford upon his promotion from detective sergeant, was a temporary replacement for DS Philip Richmond, who had gone to Scotland Yard to join a special computer unit.

Banks took a deep breath and walked behind the screen. Dr Glendenning looked up, cigarette dangling from his mouth, its smoke indistinguishable from the fog that surrounded them.

'Ah, Banks . . .' he said in his lilting Edinburgh accent, then he shook his head slowly.

Banks looked down at the body. In all his years in Eastvale, he hadn't had to deal with a crime like this. He had seen worse in London, of course, which was part of the reason he had left the Met and transferred up north. But you clearly couldn't hide from it any more now. Not anywhere. George Orwell was right about the decline of the English murder, and this was exactly the kind of thing it had declined into.

The girl, about fifteen or sixteen by the look of her, lay on her back in the long grass behind a huge Victorian sepulchre, upon which stood a marble statue of an angel. The angel had its back turned to her, and through the fog Banks could make out the chipped feathers of its wings.

Her eyes stared into the fog, her long blonde hair lay

fanned out around her head like a halo, and her face had a reddish-purple hue. There was a little cut by her left eye and some discolouration around her neck. A trickle of blood the shape of a large teardrop ran out of her left nostril.

Her maroon school blazer lay bunched up on the ground beside her, and her white blouse had been ripped open at the front; her bra had then been removed – roughly, by the looks of it.

Banks felt the urge to cover her. In his job, he had already seen far more than a man should, and it was little things like this that sometimes affected him more than the blood and guts. The girl looked so vulnerable, so callously violated. He could imagine her shame at being exposed in this way, how she would blush and hurry to cover herself if she were alive. But she was beyond shame now.

Below her waist, someone had pulled her skirt up to reveal her thighs and pubic region. Her long legs lay open at a forty-five-degree angle. Her white socks were down around her ankles. She wore shiny black shoes with buckles fastened at the sides.

Lying beside her was an open satchel. The strap had come free of the metal ring at one end. Using his pen, Banks pushed back the flap and read the neatly inked address:

Miss Deborah Catherine Harrison
28 Hawthorn Close
Eastvale
North Yorkshire
England
United Kingdom of Great Britain and Northern Ireland
European Community
Earth

Solar System
Milky Way
The Universe.

He smiled sadly to himself. It was a typical teenager's sense of playfulness, exactly the same thing he had done at school.

Hawthorn Close meant money, as did St Mary's in general. It was an area of large, mostly detached houses, each with an acre or two of garden, long drives and croquet lawns shaded by copper beeches. To live there, you had to make enough money to employ a gardener, at the very least. St Mary's School required money, too – about £1200 per term. Banks had checked when he first arrived in town, but soon found he couldn't afford to send his daughter, Tracy, there.

Banks cadged some evidence bags from one of the SOCOs and, holding the satchel by its edges, tipped the contents inside one of them. All he found were a couple of exercise books with the name 'Deborah Catherine Harrison' written on the cover, a portable chess set, a few cosmetic items and three loose tampons in cellophane wrappers. But why had the satchel been open? he wondered. The buckles seemed strong enough, so he doubted it came open during a struggle. Had someone been looking for something?

Glendenning directed one of his underlings to take oral, vaginal and anal swabs and comb the pubic hair. Then he groaned and got to his feet. 'I'm getting old, Banks,' he said, massaging his knees. 'Too old for this sort of thing.' He jerked his head towards the body. Tall and white-haired, with a nicotine-stained moustache, the doctor was probably in his late fifties, Banks guessed.

They moved away, letting the screen block their view of the victim. Every so often, Peter Darby's flash exploded, creating a strobe-light effect in the fog. Banks accepted one of Glendenning's Senior Service. Normally he smoked Silk Cut tipped, but he had cut down drastically on his smoking over the last few months and wasn't even carrying a packet with him. Well, he thought, as Glendenning proffered a gold, initialled lighter, cutting down had been easy enough to do in a lazy summer with no murders to investigate. Now it was November and there was a body at his feet. He lit up and coughed.

'Ought to get that cough seen to, laddie,' said Glendenning. 'Might be a touch of lung cancer, you know.'

'It's nothing. I'm just getting a cold, that's all.'

'Aye . . . Well, I don't suppose you dragged me out here on a mucky night like this just to talk about your health, did you?'

'No,' said Banks. 'What do you make of it?'

'I can't tell you much yet, but judging by her colour and the marks on her throat, I'd say asphyxia due to ligature strangulation.'

'Any sign of the ligature?'

'Off the record, that satchel strap fits the bill pretty nicely.'

'What about time of death?'

'Oh, come off it, laddie.'

'Vaguely?'

'Not more than two or three hours ago. But don't quote me on that.'

Banks looked at his watch. Eight o'clock. Which meant she was probably killed between five and six. Not on her way home from school, then. At least not directly.

'Was she killed here?'

'Aye. Almost certainly. Hypostasis is entirely consistent with the position of the body.'

'Any sign of the rest of her underwear?'

Glendenning shook his head. 'Only the brassiere.'

'When can you get her on the table?'

'First thing in the morning. Coming?'

Banks swallowed; the fog scratched his throat. 'Wouldn't miss it for the world.'

'Fine. I'll reserve you the best seat in the house. I'm off home. You can get her to the mortuary now.'

And with that, Glendenning turned and faded into the fog.

Banks stood alone for a moment trying to forget the girl he had just seen spread-eagled so cruelly before him, trying desperately not to see Tracy in her place. He stubbed out his cigarette carefully on the side of the Inchcliffe Mausoleum and pocketed the butt. No point leaving red herrings at the crime scene.

A couple of yards away, he noticed a light patch on the grass. He walked over and squatted to get a closer look. It looked and smelled as if someone had been sick. He could also make out the stem and fragments of a wineglass, which seemed to have smashed on the stone edging of a grave. He picked up one of the slivers carefully between thumb and forefinger. It was stained with blood or wine; he couldn't be certain which.

He saw DI Stott within hearing range and called him over.

'Know anything about this?' he asked.

Stott looked at the glass and vomit. 'Rebecca Charters. Woman who discovered the body,' he said. 'Bit of an oddball. She's in the vicarage. WPC Kemp is with her.'

'Okay. I'll talk to her later.' Banks pointed to the

mausoleum. 'Anyone had a look in there yet?'

'Not yet. I sent PC Aiken to see if he could come up with a key from the vicar.'

Banks nodded. 'Look, Barry, someone's got to break the news to the girl's parents.'

'And seeing as I'm the new lad on the block . . .'

'That's not what I meant. If you're not comfortable with the job, then get someone else to do it. But get it done.'

'Sorry,' said Stott, taking his glasses off and wiping them on a white handkerchief. 'I'm a bit . . .' He gestured towards the body. 'Of course I'll go.'

'Sure?'

'Yes.'

'Okay. I'll join you there soon. Before you go, call in DC Gay and DS Hatchley and tell them to get down here. Someone might have to drag Jim out of The Oak.'

Stott raised his eyebrows. Banks noticed his little moue of distaste at the mention of Detective Sergeant Hatchley. Well, he thought, that's *his* cross to bear.

'And get as many officers out on the streets as you can. I want every house in the area canvassed as soon as possible. It's going to be a long, busy night, but we'd better work fast. People forget quickly. Besides, by tomorrow the vultures will be here.'

'Vultures?'

'Press, TV people, sightseers. It's going to be a circus, Barry. Prepare yourself.'

Stott nodded. PC Aiken turned up with the key to the mausoleum. Banks borrowed a torch from one of the search team, and he and Stott trod carefully down the weed-covered steps.

The heavy wooden door opened after a brief struggle with the key, and they found themselves in the dark with the dead; six sturdy coffins rested on trestles. A few tentacles of fog slid down the stairs and through the door after them, wreathing around their feet.

The small tomb didn't smell of death, only of earth and mould. Fortunately, there were no fresh Inchcliffes buried there; the family had left Eastvale fifty years ago.

All Banks could see on his first glance around were the spider-webs that seemed to be spun in the very air itself. He gave a little shudder and shone his torch over the floor. There, in the corner furthest from the entrance, lay two empty vodka bottles and a pile of cigarette ends. It was hard to tell how recent they were, but they certainly weren't fifty years old.

They found nothing else of interest down there, and it was with great relief that Banks emerged into the open air again; foggy as it was, it felt like a clear night after the inside of the tomb. Banks asked the SOCOs to bag the empty bottles and cigarette ends and search the place thoroughly.

'We'll need a murder room set up at the station,' he said, turning to Stott again, 'and a van parked near the scene; make it easy for people to come forward. Exhibits Officer, phone lines, civilian staff, the usual thing. Get Susan Gay to see to it. Better inform the Chief Constable, too,' Banks added with a sinking feeling.

At the moment, Banks was senior man in Eastvale CID, as Detective Superintendent Gristhorpe had broken his leg while fixing his dry-stone wall. Technically, Detective Chief Superintendent Jack Wormsley, from North Yorkshire Regional HQ at Northallerton, was supposed to be in charge of a murder investigation. However, Banks knew from experience not to expect much beyond the occasional phone call from DCS Wormsley; he was rumoured to be far too close to finishing his scale matchstick model of the Taj Mahal to be bothered with a mere murder. If it came from anywhere, Banks knew, the main hindrance would come from the new chief constable: Jeremiah 'Jimmy' Riddle, a high-flier of the pushy, breathe-down-your-neck school of police management.

'We'll also need a thorough ground-search of the graveyard,' Banks went on, 'but we might be better doing that in daylight, especially if this fog disperses a bit during the night. Anyway, make sure the place is well secured.' Banks looked around. 'How many entrances are there?'

'Two. One off North Market Street and one off Kendal Road, just by bridge.'

'Should be easy to secure, then. The wall looks high enough to deter any interlopers, but we'd better have a couple of men on perimeter patrol, just to make sure. The last thing we need is some intrepid reporter splashing crime-scene photos all over the morning papers. Is there any access from the riverside?'

Stott shook his head. 'The wall's high there, too, and it's topped with broken glass.'

'Welcoming sort of place, isn't it?'

'I understand they've had a bit of vandalism.'

Banks peered through the fog at the lights in the vicarage. They looked like disembodied eyes. 'You're a bit of a churchman, aren't you, Barry?'

Stott nodded. 'Yes. St Cuthbert's, though, not St Mary's.'

Banks nodded towards the vicarage. 'Do you know who the vicar is here?'

'Father Daniel Charters.'

Banks raised his eyebrows. 'I thought so. I don't know all the details, but isn't he the one who's been in the news a bit lately?'

'He is,' Stott said through gritted teeth.

'Interesting,' said Banks. 'Very interesting.' And he wandered off towards the vicarage.

THREE

The woman who answered Banks's knock at the back door was in her mid-thirties, he guessed, with a lustrous cascade of auburn hair spilling over her shoulders, an olive complexion, large hazel eyes and the fullest, most sensuous lips he had ever seen. She also had a stunned, unfocused look on her face.

'I'm Rebecca Charters,' she said, shaking his hand. 'Please come through.'

Banks followed her down the hall. A tall woman, she was wearing a heavy black shawl draped over her shoulders and a loose, long blue skirt that flowed over the swell of her hips almost down to the stone flags of the hallway. Her feet were bare and dirty, with blades of grass stuck to her ankles and instep. There was also a fresh cut by the Achilles tendon of her right foot. As she walked, her hips swayed just a little more than he would have expected in a vicar's wife. And was it his imagination, or did she seem a little unsteady on her pins?

She led him into a living-room with a high ceiling and dull, striped wallpaper. WPC Kemp stood by the door, and Banks told her she could leave now.

Bottle-green velour curtains were drawn across the bay window against the fog. An empty tiled fireplace stood directly across from the door, and in front of it lay a huge bundle of brown-and-white fur that Banks took to be a large dog of some kind. Whatever it was, he hoped it stayed there. Not that he disliked dogs, but he couldn't stand the way they slobbered and fussed over him. Cats were much more Banks's kind of animal. He liked their arrogance, their independence and their sense of mischief, and would have one for a pet were it not that Sandra, his wife, was violently allergic.

The only heat was provided by a small white radiator against the far wall. Banks was glad he hadn't taken off his raincoat yet; he was thankful for the extra layer of warmth.

A three-piece suite upholstered in worn brown corduroy ranged around the coffee-table, and in one of the armchairs sat a man with thick black eyebrows that almost met in the middle, a furrowed brow, a long, pale face and prominent cheekbones. He had the haunted look of a troubled young priest from an old movie.

As Banks came in, the man stood up, a manoeuvre that resembled some large, long-limbed animal uncurling from its lair, and reached out his slender hand.

'Daniel Charters. Would you like some coffee?'

Shaking his hand, Banks noticed the carafe on the table and nodded. 'Love some,' he said. 'Black, no sugar.'

Banks sat on the sofa, Rebecca Charters next to him. Also on the coffee-table stood an empty bottle of Sainsbury's Romanian Pinot Noir.

As Daniel Charters poured the coffee, Rebecca walked over to a glass-fronted cabinet, brought out a bottle and a brandy balloon and poured herself a large one. Banks noticed her husband give her an angry look, which she ignored. The coffee was good. Almost as soon as he sipped it Banks felt the scratchiness in his throat ease up a little.

'I realize you've had a terrible shock,' Banks said, 'but do you think you could answer a few questions?'

Rebecca nodded.

'Good. Did you report finding the body immediately?'

'Almost. When I saw the shape, what it was, I . . . I was sick first. Then I ran back here and telephoned the police.'

'What were you doing in the graveyard at that time, on such a miserable night?'

'I went to see the angel.'

Her voice was such a low whisper, Banks didn't believe he could have heard right. 'You what?' he asked.

'I said I went to see the angel.' Her large, moist eyes held his defiantly. They were red-rimmed with crying. 'What's wrong with that? I like graveyards. At least I did.'

'What about the glass?'

'I had a glass of wine. I dropped it, then I fell. Look.' She lifted her skirt as far as her knees. Both of them were bandaged, but the blood was already seeping through.

'Perhaps you should see a doctor?' Banks suggested.

Rebecca shook her head. 'I'm all right.'

'Did you disturb the body in any way?' Banks asked.

'No. I didn't touch anything. I didn't go near her.'

'Did you recognize her?'

'Just that she was a St Mary's girl.'

'Did you know a girl called Deborah Catherine Harrison?'

Rebecca put her hand to her mouth and nodded. For a moment Banks thought she was going to be sick again. Her husband didn't make a move, but Banks could tell from his expression that he recognized the name, too.

'Is that who it was?' Rebecca asked.

'We think so. I'll have to ask you not to say anything to anyone until the identity has been confirmed.'

'Of course not. Poor Deborah.'

'So you knew her?'

'She sang in the choir,' Daniel Charters said. 'The

school and the church are very closely linked. They don't have a chapel of their own, so they come here for services. A number of them also sing in the choir.'

'Have you any idea what she might have been doing in the graveyard around five or six o'clock?'

'It's a short cut,' Rebecca said. 'From the school to her house.'

'But school finishes at half past three.'

Rebecca shrugged. 'They have clubs, societies, activities. You'd have to ask Dr Green, the head.' She took another gulp of brandy. The dog on the hearth hadn't moved. For a moment Banks thought it might have died, then he noticed the fur moving slowly as it breathed. Just old, most likely. The way he was feeling.

'Did either of you see or hear anything outside earlier this evening?' he asked.

Daniel shook his head, and Rebecca said, 'I *thought* I did. When I was in the kitchen opening the wine. It sounded like a stifled cry or something.'

'What did you do?'

'I went over to the window. Of course, I couldn't see a damn thing in this fog, and when I didn't hear anything else for a couple of minutes I decided it must have been a bird or a small animal.'

'Can you remember what time that was?'

'Around six o'clock, maybe a few minutes after. The local news was just starting on television.'

'And even though you thought you heard a cry, you still went out into the dark, foggy graveyard alone forty minutes later?'

Rebecca cast her eyes on the empty wine bottle. 'I'd forgotten all about it by then,' she said. 'Besides, I told you, I assumed it was an animal.'

Banks turned to Daniel Charters. 'Did you hear anything?'

'He was in his study until I came back screaming about the body,' Rebecca answered. 'That's the other room at the front, the far side. He couldn't have heard a thing from there.'

'Mr Charters?'

Daniel Charters nodded. 'That's right. I was working on a sermon. I'm afraid my wife is correct. I didn't hear anything.'

'Have either of you seen any strangers hanging around the area recently?'

They both shook their heads.

'Has anyone been inside the Inchcliffe Mausoleum lately?'

Charters frowned. 'No. As far as I know no-one's been in there for fifty years. I just gave the key to one of your men.'

'Where do you usually keep it?'

'In the church. On a hook in the vestry.'

'So it's accessible to anyone?'

'Yes. But I can't see—'

'Someone's been down there recently. We found vodka bottles and cigarette ends. Have you any idea who it might be?'

'I can't . . .' Then he stopped and turned pale. 'Unless . . .'

'Unless what, Mr Charters?' Banks drank some more coffee.

'As you probably know,' Charters said, 'I've been under a bit of a cloud these past two months. Do you know the details?'

Banks shrugged. 'Only vaguely.'

'The whole thing *is* only vague. Anyway, we employed a Croatian refugee here as a sexton. He turned out to be a complete mistake. He drank, he was abusive and he frightened people.'

'In what way?'

'He used to leer at the schoolgirls, make lewd gestures. One girl even saw him urinating on a grave.' Charters shook his head. 'That sort of thing. He never actually touched anyone as far as we know, but some of the girls complained to Dr Green, and she and I had a long talk. The upshot was, I decided to get rid of him. As soon as he'd gone, he went to the church authorities and claimed that I fired him because he refused to have sex with me.'

'And the church authorities believed him?'

'It doesn't matter what they believed,' said Charters, with a bitter glance at his wife. 'Once the accusation is made, the wheels start to grind, enquiries have to be made. And the accused is put immediately on the defensive. You ought to know how it works, Chief Inspector.'

'Like "when did you stop beating your wife?"'

'Exactly.'

'And you think he might have been in the mausoleum?'

'He's the only one I can think of. And he had better access to the key than most. Also, as I remember, vodka was his drink of preference because he believed people couldn't smell it on his breath.'

'What do you think of all this, Mrs Charters?'

Rebecca shook her head, looked away and drank more brandy.

'My wife, as you can see,' said Charters, 'has been a pillar of strength.'

Banks decided to leave that one well alone. 'What's he called, this man you fired?'

'Ive Jelačić.'

'How do you spell that?'

Charters told him, explaining the diacritical marks. Banks wrote it down.

'What does he look like?'

'He's tall, about my height, solidly built. He has black hair, which always needs cutting, a dark complexion, a slightly hooked nose.' He shrugged. 'I don't know what else to say.'

'Where is he now?'

'Leeds.'

'Has he ever threatened or bothered you at all since you fired him?'

'Yes. He's been back a couple of times.'

'Why?'

'To offer me a deal. He suggested that he would drop the charges if I gave him money.'

'How much?'

Charters snorted. 'More than I can afford, I'm afraid.'

'And how would he get the charges dropped?'

'Say he misinterpreted my gesture. Cultural differences. I told him to go away. The man's a liar and a drunk, Chief Inspector. What difference does it make?'

'It might make a lot of difference,' said Banks slowly, 'if he had a reputation for bothering the St Mary's girls and he had a grudge against you. Do you know his address?'

Charters went over and opened a sideboard drawer. 'I ought to,' he muttered, flipping through a pile of envelopes. 'There's been enough correspondence on the matter. Ah, here it is.'

Banks looked at the address. It was in the Burmantofts area of Leeds, but he didn't recognize the street. 'Mind if I use your phone?' he asked.

'Go ahead,' said Charters. 'There's an extension in my study, if you want some privacy. It's just across the hall.'

Banks went into the study and sat at the desk. He was impressed how tidy it was – no papers scattered all around, no chewed pencils, no reference books open face down, no errant paperclips or rubber bands, the way his own desk usually looked when he was working on something. Even the ruler was lined up parallel with the edge of the blotter. A neat man, the Reverend Charters. So neat that he had even tidied his desk *after* his wife came in screaming about a murder in the graveyard?

Banks consulted his notebook and phoned Detective Inspector Ken Blackstone at home. Blackstone, a good friend, worked for West Yorkshire CID out of Millgarth, Leeds. Banks explained what had happened and asked Blackstone if he could arrange to have a couple of officers go around to the address Charters had given him. First, he wanted to know if Jelačić was at home, and secondly, whether he had an alibi for this evening. Blackstone said it would be no problem, and Banks hung up.

When he went back into the living-room he obviously interrupted Daniel and Rebecca Charters in the midst of a hissed argument. Rebecca, he noticed, had refilled her brandy glass.

Banks had nothing more to ask, so he knocked back the rest of his lukewarm coffee and headed out into the grave-yard.

FOUR

As soon as Banks had gone, Daniel Charters looked dis-gustedly at the empty wine bottle and the remains of the brandy, then at Rebecca. 'I asked you why you did that,' he said. 'Why on earth did you lie to him?'

'You know why.'

Daniel leaned forward in his chair, hands clasped between his knees. 'No, I don't. You didn't even give me a chance to answer. You just jumped right in with your stupid lie.'

Rebecca sipped her brandy. 'I didn't notice you rushing to correct me.'

Daniel reddened. 'It was too late by then. It would have looked suspicious.'

'Shpicious? Oh, that's a good one, Daniel. And how do you think it looks *already*?'

Daniel's face contorted in pain. 'Do you think I did it? Do you really believe *I* killed that girl out there?' He pointed a long, bony finger towards the graveyard. 'Is that what you think you were protecting me from? Giving me an alibi for?'

Rebecca turned away. 'Don't be silly.'

'Then why did you lie?'

'To make things easier.'

'Lies never make things easier.'

Oh, don't they? Rebecca thought. Shows what you know. 'We've got enough problems,' she said with a sigh, 'without having you as a suspect in a murder investigation.'

'Don't you want to know where I was?'

'No. I don't care where you were.'

'But you lied for me.'

'For us. Yes.' She ran her hand through her hair. 'Look, Daniel, I saw something horrible out there in the graveyard. I'm tired, I'm upset and I feel sick. Can't you just leave me alone?'

Daniel remained silent for a moment. Rebecca could hear the clock ticking on the mantelpiece. Ezekiel stirred briefly then settled down to sleep again.

'You think I did it, don't you?' Daniel persisted.

'Please, Daniel, just let it drop. Of course I don't think you did it.'

'Not the murder. The other business.'

'I don't think anything of the kind. I told you. Haven't I stuck by you? Do you think I'd still be here if I thought you did it?'

'*Here*? You're not *here*. You haven't been *here* since it happened. Oh, you may actually be physically present in this room. Yes, I'll admit that. But you're not really *here*, not with me. Most of the time you're in the bottle, the rest you're . . . God knows where.'

'Oh, right, and we all know you're such a bloody saint you haven't touched a drop throughout all our troubles. Well, maybe I'm not as *strong* as you, Daniel. Maybe we're not all so bloody *devout*. Some of us might just show a little human *weakness* every now and then. But you wouldn't know about that, would you?'

Rebecca topped up her brandy. Daniel reached forward and knocked the glass out of her hand. The brandy spilled on the coffee-table and the sofa, and the glass bounced on the carpet.

Rebecca didn't know what to say. Her breath caught in her throat. It was the first time since she had known him that Daniel had shown even the slightest sign of violence.

His face was red, and his frown knitted his thick dark eyebrows together at the bridge of his nose. 'You have your doubts don't you?' he insisted. 'Go on. Admit it. I'm waiting.'

Rebecca bent down, picked up the glass and poured

herself another shot with shaking hands. This time Daniel did nothing.

'Answer me,' he said. 'Tell me the truth.'

Rebecca let the silence stretch, then she took a long sip of brandy and said, in a parody of a prostitute's tone, 'Well, you know what they say, don't you, ducky? There's no smoke without fire.'

FIVE

Banks left his car parked on North Market Street, outside St Mary's, and set off on foot to Hawthorn Close. The fog appeared less menacing on the main road than it had in the unlit graveyard, though the high amber street-lights and the flashing Belisha beacons at the zebra crossing looked like the Martian machines out of *War of the Worlds*.

Why had Rebecca Charters lied for her husband? She *had* lied, of that Banks was certain, even without the evidence of the tidy desk. Was she giving him an alibi? Perhaps tomorrow he would call on them again. She was certainly an odd one. *Going to see the angel*, indeed!

Banks looked at his watch. Luckily, it was just after nine o'clock, and he still had time to nip into the off-licence at the corner of Hawthorn Road and buy twenty Silk Cut.

After he had walked about two hundred yards down Hawthorn Road, he took Hawthorn Close to the right, a winding street of big, stone houses that traditionally housed Eastvale's gentry.

He found number 28, stubbed out his cigarette and walked up the gravel drive, noting the 'P' registration

Jaguar parked outside the front door. On impulse, he put his hand on the bonnet. Still a little warm.

Barry Stott answered the door, looking grim. Banks thanked him for doing the dirty work and told him he could return to the station and get things organized; then he walked down the hall alone into a spacious white room, complete with a white grand piano. The only contrasting elements were the Turkish carpets and what looked like a genuine Chagall on the wall over the Adam fireplace, where a thick log burned and crackled. A white book-case held Folio Society editions of the classics, and french windows with white trim led out to the dark garden.

There were three people in the room, all sitting down, and all, by the looks of it, in a state of shock. The woman wore a grey skirt and a blue silk blouse, both of a quality you'd be hard-pushed to find in Eastvale. Her shaggy blonde hair was the expensive kind of shaggy, and it framed an oval face with a pale, flawless complexion, pale blue eyes and beautifully proportioned nose and mouth. All in all, an elegant and attractive woman.

She got up and floated towards him as if in a trance. 'Has there been a mistake?' she asked. 'Please tell me there's been a mistake.' She had a hint of a French accent.

Before Banks could say anything, one of the men took her by the elbow and said, 'Come on, Sylvie. Sit down.' Then he turned to Banks. 'I'm Geoffrey Harrison,' he said. 'Deborah's father. I suppose it's too much to hope there *has* been a mistake?'

Banks shook his head.

Geoffrey was about six foot two, with the long arms and broad shoulders of a fast bowler. In fact he looked a bit like a famous test cricketer, but Banks couldn't put a name to him. He was wearing grey trousers with sharp creases and a knitted green V-neck sweater over a white shirt. No tie. He had curly fair hair, with some grey visible around the ears, and a strong, cleft chin, a bit like Kirk Douglas. Everything about his movements and features spoke of power, of someone used to getting his own way. Banks put his age at about forty-five, probably a good ten years older than his wife.

All of a sudden, the realization hit Banks like a bucket of cold water. Christ, he should have known. Should have been able to add it all up. This damn cold must be addling his brain. The man in front of him was Sir Geoffrey Harrison. *Sir*. He had been knighted for services to industry – something to do with leading-edge computers, electronics, microchips and the like – about three years ago. And Deborah Harrison was his daughter.

'Do you have a recent photograph of your daughter, sir?' he asked.

'Over there on the mantelpiece. It was taken last summer.'

Banks walked over and looked at the photograph of the young girl posing on the deck of a yacht. It was probably her first year in a bikini, Banks guessed, and while she hardly had the figure to fill it out, it still looked good on her. But then anything would probably have looked good on such youth, such energy, such potential.

Deborah was smiling and holding the mast with one hand; with the other she held back a long strand of blonde hair from her face, as if the wind were blowing it out of place. Even though the girl in the picture glowed with health and life, it was the same one who now lay in Eastvale mortuary.

'I'm afraid it's not a mistake,' he said, glancing at the photograph beside it. It showed two smiling young men in cricket whites, one of them unmistakably Sir Geoffrey, standing together in a quadrangle. The other man, who had his arm casually draped over Sir Geoffrey's shoulder, could easily have been the other person in the room about twenty-five years ago. Even now, he was still slim and good-looking, though the sandy hair above his high forehead was receding fast and thinning on top. He was wearing what looked like very expensive casual clothes – black cords and a rust-coloured cotton shirt – and a pair of gold-rimmed spectacles hung around his neck on a chain. 'Michael Clayton,' he said, getting up and shaking Banks's hand.

'Michael's my business partner,' said Sir Geoffrey. 'And my oldest friend. He's also Deborah's godfather.'

'I live just around the corner,' said Clayton. 'As soon as Geoff heard the news . . . well, they phoned me and I came over. Have there been any developments?'

'It's too early to say,' said Banks. Then he turned to Sir Geoffrey and Lady Harrison. 'Did you know if Deborah was planning on going anywhere after school?'

Sir Geoffrey took a second to refocus, then said, 'Only the chess club.'

'Chess club?'

'Yes. At school. They meet every Monday.'

'What time is she usually home?'

Sir Geoffrey looked at his wife. 'It's usually over by six,' Lady Harrison said. 'She gets home about quarter past. Sometimes twenty past, if she dawdles with her friends.'

Banks frowned. 'It must have been after eight o'clock when Detective Inspector Stott came to break the bad news,' he said. 'But you hadn't reported Deborah missing. Weren't you worried? Where did you think she was?'

Lady Harrison started to cry. Sir Geoffrey gripped her

hand. 'We'd only just got in ourselves,' he explained. 'I was at a business reception at the Royal Hotel, in York, and the damn fog delayed me. Sylvie was at her health club. Deborah has a key. She *is* sixteen, after all.'

'What time did you get back?'

'About eight o'clock. Within minutes of each other. We thought Deborah might have been home and gone out again, but that wasn't like her, not without letting us know, and certainly not on a night like this. There was no note, no sign she'd been here. Deborah's not . . . well, she usually leaves her school blazer over the back of a chair, if you see what I mean.'

'I do.' Banks's daughter Tracy was just as untidy.

'Anyway, we were worried she might have been kidnapped or something. We were just about to phone the police when Inspector Stott arrived.'

'Have there ever been any kidnap threats?'

'No, but one hears about such things.'

'Could your daughter have been carrying anything of value? Cash, credit cards, anything?'

'No. Why do you ask?'

'Her satchel was open. I was just wondering why.'

Sir Geoffrey shook his head.

Banks turned to Michael Clayton. 'Did you see Deborah at all this evening?'

'No. I was at home until I got Geoff's phone call.'

Sir Geoffrey and Lady Harrison sat on the white sofa, shoulders slumped, holding hands like a couple of teenagers. Banks sat on the edge of the armchair and leaned forward, resting his hands on his knees.

'Inspector Stott says Deborah was found in St Mary's graveyard,' Sir Geoffrey said. 'Is that true?'

Banks nodded.

Anger suffused Sir Geoffrey's face. 'Have you talked to that bloody vicar yet? That pervert?'

'Daniel Charters?'

'That's him. You know what he's been accused of, don't you?'

'Making a homosexual advance.'

Sir Geoffrey nodded. 'Exactly. If I were you, I'd—'

'Please, Geoffrey,' Sylvie said, plucking at his sleeve. 'Calm down. Let the chief inspector talk.'

Sir Geoffrey ran his hand through his hair. 'Yes, of course. I apologize.'

Why such animosity towards Charters? Banks wondered. But that was best left for later. Sir Geoffrey was distraught; it wouldn't be a good idea to press him any further just now.

'May I have a look at Deborah's room?' he asked.

Sylvie nodded and stood up. 'I'll show you.'

Banks followed her up a broad, white-carpeted staircase. What a hell of a job it would be to keep the place clean, he found himself thinking. Sandra would never put up with white carpets or upholstery. Still, he didn't suppose the Harrisons did the cleaning themselves.

Sylvie opened the door to Deborah's room, then excused herself and went back downstairs. Banks turned on the light. It was bigger, but in much the same state of disarray as Tracy's. Clothes lay tossed all over the floor, the bed was unmade, a mound of rumpled sheets, and the closet door stood open on a long rail of dresses, blouses, jackets and jeans. Expensive stuff, too, Banks saw as he looked at some of the designer labels.

Deborah's computer, complete with CD-ROM, sat on the desk under the window. Beside that stood a bookcase filled mostly with science and computer textbooks and

26

a few bodice-rippers. Banks searched through all the drawers but found nothing of interest. Of course, it would have helped if he had known what he was looking for.

Arranged in custom shelving on a table by the foot of the bed were a mini hi-fi system, a small colour television and a video – all with remote controls. Banks glanced through some of the CDs. Unlike Tracy, Deborah seemed to favour the rough, grungy style of popular music: Hole, Pearl Jam, Nirvana. A large poster of Kurt Cobain was tacked to the wall next to a small poster of River Phoenix.

Banks closed the door behind him and walked back down the stairs. He could hear Sylvie crying in the white room and Sir Geoffrey and Michael Clayton in muffled conversation. He couldn't hear what they were saying, and when he moved close, they saw him through the open door and asked him back in.

'I have just one more question, Sir Geoffrey, if I may?' he said.

'Go ahead.'

'Did your daughter keep a diary? I know mine does. They seem to be very popular among teenage girls.'

Sir Geoffrey thought for a moment. 'Yes,' he said. 'I think so. Michael bought her one last Christmas.'

Clayton nodded. 'Yes. One of the leather-bound kind, a page per day.'

Banks turned back to Sir Geoffrey. 'Do you know where she kept it?'

He frowned. 'I'm afraid I don't. Sylvie?'

Sylvie shook her head. 'She told me she lost it.'

'When was this?'

'About the beginning of term. I hadn't seen it for a while, so I asked her if she'd stopped writing it. Why? Is it important?'

'Probably not,' said Banks. 'It's just that sometimes what we don't find is as important as what we do. Trouble is, we never really know until later. Anyway, I won't bother you any further tonight.'

'Inspector Stott said I'd have to identify the body,' Sir Geoffrey said. 'You'll make the arrangements?'

'Of course. Again, sir, my condolences.'

Sir Geoffrey nodded, then he turned back to his wife. Like a butler, Banks was dismissed.

SIX

What with one thing and another, it was after two in the morning when Banks parked the dark-blue Cavalier he had finally bought to replace his clapped-out Cortina in front of his house. After Hawthorn Close, it was good to be back in the normal world of semis with postage-stamp gardens, Fiestas and Astras parked in the street.

The first thing he did was tiptoe upstairs to check on Tracy. It was foolish, he knew, but after seeing Deborah Harrison's body, he felt the need to see his own daughter alive and breathing.

The amber glow from the street-lamp outside her window lit the faint outline of Tracy's sleeping figure. Every so often, she would turn and give a little sigh, as if she were dreaming. Softly, Banks closed her door again and went back downstairs to the living-room, careful to bypass the creaky third stair from the top. Despite the late hour, he didn't feel at all tired.

He turned on the shaded table lamp and poured himself a stiff Laphroaig, hoping to put the image of Deborah Harrison spread-eagled in the graveyard out of his mind.

After five minutes, Banks hadn't succeeded in getting his mind off the subject. Music would help. 'Music alone with sudden charms can bind / The wand'ring sense, and calm the troubled mind,' as Congreve had said. Surely it wouldn't wake Sandra or Tracy if he played a classical CD quietly?

He flipped through his quickly growing collection – he was sure that they multiplied overnight – and settled finally on Richard Strauss's *Four Last Songs*.

In the middle of the second song, 'September,' when Gundula Janowitz's crystalline soprano was soaring away with the melody, Banks topped up his Laphroaig and lit a cigarette.

Before he had taken more than three or four drags, the door opened and Tracy popped her head around.

'What are you doing up?' Banks whispered.

Tracy rubbed her eyes and walked into the room. She was wearing a long, sloppy nightshirt with a picture of a giant panda on the front. Though she was seventeen, it made her look like a little girl.

'I thought I heard someone in my room,' Tracy muttered. 'I couldn't get back to sleep so I came down for some milk. Oh, Dad! You're smoking again.'

Banks put his finger to his lips. 'Shhh! Your mother.' He looked at the cigarette guiltily. 'So I am.'

'And you promised.'

'I never did.' Banks hung his head in shame. There was nothing like a teenage daughter to make you feel guilty about your bad habits, especially with all the anti-smoking propaganda they were brainwashed with at school these days.

'You did, too.' Tracy came closer. 'Is something wrong? Is that why you're up so late smoking and drinking?'

She sat on the arm of the sofa and looked at him, sleep-filled eyes full of concern, long blonde hair straggling over her narrow shoulders. Banks's son, Brian, who was away studying architecture in Portsmouth, took after his father, but Tracy took after her mother.

They had come a long way since the bitter arguments over her first boyfriend, long since dumped, and too many late nights over the summer. Now Tracy had determined not to have a boyfriend at all this year, but to put all her efforts into getting good A-level results so she could go to university, where she wanted to study history. Banks couldn't help but approve. As he looked at her perching so frail and vulnerable on the edge of the sofa his heart swelled with pride in her, and with fear for her.

'No,' he said, getting up and patting her head. 'There's nothing wrong. I'm just an old fool set in his ways, that's all. Shall I make us both some cocoa?'

Tracy nodded, then yawned and stretched her arms high in the air.

Banks smiled. Gundula Janowitz sang Hermann Hesse's words. Banks had listened to the songs so many times, he knew the translation by heart:

> The day has tired me,
> and my spirits yearn
> for the starry night
> to gather them up
> like a tired child.

You can say that again, thought Banks. He looked back at Tracy as he walked to the kitchen. She was examining the small-print CD liner notes with squinting eyes trying to make out the words.

She would find out soon enough what had happened to

Deborah Harrison, Banks thought. It would be all over town tomorrow. But not tonight. Tonight father and daughter would enjoy a quiet, innocent cup of cocoa in the middle of the night in their safe, warm house floating like an island in the fog.

2

ONE

Chief Constable Jeremiah Riddle was already pacing the lino when Banks arrived at his office early the next morning. Bald head shining like a new cricket ball freshly rubbed on the bowler's crotch, black eyes glowing like a Whitby jet, clean-shaven chin jutting out like the prow of a boat, uniform sharply creased, not a speck of fluff or cotton anywhere to be seen, and a poppy placed ostentatiously in his lapel, he looked alert, wide-awake and ready for anything.

Which was more than Banks looked, or felt for that matter. All told, he had got no more than about three hours' uneasy sleep, especially as an early telephone call from Ken Blackstone had woken him up. Though the fog was quickly turning to drizzle this morning, he had walked the mile to work simply to get the cobwebs out of his brain. He wasn't sure whether he had succeeded. It didn't help that his cold was getting worse, either, filling his head with damp cotton wool.

'Ah, Banks, about bloody time,' said Riddle.

Banks removed his headphones and switched off the Jimi Hendrix tape he had been listening to. The breakneck arpeggios of 'Pali Gap' were still ringing in his stuffed-up ears.

'And do you have to go around with those bloody

things stuck in your ears?' Riddle went on. 'Don't you know how silly you look?'

Banks knew a rhetorical question when he heard one.

'I suppose you're aware who the victim's father is?'

'Sir Geoffrey Harrison, sir. I talked to him last night.'

'In that case you'll realize how important this is. This . . . this . . . terrible tragedy.' Never at a loss for a cliché wasn't Jimmy Riddle, Banks reflected. Riddle slid his hand over his head and went on. 'I want a hundred per cent on this one, Banks. No. *Two* hundred per cent. Do you understand? No shirking. No dragging of feet.'

Banks nodded. 'Yes, sir.'

'Now what about this Bosnian fellow? Jurassic, is it?'

'Jelačić, sir. And he's Croatian.'

'Whatever. Think he's our man?'

'We'll certainly be talking to him. Ken Blackstone has just reported that Jelačić's known to the Leeds police. Drunk and disorderly, one charge of assault in a pub. And he didn't get home until after two this morning. They've got his prints, so we should be able to compare them if Vic gets anything from the vodka bottle.'

'Good.' Riddle grinned. 'That's the kind of thing I like to hear. I want a quick arrest on this one, Banks. Sire Geoffrey's a personal friend of mine. Do you understand?'

'Yes, sir.'

'Right. And take it easy on the family. I don't want you pestering them in their time of grief. Am I clear?'

'Yes, sir.'

Riddle straightened his uniform, which didn't need it, and brushed imaginary dandruff from his shoulders. Wishful thinking, Banks guessed. 'Now I'm off to give a press conference,' he said. 'Anything I ought to know to stop me looking a prize berk?'

Nothing could stop you looking like a prize berk, Banks thought. 'No, sir,' he said. 'But you might like to drop by the murder room and see if there's anything fresh come in.'

'I've already done that. What do you think I am, a bloody moron?'

Banks let the silence stretch.

Riddle kept pacing, though he seemed to have run out of things to say for the present. At last he headed for the door. 'Right, then. Remember what I said, Banks,' he said, pointing a finger. 'Results. Fast.'

Banks felt himself relax and breathe easier when Riddle had gone, like a Victorian lady when she takes her corsets off. He had read about 'Type A' personalities in a magazine article – all push and shove, ambition and self-importance, and bloody exhausting to be in the same room with.

Banks lit a cigarette, read the reports on his desk and looked at the *Dalesman* calendar on his wall. November showed the village of Muker, in Swaledale, a cluster of grey limestone buildings cupped in a valley of muted autumn colours. He walked over to the window where the early morning light was leaking through the cloud cover like dirty dishwater.

The market square, with its Norman church to his left, bank, shops and cafés opposite and Queen's Arms to the right, was a study in slate-grey, except for one bright red Honda parked by the weathered market cross. Banks watched a bent old lady hobble across the cobbles under a black umbrella. He checked his watch with the church tower clock: five to eight, time to gather his papers and head for the morning meeting.

DI Stott was already waiting and raring to go in the 'Boardroom,' so called because of its well-polished oval table, ten matching stiff-backed chairs and dark-burgundy wallpaper above the wainscoting.

Detective Constable Susan Gay arrived two minutes later. Her make-up almost hid the bags under her eyes, the gel made her short curly hair look as if it were still wet from the shower, and her subtle perfume brought a whiff of spring to the room.

Detective Sergeant Jim Hatchley, big and heavy, like a rugby prop-forward gone to seed, came in last. He hadn't freshened up. His face looked like a lump of dough with tufts of stubble sticking out of it, his eyes were bloodshot and his strawy hair uncombed. His navy-blue suit was creased and shiny.

'Okay,' said Banks, shuffling the papers in front of him, 'we've got two new pieces of information to deal with. I'd hesitate to call them leads, but you never know. First off, for what it's worth, one of our diuretically challenged constables found the missing underwear while nipping behind a handy yew to drain the dragon. They're with the rest of her clothing at the mortuary. The second item might be even more significant,' he went on. 'Some of you may already know that a Croatian refugee called Ive Jelačić was recently fired by Daniel Charters, vicar of St Mary's, and subsequently brought charges of sexual harassment against him. By the sound of it, this Jelačić's an unsavoury character. According to West Yorkshire CID, Mr Jelačić didn't get home until after two o'clock last night, plenty of time to get back from committing a murder in Eastvale, even in the fog. He said he'd been playing cards with some fellow countrymen at a friend's house.'

Hatchley grunted. 'These foreigners would lie as soon as look at you,' he said. 'Especially to cover up for one another.'

'West Yorkshire CID are already checking it out,' Banks went on, 'but I'm afraid Detective Sergeant Hatchley has, in his inimitable fashion, probably put his finger on the truth of the matter. So we'll take this alibi with a large pinch of salt. DI Blackstone said they'll sit on Jelačić until we get there. I think we'll let him sweat for a couple more hours.

'Now we don't have anything in from the lab yet, but from my observations of the scene, what we've got here looks like a sex murder. There was an *arranged* quality to it all. But I want to stress *looks like*. Right now, we just don't know enough. There are several other avenues we simply can't afford to overlook.' He counted them off on his fingers. 'School, family, Jelačić, boyfriends and the couple at the vicarage, for starters. Rebecca Charters lied to me last night when I asked where her husband had been at the time of the crime. She gave him a false alibi and I'd like to know why he needed it, especially given the recent scandal involving him. We also need to know a lot more about Deborah Harrison's life. Not just her movements yesterday, but her interests, her activities, her sex life, if she had one, and her past. We need to know what made her tick, what kind of person she was. Any questions?'

They all shook their heads.

'Good. Barry, I'd like you and Sergeant Hatchley to spend the morning going through the records of all known sex offenders in the county. You know the procedure. If anyone sounds likely, make enquiries. After that, ask around at some of the restaurants and cafés in the St Mary's area, places that might have been closed after eight or nine last night, when the uniforms did their house-to-house. You never know, our man might have stopped off for a cup of tea on his way to the graveyard.'

Stott nodded.

'And, I'd also like you to try and find out anything you can about Jelačić from records, immigration, wherever. Does he have form back home? Has he ever committed a sex offence of any kind there?'

Stott scribbled notes on his pad.

'Susan, I'd like you to team up with me and check out a few things closer to home. For a start we've got to find out exactly what Deborah's movements were yesterday, who saw her last. Okay?'

'Yes, sir.'

'So if there's nothing else,' Banks said, 'let's get on with it. Everyone check in with the murder room at regular intervals.'

Given their tasks, they drifted away. Except DC Susan Gay, who topped up her milky coffee and sat down again.

'Why me, sir?' she asked.

'Pardon?'

'Why am I teamed up with you on this? I'm only a DC. By rights it should—'

'Susan, whatever your rank, you're a good detective. You've proved that often enough. Think about it. Taking Jim Hatchley around to a girls' school, a vicarage and Sir Geoffrey Harrison's . . . It would be like letting a bull loose in a china shop.'

Susan's lips twitched in a smile. 'What exactly will we be doing?'

'Talking to the family, friends, teachers. Trying to find out if this isn't just the sex murder it seems, and if someone had a *reason* to want Deborah Harrison dead.'

'Are you going to check her parents' alibis?'

Banks paused for a moment, then said, 'Yes. Probably.'

'The chief constable won't like it, will he?'

'Won't like what?'

'Any of it. Us going around poking our noses into the Harrison family background.'

'Maybe not.'

'I mean, it's pretty common knowledge around the station that they're in the same funny-handshake brigade, sir. The chief constable and Sir Geoffrey, that is.'

'Oh, is it?'

'So rumour has it, sir.'

'And you're worried about your career.'

'Well, I've passed my sergeant's exam, as you know. I'm just waiting for an opening. I mean, I'm with you all the way, sir, but I wouldn't want to make enemies in the wrong places, not just at the moment.'

Banks smiled. 'Don't worry,' he said, 'it's my balls on the chopping-block, not yours. I'll cover you. My word on it.'

Susan smiled back. 'Well, that's the first time not having any balls has ever done me any good.'

TWO

When she woke up shortly after eight o'clock on Tuesday morning, Rebecca Charters felt the hammering pain behind her eyes that signalled another hangover.

It hadn't always been like this, she reminded herself. When she had married Daniel twelve years ago, he had been a dynamic young cleric. She had loved his passionate faith and his dedication just as she had loved his sense of humour and his joy in the sensual world. Love-making had always been a pleasure for both of them. Until recently.

She got up, put on her dressing-gown against the chill and walked over to the window. When they had first moved to St Mary's six years ago, her friends had all said how depressing and unhealthy it would be living in a graveyard. Just like the Brontës, darling, they said, and look what happened to them.

But Rebecca didn't find it at all depressing. She found it strangely comforting and peaceful to consider the worms seething at their work just below the overgrown surface. It put things in perspective. It also reminded her of that Marvell poem Patrick had quoted for her just on the brink of their affair, when things could have gone either way:

> But at my back I always hear
> Time's wingèd chariot hurrying near;
> And yonder all before us lie
> Deserts of vast eternity.
> Thy beauty shall no more be found;
> Nor, in thy marble vault, shall sound
> My echoing song; then worms shall try
> That long preserv'd virginity:
> And your quaint honour turn to dust;
> And into ashes all my lust.
> The grave's a fine and private place,
> But none I think do there embrace.

What an easy seduction it had been, after all. The poem worked. Marvell would have been proud of himself.

Rebecca pulled back the curtain. Some fog still drifted around the yew trunks and the heavy grey headstones, but the drizzle seemed to have settled in now. From her window, she could see uniformed policemen methodically searching the ground around the church in a grid pattern.

Deborah Harrison. She had often seen Deborah taking a

short cut through the churchyard; she had also seen her in church and at choir practice, too, before the trouble began.

Deborah's father, Sir Geoffrey, had deserted St Mary's at the first hint of a scandal. The school had stuck with Daniel, but Sir Geoffrey, to whom appearances were far more important than truth, had made a point of turning his back, taking his family and a number of other wealthy and influential members of the congregation with him. And St Mary's was the wealthiest parish in Eastvale. Had been. Now the coffers were emptying fast.

Rebecca rested her forehead against the cool glass and watched her breath mist up the window. She found herself doodling Patrick's name with her fingernail and felt the need for him burn in her loins. She hated herself for feeling this way. Patrick was ten years younger than she was, a mere twenty-six, but he was so ardent, so passionate, always talking so excitedly about life and poetry and love. Though she needed him, she hated her need; though she determined every day to call it off, she desired nothing more than to lose herself completely in him.

Like drinking, Patrick was an escape; she had enough self-knowledge to work that out, at any rate. An escape from the poisoned atmosphere at St Mary's, from what she and Daniel had become, and, as she admitted in her darkest moment, an escape from her own fears and suspicions.

Now this. It didn't make sense, she tried to convince herself. Daniel couldn't possibly be a murderer. Why would he want to murder someone as innocent as Deborah Harrison? Just because you feared a person might be guilty of one thing, did that mean he had to be guilty of something else, too?

As she watched the policemen in their capes and

wellingtons poke through the long grass, she had to face the facts: Daniel had come home only *after* she had gone to see the angel; he had gone out *before* she thought she heard the scream; she hadn't known where he was, and when he came back his shoes were muddy, with leaves and gravel stuck to their soles.

THREE

The mortuary was in the basement of Eastvale General Infirmary, an austere Victorian brick building with high draughty corridors and wards that Susan had always thought were guaranteed to make you ill if you weren't already.

The white-tiled post-mortem room, though, had recently been modernized, as if, she thought, the dead somehow deserved a healthier environment than the living.

Chilled by the cooling unit rather than by the wind from outside, it had two shiny metal tables with guttered edges and a long lab bench along one wall, with glass-fronted cabinets for specimen jars. Susan had never dared ask about the two jars that looked as if they contained human brains.

Dr Glendenning's assistants had already removed Deborah Harrison's body from its plastic bag, and she lay, clothed as she had been in the graveyard, on one of the tables.

It was nine o'clock, and the radio was tuned to *Wake up to Wogan*. 'Do we have to listen to that rubbish?' Banks asked.

'It's *normal*, Banks,' said Glendenning. 'That's why we have it on. Millions of people in houses all around the country will be listening to Wogan now. People who aren't just about to cut open the body of a sixteen-year-old girl. I suppose you'd like some fancy classical concert on Radio 3, wouldn't you? I can't say that the thought of performing a post-mortem to Elgar' *Enigma Variations* would do a hell of a lot for me.' Glendenning stuck a cigarette in the corner of his mouth and pulled on his surgical gloves.

Susan smiled. Banks looked at her and shrugged.

The girl on the slab wasn't a human being, Susan kept telling herself. She was just a piece of dead meat, like at the butcher's. She remembered June Walker, the butcher's daughter, from school in Sheffield, and recalled the peculiar smell that always seemed to emanate from her. Odd, she hadn't thought of June Walker in years.

The smell – stale and sharp, but sweet, too – was here, all right, but it was buried under layers of formaldehyde and cigarette smoke, for both Glendenning and Banks were smoking furiously. She didn't blame them. She had once seen a film on television in which an American woman cop rubbed some Vick's or something under her nose to mask the smell of a decomposing body. Susan didn't dare do such a thing herself for fear the others would laugh at her. After all, this was Yorkshire, not America.

Still, as she watched Glendenning cut and probe at the girl's clothing, then remove it for air-drying and storage, she almost wished she were a smoker. At least that smell was easier to wash away than the smell of death; which seemed to linger in her clothes and hair for days after.

Deborah's panties lay in a plastic bag on the lab bench. They weren't at all like the navy-blue knickers, the 'passion-killers,' that Susan had worn at school, but expensive, silky and rather sexy black panties. Maybe such things were *de rigueur* for St Mary's girls, Susan thought. Or had

Deborah been hoping to impress someone? They still didn't know if she'd had a boyfriend.

Her school blazer lay next to the panties in a separate bag, and beside that lay her satchel. Vic Manson, the fingerprints expert, had sent it back early that morning, saying he had found clear prints on one of the vodka bottles but only blurred partials on the smooth leather surface of the satchel. DI Stott had been through Deborah's blazer pockets and found only a purse with six pounds thirty-three pence in it, an old chewing-gum wrapper, her house keys, a cinema ticket stub and a half-eaten roll of Polo mints.

After one of his assistants had taken photographs, Glendenning examined the face, noting the pinpoint haemorrhages in the whites of the eyes, eyelids and skin of the cheeks. Then he examined the weal on the neck.

'As I said last night,' he began, 'it looks like a clear case of asphyxia by ligature strangulation. Look here.'

Banks and Susan bent over the body. Susan tried not to look into the eyes. Glendenning's probe indicated the discoloured weal around the front of the throat. 'Whoever did this was pretty strong,' he said. 'You can see how deeply the strap bit into the flesh. And I'd say our chappie was a good few inches taller than his victim. And she was tall for her age. Five foot six.' He turned to Susan. 'That's almost 168 centimetres, to the younger generation. See how the wound is deeper at the bottom, the way it would be if you were pulling a leather strap upwards?' He moved away and demonstrated on one of the assistants. 'See?' Banks and Susan nodded.

'Are you sure the satchel strap was the weapon?' Banks asked.

Glendenning nodded. He picked it up and held it out.

'You can see traces of blood on the edge here, where it broke the skin. We're having it typed, of course, but I'd put money on this being your weapon.'

Next, he set about removing the plastic bags that covered the hands. Gently – almost, Susan thought, like a manicurist – he held up each hand and peered at the fingernails. Deborah's nails had been quite long, Susan noticed, not the bitten-to-the-quick mess hers had been when she was at school.

When Glendenning got to the middle finger of her right hand, he murmured to himself, then took a shiny instrument from the tray and ran it under the top of the nail, calling to one of his assistants for a glassine envelope.

'What is it?' Banks asked. 'Did she put up a fight?'

'Looks like she got at least one good scratch in. With a bit of luck we'll be able to get DNA from this.'

Passing quickly over the chest and stomach, Glendenning next picked up a probe and turned his attention to the pubic region. Susan looked away; she didn't want to witness this indignity, and she didn't care what anyone said or thought of her.

But she couldn't shut out the sound of Glendenning's voice.

'Hmm. Interesting,' he said. 'No obvious signs of sexual interference. No bruising. No lacerations. Let's have a look behind.'

He flipped the body over; it slapped against the table like meat on a butcher's block. Susan heard her heart beating fast and loud during the silence that followed.

'No. Nothing,' Glendenning announced at last. 'At least nothing obvious. I'm waiting for the test results on the swabs but I'd bet you a pound to a penny they'll turn up nothing.'

Susan turned back to face the two of them. 'So she wasn't raped?' she asked.

'Doesn't look like it,' Glendenning answered. 'Of course, we won't know for sure until we've had a good look around inside. And in order to do that . . .' He picked up a large scalpel.

Glendenning bent over the body and started to make the Y incision from shoulders to pubes. He detoured around the tough tissue of the navel with a practised flick of the wrist.

'Right,' said Banks, turning to Susan. 'We'd better go.'

Glendenning looked up from the gaping incision and raised his eyebrows. 'Not staying for the rest of the show?'

'No time. We don't want to be late for school.'

Glendenning looked at the corpse and shook his head. 'Can't say I blame you. Some days I wish I'd stayed in bed.'

As they left Glendenning to sort through the inner organs of Deborah Harrison, Susan had never felt quite so grateful to Banks in her life. Next time they were in the Queen's Arms, she vowed she would buy him a pint. But she wouldn't tell him why.

3

ONE

St Mary's School wasn't exactly Castle Howard, but it
certainly looked impressive enough to be used as a
location in a BBC classic drama.

Banks and Susan turned through the high, wrought-
iron gates and drove along a winding driveway; sycamores
bordered both sides, laying down a carpet of rust and gold
leaves; double-winged seeds spun down like helicopter
blades in the drizzle.

Through the trees, they first glimpsed the imposing grey
stone building, with its central cupola, high windows and
columns flanking the front entrance. Statues stood on the
tops of the columns, against a frieze, and double stairs
curled out at the front like lobster claws.

St Mary's School for Girls, Banks had read, was
founded in 1823 on forty acres of woodland by the River
Swain. The main building, completed in 1773, had been
intended as a country house but had never been lived in.
Rumour had it that Lord Satterthwait, for whom the house
had been built, lost much of his fortune in an ill-advised
business venture abroad, along with the money of a
number of other county luminaries, and was forced to flee
the area in disgrace for America.

The grounds were quiet this morning, but a group of girls in maroon blazers saw Banks pull up and started whispering among themselves. The car was unmarked, but Banks and Susan were strangers, and by now everyone must know that Deborah Harrison had been murdered.

Banks asked one of the girls where they might find the head, and she directed him through the front door, right down to the back of the building, then along the last corridor to the right. Inside, the place was all high ornate ceilings and dark, polished wainscoting. Susan's footsteps echoed as they walked. It was certainly a far cry from the institutional gloom of Eastvale Comprehensive, or from Banks's old redbrick school in Peterborough, for that matter.

They walked along the narrow corridor, noting the gilt-framed paintings of past heads on the walls. Most of them were men. When they reached the door marked 'Dr JS Green: Principal,' Banks knocked sharply.

Expecting to be asked into an anteroom and vetted by a secretary first, Banks was surprised when he and Susan found themselves in the head's office. Like the rest of the building, it had a high ceiling with elaborate cornices, but there its ancient character ended.

The wainscoting, if there had been any, had been removed and the walls were papered in an attractive Laura Ashley print. A shaded electric light hung from the old chandelier fixture, and several gunmetal filing cabinets stood against the wall. The bay window dominated the room, its window seat scattered with cushions that matched the wallpaper. The view through the trees to the river, Banks noticed, was magnificent, even on a drizzly November morning. Across the river was St Mary's Park, with its pond, trees, benches and children's playground.

'What do you think?' Dr Green asked, after they had introduced themselves and shaken hands.

'Pardon?' said Banks.

She took their raincoats and hung them on a rack in the corner. 'I couldn't help but notice that you were "casing the joint" as they say,' she said.

'Hardly,' said Banks. 'That's what the bad guys do.'

She blushed slightly. 'Oh, dear. My gaffe. I suppose criminal parlance is not my forte.'

Banks smiled. 'Just as well. Anyway, it's very nice.'

The tall, elegant Dr Julia Green looked every bit as Laura Ashley as her walls. The skirt and waistcoat she wore over her white blouse were made of heavy cloth; earth colours dominated, browns and greens, mixed with the odd flash of muted pink or yellow, like wildflowers poking their way through the undergrowth.

Her ash-blonde hair lay neatly piled and curled on her head, with only one or two loose strands. She had a narrow face, high cheekbones and a small nose. There was also a remote, unattainable quality about her that intrigued Banks. She might be one of the pale and distant beauties, but there was no mistaking the sharp glint of intelligence in her apple-green eyes. Right now, they also looked red from crying.

'This is a terrible business,' she said. 'Though I suppose you have to deal with it all the time.'

'Not often,' said Banks. 'And you never get used to it.'

'Please sit down.'

Banks and Susan sat in the two chairs opposite the small, solid desk. Susan took her notebook out.

'I don't know how I can help you,' Dr Green went on, 'but I'll do my best.'

'Maybe you could start by telling us what kind of a girl Deborah was.'

She rested her hands on the desk, tapered fingers laced together. 'I can't tell you very much,' she said. 'Deborah is . . . was . . . a day-girl. Do you know how the system works?'

'I don't know much about public schools at all.'

'*Independent* school,' she corrected him. 'Public school sounds so Victorian, don't you think? Well, you see, we have a mix of day-girls and boarders. The actual balance changes slightly from year to year, but at the moment, we have 65 day-pupils and 286 boarding. When I say that Deborah was a day-girl I don't describe her status in any way, just note the simple fact that she came and went each day, so one didn't develop any special relationship with her.'

'Relationship?'

'Yes. Well, when you live in such close proximity to the pupils, you're bound to get to know more about them, aren't you?'

'In what way?'

'In any number of ways. Whether it be the crisis of Elizabeth's first period, Meredith's parents' divorce or Barbara's estrangement from her mother. These things can't help but come out from time to time with the boarding pupils.'

'So you'd soon find out who's a troublemaker, for example?'

'Yes. Not that we have any troublemakers. Nothing serious, anyway. We did catch one girl smoking marijuana in the dorm last year, and some years ago one of our upper-sixth girls got pregnant. But these are extremes, you understand, quite rare.'

'Have you ever had any inkling of widespread problems here?'

'Such as what?'

'Drugs, perhaps, or pornography.'

'Chief Inspector, this isn't a comprehensive, you know.'

'Perhaps not. But girls will be girls.'

'I don't know what you mean by that, but to answer your question, no, there's been nothing of that nature at St Mary's.'

'Do *you* live on the school grounds?'

Dr Green nodded. 'There's a small block of flats for members of staff – for some of us, anyway – and I live there.'

'Alone?'

'Yes. Alone.'

'So what can you tell me about Deborah Harrison?'

Dr Green shrugged. 'Just superficial things, really. She was a bright girl. Very intelligent. I don't think there's much doubt she would have ended up at Oxford or Cambridge, had she lived.'

'Where did her strengths lie?'

'She was something of an all-rounder, but she excelled in the sciences – maths and physics, in particular. She was also good at modern languages. She had just entered the lower sixth this year. The school offers twenty-three subjects at A-level. Deborah was taking four: mathematics, French, German and physics.'

'What about her personality?'

Dr Green leaned back and put her hands on the arms of her chair. 'Again, I can only be fairly superficial.'

'That's all right.'

'She always seemed cheerful and lively. You know, some girls can get very moody and withdrawn in the lower sixth – they go through a very difficult period in their lives – but Deborah seemed to be outgoing. She was an outstanding athlete. Swimming, tennis, running, field events. She was a good equestrian, too.'

'I understand she belonged to the chess club?'

'Yes. She was a fine player. A superb strategist.'

'You sound as if you play yourself.'

She smiled. 'Moderately well.'

'I'd appreciate it if you could provide me with a list of the other members.'

'Of course.' Dr Green searched through one of the filing cabinets and handed Banks a sheet of paper with ten names on it. Then she paused, scratched her cheek, and said, 'I must admit, Chief Inspector, the questions you're asking surprise me.'

'They do? Why?'

'Well, I know nothing of police work, of course, but I fail to understand why you should require *my* impressions of Deborah in order to apprehend the criminal who attacked and murdered her.'

'What kind of questions do you think I should be asking?'

She frowned. 'I don't know. About strangers in the area, that sort of thing.'

'Have you noticed any suspicious strangers hanging around the area lately?'

'No.'

Banks blew his nose. 'Sorry. Well, that covers that one, doesn't it? Now, what about Deborah's faults?'

'Faults?'

'Yes, was she mischievous, disobedient, dishonest, wilful?'

'No more than any other child of her age. Less than

most, actually.' She thought for a moment. 'No, I'd say if Deborah did have a fault it was that she tended to show off her abilities to some extent. She could sometimes make the other girls feel small, or awkward and clumsy. She had a tendency to belittle people.'

'Was she boastful?'

'Not at all. No, that's not what I mean. She never *boasted* about her abilities, she just used them to the full. She wasn't the kind to hide her light under a bushel. Half the time it was as if she didn't even realize she was so much brighter and more fortunate than many. She liked the way her quickness with figures impressed people, for example, so she would add up or multiply things in her head quicker than some of the other girls could do it with a calculator.'

'That's one good way to make enemies.' Banks remembered his own school maths reports: *Could do better than this; Harder work needed; Watch that arithmetic!*

'It was hardly serious,' Dr Green went on, shrugging. 'Simply a matter of girlish exuberance, a young woman taking full joy in her talents.' Her eyes sparkled for a moment. 'Have you forgotten what it was like to be young, to be popular, gifted?'

'I don't know that I was ever gifted or popular,' Banks said, with a sidelong glance at Susan, who was smiling down into her notebook. 'But I do remember what it was like to be young. I thought I would live forever.'

After the awkward silence that followed, Banks asked, 'Was Deborah popular with the other girls?'

'What do you mean?'

'She sounds like a right little madam to me, a proper pain in the neck. I was wondering how she got on with her classmates.'

'Really, Chief Inspector,' Dr Green said through tight lips. 'These were very minor faults I'm talking about. Mostly, Deborah was friendly, cheerful and helpful.'

'Was there any friend in particular?'

'Yes. Megan Preece. Her name's on the list I gave you.'

'I understand from Daniel Charters,' Banks went on, 'that there was some trouble with Ive Jelačić, the sexton.'

'Yes,' Julia Green rubbed her cheek. 'He'd been bothering the girls. Saying things, making lewd gestures, that sort of thing.'

'Had Deborah, in particular, complained about him?'

'I believe she had.'

'Did she continue going to the church after Mr Jelačić made his accusations against Daniel Charters? It was my impression that her father seemed more upset about what Charters had been accused of, rather than what Jelačić *did*.'

Julia Green paused for a moment, then said, 'Yes, yes he was. I don't understand it myself. The school stands one hundred per cent behind Father Charters, but Sir Geoffrey forbade Deborah from singing with the choir or attending any services.'

'Why do you think he did that?'

'I don't know. Some people are just . . . well, very funny about any hint of homosexuality in the ministry.'

'Did Deborah obey him?'

'As far as I know she did. I never saw her there, anyway.'

'Did Deborah keep any of her belongings here at school?'

'All the girls have desks.'

'No lockers or anything?'

She shook her head. 'Not the day-girls. They bring what they need from day to day, mostly.'

'Might we have a look?'

'Of course. We've cancelled classes for the day, so the room should be empty.'

She led them through a maze of high corridors to a small room. It wasn't like any classroom Banks had ever seen before, with its well-polished woodwork and nicely spaced desks.

'This one,' said Dr Green, pointing to a desk.

Banks lifted the hinged flap. He hadn't expected much – school desks are hardly the most private of places – but he was disappointed by how little there was: a couple of school exercise books, a computer magazine, textbooks, pens and pencils. There was also a tattered paperback by Jeffrey Archer. Deborah's intelligence obviously hadn't stretched as far as her literary taste.

Under the flap, Deborah had taped a photograph of a scruffy pop star Banks didn't recognize.

Dr Green saw it and said, with a smile, 'We discourage such things, but what can you do?'

Banks nodded. Then he examined the desk surface to see if Deborah had carved any initials, the way he had at school. Again, nothing. Strongly discouraged, no doubt.

'Thanks,' he said to Dr Green. 'Can we have a word with Megan Preece now? Is she here?'

Dr Green nodded. After stopping back at her office for their raincoats and her umbrella, she led them outside.

'Where are we going?' Banks said.

'The school infirmary. That's where Megan is. I'm afraid she had rather a nasty turn when I broke the news in assembly this morning.'

TWO

The brick shattered the vicarage window at nine-thirty that morning, waking Rebecca from the uneasy doze she had slipped into after taking three aspirin and a glass of water.

At first she lay there terrified, fearing that someone had broken in. Then, slowly, so as not to make the bedsprings creak, she sat up, ears pricked for any sounds. But nothing came.

She put on her dressing-gown and looked out of the bedroom window. Nothing but the drizzle on the trees and graves, and policemen in capes searching the grounds. She tiptoed downstairs, and when she got to the front room she saw the damage.

Shards of glass lay all over the floor, and some had even got as far as the sofa and coffee-table. The brick had clearly been thrown from the river path, beyond the small garden, an area that was unguarded because it didn't provide access to the graveyard.

The brick had bounced off the coffee-table and ended up in the far corner by the sideboard. It had a piece of paper wrapped around it, fixed by a rubber band. Slowly, Rebecca bent, picked up the brick and unfolded the paper:

Once you let the devil into your heart he will corrupt every cell in your body and this is what has happened it is clear. You must confess your sins. It is the only way. Or else we must take things into our own hands.

Someone knocked at the back door. Crumpling the note in her pocket, Rebecca gathered her dressing-gown around her and went to see who it was.

'Is everything all right, ma'am?' asked one of the uniformed constables who had been searching the grave-yard. 'I thought I heard breaking glass.'

'You did,' Rebecca said. 'But everything's fine. Just a little domestic accident.'

'Are you sure?'

'Yes.' Rebecca started closing the door on him. 'Thank you, everything's fine.' When she had shut the door she leaned her back against it and listened. In a few seconds, she heard his footsteps going along the path.

She took out a dustpan and broom and busied herself sweeping up the glass, wondering what she could use to cover the broken window before she caught a chill and died. Maybe that would be best for everyone, she thought. It would be very fitting, too. Hadn't Emily Brontë died after catching a chill at her brother's funeral? But no. She wasn't going to give the miserable, mean-spirited bastards the satisfaction.

Just as she was trying to tape up a piece of cardboard over the window, the phone rang.

'Can you talk?' the familiar voice asked.

'Patrick. Yes. Yes, I can.'

'We've been given the day off, pupils and staff. That terrible business with the girl. It must have been especially awful for you. How are you bearing up?'

'Oh, not bad, I suppose.'

'Is Daniel . . .?'

'He's out. Meeting in York. Said he couldn't get out of it.'

'Could we see one another? I could come over.'

'I don't know,' Rebecca said, feeling herself flush with desire like a silly schoolgirl as she spoke. 'No, I don't think we should. Not the way things are around here.'

'But I want you.'

Rebecca put her hand over the mouthpiece and took a deep breath.

'Don't you want me?' he went on.

'Of course I want you, Patrick. You know I do. It's just . . . there's police all over the place.'

'We could go for a drive.'

Rebecca paused and looked around her. She couldn't stay here, not with this mess, not after the threatening note; she would go insane. And she couldn't deal with the police, either. On the other hand, the very thought of Patrick made her tingle. God, how she hated herself, hated the way her body could so easily betray her morality and her good intentions, how her defective conscience found ways of rationalizing it all.

'All right,' she said. 'But you mustn't come here. I mean it about the police. We shouldn't be seen together.'

'I'll pick you up at the—'

'No. Let's meet at the hotel.' She looked at her watch. 'There's a bus at ten-fifteen.'

'All right. I'll be waiting for you.'

THREE

'These are the dormitories for the boarding pupils,' Dr Green pointed out as they walked through the school grounds. The two large buildings ahead were of far more recent construction than the main school building, red-brick for the most part, with some stone at their bases, functional rather than aesthetically pleasing. 'As I said earlier, we have 286 boarders. They have showers, central heating, all the comforts the modern child requires. You'll also notice we have installed a number of lamps along all the major pathways. They're kept on until ten o'clock every night, by which time all the girls are expected to be in bed. This isn't Lowood or Dotheboys, you realize. Parents spend a lot of money to send their children here.'

'Television?'

She smiled. 'Yes, that too.'

'What's that building over there?' Banks pointed through the trees to a three-storey rectangular building that seemed to be made of some sort of prefabricated concrete the colour of porridge.

'That's the staff residence, I'm afraid,' said Dr Green. 'Ugly, isn't it? Actually, it's quite nice inside. The flats are quite spacious: living-room, bedroom, storage heaters. Luxury.'

'Who lives there, apart from you?'

'At the moment, six of the flats are occupied. It all depends. We have thirty members of staff, a very good ratio, and some of our teachers live in or near town. The flats are essentially for single members of staff who have recently moved into the area, or, as in my case, single teachers who want to maintain close contact with the school.' She tilted her umbrella and gave Banks a chal-lenging glance from under the rim. 'You asked me rather impertinently not so long ago whether I lived alone. The school is my life, Chief Inspector. I have neither the incli-nation nor the time for anyone or anything else.'

Banks nodded. Then he sneezed. Susan blessed him.

'Here we are,' Dr Green went on, stepping under the porch of the dormitory and lowering her umbrella. She shook it carefully before rolling it up. 'The infirmary is on the ground floor. We have one full-time nurse on staff and a local doctor on call.'

They walked down the hall and entered the infirmary.

It smelled of disinfectant. After a brief word with the nurse, Dr Green directed Banks and Susan towards a row of curtained cubicles, in one of which Megan Preece lay on a narrow bed.

'Megan's fine, nurse says,' Dr Green whispered. 'But she's had a terrible shock and she's been given a mild tranquilliser, so please go slowly.'

Banks nodded. There clearly wasn't room for all of them in the cubicle, yet Dr Green seemed to want to stay.

'It's all right,' Banks said, ushering Susan to Megan's bedside chair. 'We'll find our way out when we've finished.'

Dr Green stood for a moment and frowned, then she nodded, turned on her heel and clicked away down the corridor.

When Banks found a chair for himself, Susan was already talking to Megan, reassuring her that everything would be all right. From what Banks could see of the head poking above the grey blanket, Megan was a slight, thin girl of about Deborah Harrison's age, with dark curly hair and a dark complexion.

But Megan's features lacked whatever cohesion or symmetry it took to make her conventionally pretty, unlike her friend Deborah, who had been beautiful in that lissom, blonde, athletic sort of way. Megan's nose was a little too big, and slightly crooked; her lips were too thin, and her mouth was too small for her teeth. But her big, serious earth-brown eyes were striking; they seemed to capture you at first glance and draw you to her.

Banks introduced himself, noting that Megan seemed comfortable enough in the presence of a male policeman, and said he wanted to ask her a few questions about Deborah. Megan nodded, eyes turning a little glassy at the mention of her friend's name.

'Were you very close friends?' he began.

She nodded. 'We're both day-girls and we've known each other for years. We both live in the same area.'

'I thought you must be boarding,' said Banks. 'Why aren't you at home?'

'I had a dizzy spell at assembly, then I . . . I got all upset. Nurse says I should rest here for a while, then I can go home at lunchtime. There'll be nobody there, anyway. Mummy's away in America and Daddy's at work.'

'I see. Now can you tell me what happened yesterday after the chess club. Go as slowly as you want, there's no hurry.'

Megan chewed her lower lip, then began, 'Well, when we'd put all the boards and pieces away in the cupboard and made sure the room was tidy, we left the school—'

'Was this the main building?'

'Yes. We hold the chess club in one of the upstairs classrooms.'

'What time?'

'Just before six o'clock.'

'How many attended last night?'

'Only eight. Lesley and Carol are doing a play with the theatre department, so they had rehearsals. The others are all boarders.'

'I see. Was there anyone else around?'

'A few people, coming and going, as usual. The school is always well lit and there are always people around.'

'Okay. Go on.'

'Well, we walked down the drive to Kendal Road. There's only one main gate, you see. The school's sur-rounded by woods, and there's the river on the west side. It was so foggy we could hardly see the trees around us. I must admit I was getting a bit scared, but Debs seemed to be enjoying herself.'

'What do you mean?'

'Oh, she liked things like that. Spooky things. She liked to tell ghost stories in graveyards, just for fun.'

'Do you know if she ever went inside the Inchcliffe Mausoleum?'

'She never said anything to me about it if she did.'

'Okay. Go on.'

'We crossed the road. I live on St Mary's Hill, behind the shops, so Debs and I always said goodbye at the bridge.' She put her hand over her eyes.

'Take it easy,' Susan said. 'Take your time.' When Banks looked down, he noticed that Megan was gripping Susan's hand at the side of the bed.

Megan took a deep breath and went on. 'That's all,' she said. 'We said goodbye. Debs was running backwards, just showing off, like, then she disappeared into the fog.' She frowned.

'Was there something else?' Banks asked. 'Did you notice anyone else around?'

'Well, like I said, it was so foggy you couldn't really see more than a few feet, but I saw a shape behind her. I remember thinking at the time there was something odd about it, but I put it down to the way Debs had been scaring me with her stories of ghosts taking shape from the fog.'

'You mean you thought you were imagining it?'

'Yes. Seeing things. But I know I wasn't, if that makes any sense.'

'You're doing fine, Megan. What kind of shape was it?'

'It was a man's shape. A tall man.'

'What was he doing?'

'Nothing. He was just standing on the bridge looking down the river towards the town.' She paused and her eyes lit up. 'That's it. That's what was strange. He was looking over the bridge towards the town, but he couldn't possibly see anything, could he, because of the fog. So why was he standing there?'

'Did you think that at the time?'

'No. It just came to me.'

'Did you see what he looked like?'

'Not really, because of the fog. I mean, he was like a silhouette, a dark figure. His features weren't clear, and he was in profile. He did have a bit of a big nose, though.'

'Could you see what he was wearing?'

'An anorak, I think. A bright colour. Orange or red, maybe.'

'Did you see him approach Deborah?'

'No. He was just behind her. I don't think she'd seen him because she was still running backwards and waving goodbye. I remember thinking if she wasn't careful she'd bump into him and that would give her a shock, but I really didn't think much of it. I mean, it wasn't the only person we'd seen.'

'Who else did you see?'

'Just ordinary people, you know, crossing the road and such. I mean, life goes on, doesn't it? Just because it's foggy you can't stop doing everything, can you?'

'That's true,' said Banks. 'Can you remember anything else?'

Megan squeezed her eyes shut. 'I think he had dark hair,' she said. 'Then I turned away and went home. I never thought anything of it. Until . . . until this morning, when I heard . . . I should have known something was going to happen, shouldn't I?'

'How could you?'

'I just should. Poor Debs. It could have been me. It *should* have been me.'

'Don't be silly, Megan.'

'But it's true! Debs was so good, so wonderful and pretty and talented. And just look at me. I'm nothing. I'm not pretty. She should have lived. I'm the one who should have died. It's not fair. Why does God always take the best?'

'I don't know the answer to that,' Banks replied softly. 'But I do know that *every* life is important, every life has its value, and *nobody* has the right to decide who lives and who dies.'

'Only God.'

'Only God,' Banks repeated, and blew his nose in the ensuing silence.

Megan took a tissue from the box on the table beside her and wiped her eyes. 'I must look a sight,' she said.

Banks smiled. 'Just like me first thing in the morning,' he said. 'Now, when we found Deborah, she had about six pounds in her purse. Did she ever have a lot of money to flash around?'

'Money? No. None of us ever carried more than a few pounds.'

'Do you know if she kept anything valuable in her satchel?'

Megan frowned. 'No. Just the usual stuff. Exercise books, text-books, that sort of thing.'

'Did she say if she was intending to meet anyone after the chess club or go anywhere else before she went home?'

'No. As far as I know, she was going straight home.'

'Can you tell us anything else about her?'

'Like what?'

'You were her best friend, weren't you?'

'Yes.'

'Did you ever fall out?'

'Sometimes.'

'Why?'

'Nothing, really. Maybe Debs would tease me about a lad she thought I liked, or something, or about not being good at arithmetic, and I'd get mad. But it wouldn't last long.'

'Is that all?'

'Yes. She can be quite a tease, can Debs. She gets her little needle in where she knows it hurts and just keeps pushing.' She put her hand to her mouth. 'Oh, I didn't mean that to sound as bad as it did, honest I didn't. All I mean is that she had an eye for a weakness and she could be a bit nasty about it. It was never anything serious.'

'Do you know if anything had been bothering her lately?'

'I don't think so. She'd been a bit moody, that's all.'

'Since when?'

'The beginning of term.'

'Did she say why?'

'No. We have a lot on our minds. A lot of work. And she's been moody before.'

'She didn't mention any problems; anything that might have been worrying her?'

'No.'

'Did she have any enemies, anyone who might have wanted to harm her?'

'No. Everyone loved Debs. It must have been a stranger.'

'Did she ever mention Mr Jelačić, the sexton at St Mary's?'

'The man who got fired?'

'That's the one.'

'She said he was gross, always sticking his tongue out and licking his lips when she went past.'

'Did he ever bother you?'

'I never went in the churchyard. I live this side of the river, over Kendal Road. It was a short cut for Debs.'

'Are you sure Deborah didn't have any other problems, any worries? Maybe at home?'

'No. She didn't complain about anything in particular. Only the usual stuff. Too much homework. That sort of thing.'

Banks realized that Deborah Harrison would probably have fewer practical causes for concern than his own daughter, Tracy, who, at one time anyway, had been constantly moaning about some new style of jacket or jeans she just had to have because everyone else was wearing it, and the Doc Martens that were just *essential* these days.

Banks had been like that himself, and he gave Tracy the same answer his mother and father gave him when they bought him a pair of heavy workboots for school instead of the thin-soled winkle-pickers he had asked for. 'We can't afford it. You'll just have to make do. These will last a lot longer.'

But Deborah Harrison had wanted for nothing, at least nothing that had a monetary value.

'What about boyfriends?' Banks asked.

Megan blushed. 'We don't have time, not in the lower sixth. And Debs was always involved in some school event: equestrian, sports or quizzes or whatever.'

'So she didn't have a boyfriend?'

'I'm not saying she *never* had one.'

'When was the last one?'

'In the summer.'

'What was his name?'

'She told me his name was John, that's all. They didn't go out together for long. She said he was really cool but too thick, so she chucked him.'

'Did she tell you anything else about him?'

Megan blushed. 'No.'

'Are you sure?'

'Yes. That's all I know. His name was John and he was a thickie.'

'Where did she meet him?'

'I don't know. She didn't say. I was away in America all summer with my parents, so I didn't see her until school started. By then she'd already chucked him.'

'Was he her first boyfriend?'

'I don't think so, but there was never anyone serious.'

'How do you know?'

'She would have told me.'

'Does she tell you everything?'

Megan considered the question seriously for a moment or so, then said, 'No, I don't think so. She can be secretive, can Debs. But she'd tell me if she had a boyfriend. Or I'd just *know*.'

'Was she being secretive about anything recently?'

Megan frowned. 'Yes, she was. I was getting fed up of it.'

'Did she tell you anything about it?'

'No. It wouldn't be a secret then, would it?'

'Did she tell you who or what it concerned?'

Megan shook her head. 'No.'

'Did she say *anything* about it?'

'Just that she thought it was time to tell someone, and

then to watch what happened when the sh—. Just to see what happened.'

'When did she tell you this?'

'Just as she was leaving, on the bridge.'

'While she was running backwards?'

'Yes. It's . . . it was the last thing she said.' Her eyes filled with tears. 'I'm tired.'

'All right,' said Banks. 'I'm sorry, Megan. You're doing really well. I'll try not to be much longer. But you must realize how important it is. If it was a secret about some-body who didn't want it known . . . And if that somebody knew that Deborah knew . . . Do you see what I mean?'

Megan nodded.

'How long had she been talking about this secret?'

'Since the beginning of term.'

'That's quite a long time.'

'Yes. She'd let it drop for a week or two, then bring it up again.'

'Would she have told anyone else?'

'No. I'm her *best* friend.'

'Is there anything else you can tell us, Megan? Anything at all.'

Megan shook her head. 'I don't think so.'

Banks and Susan stood up. 'Get some rest now,' Banks said. 'And believe me, we'll be doing our best to find out who did this.'

They said goodbye to the nurse, picked up their rain-coats and headed out into the drizzle.

'What did you think?' Banks asked Susan as they walked back to the car.

'About Megan? I think she told us pretty much all she knew.'

'Notice the way she blushed and turned her eyes away

when I pushed her about the boyfriend? I'd say there's more to that relationship than she's told us.'

'Well, sir,' said Susan, 'from my experience I'd say Deborah probably said he had his uses but he was thick.'

'You think Deborah might have slept with this John?'

'She might have, but that's not what I mean. What I mean is, she'd say that, or hint that she had, the way kids do. It doesn't mean they actually *did* anything.'

'And Megan was embarrassed by it?'

'Yes. I'd guess Megan is a bit shy around boys.'

'Would you agree she was the ugly one in that relationship?'

'I wouldn't put it quite that way, sir.'

Banks smiled. 'I'm sorry. It must be something to do with being on school grounds again. It takes me back. But when you were a teenager and you met two girls, one of them was bound to be the ugly one.'

'And when you met two boys, one of them was certain to be a drip and the other an octopus. If you were really lucky, you got a combination of the two.'

Banks laughed.

'I'm sorry, sir,' Susan went on, 'I don't get your point. Surely you're not suggesting that Megan Preece had anything to do with Deborah's murder?'

'No. Of course not. Just thinking out loud, is all.'

They got in the unmarked police car. When it started up, Vaughan Williams's *Suite for Viola and Orchestra* was playing on the radio: the beautiful, melancholy 'Ballad.' It suited the falling leaves and the November drizzle perfectly, Banks thought.

'I'm just trying to understand the relationship so that I can understand the way Deborah related to people,' he said. 'The way I see it is that Megan was the less attractive of the two friends. That would probably make her adoring and resentful in equal measures. She knew she was over-shadowed and outclassed by Deborah's looks and talent, and for the most part she was probably content to bask in the glory of being the chosen one, best friend of the goddess. Are you with me so far?'

'Yes, sir. Megan was the kind of friend who could only make Deborah look even better.'

'Right. But it also sounded as if Deborah could twist the knife, too, could be cruel. If she could annoy her best friend the way she did, then she could have angered a more dangerous enemy, don't you think?'

'It's possible, sir. But a bit far-fetched, if you don't mind me saying so. I still say we're looking for a stranger. And from what we know already, that stranger on the bridge could have been Ive Jelačić.'

'True,' said Banks. 'It could also have been a figment of Megan's imagination, at least in part. But we'll sort out Mr Jelačić later. He's not going anywhere. Ken Blackstone's got him under surveillance. What do you think about the secret?'

'Not much. A lot of schoolgirls are like that. As Megan said, it probably didn't mean anything.'

'Not to her, perhaps. But maybe to someone else. Look, isn't that . . .' He pointed.

As they were turning left onto North Market Street, Banks noticed a woman in a long navy raincoat standing at the bus-stop over the road.

'Isn't it who?' Susan asked.

'Oh, I forgot. You haven't met her. Rebecca Charters, the vicar's wife. I'm sure it was her. I wonder where she's going?'

'Curiouser and curiouser,' said Susan.

4

ONE

'**Well, sir,**' said Sergeant Hatchley, looking at his watch. 'Don't you think we might as well have a spot of lunch?'

Barry Stott sighed. 'Oh, all right. Come on.'

This was the detective inspector's first major case after his promotion and transfer, and he intended to make the most of it. The only thorn in the ointment was this idle, thick lump of Yorkshire blubber beside him: Detective Sergeant Hatchley.

Stott would have preferred DC Susan Gay. Not because she was prettier than Hatchley – he didn't find her attractive in that way – but because she was smarter, keener and a lot less trouble.

Like now. Left to himself, Stott would have skipped lunch, or bought a take-away from one of the cafés on North Market Street. The morning had been a waste of time; they had found no leads in the sex offender files, and all Stott could find out from immigration about Jelačić was that he was an engineer from Split, who had come to England two years ago. And since then, he had worked at a variety of odd jobs, never lasting long in any one place. Short of going to Croatia himself, Stott thought, it didn't look as if it would be an easy task getting hold of a criminal record, if there was one.

At least out there, near the crime scene, he felt he had

a good chance of scoring some success. *Somebody* had to have noticed a stranger in the area, fog or no fog. Or a car parked where it shouldn't be. St Mary's was, after all, an upper-crust area, and people who could afford to live there were very wary of strangers. And Stott was sure that a stranger had murdered Deborah Harrison.

They were standing in the rain outside the Nag's Head at the north-west corner of Kendal Road and North Market Street, diagonally across from St Mary's Church, and Stott was ready to do just about anything to shut Hatchley up.

It wasn't the kind of pub you'd expect in such a wealthy area, Stott thought: no thick carpet, polished brass and gleaming wood, pot of mulled wine heating on the bar. In fact, it looked distinctly shabby. He guessed it was probably a traveller's pub, being situated at such an important junction. In one form or another, Kendal Road ran all the way from the Lake District to the east coast and Market Street was a major north-south route. The locals would have their own tasteful pubs hidden away in the residential streets. Either that or they drove out to the country pubs.

There were about six people in the lounge bar. Stott noted with distaste that the room smelled of smoke and beer. This certainly wasn't his kind of pub, if there was such a place. He far preferred churches. Pubs, as far as Stott was concerned, were simply breeding grounds for trouble.

Pubs were where fights started – and he had a couple of scars from his beat days to prove that – they were where crooked deals took place, dodgy goods traded hands, places where drugs were openly sold, where prostitutes plied their filthy trade, spreading disease and misery. Close all the pubs and you'd force the criminals into the open, right into the waiting arms of the police. At least that was what DI Barry Stott thought as he turned up his nose in the Nag's Head that lunch-time.

Sergeant Hatchley, on the other hand, looked quite at home. He rubbed his ham-like hands together and said, 'Ah, this is better. Nowt like a bit of pub grub to take away the chill, don't you think, sir?'

'Let's make it quick, Sergeant.'

'Yes, sir. Alf! Over here, mate. Let's have a bit of service. A person could die of thirst.'

If there were a landlord Hatchley didn't know by name in all of the Eastvale – nay, all of Swainsdale – Stott would have been surprised.

When Alf finally turned up, Stott waited while he and Hatchley exchanged a few pleasantries, then ordered a ham and cheese sandwich and a cup of tea. Alf raised his eyebrows but said nothing.

'I'll have one of those bloody great big Yorkshire puddings full of roast beef, peas and gravy,' said Hatchley. 'And a pint of bitter, of course.'

This seemed to please Alf more.

Pint in hand, Hatchley marched over to a table by the window. Through the streaked glass, they could see the rain-darkened trees in the park and the walls of St Mary's church across the intersection, square tower poking out above the trees.

The drizzle hadn't kept the ghouls away. Here and there along the six-foot stone wall, people would jump up every now and then and hold themselves up by the finger-tips for a glimpse into the graveyard.

A group of about ten people stood by the Kendal Road entrance. Journalists. One of them, a woman, stood talking into a microphone and looking into a video camera wrapped in a black plastic bag to protect it from the rain. Someone else held a bright light over her head. Yorkshire Television, Stott thought. Or BBC North. And newspaper reporters. Pretty soon they'd be doing re-enactments for *Crimewatch*. Banks was right; the vultures had come.

'We haven't had much of a chance to get to know one another since you got here, have we, sir?' said Hatchley, lighting a cigarette. 'And I always find it helps to know a bit about one another if you're going to work together, don't you?'

'I suppose so,' said Stott, inwardly grimacing, trying to sit downwind of the drifting smoke. It didn't work. He thought it must be one of those laws, like Sod's and Murphy's: wherever a non-smoker sat, the smoke was going to come his way, no matter which way the draught was blowing.

'Where are you from, sir?' Hatchley asked.

'Spalding, Lincolnshire.'

'I'd never have guessed it. Not from the accent, like.'

'We moved away when I was just a boy.'

'Where?'

'All over the place. Cyprus, Germany. My father was in the army.' Stott remembered the misery of each move. It seemed that as soon as he had made friends anywhere, he had to abandon them and start all over again. His child-hood had consisted of a never-ending succession of new groups of strangers to whom he had to prove himself. Cruel strangers with their own initiation rights, just wait-ing to humiliate him. He remembered the beatings, the name-calling, the loneliness.

'A squaddie, eh?'

'Major, actually.'

'Pretty high up, then?' Hatchley swigged some beer. 'Where does he live now?'

'Worthing. He retired a few years ago.'

'Not a dishonourable discharge, I hope, sir.'

'No.'

'Look, sir,' said Hatchley, 'I've been wondering about this here inspector's exam. I've been thinking of giving it a go, like. Is it easy?'

Stott shook his head. All promotional exams were tough and involved several stages, from the multi-choice law test and the role-playing scenarios to the final oral in front of an assistant chief constable and a chief super-intendent. How Hatchley had even passed the sergeant's exam was a mystery to Stott.

'Good luck,' he muttered as a pasty-faced young woman delivered their food and Stott's pot of tea, which was actually just a pot of lukewarm water and a teabag on a string to dunk in it. And they were stingy with the ham, too. 'About one in four get through,' he added.

How old was Hatchley? he wondered. He couldn't be older than his mid-thirties. Maybe five or six years older than Stott himself. And just look at him: unfit, a bulky man with hair like straw, piggy eyes, freckles spattered across his fleshy nose, tobacco-stained teeth. He also seemed to own only one suit – shiny and wrinkled – and there were egg stains on his tie. Stott could hardly imagine Hatchley going up before the chief for his formal promotion dressed like that.

Stott prided himself on his dress. He had five suits – two grey, two navy blue and one brown herring-bone – and he wore them in rotation. If it's Thursday, it must be her-ring-bone. He also wore his father's old striped regimental tie and, usually, a crisply laundered white shirt with a starched collar.

He always made sure that he was clean shaven and that

his hair was neatly parted on the left and combed diagonally across his skull on each side, then fixed in place with spray or cream if need be. He knew that the way his ears stuck out still made him look odd, especially with his glasses hooked over them, just as they had when he was a young boy, and that people called him names behind his back. There was an operation you could have for sticking-out ears these days, he had heard. Maybe if it wasn't too late he'd have his ears done soon. A freakish appearance could, after all, be detrimental to one's career path. And Barry Stott felt destined for the chief constable's office.

Hatchley tucked into his Yorkie with great relish, adding a gravy stain to the egg on his tie. When he had finished, he lit another cigarette, inhaled deeply and blew out the smoke with a sigh of such deep satisfaction as Stott had never encountered before over a mere physical function – and an unpleasant one at that. One of nature's true primitives, Sergeant Hatchley.

'We'd better be getting along, Sergeant,' he said, pushing his plate aside and standing up.

'Can't I finish my fag first, sir? Best part of the meal the cigarette after, if you know what I mean.' He winked.

Stott felt himself flush. 'You can smoke it outside,' he said rather harshly.

Hatchley shrugged, slurped down the rest of his pint, then followed Stott towards the door.

'Bye, Alf,' he said on the way to the door. 'I hope our lads didn't catch you serving drinks after hours last night.'

'What lads?' said Alf.

Hatchley turned and walked towards the bar. 'Police. Didn't they come and ask you some questions last night? Whether you'd seen any strangers, that sort of thing?'

Alf shook his head. 'Nah. Nobody in last night. I shut up at ten o'clock. Filthy weather.'

By the time Stott got to the bar, Hatchley seemed to have magically acquired another pint, and his cigarette had grown back to its original length.

Stott swallowed his anger.

'Were you open earlier?' Hatchley asked.

Alf snorted. 'Aye, for what it were worth.'

'Any strangers?'

'We get a lot of strangers,' he said. 'You know, commercial travellers and the like. Tourists. Ramblers.'

'Aye, I know that,' said Hatchley. 'But how about yesterday, late afternoon, early evening?'

'Nah. Weather were too bad for driving.'

'Anyone at all?'

Alf scratched his stubbly cheek. 'One bloke. He had nobbut two pints and a whisky and left. That were it.'

'A regular?'

'Nah. Don't have many regulars. People round here are too stuck-up for the likes of this place.'

Stott was beginning to feel frustrated. This Alf was obviously a moron; they would get nothing useful out of him. 'But you said you hadn't had any strangers in lately,' he said.

'He weren't a stranger, either.'

'Who was he, then?'

'Nay, don't ask me.'

'But you said you knew him.'

Alf looked over at Hatchley and gave a sniff of disgust before turning back to Stott and answering. 'No, I didn't,' he said. 'I said he weren't a regular, but he weren't exactly a stranger, either. Different thing.'

'So you've seen him before?'

Alf spat on the floor behind the bar. 'Well, of course I bloody have. Stands to reason, doesn't it? He'd have been a stranger if I hadn't seen him before, wouldn't he?'

Hatchley took over again. 'All right, Alf,' he said. 'You're right. Good point. How often have you seen him?'

'Not often. But he's been in three or four times this past year or so. Used to come in with a lass. A right bonnie lass, and all. But not the last few times.'

'Do you know who he is?'

'No. He always stuck to himself.'

'Any idea where he lives?'

'Could be bloody Timbuktu, for all I know.'

'Are you saying he was African-English?' Stott cut in.

Alf gave him a withering look. 'It's just a saying, like. Summat me mother used to say.'

'What did he look like?' Hatchley asked.

'Well, he were a tall bloke, I remember that. A bit over six foot, anyroad. Thick black hair, a bit too long over t'collar, if you ask me. Bit of a long nose, too.'

'Did you talk to him?'

'No more than to serve him and make a few remarks about the weather. He didn't seem to want to talk. Took his pint over by the fire and just sat there staring into his glass. Muttered to himself now and then, too, as I recall.'

'He talked to himself?'

'Well, not all the time. And not like he was having a conversation or anything. No, he'd just say something once in a while, as if he were thinking out loud, like you do sometimes.'

'Did you hear anything he said?'

'Nay. He were too far away.'

'Did he have any sort of an accent?' Stott cut in.

'Couldn't say.'

'Did you know Ive Jelačić, the sexton over the road at St Mary's.'

'Nah. He drank at t'Pig and Whistle.'

'How do you know?'

'Landlord, Stan, told me, after it was in t'papers, like, about him and that dodgy vicar.'

'Did you ever see Mr Jelačić?'

'Only from a distance.'

'Could this have been him?'

'Could've been, I suppose. Same height and hair colour.'

'Do you know if this customer had a car?'

'How would I know that?' Alf rubbed his chin. 'Come to think of it, he looked more like he'd been walking. You know, a bit damp, short of breath.'

'What time was this, Alf?' Hatchley asked.

'About five o'clock.'

'What time did he leave?'

'Just afore six. Like I said, he had nobbut two pints and a double whisky. One for the road, he said, and knocked it back in one, then he was out the door.' Alf mimicked the drinking action.

Stott pricked up his ears. The timing worked, assuming the girl had been killed on her way from the school chess club. Was that the way a person might act before raping and murdering a sixteen-year-old schoolgirl in a foggy graveyard? Stott wondered. A dram of Dutch courage? He tried to remember what he'd learned in the criminal psychology course.

The trouble was, you could justify just about any sort of behaviour if you were talking about a psycho. Some of them liked to sit and have a beer and a fag before a nice little dismemberment; others liked to buy a box of chocolates or bunch of flowers for their mothers. You could never predict. So maybe the killer would have dropped in at the Nag's Head. Why not? Maybe he just needed to sit there for a while, have a little chat with himself about what he was going to do?

'Did you see which direction he went?' Stott asked.

'Nay. You don't expect me to chase outside after my customers and see which way they're going, do you?'

'What was he wearing?' Stott asked.

'Orange anorak. Expensive type, by the looks of it. That Gore-Tex stuff. Lots of pockets and zips.'

'Can you remember anything else about his appearance?'

'I'm not good at describing people. Never was.'

'Do you think you could work with a police artist?'

'Dunno. Never tried it.'

'Will you give it a try?'

Alf shrugged.

'Sergeant,' Stott said, 'go and see if you can get a police artist out as soon as possible, will you? I'll wait here.'

It was almost worth suffering the stale smoke and booze atmosphere of the Nag's Head for another hour or so to see the expression on Sergeant Hatchley's face as he trudged out into the rain.

TWO

They had made love in every position imaginable: side-ways, backwards, forwards, upside down. They had also done it in just about every place they could think of: her bed, his bed, hotels, a field, his cramped Orion, up against a wall, under the kitchen table. Sometimes, it seemed to last forever; other times, it was over almost before it began. Sometimes, the foreplay went on so long Rebecca thought she would burst; other times, they were overtaken by a sense of urgency and didn't even have time to get all their clothes off.

This time, it had been urgent. Afterwards, Rebecca lay on the bed of a hotel room in Richmond panting for breath, covered by a film of sweat. Her skirt was bunched up around her waist, her knickers down, still hanging around one bare ankle; her blouse was open at the front, a couple of the buttons torn off in the heat of the moment, and her bra was pushed up to expose her breasts.

Patrick's head lay against her shoulder. She could feel his breath warm against her skin. Both their hearts were beating fast. Rebecca rested one hand over his broad, strong shoulders, and with the other she stroked the hair over his ear, felt the stubbly down at the back of his neck, where it had been recently cut. It wasn't love – she knew enough to realize that – but it was one hell of a fine substitute.

But all too soon the sense of shame and melancholy that always came to her after sex with Patrick began to descend like a thick fog, numbing the nerve-ends that, only minutes before, had thrilled to such exquisite pleasure, and guilt began to overwhelm the vestiges of her joy.

Patrick moved away and reached for a cigarette. It was the one thing she disliked, his smoking after sex, but she didn't have the heart to tell him not to. He also put his glasses on. She knew he couldn't see a thing without them, but sometimes she laughed because he looked so funny naked except for his glasses.

'What is it?' Patrick asked, clearly sensing something was wrong. 'Didn't you enjoy it?'

'Of course I did. You know that. I always do . . . with you. No . . . it's just that I feel so . . . so damn guilty.'

'Then leave him. Come and live with me.'

'Don't be foolish, Patrick. Just imagine the scandal. Schoolteacher shacks up with minister's wife. You'd lose your job, for a start. And where would we live?'

'Oh, don't be so practical. We'd manage. We'll get a flat in town. I can get another job. We'll move away.'

Rebecca shook her head. 'No. No. No.'

'Why not? Don't you love me?'

Rebecca didn't answer.

'You do love me, don't you?' he persisted.

'Of course I do,' Rebecca lied. It was easier that way.

'Then leave him.'

'I can't.'

'You don't love him.'

'I . . . I . . . don't know.' Rebecca *did* love Daniel. Somewhere inside her, the feeling was still there, she knew; battered, bruised, half-evaporated, but still there. She couldn't explain that to Patrick.

'I shouldn't tell you this, but . . .'

Rebecca felt a tingle run up her spine at the words, nothing to do with sex. 'Yes?' she prompted him. 'Go on.'

'Yesterday evening your husband came to see me.'

'Daniel went to see you? Why?'

'He came to talk to me.'

Rebecca sat up. She quickly slipped her bra down and rearranged her skirt to cover herself, holding the front of her blouse together as best she could. 'What about?' she asked, feeling awkward and stupid.

'About us.' Patrick flicked his ash into the ashtray on the bedside table. It was a small room, with the curtains drawn, and Rebecca already felt claustrophobic.

'But he doesn't know about us.'

'Oh, but he does. He says he's known for a while. He suspected something, then he watched you. He's seen us together.'

'My God.'

'He told me not to tell you he'd been to see me.'

'What did he want?'

'He asked me to stop seeing you.'

'What did you say?'

'I told him the truth. That we were in love. That you were discovering for the first time your true erotic nature. And that as soon as we could manage it you were going to leave him and we were going to live together.'

Rebecca couldn't believe what she was hearing. Daniel knew? Had known for ages? 'You bloody fool.' She swung her legs over the side of the bed and pulled up her knickers. Then she put on her jacket over her torn blouse and went to the wardrobe where her raincoat was hanging. 'You bloody fool,' she muttered again under her breath. 'Daniel. I must go to him.'

Patrick sat up and stubbed out his cigarette. 'What do you mean? It *is* the truth, isn't it?'

'You idiot. You've ruined everything.'

He got up and walked over to her. She thought he suddenly looked ridiculous with his glasses on, the limp penis hanging between his thin, hairy legs.

'Rebecca,' he said, grasping her arms. 'He's only concerned about how it looks. With appearances. Don't you see? He wants everything to seem normal, for you to act like the dutiful vicar's wife. But it's not you. It's really not you. I *know* you, Rebecca. I know your true nature. We've discovered it together. You're a wild, passionate, sensual creature, not a bloody dried-up vicar's wife.'

'Let me go!'

She tore herself out of his grasp, finished putting her raincoat on and grabbed the door-handle.

'Don't do this, Rebecca,' he said. 'Stay with me. Don't be afraid of finding out who you really are. Follow your passion, your *feelings*.'

'Oh, shut up, you pompous bastard. It was just a fuck, that's all. You don't know a bloody thing, do you?'

'Wait. I'll drive you,' he called out as she walked through the door.

'Don't bother,' she said over her shoulder. 'I'll catch a bus.' And she slammed the door behind her.

THREE

A couple of uniformed policemen kept the press away from Sir Geoffrey's house. When Banks and Susan got there early in the afternoon, there were only about six reporters hanging around at the end of the driveway. They fired off a few questions, but Banks ignored them. Too early to start giving statements to the press. Unless you were Chief Constable Riddle, of course.

The only new information Banks had was that the swabs taken from Deborah had revealed no traces of semen, and he certainly wasn't going to tell the media that. He had also discovered that Sir Geoffrey's reception at the Royal Hotel in York had ended at four o'clock, plenty of time to get back home by six, even in the fog. Lady Harrison had, indeed, been at the health club; but she hadn't arrived there until almost six-thirty.

Banks hadn't noticed in the fog last night, but the house had a large lawn and beautiful flower-beds, clearly the work of a gardener. Even keeping the lawn trimmed would have been a full-time job. The house itself was an ostentatious pile of Victorian stone, complete with gables, probably built for one of the get-rich-quick wool merchants in the last century.

Sir Geoffrey himself answered Banks's ring and beckoned the two of them in. Banks introduced Susan.

'Is there any news?' Sir Geoffrey asked.

Banks shook his head. 'Not yet, sir. Sorry.'

Sir Geoffrey looked drawn and stooped, and he had large bags, like bruises, under his eyes. Banks followed him through to the white room with the bookcases, the Chagall and the grand piano. Michael Clayton was sitting in one of the armchairs, also looking as if he had gone without sleep for a week.

'Michael, I believe you met Detective Chief Inspector Banks last night,' Sir Geoffrey said.

'Yes,' said Clayton, 'and I know Detective Constable Gay, too. I don't know if I ever thanked you.'

Susan smiled. 'All part of the service, sir.'

Banks gave her a quizzical look.

'Mr Clayton had his car and a valuable notebook computer stolen in August,' she explained. 'We got them back for him. Someone was trying to sell the computer at Eastvale market.'

'I don't think I explained last night,' Sir Geoffrey went on, 'but in addition to being a dear friend, Michael's the scientific genius behind HarClay Industries. I simply provide the sales and marketing strategies.' He clapped Clayton on the shoulder. 'I don't know what we'd do without him. Please, sit down.'

'Where's your wife, sir?' Banks asked.

'Sylvie's resting. She . . . we didn't get much sleep last

night. She's exhausted. Me, too. Look, we . . . er . . . I'm sorry. Things are a bit of a mess around here. How can I help you?'

'We won't keep you long. Just a couple of questions.'

Sir Geoffrey nodded wearily. 'I'll do the best I can.'

'Thank you,' said Banks. 'We've talked to a few people at Deborah's school, and everyone seems to agree that Deborah was a cheerful and talented girl.'

Sir Geoffrey nodded. 'Sylvie and I are very proud of her.'

'But even the best of people make enemies,' Banks went on. 'Often inadvertently. Can you think of any enemies Deborah might have made?'

Sir Geoffrey closed his eyes and thought for a moment, then shook his head. 'No. She got along well with her schoolfriends and teachers – I'm sure they'll all bear that out – and there wasn't really anyone else in her life aside from family.'

'I heard that she had a tendency to show off at times. Would you say that's fair?'

Sir Geoffrey smiled. 'Yes, Deborah can be a show-off, and a bit of a devil at times. But what child can't be?'

Banks smiled, thinking of Tracy. 'And Deborah *was* still a child in some ways,' he said. 'She might not always have realized the effects of her actions on others. Do you see what I mean?'

Sir Geoffrey nodded. 'But I can't see us getting any-where with this,' he said. 'Unless you're implying that someone at the school had something to do with her death. Or that bloody minister at St Mary's.'

'Daniel Charters?'

'That's the one.'

'Why do you dislike him so?'

'The man's a pervert. He abused his power.'

Banks shook his head. 'But nothing's been proved against him. Isn't he entitled to be presumed innocent until proven guilty?'

'In theory, perhaps. But a man in his position should be above suspicion.'

'The man who accused Father Charters is called Ive Jelačić. Would it surprise you to know that he made lewd gestures towards your daughter, and that she complained to Dr Green, the head of St Mary's?'

'She never told me that. If she had, I'd have broken his bloody neck.'

Banks turned to Clayton. 'Did Deborah ever confide in you about anything?'

Clayton raised his eyebrows. 'Me? Good heavens, no. I suppose I was just as uncool as her parents as far as she was concerned.'

'Uncool?'

'You know teenagers, Chief Inspector. We're ancient and decrepit creatures to them.'

'I suppose we are.' Banks took a deep breath and turned back to Sir Geoffrey. 'This is a little delicate, I'm afraid, but I have to ask where you went after the Royal Hotel reception ended at four o'clock yesterday.'

'Good God, man! You can't poss—'

'Geoff, he has to ask. He's just doing his job,' said Michael Clayton, putting his hand on Sir Geoffrey's arm. 'Offensive though it may be.'

Sir Geoffrey ran his hand over his hair. 'I suppose so. I had a private meeting with a client, if you must know. A man from the government called Oliver Jackson. It's a very confidential matter, and I don't want *anyone* else to know about the meeting. Things like this can have an effect on share prices and any number of market factors. Not to mention international affairs. Do you understand?'

Banks nodded. 'There is just one more thing . . .'

Sir Geoffrey sighed. 'Go ahead, if you must.'

'I was wondering about any boyfriends Deborah might have had.'

'Boyfriends?'

'Yes. It would be perfectly natural for a girl of sixteen to have an interest in the opposite sex. Perfectly innocent things, like going to the pictures with a boy, maybe. She did have a ticket stub from the Regal in her blazer pocket.'

Sir Geoffrey shook his head. 'She used to go to the pictures with her mother a lot. The two of them . . . Deborah didn't have any boyfriends, Chief Inspector. You're barking up quite the wrong tree there. She didn't have time for boys.'

'Had she never had a boyfriend?'

'Only Pierre, if that counts at all.'

'Pierre?'

'In Bordeaux, or rather at Montclair. My wife's family owns a chateau in the country near Bordeaux. We often spend holidays there. Pierre is a neighbour's son. All quite innocent, of course.'

'Of course,' Banks agreed. 'And a long way away.'

'Yes . . . well. Look, about this Jelačić character. That's a disturbing piece of news. Are you going to bring him in?'

'We're pursuing enquiries in a number of directions,' Banks said as he and Susan walked to the door, annoyed at himself for sounding as if he were talking to the press.

Outside, they ducked through the reporters beyond the gate and got back into Banks's car out of the rain.

'Interesting, don't you think?' Banks said. 'About the boyfriend.'

'Yes, sir. Either he really didn't know, or he was lying.'

'But why lie?'

'Perhaps Deborah really did keep it a secret from him? If he's a strict father, I could see her doing that.'

'Possibly. What about his alibi?'

'Very plausible,' said Susan. 'I noticed you didn't ask his wife for hers.'

'One at a time, Susan. One at a time. Besides, I hardly think Sylvie Harrison murdered her own daughter. She's not tall or strong enough, for a start.'

'If she goes to a health club, she's probably strong enough,' Susan pointed out. 'Maybe she stood on a stone?'

Banks sneezed into his handkerchief.

'Bless you, sir,' Susan said.

They headed towards North Market Street. 'You know,' said Banks, 'I think there's a lot more to Deborah's life than people know, or are saying. I'd like to have another talk with her mother, alone if possible. Michael Clayton was right, teenagers don't have a lot of time for adults, but daughters do sometimes confide in their mothers. And I'd like to find this John, if he exists.'

'Oh, I'm sure he does, sir. Deborah was an attractive girl. And she was sixteen. I'd be very surprised indeed if she had nothing at all to do with boys.'

Banks's car phone beeped. He picked it up.

'DI Stott here.'

'What's up, Barry?'

'I think we should meet up back at the station. We've got a description of a possible suspect in the Deborah Harrison murder, and it could be Jelačić. Vic Manson called, too. Jelačić's prints are all over the vodka bottles.'

'We're on our way.' Banks switched off the phone and put his foot down.

FOUR

All the way home on the rickety bus, Rebecca chewed her nails. She didn't look once at the fading autumn scenery beyond the rain-streaked windows: the muted gold, russet and lemon leaves still clinging to the roadside trees, fragile and insubstantial as the moon's halo; the soft greens and browns of the fields; the runic patterns of the drystone walls. She didn't notice the way that the dale to her west, with its gradually steepening valley sides, was partially lost in mist and drizzle, making it look just like a Chinese water-colour.

Rebecca chewed her nails and wished that tight, tearing, churning feeling inside her would go away. She felt constantly on the verge of screaming, and she knew if she started she could never stop. She took deep breaths and held them to calm herself. They helped.

By the time the bus lumbered into Eastvale, she had regained some control of her emotions, but she still felt devastated, as if her world had been suddenly blown apart. She supposed it had to happen, that she had been living a lie, living on borrowed time, or whatever other cliché she could come up with to describe the last few months of her life.

Looking at it now, her life had simply become one hangover after another; either from booze or infidelity, it didn't seem to make any difference. What pleasures she had found in getting drunk or having sex were so fleeting and so quickly overwhelmed by the pains – headaches, stomach-ache, guilt, shame – that they no longer seemed worthwhile. But was it too late now? Had she lost Daniel?

Almost there.

She pushed the bell and felt the driver and other passengers giving her strange looks as she waited for the bus to stop. What could they sense about her? Could they smell sex on her? She hadn't washed before leaving Patrick in Richmond; she had simply pulled her clothes on as quickly as possible and left. But her raincoat covered the torn blouse. God, what could she do about that? If Daniel were home, he would notice. But what did it matter now? He knew anyway. Even so, she couldn't stand the thought of his knowing she had been with Patrick this afternoon.

As the bus approached the stop, she saw the knot of reporters hanging about by the church walls and knew why the passengers were looking at her. She was getting off at St Mary's, the scene of the most horrible crime Eastvale had experienced in decades.

The bus came to a sharp halt and Rebecca would have tumbled forwards if she hadn't been holding onto the metal pole. When the doors opened, she jumped off and dashed past the policeman at the gate, then ran through the churchyard to the vicarage.

When she got there she flung open the door and called out for Daniel. Silence. Thank God, he wasn't home. Pulling off her torn blouse, she ran upstairs to the bathroom to wash the smell of sex from her body. Then she would be ready to face Daniel. She would have to be.

FIVE

Ive Jelačić lived on the sixth floor of a ten-storey block of flats in Burmantofts, off York Road. In the grey November drizzle, the maze of tall buildings reminded Banks of a newspaper picture he'd seen of workers' quarters in some Siberian city.

'Charming, isn't it?' said Detective Inspector Ken Blackstone, waiting for them outside. He looked at his watch. 'Do you know, the council had to put slippery domes on all the roofs to stop kids climbing down on the upper balconies and breaking in through people's windows?'

Immaculately dressed as usual, Blackstone made Banks aware that his top collar button was undone and his tie a little askew. Blackstone looked like an academic, with his wire-rimmed glasses, bookworm's complexion and thinning sandy hair, a little curly around the ears, and he was, in fact, something of an expert on art and art fraud. Not that there was often much call for his area of expertise in Leeds. Nobody had knocked off any Atkinson Grimshaws recently, and only an idiot would try to fake a Henry Moore sculpture.

'Jelačić's alibi checks out,' Blackstone said as they walked towards the entrance. 'For what it's worth. And we've had a poke about his flat. Nothing.'

'What do *you* think it's worth?' Banks asked.

Blackstone pursed his cupid's-bow lips. 'Me? About as much as a fart in a bathtub. There were three of them – all Croatian. Stipe Pavič, Mile Paveliči and Vjeko Batorac. They'd probably swear night was day to protect one another from the police. Here it is. Take my word, the lift doesn't work.'

Banks looked through the open sliding doors. The walls of the lift were covered in bright, spray-painted graffiti, and even from where he stood he could smell glue and urine. They took the stairs instead, surprising a couple of kids sniffing solvent on the third-floor stairwell. The kids ran. They knew the only people dressed like

Blackstone in that neighbourhood were likely to be coppers.

There were a few times when Banks regretted smoking, and the climb to the sixth-floor flat was one of them. Puffing for breath and sweating a little, he finally arrived at the outside walkway that went past the front doors.

Number 604 had once been red, but most of the paint had peeled off. It also looked as if it had been used for knife-throwing practice. Jelačić answered the first knock, wearing jeans and a string vest. His upper body looked strong and muscular, and tufts of thick black hair spilled through the holes in the vest. With his height, longish hair and hooked nose, he certainly resembled the descriptions of the man seen in St Mary's yesterday evening.

'Why you bother me?' he said, standing aside to let them in and letting his eyes rest on Susan for longer than necessary. 'I tell you already, I have done nothing.'

Inside, the flat was small enough to feel crowded with four people in it and tidy enough to surprise Banks. If nothing else, Ive Jelačić was a good housekeeper. An ironing board stood in one corner, with a shirt spread on it, and there was a small television set in the opposite corner. No video or stereo equipment in sight. The only other furniture in the room consisted of a battered sofa and a table with three chairs. Family photographs and a couple of religious icons stood on the mantelpiece over the electric fire.

'How are you making a living now, Mr Jelačić?' Banks asked.

'Dole.'

'Do you own a car?'

'Why?'

'Just answer the question.'

'*Da*. Is old Ford Fiesta.'

'Did you drive it to Eastvale yesterday?'

Jelačić looked at Blackstone. '*Ne*. I tell him already. I play cards. Vjeko tells you. And Stipe and Mile.'

Jelačić sat down on his sofa, taking up most of it, and lit a cigarette. The room quickly began to fill with smoke. Blackstone stood with his back against the door, and Banks and Susan sat on the wooden chairs. Banks soon noticed the way Jelačić was sliding his eyes over Susan's body, and he could tell Susan noticed it too, the way she made sure her skirt was pulled down as far over her knees as it would go and the way she kept her knees pressed tight together. But still Jelačić ogled.

'The thing is,' Banks said, 'that people will often lie to cover for their friends, if they think a friend is in trouble.'

Jelačić leaned forward aggressively, muscles bulging in his arms and shoulders. 'You call my friends liars! *Jebem ti mater!* You tell that to their face. Fascist police. *Šupak!*'

Banks held out a photograph of Deborah Harrison. 'Did you know this girl?'

Jelačić glared at Banks for a moment before glancing towards the photo. He shook his head.

'Are you sure.'

'*Da.*'

'She went to St Mary's, sang in the church choir, used to walk through the graveyard on her way home.'

He shook his head again.

'I think you're lying, Mr Jelačić. You see, she complained about you. She said you used to make lewd, sexual comments and gestures towards her. What do you think about that?'

'Is not true.'

'Father Charters said you were drunk most of the time,

you didn't do your job properly and you bothered the girls. Is that true?'

'*Ne.* He is liar. All St Mary's people lie, get Ive in trouble, make him lose job.'

'Did you ever enter the Inchcliffe Mausoleum?'

'*Nikada.* Is always locked.'

Banks looked at Ken Blackstone and rolled his eyes. 'Oh, come on, Ive. We found your fingerprints all over the empty vodka bottles in there.'

'*Vrag ti nosi!*'

'We know you went down there. Why?'

Jelačić paused to sulk for a moment, then said, 'All right. So I go down there sometime in summer when it get too hot. Just for cool, you understand? Maybe I have a little drink and smoke. Is not crime.'

'Did you ever take anyone else down there? Any girls?'

'*Nikada.*'

Banks waved the photograph. 'And you swear you didn't know this girl?'

Jelačić leaned back on the sofa. 'Maybe I just see her, you know, if I am working and she walk past.'

'So you do admit you might have seen her?'

'*Da.* But that is all.'

'Jelačić, what were you wearing last night?'

Jelačić pointed towards a coat-hook by the door. A red windcheater hung on it.

'Shoes?'

Frowning, Jelačić got to his feet and picked up a pair of old trainers from the mat below the hook. Banks looked at the soles and thought he could see gravel trapped in the tread and, perhaps, bits of leaves. There was also mud on the sides.

'How did your shoes get in this state?' he asked.

'I walk back from Mile's.'

'You didn't drive?'

Jelačić shrugged. 'Is not far.'

'We'd like to take your shoes and windcheater in for testing,' Banks said. 'It would be easiest if you gave us permission. You'll get a receipt.'

'If I do not?'

'Then we'll get a court order.'

'Is okay. You take them. I have nothing to hide.'

'Were you standing on the Kendal bridge around six o'clock yesterday evening?'

'*Ne.* I go to Mile's house. We play cards until late.'

'Did you have two pints of beer and a double whisky in the Nag's Head, opposite St Mary's Park?'

'I tell you. I go to Mile's and we play cards and drink.'

'Daniel Charters told us you'd been back to Eastvale to extort money from him. Is that true?'

'*Vražje!* I tell you, that man, he is Satan's tool, an evil liar.'

'So it's not true that you offered to withdraw the charges in exchange for money?'

'Is not true. *Ne.* And I have nothing more to say.' Jelačić looked at Susan again, letting his eyes travel slowly from her feet all the way up to her breasts, where they lingered. He didn't exactly lick his lips, but he might as well have done. Banks saw Susan flush with embarrassment and rage.

'Well, let me just get clear what you *have* told us,' Banks said. 'Last night, you were playing cards with friends who will vouch for you, right?'

Jelačić nodded.

'You didn't know the girl in the photograph, though you might have seen her in passing.'

'*Da.*'

'But you certainly didn't leer at her or make any suggestive gestures.'

'*Ne.*'

'And after you were unjustly fired you never went back to Eastvale and tried to extort money out of Father Daniel Charters.'

'*Nikada.*'

'Fine, then,' said Banks, standing up. 'That'll be all. We'll be off now.'

Jelačić looked surprised. 'You leave now?'

'Don't worry, we'll take good care of the clothing and get it back to you as soon as we've run our tests. Thank you for your co-operation, Mr Jelačić. Good day.'

And they left him gaping after them.

'Biggest load of bollocks I've ever heard in my life,' said Ken Blackstone as they walked down the stairs. A dog went on pissing nonchalantly against the wall as they passed by.

Banks lit a cigarette. 'Yes, it was, wasn't it? What do you think Susan?'

'Whether he did it or not,' Susan Gay said between gritted teeth, 'I think the bastard should be hung over the balcony by his balls. Sir.'

5

ONE

It was after six and Daniel still wasn't back. Rebecca paced. She should make a start on dinner. At least it would take her mind off things. Had all this happened just a couple of days ago, she would have gone to see the angel, blabbed her fears and feelings out to its marble heavenward gaze, but the Inchcliffe Mausoleum was soured for her now by what she had seen there.

She put on her striped butcher's apron – a birthday present from Daniel, when he still had his sense of humour – and searched in the fridge for the remains of the weekend's roast. She would make shepherd's pie. There was a bottle of Marks and Sparks Sauvignon Blanc in the fridge, lying on its side near the front. After a moment's hesitation, Rebecca opened it and poured herself a generous glass before setting about grinding the leftover meat.

She was halfway through her second glass, and had just put the potatoes on, when she heard the door open. Daniel. Her legs turned to water. Suddenly she couldn't face him, didn't know what to say. He called out her name and she managed to tell him she was in the kitchen. Quickly, she knocked back the rest of the wine and poured herself another glass. Her hand was shaking so much she spilled some of it on the table. Sometimes you just couldn't get drunk enough quick enough.

'What happened to the front window?' Daniel asked when he came through.

Rebecca stared down at the potatoes in the pan, waiting for the water to boil. 'Someone chucked a brick through it,' she said. She didn't tell him about the note.

'Where were the police?'

'Up around the Inchcliffe Mausoleum.'

'Isn't it marvellous? Police all over the place but still a crime gets committed.' Daniel rested the backs of his thighs against the solid wood table.

'Daniel, a young girl's been killed. And I found her.'

Daniel rubbed his brow. 'I know. I'm sorry. I wasn't thinking clearly. Bad day.'

'How was the meeting?'

'At least they're resolved on not kicking me out for the present,' Daniel said. Over the past month, he had developed a tick beside his left eye. It was jumping now. 'But the bishop is very upset about the murder, especially about its happening on church property. That's another nail in my coffin. Things could hardly get much worse.'

'Don't tempt providence.'

'Providence? Hah. I don't know if I still believe in providence any more. Or in anything, for that matter. I'm hungry.' He went to the fridge, found some old cheddar and cut himself a chunk. 'How about you?'

Rebecca shook her head. The way her stomach felt, she thought she might never be able to eat again. The potatoes came to a boil. She turned down the heat and wiped her hands on her apron. The tension inside her had built so high that she felt like a volcano about to erupt. She couldn't stand it any longer.

'Daniel?' She turned to face him.

'What?'

'I . . . I don't . . . Today. I—'

The front doorbell rang.

'Damn!' Rebecca banged her fist on the table. 'Who could that be?'

'I'll go and see.' Daniel went off to answer it.

Rebecca grasped the edge of the table. She could feel the room spinning around her, and it wasn't the booze this time.

'Becky!' The note of concern in his voice brought her back. 'Are you all right?'

She closed her eyes and shook her head. Not so bad. 'I'm fine. Sorry. I just came over a bit funny, that's all.' When she opened her eyes, she saw Daniel standing next to the detective who had visited them last night.

He was smaller than you'd expect for a policeman, she noticed, compact, lean and wiry, with an aura of pent-up strength. His closely cropped black hair showed just a little grey at the temples, and his blue eyes danced and sparkled with energy. There was a little crescent scar beside his right eye.

'Detective Chief Inspector Banks is back,' Daniel said. 'He wants to ask us some more questions.'

Rebecca nodded, took off her apron and followed them through to the living-room. She left the glass of wine on the kitchen table. Another postponement. Maybe she could drink herself through yet another night of guilt and misery.

'I'm sorry to intrude again,' Banks said when they had all sat down. He sneezed, took out a large handkerchief and blew his nose. 'Sorry. I seem to be catching a cold. Look, I'll come straight to the point. I can see you were busy getting dinner ready. I was just wondering if maybe you'd decided to tell me the truth about last night?'

For a moment, Rebecca was stunned by the matter-of-fact way Banks spoke. 'The truth?' she echoed.

'Yes. You're a poor liar, Mrs Charters. And you can take that as a compliment.' He glanced towards Daniel. 'When I asked your husband where he had been at the time you said you heard a cry, you jumped in a bit too quickly and answered for him.'

'I did?'

'Yes. Then he felt duty-bound to lie to cover for you. It's all very admirable in some ways, but it won't do. Not when there's a sixteen-year-old girl lying dead in Eastvale mortuary.'

Rebecca felt completely tongue-tied. What the hell was going on? Her mind whirled, searching for things to say, but before she could say anything a voice far calmer than her own cut in.

'Chief Inspector,' Daniel Charters said. 'I'm afraid that's my fault. I should have corrected Rebecca rather than let the deceit stand. Believe me, there was no need for a lie. I have nothing to hide.'

Banks nodded. He seemed to be waiting for something else.

Daniel sighed and went on. 'Yes, I was out at the time my wife heard the cry, but I can assure you that my whereabouts had absolutely nothing at all to do with the poor girl's murder.'

'Where were you?' Banks asked.

Rebecca noticed Daniel's lips tighten for a moment as he tensed in thought. 'I'd rather not say.'

'It would help us a lot if we could verify your story.'

Daniel shook his head. 'I'm afraid I wouldn't be able to prove my alibi, even if I told you.'

'You could let *us* try.'

He smiled sadly. 'It's a kind offer, but—'

The doorbell rang again.

'I'll go,' said Rebecca.

'Whoever it is,' Daniel told her, 'get rid of them.'

Leaving them in silence, Rebecca went to open the front door. Patrick Metcalfe was standing there. He looked as if he had been walking around in the rain without a raincoat for hours.

'Oh, my God,' Rebecca cried, trying to shut the door against his shoulder. 'Please, go away. Can't you see you've caused enough trouble already?'

'Let me in, Rebecca. I want to come in. I must come in. I want to talk to both of you. You must listen to me.'

He kept pushing at the door and Rebecca wasn't strong enough to hold him back. Suddenly, Banks's calm voice behind her said, 'Why don't you let him in, Mrs Charters? Whoever he is. The more the merrier.'

TWO

Even Barry Stott was almost ready to call it a day by six-thirty. The drizzle that, at one time, had looked like ending, had turned into a much harder downpour as darkness fell, and now both he and Sergeant Hatchley were soaked to the skin. Even the best raincoat and shoes, which Stott's were, could only take so much without springing leaks. If only Jelačić had broken down and confessed instead of stubbornly protesting his innocence, the way Banks said he had, how much easier life would have been.

They were showing the police artist's impression, based on Alf's description – and what a lengthy and frustrating experience getting that done had been – along the rather twee row of shops set back from Kendal Road opposite the school. The newsagent hadn't seen anyone, the grocer was closed and the hairdresser gave a lengthy opinion as to the sorry state of the suspect's locks, but said she was closed on Mondays, and no, she hadn't noticed anyone strange hanging around on any other days.

The teashop was also closed, the way most Yorkshire teashops close at teatime, but the Peking Moon, the Chinese restaurant next door, had just opened. It was, as Hatchley explained, a rather pricey, up-market sort of Chinese restaurant, not the kind of place that yobbos go for a quick chop suey after a skinful of ale on a Friday night.

'I wonder why they don't change the name,' Sergeant Hatchley said as they approached the door. 'Isn't Peking called Beijing now? A real Chinaman wouldn't have a clue where he was if he saw this.'

Stott turned to Hatchley before he pushed the door open. 'I know what you're thinking, Sergeant. And you can forget it. We're not staying here for dinner. Definitely not. Got it?'

Hatchley looked hurt. 'Furthest thing from my mind, sir. I don't even like Chinese food. It's got no sticking power. I'm always hungry again ten minutes after I've eaten it.'

'Right. Just as long as we understand each other . . .'

The bell at the top of the door jingled as they went in. Like many Chinese restaurants, its decor was simple and relaxing, with a series of ancient Chinese landscapes – tiny human figures dwarfed by evergreen-covered mountains – on the walls, and plain red tablecloths. Soft, tinkling music played in the background. So soft that Stott couldn't even figure out whether it was pop or classical. Or Chinese. Not that he cared much for music.

A waiter in a white jacket walked towards them. 'Jim, me old mate. What can I do you for?' he asked in a cockney accent you could cut with a knife, despite the oriental eyes and complexion.

'DI Stott,' Hatchley introduced them. 'This is Well Hung Low.' He laughed, and the waiter laughed with him.

Stott seethed inside, his rage, as it always did, crystallizing quickly from fire to ice.

'Just a joke, sir,' Hatchley went on. 'His name's Joe Sung. Deserted the bright lights of Whitechapel for the greener pastures of Eastvale. Joe wanted to be a copper once, too, sir, but I managed to persuade him he was better off where he was. His father owns this place. It's a little gold-mine.'

'Perhaps you should reconsider,' Stott said with a smile, shaking Joe's hand. 'We need more . . . a more ethnically diverse police force. Especially in Yorkshire.'

'Aye,' said Hatchley. 'I told him he wouldn't know what was worse, the prejudice or the patronizing.'

Joe laughed.

Again, Stott felt his anger boil up and freeze. Oafs like Hatchley symbolized all that was wrong in today's police force. His type's days were numbered. 'I wonder if we might ask you a few questions?' he said to Joe Sung.

'Fire away, mate.' Joe gestured to the empty restaurant. 'See how busy we are. Here, take the weight off.' He beckoned them to join him at one of the tables.

'Remember what I said, Sergeant,' Stott hissed in Hatchley's ear as they followed. 'This isn't another meal break.'

'No, sir.' But Hatchley took the ashtray on the table as an invitation to light up.

'What is it, then?' Joe asked when they'd sat down. 'Official business? About that murder?'

'Yes,' said Stott.

Joe shook his head. 'Terrible business. I knew the girl, too, you know.'

'Knew her?'

'Well, not in the real sense of the word. Not to talk to, like. I mean she'd eaten in here with her mates, that's all. I couldn't believe my eyes when I saw that photo in the *Evening Post*.'

Stott couldn't understand how it happened, but a tray of appetizers suddenly appeared on the table in front of them: spring rolls, garlic shrimp, chicken balls. All Stott noticed was the retreating back of another waiter. He hadn't heard a thing. Hatchley picked up a shrimp and popped it in his mouth between drags on his cigarette.

'When did she eat here?' Stott asked.

'They come here every now and then. A bunch of girls from the school, that is. Maybe when one of their daddies sends the monthly cheque. Anyway, they generally keep quiet, don't cause any trouble, and they don't expect to be served beer. She was with them once or twice, that Deborah Harrison who got killed. I recognized her.'

'Do you remember anything about her?'

'Nah, not really. 'Cept that she was a good-looking girl. That's why I remembered her in particular.'

'Ever noticed anyone take an unusual interest in her, or the other St Mary's girls?'

'Well, they've caught the odd eye or two. There's a couple of right corkers among them, and there's always something about a girl in a school uniform. Sorry. That was in bad taste.'

'Not at all, Joe,' said Hatchley. 'I know what you mean, and I'm sure the inspector does, too.'

Stott said nothing. Three bottles of beer materialized with three glasses on the table before them, as if by magic.

'Somefink to wash the food down,' Joe said with a grin. 'My treat.'

Stott ignored the beer. Hatchley grabbed a bottle and ignored the glass. Well, let him drink it, Stott thought. Fine. He wasn't going to touch any himself. Give Hatchley enough rope and he'll surely hang himself. If only he didn't have a strong ally in Chief Inspector Banks. Stott couldn't understand that relationship at all. Banks seemed like an intelligent, civilized sort of copper. What could he possibly see in a boor like Hatchley?

Right now, though, there were more important things to think about than Hatchley's eating and drinking habits. 'So you noticed nothing unusual about the girl and nobody taking any undue interest in her or her friends?' Stott asked.

'That's right,' said Joe. 'Noffink out of the ordinary.'

'Did she ever meet anyone here? Anyone other than her schoolfriends?'

'No. They always came and left together as a group. Never had any boys with them, if that's what you mean. Too close to the school, if you ask me. You never know when one of the teachers might drop in and catch them. They eat here, too, sometimes.'

Stott glanced over at Hatchley, who took out the artist's impression of the stranger in the Nag's Head. 'Ever seen this man?' he asked.

Joe stared at the picture, shaking his head. 'It doesn't

look much like him, except for the hair,' he said, 'but we had a bloke looked a bit like that in here just last night.'

Stott's pulse began to race. 'What was he wearing?'

'An orange anorak.'

'Tall?'

'Yeah, tall-ish. Bit over six feet, anyway.'

'What time did he come in?'

'About half six. I remember because he was the only man in at that time. Miserable night.'

The time fitted, Stott thought, feeling his excitement rise. The killer had a couple of drinks at the Nag's Head, murdered Deborah Harrison, and then he came here for dinner.

'Did he do or say anything unusual?'

'He seemed a bit restless. I saw him muttering to himself once or twice.'

'Hear what he said?'

'Sorry.'

'Who waited on his table?'

'I did. We were short-staffed because of the fog. He was certainly hungry, I'll say that. First he had spring rolls, then he ordered orange beef *and* Szechuan shrimp, a bowl of rice and a pint of lager. Ate it all, too.'

'Did you talk to him?'

'Only to take his order. He didn't seem communicative, so I didn't push it. You learn how to behave in this business, who wants to chat and who just wants to be left alone. This bloke wanted to be left alone.'

Stott saw his bottle of beer disappear into Hatchley's hand. He let it pass. 'Did you notice anything else about him?'

'Yeah. He had a little cut, just up there, high on his left cheek.' Joe touched the spot on his own cheek.

Stott could hardly contain his excitement. The post-mortem had reported skin and tissue under the middle fingernail of Deborah Harrison's right hand. She had scratched her attacker. It had to be Jelačić. 'How long did he stay?' Stott asked.

'Just as long as it took to order and eat. About three-quarters of an hour.'

'Did he have a car?'

'If he did, I didn't see it. Somehow, I got the impression he was on foot. I mean, who'd take the car out by himself on a night like that, just to go out alone for a Chinese meal? Fine as the food here is. Me, I'd order a take-away and let some other poor bugger do the driving.'

'Good point,' said Stott. 'See where he went?'

'Afraid not.'

From the corner of his eye, Stott noticed the last spring roll disappear between two sausage-like fingers.

'Had you ever seen him before?' he asked.

Joe shook his head.

Stott smiled. 'I don't suppose he happened to mention his name, did he?'

Joe grinned back. 'Sorry. Didn't mention his address, either. No. Like I said, some of them are chatty, this one wasn't.' He paused. 'I'll tell you what, though.'

'What?'

Joe stood up. 'If my memory serves me right, he paid by card. You might be able to get his name from that. I haven't done the returns yet. Shall I go get it for you?'

Stott sent up a silent prayer of thanks to God.

Joe came back with a sheaf of Visa slips in his hand and started going through them. 'Not this one. Not that . . . no . . . no. Yeah. Right, this is the one.' And he passed it over.

Anxiously, Stott grabbed the slip of paper, but as soon

as he looked at it, his spirits sank. He couldn't read the signature – that was just a mess of loops and whirls – but the name was printed clearly enough in the top left corner. And it *wasn't* Ive Jelačić.

Beside him, he heard the glug of an emptying beer bottle followed by a resonant burp.

THREE

'Right,' said Banks, 'now that we've all calmed down a bit, maybe we can play truth or consequences. And I'm telling you, the consequences will be bloody severe if you don't play. Got it?'

The three pale, miserable-looking people in the chilly vicarage living-room nodded in unison. The brown-and-white bundle of fur on the hearth scratched and fell still again.

As soon as Banks had appeared in the hall, Patrick Metcalfe had tried to make a break for it. Perhaps he believed that the power of his love could vanquish unhappy husbands, but he must have known it didn't stand a chance against the long arm of the law. As he turned to run away, he slipped on the doorstep and fell down three stone steps onto the garden path, sprawling in the rain on the worn paving-stones, holding his knee and cursing. Banks helped him inside with a firm hand and sat him down in one of the armchairs.

Now he sat there, hair plastered to his skull, looking sullen. The 'consumptive' look wasn't hard for him to cultivate, given his lanky frame and hollow cheeks. He kept giving Rebecca Charters significant stares with his soulful eyes, but she averted her gaze.

By this time, Rebecca had brought the bottle of wine from the kitchen and topped up her glass. She was beginning to look a little blurred around the edges. Daniel Charters, permanent frown etched in his high brow, muscle twitching beside his left eye, just sat there, long legs crossed, his face growing steadily paler, looking like a man old before his time.

'Now, then, Mr Charters,' Banks said. 'You were trying to tell me where you were last night before we were so rudely interrupted.'

'He was with me,' the newcomer burst out.

'And you are?'

'Patrick Metcalfe. I'm the history teacher at St Mary's.'

'So you knew Deborah Harrison?'

'I wouldn't say I *knew* her. I taught her history last year.'

'And you say Mr Charters was with you yesterday evening?'

'He was.'

'What time did he arrive?'

Metcalfe shrugged. 'About quarter to six. I was just thinking about putting something in the microwave for dinner, and I usually eat at about six.'

'Does that time sound right to you, Mr Charters?'

Charters nodded glumly.

Banks turned back to Metcalfe. 'Where do you live?'

'One of the school flats. On St Mary's grounds.'

'Alone?'

'Yes. Alone.' Metcalfe looked longingly at Rebecca Charters, who stared down into her wineglass.

'What time did Mr Charters leave?' Banks asked.

'Around ten to six. He didn't stay more than five minutes. He could see I wasn't interested in what he had to say.'

Which meant that Charters was unaccounted-for during the crucial period around six o'clock. Banks could see Rebecca frowning at this information. She had lied for her husband, only to have someone give him what seemed like an alibi, then immediately snatch it away again. Did *she* know where he had been between ten to six and whenever he got back home?

And, Banks realized, this also left Patrick Metcalfe without an alibi. Rebecca, too, for that matter; he only had her word that she had heard something like a cry around six o'clock.

'What were you wearing?' Banks asked Charters.

'Wearing? A raincoat.'

'Colour?'

'Beige.'

'May I see it.'

Charters went and brought the raincoat in from the hall closet. Banks examined it closely but could see no traces of blood or earth. 'Do you mind if I take this for further testing?' he asked. 'I'll give you a receipt of course.'

Charters looked alarmed. 'Should I call my lawyer?'

'Not if you've got nothing to hide.'

'I've got nothing to hide. Go ahead. Take it.'

'Thank you.'

'Where did you go after you left Mr Metcalfe?'

'Nowhere in particular. I just walked.'

'Where?'

'In the school grounds. By the river.'

'Did you see anyone?'

'There were a few people about, yes.'

'What about on or near the bridge?'

He thought for a moment, then said, 'Yes, come to think of it, I did see someone. When I came out of the main school gate and crossed the road, there was a man in front of me walking along Kendal road towards the bridge.'

'Did you get a good look at him?'

'No. He stopped on the bridge and I walked past him. He was about my height – six foot two – and he was wearing an orange anorak. I could see that much from behind. His hair was dark and rather long.'

'Are you sure it was a man?'

'Certain. Even in the fog I could tell by the way he walked. There's something . . . I don't know how to explain it . . . but I'm *certain* it was a man.'

Another sighting of the mysterious stranger that Stott and Hatchley had unearthed in the Nag's Head. Interesting. 'Can you tell me anything more about him?'

'I'm afraid not,' said Charters. 'I had other things on my mind.'

'Could it have been a red windcheater rather than an orange anorak?'

Charters frowned. 'I suppose it *could* have been. I wasn't paying really close attention.'

'I hope you realize, Mr Charters, that if you'd continued lying to us you would also have been withholding what could be an important piece of evidence.'

Charters said nothing.

'Where did you go next?' Banks asked.

'I walked up to North Market Street, carried along there for a while, then took Constance Avenue back down to the river path and home.' He looked at Rebecca, then looked away again. 'But when I got here I . . . I . . . didn't want to go in and . . . Not just yet. So I kept on walking for a good ten minutes or so, then turned back and came home.'

'Is that everything?'

'Yes.'

'Did you go into the churchyard at any time?'

'No. I wish I had. I might have been able to prevent the poor girl's murder.'

'What time *did* your husband get home, Mrs Charters?'

'He was home when I got back from the graveyard.'

'And that was about a quarter to seven?'

'Yes.'

'And what did you do after Mr Charters left your flat?' Banks said to Metcalfe.

'Nothing much. Heated up my dinner. I considered coming over here and putting an end to the ridiculous charade, but decided against it.'

'What ridiculous charade?'

They were all silent for a moment, as if someone had finally gone too far and they were deciding how to cover up, then Daniel Charters spoke up. 'I went to talk to Metcalfe,' he said, 'to try to persuade him to stop seeing my wife.'

Banks looked at Metcalfe. 'Is this true?'

'Yes.'

'And what was your response?'

Metcalfe sneered at Charters. 'I told him I wasn't interested, that it was too late. Rebecca and I are in love and we're going away together.'

Banks looked towards Rebecca. She had lowered her head, so he couldn't see her expression, only the mass of auburn hair hanging down to her knees. Her glass of wine had sat untouched for several minutes on the table.

'Tell him,' Metcalfe urged her. 'Go on, Rebecca. Tell him it's true. Tell him how this marriage is a sham, how it's stifling you, destroying your true nature. Tell him you don't love your—'

'No!'

'What?'

Rebecca Charters held her head up and stared directly at Metcalfe. Her dark eyes flashed with angry tears. 'I said no, Patrick.' She seemed to gain control of the situation; the welling tears remained at the edges of her eyes. She spoke quietly: 'I tried to tell you before, but you wouldn't listen. You didn't want to understand. I'm not defending myself. What I've done is wrong. Terribly wrong.' She looked at her husband, who showed no expression, then back at Metcalfe. 'But it's *my* guilt, *my* sin. If I wasn't strong enough to stand by my husband when he needed me most, if I let a hint of scandal and suspicion poison our marriage, then it's my mistake, my fault. But I won't compound it with lies.'

She turned to Banks. 'Yes, Chief Inspector, I had an affair with Patrick. I met him at a social evening we put on for the staff and upper sixth of St Mary's School around the middle of last month. He was charming, interesting, passionate, and I became infatuated with him. Daniel and I were already going through a difficult time, as I think you know, and when I should have been strong, I was weak. I'm not proud of myself, but I want you to know that's why I lied to you, because I was afraid that too many questions would lead to exactly this kind of situation. Now it's happened, I'm glad, believe me, though I've been trying to avoid it at all costs. There's been far too much distrust and suspicion around this house lately. I can't believe that my husband had anything to do with this murder, any more than I can believe he's capable of doing what that vile man accused him of.'

She turned back to Metcalfe, tears still hanging on the rims of her eyes, dampening the long, dark lashes. 'I'm sorry, Patrick, if I misled you. I didn't intend to. Just put it down to a foolish woman seeking temporary escape. But you were only a distraction. I didn't mean for you to fall in love with me. And, if you're honest with yourself, I think you'd have to admit that you're not in love with me at all. I think you're in love with the idea of being in love, but you're far too self-absorbed to ever love anyone but yourself.'

Metcalfe stood up. 'It's not true, Rebecca. I do love you. Can't you see how you're blinding yourself? If you stay, you'll wither up and die before your time, before you've even—'

A harsh sound came from one of the armchairs, and Banks saw Daniel Charters bend forward, cup his head in his hands and start to cry like a child. Rebecca jumped up and went over to him, putting her arm around his shoulder.

'He doesn't even like women,' Metcalfe went on. 'You can't possibly—'

Banks picked up Charters's raincoat, grasped Metcalfe by the back of the collar and shoved him towards the front door. Even though Metcalfe was a few inches taller than Banks, he didn't put up much of a struggle, just muttered something about police brutality.

Once outside, Banks shut the door behind him, guided Metcalfe down the path and tossed him out of the gate onto the river path. 'On your bike,' he said.

Still muttering, Metcalfe walked towards the school. Banks glanced back as he closed the gate and saw Rebecca and Daniel framed in the window. Rebecca was cradling her husband's head against her breast, like a baby's, stroking his hair. Her mouth was opening and closing, as if she were uttering soothing words.

Banks had unfinished business at the vicarage – they

weren't off the hook yet – but it could wait. He looked up into the dark sky, as if searching for enlightenment, but felt only the cool raindrops on his face. He sneezed. Then he pulled his collar up and set off along the river path for the Kendal Road bridge.

6

ONE

Owen Pierce had just opened a bottle of wine and taken the heated remains of last week's beef stew out of the oven when the doorbell rang.

Muttering a curse, he put his stew back in the oven to keep warm and trotted to the front door. At the end of the hall, he could make out two figures through the frosted glass: one tall and heavy-set, one shorter and slim.

When he opened the door, he first thought they were Jehovah's Witnesses or Mormons – who else came to the door in pairs, wearing suits? But these two didn't quite look the part. True, one of them did look like a bible salesman – sticking-out ears, glasses, not a hair out of place, freshly scrubbed look – but the other looked more like a thug.

'Mr Pierce? Mr Owen Pierce?' asked the bible salesman.

'Yes, that's me. Look, I was just about to eat my dinner. What is it? What do you want? If you're selling—'

'We're police officers, sir,' the man went on. 'My name is Detective Inspector Stott and this is Detective Sergeant Hatchley. Mind if we come in?' They flashed their warrant cards and Owen stood back to let them in.

As soon as they got into the living-room, the big one started poking around.

'Nice place you've got,' Stott said, while his partner

prowled the room, picking up vases and looking inside them, opening drawers an inch or two, inspecting books.

'Look, what is this?' Owen said. 'Is he supposed to be going through my things like that? There are no drugs here, if that's what you're looking for.'

'Oh, don't mind Sergeant Hatchley. He's just like that. Insatiable curiosity.'

'Don't you need a search warrant or something?'

'Well, Owen,' said Stott, 'the way it works is like this. We *could* go to a magistrate, and we *could* apply for a warrant to search your premises, but it takes a lot of time. Sergeant Hatchley would have to stay here with you while I took care of the formalities. I think this way is much better all round. Anyway, you've nothing to hide, have you?'

'No, no, it's not that. It's just . . .'

'Well,' said Stott with a smile. 'That's all right, then, isn't it?'

'I suppose so.'

'Mind if I sit down?'

'Be my guest.'

Stott sat in the chair by the fake coals and Owen sat opposite him on the sofa. A mug of half-finished coffee stood between them on the glass-topped table beside a couple of unpaid bills and the latest *Radio Times*.

'Look,' Owen said, 'I'm afraid you've got me at a disadvantage here. What's it all about?'

'Just routine enquiries, sir. That's a nasty scratch on your face. Mind telling me where you got it?'

Owen put his hands up to his cheek. 'I've no idea,' he said. 'I woke up this morning and there it was.'

'Were you in the St Mary's area of Eastvale yesterday evening?'

'Let me think . . . Yes, yes, I believe I was.' He glanced at Hatchley, who seemed fascinated by the print of Renoir's *Bathers* over the fireplace.

'Why?'

'What? Sorry.'

'Look, just ignore Sergeant Hatchley for the moment,' Stott said. 'Look at me. I asked you *why* you were in St Mary's.'

Owen shrugged. 'No particular reason. I was just walking.'

'Walking? On a miserable night like that?'

'Well, if you let the weather dictate it, you wouldn't get much walking done in Yorkshire, would you?'

'Even so. St Mary's is quite a distance from here.'

'No more than three miles each way. And it's a very pleasant walk along the river. Even in the fog.'

Hatchley fished a copy of *Playboy* out of the magazine rack and held it up for Stott to see. Stott frowned and reached over for it. The cover showed a shapely blonde in skimpy pink lace panties, bordered in black, a flimsy slip, stockings and suspender belt. She was on her knees on a sofa, and her round behind faced the viewer. Her face was also turned towards the camera: glossy red lips, eyes an impossible shade of green, unfocused, as if she had just woken from a deep sleep. One thin strap had slipped over her upper right arm.

'I bought it because of one of the stories I wanted to read,' Owen said, immediately feeling himself turn red. It wasn't so much that he had been caught with something warped and perverted, but with something sub-literary, something beneath his intelligence and dignity. 'It's not illegal, you know. You can buy it at any newsagent's. It's not pornography.'

'That's a matter of opinion, sir, isn't it?' said Stott. He handed the magazine back to Hatchley as if he were dropping something in a rubbish bin, holding it between his thumb and forefinger.

'And there's a video tape full of what sounds like sexy stuff to me, sir, judging by the titles,' said Hatchley. 'One of them's called *School's Out*. And you should have a butcher's at some of the poses in these here so-called art books.'

'I'm an amateur photographer,' Owen said. 'It's my hobby. For Christ's sake, what do you expect? Is that what all this is about? Pornography? Because if it is—'

Stott waved his hand. 'No,' he said. 'It's of no matter, really. It might be relevant. We'll have to see. Do you live here by yourself, Mr Pierce?'

'Yes.'

'What kind of work do you do?'

'I'm a lecturer at Eastvale College. English.'

'Ever been married?'

'No.'

'Girlfriends?'

'Some.'

'But not to live with?'

'No.'

'Videos and magazines enough to satisfy you, eh?'

'Now just a min—'

Stott held up his hand. 'Sorry,' he said. 'Sorry, I shouldn't have said that. Tasteless of me. Out of line.'

Why couldn't Owen quite believe the apology? He sensed very strongly that Stott had made the remark on purpose to nettle him. He hoped he had passed the test, even though he couldn't be sure what the question was. Feeling more like Kafka's Joseph K every minute, he shifted in his chair. 'Why do you want to know all this?' he asked again. 'You said you were going to tell me what it's all about.'

'Did I? Well, first, would you mind if we had a quick look around the rest of the place? It might save us coming back.'

'Go ahead,' Owen said, and accompanied them as they did the rounds. It wasn't a thorough search, and Owen felt that by granting them permission he had probably saved himself a lot of trouble. He had seen on television the way search teams messed up places. They gave the bedrooms, one of which was completely empty, a cursory glance, poked about in his clothing drawers and wardrobe. In the study, Stott admired the aquarium of tropical fish and, of course, Hatchley rummaged through some of Owen's photo files and found the black-and-white nude studies of Michelle. He showed them to Stott, who frowned.

'Who's this?' Stott asked.

Owen shrugged. 'Just a model.'

'What's her name?'

'I'm sorry. I don't remember.'

'She looks very young.'

'She was twenty-two when those were taken.'

'Hmm, was she now?' muttered Stott, handing the photos back to Hatchley. 'Must be artistic licence. Notice any resemblance, Sergeant?' he asked Hatchley.

'Aye, sir, I do.'

'Resemblance to who?'

'Mind if we take these, too?' Stott asked.

'As a matter of fact, I do. They're the only prints I've got, and I've lost the negatives.'

'I understand, sir. You want to hang onto them for sentimental reasons. We'll take good care of them. Wait a minute, though . . . didn't you say she was just a model?'

'I did. And I didn't say I wanted to keep them for sentimental reasons. They're part of my portfolio. For exhibitions and such like.'

'Ah, I see. Might we just take one of them, perhaps, then?'

'Oh, all right. If you must.'

Hatchley leafed through some more art books on a shelf over the filing cabinet. One of them dealt with Japanese erotic art, and he opened it at a charcoal sketch of two young girls entwined together on a bed. They had either shaved off their pubic hair, or they were too young to have grown any. It was difficult to tell. He shoved it under Stott's nose.

'A bit like those books in the other room, sir,' he said.

Stott turned up his nose.

'And some of them novels he reads have been on trial,' Hatchley went on. '*Lady Chatterley's Lover, Naked Lunch, Ulysses, Delta of Venus*, a bit of De Sade . . .'

'For Christ's sake!' Owen cut in. 'I can't believe this. I'm an English teacher, you fucking moron. That's what I do for a living.'

'Now, you look here, mate,' said Hatchley, squaring up to him. 'The last bloke used that kind of language with me had a nasty accident on his way down the police station steps.'

'Are you threatening me?'

Hatchley thrust his chin out. 'Take it any way you want.'

'Stop it, Sergeant!' Stott cut in. 'I'll not have you talking to a member of the public this way. Apologize to Mr Pierce at once.'

'Yes, sir,' said Hatchley. He looked at Pierce and said, 'Sorry, sir.'

'If you ask me,' Owen said, 'you're the ones who are sick. Like witch-hunters, seeing the devil's work everywhere.'

'Maybe it is everywhere,' Stott said calmly. 'Have you ever thought about that?'

'It's just hard to believe there's someone who still thinks *Lady Chatterley's Lover* and *Ulysses* are dirty books, that's all.'

They sat down in the living-room again. 'Now why don't you tell me all about what you did in St Mary's yesterday evening,' Stott said. 'Sergeant Hatchley will take notes. No hurry. Take your time.'

Owen told them about his walk, the drinks at the Nag's Head, the meal at the Peking Moon and the walk home. As he spoke, Stott looked directly at him. The stern, triangular face showed no expression; and the eyes behind the lenses seemed cool. The man's ears almost made Owen want to laugh out loud, but he restrained himself. The big one, Hatchley, scribbled away in a spiral-bound notebook. Owen was surprised he could even write.

'Are you in the habit of talking to yourself, Mr Pierce?' asked Stott when he had finished.

Owen reddened. 'I wouldn't say *talking* to myself exactly. Sometimes I get lost in thought and I forget there are people around. Don't you ever do that?'

'No,' said Stott, 'I don't.'

Finally, after they had asked him to go over one or two random points again, Hatchley closed his notebook and Stott got to his feet. 'That'll be all for now,' he said.

'For now?'

'We might want to talk to you again. Don't know. We have to check up on a few points first. Would you mind if we had a look in your hall cupboard on the way out?'

'Why?'

'Routine.'

'Go ahead. I don't suppose I can stop you.'

Stott and Hatchley searched through the row of coats and jackets and pulled out Owen's new orange anorak. 'Is this what you were wearing last night?'

'Yes. Yes, it is. But—'

'What about these shoes?'

'Yes, those too. Look—'

'Mind if we take them with us, sir?'

'But why?'

'Purposes of elimination.'

'You mean it might help clear this business up?'

Stott smiled. 'Yes. It might. We'll let you have them back as soon as we can. Do you think you could get me a plastic bag while the sergeant here writes out a receipt.'

Owen fetched a bin-liner from the kitchen and watched Stott put the shoes and anorak inside it while Hatchley wrote out the receipt. Then he accepted the slip of paper and signed a release identifying the items as his.

Stott turned to Hatchley. 'I think we'd better be off, then, Sergeant,' he said. 'We've already taken up enough of Mr Pierce's valuable time.'

Hatchley took the plastic bag while Stott slipped the photograph into his briefcase, then they walked towards the door.

'Aren't you going to tell me what it's all about?' Owen asked again as he opened the front door for them. It was still raining.

Stott turned and frowned. 'That's the funny thing about it, Owen,' he said. 'That you don't know.' Then he shook his head slowly. 'Anybody would think you don't read the papers. Which is odd, for an educated man like yourself.'

TWO

Tracy Banks's bedroom, lit by a shaded table lamp, was a typical teenager's room, just like Deborah Harrison's, with pop-star posters on the wall, a portable cassette player, a narrow bed, usually unmade, and clothes all over the floor.

Tracy also had a desk against one wall and perhaps more books on her shelves than many girls her age. They ran the gamut from *The Wind in the Willows* to the *Pelican History of the World*. A row of dolls and teddy bears sat on the bookcase's lowest shelf; they always reminded Banks that his daughter wasn't that far away from childhood things yet. One day, they would disappear, as had most of his own toys; the fort with its soldiers, the Hornby train set, the Meccano. He had no idea where they had gone. Along with his childhood innocence.

Tracy herself sprawled on the bed in black leggings and a sloppy sweatshirt. She looked as if she had been crying. When Banks had got the message from his wife, Sandra, at his office, saying that Tracy was upset and wanted to talk to him, he had hurried straight home.

Now Banks sat on the edge of the bed and stroked his daughter's hair, which was tied back in a ponytail. 'What is it, love?' he asked.

'You didn't tell me,' Tracy said. 'Last night.'

'Are you talking about the murder?'

'Yes. Oh, it's all right. I know *why* you didn't tell me.' She sniffled. 'You wanted to spare my feelings. I don't blame you. I'm not mad at you or anything. I wish you had told me, though. It wouldn't have been such a shock when all the girls at school started talking about it.'

'I'm sorry,' said Banks. 'I knew you'd find out eventually and it would upset you. I suppose I was just trying to give you one more night of peace before you had to deal with it. Maybe it was selfish of me.'

'No. Really. It's all right.'

'So what *is* wrong?'

Tracy was silent a moment. Banks heard laughter and music from downstairs. 'I knew her,' she said finally.

'Knew who?'

'Deborah Harrison. I knew her.'

Apart from both being attractive blonde teenagers, Tracy and Deborah Harrison were about as far apart as you could get in background and class. Deborah went to the expensive, élite St Mary's School, where she was carefully groomed for Oxford or Cambridge, and Tracy went to Eastvale Comprehensive, where she had to fight her way through overcrowded classes, massive apathy and incompetent teaching to get decent enough A-levels to get into a redbrick university. Now here was Tracy saying she *knew* Deborah.

'How?' he asked.

Tracy shifted on the bed and sat cross-legged. She pulled the duvet over her shoulders like a shawl. 'You won't get mad at me, will you, Dad? Promise?'

Banks smiled. 'I've a feeling I'm not going to like this, but you've got my word.'

Tracy took a deep breath, then said, 'It was in the summer. A few times I hung around with the crowd at the Swainsdale Centre down by the bus station.'

'You hung around with those yobs? Jesus Christ, Tracy, I—'

'See! I knew you'd be mad.'

Banks took a deep breath. 'Okay. I'm not mad. Just

surprised, that's all. How could you *do* that? Those kids are into drugs, vandalism, all sorts of things.'

'Oh, we didn't do any harm, Daddy. It was just some-where to go, that's all. And they're not so bad, really. I know some of them look pretty weird and frightening, but they're not really. What did you used to do when you were a kid with nowhere to go?'

Banks would like to have answered, 'Museums, art galleries, long walks, books, classical concerts.' But he couldn't. Mostly he and his friends had hung around on street corners, on waste ground or in empty schoolyards. Sometimes they had even broken into condemned houses and played there.

'Okay,' he said. 'We'll let it pass for now. Carry on.'

'Deborah Harrison was down there shopping one day and one of the girls in the group knew her vaguely from dressage or swimming competitions or something, and they got talking. She came down a couple of days later – dressed down a bit – and started to hang out. I think she was bored with just staying at home and studying so she thought she'd slum it for a while.'

'What about her own friends?'

'I don't really think she had any. She said most of her school-friends were away for the summer. Most of the boarders had gone home, of course, and the day-girls had all jetted off to exotic places like America and the south of France. Why can't we go to places like that, Dad?'

'You were in France earlier this year.'

She slapped his arm. 'I'm only teasing. It wasn't a serious question.'

'When did Deborah first start joining in with the group?'

'Early August, I think.'

'And how did the others treat her?'

'They'd tease her about being a bit lah-de-dah, some-times, but she took it well enough. She said somebody had to be, and besides, it wasn't all it was cracked up to be.'

'What did she mean by that?'

'It was just her way of talking about things.'

'Did she ever flaunt her wealth, flash it about?'

'No. Not that I saw.'

'How long did she hang around with the group?'

'About three weeks, on and off.'

'Have you seen her since then?'

Tracy shook her head. 'Well, she wouldn't want to be seen dead with the likes of us now, would she? Not now she's back at St Mary's.' Then she put her hand over her mouth. 'I'm sorry, Dad. I just haven't got used to the idea that she's dead yet.'

Banks patted her arm. 'That's all right, love. It takes time. How well did you know her?'

'Not very well, but we chatted once or twice. She wasn't so bad, you know, when you got to know her a bit. I mean, she wasn't so snobbish. And she was quite bright.'

'Did you ever talk about school?'

'Sometimes.'

'What did she think of St Mary's?'

'She thought it was all right. At least the teachers were pretty good and the classes weren't too big. She said they had a staff to pupil ratio of one to ten. It must be more like one to five hundred where I go.'

'Did she mention any teachers in particular?'

'Not that I can remember.'

'Patrick Metcalfe. Does that name sound familiar?'

Tracy shook her head. 'No.'

'What kind of things did she say about school?'

'Nothing much, really. Just like, "You'd be surprised if you knew some of the things that go on there." That sort of thing. Very melodramatic.'

'What did you think she meant?'

Tracy looked down and rubbed her hand against her knee. 'Well, there's a lot of girls live in, you know, all together in the dormitories. I thought she meant, like, lesbians and stuff.'

'Did she imply that any of the teachers had any sort of sexual relationships with the pupils?'

'No, Dad. Honest, I don't know. I mean, she never really *said* anything. Not specific. She just implied. Hinted. But she was like that about everything.'

'Like what?'

'As if she knew more than she let on. And as if we were poor fools who saw only the surface, and she knew what *really* went on underneath. Like, *we* all swallowed the illusion, but she knew the underlying truth. I'm not trying to paint her in a bad way. She was really nice, but she just had this sort of tone, like, as if she knew more than everyone else.'

'Did she ever speak about her family?'

'She mentioned her father's business now and then.'

'What did she say about that?'

'I said once that it must be interesting having a father as famous as Sir Geoffrey Harrison, being knighted and all that.'

So much for having a mere detective for a father, Banks thought, swallowing his pride. 'What did she say?'

'The usual. Something like, "Oh, you'd be shocked if you knew some of the things I know."'

'And she didn't elaborate?'

'No. I just shrugged it off. I thought she meant the bad

128

side of technology, all the war stuff, missiles and bombs and that. We all know Sir Geoffrey Harrison's companies are involved in things like that. It's in the papers nearly every day.'

'And she didn't say any more about it?'

'No.'

'Did she ever mention Father Daniel Charters or Ive Jelačić?'

'The people from St Mary's church?'

'Yes.'

'Not to me. If you ask me, she was more interested in boys than anything else.'

'Boys? Anyone in particular?'

'Well, she sort of took up with John Spinks.' Tracy pulled a face. 'I mean, of all the boys . . .'

Banks leaned forward. The bedsprings creaked. 'Tell me about John Spinks,' he said.

7

ONE

Eastvale College of Further Education was a hodgepodge
of ugly redbrick and concrete buildings on the southern
fringe of the town, separated from the last few houses by
a stretch of marshy waste ground. There was nothing else
much around save for the Featherstone Arms across the
road, a couple of industrial estates and a large riding
stable, about half a mile away.

The college itself was a bit of a dump, too, Owen
thought over his lunch-time pint and soupy lasagne, and
he wouldn't be teaching there if he could get anything
better. The problem was, with only a BA from Leeds and
an MA from an obscure Canadian university, he *couldn't*
get anything better. So he was stuck teaching the business,
secretarial and agriculture students how to spell and write
sentences, skills they didn't even want to know. It was a
long way from the literary ambitions he had nursed not so
many years ago.

But he had more immediate problems than his teaching career: he had lied to the police, and they probably
suspected as much.

It wasn't much of a lie, admittedly. Besides, it was none
of their business. He had said he never lived with a woman,
but he had. With Michelle. For five years. And Michelle was
the woman in the black-and-white nude photographs.

So Owen wasn't exactly surprised when Stott and Hatchley walked into the pub and asked him if he would mind going to the station with them to clear up a few points. Nervous, yes, but not surprised. They said the department head had told them where they were likely to find him, and they had walked straight over.

Nobody spoke during the first part of the journey. Sergeant Hatchley drove the unmarked Rover, and Inspector Stott sat beside him. Owen could see the sharp line of his haircut at the back of his neck and the jug-handle shape of his ears, glasses hooked over them. As they approached the market square, Owen looked out of the window at the drab, shadowy figures hurrying from shop to shop, holding onto their hats.

'I wonder if you'd mind very much,' Stott said, turning slightly in his seat, 'if we arranged to take a couple of samples?'

'What kind of samples?'

'Oh, just the usual. Blood. Hair.'

'Do I have to?'

'Let me put it like this. You're not under arrest, but the crime we're investigating is very serious indeed. It would be best all around if you gave your permission and signed a release. For elimination purposes.'

'And if I refuse? What will you do? Hold me down, pull my hair out and stick a needle in me?'

'Nothing like that. We could get the superintendent to authorize it. But that wouldn't look good, would it? Especially if the matter ever went to court. Refusing to give a sample? A jury might see that as an admission to guilt. And, of course, as soon as you're eliminated from the enquiry, the samples will all be destroyed. No records. What do you say?'

'All right.'

'Thank you, sir.' Stott turned to face the front again and picked up his car phone. 'I'll just take the liberty of calling Dr Burns and asking him to meet us at the station.'

It was all handled quickly and efficiently in a private office at the police station. Owen signed the requisite forms, rolled up his sleeve and looked away. He felt only a sharp, brief pricking sensation as the needle slid out. Then the doctor pulled some hair out of his scalp. That hurt a little more.

The interview room they took him to next was a desolate place: grey metal desk; three chairs, two of them bolted to the floor; grimy windows of thick wired glass; a dead fly smeared against one institutional-green wall; and that was it.

It smelled of stale smoke. A heavy blue glass ashtray sat on the desk, empty but stained and grimy with old ash.

Stott sat opposite Owen, and Sergeant Hatchley moved the free chair and sat by the wall near to the door, out of Owen's line of vision. He sat backwards on the chair, wrapping his thick arms around its back.

First, Stott placed the buff folder he'd been carrying on the desk, smiled and adjusted his glasses. Then he switched on a double-cassette tape recorder, tested it, and gave the date, time and names of those present.

'Just a few questions, Owen,' he said. 'You've been very co-operative so far. I hope we don't have to keep you long.'

'So do I,' said Owen, looking around the grim room. 'Shouldn't I call my lawyer or something?'

'Oh, I don't think so,' said Stott. 'Of course, you can if you want. It's your right.' He smiled. 'But it's not as if you're under arrest or anything. You're free to leave anytime you want. Besides, do you actually have a solicitor? Most people don't.'

Come to think of it, Owen didn't have a solicitor. He knew one, though. An old university acquaintance had switched from English to law after his first year and now practised in Eastvale. They hadn't seen each other in years, until Owen had bumped into him in a pub a few months back. Gordon Wharton, that was his name. Owen couldn't remember what kind of law he specialized in, but at least it was a start, if things went that far. For the moment, though, Stott was right. Owen hadn't been arrested, and he didn't see why he should have to pay a solicitor.

'Let me lay my cards on the table, Owen. You have admitted to us that you were in the area of St Mary's on Monday evening. Is that true?'

'Yes.'

'Why?'

'I told you. I went for a walk.'

'Shall we just go over it again, for the record?'

Owen shrugged. 'There's really nothing to go over.' He could see the sheet of paper in front of Stott, laid out like an appointment book. Some of the times and notes had question marks in red.

'What time did you set off on this walk?'

'Just after I got back from work. About four. Maybe as late as half past.'

'How far is it to St Mary's?'

'Along the river? About three miles from my house. And the house is about half a mile from the river.'

'About seven miles there and back, then?'

'Yes. About that.'

'Now, before you ate at the Peking Moon you drank two

pints of bitter and a Scotch whisky at the Nag's Head, right?'

'I wasn't counting, but yes, I had a couple of drinks.'

'And you left the pub at about a quarter to six?'

'I wasn't especially aware of the time.'

'That's what the landlord told us.'

'I suppose it must be true, then.'

'And you ate at the Peking Moon at approximately six-thirty, is that correct?'

'About then, yes. Again, I didn't notice the actual time.'

'What did you do between a quarter to and half past six?'

'Walked around. Stood on the bridge.'

'Did you go into St Mary's graveyard?'

'No, I didn't. Look, if you're trying to tie me in to that girl's murder, then you're way off beam. Why would I do something like that? Perhaps I *had* better call a solicitor, after all.'

'Ah!' Stott glanced over Owen's shoulder towards Sergeant Hatchley. 'So he *does* read the papers, after all.'

'I did after you left. Of course I did.'

Stott looked back at him. 'But not before?'

'I'd have known what you were talking about then, wouldn't I?'

Stott straightened his glasses. 'What made you connect our visit with that particular item of news?'

Owen hesitated. Was it a trick question? 'It didn't take much,' he answered slowly, 'given the kind of questions you asked me. Even though I know nothing about what happened, I know I was in St Mary's that evening. I never denied it. And while we're on the subject, what led you to me?'

Stott smiled. 'Easy, really. We asked around. Small, wealthy neighbourhood like St Mary's, people notice strangers. Plus you were wearing an orange anorak and you used your Visa card in the Peking Moon.'

Owen leaned forward and slapped his palms on the cool metal surface. 'There!' he said. 'That proves it, then, doesn't it?'

Stott gave him a blank look. 'Proves what?'

'That I didn't do it. If I *had* done it, what you seem to be accusing me of, I would hardly have been so foolish as to leave my calling card, would I?'

Stott shrugged. 'Criminals make mistakes, just like everybody else. Otherwise we'd never catch any, would we? And I'm not accusing you of anything at the moment, Owen. You can see our problem, though, can't you? Your story sounds thin, very thin. I mean, if you were in the area for some real, believable reason . . . Maybe to meet someone? Did you *know* Deborah Harrison, Owen?'

'No.'

'Had you been watching her, following her?'

Owen sat back. 'I've told you why I was there. I can't help it if you don't like my reason, can I? I never thought I'd have to explain myself to anyone.'

'Did you see anyone acting suspiciously?'

'Not that I remember.'

'Did you see Deborah Harrison?'

'No.'

'About that scratch on your cheek,' Stott said. 'Remember yet where you got it?'

Owen put his hand to his cheek and shrugged. 'Cut myself shaving, I suppose.'

'Bit high up to be shaving, isn't it?'

'I told you. I don't remember. Why?'

'What about the nude photos, Owen? The ones we found at your house?'

'What about them? They're figure studies, that's all.'

Sergeant Hatchley spoke for the first time, and the rough voice coming from behind startled Owen. 'Come on, lad, don't be shy. What's wrong with you? Don't you like looking at a nice pair of tits? You're not queer, are you?'

Owen half-twisted in his seat. 'No. I didn't say I didn't like looking at naked women. Of course I do. I'm perfectly normal.'

'And some of the girls in that magazine seemed very young to me,' said Stott.

Owen turned to face him again. 'Since when has it been a crime to buy *Playboy*? You people are still living in the middle ages. For Christ's sake, they're models. They get paid for posing like that.'

'And you like videos, too, don't you, Owen? There was that one in your cabinet, your own private video to keep, to watch whenever you want. Including *School's Out*.'

'A friend gave me it, as a sort of joke. I told him I'd never seen any porn – any sexy videos before, and he gave me that, said I'd enjoy it.'

'Well, I'll tell you, Owen,' said Stott. 'I've got to wonder about a bloke who watches stuff like that and likes the sort of art books and pictures you like. Especially if he takes nude photos of young girls, too.'

'It's a free country. I'm a normal single male. I also happen to be an amateur photographer. And I have a right to watch whatever kind of videos I want as long as they're legal.' Owen felt himself flushing with embarrassment. Christ how he wished Chris Lorimer at the college hadn't given him the bloody video.

'*School's Out*,' Hatchley said quietly from behind. 'A bit over the top, that, wouldn't you say?'

'I haven't even watched that one.'

'You can see what Sergeant Hatchley's getting at, though, can't you, Owen?' said Stott. 'It looks bad: the subject-matter, the image. It all looks a bit odd. Distinctly fishy.'

'Well, I can't help that. It's not fishy. I'm perfectly innocent, and that's the truth.'

'Who's the girl in the photographs? The one who looks about fifteen.'

'She was twenty-two. Just a model. It was a couple of years ago. I can't remember her name.'

'Funny, that.'

'What is?'

'That you remember her age but not her name.'

Owen felt his heart pounding. Stott scrutinized him closely for a few seconds, then stood up abruptly. 'You can go now,' he said. 'I'm glad we could have our little chat.'

Owen was confused. 'That's it?'

'For the moment, yes. We'll be in touch.'

Owen could hardly stand up quickly enough. He banged his knee on the underside of the metal desk and swore. He rubbed his knee and started to back towards the door. His face was burning. 'I can really go?'

'Yes. But stay available.'

Owen was shaking when he got out of the police station and turned down Market Street towards home. Could they really treat you like that when you went along with them of your own free will? He had a feeling his rights were being trampled on and maybe it *was* time to look up Gordon Wharton.

The first thing he did when he got into the house was

tear up the copy of *Playboy* and burn the pieces in the waste-bin, Cormac McCarthy story and all. Next, he took the video that Chris Lorimer had given him, pulled the tape out, broke the plastic casing and dumped it in the rubbish bin to burn too. At least they couldn't use it as evidence against him now.

Finally, he went into the spare room and took the rest of the nude photographs of Michelle from his filing cabinet. He held them in his hands, ready to rip them into tiny pieces and burn them along with the rest, but as he held them he couldn't help but look at them.

They were simple, tasteful chiaroscuro studies, and he could tell from the way Michelle's eyes glittered and her mouth was set that she was holding back her laughter. He remembered how she had complained about goose-bumps, that he was taking so long setting up the lighting, then he remembered the wine and the wild lovemaking afterwards. She had liked being photographed naked; it had excited her.

His hands started to shake again. God, she looked so beautiful, so perfect, so young, so bloody innocent. Still shaking, he thrust the photos back in the cabinet and turned away, tears burning in his eyes.

TWO

While Stott and Hatchley were interviewing Owen Pierce, Banks drove out to St Mary's to see Lady Sylvie Harrison. He would have liked Susan with him, for her reactions and observations, but he knew he was risking Chief Constable Riddle's wrath by having anything more to do with the Harrisons, and he didn't want to get Susan into trouble.

She was right; she had worked hard and passed her sergeant's exam, all but the rubber stamp, and he wouldn't forgive himself easily if he ruined her chances of a quick promotion. He would be sad to lose her, though. Detective constables were rarely promoted straight to the rank of detective sergeant, and almost never in the same station; they usually went back in uniform for at least a year, then they had to reapply to the CID.

Before setting off, Banks had phoned the Harrison household and could hardly believe his luck. Sir Geoffrey was out with Michael Clayton, and Lady Harrison was at home alone. No, she said, with that faint trace of French accent, she would have no objections to talking to Banks without her husband present.

As he drove along North Market Street past the tourist shops and the community centre where Sandra worked, Banks played the tape of Ute Lemper singing Michael Nyman's musical adaptations of Paul Celan's poems. It was odd music, and it had taken him some time to get used to it, but now he adored them all, found them pervaded by a sort of sinister melancholy.

It was a chilly day outside, grey and windy, skittering the leaves along the pavements. But at least the rain had stopped. Just as 'Corona' was coming to an end, Banks pulled up at the end of the Harrisons' drive.

Lady Harrison must have heard him coming because she opened the large white door for him as soon as he got out of the car. She wore jeans and a blue cashmere pullover. She hugged herself against the cold as she stood in the doorway.

She had done her best to cover up the marks of misery and pain on her face, but they were still apparent through the make-up, like distant figures looming in the fog.

This time, instead of heading for the white room, she hung up his overcoat and led him to the kitchen, which was done in what Banks thought of as a sort of rustic French style: lots of wood panelling and cupboards, copper-bottomed pots and pans hanging on hooks on the wall, flower-patterned mugs on wooden pegs, a few potted plants, a vase of chrysanthemums on the table and a red-and-white checked tablecloth. The room smelled of herbs and spices, cinnamon and rosemary being the two most prominent. A kettle was just coming to the boil on the red Aga.

'Please sit down,' she said.

Banks sat on a wooden chair at the kitchen table. Its legs scraped along the terracotta floor.

'Tea? I was just going to make some.'

'Fine,' said Banks.

'Ceylon, Darjeeling, Earl Grey or Lapsang Souchong?'

'Lapsang, if that's all right.'

She smiled. 'Exactly what I was going to have.'

Her movements were listless and Banks noticed that the smile hadn't reached her eyes. It would probably be a long time before one did.

'Are you sure you're all right here alone, Lady Harrison?' he asked.

'Yes. Actually, it was *my* idea. I sent Geoffrey out. He was getting on my nerves. I needed a little quiet time to . . . to get used to things. What would be the point of us both moping around the house all day? He's used to action, to doing things. And please,' she added with a fleeting smile, 'call me Sylvie.'

'Fine,' he said. 'Sylvie it is.'

She measured out the leaves into a warmed pot – a rather squat, ugly piece with blue squiggles and a thick, straight spout – then sat down opposite Banks and let it brew.

'I'm sorry to intrude on your grief,' Banks said. 'But there are still a lot of questions need answering.'

'Of course,' said Sylvie. 'But Geoffrey told me this morning that you already have a suspect. Is it true?'

Interesting, Banks thought. He hadn't realized there was a lodge meeting last night. Of course, as soon as Stott had tracked down Owen Pierce and sent his anorak off to the lab for analysis, Banks had let the chief constable know what was happening, and Riddle obviously hadn't wasted much time in reporting to Sir Geoffrey. Ah, privilege.

'Someone's helping us with our enquiries, yes,' he said, immediately regretting the trite phrase. 'I mean, last night we talked to someone who was seen in the area on Monday evening. Detective Inspector Stott is interviewing him again now.'

'It's not that man from the church, the one who was fired?'

'We don't think so, but we're still keeping an open mind about him.'

'Do you think this other person did it?'

'I don't know. I haven't talked to him yet. We're playing it very cautiously, very carefully. If he is the one, we want to be certain we don't make any mistakes that will come back to haunt us when the case goes to court.'

'Sometimes,' mused Sylvie, 'it seems that the system favours the criminal rather than the victim. Don't you think?'

Tell me about it, thought Banks wearily. If they did think they'd got their man, next they would have to convince the Crown Prosecution Service they had a case –

not always an easy job – then, after they had jumped
through all the hoops, as often as not they could look
forward to watching the accused's lawyer tear the evidence to shreds. 'Sometimes,' he agreed. 'Did Deborah
ever mention anyone called Owen Pierce?'

Sylvie frowned. 'No. I've never heard the name before.'

Banks described Pierce, but it meant nothing to her.

She poured the tea, tilting her head slightly and biting
the end of her tongue as she did so. The Lapsang smelled
and tasted good, it's smoky flavour a perfect foil for a grey,
cold November day. Outside, the wind whistled through
the trees and rattled the windows, creating dust devils
and gathering the fallen leaves into whirlwinds. Sylvie
Harrison put both hands around her mug, as if keeping
them warm. 'What do you want to know from me?' she
asked.

'I'm trying to find out as much as I can about what
Deborah was like. There are still a few gaps.'

'Such as?'

'Boyfriends, for example.'

'Ah, boyfriends. But Deborah was far too busy at school
for boys. There was plenty of time for that later. After she
finished her education.'

'Even so. There was the summer.'

Sylvie held his gaze. 'She didn't have a boyfriend.'

Banks paused, then said slowly, feeling as if he were
digging his career grave with every word. 'That's not what
I heard. Someone told me she had a boyfriend in August.'

Sylvie paled. She pressed her lips so tight together they
almost turned white.

'*Did* she have a boyfriend?' Banks asked again.

Sylvie sighed, then nodded. 'Yes. In the summer. But
she finished with him.'

'Was his name John Spinks?'

She raised her eyebrows. 'How did you know that?'

'You knew about him?'

She nodded. 'Yes. He was a most unpleasant character.'

'Why do you think a bright, pretty girl like Deborah would go out with someone like that?'

A distant look came into her eyes. 'I don't know. I suppose he was good-looking, perhaps exciting in a way. Sometimes one makes mistakes,' she said, with a shrug that Banks thought of as very Gallic. 'Sometimes one makes a fool of oneself, does something with the wrong person for all the wrong reasons.'

'What reasons?'

She shrugged again. 'A woman's reasons. A young woman's reasons.'

'Was Deborah having sex with John Spinks?'

Sylvie paused for a moment, then nodded and said with a sigh, 'Yes. One day I came home unexpectedly and I caught them in Deborah's bedroom. I was crazy with anger. I shouted at him and threw him out of the house and told him never to come back.'

'How did he react?'

She reddened. 'He called me names I will not repeat in front of you.'

'Was he violent?'

'He didn't hit me, if that's what you mean.' She nodded in the direction of the hall. 'There was a vase, not a very valuable vase, but a pretty one, a present from my father, on a stand by the door. He lifted it with both hands and threw it hard against the wall. One small chip of pottery broke off and cut my chin, that's all.' She fingered the tiny scar.

'Did he leave after that?'

'Yes.'

'Did you tell Sir Geoffrey about him?'

'No.'

'Why not?'

She paused before answering. 'You must understand that Geoffrey can be very Victorian in some ways, especially concerning Deborah. I hadn't even told him she was seeing the boy in the first place. He would have made things very uncomfortable for her if he'd known, given Spinks's character and background. I . . . well . . . I'm a woman and I think in some ways I understood what she was going through, more than Geoffrey would have, anyway. I'm not saying I approved, but it was something she had to get out of her system. Stopping her would only have made her more determined. In the long run it would probably have resulted in even more damage. Do you know what I mean?'

'I think so. Did Deborah go on seeing Spinks?'

'No. I don't think so. Not after he threw the vase. She was very upset about what happened and we had a long talk. She said she was really sorry, and she apologized to me. I like to think that she understood what I was telling her, what a waste of time seeing this Spinks boy was. She said she realized now what kind of person he was and she would never go near him again. She'd heard him curse me in the most vile manner. She'd seen him throw the vase at the wall, seen the sliver cut me, draw blood.' Sylvie touched the small scar again. 'I think it truly shocked her, made her see him in a new light. Deborah is a good girl inside, Chief Inspector. Stubborn, wilful, perhaps, but ultimately sensible too. And like a lot of girls her age, she is very naïve about men.'

'In what ways?'

'She didn't understand the way they use women, manipulate them, or the power of their lust. I wanted her to learn to value herself. In sex, when the time came, as much as in everything else. Unless a woman respects her sexual self, she's going to be every man's victim all her life. Giving herself away to that . . . that *animal* was a bad way for her to start. You men don't always understand how important that time of a woman's life is.'

'Was she a virgin before she met Spinks?'

Sylvie nodded and curled her lip in disgust. 'She told me all about it that night after the row. He stole a car, like so many youths do these days. They went for a ride out on the moors . . .' Her fists clenched as she talked. 'And he did it to her in the back of the car.'

'Had you met him before that time?'

She nodded. 'Just once. It was two or three weeks earlier. Deborah brought him to the house. It was a sunny day. They were out making a barbecue when I got back from shopping in Leeds.'

'What happened?'

'That time? Oh, nothing much. They were drinking. No doubt at the boy's instigation. Deborah had taken a bottle of my father's estate wine from the cellar. I was a little angry with them, but not too much. You must remember, Chief Inspector, that I grew up in France. We had wine with every meal, taken with a little water when we were children, so drinking under age hardly seems the great sin it does to you English.'

'What was your impression of John Spinks?'

'He was very much a boy of single syllables. He didn't have much to say for himself at all. I'll admit I didn't like him right from the start. Call me a snob, if you like, but it's true. After he'd gone, I told her he wasn't good enough for her and that she should consider breaking off with him.'

'How did she react to that?'

Sylvie smiled sadly. 'The way any sixteen-year-old girl would. She told me she'd see who she wanted and that I should mind my own business and stop trying to run her life.'

'Exactly what my daughter said in the same situation,' said Banks. 'Is there anything else you can tell me about Spinks?'

Sylvie sipped some tea, then she went to fetch her handbag. She slipped her hand inside and pulled out a packet of Dunhill. 'You don't mind if I smoke, do you?' she asked. 'Why I should ask permission in my own house, I don't know. It's just, these days . . . the anti-smoking brigade . . . they get to you. It's only in moments of stress I revert to the habit.'

'I know what you mean,' said Banks, pulling his Silk Cut out with a conspiratorial smile. 'May I join you?'

'That would be even better. Geoffrey will go spare, of course. He thinks I've stopped.'

The phrase 'go spare' sounded odd with that slight French lilt to it; such a Yorkshire phrase, Banks thought.

'Your husband told me you're from Bordeaux,' Banks said, accepting a light from her slim gold lighter.

Sylvie nodded. 'My father is in the wine business. A *négociant*. One of *la noblesse du bouchon*.'

'I'm afraid my French is very rusty.'

'Literally, it means "the bottle-cork nobility." It's a collective term for the *négociants* of a great wine centre, like Bordeaux.'

'I suppose it means he's rich?'

She wrinkled her nose. 'Very. Anyway, I met Geoffrey when he was on a wine-tasting tour of the area. It must have been, oh, seventeen years ago. I was only nineteen at the time. Geoffrey was thirty.'

'And Sir Geoffrey fell in love with the *négociant*'s daughter? How romantic.'

Sylvie dredged up another sad smile. 'Yes, it was romantic.' Then she drew deep on her cigarette and let the smoke out of her nose. 'You asked if there was anything else about Spinks, Chief Inspector. Yes, there was. Things had been going missing from the house.'

'Missing? Like what?'

She shrugged. 'A silver snuffbox. Not very valuable, though it might look antique to the untrained eye. Some foreign currency. A pair of silver earrings. Little things like that.'

'Since Deborah had been seeing Spinks?'

She nodded. 'Yes. I'm almost certain of it. Deborah wouldn't do anything like that. I'm not saying she was a saint – obviously not – but at least she was honest. She was no thief.'

'Did you challenge her about the stolen articles?'

'Yes.'

'And what did she say?'

'She said she didn't know about the missing things but she would talk to him.'

'Did she tell you what he said?'

'She said he denied it.'

'Did Spinks ever bother either of you after that day you threw him out?'

Sylvie frowned and stubbed out her cigarette. She rubbed the back of her hand over her lips as if to get rid of the taste. 'He made threats. One day, he came to the house when both Deborah and Geoffrey were out.'

'What did he do?'

'He didn't *do* anything. Nothing physical, if that's what you mean. If he had, I wouldn't have hesitated to call the police. I tried to close the door on him, but he pushed his way in and asked for money.'

'Did you give him any?'

'No.'

'What did he say?'

'He said if I didn't give him money, he would keep on seeing Deborah, and that he would get her pregnant, make himself part of the family.' She shuddered. 'He was disgusting.'

'And you still didn't give him anything.'

'No. Then he said if I didn't give him money he would start spreading the word around that he had deflowered Sir Geoffrey Harrison's daughter. That she was nothing but a slut. He said he would spread it around St Mary's and get her expelled, and he would make sure people in the business community knew so that they would all laugh at Geoffrey behind his back.'

'What did you do?'

'Nothing. I was too shocked. Luckily, Michael was here at the time. He handled it.'

'What did he do?'

'I don't know. You'll have to ask him. I was so upset I went upstairs. All I can say is that I heard nothing more of the matter after that. Spinks disappeared from our lives just as if he had never been there in the first place. Not without leaving some damage, of course.'

'Did he ever threaten to harm Deborah physically?'

Sylvie shook her head. 'Not that I heard.'

'But he certainly seemed capable of acting violently?'

She touched her scar again. 'Yes. Do you think . . .?'

'I honestly don't know,' said Banks. 'But anything's

possible. Did Mr Clayton know about Spinks from the start?'

'Yes. He dropped by the house that time when they were having the barbecue. He said something to Spinks about the drinking and Spinks was very rude. Michael agreed with me then that Deborah was wasted on the boy. And I told him about . . . when I found them together in bed. I had to tell someone.'

Clayton seemed to be dropping by Sir Geoffrey's house an awful lot, Banks thought. Especially when Sir Geoffrey wasn't there but Sylvie was.

'Does Mr Clayton have any family of his own?' he asked.

'Michael? No. He and his wife, Gillian, split up three years ago. It was a childless marriage.' She smiled. 'I think part of the problem was that Michael is married to his work. Sometimes I think he has his computers wired directly to his brain. He has a girlfriend in Seattle now, and that seems ideal for him. Long-distance romance. He travels there quite often on company business.'

'How long have he and Sir Geoffrey known one another?'

'Since Oxford. They've always been inseparable. In fact, Michael was with Geoffrey when we met.'

Banks paused for a moment and sipped some lukewarm tea. 'Do you know any of the teachers at St Mary's?' he asked.

'Some of them. When you pay as much money to send your child to school as we do, you tend to have some say in the way the place is run.'

'And?'

'And St Mary's is an excellent school. Wonderful facilities, good staff, a healthy atmosphere . . . I could go on.'

'Did you ever get the sense there was anything unpleasant going on there?'

'Unpleasant?'

'I'm sorry I can't be any more precise than that. But if anyone, or any group, was up to something at school – something illegal, such as drugs – and if Deborah found out about it . . . She was attacked on her way home from school, after all. Someone could have followed her from there.'

Sylvie shook her head slowly. 'The things you policemen dream up. No, I never heard the slightest hint of a rumour of anything wrong at St Mary's. And I believe one *does* hear about these things, if they are going on.'

'Did you have any reason to think John Spinks or anyone else might have introduced Deborah to drugs?'

She sighed. 'I can't say I didn't worry about it.' Then she shook her head. 'But I don't think so. I never saw any signs. Deborah was a very active girl. She valued her physical health, her athletic prowess, far too much to damage it with drugs.'

'Do you know Patrick Metcalfe?'

'I've met him, yes.'

'Did Deborah ever talk about him?'

'No, not that I recall.'

'Did she like him?'

'She didn't say one way or the other. She did quite well at history, though it wasn't her best subject. But why do you ask?'

'He's just part of the tapestry, that's all. Maybe not an important part. Did Deborah have any contact with the church after you and your husband stopped going?'

'I don't think so. Geoffrey was quite adamant that we all stay away. But the school and the church remained close. She may have had some contact.' She rubbed her eyes and stood up. 'Please excuse me, Chief Inspector, but I'm feeling very tired. I think I've told you all I can for the moment. And I hope you'll be discreet. I'd prefer it if you didn't let Geoffrey know about what I've told you today.'

Banks smiled. 'Of course not. Not if you don't tell him I've been here. I'm afraid my boss—'

But before he could get the words out, the front door opened and shut and Sir Geoffrey shouted out, 'I'm home, darling. How is everything?'

THREE

At the back of Eastvale bus station, past the noise of revving engines and the stink of diesel fumes, a pair of heavy glass doors led past the small newsagent's booth to an escalator that rarely worked.

At the top of the staircase, a shop-lined corridor ended in an open, glass-roofed area with a central fountain surrounded by a few small, tatty trees in wooden planters. The Swainsdale Centre.

Several other corridors, leading from other street entrances, also converged like spokes at the hub. There were shops all around – HMV, Boots, W. H. Smith, Curry's, Dixon's – but at six-thirty that Wednesday evening, none of them were open. Only the small coffee shop was doing any business at all – if you could call two cups of tea and a Penguin biscuit in the last two hours 'business.'

The teenagers hung out around the fountain, usually leaning against the trees or sitting on the benches that had been put up for the little old ladies to rest their feet. No little old ladies dared go near them now.

A number of pennies gleamed at the bottom of the pool into which the fountain ran. God knew why people felt they had to chuck coins in water, Banks thought. But the small pool was mostly full of floating cigarette ends, cellophane, Mars bar wrappers, beer tins, plastic bags containing traces of solvent, and the occasional used condom.

Banks experienced a brief flash of anger as he approached, imagining Tracy standing there as one of this motley crowd, smoking, drinking beer, pushing one another playfully, raising their voices in occasional obscenities or sudden whoops, and generally behaving as teenagers do.

Then he reminded himself, as he constantly had to do these days, that he hadn't been much different himself at their age, and that as often as not, beneath the braggadocio and the rough exteriors, most of them were pretty decent kids at heart.

Except John Spinks.

According to Tracy, Spinks was a hero of sorts among the group because of his oft-recounted but never-detected criminal exploits. She thought he made most of them up, but even she had to admit that he occasionally shared his ill-gotten gains with the others in the form of cigarettes and beer. As he didn't work and couldn't have got very much from the dole, he clearly had to supplement his income through criminal activities. And he never seemed short of a few quid for a new leather jacket.

He lived with his mum on the East Side Estate, a decaying monument to the sixties' social optimism, but he never talked much about his home life.

He had boasted of going to an 'Acid House' party in Manchester once, Tracy said, and claimed he took Ecstasy there. He had also tried glue-sniffing, but thought it was kids' stuff and it gave you spots. He was proud of his clear complexion.

Spinks, standing a head taller than the rest, was immediately recognizable from Tracy's description. His light-brown hair was short at the back and sides, and long on top, with one long lock half-covering the left side of his face. He wore jeans, trainers with the laces untied and a mid-length flak jacket.

When Banks and Hatchley approached, showed their warrant cards and asked for a private little chat, he didn't run, curse them or protest, but simply shrugged and said, 'Sure,' then he gave his mates a sideways grin as he went.

They went into the coffee shop, took a table, and Hatchley fetched three coffees and a couple of chocolate biscuits. The owner's face lit up; it was more business than she'd done in ages.

In a way, Tracy was right; Spinks did resemble someone from *Neighbours*. Clean cut, with that smooth complexion, he had full lips, perhaps a shade too red for a boy, brown eyes that could probably melt a young girl's heart, and straight, white teeth, the front ones stained only slightly by tobacco. He accepted the cigarette Banks offered and broke off the filter before smoking it.

'You Tracy Banks's dad, then?' he said.

'That's right.'

'She said her father were a copper. Nice bit of stuff, Tracy is. I've had my eyes on her for a while. Come to think of it, I haven't seen her for a few weeks. What's she up to, these days?'

Banks smiled. It hadn't taken long to get past the good looks to the slimy, vain and cocky little creep underneath. Now he knew he wouldn't feel bad, no matter what he had to do to get Spinks to talk.

When Banks didn't answer, Spinks faltered only slightly before saying, 'Why don't you ask her to drop by one evening? She knows where I am. We could have a really good time. Know what I mean?'

'One more remark like that,' Hatchley cut in, 'and you'll be mopping blood from your face for the rest of our little chat.'

'Threats now, is it?' He shrugged. 'What's it matter, anyway? I've already had the little bitch and she's not—'

The woman behind the counter looked over just after Spinks's face bounced off the table, and she hurried over with a cloth to stem the flow of blood from his nose.

'That's police brutality,' Spinks protested, his words muffled by the cool, wet cloth. 'Broke my fucking nose. Did you see that?'

'Me?' said the woman. 'Didn't see nothing. And there's no call for that sort of language in here. You can keep the cloth.' Then she scurried back behind the counter.

'Funny,' said Banks. 'I was looking the other way, too.' He leaned forward. 'Now listen you little arse-wipe, let's start again. Only this time, I ask the questions and you answer them. Okay?'

Spinks muttered a curse through the rag.

'Okay?' Banks asked again.

Spinks took the cloth away. The flow of blood seemed to have abated, and he only dabbed at it sulkily now and then throughout the interview. 'You've broken my tooth,' he whined. 'That'll cost money. I was only joking, anyway, about your—'

'Deborah Harrison,' Banks said. 'Name ring a bell?'

Spinks averted his eyes. 'Sure. It's that schoolkid from St Mary's got herself killed the other day. All over the news.'

'She didn't "get herself" killed. Someone murdered her.'

'Whatever.' The lock of hair kept slipping down over Spinks's eye, and he had developed the habit of twitching his head to flick it back in place. 'Don't look at me. I didn't kill her.'

'Where were you on Monday around six o'clock?'

'Was that the day it was really foggy?'

'Yes.'

'I was here.' He pointed to the group outside. 'Ask anyone. Go on, ask them.'

Banks nodded at Sergeant Hatchley, who went out to talk to the youths.

'Besides,' Spinks went on, 'why would I want to kill her?'

'You went out together over the summer and you parted on bad terms. You were angry with her, you wanted revenge.'

He probed his tooth and winced. 'That's a load of old knob-rot, that is. Besides, they wasn't supposed to tell you that.'

'Who wasn't?'

'*Them*. The French tart and that bloody Clayton. They went to enough trouble to stop *me* from telling anyone, now they go and tell you themselves. Bloody stupid, it is. Doesn't make sense. Unless they just wanted to drop me in it.' He dabbed at his red nose.

Hatchley came back inside and nodded.

'They telling the truth?' Banks asked.

'Hard to say. Like Jelačić's mates, they'd probably say black was white if young Lochinvar over here told them to.'

Banks studied Spinks, who showed no emotion, but

kept dabbing at his nose and probing his tooth with his tongue. 'What did Michael Clayton do to stop you from talking?' he asked.

Spinks looked down into the bloodstained rag. 'Imagine how it would sound if some newspaper got hold of the story that an East Side Estate yobbo like me had been sticking it to Sir Geoffrey Harrison's daughter.'

'That's *why*. I asked you *what*.'

'Gave me some money.'

'Who did?'

'Clayton.'

'Michael Clayton gave you money to stay away from Deborah?'

'That's what I said.'

'How much?'

'Hundred quid.'

'So you admit to blackmailing Lady Harrison?'

'Nothing of the sort. Look, if you sell a story to the papers, they pay you for it, don't they? So why shouldn't you get paid if you *don't* sell the papers a story?'

'Your logic is impeccable, John. I can see you didn't waste your time in school.'

Spinks laughed. 'School? Hardly ever there, was I?'

'Was Deborah there when you went to ask for money?'

'Nah. Just the two of them. Clayton and the old bag.' He put on a posh accent. 'It was Deborah's day for riding, don't you know. *Dressage.* Got a horse out Middleham way. Always did like hot flesh throbbing between her legs, did Deborah.'

'So the two of them had a talk with you?'

'That's right.'

'And after Lady Harrison had gone upstairs, Michael Clayton hit you and gave you a hundred pounds.'

'Like I said, we came to an arrangement. Then her ladyship came back and said if she ever heard I'd been talking about her daughter, she *would* tell Sir Geoffrey and he'd probably have me killed.'

'You blackmailed her and she threatened you with murder?'

'Yeah. Get away with anything, those rich fuckers. Just like the pigs.'

'You've been listening to too many Jefferson Airplane records, John. They don't call us pigs now.'

'Once a pig, always a pig. And it's compact discs now, not *records*. Jefferson Airplane, indeed. You're showing your age.'

'Oh, spare us the witty repartee. Did you see Deborah again after that?'

'No.'

'Did you ever have anything to do with St Mary's Church, with Daniel Charters and his wife, or with Ive Jelačić?'

'Church? Me? You must be fucking joking.'

'Did Deborah ever mention an important secret she had?'

'What secret?'

'You're not being very co-operative, Johnny.'

'I don't know anything about no secret. And my name's John. What you gonna do? Arrest me?'

Banks took a sip of coffee. 'I don't know yet. If you didn't kill Deborah, who do you think did?'

'Some psycho.'

'Why are you so sure?'

'I saw it on telly. That's what they said.'

'You believe everything you hear on telly?'

'Well if it wasn't a psycho, who was it?'

Banks sighed and lit another cigarette. This time he didn't offer Spinks one. 'That's what *I'm* asking *you*.' He snapped his fingers. 'Come on, wake up, John boy.'

Spinks dabbed at his nose; it had stopped bleeding now. 'How should I know?'

'You knew her. You spent time with her. Did she have any enemies? Did she ever talk to you about her life?'

'What? No. Mostly we just fucked, if you want to know the truth. Apart from that, she was boring. Always on about horses and school. And always bloody picking on things I said and the way I said them.'

'Well, she was an educated woman, John. I realize it would have been hard for you to keep up with her intellectually.'

'Like I said, she was only good for one thing.'

'I understand you once stole a car and took Deborah for a joyride?'

'I . . . now, hang on just a minute. I don't know who's been spreading vicious rumours about me, but I never stole no car. Can't even drive, can I?' He took a pouch of Drum from his flak-jacket pocket and rolled a cigarette.

'What about drugs?'

'Never touch them. Stay clean. That's my motto.'

'I'll bet if we had a look through his pockets,' said Sergeant Hatchley, 'we'd probably find enough to lock him up for.'

Banks stared at Spinks for a moment, as if considering the idea. He saw something shift in the boy's eyes. Guilt. Fear.

'No,' he said, standing up. 'He's not worth the paper-work. We'll leave him be for the moment. But,' he went on, 'we'll probably be back, so don't wander too far. I want you to know you're looking good for this, John.

You've got quite a temper, so we hear, and you have every reason to hold a grudge against the victim. And one more thing.'

Spinks raised his eyebrows. Banks leaned forward, rested his hands on the table and lowered his voice. 'If I ever catch you within a mile of my daughter, you'll think that bloody nose Sergeant Hatchley gave you was a friendly pat on the back.'

FOUR

At home later that evening, after dinner, when Tracy had gone up to her room to do her homework, Banks and Sandra found a couple of hours to themselves at last. With Elgar's first symphony playing quietly on the stereo, Banks poured himself a small Laphroaig and Sandra a Drambuie with ice. He wouldn't smoke tonight, not at home, he decided, even though the peaty bite of the Islay almost screamed out for an accompaniment of nicotine.

First, Banks told Sandra about John Spinks and his visit to Sylvie Harrison.

'I thought the chief constable ruled the family off-limits,' she said.

'He did,' Banks shrugged. 'Actually, I just escaped by the skin of my teeth. Sir Geoffrey came in and caught me talking to her. A word in Jimmy Riddle's ear and my name would be mud. Luckily, Lady Harrison didn't want him to know we'd been talking about Deborah's boyfriend, so she told him I'd just dropped by to give them a progress report. He was more annoyed that she'd been smoking than he was about my presence.'

'This Spinks,' Sandra said. 'He sounds like a bad

character. Do you think Tracy had anything to do with him?'

Banks shook his head. 'He was part of the crowd, that's all. She's got more sense than that.'

'Deborah Harrison obviously didn't have.'

'We all make mistakes.' Banks stood up and walked towards the hall.

'Oh, go on,' Sandra said with a smile. 'Have a cigarette if you want one. It's been a tough day at the gallery. I might even join you.' Sandra had stopped smoking some years ago, but she seemed able to cheat occasionally without falling back into the habit. Banks envied her that.

As it turned out, Banks hadn't been going for his cigarettes but for the photograph that Stott and Hatchley had got from Owen Pierce. Still, not being one to look a gift horse in the mouth, he weakened and brought the Silk Cut from his overcoat pocket.

Once they had both lit up and the Elgar was moving into the adagio, Banks slid the photograph out of the envelope and passed it to Sandra.

'What do you think?' he asked.

'Very pretty. But not your type, surely. Her breasts are too small for your taste.'

'That's not what I meant. And I've got nothing against small breasts.'

Sandra dug her elbow in his side and smiled. 'I'm teasing.'

'You think I didn't know that? Seriously, though, what do you think? Professionally.'

Sandra frowned. 'It's not *her*, is it? Not the girl who was killed?'

'No. Do you see a resemblance, though?'

Sandra shifted sideways and held the photo under the

shaded lamp. 'Yes, a bit. The newspaper photo wasn't very good, mind you. And teenage girls are still, in some ways, unformed. If they've got similar hair colour and style, and they're about the same height and shape, you can construe a likeness easily enough.'

'Apparently she's not a teenager. She was twenty-two when that was taken.'

Sandra raised her dark eyebrows. 'Would we could all look so many years younger than we are.'

'What do you think of the style?'

'As a photograph, it's good. Very good in fact. It's an excellent composition. The pose looks natural and the lighting is superb. See how it brings out that hollow below the breasts and the ever-so-slight swell of her tummy? You can even see where the light catches the tiny hairs on her skin. And it has a mood, too, a unity. There's a sort of secret smile on her face. A bit Mona Lisa-ish. A strong rapport with the photographer.'

'Do you think she knew him?'

Sandra studied the photograph for a few seconds in silence, Elgar playing softly in the background. 'They were lovers,' she said finally. 'I'll bet you a pound to a penny they were lovers.'

'Women's intuition?'

Sandra gave him another dig in the ribs. Harder this time. Then she passed him the photo. 'No. Just look at her eyes, Alan, the laughter, the way she's looking at him. It's obvious.'

When he looked more closely, Banks knew that Sandra was right. It *was* obvious. Men and women only looked like that at one another when they had slept together, or were about to. He couldn't explain why, certainly couldn't offer any proof or evidence, but like Sandra, he *knew*. And

Barry Stott had said that Pierce denied knowing the woman. The next job, then, was to find her and discover why. Banks would wait for the initial forensic results, then he'd have a long chat with Owen Pierce himself.

8

ONE

The man who sat before Banks in the interview room at two o'clock that Saturday afternoon looked very angry. Banks didn't blame him. He would have been angry, himself, if two hulking great coppers had come and dragged him off to the police station on his day off, especially with it being Remembrance Day, too.

But it couldn't be helped. Banks would rather have been at home listening to Britten's *War Requiem* as he did every 11 November, but it would have to wait. New information had come in. It was time for him to talk to Owen Pierce in person.

'Relax, Owen,' said Banks. 'We're probably going to be here for a while, so there's no point letting your blood pressure go right off the scale.'

'Why don't you just get on with it,' Owen said. 'I've got better things to do with my time.'

Banks sighed. 'Me, too, Owen. Me too.' He put new tapes in the double-cassette recorder, then he told Owen that the interview was being taped, and, as before, stated the names of everyone in the room, along with the time, place and date.

Susan Gay was the only other person present. Her role was mostly to observe, but Banks would give her the chance to ask a question or two. They were taking a 'fresh team' approach – so far only Stott and Hatchley had interviewed Pierce – and Banks had already spent a couple of hours that morning going over the previous interview transcripts.

'Okay,' Banks began, 'first let me caution you that you do not *have* to say anything, but if you do not mention now something which you later use in your defence, the court may decide that your failure to mention it strengthens the case against you. A record will be made of anything you say and it may be given in evidence if you are brought to trial.'

Owen swallowed. 'Does this mean I'm under arrest?'

'No,' said Banks. 'It's just a formality, so we all know what's what. I understand you've been informed about your right to a solicitor?'

'Yes.'

'And you've waived it?'

'For the moment, yes. I keep telling you, I haven't done anything. Why should I have to pay for a solicitor?'

'Good point. They can be very expensive. Now then, Owen, can we just go over last Monday evening one more time, please?'

Owen sighed and told them exactly the same as he had told Stott the last time and the time before that.

'And you never, at any time that day, had contact with the victim, Deborah Harrison?'

'No. How could I? I had no idea who she was.'

'You're quite sure you didn't meet her?'

'I told you, no.'

'Why were you in the area?'

'Just walking.'

'Oh, come on. Do you think I was born yesterday, Owen? Hey? You had a meeting with Deborah, didn't you? You knew her.'

'Don't be ridiculous. How could I know someone like her?'

Banks reached down into his briefcase and pushed the photograph across the desk. 'Who's this?' he asked.

'Just a model.'

'Look at it, Owen. Look closely. You *know* her. Any idiot can see that.'

Banks watched Owen turn pale and lick his lips. 'I don't know what you mean,' he said. 'She was just a model.'

'Bollocks she was just a model. Have you noticed her resemblance to the murdered girl?' Banks set a photograph of Deborah Harrison next to it.

Owen looked away. 'I can't say I have.'

'Look again.'

Owen looked and shook his head. 'No.'

'And you still maintain that you've never met Deborah Harrison?'

'That's right.' He looked at his watch. 'Look, when is this farce going to end? I've got work to do.'

Banks glanced over at Susan and nodded. She leaned forward and placed two labelled packages on the desk. 'The thing is, Owen,' Banks said, 'that this evidence shows otherwise.'

'Evidence? What evidence?'

'Hair, Owen. Hair.' Banks tapped the first envelope. 'To cut a long story short, this envelope contains samples of hairs taken from those we found on the anorak you were wearing on Monday evening when you went for a walk, the one you gave us permission to test. There are a number of hairs that our experts have identified as coming from the head of Deborah Harrison.'

Owen grasped the edge of the desk. 'But they can't be! You must be mistaken.'

165

Banks shook his head gravely. 'Oh, I could bore you with the scientific details about the medulla and the cortex and so on, but you can take my word for it – they match.'

Owen said nothing. Susan pushed the other package forward. 'Now this,' Banks said, 'contains hair samples taken from Deborah Harrison's school blazer. Oddly enough, some of these hairs have been positively identified as yours, again matched with the samples you freely allowed us to take the other day.' Banks sat back and folded his arms. 'I think you've got quite a bit of explaining to do, haven't you, Owen?'

'You're trying to set me up. Those hairs aren't mine. They can't be. You're lying to get me to confess, aren't you?'

'Confess to what, Owen?'

Owen smiled. 'You're not going to catch me out as easily as that.'

Banks leaned forward and rested his palm on the desk. 'Read my lips, Owen,' he said. 'We're not lying. The hairs are yours.'

Owen ran his hand through his hair. 'Wait a minute. There must be some simple explanation for this. There's got to be.'

'I hope so,' said Banks. 'I'd really like to hear it.'

Owen bit his lip and concentrated. 'The only thing I can think of,' he said after a few moments, 'is that when I was on the bridge, someone bumped into me. It all happened so fast. I was turning from looking over the river, and she knocked the wind out of me. I didn't get a really good look because she disappeared into the fog and I only saw her from behind, but I think she had long fair hair and wore a maroon blazer and skirt. It could have been her, couldn't it? That *could* have been how it happened, couldn't it?'

Banks frowned and looked through the notes in front of him. 'I don't understand, Owen. When you talked to DI Stott and DS Hatchley you didn't say anything about this.'

'I know.' Owen looked away. 'At first I just forgot, then, well . . . when I remembered, when I'd seen the paper and knew why they'd been questioning me . . . Well, I'd already not said anything, so I suppose I was worried it would look bad if I spoke up then.'

'Look bad? But how could it, Owen? How could it look bad if you simply said the girl might have bumped into you? What were you afraid of?'

'Yes, but I mean, if it really *had* been Deborah Harrison . . . I don't know. Besides, I couldn't be *sure* it was her. It just seemed like the best thing to do at the time. Keep quiet. It didn't seem important. I'm sorry if it caused you any problems.'

'Caused *us* any problems? Not really, Owen. But it has caused you quite a few. It's funny you should mention it now, though, isn't it, now we've matched the hair samples?'

'Yes, well . . . I told you. Look, you can check, can't you? Didn't her friend see me? I could just see her through the fog.'

Banks tapped the two envelopes. 'What if she did see you? That doesn't help your case at all, does it? In fact, it makes things worse.'

'But I never denied being on the bridge.'

'No. But you led us to believe you didn't see Deborah Harrison. Now you're changing your story. I'd like to know why.'

'I was confused that's all.'

'I understand that, Owen. But why didn't you tell the

detectives who first interviewed you that you'd seen Deborah that night?'

'I told you. It slipped my mind. After all, I had no idea *why* the detectives were talking to me. Then later, when I knew . . . well, I was worried that this was exactly the kind of thing that would happen if I did tell you, that you would misconstrue it.'

'Misconstrue?'

'Yes. Misinterpret, distort, misunderstand.'

'I know what the word means, Owen,' said Banks. 'I don't need a bloody thesaurus, thank you very much. I just don't see how it applies in your case.'

'I'm sorry. Just put it down to an English teacher's pedantry. What I mean is, I thought you'd read more into it, that's all. When you get right down to it, it's not very much in the way of evidence, is it? You have to admit.' Owen attempted a smile, but it came out crooked. 'I mean, a couple of hairs. Hardly enough to stand up in court, is it?'

'Don't get clever with me, sonny.'

'I . . . I wasn't. I was just pointing it out, that's all.'

'But we don't know *how* the hairs got where they did, do we?'

'That's what I'm saying. Maybe it happened when she bumped into me.'

'If it was her who bumped into you.'

'I can't think of any other explanation.'

'But I can. See, you've lied to us before, Owen. To DI Scott and DS Hatchley. Why should we believe you now?'

Owen swallowed. His Adam's apple bumped up and down. 'Lied?'

'Well, you never told us about seeing Deborah, or about bumping into her for that matter. That's a lie of a kind, isn't it? You might call it a lie of omission. And you also said you didn't know the girl in the photo, but you do know her, don't you?'

'No. I –'

Banks sighed. 'Look, Owen, I'm giving you a chance to dig yourself out of this hole before it's too late. We've talked to the landlord of the Nag's Head again, showed him the picture of this "model." He says you've been in the pub with her on a number of occasions. He's *seen* you together. What do you have to say about that?'

Banks noticed the sweat start beading on Owen's forehead. 'All right, I know her. Knew her. But I don't see how it's relevant in any way. She was my girlfriend. We lived together. Does that satisfy you?'

'Who is she? Where is she now? What happened to her?'

Owen put his hands over his ears. 'I don't believe I'm hearing this. Surely you can't think that I've killed Michelle, too?'

'Too? As well as who?'

'For Christ's sake. It's a figure of speech.'

'I'd have thought a pedantic English teacher like yourself would be more careful with his figures of speech.'

'Yes, well, I'm upset.'

'This Michelle, what happened?'

'We lived together for nearly five years, then we split up over the summer. Simple as that.'

'And where is she now?'

'She lives in London. In Swiss Cottage.'

'Why did you split up?'

'Why does anyone split up?'

'Irreconcilable differences?' Banks suggested.

Owen laughed harshly. 'Yes. That'll do. Irreconcilable differences. You could call it that.'

'What would *you* call it?'

'It's none of your business. But there is something else. It's got nothing to do with this at all, but if it'll help . . .'

'Yes?'

'Well, it's the reason I was out walking. It was the anniversary. The anniversary of the day we met. I was a little down, a bit sad. We used to go for walks by the river, as far as St Mary's, or even further, and we'd sometimes drop in at the Nag's Head to wet our whistles. So I just went for that long walk to get it out of my system.'

'You were upset?'

'Of course I was upset. I loved her.'

'And did you get it out of your system?'

'To a certain extent.'

'How did you get it out of your system?'

'Oh, this is absurd. You've got a one-track mind. There's no point talking to you any more.'

'Maybe not, Owen. But you've got to admit things are looking pretty bleak. You lied to us *four* times.' He counted them off on his fingers. 'Once about why you were out walking, once about never meeting Deborah Harrison, once about not knowing the girl in the photo and once again about never having lived with anyone. All lies, Owen. You see what a position it puts me in?'

'But they were all so . . . such small lies. Yes, all right, I lied. I admit it. But that's all. I haven't harmed anyone.'

At that point came the soft knock at the door that Banks had arranged earlier. He turned off the tape recorders and told the person to come in. DI Stott entered, nodded quickly at Owen Pierce and apologized for disturbing them. Then he handed a report to Banks and stood by the door.

Banks glanced over the sheets of paper, taking his time, pretending he didn't already know the information they contained. When he had finished, he passed them to Susan. All the time, he was aware of Owen's discomfort and restlessness. Susan read the report and raised her eyebrows. Banks thought they were overacting a bit, behaving like doctors who had just looked at the X-rays and found out their patient had an inoperable tumour. But it was working. Pierce was really sweating now.

Banks turned the tape recorders on again, explaining briefly why he had turned them off and adding that DI Stott was now also in the room. 'Results of the blood tests,' he said to Owen.

'What blood tests?'

'Remember, we took samples the other day?'

'Yes, but . . .'

'With your permission.'

'I know, but—'

'Well, we also found a small dried bloodstain on your anorak, and according to this report, Owen, it's Deborah Harrison's blood group, not yours. Can you explain that?'

'I . . . I . . .'

The three detectives remained silent for a few moments as Owen struggled for an explanation. Then Banks spoke up again. 'Come on, Owen,' he said. 'Tell us about it. It'll do you good.'

Owen slammed his fist on the table. 'There's nothing to tell! I saw a girl. She bumped into me. Then she ran off. She *might* have been Deborah Harrison. It was foggy. I didn't get a clear enough look. That's all that happened. I don't know how her blood got there. You're trying to frame me. You're planting evidence.'

'You're starting to sound a bit desperate now, Owen,' Banks said. 'Clutching at straws. Why don't you calm down and tell us all about it?'

'But *why* would I have killed the girl? What possible reason could I have? Why don't you believe me?'

'Because you didn't tell us the truth. That means you had something to hide. And there's something else, too.'

'What?'

'We found your blood under Deborah Harrison's finger-nails. What do you have to say to that?'

'Nothing,' Owen said, 'I want a solicitor. Now. I'm not saying another word until I get a solicitor.'

'That's your right,' said Banks. 'But just hear me out for a moment before you do or say anything else. You'll feel much better if you just tell us what happened. And it'll go better for you in the long run. When you saw Deborah Harrison on the bridge, she reminded you of this Michelle, didn't she? The girl you were upset about. Were you punishing Michelle through Deborah, Owen? Is that what all this was about? What did she do to you?'

Owen broke off eye contact. 'Nothing,' he said. 'This is all just speculation. It's rubbish.'

'You followed her into the graveyard and you approached her, didn't you?' Banks went on, resting his elbows on the desk and speaking softly. 'Maybe you offered her a fiver to toss you off so you could pretend it was Michelle doing it. Whatever. It doesn't matter. But she reacted badly. She got scared. You dragged her off the path, behind the Inchcliffe Mausoleum. It was dark and foggy and quiet there. You were going to give her what for, weren't you? Give it to her good and proper just to show her she couldn't do what she did to you and get away with it? All your anger burst out, didn't it, Owen? What happened? Couldn't you get it up? What did Michelle do to you? It *was* her you were strangling, wasn't it? Why did you lie about knowing her?'

Owen put his head in his hands and groaned. Banks packed up his papers, stood and nodded to Stott, who said, 'Owen Pierce, you have already been cautioned and now we're going to put you under arrest. I'm going to ask you to come with me to the custody officer. Do you understand me, Owen?'

TWO

Stott had called it the 'custody suite' on the way down, and the sign on the door said 'Charge Room,' but to Owen it resembled nothing less than the entrance to hell. Abandon all hope . . .

It was a cavernous room in the basement of the old Tudor-fronted Eastvale Regional HQ, full of noise and activity. Saturday afternoon was one of the busiest times in the Eastvale custody suite. Today, in addition to the usual Saturday bouts of shoplifting, hooliganism and drunkenness, Eastvale United were playing at home to arch-rivals, Ripon, and there had already been plenty of violence both on and off the field.

The flaking paint had obviously once been an attempt at a cheerful lemon colour; now it looked like a nicotine stain. Owen sat between Stott and Hatchley on a hard bench opposite elevated, joined desks, screwed to the floor, that ran the whole length of the room like a counter. Behind the desks, about six or seven uniformed police officers typed, bustled about, shouted, laughed, filled in forms and questioned people, presided over by the custody sergeant himself. The contrast between the real smell of fear and this slick, bureaucratic activity brought for Owen its special brand of terror, like a hospital casualty department where ripped flesh bleeds and pristine machines hiss and beep.

At the moment, a drunk with a bloody face leaned over the desk singing 'Danny Boy' at the custody sergeant, who was trying to get his personal details. On the benches near Owen sat a couple of gloomy skinheads, laces missing from their bovver boots; a man who resembled nothing more than a bank clerk, perhaps an embezzler, Owen thought; and a nervous-looking young woman, smartly dressed, biting her lip. A kleptomaniac?

Another man at the desk started arguing with one of the officers about being picked on because he was black. The drunk paused in his song to look over and shout, 'Bloody right, too. Ought to go back to the bloody jungle where you came from, Sambo,' then he emitted a technicolour whoosh of vomit all over the desk and sank to his knees on the floor to clutch his stomach and whimper. The sergeant swore and jumped backwards, but he wasn't quick enough to prevent some of the vomit from spattering the front of his uniform.

'Get that bastard out of here!' he yelled. In the room's eerie acoustics, his voice rose, echoed wildly, then fell dead.

Adrenalin pumped through Owen's system. He took a couple of deep breaths to calm himself and almost gagged on the stink of vomit and ammonia cleaning fluid that permeated the stale air.

An officer filled in names, numbers, charges and times with a black marker on a white board. Posters covered the walls: one gave a graphic warning about the possible consequences of driving while drunk; one informed prisoners of their rights; a third showed sign language; another advised officers to wear gloves when dealing with vomit and blood due to possible AIDS and Hepatitis B exposure.

Two officers dragged the drunk out and another started clearing up the mess with a mop, cloth and a bucket of Lysol. He was wearing plastic gloves. Blood had dripped on the pale green linoleum. Even the skinheads looked cowed by it all.

Owen kept trying to convince himself that the nightmare would end any moment and he would wake up and find himself out shopping with the rest of the Saturday crowd. Perhaps he would go to HMV in the Swainsdale Centre and buy the new Van Morrison CD. Then, maybe a pint or two and a nice dinner out, Chinese or Indian, just to celebrate. Alone, the way he liked it best.

Or perhaps the policemen would rip off their uniforms to reveal clowns' costumes underneath, and Stott would break into a song and dance number, like characters out of a Dennis Potter play.

As soon as the custody sergeant was free, Stott went over and had a brief word, then gestured for Owen to approach the desk. Stott disappeared through the far door.

'Empty your pockets, please, sunshine,' said the sergeant, after taking Owen's personal details.

Owen emptied his pockets onto the desk. There wasn't much in them: keys, wallet, three pounds sixty-eight pence in change, cheque book, bank machine and credit cards, a few crumpled shopping lists and old bus tickets that had been through the washer and dryer a couple of times, his gold Cross fountain-pen, the small Lett's appointment diary-cum-address book with the pencil tucked down the spine, three pieces of Dentyne chewing-gum and a few balls of fluff.

The sergeant flipped through Owen's diary. It was

empty apart from a few addresses. Next he looked through Owen's wallet. 'Nothing much there,' he said, placing it in the plastic bag with the other items. He held the pen between thumb and forefinger and said, 'Gold-looking fountain-pen.'

'It *is* gold,' Owen said. 'It's not just gold-looking.'

'Well we're not going to get a bloody appraiser in, mate, are we?' the sergeant said. 'Gold-looking.' He dropped it in the bag.

Before they sealed the bag, a constable patted Owen down to see if he had anything else hidden.

'Shall we have a look up his arse, sir?' he asked the custody sergeant when he had finished.

The sergeant looked at Owen, then back at the constable, as if he were seriously considering the proposition. 'Nah,' he said. 'I never did like rectal searches, myself. Messy business. Never know what you might find. Take him to the studio.'

Jesus Christ, thought Owen, they're enjoying this! They don't need to be rude, violent and brutal; they get their kicks better this way, the vicious tease, the cruel joke. They had already judged and condemned him. In their minds, he was guilty, and the rest would be mere formality. And if they believed it, wouldn't everyone else?

When they put him in jail, he thought with a stab of fear, it would be even worse. He had heard about the things that went on, how people like the Yorkshire Ripper and Dennis Nilsen had to be kept in solitary for their own good, how Jeffrey Dahmer had been murdered in prison and Frederick West had hanged himself.

Solitary confinement would probably be better than a poke up the bum from a three-hundred-pound Hell's Angel with tattoos on his cock, Owen thought. But could he stand the loneliness, the feeling of being hopelessly cut off from everything he held dear, abandoned by the whole civilized world? He liked the solitary life, but that was his choice. Could he stand it when it was imposed on him?

The constable led him into another room for finger-printing and mug shots taken by a mounted camera. The 'studio.' Another cruel joke.

'Now then, mate,' the constable said, 'let's have your belt and shoelaces.'

'What? Why on earth—'

'Regulations. So's you don't top yourself, see.'

'But I'm not going to do away with myself. I've told you all. I'm innocent.'

'Aye. Well, it doesn't matter. It's more than my job's worth. We'd have your tie too if you were wearing one. Saw a fellow once topped himself with his tie. Polka-dot tie it was. A nice one. You should've seen him, eyes all bulging and his tongue sticking out. And the pong, you wouldn't believe it! Aye, nasty business, it was. Don't worry, mate, you'll get your things back – that's if you're ever in a position to need them again.'

He had a good laugh at that while Owen took the belt off his jeans and the long white laces from his trainers.

Back at the desk, the custody sergeant gave Owen a pamphlet on legal aid and a sheet of paper that advised him of his rights: to call a solicitor, to inform a friend, and to consult the Codes of Practice. Then he went over to scrawl details on the board.

'I want to call my solicitor,' Owen said.

The sergeant shrugged and gestured to the constable again, who escorted Owen to a telephone. He felt in his inside pocket for his address-book, where he had politely jotted down Wharton's number, but realized it had been taken away along with all his other possessions. He turned to the constable.

'The phone number,' he said. 'it's in my diary. Can I get it back for a minute?'

'Sorry,' the constable replied. 'Against regulations. It's all been entered and bagged.'

'But I can't remember my solicitor's number.'

'Best try this, then.' He pulled a dog-eared telephone directory from the desk drawer. 'It usually works.'

Owen flipped through and managed to find Gordon Wharton's office number. He got an answering machine, and even though it was late on Saturday afternoon, left an urgent message anyway, just in case. Then he tried the listed home number, but got no answer. 'What now?' he asked the constable.

'Cells.' Another constable appeared beside them. They took Owen gently by the elbows and led him back into the corridor. 'Nothing to worry about,' the first officer said. 'Quite comfortable really. More like a hospital ward. Most modern part of the whole building.'

Police boots echoed from the greenish-blue walls and high ceiling as the three of them walked down the hallway. At the end, the constable took out a key and opened a heavy, hinged door.

True, the cell wasn't the dank, dripping dungeon Owen had imagined; it was actually very clean, all white tiles, like a public urinal, and bright light from bulbs covered by wire mesh.

It contained a narrow bed, fixed to the wall and floor, with a thin mattress, a washstand and a seatless toilet made of moulded orange plastic. There was only one window, set high and deep in the wall, about a foot square and almost as thick. The door had a flap for observation.

A faint odour of dead skin and old sweat lurked under the smell of disinfectant.

'Sorry there's no telly,' said one of the jailers, 'but you can have something to read if you like. A book, maybe, or a magazine?' He turned to his companion. 'Jock here's probably got an issue or two of *Playboy* hidden away at the back of his desk.'

Owen ignored the taunt. He simply shook his head and stared around in amazement at the cell.

'Owt to eat?' the jailer asked.

When he thought about it, Owen realized that he *was* hungry. He said yes.

'The special's steak and kidney pud today. Or there's fish and chips, sausage and—'

'Steak and kidney pud sounds just fine,' Owen said.

'Mug of tea? Milk and sugar?'

Owen nodded. This is bloody absurd, he thought, almost unable to contain his laughter. Here I am, sitting in a cell in the bowels of the Eastvale police station putting in an order for steak and kidney pudding and a mug of tea!

'You won't be here long,' said the jailer. 'And if it wasn't a weekend we'd have you up before the beak tomorrow. Anyway, just so's you know, you'll be well treated. You'll get three square meals a day, a bit of exercise if you want it, reading material, pen and paper if you want—'

'We can't give him a pen, Ted,' said Jock. 'He might . . . you know . . . Remember that bloke who . . .?' He drew his forefinger across his throat and made a gurgling sound.

'Aye, you're right.' Ted turned back to Owen. 'We had a bloke once tried to cut his throat with a fountain-pen. Messy. And another jabbed a pencil right through his eye socket. A yellow HB, if I recollect it right.' He shook his head slowly. 'Sorry, lad, you'll have to wait for writing privileges. It's our responsibility, see. Anything else you want, though, just let us know. As I always say, just ring the bell and ask for room service.'

They laughed and walked out into the corridor. The heavy door slammed shut behind them.

THREE

'So what do you think, sir?' Susan Gay asked over the noise, handing Banks the pint she had just bought him.

'Thanks. Looks like I was wrong, doesn't it?' Banks said, with a shrug.

The Queen's Arms was buzzing with conversation and ringing with laughter that Saturday evening. Rumours had leaked out that the 'Eastvale Strangler' was in the holding cells and all was well with the world. Parents could once again rest easy in their beds; just about every phone, fax and modem in town was tied up by the press; and those police who were off duty were celebrating their success. The only things missing were the fireworks and the brass band.

Banks sat next to Susan Gay, with Hatchley and Stott not far away. Stott looked like the cat that got the cream.

Chief Constable Riddle had visited the station earlier, patting backs and bragging to the media. He hadn't wasted the opportunity to admonish Banks for pestering the Harrisons; nor had he neglected to praise Stott for his major role in what was probably the quickest arrest of a sex murderer ever.

This time, Riddle was going to go and tell the Harrisons personally that he had a man in custody for Deborah's murder, largely due to the efforts of a new member of Eastvale CID, DI Barry Stott. Of course, Riddle wouldn't be seen dead drinking in a pub with the common foot-soldiers, even if he didn't have a couple of TV interviews lined up. Thank God for small mercies, Banks thought.

As he sipped his pint and let the conversation and laughter ebb and flow around him, Banks wondered why he felt so depressed. Never one to shy away from self-examination, he considered professional jealousy first.

But was that really true? Banks had to admit that it would only look that way to the chief constable and one or two others who had it in for him. As far as the media were concerned, Detective Chief Inspector Alan Banks had headed the most successful investigation in the history of Eastvale Divisional Headquarters. *His* troops had won the battle. He was the general. So why did he feel so depressed?

'The evidence is pretty solid, isn't it?' Susan shouted in his ear.

Banks nodded. It was. Nothing on the shoes that Pierce couldn't have picked up on the river path, but positive blood and hair matches both ways. His and hers. Suspect a bit of an oddball. A liar, to boot. Seen in the area, with no good reason, around the time of the murder. Oh, yes, Banks admitted, even the Crown Prosecution Service should have no trouble with this one. What could be better? And if the DNA results were positive when they came through . . .

He looked at Susan. Earnest expression on her round face, with its peaches and cream complexion; short, slightly upturned nose; tight blonde curls. She had a glass of St Clement's in front of her.

Banks smiled, trying to shake off his gloom. 'Let me

buy you a drink, Susan,' he said. 'A *real* drink. What would you like?'

'I shouldn't, sir, really . . .' Susan said. 'I mean, you know, officially . . .'

'Bugger *officially*. You're off duty. Besides, this is your senior officer telling you it's time you had a real drink. What's it to be?'

Susan blushed and smiled, averting her blue-grey eyes. 'Well, in that case, sir, I'll have a port and lemon.'

'Port and lemon it is.'

'Let me go, sir.'

'No, stay there. Save my seat.'

Banks got up and edged his way through the crowd, nodding and smiling a hello here and there. One or two people clapped him on the back and congratulated him on the speed with which he had caught the killer.

With his pint in one hand and Susan's port and lemon in the other, he excuse-me'd his way back. Before he had got halfway he felt a tap on his shoulder and turned around to see Rebecca Charters standing there, long auburn hair framing her pale face.

Banks smiled. 'A bit off the beaten track, aren't you?' he said.

'I dropped by the police station first. The man on the front desk said you were all over here celebrating. I've heard that you've got someone under arrest for Deborah Harrison's murder. Is it true?'

Banks nodded. 'Yes. A suspect, at least.'

'Does that mean you'll be leaving us alone now? Things can get back to normal?'

'Whatever that is,' Banks said. 'Why? What are you worried about?'

'I'm not worried about anything. It would just be nice

to know we could get on with our lives in private now rather than sharing every significant emotional event with the local police.'

'That was never my intention, Mrs Charters. Look, it's a bit silly just standing here like this. Would you like a drink?'

He could see Rebecca consider the offer seriously, needily. She eyed the bottles ranged behind the bar, then suddenly she shook her head. 'No. No thank you. That's another thing I'm trying to put behind me.'

'Good,' said Banks. 'Good for you.'

'How the hell would *you* know?' she said, and stormed out.

Banks shrugged and headed back to the table, where everyone, even DI Stott, was laughing at one of Hatchley's jokes. Banks didn't mind missing it; he had heard them all before, at least five times.

When he slid into his seat again, Susan thanked him for the drink. 'What was all that about?' she asked.

'I'm not sure,' said Banks. 'I think I offended her. Or maybe abstinence has made her irritable.'

'As long as she doesn't complain to the chief constable. What next, sir?'

'Next, I think we've got to find out a bit more about what makes Pierce tick. We've still got no motive, have we? He asked us why he should have committed such a crime, and I think we have a duty to try and answer that. If not for his sake, then for a jury's.'

'But, sir, if it was a sex murder we don't really need a motive, do we? We wouldn't expect a rational one.'

'Did Owen Pierce seem mad to you?'

'That's a very difficult question,' Susan said slowly. 'The kind of thing experts argue about in court.'

PETER ROBINSON

'I'm not asking for an official statement. This is off the record. Your personal observations, your copper's intuition.'

Susan sipped her port and lemon. 'Well, to start with, he was nervous, edgy, hostile and confused.'

'Isn't that how you would feel if you were accused of murder and subjected to an interrogation?'

Susan shrugged. 'I don't know, sir. I've never been in that position. I mean, if you've got nothing to hide . . . If you're telling the truth . . . Why get upset?'

'Because everyone *thinks* you did it. And they've got all the power. We have the power. We basically bullied Pierce until he was so confused he acted like a guilty man.'

'Are you saying you still don't think he did it, sir?'

Banks scratched the scar beside his right eye. It was itching; sometimes that meant something, sometimes not. He wished he knew which was which. 'No. All I'm saying is that everyone's got *something* to hide. Everyone starts to feel guilty when they're stopped and questioned by the police, whether they've done anything or not. Almost anyone would react the way Pierce did under that sort of pressure.' Banks lit a cigarette and blew out the smoke slowly, careful to blow it away from Susan, then he took a long swig of beer.

'But you still have doubts?'

Banks clicked his tongue. 'I shouldn't, should I? I mean, I *did* arrest him. This is just perfect: signed, sealed and delivered. I'm still confused, that's all. All this business with Pierce has happened so quickly. There are still too many loose ends. There was so much going on around Deborah. Remember? Jelačić's alibi still doesn't really hold water. Then there's that triangle of Daniel and Rebecca Charters and Patrick Metcalfe. That's a pretty volatile

184

combination if ever I've seen one. There's John Spinks, another character capable of violence. Add to that the open satchel, Michael Clayton spending half his time with Sylvie Harrison while her husband is out, and you've still got a lot of unanswered questions.'

'Yes, sir, but are any of them relevant now we've got Pierce with the hair and blood?'

Banks shrugged. 'Hair and blood aren't infallible. But you're probably right. Sometimes I wish I could just accept the official version.'

'But you agree Pierce *could* have done it?'

'Oh, yes. He probably *did* do it. We found no trace evidence at all on either Charters's or Jelačić's clothing. And Pierce *was* in the area. There's also something about him that *harmonizes* with the crime in an odd sort of way. I don't know how to put it any better than that.'

'You struck a nerve in him there, sir. I must admit, he gives me the creeps.'

'Yes. There's a part of him that has some sort of imaginative sympathy with what happened to Deborah Harrison. What I tried to do in that room was make contact with his dark side.' Banks gave a little shudder.

'What is it, sir?'

'Everyone has a dark side, Susan. Doesn't Owen Pierce make you wonder about your own?'

Susan's eyes widened. 'No, sir. I don't think so. I mean, we've done our job. We've got the evidence, we've got a suspect in custody. I think we should just let it lie and move on.'

Banks paused, then smiled. 'You're right, of course,' he said. 'But we've still a fair bit of work to do. How do you fancy a trip to London on Monday?'

'London? Me, sir?'

'Yes. I'd like to pay this Michelle a visit, see what her story is. He did his best to keep their relationship from us, so there has to be something in it. Besides, I'd like your impressions, woman to woman, if that's not a terribly sexist thing to say.'

'It isn't, sir. Of course. I'd love to come.'

'Good.' Banks looked at his watch and finished his pint. 'I'd better get home. Have a nice lie-in tomorrow. You'll enjoy it.'

Susan smiled. 'I think I will, sir, good-night.'

Banks put his overcoat on, said farewell to everyone and acknowledged a few more pats on the back as he walked through the crowd to the door. He stood for a moment on Market Street by the cobbled square watching his breath plume in the clear, cold air.

So much had happened today that he had hardly had time to notice the clear blue sky, the autumn wind stripping leaves from the trees. Now it was dark and the stars shone for the first time in days. A line from last month's Eastvale Amateur Dramatic Society production tripped through his mind: 'The fault, dear Brutus, is not in our stars, / But in ourselves.' Again, Banks thought of that foggy night in the graveyard and wondered what had really happened there. Perhaps he would never know.

It was a cold night to walk home, but he had drunk three pints, too much for driving, and he decided he wanted to clear his head anyway. With numb hands, he managed to put on his headphones and flip the switch of the Walkman in his pocket. After a second or two of hiss, he was shocked by the assault of a loud, distorted electric guitar. He had forgotten about the Jimi Hendrix tape he had put in earlier in the week to wake him up on his way to work. He hadn't listened to it since then. Then he smiled and started walking home. Why not? 'Hear My Train a' Coming' would do just fine; he would listen to Britten's *War Requiem* later.

9

ONE

The 9:36 InterCity from York pulled into London King's Cross at 12:05 on Monday, 13 November, twenty minutes late. A problem with points outside Peterborough, the conductor explained over the PA system. Not for the first time, Banks regarded the bleak, post-industrial landscape of his hometown with a mixture of nostalgia and horror. *Peterborough.* Of all the places to come from. Even if the football team he had supported as a teenager had recently edged about halfway up the second division.

As forecast, the rain came. Not a shower or a storm, but steady November drizzle that looked as if it would keep falling forever from a leaden sky. It was raining in Eastvale when Banks and Susan drove out to York that morning; it was raining in York when they caught the train; and it was raining in London when they got off the underground at Oxford Circus. At least it was a little warmer than the weekend: raincoat weather, not heavy overcoat.

To make it easy all around, Michelle Chappel had suggested over the telephone that she talk to them during her lunch-hour, which started at 12:30, in a small pasta restaurant off Regent Street, near where she worked as office administrator for a quality stationery company.

As the questioning was to be informal, and Michelle herself certainly wasn't suspected of any crime, Banks agreed. It meant they could get the job done and be back in Eastvale by late afternoon if they were lucky.

As usual, Regent Street was crowded, even in the rain, and Banks found he had to dodge many an eye-threatening umbrella spoke as he and Susan made their way to the rendezvous in a sidestreet not far from Dickins & Jones.

They got there about five minutes late, and Banks spotted Michelle Chappel at a window table. With a skill that Peterborough United could have used the previous weekend, he managed to sidestep the waiter, who was blocking the way, holding out large menus and muttering about a fifteen-to-twenty-minute wait.

The restaurant was unpretentious in appearance – rickety tables and chairs, plenty of scratched woodwork, gilt-framed water-colours of Venice and Florence, stained white tablecloths – but when Banks looked at the list of specials chalked on the blackboard, he soon realized it was the kind of London unpretentiousness you pay for through the nose.

The small dining-room was crowded, but Michelle had saved two places for them. Waiters scurried around, sweaty-browed; carafes of wine appeared on tables; and the smell of garlic, tomatoes and oregano permeated the air. Despite the bustle, though, it wasn't unduly noisy, and when they had introduced themselves and sat down, they didn't have to shout to be heard.

'I've told Mr Littlewood I might be a few minutes late getting back,' Michelle said. 'He said he didn't mind.'

'Good,' said Banks. 'We'll certainly try not to take up too much of your time.'

'That's all right.'

Physically, Michelle resembled her photograph very closely except for her hair, which was now cut short, razorsculpted round her delicate ears, and hung in a ragged fringe. The strong bone structure was still apparent in her cheeks and jaw, the pale, almost translucent skin still flawless, and although she was sitting, it was clear that she maintained her slim, athletic figure. She wore a tailored red jacket over a black silk blouse buttoned up to the hollow of her long, swan-like neck. From her tiny, pale ears two silver angel earrings danced every time she moved her head.

'You said on the telephone that you would recognize me from one of Owen's photographs,' Michelle said to Banks, clearly aware of his scrutiny. 'That was two years ago. Have I changed very much?'

Banks shook his head.

'It was one of the nudes, I suppose.'

'Yes.'

'Then I'm afraid you'll have to take my word on the rest.' She smiled, and the humour flickered in her eyes for a moment just as Owen Pierce had captured it on film. She touched her hair. 'I had this cut six months ago. Just for a change. Would you like to eat?'

Both Banks and Susan had skipped the train food and were starving. After much study and some consultation, Banks decided on the gourmet pizza with goat cheese, olives, sun-dried tomatoes and Italian sausage. It was London, after all, he thought, and London prices, so why not? Susan went for the cannelloni. They ordered a half-litre of red wine for the two of them. Michelle was already drinking white. She ordered linguine with clam sauce.

That done, they settled back to talk. Customers came and went, more leaving than arriving as it got close to one o'clock, and the drizzle continued to streak the window behind the slightly dirty white lace curtains.

'I'm not sure what you want from me,' Michelle said.

'You didn't tell me very much on the telephone.'

'I'm not certain myself, Miss Chappel,' said Banks. 'I just hope I'll know it when I hear it.'

'Call me Michelle. Please.'

Banks nodded.

'You said Owen has been arrested?'

'That's right.'

'On what charge?'

'You mean you don't know?'

'Well, his name's not been in the papers, and you didn't tell me over the phone. How could I know?'

'Of course not.' Banks looked at Susan and nodded.

'I'm afraid it's very serious, Michelle,' Susan said. 'Owen's been arrested for murder. I'm sorry.'

'Murder? But who . . . Wait a minute . . . Not that schoolgirl?'

'Deborah Harrison. Yes.'

'I read about it.' Michelle shook her head slowly. 'Bloody hell. So he's . . .' She looked back at Banks. 'And what do you think I can do for you?'

'We'd like to know what you can tell us about him. He didn't seem willing to admit he knew you, or tell us who you were.'

'I'll bet he didn't.'

'Did something happen between you?'

Michelle frowned. 'What do you know already?'

'Not much. Given the nature of the crime, we need to get some sort of grasp on what kind of person he is. We understand already that he's a bit of a loner, something of an oddball, according to some people.'

'Is he? He wasn't always, you know. Not at first. He could be fun, could Owen. For a while, anyway, then . . .' her eyes darkened.

'Then what?'

'Oh, just . . . things change. People change. That's all.'

'Well, you can see our problem, can't you?' Banks said. 'He's got no close family, and no-one in Eastvale seems to know him very well. We were hoping you might be able to throw some light on his character.'

'Is he going to plead insanity?'

'It's nothing like that. Why do you ask?'

'I mean, what do you want to know about him for?'

'Look, don't worry. We're not going to drag you into court or anything.'

'Oh, I don't mind that.'

'Then what?'

Michelle leaned forward and rested her elbows on the table. 'In fact,' she said, lowering her voice, 'I'd be more than happy to go into court.'

Banks frowned. 'I don't understand, Michelle. What happened between you? All we know is that the two of you split in the summer and that Owen seemed reluctant to admit he knew you. In fact he tried to tell us the photographs were of some anonymous model.'

Michelle snorted. 'I'll bet he did.'

'Why would he do that?'

'Why? I'll tell you why. Because he tried to kill me, too, that's why.'

TWO

It was less than a mile from the police station to the Town Hall, and Owen would have appreciated the walk after being cooped up in a cell all weekend. But two officers escorted him straight to a van in front of the station. Before they went out of the doors, one of them threw a musty old raincoat over his head.

It was no distance from the front doors to the van, either, but on the way Owen had the awful sensation of being swallowed up by a huge mob, and he had to struggle to stop his bowels from loosening.

He could hear people shouting questions, yelling insults and cursing him. One group, all women by the sound of them, were chanting, 'Hang him! Hang him!' Owen had always feared crowds, had never been able to attend a football match or a music concert in comfort. To Owen, crowds weren't really human; they were a mindless beast with the power of an elemental force. The raincoat over his head smelled of other people's fear.

Luckily the jostling didn't last. Before Owen actually lost control of his bowels and made a fool of himself, he felt himself pushed into the back of a van and heard the door slam. The shouts and chants were muffled now, and the van's engine soon drowned them out completely.

Things weren't quite as bad at the other end, where he was hustled through a smaller crowd, then taken to an antechamber. When Owen was finally able to remove the raincoat, the first person he saw was Gordon Wharton. Not the prettiest sight in the world, but a welcome one under the circumstances.

Wharton leaned back in his chair, plucked up the crease of his pinstripe trousers and crossed his legs. It was a prissy sort of gesture, Owen thought, and one that went with his supercilious expression, the pink, well-scrubbed cheeks and the way he wore his few remaining strands of oily hair combed across his gleaming skull. Though he was probably about the same age as Owen, he looked much older. It was partly the fat, Owen thought, and the baldness, and maybe the strain of overwork. Why did the only solicitor he knew turn out to be Wharton?

He had been the university swot, never time for a drink in the local or a film in town, and Owen had never much liked him. He sensed the feeling was mutual. The only reason they had first come into contact at all was a shared subsidiary subject in their first year, and then they had both ended up working in Eastvale and met by chance that day.

Wharton had finally arrived to see Owen on Sunday morning, having been out of town on Saturday, and had been unable to get him out on police bail.

'All right?' Wharton asked.

Owen took a few deep breaths. 'I suppose so. What are they trying to do, get me torn to pieces?'

Wharton shrugged.

'What nobody seems to realize is that I'm *innocent*.'

Wharton made a steeple of his fingers and looked down. 'Owen, you're not the first innocent man to be arrested for some offence or other, and you won't be the last. That's why we have the law. Everyone's innocent until they're proven guilty. The police are only concerned with whether they can prove a case. It's up to the courts to decide now. Trust in justice.'

Owen snorted. 'The British justice system? It hasn't done me a lot of good so far, has it?'

'Carp all you may, Owen, but it *is* the best justice system in the world. In many other countries you'd be on your way to the executioner already, or languishing forever in some smelly cell. Look, I suggest that you accept your situation. Complaining will do you no good at all in your present circumstances. It will only lead to self-pity. Now let us see if there's anything else we need to consider.'

Pompous bastard, Owen thought. 'It's all very well advising me not to complain,' he said. 'You're not the one who's in jail. Will I get bail at court this morning?'

Wharton shook his head. 'I doubt it. Not on a charge like this one.'

'Look, I'm sure if you could persuade the police to do a bit more digging around, they'll come up with the real killer.'

Wharton leaned forward and rested his hands on the desk. Owen noticed the gold cufflinks flash in the light. 'Owen,' he said, pausing for emphasis, 'you still don't seem to realize the gravity of your situation. You have been arrested for the most serious crime there is: murder. Nobody's going to let you simply walk away.'

'Whose side are you on?'

Wharton held his hand up. 'Let me finish. As far as the police are concerned, they have already got their man. Why would they waste their time looking for an alternative? You'll have to face up to the facts, Owen, you've been arrested for murder, you're being held, in a week or two the Crown Prosecution Service will start building a case against you, and you're going to be tried in court. I will do everything in my power to help you, including engaging the services of the best barrister I can find to represent you, but you *must* accept the situation. Do you understand me?'

Owen wasn't sure that he did, but he nodded anyway.

'Good,' said Wharton.

'So what *will* happen in court? What's the point of coming here if they're only going to send me back to jail?'

'For remand. They'll either grant it or release you. As I've already said, I wouldn't depend on the latter. Then they'll set a date for the preliminary hearing.'

'How long will I have to wait before that?'

'Hmm. It's hard to say. There's supposed to be a time limit of fifty-six days.' Wharton gave a twisted smile. 'Unfortunately, you're not the only alleged criminal in the system. We get backlogs.'

Owen felt his chest tighten. 'Are you saying I could be in jail until February before I even get a preliminary hearing?'

'Oh, at least. Not in Eastvale nick, though. No. Probably somewhere like Armley. And don't worry, they know well enough to keep the other prisoners away from you. Everyone knows how moral criminals get when sex crimes are involved. You'll be isolated. But don't worry about that now. Take things as they come, Owen. One day at a time. That's my advice. I'll be working for you, never fear.'

Why didn't that thought comfort Owen as much as it should have? he wondered.

A clerk popped his head around the door. 'Time, gentlemen.'

Wharton smiled and picked up his black leather briefcase. 'Come on then, Owen,' he said. 'Better gird up your loins.'

THREE

The food arrived just after Michelle's remark about Owen Pierce trying to kill her, and they kept silent as the waiter passed them the hot plates and refilled the baskets of bread. It was after one o'clock now. Michelle was going to be late back for work, Banks knew, but she didn't seem to mind. She clearly wanted to tell them the worst about Owen Pierce.

Banks waited until they had all sampled their food and commented on its quality, then went on. 'There was something you said earlier, about Owen being fun at first, then changing. How did he change? Was that anything to do with what happened? Did he become violent?'

'No. Well, not really *violent*. Not until the end, that is.'

'The end?'

'The day I left him. The night before, rather.'

'If he wasn't violent before that, then what *was* wrong? How did he change?'

'He was just becoming impossible, that's all. Bad-tempered. Complaining. Irrational. Jealous.' She paused and took a mouthful of her linguine, following it with a sip of white wine.

'Did he have a violent temper?'

Michelle nodded. Her angel earrings danced. 'He started developing one. It got worse towards the end. He just became so possessive, so jealous. He'd fly into rages over nothing.'

'Is that why you left him? Fear of violence?' Susan cut in. 'Were you frightened he'd hurt you?'

Michelle looked at Susan. 'No,' she said. 'Well, not really. It *was* frightening, especially the last night, but . . . how can I make you understand?'

'We're listening.' Susan watched Banks nibble at his pizza out of the corner of her eye. 'What happened? Will you tell us?'

Michelle gulped a little more wine, looked at her, then nodded. When she spoke, she looked back and forth between the two of them. 'All right. Yes. I'd been out late with a friend. Owen was waiting up for me. And he'd been drinking.'

'Did he usually drink much?' Banks asked.

Michelle speared some linguine and twisted it on her fork. 'No, not usually, though he had been doing more lately. Especially if he was brooding about something, which he always seemed to be. Anyway, I could definitely smell the whisky on his breath that night.'

Banks sipped his red wine. It tasted watery. 'Had you been drinking much, too?' he asked.

'Only a couple of glasses of wine.'

Banks nodded. 'What happened next?'

'He started calling me terrible names and accusing me of all kinds of disgusting things and then he . . . he . . .'

'He what Michelle?'

'Oh, bugger it. Get it out, Michelle.' She took a deep breath and rubbed the back of her hand across her eyes. 'He tried to force himself on me, that's what he did.'

'He tried to rape you?'

'Yes. He tried to rape me.' She wasn't crying, but her eyes glittered with anger.

'Was this the first time he had ever tried such a thing?'

'Of course it was. Do you think I'd willingly stay a moment longer than I had to with anyone who did that to me?' She hadn't finished her meal, but she pushed her plate aside and sipped some more wine.

'I don't know what your situation was,' Banks said. 'Sometimes people, women especially, get stuck in abusive situations. They don't know what to do.'

'Yes, well, not me. I'm not like that. Oh, I'd done my best, tried to please him, given in to his . . . but it was getting impossible. I was at my wits' end. His demands were getting too much for me. This was the last straw. And I was especially upset by the names he called me and the dirty things he accused me of.'

'So you resisted him?'

'Yes. I thought it was awful that someone would say such horrible things to me, call me such vile names and then want to do it to me . . . you know . . . like animals.'

'Did you struggle?'

Michelle nodded.

'Then what happened?'

'It's not very clear after that. I know he hit me at least once and then everything went dark.'

'He hit you when you refused to have sex with him?'

'Yes. I just remember falling and my head hurting and everything going dark for . . . I don't know . . . maybe only a few seconds.'

'What happened next?'

'I felt his hands around my neck.'

'Owen was trying to strangle you?'

'Yes. He had his hands on my throat and he was pressing.'

'How did you stop him?'

'I didn't. I hadn't the strength. I must have passed out again.'

'Then what?'

'I woke up. It was light, early morning, and I was still on the floor, where I'd fallen. I felt all stiff and my head hurt. My clothes were torn. I had an awful headache.'

'Where was Owen?'

'He was in bed asleep, or passed out. I heard him snoring and went to look.'

'Had he interfered with you sexually in any way?'

'Yes. I think he'd had sex with me.'

'You can't be certain?'

'No. I wasn't conscious. But I'm pretty sure he had.'

'How did you know?'

She looked directly at Banks. He couldn't detect any

strong emotion in her eyes now, despite the events she was relating. She wasn't exactly being cold and clinical about it all, but she wasn't overly agitated, either. The few remaining diners would never have guessed what horrors the trio near the window were talking about.

'A woman can tell about those things,' she said, then she turned to Susan. 'I felt sore . . . you know . . . down there.'

Susan nodded and touched her arm.

Banks finished his pizza and looked around to see if anyone was smoking. Miraculously, one or two people were. The restaurant had quietened down a lot, and when Banks beckoned the waiter to bring him an ashtray, he did.

'What did you do next?' Banks asked Michelle.

'I packed up my things, what little I had, and I left.'

'Where did you go?'

'I just walked and walked. I had nowhere *to* go. At least it was summer. And it wasn't raining. I remember sleeping in the sun in a park.'

'And that night?'

'I tried to sleep at the railway station, but the police kept moving me on. I went in shop doorways, wherever I could find shelter. I was scared.'

'And the next day?'

'I swallowed my pride, went back to my parents and faced the music. A month later I got the job down here.'

'What did you tell them?' Susan asked.

'I couldn't tell them the truth, could I? I was too ashamed. I couldn't tell anyone that. I made up a story about just not, you know, being happy with Owen, and they believed it. It was what they wanted to hear. They'd only met him once and didn't like him anyway. Thought he was too old for me. All I had to do was tell them what they wanted to hear and eat enough crow. They always believed what I told them.'

'Why didn't you report the incident to the police?' Banks asked.

'I told you. I was too ashamed. I'm sure Detective Constable Gay will understand that.'

Susan nodded. 'Yes.'

'Oh, I know what I *should* have done,' Michelle went on. 'Especially now, after what's happened to that poor schoolgirl. In a way, I feel terribly guilty, almost responsible. But you can't really predict what a person will do, can you, how far he will go? I knew Owen was a bit unbalanced, that he could be dangerous. I should have known just *how* dangerous, and I should have reported him to the police. But I was scared.' She looked at Susan again. 'And I'd heard such awful things about what they do, you know, in court, to girls who make such complaints. How they make out you're the guilty one, that you're just a slut, and how they get all sorts of doctors and . . . I . . . just didn't think I could go through with it. I mean, I *was* living with Owen, wasn't I? And I had given in to him willingly before. What would they have said about that? They'd have said I led him on, that's what.'

'The courts aren't so easy on rapists these days, Michelle,' said Susan. 'It wouldn't have been like that.'

'But how was I to know?'

'Was that the only reason you didn't report the incident?' Banks asked. 'Fear of the police and the courts?'

'Well, mostly. But there was Owen, too, wasn't there? I mean, after someone's done something like that to you, something violent, you have to wonder, don't you, whether they're capable of anything. You hear about men stalking women and all the things they do to them. I was ashamed, but I was scared as well. Scared of what he might do.' She looked at her watch. 'My God, it's after two,' she said. 'Look, I really must go now. Mr Littlewood is only liberal to a degree.'

'In the light of what you've just told us,' Banks said, 'we'd like to get a full statement from you. We can do it after you've finished work this evening, if you've got no objection.'

Michelle bit her lip and thought for moment.

'No,' she said. 'I've got no objection. Yes. Let's do it. Let's get it over with. I finish at five-thirty.'

'We'll be waiting.'

They watched her go, then Banks lit another cigarette and they each ordered a cappuccino. 'Well,' said Banks, 'it looks like we're stuck in the big city for the afternoon. Want to see the crown jewels? Maybe tour the Black Museum? Or we could always do some early Christmas shopping.'

Susan laughed. 'No thanks, sir. Perhaps we could give Phil Richmond a call at the Yard? He might be able to sneak away for an hour or so.'

'All right,' said Banks. 'Why don't you phone him?'

'Yes, sir. Got a ten-pee piece?'

FOUR

Armley Jail loomed ahead like a medieval fortress. Owen could only see part of it through the mesh window between himself and the van's driver, but he knew the building well enough; he'd seen it many times when he was at Leeds University.

Standing on a hill to the west of the city centre, it was an enormous, sprawling Victorian edifice of black granite, complete with battlements and towers and newer sections that seemed constantly under construction. The place was practically a tourist attraction. They had kept Peter Sutcliffe, the 'Yorkshire Ripper' on remand there for a while in 1981.

At least the van driver had a sense of humour. Elvis Presley belted out 'Jailhouse Rock' as the van passed through the huge gates with its load of prisoners shackled in heavy cuffs. Owen wondered if he did that every trip, the way tour guides always made the same jokes.

In a low-ceilinged reception room, the cuffs were removed, and Owen found himself signed over from the police to the jailers. He might easily have been a cow or pig sold at market. Next he was given a number he made no attempt to memorize, then, after his belongings had been catalogued and placed in a box, much as in the charge room at the police station, he was taken to a cubicle and strip-searched.

After that, the governor explained that as Owen was regarded as a Category A inmate, he would spend twenty-three and a half out of twenty-four hours alone in his cell, the other half-hour being set aside for supervised exercise. He would be allowed to purchase as many cigarettes as he wanted – not that this appealed to Owen at all – and given access to writing paper and books.

The whole thing reminded Owen of the scene from Kubrick's film, *A Clockwork Orange*, where Alex is inducted into jail. This room had the same grey inhuman feel, a perfect setting for humiliation. He was now a number, no longer a man.

After a cursory medical ('Ever suffered from

palpitations, shortness of breath?') no doubt required to protect the authorities should he drop dead tonight in his cell, he was ordered to take a bath in about six inches of lukewarm water. The tub was an old, Victorian model, with stained sides and claw feet. When he had dried off, he was given his prison uniform: brown trousers and a blue striped shirt that felt coarse and scratchy next to his skin.

After this, he was handed his equally rough bedding and escorted to his cell. It was in a special wing of the prison with black metal stairs and catwalks like something out of an M.C. Escher print. The walls were covered in flecked institutional-green paint, and high ceilings echoed every footstep.

His cell was slightly larger than the one in Eastvale police station, but a lot more gloomy. The whitewashed walls had turned grey with age and dirt; the floor was cold stone. The only window stood high in the wall. About as big as a handkerchief, it seemed to be made of reinforced glass. Light shone from a low-wattage bulb hanging from a ceiling outlet; the shade was covered by wire mesh. Though a washstand, soap and a towel stood in the corner behind the door, there was no toilet. Looking around, Owen located a bucket and some toilet paper beside his bed.

One added feature was the table and chair. They were so small that he could hardly get his knees underneath comfortably. The scored table was a bit rickety, but a couple of sheets of toilet paper, folded and wadded beneath one of the legs, soon fixed that.

He had asked for paper and books from the prison library – science-fiction if possible, to let him escape, at least in mind, from his dreary surroundings. Sci-fi had been a passion during his adolescence, though he hadn't read any since. Now, curiously, he felt an urge to start reading it again. Wharton would also be bringing him his Walkman and a few cassettes as soon as possible.

He paced for a while, then tried to take approximate measure of his cell. He concluded that it was about eight feet by ten. Next he slouched on his hard, narrow mattress and stared up at the cracks on the ceiling. He had expected to find days crossed off all over the walls, just like he had seen in films, but there were none. There wasn't even a trace of graffiti, a name scratched by fingernail, to show who had been here last.

Perhaps it had been the Ripper himself. Owen shivered. That was a foolish thought, he told himself. It was years ago that Sutcliffe had been held here. Dozens of people must have been in and out since then. Still . . . a haunted cell, that would just about make his day.

It was time to keep his imagination in check and take stock of his situation. Certainly he was aware of what *could* happen to him, the 'worst case scenario' as Wharton had put it earlier that morning, and that didn't bear thinking about.

Wharton had already been right about the Magistrates' Court; the whole thing had been over in a couple of minutes and Owen found himself on remand awaiting trial for the crime of murder. So much for truth and justice.

What worried him most now were the practical things: his job, the house, the fish, his car. Wharton had taken his keys and said he would take care of things, but still . . . Had anyone let the department at college know? If so, what had the chairman done? It wouldn't be too difficult to share out his classes among his colleagues until a temporary lecturer could be brought in, but what if this thing dragged on for months? He didn't have tenure, so the college could let him go whenever they felt like it. If he lost his job because of this farce, this absurd mistake, he wondered if he could seek any kind of compensation.

The house would remain his as long as his bank account could stand the strain of the standing payment order for his mortgage, and that should be long enough. After all, he had been making fairly decent money for some time and had very little in the way of expenses. He hoped that his neighbour Ivor, who also had a key, would take good care of the fish.

The sound of footsteps disturbed his train of thought, then he heard the key turn in the lock. It was meal-time already. The warder had also brought him a felt-tipped pen, writing pad and envelopes, a surprisingly well-thumbed copy of Wordsworth's *Collected Poems* and Isaac Asimov's *Foundation* trilogy.

When he had finished his meal and the door closed again behind the warder, Owen picked up the pen and sat at the desk. He had no-one to write to, but he could certainly pass time on a journal of his experiences and impressions. Maybe someday someone would want to publish it.

Fifty-six days or longer, Wharton had said. Well, there was nothing he could do about it, was there, so he might as well just get used to it.

10

ONE

The offices of the Eastvale Crown Prosecution Service were located on the top floor of a draughty old three-storey building on North Market Street, straddling two shops between the community centre and the Town Hall. The lower floor was taken up by a clothes boutique catering for oversize people and a shop that sold imported Belgian chocolate. Somewhere else in the building, a dentist had managed to squeeze in his surgery. Sometimes you could hear the drill while discussing a case.

The chief CPS lawyer assigned to the Pierce file was Stafford Oakes, a shabby little fellow with elbow patches, greasy hair, a sharp nose and eagle eyes. Banks had worked with Oakes before on a number of occasions and had developed great respect for him.

Banks was with DI Stott, and beside Oakes sat Denise Campbell, his colleague, whose expensive and stylish designer clothes stood in stark contrast to Oakes's off-the-peg bargain items. Denise was an attractive and ambitious young lawyer with short black hair and pale skin. Banks had never once seen her smile, and she seemed far too stiff, prim and proper for her age.

In general, the police were wary of the CPS because of its negative attitude towards bringing cases to court, and indeed Banks had had more than one argument with Oakes on this subject. On the whole, though, Oakes was a fair man, and he didn't usually – like so many Crown Prosecutors – do more damage to the case than the defence did. Banks had even had a pint with him on a couple of occasions and swopped stories of life in the trenches of London, where they had both spent time.

Oakes's office was as untidy as the man himself, briefs and files all over the place. Many of them bore his trademark – linked coffee-rings, like the Olympic games symbol – for Oakes was a caffeine addict and didn't care where he rested his mug. Today it sat on top of the post-mortem report on Deborah Harrison.

It was already only a couple of weeks before Christmas, more than two weeks since they had first consulted by telephone. DNA tests had confirmed that it was, indeed, Deborah's blood on Owen's anorak and Owen's tissue under her fingernail. Banks had sent over all the witness statements and forensic test results collected in the Initial Case File. Owen Pierce's defence team would also have copies of them by now.

'I like this,' Oakes was saying, tapping the foot-thick heap of files on his desk. 'I particularly like this DNA analysis. Something I can really get my teeth into. No confession, you say?'

'No,' Banks answered.

'Good.' He slurped some coffee. 'Nothing but trouble, confessions, if you ask me. You're better off without them. What do you think, Denise?'

'We've had *some* success with confessions. Limited, I'll admit. As often as not they'll retract, say the police falsified it or beat it out of them.' She gave Banks a stern look. 'But even scientific evidence isn't entirely problem-free. Depends very much on how it was gathered and who's presenting it.'

'Oh, I know that,' said Oakes, waving his hand in the air. 'Remember that dithering twit in the Innes case we did in Richmond?' He looked at Banks and Stott and rolled his eyes. 'Open and shut. Or should have been. Simple matter of blood-stains. By the time the defence had finished with this chap, he was a nervous wreck, not even sure any more that two and two made four. But what I mean is, a good, solid case rests on facts. Like DNA. That's what judges like and that's what juries like. Facts. Indisputable. Beautiful. Facts. Am I right, Denise?'

Denise Campbell nodded.

'Now,' Oakes went on after another slug of coffee, 'I trust that Mr Pierce gave his permission for the blood and hair samples to be taken?'

'Yes,' said Banks. 'They were taken by a registered police surgeon. You should have copies of the signed consent forms.'

Oakes frowned and dug around deeper in the pile. 'Ah, yes,' he muttered, pulling out a few coffee-ringed sheets. 'Here they are. Good. Good. And I trust this anorak was legally obtained in the first place?'

Banks looked at Stott, who said, 'Yes. He gave us his permission to take it in for tests and we gave him a receipt.'

'But you didn't go into his home with a search warrant?'

'No,' said Stott. 'At that stage in our enquiries we merely wanted to talk to Mr Pierce. Then, when I saw the orange anorak, having heard descriptions of a man in a similar orange anorak in the vicinity of the crime scene, I took the initiative and—'

Oakes flapped his hand again. 'Yes, yes, yes, Inspector. All right. You're not giving evidence in court. Spare me the formalities. It's a bit flimsy, but it'll have to do.'

Stott sat stiffly in his chair, red-faced, mouth tight. Banks couldn't resist a smile. It was the new lad's first taste of Stafford Oakes.

Oakes went on, thumbing through the pile on his desk. 'Good stuff, most of this,' he said. 'DNA, hair, blood analysis. Good stuff. Can't understand a word of it myself, of course, but get the right man in the box and we'd even be able to sell it to your average *Sun* reader. That's the key, you know: plain language, without talking down.' He put a thick wad of papers aside and flapped a few statements in the air. 'And this,' he went on. 'Not so bad, either. Your vicar, what's his name . . . Daniel Charters . . . places our man on the bridge around the right time.' He touched his index finger to the side of his nose. 'Must say though, Banks, there's a hint of moral turpitude about the fellow.'

'Daniel Charters was accused of making a homosexual advance to a church worker,' said Banks. 'A Croatian refugee called Ive Jelačić, who was also a suspect in this case, until we turned up Pierce. If it's of any interest, I don't believe Charters did it.'

'Doesn't matter what *you* believe. Does it, Denise?'

'No,' said Denise.

'See, my learned colleague agrees. No, what matters, Banks, is what the jury believes. Vicar with a whiff of scandal lingering around the dog-collar like a particularly virulent fart.' He shook his head and tut-tutted. 'Now, there, they say to themselves, goes a true hypocrite, a man who preaches the virtue of chastity, a man who belongs to a church that won't even ordain homosexual ministers, caught with his hand up the choirboy's surplice, so to speak. Well, you see what I mean? It's tabloid scandal-sheet material, that's what it is.'

'The point is academic, anyway,' Banks said, 'as Owen Pierce openly admits to being on the bridge at the time.'

'Ah-hah,' said Oakes, raising a finger. 'I wouldn't take too much notice of that. It's about as useful as a confession. And remember, that's what he said *before* he talked to his solicitor. A lot can change between now and the trial. Believe me, we need as much evidence as we can get.'

'Charters isn't the only one who can place Pierce on the bridge around the right time. Deborah's friend Megan Preece saw him, too.'

Oakes shook his head. 'I've read her statement. She's not entirely *sure* it was him. Damn good thing, too. Nothing worse than children in the box. Oh, we'll use your vicar. Don't worry about that. Just playing devil's advocate. Have to anticipate all eventualities.' He glanced at more statements. 'The landlord of the Nag's Head places Pierce in the pub a short while before, too, I see. He's reliable, I suppose?'

Banks looked at Stott again. 'Well,' the latter said stiffly. 'He seems a bit slow to me, but given that it wasn't a busy night and Pierce seems to have been about his only customer, I think we can rely on him, yes.'

'Good. And what's this other place now . . . Ah, the Peking Moon. A Chinese restaurant.' He wrinkled his nose. 'Chinaman, I suppose?'

'Born and bred in Whitechapel,' said Stott.

'Chinaman with a cockney accent, then?'

'Yes.'

Oakes shook his head. 'Juries don't like Chinamen.

Don't trust them. Still think of the old Fu Manchu image, you know, inscrutable, yellow peril and all that. Don't go for it myself, but you can't seem to get these racist attitudes out of people's minds as quickly as you'd like, and you certainly can't legislate them away. Still, we'll do our best. Bright fellow, is he?'

'He's very articulate,' said Stott.

'Good, that'll help. Unless he seems too bright, of course. Juries don't like people who come across as being *too* clever. Especially foreigners. They expect it of the boffins, of course, but not of your common-or-garden sort of restaurateur. Well, can't be helped.' He got up and refilled his coffee mug from the machine on the filing cabinet. 'Now what really bothers me,' he went on, 'is this other stuff here.' He reached into the pile again and pulled out more papers. 'You took a statement from a woman called Michelle Chappel, an ex-girlfriend of Pierce's. It's all above board, of course, but the whole issue's dodgy.' He clicked his tongue and rested his hand on the papers, as if ready to swear on the Bible. 'Dodgy in the extreme.'

'In what way?' asked Banks.

Oakes sat back in his chair, linked his hands behind his head and quoted at the cracked ceiling. '"A trial judge in a criminal trial has always a discretion to refuse to admit evidence if in his opinion its prejudicial effect outweighs its probative value." Lord Diplock, Regina v. Sang, 1979.'

'And do you think this is the case with Michelle Chappel's statement?' Banks asked.

'I'm saying it could be a problem. "There should be excluded from the jury information about the accused which is likely to have an influence on their minds prejudicial to the accused which is out of proportion to the true probative value of admissible evidence conveying that information." Same source. And it usually relates to evidence of similar fact. You're implying here, by trying to introduce the woman's statement as evidence, that Pierce was just the kind of person who would commit such a crime. Freudian mumbo-jumbo, and juries don't like it, except on television. And, more to the point, a lot of judges don't like it, either.'

Banks shrugged. 'I'm aware of the similar fact rule,' he said, 'but what we're trying to establish here is a history of violence against women. And there's a marked physical similarity between the two victims. We're trying to get at a motive.'

Oakes's eyebrows shot up. 'Ah, yes, that's all very well and good, Banks. But then you're an imaginative sort of chap, kind who reads a lot of fiction, aren't you? If you understand the problem of similar fact evidence, then you must see that what you're doing is saying that Pierce was the sort of person who would commit such a crime because he once acted in a way *similar* to the perpetrator of the crime under consideration. And, what's more, it's an unreported crime based purely on the evidence of a woman who no doubt despises the man for rejecting her.' He tut-tutted again and drank some coffee. 'Still,' he mused, 'stranger things have happened.'

'So what's your conclusion?' Banks asked.

'My conclusion?' He slapped the stack of coffee-stained files. 'Oh we'll give it a try. Why not? At worst, her evidence can only be declared inadmissible.' He chuckled. 'It used to be that the definition of inadmissible evidence was anything that might help the defence. That was in the good old days. Sometimes, depending on the judge, you can get a bit of leeway on these matters, especially in a case as serious as this one. I've seen similar fact evidence admitted more than once. What the rule actually states is that the *mere fact* that the accused has previously acted in a similar way to the crime he is standing trial for its not relevant. However, if there's a *very close* similarity, something that links the two events in a convincing way as part of a whole system of actions, an emerging *pattern*, so much so that it becomes more than a matter of mere coincidence, then such evidence may be admissible. Do you follow me?'

'I think so,' said Banks.

'If we attempt to show that the two assaults are part of such a pattern,' Oakes continued, 'then we might just be able to squeeze it in. Depending on the judge, of course. Have you got a psychologist you can consult on this? What about that young woman I've seen you with in the Queen's Arms? Pretty young thing. Redhead. Isn't she a psychologist?'

'Jenny Fuller?'

'That's the one.'

'Yes. But Jenny's still teaching in America. She won't be back until after Christmas.'

'That'll do fine. No hurry, dear boy, no hurry. We've got enough for committal already. Just need something to beef up the admissibility quotient, if we can.'

'Are you going to prosecute, then?'

Oakes drank more coffee, looked at the papers and sniffed a few times. 'Oh, I think so,' he said, after what seemed like an eternity. Then he nodded. 'Yes, yes, I think we've got a good case. What about you, Denise?'

Denise Campbell nodded. 'Let's nail the bastard,' she said. Then she blushed and put her hand over her mouth as if she had just burped.

TWO

Owen's committal proceeding occurred in early February. The whole affair was about as exciting as a damp squib, more reminiscent of a college faculty meeting than an affair at which grave matters were decided. Nobody was even wearing wigs and robes.

He appeared before three JPs one bitter cold morning, and on Wharton's advice, they heard the 'new-style committal.' That is, they read all the prosecution's statements and the defence offered no case. It was basically committal by consent. And just as Wharton had guaranteed, the JPs agreed there was *prima facie* case and Owen was bound over for trial in the Crown Court. A trial date was set for late March. There were a few spectators in court, and Owen's name was now known to the general public, but only the charges and bare details were made known to the press, not the actual evidence.

Luckily, Owen had quickly got used to the monotony of prison routine: lights on, slop out, lights out, sleep. After the first few weeks, he had lost track of time. He was allowed out of his cell only to exercise in the dreary yard for half an hour each day. He hardly saw another soul there but for his guards, and it was no pleasure walking around in circles alone.

The food reminded him of school dinners: bread-and-butter pudding, grey leathery beef, lumpy custard, Spam fritters. Usually he left most of it. Even so, he felt constipated much of the time.

The cells around him were all occupied. At night he heard voices, even crying sometimes, and one evening the person in the next cell tried to strike up a conversation, asking him what he'd done. But Owen didn't answer. What could the man possibly want to talk about? Compare notes on rape and mutilation?'

Mostly, he listened to the tapes Wharton brought him and read poetry and science-fiction. He had Wordsworth almost by heart after the first month.

Every few days, for some unknown reason, the prison authorities played musical cells with him. Only the smells were different. One place had a mattress acrid with spilled semen; one of the washstands seemed to breathe vomit fumes from its depths. But maybe that was his imagination. The predominating odour was of disinfectant and slops. In one cell, he discovered in the middle of the night that there was no chamber pot or bucket. He called a warder, who told him to piss on the floor. He pissed down the sink. That wasn't his imagination.

As time went on, it was the little things that began to get him down: the rough feel of his prison clothes, the lack of cooking or tea-making facilities, the lousy coffee, the dreadful food . . . The more he thought about them, the less petty they seemed. These were the essential parts of the tapestry of his liberty, things he took for granted normally. Now he had no access to them, they assumed greater importance in his mind.

It was all relative, of course. For a starving child in an Ethiopian village, for example, prison food would be a luxury and freedom might simply be defined as the hour or two's relief from the agony of hunger. When people are starving, they have no true freedom. But for someone like Owen – middle-class, reasonably well-off, well-educated, living in England – freedom was made up of myriad things, some more abstract than others, but it all came down to *having a choice*.

Locked in his small, lonely cell once again, Owen actually felt relieved to be left alone at last, to be shut away from the bureaucrats, the reporters and the women who stared at him with such naked hatred in their eyes. He was protected here from the crowds outside eager for his blood, and from the policemen so anxious to rip off the surface of his life and dig their hands deep into the slimy darkness below.

His cell was the only place he felt safe now; its routine and isolation sheltered him from the malevolent absurdity of the world outside.

THREE

Jenny Fuller dashed into the Queen's Arms ten minutes late, shucked off her black overcoat and folded it carefully over the back of the adjacent chair. She gave her head a shake to toss back her mass of flame-coloured hair, then sat down and patted her chest. 'Out of breath. Sorry I'm late. Are we on expenses?'

Dr Jennifer Fuller was a lecturer in psychology at the University of York, and over the years her focus had shifted towards criminal and deviant psychology. Now, she had even started publishing in the field and was quickly making a name for herself. Hence the summer in America. Banks had worked with her on several cases before, and an initial attraction had transformed into an enduring friendship that delighted and surprised both of them.

Banks laughed. 'Afraid not.'

'Pity. I was getting sort of used to that in America. Everyone's on expenses there.'

'Let me buy the first one, at least.'

'How kind. I'll have a small brandy please, to take the chill off.'

'And to eat?'

'Chicken in a basket.'

On his way to the bar, Banks recognized one or two of the local shop-owners and the manager of the NatWest bank on his lunch-break. Cyril had also got the coal fire going nicely. The closest table to it was already taken by a group of ramblers in hiking boots and waterproof gear, so Banks and Jenny sat off to one side, near the window. Rain spattered the red and amber diamonds and blurred the clear panes. Along with the drinks, Banks ordered Jenny's chicken, and scampi and chips for himself.

Jenny rubbed her hands together and gave a mock shiver when Banks came back with the drinks, then she picked up her small glass and said, 'Cheers.' They clinked glasses. 'Have a good Christmas?'

'The usual. My parents for Christmas Eve, Sandra's for Christmas Day and Boxing Day.'

'And how is Sandra?'

'She's fine.'

Jenny took another sip of brandy. 'So,' she said, 'I see you've got your man under lock and key. Another notch in your truncheon.'

Banks nodded. 'It looks that way.'

'I take it that's what you *do* want to pick my brains about, and this isn't just a ruse to secure the pleasure of my company?'

Banks smiled. 'Yes to the first. Not that I'd be averse to the latter.'

'Stop it, you sweet man. You'll make the lady blush. How can I help?'

Banks lit a cigarette. 'I don't know if you can. Or if you will, rather. Just listen, first of all, and tell me if I'm going way off the tracks.'

Jenny nodded. 'Okay.'

Banks told her what they knew about Owen Pierce and Michelle Chappel, stressing Owen's reluctance to admit to knowing Michelle, her resemblance to Deborah Harrison, and what she said Owen had done to her.

When he had finished, Jenny sat quietly for a moment, sucking her lower lip and thinking. Banks sipped some beer and said, 'I've been trying to work up some sort of psychological scenario for this crime. Owen Pierce had means and opportunity, and the DNA evidence is pretty damning. I suppose I'm looking for a *motive*.'

'You should know by now that you don't always get one with crimes like this, Alan. Motiveless, stranger killings. At least not what you or I would regard as a logical or even a reasonable motive, like anger or revenge.'

'True. But bear with me, Jenny. Say he's upset about the girl, Michelle, angry at her. He goes for a walk and there, out of the fog, this vision appears. Michelle. Well, maybe not *exactly* Michelle, but an approximation. A younger model, more innocent, perhaps more vulnerable, less threatening. So he follows her into the graveyard, approaches her, she says something and sparks his anger. He's already been violent towards Michelle, remember, so there's a precedent. Does it make sense?'

Jenny frowned. 'It could do,' she said. 'Sometimes, we act out, we behave towards people as if they were some-one else. It's called "displacement," an unconscious defence mechanism where emotions or ideas are trans-ferred from one object or person to another that seems less threatening. I think Freud defined it as one of the neuroses, but my Freud's a bit rusty at the moment. What you're asking is whether I think Owen Pierce could have displaced his feelings for Michelle to Deborah because of some vague superficial resemblance—'

'And because of his mental state at the time.'

'All right, that too. And that this led him to kill her. Really he was killing Michelle.'

'Yes. What do you think?'

'I think you've got a point, or the beginning of one.'

'You don't think I'm way off beam?'

'Not at all.' Their food came. 'How about another drink to wash this down?'

'Please. I never argue when a woman wants to buy me a drink.'

Banks watched Jenny walk to the bar. She moved well and had a superb figure: long legs, narrow waist and a bum like two plums in a wet paper bag. She had a new energy and confidence in her stride, too, and it looked as if the summer in California had done her good.

She was wearing tight black jeans and a jade-green jacket, made of raw silk, over a white shirt. Judging by the cut and the material of the jacket, the way it narrowed at her waist and flared slightly over the swell of her hips, it had probably cost her a small fortune on Rodeo Drive or some such place. But Jenny always had liked nice clothes.

Banks noticed her exchange a few words with a young man who looked like a trainee bank manager while she waited for Cyril to pour the pint. Poor fellow, Banks thought; he didn't stand a chance. But Jenny was smiling. Why did he feel a pang of jealousy when he saw her flirt with another man, even to this day?

She came back with a pint of bitter for Banks and a

Campari and soda for herself. He thanked her. 'Making a date?' he said, nodding towards the man.

Jenny laughed. 'What do you think I am, a cradle-snatcher? Besides, he's not my type.' Jenny was thirty-five in December; the young man about twenty-four. As yet, Banks knew, Jenny hadn't quite figured out what her 'type' was.

When Jenny smiled, her green eyes lit up and the lines around them crinkled into a map of her humour. Her tan brought out the freckles across her nose and cheeks.

'How was California?' he asked.

'All sun and surf. Just like *Baywatch*.'

'Really?'

She wrinkled her nose. 'No, not really. You'd hate it,' she said. 'Can't smoke anywhere.'

'And they call it the Garden of Eden. Is that where you developed a taste for fried chicken?'

'Not at all. I've always had a weakness for lean, relatively fat-free meat deep-fried in batter and cholesterol. It appeases both conflicting sides of my nature.' She sliced off a chunk of deep-fried chicken breast and popped it in her mouth.

Banks laughed. They finished their meal in silence, then Banks lit a cigarette and said, 'Back to Pierce. Look, I know I'm putting you on the spot, Jenny, but I'd like you to work something up for the CPS.'

'Like what?'

'The kind of thing we were talking about. Displacement, for example. Tell me more.'

Jenny sipped her Campari and soda. Banks still had half a pint left, and he wasn't allowing himself another drink this lunch-time.

'Okay,' Jenny said, 'let's say that he has poor control

over his anger. It's pretty much a commonplace that people often respond to frustration by getting angry, and if their anger is really intense and their inner controls are weakened even further – say by alcohol or tiredness – then it can result in physical assault, even murder. That seems to be what happened with Michelle, but what about Deborah? Had he been drinking?'

'He'd had two pints and a whisky.'

'Okay. Let's say then, that we *are* dealing with displacement, which is a coping pattern. A defence mechanism, if you like.'

'Defence against what?'

'Stress, basically. If a situation really threatens your sense of adequacy, your ego, your self-esteem, then your reactions become defence-orientated, you defend your *self* from devaluation.'

'How?'

'Any number of ways. Denial. Rationalization. Fantasy. Repression. Things we all do. What it basically comes down to is ridding yourself of the anxiety and the tensions that are causing the pain.'

'Sexual tension?'

'Could be. But that's just one kind.'

'And displacement is one of these defence mechanisms?'

'Yes. You shift the strong feelings you have from the person or object towards which they were originally intended to another person or object. Often very difficult emotions are involved, like hostility and anxiety. It's an unconscious process.'

'Are you suggesting he wasn't responsible?'

'Interesting point. But I don't think so. I don't know exactly what the law is, but I'm not saying a person suffering displacement isn't responsible for his actions, especially violent ones. Just that he might not know the inner processes that are leading him to want to do what he does.'

'Which you can probably say for most of us most of the time?'

'Yes. In less extreme ways.'

'Okay. Go on.'

'Displacement is often combined with projection, where you put the blame for your own problems on someone else, or some group.'

'Women?'

'Could be. In extreme cases it leads to a form of paranoia. People become convinced that forces or groups are working against them. He *could* have formed such a projection of his anxieties and hostilities against women in general. Plenty of men do. That French Canadian who shot all those women at the college in Montreal, for example.'

'And could he also have displaced his hostile feelings for Michelle onto Deborah, given the stress of the anniversary, the effect of alcohol and the resemblance between the two women?'

'Possibly. Yes. There's a study by a psychologist called Masserman, done in 1961, where he manages to show that under sustained frustration people become more willing to accept substitute goals.'

'Deborah for Michelle?'

'Yes. Look, I'm a bit rusty on this. I'll need a few days to come up with something.'

'How about next week?'

Jenny smiled. 'I'll see what I can do.'

'If there's anything else you want to know, give me a call.'

'Can you get copies of the statements to me?'

'No problem.'

'Okay. Now I really must go.' She stood up and reached for her raincoat. Then she leaned forward and gave Banks a quick peck on the cheek.

When she had gone, he lit another cigarette, vowing it would be his last for the day, and contemplated the remains of his pint. Another half wouldn't do any harm, he decided, so he went and got one, pouring it into the pint glass because he didn't like drinking beer from small glasses.

FOUR

One afternoon about three or four weeks after his committal – he was losing track of time – Owen was taken from his cell to a prison interview room, where he met for the first time the barrister Gordon Wharton had engaged to lead his defence.

In her early forties, Owen guessed, Shirley Castle, QC, was an attractive woman by any standards. She was also the first woman he had seen since his trip to the Magistrates' Court. She had glossy dark hair that fell over her shoulders and framed a pale, oval face. Her almond-shaped eyes were a peculiar shade of violet, so unusual that Owen wondered if she were wearing tinted contact lenses. She had on a grey pleated skirt and a pale pink blouse buttoned up to her chin. Her perfume smelled subtle and expensive.

Wharton sat beside her with a smug, proprietorial air about him, basking in the glory of her presence, as if to say, 'Just look who I've got for you, my boy. What a treat!'

Shirley Castle took the cap off her Montblanc fountain-pen, shuffled some papers in front of her and began.

'It doesn't look very good, Owen,' she said. 'I don't want to give you any false hopes or illusions. We'll have an uphill struggle on our hands with this one.'

'But all they've got is circumstantial evidence.'

She looked at him. 'The point is, that they can build a very good case on that. Look at it this way.' She started to count off the points on her long fingers. 'One, you had the opportunity. Two, motive in such crimes is so obscure, to say the least, that they don't really need to establish one. And, three, there's the DNA, hairs and blood.'

'But I can explain it all. I have done. I never denied being in the area from the start, and I told them the girl bumped into me. Maybe that's how the hair and blood were exchanged.'

'Maybe. But the police don't believe you,' she said. 'And quite frankly, I don't blame them, especially given that you only came up with that explanation at the eleventh hour. No, Owen, I'm afraid we're going to have to fight tooth and nail for this one.'

'Are they still looking for the real murderer?'

'Why should they? They think they've already got him.'

'So there's nobody out there trying to prove my innocence?'

'I'm afraid not.'

'Can't you employ a private detective or someone?'

Shirley Castle laughed. It was a lighter, frothier, more vivacious sound than he would have imagined, given her overall gravity. But it was a nervous laugh, no doubt about that. 'To do what?' she asked.

'Find the real murderer. Prove me innocent.'

'Things don't work quite like that.'

'Well, how *do* they work?'

She leaned back in her chair and frowned. 'We go to court and we give them the best fight we can. There's no other way. It's only on *Perry Mason* that the lawyer and the private eye get out on the mean streets and track down the *real* killer.'

'Just let me tell them my story. I'm sure they'll believe me.'

'I'm not sure yet if I'm going to put you in the witness box at all.'

'Why not?'

Shirley Castle frowned. 'Cross-examination can be really tough.'

'Is something bothering you?'

'Yes, as a matter of fact it is. The CPS file suggests an approach to the case that involves similar fact to try and establish a *motive* for the murder, too.'

'But you said they didn't need one.'

'Their case will be all that much stronger if they can come up with one.'

'What are they saying?'

Shirley Castle rested her chin in her hand. 'Tell me about Michelle Chappel, Owen.'

Owen swallowed. His mouth felt dry. 'What about her?'

'About your relationship. And why you lied to the police about the nude photographs, denied you knew her. You didn't want them to find her and talk to her, did you?'

'No, I can't say I did. Michelle . . . well, let's say we parted on bad terms. She'd have nothing good to say about me.'

'As I understand it, there was violence, perhaps attempted murder?'

'That's absurd! Have you talked to her?'

'No,' she said. 'The police have. I've just been reviewing the statement, and it's very interesting. Read for yourself.' She dropped a sheaf of papers in front of him.

Owen felt rising panic as he read the transcript of the taped interview with Michelle:

Q: Miss Chappel, could you tell us how and when you first met Mr Pierce?

A: Yes. In class. He was my teacher. I was his student.

Q: How old were you at the time?

A: Seventeen.

Q: Was this at Eastvale College of Further Education?

A: Yes.

Q: How old was Owen Pierce when you met?

A: Thirty-two, thirty-three. I'm not exactly sure.

Q: So he was almost old enough to be your father?

A: Technically. I suppose a sixteen-year-old could be a father.

Q: Did you live at home?

A: Yes. Until I was eighteen.

Q: Where did you go then?

A: I moved in with Owen.

Q: How long did you live with him?

A: Five years.

Q: How did Mr Pierce approach you?

A: He suggested a coffee after class, one day, then he asked me out to dinner.

Q: Were your marks good?

A: Yes.

Q: Did you start seeing one another regularly?

A: Yes. We went out together a few times for dinner, to the pictures or for a drink. Sometimes he took me out for a ride in the country in his car, and we'd find a little village pub somewhere.

Q: How soon did you become lovers?

A: Very soon after we first went out.

Q: Weeks? Days?

A: Days.

Q: And the relationship went well after you moved in with him?

A: At first it did, yes. Look, I mean, you have to realize, I was very young. A bit of a misfit, too, I suppose. I wasn't very happy at home, and I didn't really have any close friends. I found most people my own age immature. I was also very shy and Owen was nice to me. I suppose I was flattered, too, by the attention. When I talked about leaving home, he asked if I'd like to move in with him, and it seemed like a good idea. I felt safe with him.

Q: Were you still his student when you moved in with him?

A: I was in his business communications class, yes.

Q: Did you continue to do well in that course?

A: Very well.

Q: Deservedly?

A: I think so. Look, I'm not stupid, but I also admit it may have helped, sleeping with my teacher.

Q: Do you think there was a price to pay for your success?

A: What do you mean?

Q: Did Owen ever suggest or attempt to commit any unnatural acts?

A: Do you mean was he kinky?

Q: Something like that.

A: No. I wouldn't say that. I mean, he liked me to wear

certain underclothes. You know, black silky things, thigh stockings, skimpy things. He liked me to keep them on when we . . . you know.

Q: During intercourse?

A: Yes.

Q: Was that all?

A: All? Was what all?

Q: The skimpy clothes. Did he ever make you do anything you didn't want to?

A: He wanted to do it to me from behind, like dogs. I didn't like that.

Q: But did you do as he wished?

A: Well, I . . . yes, at first I did. I wanted to please him.

Q: Because you were worried about your marks?

A: A bit, I suppose.

Q: Did he show any interest in pornography?

A: We watched a dirty video once. You know the sort of thing. I didn't really enjoy it. In fact, I thought it was dead gross, but it seemed to turn him on.

Q: How did he behave when you were watching the video?

A: Well, he was, you know, maybe a bit more ardent than usual. He wanted to try out things they were doing, you know, on the video.

Q: Against your will?

A: No, but I thought it was a bit weird.

Q: Did he ever resort to violence for the purpose of sexual stimulation?

A: He used to like to tie me up sometimes.

Q: How did you react to this?

A: What could I do? He was stronger than me. I wanted to please him. It was uncomfortable and it frightened me a bit, but it didn't really hurt. It was just a game, really. It was something he'd seen in that silly film and it turned him on.

Q: Did he beat you at all? Flagellation?

A: No.

Q: So apart from the tying up he wasn't violent?

A: No . . . not until the end. Then living with him became sort of like being in prison. Every time I went out I had to account for my movements. Some nights he wouldn't even let me go out.

Q: How did he keep you in?

A: He just made such a fuss it wasn't worth it. I felt shut in, always under observation. I couldn't breathe. I was frightened of his temper. I started rebelling in small ways, like seeing other friends and stuff, and it made him more and more possessive.

Q: Is that why you left him? Fear of violence?

A: Partly . . . it was frightening, especially the last night, but . . .

Q: Can you tell us about the last night, Michelle?

Michelle went on to tell about the night she claimed Owen had raped and tried to strangle her. Pale, Owen shoved the papers aside and looked at Shirley Castle.

'Well?' she asked. 'What do you think of it?'

Owen shook his head slowly. 'I don't know what to say.'

'It's not true, then?

'Some of it, maybe. But she even makes the truth sound different, sound bad for me, the way she slants it.'

'In what way?'

'Every way. The sex, for example. She makes me sound like a pervert, but most of it was her idea. She loved it, the tying up, the talking dirty. It really got her going. And she liked the video.'

'Did you hit her that last night?'

'I pushed her. I was protecting myself. She was berserk, out of control. She'd have killed me if I hadn't pushed her away.'

'And she hit her head as she fell?'

'Yes.'

'Knocking her unconscious?'

'Yes, but . . . Oh, God.' Owen held his head in his hands. 'I know how it sounds, but I've never hurt anyone in my life, never on purpose.'

'Did you have sex with her after she'd knocked herself out?'

'No, I didn't. That's a lie. What do you take me for?'

'I'm just trying to get at the truth, Owen. Did you try to force her to have sex at any time that evening?'

'No, I mean, yes. No, I didn't try to force her, but I suggested it. I just wanted to see how she would react. It was a test. I didn't force her.'

Shirley frowned. 'You made advances? I'm afraid I don't understand you, Owen. You'll have to explain it to me.'

How could he tell her about that night? Still vivid in his mind, it was like watching a cartoon play, the gaudy colours, the exaggerated violence, the sense of being a spectator, unable to stop the film, unable even to walk out of the cinema.

'How did it start, Owen?'

Owen tried to explain. He had grown suspicious of Michelle over the last year or so, he said, suspected that she was seeing another man, or other men. That night, when she said she was going to meet a girlfriend, he followed her into Eastvale town centre and watched her meet someone in a pub. As they talked and drank, rubbing close together, Owen sat, shielded by a frosted-glass partition and watched the shadows. At closing time, he followed them to a house not far from his own and watched outside as the bedroom light went on, then the curtains closed, and someone turned out the light.

He went home and paced and drank whisky until Michelle got in after two-thirty in the morning. Instead of challenging her immediately with what he'd found out, he made sexual advances to see how she would react.

She pushed him away and told him she was too tired; listening to her girlfriend's tales of woe till so late. He could smell the other man on her, the stale beer and smoke on her clothes, in her hair, mingled with the reek of sex. She hadn't even had the decency to take a shower afterwards.

Then he told her what he'd seen, what he had watched. She went wild, flew at him, screamed that he didn't own her and if he was no good in bed she had every damn right to find someone who was. It was like watching another person emerge from the shell of someone you thought you knew.

He called her a bitch, a whore, told her he knew she'd been at it all the time they'd been together, that she had just used him, had never really loved him. For a moment, she paused in her attack and a different look came into her eyes: hard, cold hatred. She picked up a pair of scissors from the table and lunged at him. He grabbed her hand and twisted until she dropped them.

Then she renewed the attack, kicking, scratching, flailing out wildly. He held his hands in front of his face to ward off the blows and tried to talk her down. But she wouldn't stop. Finally, out of desperation, he pushed her away, just to give himself some space to manoeuvre and she fell over and hit her head on the chair leg.

He tried to tell Shirley Castle all this, as calmly as he could. He knew it sounded thin without the whole background of the relationship, from the early innocence to the bitter knowledge that it had all been a lie.

What he couldn't tell her, though, what he hardly dared even admit to himself, was that after Michelle had fallen on the floor, arms spread out, one leg crooked over the other, he had wanted her. Hating her even then, he had torn at her clothing, then, half-mad with jealousy and hatred, had put his hands around her throat and wanted to choke the life out of her for what she had done to him, for ruining, for defiling what he had thought was the love of a lifetime. He hated himself for wanting her, and he hated her for making him.

At that moment, the full power of his love turned to hate and overwhelmed him, and he knew that everything, her words, her gestures, her lovemaking, her promises, had all been a lie. But he let go; he couldn't kill her. He stood up, steadied himself and went to collapse on the bed. She was still breathing; there was no blood; he hadn't raped her.

In the morning he found her sulking in the spare room, nursing the bump on her head. She tried to make up to him, told him she would do anything he wanted . . . *anything* . . . and started squirming around under the thin sheet. It had always worked before, but this time Owen had had more than enough.

He knew that if he took her back, if he lived with her for just one more day he would lose his self-respect forever. When he told her to go, she screamed and begged, but he threw her out in the street with only her suitcase. The next thing he knew, he got a letter with a Swiss Cottage address to send on the rest of her things. He did so.

Shirley Castle let the silence stretch after his explanation. Owen couldn't read the way she looked at him. He didn't know whether she believed him or not.

'Owen,' she said finally. 'Whatever the truth, Michelle's is a very damning statement. You can imagine the case the Crown is trying to build up. A man obsessed with pornography, especially if it features young girls, capable of sexual violence against women . . . You see my point?'

'But it's not true!' Owen argued. 'None of it. I'm not obsessed with pornography.'

Shirley held up her hand. 'I'm not attacking you, Owen. I'm simply trying to demonstrate the spin the prosecution will try and put on the facts, given the chance.'

Owen laid his hands on the desk and stared at the veins in his wrists. 'I don't know what you must think of me,' he said, his voice hardly more than a whisper, 'but I want you to know that I'm not the monster they say I am. It's a distortion. If I knew only *certain* facts about your life, or anyone's, if your fantasies were laid bare for all to see . . . well, I might form a picture, and it might be the wrong one. Do you know what I mean?'

He could have sworn there was an amused glint in her eyes, and perhaps a faint flush on her cheeks. 'You don't need to please me, Owen,' she said. 'I'm here as a professional. It's not my place to make judgements about your private life, only to prove reasonable doubt. You don't need to seek my approval.'

'But I want it,' Owen said. 'Damn it, I want it! You're

not a machine, are you? You must have opinions, feelings.'

Shirley Castle didn't answer. Instead, she shuffled the papers back towards her briefcase and said, 'There's one more important question before I go, Owen. Why would Michelle do what she did? Why would she say all those things about you to the police if they're not true? What reason has she to want you to go to jail?'

'Don't you understand? Michelle's a user. She used me from the start, for her education, her escape from her overbearing parents, for her living-quarters, the good life. I was her passport through college. She threw me a few crumbs and I took them for love. Even now I have a hard time believing that you can live with someone for so long and not really see them for what they are, not know them at all. But it's true. Maybe I didn't *want* to see. All the time she was with me, she was going with other men, and I admit I got jealous and possessive. But she didn't care. She thought she could get away with everything, just take her clothes off for me and make it all right. At heart she's a cold, calculating monster. She has no conscience. Do you understand? Sometimes, it's only when the final piece falls into place that you see there was ever a pattern at all. That was what happened that last night. The final piece. She'd been doing it all along, lying to me, seeing other men, doing exactly what she wanted, using my home – *our* home – as a squat. I gave her all the freedom she wanted at first, before I started to suspect the truth. She was young after all. How can you keep the love of a younger woman if you try to put her in a cage? As soon as I became more vigilant, the cracks started to appear.'

Shirley Castle shook her head. 'I can accept all that,

Owen, but it doesn't really answer my question. Why does she wish you so much harm?'

'Why? Because I found her out,' Owen answered, remembering that one calm moment in the final battle, when he had seen her for what she really was. 'Because I saw through her. I saw her true face. And because I rejected her. I threw her out. Though she denied me the night before, just after she'd been with her boyfriend, she offered me her body the next morning. But I wouldn't take it. She begged me to forgive her and let her stay. But I threw her out. She was like a spiteful child if she didn't get her own way. She can't forgive me for seeing the truth and having the courage to throw her out before she dumped me.'

Shirley Castle nodded slowly. 'Well, Owen, that's all very well,' she said. 'But we'd just better hope, for your sake, that she doesn't get anywhere near the witness-box.'

11

ONE

Wood creaked as those present in court got to their feet one rainy April day. Judge Simmonds entered, resplendent in scarlet moire and white linen. He was a wizened old man with reptilian eyes buried deep in wrinkles and folds of flesh. His face was expressionless as he looked around the courtroom before sitting.

The benches groaned as everyone in the crowded room sat down. Owen noticed that the courtroom smelled of the same lemon-scented polish his mother used to use; it made him feel sad.

'The prisoner will stand.'

So this was it. Owen stood.

'Is your name Owen Pierce?' asked the Clerk of the Court.

'It is.'

The clerk then read out the indictment and asked Owen how he pleaded.

'Not guilty,' Owen answered, as firmly and confidently as he could manage with all eyes on him.

He scrutinized the jury as he spoke: seven men and five women, all dressed for a day at the office. A pudgy man with a slack, flabby jaw looked at him with something like awe. A pursed-lipped young woman wouldn't meet his eyes at all, but looked down at her hands folded in her lap.

Most of them at least glanced at him in passing. Some were nervous; others looked as if they had already made up their minds.

It was irrational, he knew, but he decided to pick one of them to be his barometer throughout the trial, one whose expressions he would chart to tell how the case was going – for or against him. Not the frowning woman in the powder-blue suit, nor the balding chap who reminded him of his insurance agent; not the conventionally pretty girl with the pageboy cut, nor the burly wrestler-type with his brick-red neck bulging out of his tight collar. It was difficult to find someone.

At last, he decided on a woman; for some reason, it had to be a woman. She was in her late thirties, he guessed, with a moonshaped face and short mousy hair. She had a wide red slash of a mouth and large eyes.

But it wasn't her physical appearance so much as her aura that caused him to pick her out. For some reason, he decided, this woman was good and honest. What was more, she could tell the truth from lies. At the moment, she looked puzzled and confused to find herself in such a frightening role, but she would, he knew, as soon as the trial progressed, listen carefully, weigh, judge and decide. Her decision would be the right one, and he would be able to tell from her expression what it was. Yes, he would keep a close eye on her. He would call her 'Minerva.'

Almost before Owen realized it, Jerome Lawrence, QC, had launched into his opening address. Lawrence was a small, dark-complexioned man with beady, restless black eyes and a perpetual five-o'clock shadow, shiny as shoe-polish on his cheeks and chin. Somehow, he seemed to fit perfectly into his robes, looking even more like a bat ready to flap its wings and take off into the night than anyone else in the room. Like Shirley Castle, he spoke with his hands a lot, and his robe swished about in a most distracting way.

'The Crown shall seek to prove,' Lawrence said in his oiliest public-school voice, 'that the accused is guilty of the most heinous, the most despicable, brutal, inhuman crime of all – the murder of a child, an innocent, a mere sixteen-year-old girl with her whole life before her.'

And for the rest of the day, Owen could only listen, openmouthed, to the depiction of himself as a barely human monster.

Though the parade of witnesses began dramatically enough, with Rebecca Charters tearfully recounting how she discovered Deborah Harrison's body, several things became clear to him in the first days. Probably the first and foremost of these was that you could be bored even at your own murder trial.

Witnesses came and went, people he had never met, people who didn't know him: vicars, shopkeepers, teachers, schoolgirls, policemen, pub landlords. Some of them seemed to spend hours in the box for no reason Owen could think of. Jerome Lawrence or Shirley Castle questioned most of them, but sometimes their juniors took over.

With unfailing regularity one lawyer or another would raise points of law that meant the jury had to be sent out, sometimes for hours, and all sides seemed to like nothing better than the kind of delay that meant an early adjournment for the day. Also, there were one or two days off due to illness of a jury member and another for a family bereavement. Every night, without fail, Owen was shipped back to his little cell at Armley Jail. He was becoming so used to it by now that he almost thought of it as his home. He had forgotten what his real home looked like.

As far as Owen could tell, things seemed to be going quite well over the first few weeks. Shirley Castle made mincemeat of the policeman with the jug-ears for not explaining why he was visiting Owen in the first place. Detective Inspector Stott came out looking like a member of the Gestapo.

By the time Detective Chief Inspector Banks was called, Owen had lost track of the days.

TWO

'In the same situation, Chief Inspector, do you think you would bother to mention *everyone* you saw on the streets during a certain period?'

Banks shrugged. It was his second day giving evidence and Shirley Castle was cross-examining him. 'I would hope I would do my duty and try to recall *everything* that happened around the crucial time,' he answered finally.

'But you are a policeman, Chief Inspector. You have special training. Such facts and fine details are part of your job. I'm sure I wouldn't even remember most of the people I passed in the street. Nor, I imagine, would most members of the jury.' And here, Shirley Castle paused long enough to look over at the jury. Most of them seemed to agree with her, Banks thought. 'Yet you expect Mr Pierce to remember every face, every detail,' she went on. 'I ask you again, Chief Inspector, do you really think this is reasonable?'

'Perhaps not on a busy thoroughfare at rush hour,' said Banks, 'but this was a foggy night in a quiet suburb. Yes, I think I would remember if I had seen a particular person. And Mr Pierce remembered as soon as—'

'That's enough, Chief Inspector. You have answered my question.'

Banks couldn't help but allow himself a slight feeling of satisfaction when he saw Shirley Castle reel from his answer. She had made a small mistake; she hadn't already known the answer to the question she asked.

She hurried on. 'Now, as Mr Sung, proprietor of the Peking Moon restaurant, has already testified, and as my learned friend brought out during his examination-in-chief, Mr Pierce used his credit card to pay for his meal there. If the timing of events is correct – and I stress *if* – this would have occurred shortly *after* the murder of Deborah Harrison, would it not?'

'Yes.'

'Now, in your professional experience, Chief Inspector, would you not say that a criminal, someone who has just committed an attack of the most vile and brutal kind, would be a little more careful to cover his tracks?'

'Most criminals aren't that clever,' said Banks. 'That's why they get caught.'

The members of the gallery laughed.

'But my client is *not* stupid,' she went on, ignoring the interruption. 'It is hardly likely that he would go and eat Chinese food and pay for it with a credit card after murdering someone, now, is it? Not to mention do it all wearing a bright orange anorak. Why would he be so foolish as to draw attention to himself in such an obvious way if he had committed the crime of which he is accused?'

'Perhaps he was distraught,' Banks answered. 'Not thinking clearly. Mr Sung did say he was talking to—'

'"Not thinking clearly,"' she repeated, with exactly the right tone of disdain. 'Is it not a fact, Chief Inspector, that perpetrators of such random crimes are usually, in fact, thinking very clearly indeed? That they rarely get caught, unless by accident? That they take great care to avoid discovery?'

Banks fiddled with his tie. He hated having it fastened up and could only bear it if he kept the top button of his shirt undone. 'There are certain schools would say that, yes. But a criminal's behaviour is not easily predictable. If it were, we'd have an easier job on our hands.' He smiled at the jury; one or two of them smiled back.

'Come on, Chief Inspector Banks, you can't have it both ways. Either they're stupid and easy to catch, as you said earlier, or they're unpredictable and impossible to catch. Which is it?'

'Some are stupid; some are not. As I said before, murderers don't always act rationally. This wasn't a rational crime. There's no way of predicting what the killer would do, or why he did things the way he did.'

'But aren't you in the business of reconstructing crimes, Chief Inspector?'

'Nowadays we leave that to *Crimewatch*.'

Laughter rose up from the gallery. Judge Simmonds admonished Banks for his flippancy.

'My point is,' Shirley Castle went on without cracking a smile, 'that you seem to know so very little of what went on in St Mary's graveyard, or indeed, of what kind of criminal you're dealing with. Isn't that true?'

'We know that Deborah Harrison was strangled with the strap of her school satchel and that her clothing was rearranged.'

'But isn't it true that you simply picked on the first person seen in the area whom you thought fitted the bill, that Owen Pierce was unfortunate enough to be in the wrong place at the wrong time?'

'I'd say it was Deborah Harrison who was in the wrong place at the wrong time.'

'Were there not certain elements of the crime scene that struck you as odd?'

'What elements?'

Shirley Castle consulted her notes. 'As I understand it,' she said, 'the victim's school satchel was *open*. Doesn't that strike you as odd?'

'It could have come open during the struggle.'

'Hardly,' scoffed Shirley Castle. 'It was fastened by two good-quality buckles. We've tested it, believe me, and it won't open unless someone *deliberately* unfastens it.'

'Perhaps the murderer wanted something from her.'

'Like what, Chief Inspector? Surely you're not suggesting robbery? From a schoolgirl's satchel?'

'It's possible. But I—'

'But what money could a schoolgirl have worth stealing? I understand Deborah Harrison had six pounds in her purse when she was found. If robbery were the motive, why not take that too? And wouldn't it make more sense to take the entire satchel? Why hang around the crime scene any longer than necessary?'

'Which question do you want me to answer first?'

Shirley Castle scowled. 'Why would Deborah Harrison's killer remain at the scene and go through her satchel rather than take it with him?'

'I don't know. Perhaps he was looking for a trophy of some kind. Something personal to the victim.'

'But was anything missing?'

'We don't know. No-one knew exact—'

'You don't know. We have heard a great deal of evidence,' she went on, 'placing Mr Pierce in the vicinity of St Mary's at the time of the crime, but let me ask you this, Chief Inspector: did anyone actually *see* Mr Pierce enter St Mary's graveyard?'

'He was seen—'

'A simple yes or no will suffice.'

Banks was silent a moment, then said, 'No.'

'Is it not also possible, Chief Inspector, that Deborah went somewhere else first and returned to the graveyard later, after Mr Pierce had gone to the Peking Moon?'

'It's possible. But—'

'And that Deborah Harrison was murdered by someone she knew, perhaps because of something she was carrying in her satchel?'

Exactly what I thought at first, Banks agreed. 'I think that's a rather far-fetched explanation,' he said.

'More far-fetched than charging Mr Pierce here with murder?' She pointed at Pierce theatrically. 'While you were busy harassing my client, did you pursue the investigation in other directions?'

'We continued with our enquiries. And we didn't har—'

She sniffed. 'You continued with your enquiries. What does that mean?'

'We tried to find out as much about the victim and her movements as possible. We tried to discover, through talking to friends and family, if she had any enemies, anyone who would want to kill her. We collected all the trace evidence we could find and had it analysed as quickly as possible. We found nothing concrete until we came up with Mr Pierce.'

'And after Mr Pierce's name came up?'

Banks knew that most investigations tend to wind down once the police think they've got their man. And much as he would have liked to pursue other possibilities, there was other work to do, and there was also Chief

Constable Riddle. 'I continued other lines of enquiry until it became app—'

'You continued other lines of enquiry? As soon as you first interviewed him, you decided on Mr Pierce's guilt, didn't you?'

'Objection!'

'Sustained. Ms Castle, please stop insulting the witness.'

Shirley Castle bowed. 'My apologies, Your Honour, Chief Inspector Banks. Let me rephrase the question: what was your attitude to Mr Pierce from the start?'

'We decided he was a definite suspect, and in the absence of any evidence to the contrary, we proceeded to build up our case against him in the usual, accepted manner.'

'Thank you, Chief Inspector,' Shirley Castle said, sitting down and trying to look bored. 'No further questions.'

'Then I suggest,' said Judge Simmonds, 'that we adjourn for the weekend. Court will be in session again at ten-thirty Monday morning.'

THREE

On Monday morning, it happened: exactly what Owen had been fearing.

When he tried to reconstruct the sequence of events later, back in his cell, he couldn't be sure whether Jerome Lawrence had actually managed to call out Michelle's name before Shirley Castle jumped to her feet. Either way, Judge Simmonds listened patiently to the objection, then he dismissed the jury for yet another *voir dire*.

What followed was a legal wrangle that Owen,

educated as he was, could only half follow, so mired was it in tortured English and in citing of precedents. As far as he could gather, though, both sides put their points of view to the judge. Jerome Lawrence argued that Michelle's evidence was relevant because it established a *pattern* of violent behaviour that had its natural outcome in Deborah Harrison's murder, and Shirley Castle countered that the proposed evidence was nothing but vindictive fantasy from an unreliable witness, that it proved nothing, and that its prejudicial effect by far outweighed any probative value it might have.

Owen held his breath as Judge Simmonds paused to consider the arguments; he knew that his entire future might be hanging in the balance here. His mouth felt dry; his jaw clenched; his stomach churned. If Simmonds disallowed the evidence, Owen knew, there could be no reporting of what had gone on in the jury's absence. Only a very few people would ever know about what had happened between him and Michelle. If Simmonds admitted it, though, the whole world would know. And the jury. He crossed his fingers so tightly they turned white.

Finally, Simmonds puckered his lips, frowned, and declared the evidence inadmissible.

Owen let out his breath. The blood roared in his ears, and he felt his whole body relax: jaw, stomach, fingers. He thought he was going to faint.

Shirley Castle flashed him a discreet thumbs-up sign and a quick smile of victory. The jury was brought back in, and Jerome Lawrence called his next witness.

Dr Charles Stewart Glendenning made an imposing figure. Tall, with a full head of white hair and a nicotine-stained moustache, the Home Office pathologist carried himself erectly and had just the right amount of Scottish burr in his accent to make him come across as a no-nonsense sort of person. The serious expression on his face, which had etched its lines over the years, added to the look of the consummate expert witness.

He entered the witness-box as if it were his second home and spoke the oath. Owen noticed that he didn't rest his hand on a copy of the New Testament and that the wording was slightly different from everyone else's. An atheist, then? Not surprising, Owen thought, given the evidence of man's inhumanity to man he must have seen over the years.

After spending what remained of the morning establishing Dr Glendenning's credentials and responsibilities, Jerome Lawrence finally began his examination-in-chief after lunch.

'Rebecca Charters has already described finding the body and calling the police,' he said. 'Could you please describe, Doctor, the condition of the body at the scene?'

'The victim lay on her back. Her blouse was open, her brassiere torn and her breasts exposed. Her skirt had been lifted above her waist, exposing the pubic region, in the manner typical of a sex murder. Her underwear was missing. I understand it was later found nearby. On closer examination of the face, I noticed a reddish-purple colour and traces of bleeding from the nose, consistent with death by asphyxia. There was also a small, fresh scratch by her left eye.'

'Could you tell us what you discovered at the post-mortem?'

'The girl was – had been – in good general health, to be expected in a girl of sixteen. There were no signs of toxicity in her organs. On further examination, I concluded as I had earlier, that death was caused by asphyxia due to strangulation.'

'Would you care to elaborate on asphyxia for the members of the jury, Doctor?' Jerome Lawrence went on.

Glendenning nodded briefly. 'Some strangulation victims die from vagal inhibition, which means heart stoppage caused by pressure on the carotid arteries in the neck.' He touched the spot beside his jaw. 'The victim in this case, however, died because of obstruction to the veins in her neck and the forcing of the tongue against the back of the throat, cutting off her air intake. There are certain tell tale signs. People who die from vagal inhibition are pale, those who die from asphyxia have reddish-purple colouring. There are also petechial haemorrhages, little pinpricks of blood in the whites of the eyes, eyelids, facial skin. Contrary to popular fiction, the tongue does not protrude.'

Owen glanced over at Sir Geoffrey and Lady Harrison, the victim's parents, who had attended almost every day. Lady Harrison turned to her husband and let her head touch his shoulder for a moment. Both were pale.

Owen felt he glimpsed, at that moment, the cold-blooded logic of the prosecution's strategy, like the dramatic structure of a play or a novel, and it sent a chill up his spine.

After hearing Rebecca Charters's emotional account of finding the body and then Banks's solid, professional testimony about the police investigation, if things had gone according to plan the jury would next have heard Michelle's testimony. They would have seen only a sweet, innocent young girl in the witness box and heard how this monster in the dock had attempted to strangle her. (He was certain she would have touched her long, tapered fingers to her throat as she described the attack). *Then* they would have heard the gruesome medical details of the effects of strangulation. And what would they have thought of Owen after all that?

'Thank you, Doctor,' Lawrence went on. 'Could you tell, in this case, *how* the victim was strangled?'

'Yes. With a ligature. A satchel strap, in fact.'

'And was this found close to the scene?'

'Yes. It was still attached to the victim's satchel.'

'In your expert opinion, do you have any reason to doubt it was used as the murder weapon?'

'None at all. We carried out a number of tests. The satchel strap matched the indentations in the victim's throat perfectly. It was angled slightly upwards, cutting into the skin at the bottom part, indicating that she had been strangled from behind and that her attacker was taller than her. There was also blood around the edge of the strap.'

'How much taller was the killer?' asked Jerome Lawrence.

'The victim was five foot six, so I would put the attacker at least six inches taller, perhaps more.'

'And the accused is six foot two, as has already been established?'

'So I believe, yes.'

'Would it have required a great deal of strength?'

'A certain amount, yes. But nothing superhuman.'

'Would the manner of attack make it difficult for the victim to fight off her attacker?'

'Almost impossible. There wouldn't be much she could do. She might manage a wild scratch, of course, or a backwards kick to the shins with her heel.'

'You mentioned a "wild scratch." Would this be possible if she were strangled from behind?'

'Oh, yes. It's quite conceivable she might reach behind and scratch her assailant.'

'Was it possible to tell whether she had been killed in St Mary's churchyard or elsewhere?'

'Yes, by the extent of post-mortem lividity, such as it was. This—' he turned to explain to the jury without Lawrence's prompting, 'means that when the heart stops, the blood simply obeys the force of gravity and sinks to the lowest part of the body. It gathers and stains at points where the flesh is not in contact with the ground. Parts of the body that do remain in contact with the ground will remain white, of course, because the pressure will not allow the blood to settle in the capillaries. In this case, the staining at the back of the neck, small of the back and backs of the legs indicated that the deceased had been lying in the same position since her death. Also, as lividity was in its early stages, she couldn't have been there for very long. It generally begins about thirty minutes to one hour after death, develops fully between three and four hours and becomes fixed between eight and ten hours. The lividity was still faint, and blanching still occurred.'

'Could you explain blanching for the benefit of the court?'

'Certainly. Before the blood coagulates in the vessels, if you touch an area of lividity it will turn white. When you remove your fingertip, it will resume its lividity. After four or five hours the discolouration hardens, becomes clotted, and pressure will not cause blanching.'

'And what does this tell you?'

'Amongst other things, it helps determine time of death. As I said, lividity had only just started and there was no sign of rigor mortis, which usually begins in the eyelids about two or three hours after death. I also took temperature readings, and based on a mathematical calculation, I came up with time of death somewhere between five o'clock and when she was discovered.'

'No earlier?'

'In my opinion, that would be very unlikely indeed.'

'And as the victim's friend Megan Preece reports parting with Deborah near the bridge at six o'clock, and the evidence of Daniel Charters places Owen—'

'Objection!'

'Sustained.' Judge Simmonds pointed with a bony finger. 'Mr Lawrence, behave yourself. You ought to know better.'

Lawrence bowed. 'Your Honour. Thank you, Dr Glendenning. I have no further questions.'

Shirley Castle stood up to cross-examine. 'I only have a couple of questions, Doctor,' she said briskly. 'Minor points, really. I shan't keep you long.'

Dr Glendenning inclined his head and smiled at her in a gentlemanly way.

'I assume you supervised the collection of oral, vaginal and anal swabs at the crime scene?' Shirley Castle began.

'I did.'

'And did you find any traces of semen?'

'None.'

'None at all?'

'That is correct.'

'In your post-mortem examination, did you discover any signs of forcible intercourse?'

'I found no signs of any intercourse at all, forcible or otherwise.'

Shirley Castle frowned. 'Yet you referred to this as a "sex crime" in your earlier testimony. Does that absence of evidence not strike you as unusual in such a crime?'

'Not really. There are many kinds of sex crimes. The way the clothing was disturbed was reminiscent, in my experience, of a sex-crime scene.'

'And we have already heard your enviable credentials as an expert on such matters, Doctor. How accurate is your estimate of time of death?'

'It's always an approximate business,' Glendenning admitted. 'There are so many variables.'

'Could you give the court an example of how you might determine time of death?'

'Certainly. As I have already indicated, there are a number of factors, such as rigor mortis, lividity and stomach contents, but body temperature is often the most accurate. If the temperature at the time of death is normal – thirty-seven degrees centigrade – and it takes the body twenty-four to thirty-six hours after death to fall to the temperature of the environment, then one can make a back-calculation to the time of death.'

'Twenty-four to thirty-six hours,' said Shirley Castle, frowning towards the jury. 'That's between a day and a day and a half. That's a rather broad margin for error, isn't it?'

Glendenning smiled. 'I did say it was an approximate business.'

'Yes, but you didn't say how wildly inaccurate it was.'

'Objection.'

'Sustained, Mr Lawrence.'

Shirley Castle bowed. 'My apologies. Doctor, how long would it have taken Deborah Harrison's body temperature to reach that of the environment?'

'Well, again it's hard to say precisely. She was healthy, normal, slim, partially unclothed, and it was a moist evening, with a temperature of ten degrees centigrade. I'd say quicker rather than later.'

'Say twenty-eight hours? Twenty-six?'

'Around there.'

'Around there. Very well. Does the body cool at an even, steady rate?'

'As a matter of fact, no. It falls in a sigmoid curve.'

'And how do you arrive at time of death from temperature?'

'Glaister's formula. In this case the victim's temperature was thirty-five point five degrees centigrade. One subtracts this from the normal temperature of thirty-seven degrees and multiplies by one point one. The answer, in this case, is one point six-five hours. Taking the temperature of the environment into account, that becomes between one and two hours before I arrived on the scene.'

'What might affect the rate at which temperature falls?'

'It's hard to say exactly. A number of factors.'

Shirley Castle took a deep breath and leaned forward. 'But it is *not* hard to say, is it Dr Glendenning, that thin people cool *quicker* than fat ones, and Deborah Harrison was thin. On the other hand, healthy people cool *more slowly* than weak ones, and Deborah Harrison was healthy. Naked bodies cool quicker than clothed ones, yet Deborah Harrison was only *partially* clothed. Bodies cool quicker in water than in air, yet in the humidity of the fog Deborah Harrison was subject to both. Am I right?'

'These are all relevant factors,' admitted Glendenning.

'According to evidence already given,' Shirley Castle went on, 'Deborah was last seen alive at six o'clock, which rules out her being murdered earlier, wouldn't you say?'

Glendenning raised his eyebrows. 'I would say so, yes.'

'But the body was discovered by Rebecca Charters at six forty-five. Is that correct?'

'I understand so.'

'And the first police officers arrived at six fifty-nine?'

'Objection.'

'Yes, Mr Lawrence?' Judge Simmonds asked.

'I'd like to know where Ms Castle is going with this line of questioning, Your Honour.'

'The defence requests Your Honour's indulgence. This will become clear in a short while.'

'Make it fast, Ms Castle.'

'Yes, Your Honour. Deborah Harrison was last seen at about six o'clock, and her body was discovered in St Mary's graveyard at six forty-five. That leaves forty-five minutes during which she could have been murdered. Now according to your evidence as regards time of death, Doctor, she *could* have been murdered later than six-thirty, couldn't she?'

Glendenning nodded. 'Yes, she *could* have been.'

'In fact, death *could* have occurred even as late as six-forty, couldn't it?'

'Yes. But I believe Rebecca Charters heard—'

'Please, Doctor. You should know better than that. Rebecca Charters has already admitted that what she heard could easily have been some animal or another. Now, given that nobody actually *saw* Owen Pierce enter St Mary's graveyard, and given that time of death could have occurred as late as six-forty, when Mr Pierce was already in the Peking Moon, there is no direct evidence placing him at the exact scene of the crime at the exact time the crime was committed, is there, Doctor?'

'This is not—'

'And as no-one saw either Deborah Harrison *or* Owen Pierce enter the graveyard,' Shirley Castle charged on before anyone could stop her, 'then it follows that Deborah could have gone somewhere else first, couldn't she?'

'It's not my place to speculate on such matters,' said Glendenning. 'I'm here to testify on matters of medical fact.'

'Ah, yes,' said Shirley Castle. 'Facts such as time of death. It's a lot of leeway to give the definition of a fact, isn't it, Doctor?'

'Objection.'

'Sustained. Will you get on with it, Ms Castle?'

'I have no further questions, Your Honour,' she said, and sat down.

Very clever, thought Owen, then he turned to watch the juror who looked like a wrestler try to scratch an egg stain off his club tie.

FOUR

A week later, after more legal arguments and a succession of dull, minor scientific witnesses, from the fingerprint man to the officer responsible for keeping track of the forensic exhibits, Owen watched Shirley Castle intimidate the hair expert, who ended up retreating into scientific jargon and admitting that it was virtually impossible to prove beyond a shadow of a doubt that hair found on a victim's or suspect's clothing could be positively matched to its source.

The final prosecution witness was Dr Tasker, biologist and DNA expert, a thin-faced, thin-haired academic of about forty, Owen guessed. He seemed to know his stuff, but there was a tentativeness about his delivery that threw Jerome Lawrence off kilter occasionally.

Owen wondered if the jury were as bored as he was by the interminable descriptions of autorads and enzyme scissors, by the testimony as to the scientific validity of polymerase chain reactions and the meaning of short tandem repeats, by the seeming hours spent describing the extreme care taken against the possibility of contamination of laboratory samples.

When Shirley Castle stood up to cross-examine the next afternoon, Tasker seemed a little in awe of her, and if Owen were not mistaken, perhaps a mite smitten, too. Maybe she realized this. Her tone, as she began, was relaxed, friendly, a little flirtatious even.

'Dr Tasker,' she said with a smile, 'I'm sure the court was most impressed yesterday with your account of DNA analysis. You would seem to have proved, without blinding us all with science, that the DNA derived from the bloodstain on Mr Pierce's anorak was indeed the DNA of Deborah Harrison. Is this true?'

Tasker nodded. 'The DNA extracted from the dried bloodstain on Mr Pierce's anorak was fifty million times *more likely to be hers* than anyone else's, and the DNA taken from the tissue sample discovered under the victim's fingernail was fifty million times more likely to be Owen Pierce's than anyone else's. All we can say is how rare such a result is compared to the rest of the population.'

'Still,' smiled Shirley Castle. 'Those are impressive odds, aren't they?'

'Oh, yes.' Tasker beamed. 'I certainly wouldn't bet against them.'

'Almost beyond a shadow of a doubt,' Shirley Castle said, 'and that is, after all, what this is all about, isn't it? However, Dr Tasker, there are one or two points you might be able to clarify for me.'

Owen swore that Tasker almost flushed with pleasure. 'Of course. It would be a pleasure.'

Shirley Castle acknowledged the compliment with a slight tilt of her head. 'How much of Deborah Harrison's blood did you find on my client's anorak?'

'A small amount.'

'Could you please give the court some sense of how much that might be?'

Tasker smiled. 'Well, not a great deal. But enough for polymerase chain reaction analysis, as I described earlier.'

'Yes, but how much? A thimble full?'

'Oh, good heavens, no, not that much.'

'As much, then, as might smear from a small cut or scratch?'

'Mmm. About that, yes.'

'A pinprick?'

'Possibly.'

'In other words, a spot of blood about the size of a pinhead. Am I right?'

'Perhaps a little bigger than—'

'*Approximately* the size of a pinhead?'

'I suppose so. About that, yes. But, as I said—'

'Now the court has already heard Dr Glendenning testify that there was a small scratch beside Deborah Harrison's left eye. Is this the kind of wound that might produce a similar amount of blood if some fabric brushed against it?'

Tasker shifted in his seat. 'Well, I didn't see the scratch so I can't say for certain, but it *was* a small amount, definitely commensurate with a minor injury such as the one you describe.'

'Where did you find this blood?'

'On the accused's anorak.'

'Where on the accused's anorak?'

'On the left arm. Near the shoulder.'

'Now we have already heard that Deborah Harrison was five foot six inches tall and Owen Pierce is six foot two. Would this put Deborah Harrison's left eye in the region of his upper arm?'

Tasker shrugged. 'I suppose so. I couldn't say exactly.'

'If Your Honour would allow me,' Shirley Castle addressed Judge Simmonds, 'I would like the opportunity to demonstrate to the court that this is, in fact, so.'

Owen could see her holding her breath. Most judges, she had told him, hate anything that smacks overly of theatrics. She must, however, have convinced him that she was following an important line of questioning, because he granted his permission after hardly any hesitation at all.

It was a simple enough thing to do. A man and a young girl were brought in – where Shirley had found them, Owen had no idea – the girl markedly shorter than the man. They were officially measured at five foot six and six foot two, then stood side by side. The girl's eye came level with the upper part of the man's arm. Shirley Castle thanked them and continued.

'Was that the only blood you discovered on my client's clothing?'

'Yes.'

Shirley Castle called for Owen's anorak to be shown to the jury. One feature, she pointed out, was the zippered pocket at the outside top of the sleeve. 'Did you, Dr Tasker, find any of the girl's blood on or around this zip?'

'Yes. In the vicinity.'

'Could you elaborate?'

'It was right at the end of the zip, actually.'

'Would you point to the spot on the exhibit, please?'

Tasker did so.

'The edge of the metal teeth is fairly sharp there,' Shirley Castle went on. 'Does that not indicate to you that the girl may have scraped her cheek on the zip when she collided with Mr Pierce after running backwards in the fog?'

'It could have got there in any number of ways.'

'But it could have got there in the way I suggest?'

'Yes, but—'

'And that was *all* the blood you found?'

'I've already said that. I—'

'Not very much, is it?'

'As I said, it was enough for PCR analysis.'

'Ah, yes: PCR, STR, DNA, "genetic fingerprinting." Magic words, these days. And what does that prove, Dr Tasker?'

'That the blood on the defendant's anorak is fifty million times—'

'Yes, yes. We've already been through all that, haven't we? But the defence has *never denied* that it is Deborah Harrison's blood. She bumped into my client and scratched herself on the zip of his anorak. Would you admit that the *amount* and *location* of the blood you found bear out that explanation?'

'I suppose so.'

'You suppose so. Did you find any traces of blood on the cuffs of the anorak?'

'No.'

'Wouldn't you expect to if the victim were bleeding from the nose as the accused strangled her?'

'Perhaps.'

'So he might be expected to get blood on his cuff if he did indeed strangle her from behind with the satchel strap?'

'Well, it's possible, yes, but—'

'And did you find any blood lower down his sleeve?'

'No. But she could have twisted side—'

'Thank you, Dr Tasker. You have answered my question. Now, given the life-and-death struggle that must have taken place, it would have been difficult to avoid *some* contact, wouldn't it?'

'Presumably.'

'And did you test the rest of the anorak for blood?'

'Yes. We carried out a thorough examination.'

'But you found no blood other than this infinitesimal amount high on the sleeve, at the edge of the metal teeth on the zip?'

'No.'

The infatuation seemed to be on the wane, Owen noticed. Tasker didn't even want to look Shirley Castle in the eye now. Owen glanced over at 'Minerva,' who was regarding the doctor sternly. No more would she believe the 'scientific tests have proved' commercials, if, indeed, she ever had.

'Dr Tasker, do you know where Deborah Harrison's hairs – what we have since learned only *might* in fact be Deborah Harrison's hairs – were found on Mr Pierce's anorak?'

'No, that's not my—'

'Then let me tell you. They were found on the upper left arm and on the upper left arm *only*. In fact, all three of her hairs were found in the teeth of Mr Pierce's zip, by the pinpoint bloodstain. What do you have to say to that?'

'I don't know. It's not my field.'

'Not your field? But would you not say it's consistent with the scenario I just outlined for you? A minor collision?'

'I have already agreed that is a *possible* explanation.'

'How much blood and skin did you find under the victim's fingernail?'

'A small amount. But enough for—'

'Consistent with what might be deposited from a light scratch?'

'Yes.'

'If Deborah Harrison had been fighting for her life, wouldn't you have expected to find more, in your professional judgement?'

'Possibly. But again, it's not my—'

'I understand that, Dr Tasker. But we can't have it both ways, can we? Either she did get the opportunity to defend herself by scratching, in which case she came away with a pitiful amount of skin, or she didn't. Which is it to be, in your opinion?'

Owen saw Lawrence on the verge of an objection, but he seemed to think better of it and sank down again.

'It could have been just a lucky strike,' said Tasker. 'I don't know.'

'You don't know. Very well. Would you at least agree that the presence of a small amount of Mr Pierce's skin under one of her fingernails could have got there during a minor collision, if she put out her hand to steady herself?'

'Yes.'

'Then would you also agree that it is possible that Deborah Harrison's killer could have been someone other than my client?'

'Objection!'

'Overruled, Mr Lawrence. Witness will please answer the question.'

Tasker fiddled with his tie. 'Well, theoretically, yes. Of course,' he gave a nervous titter. 'I mean, theoretically, anything's possible. I wasn't there, I can't tell you exactly what happened. The DNA was a good match to the defendant's, so he can't be excluded.'

'I submit that the DNA match is irrelevant. Is your answer to my question yes?'

'I suppose so.

'Is it?'

'Yes.'

Shirley Castle turned to the judge and threw her hands in the air. 'Your Honour,' she said, 'I find myself exasperated that the prosecution's case is based on so little and such flimsy evidence. No further questions.'

For the first time, Jerome Lawrence stood up to re-examine. It must be because it's his last witness, Owen thought. He wants to leave a positive impression.

'Just two questions, Dr Tasker,' he said. 'You are fully aware of the nature of the crime, the nature of the victim's injuries. Would you say, in your expert opinion, that the amounts of the victim's blood left on the accused's clothing were in any way *too little* for him to have committed such a crime?'

'No, I wouldn't,' said Tasker.

'And could the exchange of blood and tissue have taken place during a struggle for her life?'

'Indeed it could.'

Jerome Lawrence gave an oily bow. 'Thank you very much, Dr Tasker.'

12

ONE

Nothing could have prepared Owen for the shock of seeing Michelle sitting in the gallery when he glanced nervously around the courtroom before going into the witness-box.

His heart thudded against his ribcage. He felt as if a large bird had somehow found its way inside him and was scratching and plucking at his chest and throat, beating its wings, trying to get out. She was still beautiful; she still had the power to make his heart ache and yearn.

If anything, Owen thought, Michelle looked even younger than she had when they had been together: about fifteen or sixteen. She wore no make-up to mar her delicate, alabaster complexion, a maroon blazer and a simple white blouse, very much like the St Mary's school uniform.

Her blonde hair – the same colour and length as Deborah Harrison's – hung over her shoulders in exactly the same way Deborah's had in the newspaper photographs. Her lips, the colour of the inside of a strawberry, were fixed in a childish pout. And the implication of innocence and immaturity permeated her entire bearing. Owen wondered if people knew who she was. She was sitting next to a man he had seen there often before: a reporter, Owen thought.

He tried to avoid looking at her. Why was she here? Had the Crown lured her in to upset him? He had already realized that he was participating in a drama, a theatrical event more than anything else, and that the awards would be handed out in a few days' time. Did Michelle have a part to play, too? She wasn't going into the box – Shirley Castle had taken care of that – so what was she doing in court?

He was so distracted by her presence that he didn't hear Shirley Castle calling him to give evidence at first, then the judge called him to the box.

Shirley Castle spent more than a day taking him through the events of that fateful Monday in November, as smoothly as she had before in the interview room near his cell. He felt calm as he spoke, and he hoped the jury wouldn't interpret this as lack of emotion.

'Minerva,' as far as he could tell, listened to him objectively, a slight furrow of concentration in her brow. Most of the others, he noticed, appeared to be paying attention too, but a couple had disbelieving sneers etched around their lips – that 'come on, tell us another one' look he had become so adept at perceiving of late. Occasionally, he sneaked a glance at Michelle. Once in a while she turned and spoke behind her hand to the reporter next to her.

The next day, after Shirley Castle had finished eliciting a reasonable and believable account of events from Owen, or so he thought, Jerome Lawrence dragged himself to his feet. 'There hardly seems any point,' Lawrence's weary, long-suffering movements seemed to be saying, 'in bothering with this, as you and I know he's guilty, ladies and gentlemen of the jury, but duty demands we go through the motions.' Owen looked at the gallery and saw Michelle was in court again.

Lawrence asked what seemed a lot of dull questions for most of the morning, and after lunch he finally began to zoom in on the crime. 'Mr Pierce,' he said, 'you have told the jury that between the hours of about six and six-thirty on 6 November last year, you simply walked around the area of St Mary's, Eastvale, in the fog, and stood on the bridge for some time. Is this so?'

'Yes.'

'Were you intoxicated, Mr Pierce?'

'Not at all.'

'You drank, let me see, two pints of beer and a double Scotch at the Nag's Head, is that right?'

Owen shrugged. 'I think so.'

'And you weren't intoxicated?'

'I'm not saying I didn't feel the effects at all, just that I was perfectly in control. And I was walking, not driving.'

'You had more to drink later, didn't you, at the Peking Moon?'

'Yes. With a large meal.'

'Indeed. And can you tell the court why you spent so long standing on the bridge before a fine view that you *couldn't possibly see* because of the thick fog?'

'I don't know, really. It was just what I felt like doing. I had one or two problems to mull over and I find fog helps contemplation.'

'What problems were these?'

Owen saw Shirley Castle making discreet warning signals. He looked Michelle in the eye. 'Personal matters. Of no relevance.'

'I see. And was it this same *personal matter* that led you to drink so much?'

'I didn't drink a lot. I've already told you, I wasn't drunk.'

'And led you to hide yourself away in the corner of a restaurant and mutter to yourself?'

Owen felt himself flush with embarrassment. 'That's just a habit, like when I'm adding up. I've always done it. Sometimes a thought just comes out loud, that's all. I forget that there are people around. It doesn't make me a maniac. Or a murderer.'

'Are you sure you weren't muttering in the Peking Moon about what you'd just done? Murdered Deborah Harrison?'

'Of course not. That's totally absurd. I was just reasoning with myself, to calm down.'

'*Calm down*?' There was no missing the verbal under-lining in that repetition. 'Why did you feel the need to calm down, Mr Pierce? What made you so agitated in the first place.'

'I wasn't agitated. There's a difference between being a little melancholy and being agitated, isn't there? I mean—'

'Would you please stick to answering my questions?' Lawrence butted in. 'If I need lessons in the English language, believe me, I shall ask for them.'

'I'm the one in the dock, aren't I? Why shouldn't my opinion count? You've asked everyone else's, haven't you? Why should I let you get away with distorting the meaning—'

'Mr Pierce,' Judge Simmonds grumbled. 'Please answer Mr Lawrence's questions as directly and as clearly as you can.'

'I'm sorry, Your Honour,' said Owen. He turned back to Lawrence. 'The answer is no. I wasn't agitated; I was melancholy.'

'Is it not true that you were upset and dejected about your break-up with a young lady some—'

'Objection!'

'Sustained. Mr Lawrence!'

'I apologize, Your Honour.'

What the hell was that little skirmish about? Owen wondered, his heart jumping. He glanced at Michelle again. Lawrence was trying it on; he knew damn well that evidence had been ruled inadmissible. The bastard was trying to slip it in regardless. He thanked his lucky stars Shirley Castle was so quick. Still, something had been lodged with the jury, no matter how much the judge might tell them to disregard it. He looked at 'Minerva.' She seemed puzzled. Owen's breath came a little quicker.

'Let us, then, move on to the scientific evidence,' Lawrence continued. 'You don't deny that Deborah Harrison's hair and blood were found on your clothing?'

'It's not for me to accept or deny,' Owen said. 'I'm not a scientist. If your experts have identified these things, that's their business.'

'And when faced with this fact by Detective Chief Inspector Banks, you gave him some story about bumping into the girl. Is this true?'

It was plain enough that Lawrence intended 'cock and bull' to come before 'story.'

'I didn't bump into her,' Owen said. 'She bumped into me as I was turning from the wall.'

'Answer the question.'

'I would answer it if it were correctly posed.'

Lawrence sighed and made a long-suffering gesture to the jury. 'Very well, then, Mr Pierce. You told the police that the girl bumped into you. Is this correct?'

'I told them exactly what happened.'

'Why didn't you tell them earlier?'

'It didn't seem important.'

'Come on, Mr Pierce, the police had already told you how important everything that happened that day was the second time they interviewed you. You knew you were in a serious situation. Why didn't you tell them earlier?'

'I've already told you. I didn't tell them about the time I had to bend down and refasten my left shoelace, either, or about stopping at the newsagent's for an evening paper, which, by the way, they didn't have. It just *didn't seem important*.'

'Yet you remembered it well enough later. In fact, as soon as you were challenged with evidence of your physical contact with the victim, you suddenly came up with an explanation.' Lawrence laughed and flapped like a bat. 'As if by magic. Really, Mr Pierce. Do you expect the court to believe that?'

'Objection.'

'Sustained. The witness's opinion on such matters of what the court should or should not believe is not required, as you well know, Mr Lawrence.'

'I am sorry, Your Honour. I submit to you, Mr Pierce, that you saw Deborah Harrison part from her companion, that you followed her into the graveyard, and that you—'

'No! I did nothing of the kind,' Owen cut in.

'And that you strangled Deborah Harrison with her own school satchel strap!'

Owen clenched his fists and kept them out of sight. 'I did not,' he said quietly, with as much dignity as he could muster.

Lawrence held him with his black, beady eyes, then breathed, 'No more questions,' and sat down looking pleased with himself.

It was Friday afternoon, so Judge Simmonds adjourned for the weekend and Owen was escorted back to his cell.

TWO

Back in the dock on Monday, Owen tried to keep his eyes off Michelle and concentrate on Jerome Lawrence's final address to the jury. From what he heard, it wasn't much different from the opening remarks: Owen was a monster, hardly even human, who had brutally murdered a pure and innocent young girl. Most of the time he found himself looking towards Michelle. He sensed she knew he was staring at her, but she wouldn't catch his eye.

Lawrence went on for the best part of the day, piling atrocity on atrocity, outrage upon outrage, and it wasn't until Tuesday morning that Shirley Castle got to make her closing speech. Again, Owen found himself watching Michelle most of the time, and the next thing he knew, Shirley Castle was wrapping up.

'And, above all, remember the phrase *beyond reasonable doubt*,' she said. 'It is the very foundation upon which our justice system is built. The burden of proof lies with the Crown. Ask yourselves, has the Crown proven its case *beyond reasonable doubt*? Are you yourselves sure, beyond reasonable doubt, that this man before you is anything other than an innocent victim? Do you not harbour doubts yourselves? I think you will find that you do, and that you can honestly do no other than agree with me, and say *no*, the Crown has *not* proven its case. For you see in front of you a man who was in the wrong place at the wrong time, a man confused, worried and anxious by a police investigation he could not understand and which was not explained to him. But more than anything, you see in front of you an *innocent* man who has already been punished more than enough for a crime he did not commit. Look into your hearts, ladies and gentlemen, and I'm sure you will find there the certain knowledge that my client is innocent of all charges laid against him. Thank you.'

After this carefully impassioned finale, Judge Simmonds's summing up seemed perfunctory to Owen. At least he was fair, Owen had to admit. In a detached monologue, the judge reiterated the main points of the case, careful not to indicate any bias. As the old man talked, Owen kept switching his gaze between Michelle and 'Minerva.'

'Minerva' was clearly listening, but Owen could not help getting the impression that this final speech was superfluous to her, that she had already made up her mind. Once, she caught him looking at her for a second and turned away quickly, blushing. He could have sworn, though, that her eyes held no trace of accusation, of condemnation. When Michelle finally decided to return Owen's gaze, she smiled, and he couldn't mistake the cold malicious glint in her eyes; it made him shiver.

THREE

While the jury was out, Owen sat in a cheerless room below the court with Shirley Castle and his guards drinking bitter coffee until his stomach hurt.

He had experienced anxious waiting before – after a job interview, for example, or those long nights at the window watching for Michelle to come home – but nothing as gut-wrenching as this. His stomach clenched and growled; he bit his nails; he jumped at every sound. He tried to imagine what it must have been like when the death penalty existed, but couldn't. Shirley Castle tried to make conversation but soon stopped after his terse and jumbled responses.

Hours, it seemed, went by. At last, someone came and said the jury hadn't reached a verdict yet, and as it was late, Owen was to spend the night back in his cell. He asked Shirley Castle about the jury taking so long, and she said it was a good sign.

That night, he hardly slept at all. Fear gnawed at him; the cell walls closed in. In that nether world between sleep and waking, where memories take on the aspect of dreams, he actually watched himself strangle Deborah Harrison in a foggy graveyard. Or was it Michelle? He had been told so often that he had done it that his subconscious mind had actually been tricked into believing it. He thought he screamed out in the night, but nobody came rushing to see what was wrong. When he woke from the dream, he noticed he had an erection and felt ashamed.

Morning came: slopping out, the stink of piss and shit that seemed to permeate the place, the supervised shave, breakfast. Then Owen sat around in his suit waiting to go back to the court and face the verdict. Still nothing. By mid-morning on Wednesday, he wasn't sure how much longer he could last without going mad. Just before lunch, his cell door opened and the warder said, 'Come on, lad. It looks like they're back.'

In court, Owen gripped the front of the dock until his knuckles turned white. The gallery was full: Michelle leaning forward, thumbnail between her front teeth, as she often did during thrillers or when she was concentrating hard; the Harrisons; two of the detectives, Stott and Banks; the vicar, Daniel Charters and his attractive wife, Rebecca; reporters; morbid members of the public. They were all there.

The jury filed back in. Owen looked at 'Minerva.' She didn't glance in his direction. He didn't know what to make of that.

After the hush came the legal rigmarole about charges, then the question everyone had been waiting for: 'Do you find the defendant Owen Pierce guilty or not guilty as charged?'

The split-second pause between question and answer seemed an eternity for Owen. His ears roared and he felt his head swimming. Then the spokesman, a drab-looking man Owen had guessed to be a banker, spoke the words: 'We find the defendant not guilty, Your Honour.'

There was more talk after that, but most of it was lost in the hubbub that raced through the courtroom like an explosive blast. Reporters dashed for phones. Owen swayed and clutched the dock for dear life. He couldn't seem to stop the ringing in his ears. He heard a woman yell, 'It's a travesty!' Then everything went white and he fainted.

Owen came to in a room below the court, a cool, damp cloth pressed to his brow, with Shirley Castle and Gordon Wharton standing over him. As he recovered, he felt the stirrings of joy, like the first, tentative shoots of a new plant in spring, overtake the gnawing anxiety that had burdened him before. He was *free*! Surely it would sink in soon. Shirley Castle was talking to someone, but when she stopped and walked towards him, he could feel the muscles in his face form a smile for the first time in what seemed like years.

She smiled back, curled her fist and thumped the air triumphantly. 'We did it!'

'You did it,' Owen said. 'I don't know how to thank you.'

'Winning is thanks enough.' She held out her hand. 'Congratulations, Owen. And good luck.'

He shook it, the first time he'd touched a woman in months, and he was conscious of the soft warmth under the firm grip. He felt her give a little tug and released her, embarrassed to realize he had held on too long. He wanted to kiss her. And not only because she had won his case. Instead, he turned to Wharton.

'What now?' he asked.

'What? Oh.' The solicitor glanced away from the disappearing figure. 'Wonderful woman, isn't she? I told you if anyone could do it, Shirley Castle could. It was a majority verdict, you know. Ten to two. That's what took them so long. What now? Well, you're free, that's what.'

'But . . . what do I do? I mean, my stuff and . . .'

'Tell you what.' Wharton looked at his watch. 'I'll drive you back over to the prison, if you like, and you can pick your stuff up, then I'll take you back to Eastvale.'

Owen nodded. 'Thanks. How do we . . . I mean, do we just walk out of here?'

Wharton laughed. 'Yes,' he said. 'Yes, that's exactly what we do. Hard to get used to, eh? But I think there'll be a bit of a mob out front, we'd better leave by the back way.'

'A mob?'

Wharton frowned. 'Yes. Well, you've seen the papers. Those sly innuendos about the "evidence they couldn't present in court." That not-guilty verdict won't have sunk in with them yet, will it? People lose all sense of proportion when they get carried away by chants and whatnot. Come on.'

In a daze, Owen followed Wharton through the corridors to the back exit. The sun was shining on the narrow backstreet; opposite was a refurbished Victorian pub, all black trim and etched, smoked-glass windows; under his feet, the worn paving-stones looked gold in the midday light. Freedom.

Owen breathed the air deeply; a warm, still day. When he thought about it, he realized the trial had lasted almost two months, and it was now May, the most glorious month in the Dales. Back up near Eastvale, the woods, fields and hillsides would be ablaze with wildflowers: bluebells, wild garlic, celandines, cowslips, violets and primroses; and here and there would be the fields of bright yellow rape-seed.

As they walked towards Wharton's car, Owen could vaguely hear the crowd outside the front of the court-house: women's voices mostly, he thought, chanting, 'Guilty! Guilty! Guilty!'

FOUR

'*Fuck it*,' said Barry Stott loudly. Then he said it again, banging his fist on the arm of the bench for emphasis. '*Fuck it*.' A couple standing by the pub door gave him a dirty look. 'Sorry,' he said to Banks, blushing right up to the tips of his jug-ears. 'I just had to let it out.'

Banks nodded in sympathy. It was the first time he had ever heard Barry Stott swear, and he had to admit he didn't blame him.

They were sitting on the long bench outside White-lock's in the narrow alley called Turk's Head Yard, drinks and food propped on the upturned barrel that served as a table. Along with his pint of Younger's bitter, Banks had a Cornish pasty with chips and gravy, and Stott had a Scotch egg with HP Sauce, with a half of shandy to wash it down. They had just left Leeds Crown Court after the Owen Pierce verdict.

It was a beautiful May day; the pub had lured students from their studies and encouraged office workers to linger over their lunch-hours. Not much light penetrated Turk's Head Yard because of the high walls of the buildings on both sides, but the air was warm and full of the promise of summer. Men sat with their jackets off and shirt-sleeves rolled up, while bare-legged women opened an extra button or two on their blouses.

Banks took a sip of beer before tucking into the pasty. He watched Stott pick at the Scotch egg, dip little pieces in the sauce, chew and swallow, too distracted to taste the food. It was obvious that he had no appetite. He had only eaten half when he pushed his plate away. Banks finished his own lunch quickly and lit a cigarette.

'I can't believe he got off,' Stott said. 'I just can't believe it.'

'I'm just as pissed off as you are, Barry, but it happens,' said Banks. 'You get used to it. Don't take it personally.'

'But I do. It was me who cottoned on to him, me who tracked him down. We build a solid case, and he just walks away.'

Banks didn't bother reminding him how it was team-work and hard procedural slog that had led them to Owen Pierce. 'The case obviously wasn't solid enough,' he said. 'Dr Tasker wasn't very good, for a start. Even Glendenning wasn't up to his usual form. Who knows? Maybe they were right?'

'Who?'

'The jury.'

Stott shook his head. His ears seemed to flap with the motion. 'No. I can't accept that. He did it. I know he did. I feel it in my bones. He murdered that poor girl, and he got away with it. You know, if we'd got the evidence from Michelle Chappel in, then we'd have got a conviction for certain. The judge made a hell of a mistake there.'

'Perhaps. Did you see her there, by the way?'

'Where? Who?'

'Michelle Chappel. In court. I don't know if she's been there all along but she was in the public gallery for the verdict. She'd let her hair grow since last November, too. Looked more like Deborah Harrison than ever. She was even wearing a maroon blazer. She was talking to that reporter from the *News of the World*.'

'See what I mean,' said Stott. 'If we'd been able to bring out that connection, her evidence of what he did to her, there's no jury in the country wouldn't have convicted Pierce.'

'Maybe so, but that's not the point, Barry.'

Stott flushed. 'Excuse me, but I think it is. A guilty man has just walked out of that courtroom after committing one of the most horrible murders I have ever investigated, and you tell me that's not the point. I'm sorry, but—'

'I mean it's not the point I'm trying to make.'

Stott frowned. 'I don't follow.'

'Why is Michelle Chappel so keen to stick the knife in Pierce?'

'Oh, I see. Well, maybe because he beat her up. Or perhaps because he tried to strangle her? Or could being raped by him after he knocked her out have upset her just a little bit?'

Banks sipped some more beer. 'All right, Barry, give it

a rest. I catch your drift. Perhaps you're right. But why hang around after her evidence was declared inadmissible? Just to watch him suffer? Why take time off work?'

Stott frowned. 'What makes you think there's a connection?'

'It's just odd, that's all.' Banks stubbed out his cigarette and drank some more beer. 'Her hair was short when we talked to her.'

'Women's hair,' said Stott with a shrug. 'Who knows anything about that?'

Banks smiled. 'Good point. Another pint? Half, rather?'

'Should we?'

'Yes, we damn well should. Jimmy Riddle's going to be out for our blood. Might as well put off the inevitable as long as possible.'

'Oh, all right. I'll have another half of shandy. Then I'll have to be off.'

Banks edged through the crowd to the bar, looking at his reflection in the antique mirror at the back while he waited. Not too bad for his early forties, he thought, still slim and trim, despite the pints and the poor diet; a few lines around the eyes, maybe, and a touch of grey at the temples, but that was all. Besides, they added character, Sandra said.

He intended to part company with Stott after the next drink and visit an old friend while he was in Leeds: Pamela Jeffreys, a violist with the English Northern Philharmonic orchestra. About a year ago, she had been badly hurt in an attack for which Banks still blamed himself. She wasn't back in the orchestra yet, but she was working hard and getting there fast, and this afternoon, she was playing a chamber concert at the university's music department. It might go some small way towards making up for the disappointment in court this morning.

He might also, while he was so close, drop in at the Classical Record Shop and see about the Samuel Barber song collection he had been wanting for a while. Listening to Dawn Upshaw singing 'Knoxville: Summer of 1915' on the drive down had made him think about it.

On the other hand, the not-guilty verdict changed things. While he was in Leeds, he would also phone DI Ken Blackstone and see about having a chat with one of Jelačić's card-playing cronies. He might even have another word with Jelačić himself.

Though the Crown would probably appeal the verdict, as far as Banks was concerned it was back to the drawing-board for the time being, a drawing-board he was beginning to feel he should never have left in the first place. And Ive Jelačić was certainly high on his list of loose ends.

'Damn that judge,' said Stott when he had thanked Banks for the drink. 'Just thinking about it makes my blood boil.'

'I'm not convinced Michelle Chappel's testimony would have helped as much as you think, Barry,' Banks said.

'Why not? At least it proves he had homicidal tendencies towards young women of Deborah Harrison's physical type.'

'It proves nothing of the kind,' said Banks. 'Okay, I'll admit, I was as excited about the psychological possibilities it opened up as you were. And, yes, I was bloody annoyed that Simmonds excluded it. But now I think about it, looking at her in court, I'm not so sure.'

Stott scratched the back of his left ear and frowned. 'Why not?'

'Because I think that defence lawyer, Shirley Castle, would have made mincemeat of her, that's why. In the final analysis, she'd have had the jury believing that

Michelle Chappel was lying, that she did what she did out of pure vindictiveness towards Pierce, for revenge, because she harboured a grudge for the way he treated her.'

'And rightly so, after what he did to her.'

'But don't you see how it would discredit her testimony, Barry, make her seem like a lying bitch? Especially with such criticisms coming from another woman. That could be pretty damning. She's good is Ms Castle. I've been up against her before. She'd have made sure that Pierce convinced them with *his* version of that night's events. And if they believed that he had simply been warding off the frenzied attack of a hysterical woman, then he could have gained their sympathy.'

Stott took off his glasses and polished them with a spotless handkerchief. 'I still think it would have helped us get a conviction.'

'Well there's no way of knowing now, is there?'

'I suppose not,' Stott said glumly. 'What do we do now?'

'There's not much more we can do.'

'Reopen the investigation?'

Banks sipped some beer. 'Oh, yes. I think so, don't you? After all, Barry, someone out there killed Deborah Harrison, and according to all the hallmarks, it looks very much like someone who might kill again.'

13

ONE

Vjeko Batorac was out when Banks called in the afternoon, and a neighbour said he usually came home from work at about five-thirty. Ken Blackstone, who said Batorac was probably the most believable of Jelačić's three card-playing cronies, had given Banks the address.

Grateful for the free time, Banks played truant; he went up to the university and spent a delightful hour listening to Vaughan Williams's *String Quartet No. 2*.

And he was glad he did. As he watched and listened, all the stress and disappointment of the verdict, all his fears of having persecuted the wrong man in the first place, seemed to become as insubstantial as air, at least for a while.

As he watched Pamela Jeffreys play in the bright room, prisms of light all around, her glossy raven hair dancing, skin like burnished gold, the diamond stud in her right nostril flashing in the sun, he thought not for the first time that there was something intensely, spiritually erotic about a beautiful woman playing music.

It seemed, as he watched, that Pamela first projected her spirit and emotions into her instrument, the bow an extension of her arm, fingers and strings inseparable, then she became the music, flowing and soaring with its rhythms and melodies, dipping and swooping, eyes closed, oblivious to the world outside.

Or so it seemed. Though he had taken a few hesitant steps towards learning the piano, Banks couldn't actually play an instrument, so he was willing to admit he might be romanticizing. Maybe she was thinking about her pay-cheque.

Erotic fantasies aside, it was all perfectly innocent. They had coffee and a chat afterwards, then Banks headed back to Batorac's house.

Vjeko Batorac lived in a small pre-war terrace house in Sheepscar, near the junction of Roseville Road and Round-hay Road, less than a mile from Jelačić's Burmantofts flat. There was no garden; the front door, which looked as if it had been freshly painted, opened directly onto the pavement. This time, a few minutes before six o'clock, Banks's knock was answered by a slight, hollow-cheeked young man with fair hair, wearing oil-stained jeans and a clean white T-shirt.

'*Molim*?' said Batorac, frowning.

'Mr Batorac?' Banks asked, showing his warrant card. 'I wonder if I might have a word? Do you speak English?'

Batorac nodded, looking puzzled. 'What is it about?'

'Ive Jelačić.'

Batorac rolled his eyes and opened the door wider. 'You'd better come in.'

The living-room was sunny and clean, and just a hint of baby smells mingled with those of cabbage and garlic from the kitchen. What surprised Banks most of all was the bookcase that took up most of one wall, crammed with English classics and foreign titles he couldn't read. Serbo-Croatian, he guessed. The *Six O'Clock News* was on Radio 4 in the background.

'That's quite a library you've got.'

Batorac beamed. '*Hvala lipo*. Thank you very much. Yes, I love books. In my own country I was a school-teacher. I taught English, so I have studied your language for many years. I also write poetry.'

'What do you do here?'

Batorac smiled ironically. 'I am a garage mechanic. Fortunately for me, in Croatia you had to be good at fixing your own car.' He shrugged. 'It's a good job. Not much pay, but my boss treats me well.'

A baby started crying. Batorac excused himself for a moment and went upstairs. Banks examined the titles in more detail as he waited: Dickens, Hardy, Keats, Austen, Balzac, Flaubert, Coleridge, Tolstoy, Dostoevsky, Milton, Kafka . . . Many he had read, but many were books he had promised himself to read and never got around to. The baby fell silent and Batorac came back.

'Sorry,' he said. 'We have a friend takes care of little Jelena during the day, while we work. When she comes home she . . . how do you say this . . . she misses her mother and father?'

Banks smiled. 'Yes, that's right. She has missed you.'

'*Has* missed. Yes. Sometimes I get the tenses wrong. What is it you wanted to see me about? Sit down, please.'

Banks sat. This didn't look or smell like the kind of house where one could smoke, especially with the baby around, so he resigned himself to refraining. It would no doubt do him good. 'Remember,' he asked, 'a few months ago when the local police asked you about an evening you said you played cards with Ive Jelačić?'

Batorac nodded. 'Yes. It was true. Every Monday we play cards. Dragica, my wife, she is very indulgent. But on Mondays only.' He smiled. 'Tuesday I do not have to go to work, so sometimes we talk and play until late.'

'And drink?'

'Yes. I do not drink much because I drive home. The streets are not safe at night. But I drink some, yes. A little.'

'And you are *absolutely* certain on that Monday, the sixth of November, you were playing cards with Stipe Pavič and Ive Jelačić at Mile Paveliči's house?'

'Yes. I swear on the Bible. I do not lie, Inspector.'

'No offence. Please understand we have to be very thorough about these things. Was Jelačić there the whole time?'

'Yes.'

'He said that he walked to Mr Paveliči's house and back. Did he usually do that?'

'Yes. He only lives about five hundred metres away, over the waste ground.'

'I am curious, Mr Batorac—'

'Call me Vjeko, please.'

'Very well, Vjeko. I'm curious as to how the four of you got together. If you don't mind my saying so, you and Ive Jelačić seem very different kinds of people.'

Vjeko smiled. 'There are not many of my countrymen here in Leeds,' he said. 'We have clubs and societies where we meet to get news from home and talk about politics. What you English call a very good grapevine. Ive knew Mile from the old country. They are both from Split. I met Stipe here, in Leeds. He is from Zagreb and I am from Dubrovnik, long way apart. Have you ever visited Dubrovnik, Chief Inspector?'

Banks shook his head.

'It is a very beautiful city. Very much history, ancient architecture. Many English tourists came before the war. You have missed much. Perhaps forever.'

'When did you come here?'

'In 1991, after the siege. I could not bear to see my home destroyed.' He tapped his chest. 'I am a poet, not a soldier, Chief Inspector. And my health is not strong. I have only one lung.' Vjeko shrugged. 'When Ive came from Eastvale, he came into contact with us. He told us his parents were both killed in the fighting. Many of us have lost friends and relatives in the war. I lost my sister two years ago. Raped and butchered by Serb soldiers. It gives us a common bond. The kind of bond that transcends – is that right? Yes? – that transcends personality. After that, we just started meeting to talk and play cards.' He smiled. 'Not for money, you understand. My Dragica would not be so indulgent about that.'

Almost on cue, the front door opened, and a pretty, petite young woman with dark hair and sparkling eyes walked in. 'What would your Dragica not be so indulgent about?' she asked with a smile, going over and kissing Vjeko affectionately before turning to glance curiously at Banks.

Vjeko told her who Banks was and why he was there. 'I said you would not be indulgent if I played cards for money.'

Dragica thumped him playfully on the shoulder and perched on the arm of the sofa. 'Sometimes,' she said, 'I ask myself why you must stay up most of the night playing cards with those people instead of keeping your wife warm in bed and getting up when little Jelena cries. Ive Jelačić, particularly, is nothing but a useless *pijanac*.'

'*Pijanac*?' Banks repeated. 'What is that?'

'Drunk,' said Vjeko. 'Yes, Ive is . . . he does drink too much. He is not a pleasant man in many ways, Inspector. You must not judge my fellow countrymen by Ive's example. And I do not put forward the tragedy in his life as an excuse for his behaviour. He lies. He boasts. Most of all, he is greedy. He often suggests that we play cards for money, and I know he cheats. With women he is bad, too. Dragica cannot bear him near her.'

'That is true,' Dragica told Banks, shuddering at the thought and hugging her slight frame. 'He undresses you with his eyes.'

Banks remembered Susan Gay's reaction to Jelačić's ogling and nodded.

'Please excuse me,' Dragica said. 'I must attend to Jelena.' And she went upstairs.

'He is rude, too,' Vjeko went on. 'Ill-mannered. And I have seen him behave violently in pubs, picking fights when he is drunk.' He laughed. 'When I put it like that, I wonder why I do spend time with him. It is a mystery to me. But one thing I can tell you is that Ive wouldn't kill a young girl that way. Never. Perhaps in a fight, in a pub, he could kill, but not like that, not someone weaker than himself. It is a joke with us that Ive always picks on people bigger than himself, and he usually comes off worst.'

'Do you know why Mr Jelačić left Eastvale?' Banks asked.

'He told us that a *svečenik*, a man of God, made homosexual advances towards him.'

'You said he was a liar. Do you believe his story?'

Vjeko shook his head. 'No. I do not think it is true. I have listened to him talk about it, and I think he did what he did to get revenge for losing his job.'

'If that's so,' said Banks, 'then he's caused Daniel Charters an awful lot of grief.'

Vjeko spread his hands. 'But what can anyone do? I did not know Ive back in Eastvale, when all this happened, and I do not know this Father Daniel Charters. Perhaps he is a good man; perhaps he is not. But I do think that Ive is tired with his revenge. He has had enough. The problem is that he is mixed up with lawyers and human-rights campaigners among our own people. It is not so easy for him to turn around and say to them it was all a lie, a mistake or a joke. He would lose face.'

'And face is important to him?'

'Yes.'

Dragica returned carrying a sleeping Jelena in her arms and said something in Croatian; Vjeko nodded, and she went into the kitchen.

'Dragica asked if dinner is nearly ready,' he said. 'I told her yes.'

Banks stood up. 'Then I won't use up any more of your time. You've been very helpful.' He stuck out his hand.

'Why don't you stay for dinner?' Vjeko asked. 'It is not very much, just *sarma*. Cabbage rolls. But we would be happy if you would share with us.'

Banks paused at the door. It was almost six-thirty and he hadn't had anything since lunch at Whitelock's. He would have to eat sometime. 'All right,' he said. 'Thanks very much. Yes, I'd love to stay.'

TWO

Instead of continuing along Roundhay Road towards Wetherby and the A1, Banks cut back down Roseville Road and Regent Street, then headed for Burmantofts. He had dined well with the Batoracs, and conversation had ranged from books and teaching to the Balkan war and crime. After their goodbyes, it was a quarter to eight on a fine May evening, and dusk was slowly gathering when

Banks pulled up near Jelačić's flat. In the failing, honeyed light, the shabby concrete tower blocks looked as eerie as a landscape on Mars.

There were plenty of people around in the recreation areas between the buildings, mostly teenagers congregated in little knots here and there, some of them playing on swings and roundabouts.

Banks managed to climb the six flights of graffiti-scarred concrete without incident, apart from a little shortness of breath, and rapped on Jelačić's door.

He could already hear the television blaring *Coronation Street* through the paper-thin walls, so when no-one answered the first time, he knocked even harder. Finally Jelačić answered the door, grubby shirt hanging out of his jeans, and scowled when he recognized Banks.

'You,' he said. '*Supak*. Why you come here? You already have killer.'

'Things change, Ive,' said Banks, gently shouldering his way inside. The place was as he remembered, tidy but overlaid with a patina of stale booze and cigarette smoke. Here he could light up with impunity. He turned down the sound on one of Jack and Vera Duckworth's loud public arguments.

Jelačić didn't complain. He picked up a glass of clear liquid – probably vodka, Banks guessed – from the table and flopped down on the settee. It creaked under his weight. Jelačić had put on quite a few pounds since they had last met, most of it on his gut. He looked about eight months pregnant.

'You'll be glad to hear,' Banks said, 'that your alibi still seems to hold water.'

Jelačić frowned. 'Water? Hold water? What you mean?'

'I mean we believe you were playing cards at Mile

Jelačić's house at the time Deborah Harrison was killed.'

'I already tell you that. So why you come here?'

'To ask you some questions.'

Jelačić grunted.

'First of all, when exactly did you come here from Eastvale?'

'Was last year. September.'

'So the St Mary's girls would have been back at school for a while before you left?'

'Yes. Two weeks.'

Banks leaned forward and flicked his ash into an overflowing tin ashtray, which looked as if it had been stolen from a pub. 'Now the last time we talked,' he said, 'you swore blind you'd never seen Deborah Harrison, or at most that you might just have *seen* her once or twice, in passing.'

'Is true.'

'Now I'm asking you to rethink. I'm giving you another chance to tell the truth, Ive. There's no blame attached to this now. You're not a suspect. But you might be a witness.'

'I saw nothing.'

Banks nodded towards the TV set. 'I don't suppose you watch the news,' he said. 'But for your information Owen Pierce was found not guilty and released earlier today.'

'He is free?' Jelačić stared open-mouthed, then began to laugh. 'Then you failed. You let the guilty man go free. Always that happens here.' He shook his head. 'Such a crazy country.'

'Yes, well at least we don't shoot them first and ask questions later. But that's beside the point. He may or may not have committed the crime, but officially he didn't and we're reopening the case. Which is why I'm here. Now why is trying to get the tiniest scrap of help from you like getting blood out of a stone, Ive? Can you tell me that?'

Jelačić shrugged. 'I know nothing.'

'Don't you care what happened to Deborah Harrison?'

'Deborah Harrison. Deborah Harrison. Silly little English rich girl. Why I care? More girls killed in my homeland. Who cares about them? My father and mother die. My girlfriend is killed. But to you that means nothing. Nobody cares.'

'"Any man's death diminishes me." John Donne wrote that. Have you never heard it, Ive? Have you never heard of the concept that we're all in this together, all part of mankind?'

Jelačić just looked at Banks, incomprehension written on his features.

'Why don't you answer my questions?' Banks went on. 'You saw the girl, you've admitted as much. You must have seen her quite often when you were working outside.'

'I work inside and out. Clean church. Cut grass . . .'

'Right. So you liked to watch the St Mary's girls – we know you did – and you must have noticed Deborah. She was very striking and she complained about your making lewd gestures towards her.'

'I never—'

'Ive, spare me the bullshit, please. I've heard enough of it to last a lifetime. Nobody's going to arrest you or deport you for this. Bloody hell, they might even give you a medal if you tell us anything that leads to the killer.'

Jelačić's eyes lit up. 'Medal? You mean there is reward?'

'It was a joke, Ive,' said Banks. 'No, there isn't a reward. We just expect you to do your duty like any other decent, law-abiding citizen.'

'I see nothing.'

'Did you ever notice anyone hanging around the graveyard looking suspicious?'

'No.'

'Did you ever see Deborah Harrison meet anyone in St Mary's churchyard?'

He shook his head.

'Did she ever linger around there, as if she was going to meet someone, or was up to something?'

Again, he shook his head, but not before Banks noticed something flicker behind his eyes, some memory, some sign of recognition.

'What is it?' Banks asked.

'What is what? Is nothing.'

'You remembered something?'

But it was gone. 'No,' said Jelačić. 'Like I say, I only see her when she walk home sometimes. She never stay, never meet anyone. That is all.'

He was lying about something, Banks was certain. But he was equally certain Jelačić was too stubborn to part with whatever he had remembered right now. Banks would have to find more leverage. Sometimes he wished he had the freedom and power of certain other police forces in certain other countries – the freedom and power to torture and beat the truth out of Jelačić, for example – but only sometimes.

There was no point going on. Banks said goodbye and opened the door to leave. Before he had got ten feet away from the flat, he heard the sound on Jelačić's television shoot up loud again.

THREE

It was late that Wednesday evening when Owen finally got home. After he had picked up his belongings from the prison, he decided he didn't want to spend even one or two hours of such a beautiful day – his first moments of freedom in over six months – trapped in a car with Gordon Wharton. So he begged off, walked into town and just wandered aimlessly for a while, savouring his liberty. Late in the afternoon, he went into a pub on Boar Lane and had a pint of bitter and a roast beef sandwich, which almost made him gag after months of prison food. Then he walked over to the bus station, and by a circuitous route and a surprising number of changes, he managed to get himself back to Eastvale.

When Owen finally put his key in the lock, the door swung open by itself. He stood in the silence for a moment but could hear nothing. That seemed wrong. He knew there should have been a familiar sound, even if he couldn't, right now, remember what it was. His house had never been in such complete silence. No place ever is. And there was an odd smell. Dust he had expected, after so long away, perhaps mildew, too. He couldn't expect Ivor or Siobhan next door to do his cleaning for him. But this was something else. He stayed by the door listening for a while, then went into the living-room.

It looked like the aftermath of a jumble sale. Someone had pulled the books from the shelves, then ripped out pages and tossed them on the floor. Some of the torn pages had curled up, as if they had been wet and had dried out. Compact disc cases lay strewn, shattered and cracked, along with them. The discs themselves were mostly at the other side of the room, where marks on the wall showed that they had probably been flipped like Frisbees. The TV screen had been smashed. Scrawled on the wall beside the door, in giant, spidery red letters, were the words 'JAILS TOO GOOD FOR FILTHY FUCKING PERVERTS LIKE YOU!'

Owen sagged against the wall and let his bag drop to the floor. Just for a moment, he longed for the stark simplicity of his prison cell again, the intractable order of prison life. This was too much. He didn't feel he could cope.

Taking a deep breath, he stepped over the debris and went into the study. His photos and negs lay ripped and snipped up all over the carpet. None of them looked salvageable, not even the inoffensive landscapes. His cameras lay beside them, lenses cracked in spider-web patterns. His art books had also been taken from their shelves and pages of reproductions ripped out by the handful: Gauguin, Cézanne, Renoir, Titian, Van Gogh, Vermeer, Monet, Caravaggio, Rubens, everything. That was bad enough – but the thing he hadn't dared look at until last, the thing he had sensed as soon as he entered but hadn't quite grasped, was the worst of all.

The aquarium stood in darkness and silence, lights, pumps and filters switched off. The fish floated on the water's surface – danios, guppies, angelfish, jewelfish, zebrafish – their once-bright colours faded in death. It looked as if the intruder had simply switched off their life-support and left them to die. For Owen, this was the last straw. Misguided vindictiveness against himself he could understand, but such cruelty directed against the harmless, helpless fish was beyond his ken.

Owen leaned against the tank and sobbed until he

couldn't get his breath, then he ran to the bathroom and rinsed his face in cold water. After that, he stood gripping the cool sides of the sink until he stopped shaking. In his bedroom, most of his clothes had been ripped or cut up with scissors and scattered over his bed.

In the kitchen, the contents of the fridge and cupboards had been dumped on the lino and smeared in the manner of a Jackson Pollock canvas. The resultant gooey mess of old marmalade, eggs, baked beans, instant coffee, sour milk, cheese slices, sugar, tea bags, butter, rice, treacle, cornflakes and a whole rack of herbs and spices looked like a special effect from a horror film and smelt worse than the yeast factory he had once worked in as a student. Right in the middle, on top of it all, sat what looked like a curled, dried turd.

He knew he should call the police, if only for insurance purposes, but the last people on earth he felt like dealing with right now were the bloody police.

And he couldn't face cleaning up.

Instead, he decided to give up on his first day of freedom. It was only about nine o'clock, just after dark, but Owen swept the torn and snipped-up clothes from his bed, burrowed under the sheets and pulled the covers over his head.

14

ONE

Like Canute holding back the tide, or the Trojans fighting off the Greeks, Banks could only postpone the inevitable, not avoid it altogether. In fact, the inevitable was waiting for him at eight o'clock on Thursday morning when he got to his office – coffee in hand, listening to Barber's setting of 'Dover Beach' on his Walkman – in the strutting, fretting form of Chief Constable Jeremiah Riddle.

'Banks, take those bloody things out of your ears. And where the hell do you think you were yesterday?'

Banks told him about talking to Batorac and Jelačić while he was in Leeds, but omitted Pamela's chamber music concert and his quick visit to the Classical Record Shop.

Riddle's presence called for a cigarette, he thought. He was trying to cut out the early morning smokes, but under the circumstances, lighting up now might achieve the double purpose of both soothing his nerves and aggravating Riddle into a cardiac arrest. He lit up. Riddle coughed and waved his hand about, but he wasn't about to be distracted, or to die.

'What have you got to say about that fiasco in court yesterday?' the chief constable asked.

Banks shrugged. 'There's nothing much *to* say, sir,' he replied. 'The jury found Pierce not guilty.'

'I know that. Bloody idiots.'

'That may well be, sir,' said Banks, 'but there's still nothing we can do about it. I thought we had a strong case. I'm certain the Crown will appeal. I'll be talking to Stafford Oakes about it when the fuss dies down.'

'Hmph. We're going to look like real idiots over this one, Banks, as if we haven't got enough problems already.' Riddle ran his hand over his red, shiny head. 'Anyway, I want you to know that I've asked Detective Superintendent Gristhorpe to have a look over the case files. Maybe he can bring a fresh viewpoint. Either you get more evidence on Pierce or, if he really didn't do it, you damn well find out who did. I've decided I'm going to give you a week to redeem yourself on this before we hand it over to a team of independent investigators. I don't want to do that, I know how bad it looks, an admission of failure, but we've no bloody choice if we don't get results fast. I need hardly remind you of the impact a negative result might have on your future career, need I?'

'No, sir.'

'And go easy on the Harrisons. They're bound to be upset by Pierce getting off, after everything they've been through. Tread softly. Understand?'

'I'll tread softly, sir.'

Stupid pillock, Banks cursed after Riddle had left the office. A whole bloody week. And how, he wondered, could he do his job with one hand tied behind his back, and tied because of bloody privilege, class and wealth, not by compassion for a bereaved family? Again, he had the feeling he would soon be walking on very thin ice indeed if he were to get to the bottom of things.

He walked over to the window, pulled up the venetian blind and opened the sash a couple of inches. It was too early for tourists, but the market square was busy with Eastvalers starting their day, heels clicking on the cobbles as bank cashiers, dentists and estate agents went to work in the warren of offices around the town centre. The shops were opening and the smell of fresh-baked bread spilled in with sunlight.

Looking to his right, Banks could see south along Market Street, with its teashops, boutiques, and speciality shops, and out front was the square itself, with the NatWest bank, an estate agent, the El Toro coffee bar and Joplin's newsagent's at the opposite side. Over the shops were solicitors' offices, dentists' and doctors' surgeries.

With a sigh, Banks walked over to his filing cabinet, where he kept his own records of the salient points of the Harrison case. The tons of paperwork and electromagnetic traces that a murder case generated couldn't possibly be stored in one detective's office, but most detectives had their own ways of summarizing and keeping track of the cases they worked on. Banks was no exception.

His filing cabinet contained his own notes on all the major cases he had been involved with since coming to Eastvale, plus a few he had brought with him from the Met. The notes might not mean much to anyone else, but with the use of his keen memory, Banks was able to fill in all the gaps his shorthand left out. His own notes also contained the hunches and accounts of off-the-record conversations that didn't make their way into the official files and statements.

It was time, he thought, to clear his mind of Owen Pierce for the moment and go back to basics. Two possibilities remained: either Deborah Harrison had been murdered by someone she knew, or a stranger other than Owen Pierce had killed her. Putting the second possibility aside, Banks picked up the names and strands of the first. Before the Pierce business, he had believed that Deborah might have arranged to meet someone on her way home from the chess club. He would spend the morning reading his notes and thinking, he decided, then after lunch he would go back to where it all started: St Mary's graveyard.

ONE

'Siobhan would bloody well kill me if she knew I was here with you now,' Ivor said. 'You don't understand what it's been like, mate. She's still convinced you did it.'

They were standing at the bar of the Queen's Arms on Thursday lunch-time, after Owen had spent the entire morning cleaning up his house.

'That's ridiculous,' said Owen. 'I know she never really liked me, but I thought she had more sense than that. Is that why you didn't report the break-in?'

'I told you, it only happened the other day. You don't know what it's been like for us.'

'Tell me.'

Ivor sighed and took a swig from his pint. 'You should have seen some of the things you got through your letter-box, for a start.'

'What things?'

'Shit, hate-letters, used johnnies, death threats, something that looked like a lump of kidney or liver. I had to go in and clean it all up, didn't I?'

'I'm sorry. Did you report it to the police?'

'Of course I did. They sent a man round, but he didn't do anything. What can you expect?'

'The police thought I was guilty. They still do.' Along with the rest of the world, he thought.

'Still,' Ivor said, 'you weren't living next door. You didn't have to put up with it all.'

'Right. I was safely locked up in prison, all nice and comfortable in my little cell. Fucking luxury.'

'You don't have to be so sarcastic, Owen. I'm just trying to explain what it was like on the outside, so you can understand people's attitudes.'

'Like Siobhan's?'

'Yes.'

'And yours?'

Ivor shrugged.

'What exactly is your attitude?' Owen asked.

'What's it matter? You're out now.'

'Not just out, Ivor, but not guilty. Remember?'

'Well,' he mumbled, 'you know what people say.'

'No, I don't. Tell me what people say.'

'You know, guilty people get off all the time because the system's biased in their favour. We bend over backward to help criminals and don't give a damn for their victims.'

'I'm the victim here, Ivor,' Owen thrust his thumb at his own chest. 'Me. I even found a letter from the college waiting for me. That bastard Kemp has fired me, and he did it *before* the jury even went out.'

Ivor looked away. 'Yeah, well. I'm just saying what people think, in general, that's all.'

'And what do *you* think, Ivor?'

'Look, I really don't want to get into this. All I'm saying, Owen, is that shit sticks.'

'Meaning?'

'Oh, come on! For Christ's sake, you're supposed to be the English teacher. Meaning exactly what it says. All those rumours that went around during the trial, the stuff they couldn't bring in as evidence? Do you think nobody knew about it? Hell, I found out from one of the students in the local library.'

Owen felt a shiver run up his spine. 'Found out about what?'

'Everything. Your sex life, your photographic pursuits, your taste for dirty books and magazines, the porn video, how you screwed your students.'

Owen toyed with a damp beer-mat. 'You already knew that Michelle had been one of my students, I don't think even you would call *Lady Chatterley's Lover* a dirty book these days, and, don't forget, you watched part of one of those videos with me. I'm no worse than anyone else.'

'Oh, grow up. You may not be, but the whole country doesn't know everything about anyone else, does it? You know how rumours get exaggerated. As far as they're concerned, you're the one who beats up women when they won't let you fuck them. You're the one who spends his days ogling innocent young schoolgirls and your nights dreaming about defiling and strangling virgins while you're watching video nasties.'

Owen felt himself flush. 'They're all bloody hypocrites.'

'Maybe so, but that doesn't help you, does it?'

'And what does help me?'

'I don't know. I was thinking, maybe you should go away somewhere . . .?'

'Run away? That's great advice. Thanks a lot, mate.'

Owen ordered a couple more pints. At least the barmaid didn't seem to have recognized him. She actually *smiled* as she put down the drinks. A woman smiling, something he hadn't seen in ages, apart from Shirley Castle in her moment of victory. Either she didn't watch telly or read the papers, or prison had changed his appearance enough to fool some people. Not everyone, of course, but some people.

'Look,' he went on, 'get this into your thick skull. I haven't done anything. I never beat up anyone, and I certainly never raped and murdered anyone. I've been a victim of the system. They owe me something. It's doubtful they'll pay, but they owe me. In the meantime, I've lost a few months out of my life and my reputation's taken a bit of a bashing. I've got to put things in order again, and I'm damned if I'm going to start by running away. How do you think that'll look?'

Ivor paused and scratched his beard before answering. 'It's not a bad idea, you know. It's not really like running away. New life somewhere else. Fresh start. You could even go live and teach English on the continent somewhere. France maybe. Your French is pretty good, as I remember. Or Japan.'

Owen sniffed. 'I can't believe what I'm hearing. You think that's the solution to my problems? Go live in obscurity in a foreign country? A sort of self-imposed exile. I'm telling you for the last time, Ivor, *I haven't done anything.*'

Ivor paused a little before saying, 'You might find it more difficult than you think – putting things in order.'

'What do you mean?'

'Nothing specific. I'm just pointing out that Siobhan's attitude isn't unique. There's probably a few others feel the same way. Locally, like. Feelings can get pretty strong.'

'Are you telling me I'm in danger? A lynch mob or something?'

'All I'm saying is that when people get frightened they lash out.'

'And what do you feel, Ivor? You never really answered my original question, you know. You're my neighbour. You're also supposed to be my friend. Do you think I'm a pervert?'

'What can I say? How do I know? I watched part of that video with you, like you said, didn't I? I don't think doing that turned me into a pervert. Mind you, I can't say it did a lot for me, but I watched it. More of a laugh than anything, if—'

'Fuck off, Ivor.'

'What? Look—'

'Just fuck off and leave me alone.'

Ivor banged his pint down on the bar; the barmaid glanced over anxiously. 'All right, if that's the way you want it, mate. Just don't expect any more help from me.'

Owen snorted. 'Believe me, Ivor, you've earned my undying gratitude for what you've done for me already. Now just fuck off.'

Ivor stormed out, red-faced above his beard, and the barmaid gave Owen an odd look, perhaps of recognition, or disapproval. Then the landlord, Cyril, he of the Popeye forearms, appeared from the back.

'What's all the noise about?' he said. He seemed to recognize Owen and started walking towards him.

'Well, you can fuck off, too!' Owen slammed his glass down on the bar so hard it broke and beer swilled over the counter.

'Here!' yelled Cyril, making for the hinged flap. But Owen shot out of the door and down the street, the base of his thumb stinging and bleeding from where a sliver of glass had pierced it.

He hurried along North Market Street, head down and hands thrust deep in his pockets, fists clenched. Ivor. That slimy, back-pedalling little turd. And Michelle? Just what was she trying to do to him?

But perhaps Ivor was right about moving. The thought wasn't quite as upsetting as it might have been a year or so earlier; somehow, the mess he had found on his release from prison had soured the house for him anyway. There were also, he realized, still too many memories of Michelle there. And moving would be a project, something to do, start looking for a new place, perhaps somewhere a little cheaper in a different part of the country. Not abroad, but in Devon, maybe, or Cornwall. He had always liked the south-west.

As he walked down the street, head bowed, Owen felt like an outsider, as if the rest of the world were swimming happily together in a huge tank and he was knocking on the glass unable to find a way in. One or two people gave him strange looks as he passed, and he realized he must have been mumbling to himself. Or maybe they recognized him. *Shit sticks*, Ivor had said. People would see him the way the rumours had depicted him, and would perhaps move aside and whisper to one another, 'Here comes the Eastvale Strangler. You know, the one that got off.'

When he finally looked up to see where he was, he saw he was in St Mary's. Despite all his resolutions, he had walked there, as if by instinct.

He stood at the church gate, uncertain what to do, then on an impulse he decided to go in. It was a beautiful day, and the few hawthorn trees scattered among the yews bore white, yellow or pink blossoms. Wildflowers pushed their way through the grass around some of the plots. Thriving on decomposing remains, Owen thought fancifully, before he noticed that most of the graves were from the eighteenth and nineteenth centuries. There were some recent ones, but not many.

The graveyard was peaceful; the muffled sounds of traffic on North Market Street and Kendal Road formed only a distant backdrop to the birdsongs.

Owen followed the tarmac path where it curved past the church and arrived at the Kendal Road exit. There, he walked up to the bridge and stared down at the swirling water, the colour of a pint of bitter, from the peat it picked up on its way through the dale. Ahead, facing south, he could see the formal gardens, the riverside willows and the castle high on its hill, dominating the town. It seemed so long ago he had stood here that foggy November night. No, he would not think about that again.

He took the river path home, and as he passed by the vicarage, he saw, over the garden gate, a woman hanging up washing on the line and stopped to watch her.

The plain white T-shirt she was wearing stretched taut against her heavy round breasts as she reached to peg up a sheet. Owen fancied he could see the dark nipples harden at the wind's caress.

Then she looked his way. He recognized her; he had seen her in court. She was the woman who had found the body, the one whose husband had been accused of molesting a church worker.

For a moment, she seemed about to smile and say hello, then she frowned, her jaw dropped, and she backed away inside the house, shutting the door behind her. Owen could hear the sound of a chain being fastened. She hadn't hung the sheet properly on the washing-line, and at the first light gust of wind it filled like a sail then broke free and fluttered onto the flower-bed like a shroud.

THREE

Banks saw the curtain in the bay window twitch just after he rang the vicarage bell, and a few moments later a nervous and jumpy looking Rebecca Charters answered the door. She looked relieved to see him and ushered him down the hall into the living-room.

It was a lot more cosy than on his previous visits, he noticed immediately, and it felt much more like a family home than a temporary encampment. The whole place had been redecorated: new wallpaper, cream with rose patterns; a new three-piece suite in a matching floral design; and three vases of flowers placed around the room. Ezekiel, the mound of brown-and-white fur, was in his usual place by the empty fireplace.

'How about some tea?' Rebecca asked. 'Freshly brewed. Well, five minutes ago.'

'That'll be fine,' said Banks. 'No milk or sugar, thanks.'

Rebecca went into the kitchen and returned seconds later with two mugs of tea. Today, she wore her hair tied back, fixed in place by a tooled-leather slide and a broad wooden pin. The style made her olive-complexioned face seem to bulge forward a little, emphasizing the slightly long nose, weak chin and curved brow, like a photograph through a fish-eye lens, but she still looked attractive, especially the dark eyes and full lips.

'I noticed you were in court for the verdict,' Banks began.

Rebecca cradled her mug in her hands. 'Yes,' she said. 'I can hardly believe it. He was here earlier. That was why I was a bit nervous when you rang.'

'Owen Pierce was here? Why?'

'Not actually *here*, but he walked past on the river path. I was in the garden. I saw him.'

'It's a free country, I suppose,' Banks said. 'And he's a free man.'

'But isn't he dangerous? I mean, people still think he did it, even if he did get off.'

'They're free to believe what they want. I don't think you have anything to worry about, though.'

'Easy for you to say.'

'Perhaps. Keep your doors and windows locked if it makes you feel better.'

'I'm sorry,' Rebecca said. 'I don't mean to be sharp. I . . .'

'It's all right,' said Banks. 'You're worried. You think there's a killer been set free and he's got his eyes on you. The quicker we find out whether he did it or not, the sooner you'll feel safe again.'

'Do you think he did it?'

Banks scratched the little scar beside his right eye. 'Right now, I don't know,' he admitted. 'There were times when I did, certainly, but the more I look at some of the things that struck me as odd before we latched onto Pierce, the more I start to wonder. The courts set innocent people free as well as guilty ones, sometimes, and if anyone knows the truth, he's a lucky man.'

'What brought you back here?'

'I'm not really sure, except that this is where it all started.'

'Yes,' said Rebecca. 'I remember.' She gave a small shudder and fingered the neck of her dress. 'And I'd like to apologize.'

'For what?'

'For the last time we met. In the Queen's Arms. I seem

to remember I was very rude to you. I seem to be making a habit of it.'

'Don't worry,' Banks said. 'You get used to it in my job.'

'But you shouldn't have to. I mean, I shouldn't have behaved the way I did.' She put her mug down on the table. 'I'm not that kind of person. Rude . . . I . . . Look, I don't know why I'm telling you this, except that your coming here again brings it all back.'

'Brings what back? Finding the body?'

'That, yes, certainly. But it was a terrible time for me all round. The charges against Daniel, all the turmoil they caused.' She took a deep breath. 'You see, Chief Inspector, you didn't know the half of it. Of course you didn't, it wasn't relevant, not to your enquiries, but I lost a baby about three months before that business with Jelačić, and the doctor said it would be dangerous for me to try for another. Daniel and I hadn't talked about it as much as we should, and we had started drifting apart. We had just made some tentative enquiries about adoption when Jelačić brought the charges. Of course, everything fell through. It was worse than it was before. I'm afraid I withdrew. I blamed Daniel. There was even a time when I thought he was guilty. Since I lost the baby, we hadn't been . . . well, you know . . . and I thought he'd lost interest in me. It was easier to explain that by assuming he was really interested in men. What can I say? I started to drink too much. Then there was Patrick.' She laughed nervously. 'I don't know why I'm telling you all this. Except that you witnessed the final scene.'

Banks smiled. 'You'd be surprised the things people tell us, Mrs Charters. Anyway, I hope life has improved since then.'

She beamed. 'Yes. Yes, it has. Daniel and I are stronger than we've ever been. There are still . . . well, a few problems . . . but at least we're working together now.'

'How's the Jelačić problem progressing?'

'It drags on. We've not heard anything for over a month now, but believe he's got some human-rights lawyer working on it.'

'And the drink?'

'Six months without.'

'Patrick Metcalfe?'

'Not since that time you were here, when he caused all that fuss.'

'Has he pestered you at all since then?'

She smiled. 'No. I think he realized pretty quickly how carried away with himself he was getting. And I think your interest in him helped keep him at bay, too. I should thank you for that. You don't still suspect him, do you?'

'He's not off the hook yet,' Banks said. 'Anyway, that's not why I came. Actually, I was hoping for another look at the area where the body was found.'

'Surely you don't have to ask my permission to do that?'

'No, but it's partly a matter of courtesy. And you know the area better than I do. Will you come with me?'

'Certainly.'

To retrace Deborah's steps, they walked first along the riverside path from the vicarage towards the Kendal Road bridge, where worn stone steps led up to the pavement. It was another beautiful day, and over the road in St Mary's Park, lovers lay entwined, students sat reading in the shade of the trees, and children played with balls and Frisbees.

'This is where she would enter,' said Rebecca, holding

the wooden gate open for Banks. It was a lych-gate, with a small wooden roof, where the coffin would await the arrival of the clergyman in days gone by. 'Seventeenth century,' Rebecca said. 'Isn't it superb?'

Banks agreed that it was.

'This is the main path we're on now,' Rebecca explained.

It was about a yard and a half wide and had a pitted tarmac surface. Ahead, it curved around slightly in front of the church, separated from the doors only by a swathe of grass, across which led a narrow flagstone path.

'It leads to North Market Street,' Rebecca said, 'near the zebra crossing where Deborah would cross to go home. And this path,' she said, taking Banks by the elbow and diverting him to the right, where the entrance to the path was almost obscured by shrubbery, 'is the path that leads to the Inchcliffe Mausoleum.'

It was the gravel path Banks remembered from last November. After a couple of yards, the shrubbery gave way to yews and lichen-stained graves. Warm sunlight filtered through the greenery and flying insects buzzed around the dandelions and forget-me-nots.

Some of the graves were above-ground tombs with heavy lids and flowery religious epitaphs. By far the most impressive and baroque was the Inchcliffe Mausoleum, to the right.

'Now,' said Banks, 'we were assuming that Deborah reached the junction between the main path and this one when someone either grabbed her and dragged her up here or persuaded her to go with him of her own free will.'

'But why couldn't she have come this way herself?' Rebecca asked.

'Why should she? It's out of her way.'

'She had done before. I noticed her do it once or twice.'

Banks raised his eyebrows. 'You never mentioned this before.'

Rebecca shrugged. 'You never asked. And it didn't seem relevant.'

'But didn't it strike you as odd?'

'No. I'm sorry. It wasn't something I was paying a lot of attention to. I suppose I assumed that she liked grave-yards, as I do. And this is where the most interesting old tombs are, and the Inchcliffe Mausoleum, of course.' She blushed. 'Maybe she went to talk to the angel, like I did.'

'When did she start using the path?'

'I've no idea. I don't remember *noticing* her go that way before last September, when school started up, but that doesn't mean she never did.'

'Did you ever see anyone else with her? Or anyone going along the path before or after her?'

'No. You did ask me about that before, and I would have told you if I'd seen her meeting anyone. I would have noticed something like that. Do you think it's important that she took this path?'

Banks paused. 'From the start,' he explained, 'I'd been working on the theory that if Owen Pierce or someone else hadn't followed Deborah into the graveyard, dragged her off the main path and killed her, then she might have been meeting the person who did. Now you're telling me you've seen her take this path before, I'm wondering if this is where she arranged the meeting. By the mausoleum. Her friend Megan Preece said Deborah had a morbid streak, that she liked spooky things. A rendezvous in the depths of a foggy graveyard beside an old mausoleum might have appealed to her.'

'To meet someone she knew?'

'Yes. A lover, perhaps. Or someone else. We know that Deborah had a secret. It did cross my mind that she might have arranged to meet the person involved to discuss it, what to do about it.'

'But what could she have possibly known that was so important?'

'If we knew that, then we'd probably know who the killer is.'

'And do you still believe that she was meeting someone?'

'I think it's a strong possibility. She didn't tell Megan, but perhaps she wanted to be really secretive. Ive Jelačić told me he never saw her meeting anyone, but he's a pathological liar. On the other hand, you just told me yourself that you never saw anyone else around.'

'It doesn't mean that there couldn't have been someone,' Rebecca said. 'The woods are quite deep here. And it was a foggy night. I just wish I could be of more help.'

Banks stood and looked around. Rebecca was right. You could just about see the church through the trees to the south, but to the north, between the Inchcliffe Mausoleum and Kendal Road, it was a different matter. There, the yews were thicker, the undergrowth denser. It would be an ideal place for a secret meeting. And if he had learned anything from returning to the scene, it was that Deborah might have taken the gravel path of her own accord, and that she had done so before.

He looked up at the Inchcliffe Mausoleum. It could have been the angle he was viewing it from, or perhaps a trick of the light, but he could have sworn the marble angel with the chipped wings was smiling.

15

ONE

'**Let's assume** Pierce didn't do it, just for the moment,' said Banks. 'That'll make things easier.'

It was the first Friday in June, and the rays of late morning sunlight flooded the market square. Banks sat in Gristhorpe's office trying to get a fresh perspective on the Deborah Harrison murder.

Gristhorpe, a bulky man with a pock-marked face and bushy eyebrows, sat sideways at his large teak desk, one leg stretched out and propped up on a footstool. He insisted that the broken leg had healed perfectly, but he still got the odd twinge now and then. Given that it was the same leg he had also been shot in not so long ago, that wasn't surprising, Banks thought.

Banks took a sip of coffee. 'On the generous side, I'd say we've got maybe five or six suspects. If Deborah didn't have a lover we don't know about – and I don't think she did – then the key to it all might lie in the secret she had. And if Deborah knew something about some-one, she might easily have misjudged the importance of what she knew, underestimated the desperation of that person. Adults can have some pretty nasty secrets. The Pierce trial redirected all our time and energy towards proving that the killer *didn't* know her, that she was a random victim, or became a victim because she had the misfortune of resembling Pierce's ex-girlfriend Michelle Chappel.'

'What's happening with that now?'

'I talked to Stafford Oakes about an hour ago,' Banks said, 'and he's ninety-nine per cent certain the Crown will appeal the verdict on the basis of the similar fact evidence being declared inadmissible. If they get a judge who allows it in, another trial could be disastrous for Pierce, whether he did it or not.'

Gristhorpe scratched his chin. 'As you know, Alan,' he said, 'I've been able to keep an open mind on this because I wasn't part of the original investigation. I'd just like to say in the first place that I think you did good detective work. You shouldn't flagellate yourself over the result. It may still turn out that Pierce didn't do it. But I agree we should put that aside for a moment. From what I've read so far, Barry Stott seemed particularly sold on Pierce. Any idea why?'

'It was *his* lead,' Banks said. 'Or so he thought. Actually, if it hadn't been for Jim Hatchley stopping for a pint in the Nag's Head, he might never have turned it up. But Barry's ambitious. And tenacious. And let's not forget, Jimmy Riddle was dead set on Pierce, too.'

'He's a friend of the family,' Gristhorpe said. 'I should imagine he just wanted an early conclusion, no matter who went down for it.'

Banks nodded.

'Now,' Gristhorpe went on, 'the two things we have to ask ourselves are what possible secret Deborah Harrison could have learned that was important enough to kill for, and who, given the opportunity, could have killed her because of it.'

Banks told him about his visit to Rebecca Charters and

what he had learned about Deborah's occasional detours from the main path.

'You think she had arranged to meet her killer?' Gristhorpe asked.

'Rebecca never actually saw her meet anyone, but it's one possibility.'

'Blackmail?'

'Perhaps. Though I'm not sure from what I know of Deborah that she was the type to do that. I suppose it *is* possible. After all, her satchel was open when we found her, and that has always bothered me. Perhaps she had some sort of hard evidence and the killer took it. On the other hand, maybe she just wanted to let whoever it was know that she knew the secret, or how she had found out. Perhaps she just wanted to flaunt her knowledge a little. Her friends say she could be a bit of a show-off. Anyway, let's say she didn't know the power or the value of what she was playing with.'

'Which takes us to my questions: why and who?'

'Yes.' Banks counted them on his fingers, one by one. 'For a start, there's John Spinks. He was Deborah's boyfriend for part of the summer, and he's a nasty piece of work. They parted on very bad terms and I think he's the type to bear a grudge. He also has an alibi that doesn't hold much water. Ive Jelačić has a solid alibi, I'd say, in Vjeko Batorac, but I'm still certain he's involved, he knows something.'

'Any idea what?'

'I'd guess he might have seen Deborah meeting someone.'

'Why not tell us who, then?'

'That's not Jelačić's style. If you ask me, I'd say he's trying to work out what might be in it for him first. For crying out loud, he even asked me if there was a reward.'

'What do we do, beat it out of him?'

'Believe me, that thought's crossed my mind. But no. We'll get him one way or another, don't worry about that. I'm not finished with Mr Jelačić yet.'

'Who else have we got? What about that school-teacher?'

'Patrick Metcalfe? Another possibility. Though I doubt very much that he's got the bottle, we have to consider him. He was Deborah's history teacher and he was having an affair with Rebecca Charters, the vicar's wife. One might reasonably assume that's a poor career move for a male teacher at an Anglican girls' school. If Deborah knew about the affair – and she could easily have seen Metcalfe entering or leaving the vicarage on occasion – then it could have cost Metcalfe not only his job, but his entire teaching career.'

'And as I recall from the statement,' Gristhorpe said, 'he says he stayed home alone in his flat after Daniel Charters left.'

Banks nodded. 'And we've no way of confirming or denying that unless someone saw him, which no-one has admitted to so far.'

'What about the vicar?'

'I've been wondering about him, too,' Banks said. 'In general I've been pretty sympathetic towards him, but looking at things objectively, he could be our man. He certainly has no alibi, and he's both tall and strong enough.'

'Motive?'

'We know that Ive Jelačić accused him of abusing his position by making homosexual advances. Given Jelačić's character, this is probably pure fabrication – Vjeko Batorac certainly thinks it is – but let's say it's true, or it approximates the truth. And let's say Deborah saw something that could confirm it, either involving Charters and Jelačić or Charters and someone else. If it got out, he also stood to lose everything. That might give him a powerful enough motive.'

'Or his wife?' Gristhorpe suggested.

'Yes. It *could* have been a woman,' Banks agreed. 'After all, there was no evidence of rape, and the body could have been arranged to make it look like a sex murder. Rebecca Charters is probably tall and strong enough.'

'And she could have had either of two motives,' Gristhorpe added. 'To protect the knowledge of her affair with Metcalfe, or to protect her husband from certain dismissal.' He shook his head. 'It's a real *Peyton Place* we've unearthed here, Alan. Who'd think such goings on occurred in a nice little Yorkshire town like Eastvale?'

Banks smiled. '"It is my belief, Watson, founded upon my experience, that the lowest and vilest alleys in London do not present a more dreadful record of sin than does the smiling and beautiful countryside."'

Gristhorpe smiled back. 'And what about Jimmy Riddle's mates?' he said.

'Certainly not out of the question. I was beginning to think that Michael Clayton might have been having an affair with Sylvie Harrison, unlikely as it sounds. Sir Geoffrey and Michael Clayton have been close friends since university. If Clayton *were* having an affair with his wife, and if Deborah knew about that, it could have had a devastating effect. Think of how much money and prestige were at stake there.'

'As I understand it, none of them have alibis either.'

'That's right. And they all knew Deborah went to the

chess club on a Monday, and what time she usually came home. *And* by what route. But even if we accept the horrible possibility that she was *capable* of such a crime, Sylvie Harrison is neither tall nor strong enough to have killed her daughter. Rebecca Charters is the only woman in this case who could remotely have done it.'

'Clayton, then?'

'Possible. Certainly he's the more likely of the two. Though, again, he was the child's *godfather*.'

'Let's also not forget,' Gristhorpe added, 'that HarClay Industries had a lot of MoD contracts. They do a lot of hush-hush work. If Deborah found out about any hanky-panky going on there, contracts with foreign governments and the like . . .'

'Or even something our own government didn't want the general public to know?'

'I wouldn't put it past them,' Gristhorpe agreed. 'According to your notes, at the time of his daughter's murder, Sir Geoffrey Harrison was in a private meeting with a man from the government called Oliver Jackson. I happen to know Oliver Jackson, and he's not exactly from the government, he's Special Branch.'

'Aren't we getting a bit far-fetched here?' Banks said. 'Maybe it's just someone else with the same name?'

Gristhorpe shook his head. 'I checked with the York CID. It was the same Oliver Jackson all right. They knew he was in town, but they weren't told why. It's just another aspect to consider. Any other angles?'

Banks sighed. 'Not that I can think of,' he said. 'Unless Deborah stumbled on something illegal going on in the school – something to do with sex or drugs, perhaps – but we couldn't dig anything up there.'

'It's still plenty to be going on with for the moment.'

Banks stood up and walked to the door, already reaching in his pocket for his Silk Cuts.

'By the way,' Gristhorpe asked, 'how is DI Stott doing?'

Banks paused at the door. 'He's been walking around looking like death warmed up ever since Pierce got off. I'm getting a bit worried about him.'

'Maybe he'll be better after a weekend's rest?'

'Maybe.'

As he walked back to his own office, Banks heard raised voices down the corridor and went to see what was happening. There, at the bottom of the staircase, stood John Spinks and DC Susan Gay.

TWO

'The problem is not with your teaching ability, Owen. You have demonstrated that to us quite clearly over the years.'

'Then I don't understand,' Owen said. 'Why can't I have my job back?' He was sitting in the chairman's book-lined office. Peter Kemp, with his rolled-up shirtsleeves, his freckles and ginger hair like tufts on a coconut sat behind the untidy desk. 'Kemp the Unkempt,' the staff members had nicknamed him. To one side, a computer hummed, white cursor blinking in anticipation on an empty blue screen.

Kemp leaned back in his chair and linked his hands behind his head. Owen could see a dark patch of sweat under each arm. 'Technically, Owen,' Kemp said, 'you can't demand back a job you never had. Remember, you were employed purely on a term-to-term basis, no guarantees. We simply can't use you next term.'

As he spoke, Kemp looked at Owen down his nose,

under the tortoiseshell rims of his glasses, as an entomo-
logist might regard an especially interesting but ugly new
bug. The office smelled of Polo mints and fresh paint.
Owen longed to let in some air, but he knew from
experience that none of the windows opened.

'I was depending on you,' Owen said. 'You've always
renewed my contract before.'

Kemp sat forward and rested his hairy forearms on the
desk. 'Ah, yes. But this time you left us in a bit of a mess,
didn't you? We had to bring in someone to finish your
classes. She did a good job, a very good job, under the
circumstances. We can't very well chuck her out without
so much as a by-your-leave, can we?'

'I don't see why not. You seem to be doing it to me, and
at least I've got seniority. Besides, it was hardly my fault I
got arrested.'

Kemp sniggered. 'Well, it *certainly* wasn't mine. But
that's irrelevant. There's no such thing as seniority in temporary appointments, Owen. You know that. I'm sorry,
but my hands are tied.' And he held them together, linking
his fingers as if to demonstrate.

'What about next January? I can just about get by until
then.'

Kemp pursed his lips and shook his head. 'I can't see
any vacancies opening up. Budgets are tight these days.
Very tight.'

'Look,' Owen said, sitting forward. 'I'm getting fed up
with this. Ever since I've been in your office – and I had to
wait long enough before I got to see you, by the way – I've
heard nothing but flannel. You know damn well that you
could find courses for me if you wanted to, but you won't.
If it's nothing to do with my teaching abilities, then maybe
you'd better tell me what really is the problem.' Owen had

a good idea what he would hear – he had read the letter, after all – but he wanted to put Kemp through the embarrassment of having to say it.

'I've told you—'

'You've told me bugger-all. Is it the trial? Is that it?'

'Well, you could hardly imagine something like that would endear you to the board, could you? But we all understand that you were mistakenly accused, and we deeply regret any hardship you suffered.'

Owen laughed. 'Mistakenly accused? I like that. That's a nice way of putting it.'

Kemp pursed his lips. 'Owen, we know how you suffered, believe me.'

'Do you?' Owen felt himself redden with anger. He gripped the sides of the chair. 'Do you also believe in my innocence?'

'One must put faith in the justice system, Owen, abide by the verdict of the jury.'

'So you *do* believe they were right?'

'The court found you not guilty.'

'That's not the same thing.'

'But what else are we to base our judgements on?'

'What else? On your knowledge of the person, on character. On *trust*, damn it. After all, I've worked here for eight years.'

Kemp shrugged. 'But I can hardly say I *know* you, can I? Ours has always been a professional relationship, a work relationship, if you like.'

'And my work has always been of the highest quality. So what about my job, then? If you believe I've done nothing wrong and you have faith in my teaching ability, why don't I get my job back?'

'You're making this very difficult for me, Owen.'

Owen thumped the desk. 'Oh, am I? I'm really sorry about that. Maybe it just hasn't occurred to you how fucking difficult this is for *me*.'

Kemp backed away slowly on his wheeled office-chair. 'Owen, you're not helping yourself at all by behaving in this manner.'

'Don't give me that. You've already made it clear what my position is. I want you to admit why. And please don't tell me how bloody *difficult* it is for you.'

Kemp stopped edging back and leaned forward on the desk, making a steeple of his fingers. 'All right,' he said. 'If that's the way you want it. The college has expressed its unwillingness to employ an instructor who has a reputation for bedding his female students and photographing them in the nude. It's bad for our image. It'll make parents keep their daughters away. And seeing as we depend on the students for our livelihood, and a good percentage of them are females of an impressionable age, it was felt that your presence would be detrimental to our survival. And besides that, the college also takes a dim view of its lecturers giving marks for sexual favours rather than for academic excellence.' He took a deep breath. 'There, Owen, does that suit you better?'

Owen grinned at him. 'It'll do. It certainly beats the bullshit you were giving out earlier. But none of what you say has been proven. It's all hearsay.'

Kemp looked at the blinking cursor. 'You know how rumours spread, what damage they can do. And people here were aware of your . . . er . . . relationship with Ms Chappel. Even at the time.'

'You did nothing then. Why now?'

'Circumstances have changed.'

'So I lost my job because circumstances have changed?'

'No smoke without fire.'

'You smug bastard.'

'Goodbye, Owen.' Kemp stood up. He didn't hold out his hand.

Michelle, again. Owen felt like picking up the computer monitor and hurling it through the window, then punching Kemp on the nose. But he restrained himself. His teaching career was over here, perhaps everywhere. People would know about him wherever he applied. The academic community is small enough; word gets around quickly.

Instead of hitting Kemp, Owen contented himself with slamming the door. Striding down the corridor, he almost bumped into Chris Lorimer.

'Owen.' Chris had a pile of essays under his arm and seemed to be struggling to hold onto them. 'I . . . it's . . .'

'Kemp won't take me back.'

'Hmm . . . well. I suppose you can understand his position.' Lorimer shifted from one foot to the other as if he desperately wanted to go to the toilet.

'Can you? Look, Chris, it's noon, the sun's over the yard-arm, as they used to say, and I'm a bit cheesed off. It's been a bad day, so far. How about a pint and a spot of lunch over the road? My treat.'

Lorimer contorted to glance at his watch. 'I'd like to, Owen, I really would, but I have to dash.' And he really was dashing as he spoke, edging away down the corridor as if Owen had some infectious disease. 'Maybe some other time, perhaps?' he called over his shoulder, before disappearing round a corner.

Sure, Owen thought, some other time. Fuck you, too, Chris Lorimer. You and the horse you rode in on.

THREE

'Well, well, well,' said Banks, standing at the top of the stairs overlooking the open-plan ground floor. 'Speak of the devil. Just the fellow I've been wanting to see. I've been looking over your file. And guess who's turned eighteen since we last met?'

Spinks looked at him. 'Uh?'

'No more youth court.' Banks glanced towards Susan and raised an eyebrow.

'Taking and driving away, sir,' she said. 'Under the influence.'

'Influence of what, I wonder?' said Banks. 'And so early in the day.'

Spinks struggled, but Susan managed to hold onto him. 'Not to mention crashing it through the window of Henry's fish and chip shop on Elmet Street,' she said through gritted teeth.

Banks smiled and opened the door of the nearest interview room. 'Be my guest,' he said to Spinks, stretching an arm out through the open door. 'Take a pew.'

'I need a doctor,' Spinks moaned. 'The fucking steering was fucked. I hurt my head. I got whiplash. I could've been killed.'

'Shut up and sit down,' Banks said with enough authority that Spinks paused and obeyed. 'I suppose you'll be suing the owner next?'

Spinks licked his lips. 'Maybe I will.'

There was a small cut just above his right eye. It was nothing serious, but Banks knew that if they didn't get him medical attention they'd be breaking a PACE directive and Spinks would probably succeed in getting his case dismissed.

'See if you can get Dr Burns, will you, Susan?' Banks asked, indicating by a private gesture that she should take her time.

Susan nodded, straightened her dress and left.

'What are you on?' Banks asked.

Spinks looked away. 'I don't know what you mean.'

Banks grabbed Spinks's chin with one hand and held his head up, staring at the pinpoint pupils. 'Crack, is it, John? Or solvent? Maybe heroin?'

'I don't do drugs.'

'Like hell you don't. You know taking and driving away is an arrestable offence, don't you, John?'

Spinks said nothing.

'Do you know what that means?'

Spinks gave a lopsided grin. A little drool had formed at the side of his mouth. 'It means you can arrest me for it.' He giggled.

'Good,' said Banks, patting his shoulder gently. 'Very good, John. Now, you might not know this, but to put it nice and simply that also means we can detain you for up to twenty-four hours, longer if the superintendent authorizes it. Which he will. But wait a minute. Do you know what day it is, John?'

'What do you mean? Course I know. It's Friday.'

'That's right.' Banks looked at his watch. 'Pity for you, John. See, a day like this, the magistrates will all be on the golf course by now. And they don't sit on Saturday or Sunday, so you'll have to stay with us until Monday morning.'

'So what?'

'Your arrest also gives us powers of search, John. We don't need a warrant. That means there'll be coppers all over your mum's place, if there aren't already. Bound to turn up something. Your mum will love you for that, won't she?'

'She doesn't give a fuck.'

Banks turned the free chair around and sat with his arms resting on the back. 'Anyway,' he said, 'I'm not interested in petty stuff like car theft and drug abuse. You don't think a detective chief inspector concerns himself with run-of-the-mill stuff like that, do you?'

Spinks sniffed. 'Can't say I care one way or another.'

'No. Course not. I don't suppose you do. Well, I'm not doing this by the book, John. I want you to know that. Like I said, I'm not really interested in some gormless pill-popping pillock who steals a car and can't even drive it straight.'

Spinks bristled. 'I can fucking drive! I told you, the steering was fucked. Fucking owner ought to be locked up.'

'Know what they say about a poor workman, John? He always blames his tools.'

'Fuck off.'

'Look, I'm getting sick and tired of your severely limited vocabulary. Know what I think we ought to do with people like you instead of community service or jail? I think we ought to have compulsory education for gobshites like you who spent so much time blitzed on model airplane glue that they never set foot in school more than a couple of weeks a year. Know what I'd do? I'd make you read the dictionary, for a start. At least ten new words a day. And spelling tests. Every morning, first thing after slopping out. A dozen lashes for every word you get wrong. Literature, too. Lots of it. Austen, Hardy, Dickens, Trollope, George Eliot. Long books. Poetry, as well – Wordsworth, Shelley, Dryden, Milton. And Shakespeare, John. Tons and tons of

Shakespeare. Memorizing poems and long, lovely speeches. Analysing the imagery in *Macbeth* and *Othello*. Sound like fun?'

'I'd rather be in fucking jail.'

Bank sighed. 'You will be, John. You will be. It's just a fantasy of mine. Now I'd like you to travel back in time through that addled, worm-eaten brain of yours. I'd like you, if you can negotiate through that lump of Swiss cheese you call a mind, to go back to last summer. Specifically, to last August. Can you do that?'

Spinks frowned. 'Is this about that bird what got snuffed?'

'Yes,' said Banks. 'This, as you so eloquently put it, is "about that bird what got snuffed." Remember her name, John? Deborah Harrison.'

'That's right. Yeah, Debbie.'

'Good. Now something happened, didn't it? Something nasty?'

'Don't know what you mean.'

'Her mother and her godfather warned you off, didn't they?'

'Oh, right. Stuck-up motherfuckers. Look, what's this got to do with—'

'I told you, John. I'm not doing this by the book. This is unofficial, off the record. Okay?'

Spinks nodded, a look of suspicion forming in his glazed eyes.

'One day you went around to ask Lady Sylvie Harrison to give you money to leave her daughter alone. Right?'

'So? There's no law against it. They'd got plenty. I didn't see why I shouldn't get some compensation. Bird wasn't much of a fuck, really. More like a sack of potatoes. But—'

Banks gripped the back of the chair so hard his knuckles turned white. 'Spare me your erotic memoirs, John,' he said. 'They might make me do something I'll regret. You might not realize it, but I'm exercising great restraint as it is.'

Spinks laughed. A little more drool dripped down his chin. Banks felt so much like clocking him one that he had to look away. 'Who was in the house that day?'

'What?'

'You heard. Who else was there as well as you?'

'Oh. Didn't I already tell you that? I seem to remember—'

'Humour me. Tell me again.'

'Right. There was Debbie's mother, the blonde bitch. And that stuck-up prick Clayton. Fucking snobs.'

'And Deborah wasn't there?'

'I already told you. No.' Spinks's head started to roll from side to side. The drugs, whatever they were, were wearing off. Either that or he had sustained more than superficial damage in the car crash. Just as well they had sent for Dr Burns.

'When you went to the house and found Michael Clayton there,' Banks asked, 'did you get the feeling that there was anything going on?'

Spinks closed his eyes. His head stopped lolling. 'Don't know what you mean.'

'Did you interrupt anything?'

'Interrupt?'

'Stop behaving like a parrot. Did you get the feeling there was anything going on between them?'

Spinks frowned and wiped the drool from his mouth with the back of his hand. His eyes opened again and seemed to keep shifting in and out of focus. 'Going on?' he repeated. 'You mean was he fucking her? You mean do I think Clayton was fucking the wicked witch?' He laughed out loud.

Banks waited patiently until he had stopped. 'Well,' he said. 'Do you?'

'You've got a dirty mind. Do you know that?'

'Do you?'

Spinks shrugged. 'Could've been, for all I know.'

'But you didn't notice anything special about them, the way they behaved towards one another?'

'No.'

'Were they both fully dressed?'

'Course they were.'

'Did they look dishevelled at all?'

'Come again. Dish what?'

'See what I mean about the need for compulsory education? It means messed up, ruffled, untidy.'

'Oh. No. I don't think so. Can't really remember, though.'

'Did Deborah ever say anything about them?'

He shook his head, stopped abruptly and opened his mouth as if to say something, then carried on shaking it. 'No.'

Banks leaned forward on the chair back. The two front legs raised off the floor. 'What were you going to tell me, John?'

'Nothing. She never said nothing.' He coughed and a mouthful of yellow vomit dribbled down his chin onto his T-shirt. The smell was terrible: booze, cheese-and-onion crisps and tacos. Banks stood up and stepped back.

At that moment, there was a knock on the door and Susan Gay came in, followed by Dr Burns, the police surgeon, whose surgery was just across the market square.

'Sorry, sir,' Susan said, 'but the doctor's here.'

'Right,' said Banks, shaking hands with Burns. 'He's all yours. I've had enough. Take good care of him, Nick. I might want to talk to him again.'

And as he walked back to his own office, he had the strange feeling that not only had Spinks been holding back, hiding something, but that he, himself, hadn't even been asking the right questions. Something was eluding him, and he knew from experience that it would drive him around the bend until he thought of it.

16

ONE

Banks took a deep breath outside Michael Clayton's house on Saturday morning, then he got out of his car and walked up the garden path. If Chief Constable Riddle found out about this, Banks's life probably wouldn't be worth living.

Clayton's house wasn't quite as large as the Harrisons', but it was an impressive enough construction, solidly built of redbrick and sandstone, detached and surrounded by an unkempt garden. The lawn looked as if it hadn't been trimmed yet this year, and weeds choked the flower-beds.

After he rang the doorbell the first time, Banks heard nothing but silence and began to suspect that Clayton was out. He tried again. About thirty seconds later, just as he was about to head off down the path, the door opened and Clayton stuck his head out.

'Yes, what is it?' he asked crossly. 'Oh, it's you, Chief Inspector.' He moved aside and opened the door fully. 'You'd better come in. Sorry about the mess.'

Banks followed him through a door from the hallway into a room full of computer equipment. At least three computers, state-of-the-art, by the look of them, sat on their desks, two of them displaying similar graphic images. These were incomprehensible to Banks, and looked like a cross between circuit diagrams and the molecular structures he remembered from school chemistry. They were all multi-coloured, and some of the nodes and pathways between them flashed, different on each screen. The third VDU showed a deck of cards set out in what Banks recognized as the solitaire 'pyramid' fashion.

'I always have a game going when I'm working,' Clayton said, smiling. 'It helps me concentrate. Don't ask me why.'

The floor was a mass of snaking cables and Banks trod carefully not to trip over any of them.

He could almost feel the room vibrating with the electrical hum running through them.

Clayton cleared a stack of computer magazines from a hardbacked chair. Banks almost asked him what the diagrams on the screens were, but he knew that either Clayton wouldn't tell him or he wouldn't understand anyway. Best not start off looking like an ignoramus.

Sheets of paper hissed as they slid out of a laser printer. One of the computers started to emit a loud, pulsating beep. Clayton excused himself while he went over and hit a few keys.

'Diagnostic programmes,' he said when he got back.

Well, that was clear enough, Banks thought. Even he knew what diagnostic programmes were. Though what they were supposed to diagnose was another matter entirely.

'Computers,' Clayton went on. 'They've changed the world, Chief Inspector. Nothing is the same as when you and I were children. And they're still changing it. Believe me, in the not-too-distant future, nothing will be the same as it is now. But I don't suppose you came here to talk technology with me, did you? Are you coming to apologize?'

'What for?'

'For letting the bastard who killed Deborah slip through the cracks. I was there, you know, in court with Geoff and Sylvie. They're devastated. And I've hardly been able to concentrate on my work since then. How could you let it happen?'

Banks shrugged. 'I've seen it happen more often than you have. We're not living in a perfect world.'

'You can say that again. I don't know what the procedure is now, but if I can help in any way . . .' Clayton scratched his smooth chin. 'Look, I've heard one or two disturbing rumours about this Pierce fellow beating up young girls and raping them. Is that true?'

'I can't comment on that,' said Banks.

'But there *is* some evidence that wasn't admissible, isn't there? Something that might have got him convicted if it had been heard in the trial?'

'The judge rules on matters of law,' Banks said. 'So there might be a strong basis for the appeal. That's really all I can tell you at the moment.'

Clayton paused and glanced quickly around at the computer screens. 'Well, Chief Inspector, thank you for bringing me up to date. Can I help in any way?'

Banks leaned forward. 'As a matter of fact, there is something. One of the results of the court's decision is that we have decided to reopen the case and examine some of the other angles again.'

Clayton frowned. 'I don't understand. Did you get the right man or didn't you?'

'The jury thinks we didn't.'

'But what about *you*. You know more about him than you're ever allowed to tell the jury. What do *you* think?'

Banks was getting sick of that question. Now he knew

what defence barristers felt when people kept asking them how they could possibly defend people they knew must be guilty. 'I didn't see him do it,' he said, 'so there's always room for doubt.'

Clayton snorted. 'So just because the justice system fouls up yet again, you're going to run around reopening old wounds.'

'I hoped you might look at it as co-operation,' Banks said.

'About what?'

'John Spinks, for a start.'

'That moron who caused all the trouble last summer?'

'That's the one.'

'Sylvie told you about him?'

'Yes. And I talked to him again yesterday.'

'You surely don't think *he* could have done it?'

'It's possible,' Banks said.

'He doesn't have either the guts or the brains.'

'Since when did it take brains to murder someone? Outside a detective novel, that is.'

'It takes brains to do it and get away with it.'

'Brains or luck.'

Clayton shrugged. 'No point in arguing. Look at it that way and anything's possible. He was certainly angry at her about what happened. I imagine anger is a familiar enough part of his limited emotional range. I suppose he could have lain in wait for her and lost his temper.'

'Did he know she attended the chess club?'

'How should I know?'

'Somehow, I doubt it,' said Banks. 'Not if he hadn't been seeing her *after* term started. Anyway, that's beside the point. As you say, he would know the route she took and he could have simply lain in wait in the foggy graveyard ever since school came out. Now, as I understand it, Spinks came to Sir Geoffrey's house to extort money from Lady Sylvie Harrison, is that right?'

'Yes.'

'And you hit him.'

'No more than a little cuff. You're not going to arrest me for assault and battery are you?'

Banks smiled. 'No. Believe me, sir, I've felt like doing the same thing myself on more than one occasion.'

'Then you understand my feelings about him.'

'Entirely. You hit him, and later you paid him off?'

'Yes. It seemed the easiest way.'

'How much did you give him?'

'A hundred pounds.'

'That was all?'

'Yes.'

'He didn't come back for more?'

'No.'

'Why?'

Clayton leaned forward and rested his hands on his knees. 'Because I told him that if he did, I would certainly inform Sir Geoffrey, who would at the very least have him horsewhipped, no matter what vile threats he made.' Clayton frowned and sat back. 'You say you talked to Spinks again? Why? Was this in connection with reopening the case?'

'Not really. No, it was a coincidence. He stole a car and crashed it.'

'Pity he didn't break his neck. Serves the little bastard right.'

'I suppose so,' Banks said. He paused, feeling his heartbeat speed up. 'What were you doing there when Spinks came?'

'What do you mean?'

'I got the impression that you're there an awful lot. Especially when Sir Geoffrey is out and his wife is at home.'

Clayton's mouth dropped open and he started shaking his head very slowly. 'My God, you've got a mind like a sewer,' he said. 'I don't believe it. On the basis of what you're suggesting . . .' He put his fingertips to his temple. 'Let me get this clear . . . Your theory is that Sylvie and I were having a torrid affair and Deborah found out and threatened to tell her father. Instead of allowing that to happen, I waited for Deborah, my own goddaughter, in the graveyard after her school chess club one day and strangled her. Is that your theory?'

'I hadn't thought it out that far,' Banks said. 'I was just trying to get the lie of the land, that's all. But I must admit you've got a way of reducing things to their essentials. Thank you for putting it so succinctly.'

Clayton stood up. His face was red. 'This is insane, Banks. You're clutching at straws. I think you'd better leave now.'

'I was just on my way. But I do have one more question.'

Clayton gritted his teeth. 'Very well.'

'About the kind of work HarClay Industries does. Some of it is highly secret, isn't it, MoD stuff?'

'Yes. So?'

'Is there any chance that Deborah might have stumbled across something she shouldn't have, say in her father's papers?'

Clayton shook his head. 'First you practically accuse me of murder, then you bring up all this James Bond stuff. No, Chief Inspector, Deborah *couldn't* have stumbled across any government secrets that got her killed. I think you already had the killer and you let him get off. Now you're casting about wildly for some sort of scapegoat.'

Banks stood up to leave. 'Maybe,' he admitted.

'And for your information,' Clayton went on, 'I've known Geoff and Sylvie for years. I was there when they met. I was at university with Geoff. I have never had, nor am I having now, any other sort of relationship with Sylvie Harrison than that of a close friend. Am I making myself clear?'

Banks turned and met his gaze. 'Perfectly.'

'And just for this one time I'm willing to forget that this meeting ever took place. But if you ever dare come here again with your—'

Banks held his hand up. 'I get the message, sir. If I ask any more questions, you'll go tell the chief constable. Fair enough.'

When Banks got outside and back into his car, his hands were shaking as he lit his first cigarette of the day.

TWO

Rebecca Charters hadn't known what to do at first when Owen Pierce surprised her in the garden on Thursday. She had been scared, as she told Chief Inspector Banks, and her instinct had been to run inside, bolt the door and put the chain on. He hadn't tried anything after that, even though he must have known she was alone in the house, but she had looked through the window and watched him stand by the garden gate for a moment before walking off. Her heart had beat fast.

After Banks had left, she rationalized her fear away.

Pierce hadn't *done* anything, after all, or even said or threatened anything. Perhaps she was overreacting. Pierce might not be guilty of anything. Certainly Inspector Banks had his doubts, and his idea of Deborah having *arranged* to meet the person who ultimately turned out to be her murderer made sense.

But when Owen Pierce came and knocked at her door on Saturday afternoon, while Daniel was out visiting the terminally ill patients in Eastvale General Infirmary, she felt afraid all over again.

Because it was a warm day and she liked the way the scents of the flowers drifted into the living-room, Rebecca had opened the bay window. Before moving to shut it and lock it, she shouted, 'Go away or I'll call the police.'

'Please,' he said. 'Please listen to me. I'm not going to hurt you. I've never hurt anyone. I just want to talk to you.'

She left the window open but put her hands on top of the frame, ready to slam it down if he made any suspicious moves. 'What about?' she asked.

'Just talk, that's all. Please. I need someone to talk to.'

There was something in his tone that touched Rebecca, but not enough to open the door to him.

'Why me?' she asked. 'You don't even know me.'

'But I know *about* you. I know what you've been through. You're the vicar's wife. I've read about the accusations and everything. I just felt . . . I'm not trying to say I'm especially religious or anything. I don't want to lie to you about that. Please, will you just let me come in and talk? Will someone just treat me like a human being. Please.'

Rebecca could see tears in his eyes. She still didn't know why he had come. She couldn't let him in, but nor did she feel she could turn him away. After all, she was a Christian, *and* a minister's wife.

'Stay there,' she said. 'I'll come out.' She would feel safer outside in the garden, with the constant flow of people on the river path.

Why was she doing it? she asked herself as she went outside. She knew part of the answer. Not too long ago, she had allowed herself to doubt Daniel, her own husband. Instead of offering him her unqualified support and devotion, she had turned to liquor and carnality to escape her obligations. More than that. It wasn't just her obligations she was running away from, but the horrible realization that she *had* doubted Daniel, she *had* believed him guilty. And now, here was this pathetic man, found not guilty by a jury and presumed guilty by the rest of the world. Call it pity, compassion, Christian charity or mere folly, but she *couldn't* turn him away.

Daniel had put out a couple of folding chairs in the garden. When the weather was nice, he liked to sit and watch the river as he composed his sermon. There was also a beautiful view of St Mary's Hill, the fine old houses above the gentle slope of grass and trees. Here I am, Rebecca thought, sitting in the garden with a possible murderer on a warm June afternoon.

'I still don't understand why you're here,' she said.

'I told you. I want – I *need* – a friend. Or friends. Everywhere I go people turn their backs. I'm lonely and I'm scared. I heard somewhere about what your husband's been going through. But you have obviously stood by him however hard it's been. I've got nobody.'

Rebecca almost laughed out loud at the irony of it. Instead she said, 'Yes. It has been hard. But the court found you innocent. You're free now.'

Owen sniffed. 'Not innocent. Just *not guilty* as charged. It's a different thing. Anyway, it doesn't matter. I'm not really free. Everyone believes I'm guilty.'

'Are you?'

'Will you believe me if I promise to answer truthfully?'

Rebecca felt her heart speed up. It was such a simple question, but it seemed to her that so much depended on it. Not just Owen Pierce, here and now, but her whole moral reality, her sense of trust and, even, her faith itself. She became aware of Pierce looking at her and realized that she had probably been holding her breath. Finally, she let it out and took the leap.

'Yes,' she said. 'I'll believe you.'

Pierce looked her in the eye. 'No,' he said. 'No, I didn't do it.'

Somehow, Rebecca felt great relief. 'What can we do for you?' she asked.

Almost as if he didn't believe his good fortune, Pierce remained speechless for a while. His eyes filled with tears and Rebecca felt, for a moment, like taking his hand. But she didn't.

Finally, in a cracking voice, he said, 'I need help. I have to put my life back together again and I can't do it alone.' As he spoke, he regained his composure and wiped the tears away briskly. 'It may seem cold, calculated,' he said, 'but it isn't. When I found out who you were, I remembered you from court and I was drawn to you because I thought you'd understand, you know, about being thought guilty when you're innocent, about all the hypocrisy they talk about truth and justice. I'm sure your husband didn't do what he's been accused of. No more than I did.'

'But I thought you would be angry with us. My husband gave evidence against you.'

Owen shook his head. 'All he did was tell the truth. It didn't make any difference to the case. It *was* me on the bridge. I never denied that. And it must have been terrible for you finding the body. No, I hold nothing against you or your husband. Look, I have no friends, Mrs Charters. Everyone's deserted me. I have no close family. Even strangers treat me like some sort of monster if they recognize me. I need support, public support. I need it to be seen that decent, intelligent people don't think I'm a monster. I need you on my side. You and your husband.'

'You might have come to the wrong place,' Rebecca said. 'You wouldn't want to join a losing cause. Remember, my husband is still under suspicion.'

'Yes, but he has carried on in the face of it all. And I know you believe in him. You've stuck by him. So have a lot of other members of the congregation. I'm sure. Don't you see, Mrs Charters, we're both victims, your husband and I?'

Rebecca thought for a moment, remembering the hypocrisy of some parishioners. 'All right, then,' she said. 'I can't guarantee anything, but I'll talk to my husband.'

'Thank you,' breathed Owen.

'But will you do one thing for me?'

'Of course.'

'Will you come to church tomorrow morning? I'm not trying to convert you or anything, but it would be good if you could be *seen* there. The people who still come to St Mary's have, for the most part, stuck up for Daniel and believed in his innocence, as you say. If we take you into the congregation, they might do the same for you. I know it might sound hypocritical, the way people judge by appearances, but they do, you know, and perhaps if . . . Why are you laughing?'

'I'm sorry, Mrs Charters, I really am. I just can't help it. Of course I'll come to church. Believe me, it seems a very small price to pay.'

THREE

It was just after two o'clock in the morning and Banks kept waking up from disturbing dreams. He and Sandra had been out to a folk night in the Dog and Gun, in Helmthorpe, with some old friends, Harriet Slade and her husband, David. The star of the evening was Penny Cartwright, a local singer who had given up fame and fortune to settle back in Helmthorpe a few years ago. Banks had first met her while investigating the murder of Harold Steadman, a local historian, and he had seen her once or twice in the intervening years. They chatted amicably enough when they met, but there was always a tension between them, and Banks was glad when the chitchat was over.

Her singing was something to be relished, though. Alto, husky on the low notes but pure and clear in the higher range, her voice also carried the controlled emotion of a survivor. She sang a mix of traditional and contemporary – from Anon to Zimmerman – and her version of the latter's 'I Dreamed I Saw St Augustine' had made Banks's spine tingle and his eyes prickle with tears.

But now, after a little too much port and Stilton back at Harriet and David's, Banks was suffering the consequences. He had often thought that the blue bits in Stilton, being mould, had mild hallucinogenic properties and actually gave rise to restless dreams. It didn't matter that he hadn't yet found a scientist to agree with him; he was sure of it. Because every time he ate Stilton, it happened.

These weren't satisfying dreams, the kind you need to make you feel you've had a good night's sleep, but abrupt and disturbing transformations just below the threshold of consciousness: computer games turned into reality; cars crashed through monitor screens; and the ghost of a young woman walked through a foggy graveyard. In one, he had terminal cancer and couldn't remember what his children looked like. All the while, voices whispered about demon lovers, and crows picked bodies clean to the bone.

Thus Banks was not altogether upset when the phone rang. Puzzled, but relieved in a way to be rescued from the pit of dreams. At the same time, apprehension gripped his chest when he turned over and picked up the receiver. Sandra stirred beside him and he tried to keep his voice down.

'Sir?'

'Yes,' Banks mumbled. It was a woman's voice.

'This is DC Gay, sir. I'm calling from the station.'

'What are you doing there? What's happened?'

'I'm sorry to bother you, sir, but it looks like there's been another one.'

'Another what?'

'Another girl disappeared, sir. Name's Ellen Gilchrist. She went to a school dance at Eastvale Comprehensive tonight and never arrived home. Her mum and dad are climbing up the walls.'

Banks sat up and swung his legs from under the covers. Sandra turned over. 'Where are they?' he asked.

'They're here, sir, at the station. I couldn't keep them away. I said we're doing all we can, but . . .'

'Have you called her friends, boyfriends?'

'Yes, sir. That's all been done. Everyone her mum and

dad and her friends from the dance could think of. We've woken up half the town already. As far as I can gather, she left the dance alone just after eleven o'clock. Had a headache. Her parents only live on the Leaview Estate, so it's not more than a quarter of a mile down King Street. They got worried when she hadn't turned up by midnight, her curfew. Called us at twelve-thirty. Sir?'

'Yes?'

'They said normally they'd have given her till one, more likely, then given her a good talking to and packed her off to bed. But they said they'd heard about that killer who got off. Owen Pierce. That's why they called us so soon.'

Sitting on the edge of the bed, Banks rubbed his eyes, trying once and for all to rid himself of the Stilton dreams. He sighed. From one nightmare to another. 'All right,' he said. 'Get someone to put on a strong pot of coffee, will you, Susan? I'll be right over.'

17

ONE

An early rambler from Middlesbrough set off from a bed and breakfast in Skield and found the girl's body tucked away in a fold of Witch Fell, above the village, at eight o'clock on Sunday morning. An hour later, the detectives from Eastvale and the Scene-of-Crime Officers began to dribble in, closely followed by Dr Glendenning, who was out of breath by the time he had climbed up to where the body was.

Banks stood at the edge of the terrace, which he suspected was a lynchet, an ancient Anglian ploughing strip levelled on a hillside. Such lyncheted hills went up in a series of steps, of which this was the first. The strip was about ten yards wide and dipped a little in the middle.

The girl's body lay spread-eagled in the central depression, as if cupped in the petals of a flower. The little meadow was full of buttercups and daisies; flies and more delicate winged insects buzzed in the air, some pausing to light on the girl's pale, unyielding skin for a moment.

Several buttercups and daisies had been twined in her long blonde hair, which lay spread out on the bright green grass around her head like the halo in a Russian icon. Her blouse had been torn open and her bra pulled up, revealing small, pale breasts, and her short skirt was up around her thighs, her discarded panties on the grass

beside her. As Banks got closer, he noticed the discolouration around her neck, and the open shoulder-bag
by her arm, some of its contents spilled on the grass: lipstick, a purse, compact, nail-file, chewing gum, perfume,
keys, address book, earrings, hairbrush.

The similarities to the Deborah Harrison scene were too
close to be ignored. And Banks had just convinced himself
that Deborah had been murdered by someone she knew
for some sort of logical reason. Now it looked as if they
were dealing with a sexual psychopath – one who had
murdered two young girls in the area.

Banks stood back as Peter Darby took photographs and
then watched Dr Glendenning perform the on-scene
examination. By then, Superintendent Gristhorpe had
arrived and Jimmy Riddle was rumoured to be pacing at
the bottom of the hill trying to decide whether to attempt
the short climb or wait until the others came down to him.

Banks sniffed the air. It was another fine morning. A
couple of sheep stood facing the drystone wall as if just
wishing it would all go away. Well, it wouldn't, Banks
knew. No more than the tightness in his gut, which felt
like a clenched fist, would go away before tomorrow.

'Well?' he asked, after the doctor had finished his
examination.

'As we're not in court, laddie,' said Glendenning, with
a crooked grin, 'I can tell you that she probably died
between ten o'clock last night and one or two o'clock in
the morning.'

'Do you think she was killed here?'

'Looks like it from the lividity on her back and thighs.'

'So he brought her here alive all the way from
Eastvale?'

Banks made a mental calculation. The girl, Ellen

Gilchrist, had disappeared on her way home shortly after eleven o'clock last night. By car, it was about thirty miles from Eastvale to Skield, but some of that journey was on bad moorland roads where you couldn't drive very fast, especially at night. For one thing, the sheep were inclined to wander, and as anyone it has happened to will tell you, running into a sheep on a dark road is a very nasty experience indeed. Especially for the sheep.

It would probably have taken the killer over an hour, Banks estimated, particularly if he took an indirect route to avoid being seen. Why bother? Why not just dump her in Eastvale somewhere? Was location important to him, part of his profile? Did he hope the body would remain undiscovered for longer here? Not much hope of that, Banks thought. Skield and Witch Fell were popular spots for ramblers, especially with the good weather.

'There's a nasty gash behind her left ear,' Glendenning said, 'which means she was probably unconscious when he brought her here, before he strangled her. It looks like it could have been caused by a hammer or some such heavy object. Cause of death, off the record, of course, is ligature strangulation, just like the last one. Shoulder-bag strap this time, instead of a satchel.'

'And the bag's open, also like last time,' Banks mused.

'Aye,' said Glendenning. 'Well, you can have the body sent to the mortuary now.' And he walked off.

Banks tried to run the scenario in his mind as if it were a film: girl leaves friends at end of School Lane, walks onto King Street, busy during tourist hours but quiet at night, apart from the odd pub or two. Some street-lamps, but not an especially well-lit area. Most kids are still at the dance, but Ellen's going home ahead of her curfew because she has a headache, or so her friend said. She walks alone down the hill towards the Leaview Estate, not more than ten minutes at the most. Car pulls up. Or is it already waiting down the road, lights turned off, knowing there's a school dance, hoping someone will be careless enough to walk home alone?

He's standing by the car, looking harmless enough. He can't believe his luck. Another blonde, just like Deborah Harrison, and about the same age. Or did he know who he wanted? Had he been watching her? Did he *know* her?

As she passes, he grabs her and drags her into the passenger seat before she knows what's happening. She tries to scream, perhaps, but he puts his hand over her mouth to muffle her. He knocks her out. Now she's in the passenger seat, unconscious, bleeding behind her ear. He straps her in with the safety belt and sets off. Maybe someone saw the car, someone else leaving the dance? He has to get her to an isolated spot before he's seen.

All the way to Skield, he savours what he's going to do to her. The anticipation is almost as thrilling as the act itself, maybe even more so. He anticipates it, and later he relives it, replays it over and over in his mind.

He parks off the road, out of the way, car hidden behind a clump of trees, perhaps, and drags her up the hillside. It's not very far or very steep, the first lynchet, but he's sweating with the effort, and maybe she's coming round now, trying to struggle, beginning to realize that something terrible is about to happen to her. They get to the lynchet, and he lays her down on the grass and does . . . whatever he does.

'Alan?'

'What? Oh, sorry, sir. Lost in thought.'

Superintendent Gristhorpe and DC Gay had come to stand beside him as uniformed officers searched the area.

'We'd better get back to the station and get things moving,' said Gristhorpe. 'We can start by questioning all the friends who were at the dance with her again, and then do a house-to-house along King Street, check out the pubs, too. I'll get someone to ask around Skield as well. You never know. Someone might have been suffering from insomnia.'

'Sir?'

Both Banks and Gristhorpe looked around to see PC Weaver, one of the searchers, approach with something hooked over the end of a pencil. When he got closer, Banks could see that it was one of those transparent plastic containers that 35mm films come in. Living with Sandra, he had seen plenty of those.

'Found this in the grass near the body, sir,' he said.

'Near the shoulder-bag?' Gristhorpe asked.

'No, sir, that's why I thought it was odd. It was on the other side of her, a couple of yards away. Do you think it could be the killer's?'

'It could be anyone's, lad,' Gristhorpe said. 'A tourist's, maybe. But we'd better check it for prints as quickly as we can.' He turned to Banks. 'Maybe we've got one who likes to photograph his victims?'

'Possible,' Banks agreed. 'And we already know one keen amateur photographer, don't we? I'll get Vic Manson on it right away. He should be able to do a comparison before the morning's over.'

Just at that moment, a red bald head, shiny with perspiration, appeared over the rim of the meadow. 'What's going on?' grunted Chief Constable Riddle.

'Oh, we've just finished here, sir,' said Banks, smiling cheekily as he walked past Riddle and headed down the slope.

TWO

The church was hot and smelled like dust burning on the element of an electric fire. Owen remembered hearing somewhere that most household dust was just dead skin. Which meant the church smelled like dead bits of people burning. Hell? All flesh is grass. The heaps of dead, dry grass burning in allotments, or autumn stubble burning in the country fields, vast, rolling carpets of fire spread out in the distance, palls of smoke hanging and twisting in the still twilight air.

Owen took off his jacket and loosened his tie. He had never been comfortable in churches. His parents were both dyed-in-the-wool atheists, and the only times he had really been in church were for weddings and funerals. So he always wore a suit and tie.

Of course, it was all right when you were a tourist checking out the Saxon fonts and Gothic arches, but a different story altogether when there was a vicar up front prattling on about loving thy neighbour. Owen had always distrusted overly churchy types before, feeling that the church offered a public aura of respectability to many who pursued their perversions in private. But the vicar in this case was Daniel Charters, now one of the few allies Owen had in the entire world.

Today it was the hoary old chestnut about how you get nothing but bad news in the papers and how that can make you cynical about the world, but really there are wonders and miracles going on all around you all the time.

That morning, Owen could certainly relate to the first part of the sermon, if not the uplifting bit. Just before he had set off for church, he had screwed up the *News of the World* in a ball and tossed it across the room.

Judging by the looks he got when he walked into St Mary's, and by the way so many members of the congregation leaned towards one another and whispered behind cupped hands, even the upmarket clientele of St Mary's had had a butcher's at the *News of the World* over their cappuccino and croissants.

And there it was, blazoned across the front page in thick black letters: **THE STORY THEY COULDN'T TELL IN COURT**. Obviously Michelle's journalist friend had probed her thoroughly. There was reference to Owen's *liking to take photographs*, phrased in such a way that it sounded downright sinister, and a mention of his love of *kinky positions*. He also, it appeared, liked his sex rough and, as far as partners were concerned, the younger the better. Michelle came out of it sounding more like a victim than a willing lover. Which, Owen supposed, was the intention.

There was also an old, slightly blurred, photograph of the two of them and a scrap of a letter Owen had written Michelle once when he was away at a conference. The letter was a perfectly innocuous can't-wait-to-see-you-again sort of thing, but in this context, of course, it took on a far more disturbing aspect.

He recalled the day the photograph was taken. Shortly after Michelle had moved in with him, they had taken a holiday in Dorset, visiting various sites associated with Thomas Hardy's novels. In the small graveyard at Stinsford, where Hardy's heart was buried, they had asked an American tourist to take a photograph of them with Owen's camera. It turned out a little blurred because the tourist hadn't quite mastered the art of manual focusing.

Somehow, seeing the photograph and handwriting

reproduced in a Sunday tabloid angered Owen even more than the innuendos in the article. Michelle had obviously handed them over to the reporter. It was a violation, a deeper betrayal even than what she said about him. He was quickly beginning to wish that he *had* killed Michelle.

The whole article screamed out his guilt, of course, protested a miscarriage of justice, though the writer never said as much, not in so many words. Mostly, he just posed questions. Owen wondered if he should consider suing for libel. They were clever, though, these newspaper editors; they vetted everything before they printed it; they could afford a team of lawyers and they had the money put aside to finance large law suits. Still, it was worth considering.

The pew in front of Owen creaked and brought him back to the present. He realized he was sweating, *really* sweating, and beginning to feel dizzy and nauseated, too. Churches weren't supposed to be this hot. He hoped it wouldn't go on much longer; he especially hoped that Daniel wouldn't say anything about him.

They sang a hymn he remembered hearing once at a wedding, then there were more readings, prayers. It seemed to be going on forever. Owen wanted to go to the toilet now, too, and he shifted uncomfortably in his seat.

One of the readers mentioned seeing something 'as in a mirror, dimly' and it took Owen a moment or two to realize this was the approved modern version of 'through a glass darkly,' which he thought pretty much described his life. How could they, the English teacher in him wondered, utterly destroy one of the most resonant lines in the Bible, even if people did have trouble understanding what it meant? Since when had religion been about clear, literal, logical meaning anyway?

Finally, it was over. People relaxed, stood, chatted, ambled towards the doors. Many of them glanced at him as they passed. One or two managed brief, flickering smiles. Some pointedly turned away, and others whispered to one another.

Owen waited until most of them had gone. It had cooled down a little now, with the doors open and most people gone home. He still needed to go to the toilet, but not so urgently; he could wait now until he got to the vicarage. That was the plan: tea at the vicarage. He could hardly believe it.

When there were only one or two stragglers left, Owen got up and walked to the door. Daniel and Rebecca stood there chatting with a parishioner. Rebecca put her hand on his arm to stop him going immediately outside, and smiled. Daniel shook his hand and introduced him to the old woman. She looked down at her sensible shoes, muttered some greeting or other, and scurried off. This would obviously take time.

'Well,' said Daniel, taking out a handkerchief and wiping his moist brow. 'I suppose we should be grateful Sir Geoffrey and his wife weren't here.'

Owen hadn't even thought of that. If he had considered the mere possibility of bumping into Deborah Harrison's parents, he wouldn't have gone near the place.

Daniel obviously saw the alarm in Owen's expression because he reached out and touched his shoulder. 'I'm sorry,' he said. 'It was insensitive of me to say that. It's just that they used to attend. Anyway, come on, let's go.'

Owen walked outside with Daniel and Rebecca, pleased to be in the breeze again and glad to know he wasn't entirely alone against the world. Then he saw four policemen hurrying down the tarmac path from the North

Market Street gate. He told himself to run, but like Daniel and Rebecca, he simply froze to the spot.

THREE

'So, we meet again, Owen,' said Banks later that Sunday in an interview room at Eastvale Divisional Headquarters. 'Nice of you to assist us with our enquiries.'

Pierce shrugged. 'I don't think I have a lot of choice. Just for the record, I'm innocent this time, too. But I don't suppose that matters to you, does it? You won't believe me if it's not what you want to hear. You didn't last time.'

Very little light filtered through the barred, grimy window and the bare bulb hanging from the ceiling was only thirty watts. There were three people in the room: Banks, Susan Gay and Owen Pierce.

One of the public-spirited parishioners at St Mary's had heard about the Ellen Gilchrist murder on the news driving home after the morning service, and he had wasted no time in using his carphone to inform the police that the man they wanted had been at St Mary's Church that very morning, and might still be there if they hurried. They did. And he was.

In the distance, Banks could hear the mob chanting and shouting slogans outside the station. They were after Pierce's blood. Word had leaked out that he had been taken in for questioning over the Ellen Gilchrist murder, and the public were very quick when it came to adding two and two and coming up with whatever number they wanted.

People had started arriving shortly after the police delivered Pierce to the station, and the crowd had been growing ever since. Growing uglier, too. Banks feared he now had a lynch mob, and if Pierce took one step outside he'd be ripped to pieces. They would have to keep him in, if for no other reason than his own safety.

Already a few spots of blood dotted the front of his white shirt, a result of his 'resisting arrest,' according to the officers present; there was also a bruise forming just below his right eye.

Banks started the tape recorders, issued the caution and gave the details of the interview time and those present.

'They hit me, you know,' Pierce said, as soon as the tape was running. 'The policemen who brought me here. As soon as they got me alone in the car they hit me. You can see the blood on my shirt.'

'Do you want to press charges?'

'No. What good would it do? I just want you to know, that's all. I just want it on record.'

'All right. Last night, Owen, about eleven o'clock, where were you?'

'At home watching television.'

'What were you watching?'

'An old film on BBC.'

'What film?'

'*Educating Rita.*'

'What time did it start?'

'About half past ten.'

'Until?'

'I don't know. I was tired. I fell asleep before the end.'

'Do you usually do that? Start watching something and leave before the end?'

'If I'm tired. As a matter of fact I fell asleep on the sofa, in front of the television. When I woke up there was nothing on the screen but snow.'

'You didn't check the time?'

'No. Why should I? I wasn't going anywhere. It must have been after two, though. The BBC usually closes down then.'

His voice was flat, Banks noticed, responses automatic, almost as if he didn't care what happened. But still the light burned deep in his eyes. Innocence? Or madness?

'You see, Owen,' Banks went on steadily, 'there was another young girl killed last night. A seventeen-year-old schoolgirl from Eastvale Comprehensive. It's almost certain she was killed by the same person who killed Deborah Harrison – same method, same ritual elements – and we think you are that person.'

'Ridiculous. I was watching television.'

'Alone?'

'I'm always alone these days. You've seen to that.'

'So, can you see our problem, Owen? You were at home, alone, watching an old film on television. Anyone could say that.'

'But I'm not just anyone, am I?'

'How's the photography going, Owen?'

'What?'

'You're a keen photographer, aren't you? I was just asking how it was going.'

'It isn't. My house was broken into while I was on trial and the bastard who broke in killed my fish and smashed my cameras.'

Banks paused. 'I'm sorry to hear that.'

'I'll bet you are.'

Banks took out the plastic film container and held it up for Owen to see. 'Know what that is?'

'Of course I do.'

'Is it yours?'

'How would I know. There are millions of them around.'

'Thing is, Owen, we found this close to the body, and we found your fingerprints on it.'

Owen seemed to turn rigid, as if all his muscles tightened at once. The blood drained from his face. 'What?'

'We found your fingerprints on it, Owen. Can you explain to us how they got there.'

'I . . . I . . .' he started shaking his head slowly from side to side. 'It must be mine.'

'Speak up, Owen. What did you say?'

'It must be mine.'

'Any idea how it got out in the country near Skield?'

'Skield?'

'That's right.'

He shook his head. 'I went up there the other day for a walk.'

'We know,' said Susan Gay, speaking up for the first time. 'We asked around the pub and the village, and several people told us they saw you in the area on Friday. They recognized you.'

'Not surprising. Didn't you know, I'm notorious?'

'What were you doing, Owen?' Banks asked. 'Reconnoitring? Checking out the location? Do you do a lot of advance preparation? Is that part of the fun?'

'I don't know what you're talking about. I admit I was there. I went for a walk. But that's the only time I've been.'

'Is it, Owen? I'm trying to believe you, honest I am. I want to believe you. Ever since you got off, I've been telling people that maybe you didn't do it, maybe the jury was right. But this looks bad. You've disappointed me.'

'Well, excuse me.'

Banks shifted position. These hard chairs made his back ache. 'What is this thing you have for rummaging around in girls' handbags or satchels?'

'I don't know what you mean.'

'Do you like to take souvenirs?'

'Of what?'

'Something to focus on, help you replay what you did?'

'What did I do?'

'What did you do, Owen? You tell me how you get your thrills.'

Pierce said nothing. He seemed to shrink in his chair, his mouth clamped shut.

'You can tell me, Owen,' Banks went on. 'I want to know. I want to understand. But you have to help me. Do you masturbate afterwards, reliving what you've done? Or can't you contain yourself? Do you come in your trousers while you're strangling them? Help me, Owen. I want to know.'

Still Pierce kept quiet. Banks shifted again. The chair creaked.

'Why am I here?' Pierce asked.

'You know that.'

'It's because you think I did it before, isn't it?'

'Did you, Owen?'

'I got off.'

'Yes, you did.'

'So, I'd be a fool to admit it, wouldn't I? Even if I *had* done it.'

'Did you do it? Did you kill Deborah Harrison?'

'No.'

'Did you kill Ellen Gilchrist?'

'No.'

Banks sighed. 'You're not making it easy for us, Owen.'

'I'm telling you the truth.'

'I don't think so.'

'I am.'

'Owen, you're lying to us. You picked up Ellen Gilchrist on King Street last night. First you knocked her unconscious, then you drove her to Skield, where you dragged her a short distance up Witch Fell and strangled her with the strap of her handbag. Why won't you tell me about it?'

Pierce seemed agitated by the description of the crime, Banks noticed. Guilty conscience?

'What was it like, Owen?' he pressed on. 'Did she resist or did she just passively accept her fate. Know what I think? I think you're a coward, Owen. First you strangled her from behind, so you didn't have to look her in the eye. Then you lay her down on the grass and tore her clothes away. You imagined she was Michelle Chappel, didn't you, and you were getting your own back, giving her what for. She didn't have a chance. She was beyond resistance. But even then you couldn't get it up, could you? You're a coward, Owen. A coward and a pervert.'

'No!' The suddenness with which Pierce shot forward and slammed his fist into the desk startled Banks. He saw Susan Gay stand and make towards the door for help, but waved her down.

'Tell me, Owen,' he said. 'Tell me how it happened.'

Pierce flopped back in his chair again, as if the energy of his outburst had depleted his reserves. 'I want my lawyer,' he said tiredly. 'I want Wharton. I'm not saying another word. You people are destroying me. Get me Wharton. And either arrest me or I'm leaving right now.'

Banks turned to Susan and raised his eyebrows, then sighed. 'Very well, Owen,' he said. 'If that's the way you want it.'

18

ONE

By late Sunday evening, it was clear that the crowd wasn't going to storm the Bastille of Eastvale Divisional HQ, and by early Monday morning, there were only a few diehards left.

Banks turned his Walkman up loud as he passed the reporters by the front doors; Maria Callas drowned out all their questions. He said hello to Sergeant Rowe at the front desk, grabbed a coffee and headed upstairs. When he got to the CID offices, he took the earphones out and walked on tiptoe, listening for that snorting-bull sound that usually indicated the presence of Chief Constable Riddle.

Silence – except for Susan Gay's voice on the telephone, muffled behind her closed door.

Dr Glendenning's post-mortem report on Ellen Gilchrist was waiting in Banks's pigeon hole, along with a preliminary report from the forensic lab, who had put a rush on this one.

In the office, Banks closed his door and pulled up the venetian blinds on yet another fine day. Much more of this and life would start to get boring, he reflected. Still, there was a bit of cloud gathering to the south, and the weather forecast threatened rain, even the possibility of a thunderstorm.

He opened the window a couple of inches and watched

the shopkeepers open their doors and roll down their awnings against the sunshine. Then he stretched until he felt something crack pleasantly in his back, and sat down to study the report. He tuned the portable radio he kept in his office to Radio 4 and listened to *Today* as he read.

Glendenning had narrowed the time of death to between eleven and one, confirmed that the victim had been killed in the place where she was found, and matched the strap of her shoulder-bag to the weal in her throat.

The wound behind her ear was round and smooth, he also confirmed, about an inch in diameter, and most likely delivered by a metal hammer-head.

This time, unfortunately, there was no scratched tissue beneath her fingernails. In fact, her fingernails were so badly chewed they had been treated with some vile-tasting chemical to discourage her from biting them.

According to the lab, though there was no blood other than the deceased's at the scene, there were several hairs on her clothing that didn't come from her body. That was understandable, given that she had been at a crowded dance. What was damning, though, was that four of the hairs matched those found on Deborah Harrison's school blazer – the ones that had already also been tested against the sample Owen Pierce had given almost eight months ago.

Hairs could be dodgy evidence, as Pierce's trial had shown. Banks read through a fair bit of jargon about melanin and fragmented medullas, then considered the neutron activation analysis printout specifying the concentration of various elements in the hair, such as antimony, bromine, lanthanum, strontium and zinc.

The lab would need another sample of the suspect's

hair, the report said, because the ratios of these elements could have changed slightly since the last sample was taken, but even at this point, it was 4500 to one *against* the hair originating from anyone but Pierce.

Unfortunately, none of the hairs had follicular tissue adhering to their roots; in fact, there were no roots, so it was impossible to identify blood factors or carry out DNA analysis.

As in the Deborah Harrison murder, the swabs showed no signs of semen in the mouth, vagina or anus, and there was no other evidence of sexual activity.

But the hairs and the fingerprints Vic Manson had identified on the plastic film container would probably secure a conviction, Banks guessed. Pierce wasn't going to slip through the cracks this time.

In a way, Banks felt sad. He had almost convinced himself that Pierce had been an innocent victim of the system and that Deborah's killer was closer to home; now it looked as if he were wrong again.

He tuned in to Radio 3 – where *Composer of the Week* featured Gerald Finzi – and started making notes for the meeting he would soon be having with Stafford Oakes.

Things started to get noisy at around eleven-thirty, with Pierce on his way to court for his remand hearing, the phone ringing off the hook and reporters pressing their faces at every window in the building. Banks decided it was time to sneak out by the side exit and take an early lunch.

He opened the door and popped his head out to scan the corridor. Plenty of activity, but nobody was really paying him much attention. Instead of going the regular way, down to the front door, he tiptoed towards the fire exit, which came out on a narrow street opposite the Golden Grill, called Skinner's Yard.

He had hardly got to the end of the corridor, when he heard someone call out behind him. His heart lurched.

'Chief Inspector?'

Thank God it wasn't Jimmy Riddle. He turned. It was DI Barry Stott, and he was looking troubled. 'Barry. What is it? What can I do for you?'

'Can I have a word? In private.'

Banks glanced around to see if anyone else was watching them. No. The coast was clear. 'Of course,' he said, putting his hand on Stott's shoulder and guiding him towards the fire door. 'Let's go for a drink, shall we, and get away from the mêlée.'

TWO

It was a long time since Rebecca had been to talk to the angel, but that Monday she felt the need again. And this time she wasn't drunk.

As she turned off the tarmac path onto the gravel, she wondered how she could have been so wrong about Owen Pierce. She remembered how scared she was when she first saw him after his release, then how like a little boy lost he had been when he came to talk to her. When she had asked him the all-important question and he had said he would answer truthfully, she had believed him. Now it looked as if he had lied to her. How could she be sure of anything any more? Of anyone? Even Daniel?

The air around the Inchcliffe Mausoleum was warm and still, the only sounds the drone of insects and the occasional car along Kendal Road or North Market Street. The angel continued to gaze heavenward. Rebecca wished she knew what he could see there.

Sober, this time, and feeling a little self-conscious, she couldn't quite bring herself to speak out loud. But her thoughts flowed and shaped themselves as she stood there feeling silly. She wondered what the policeman, Chief Inspector Banks, would think of her.

The police had claimed that Owen Pierce had killed *another* girl. That meant they also believed he had killed Deborah Harrison. There could be no way out for him now, Rebecca thought, not with public feeling as strong as it was against him.

But he had visited her at the vicarage only that Saturday afternoon, full of talk about his innocence, the need for support and understanding. She couldn't get over that, how *convinced* she had been. Was that the behaviour of someone who was intending to go out later that night, pick up a teenage girl and murder her? Rebecca didn't think so. But what did she know? Experts had done studies on these kinds of people – serial murderers, they called them – though she didn't know if having killed only two people qualified Owen for that designation.

She had, however, seen enough television programmes about psychopaths to know that some could *appear* perfectly charming, live quite normal lives outside their need to kill. Ted Bundy, for example, had been a handsome and intelligent man who had killed God knew how many young women in America. Watch out for the nice, friendly, polite boy next door, the message seemed to be, not the raggedy man with the cruel eyes muttering to himself in a corner.

A fly settled on her bare forearm and she stared at its shiny blue and green carapace for a moment before brushing it off. Then she looked up at the angel again. If only he could make things clear for her.

Perhaps the police had arrested Owen only because they still believed he had killed Deborah Harrison. Maybe they had no real evidence that he had killed the other girl. She didn't know why she should care so much. After all, Owen was still practically a stranger to her – and for a long time she had *believed* him to be a killer. Why should she be so upset when it turned out that he really was? She still couldn't help feeling that he had let her down somehow, silly as the idea was.

'Why?' she asked, surprised to find herself speaking out loud at last, face turned up to look at the angel. 'Can you tell me why I care?'

But she got no answer.

She already knew part of the answer. Talking to Owen, taking him under her wing, had been a test for her. In a way, his presence had challenged her faith, her Christian feelings. For when it came to Christianity, Rebecca was a humanist, not one of these cold-fish theologians like some of the ministers she had met. Perhaps a better existence did await us in heaven, but to Rebecca, Christianity was useless if it forgot people in the here and now. Faith and belief, she felt, were no use without charity, love and compassion; religion was nothing if it focused entirely on the afterlife. Daniel had agreed. That was why they had done so well together. Up to last year.

'Why am I telling you this?' she asked the angel. 'What do you know of life on earth? What is it I want from you? Can you tell me?'

Still the angel gazed fixedly heaven-wards. His expression looked stern to Rebecca, but she put that down to a trick of the light.

'Am I to be a cynic now?' she asked. 'After I put so much faith in Owen and he turns out to be a killer after all?'

Again, she didn't hear any answer, but she did hear a movement coming from deeper in the woods. The area behind the Inchcliffe Mausoleum was the most overgrown in the entire graveyard, all the way back to the wall at Kendal Road. The oldest yews grew there, and the wild shrubbery was so dense in places you couldn't even walk through it easily. If there were any graves, nobody had visited them for a long time.

It must have been a small animal of some kind, Rebecca decided. Then she remembered that she had told the police and the court that the cry she heard that November evening could have come from an animal. When she really thought about it, she knew it never could have. She had simply refused to acknowledge, either to herself or to anyone else that the scream she heard was the last cry for help of a girl about to be murdered. This sound, too, was too loud to be a dog, a cat or a bird. And there were no horses or sheep in the graveyard.

She took a step towards the back of the mausoleum, aware as she did so that this was where Deborah's body had been found. 'Is anybody there?' she called out.

No answer.

Then she heard another rustling sound, this time closer to the North Market Street wall.

Rebecca turned and wandered thigh-deep into the tangled undergrowth. She felt nettles sting her legs as she walked. 'Is anyone there?' she called again.

Still no answer.

She paused and listened for a moment. All she could hear was her heart beating.

Suddenly to her left, through the trees, she saw a dark figure break into a run. It looked like a man dressed in brown and green, but she couldn't be certain because of the way the colours blended in with the background. Whoever it was, he couldn't get over the high wall before she caught up with him. His only alternative was to head along the wall to the North Market Street gate. If she hurried, perhaps she could catch a glimpse of him before he got away.

She turned back towards the back of the Inchcliffe Mausoleum and the gravel path. He was to her right now. She could hear him running towards the gate.

Before she could get out of the wooded area, something snagged at her ankle and she tripped, scratching her knees and hands on thorns. It only delayed her a few seconds, but when she got to her feet and ran past the mausoleum along the gravel path into the open area, all she saw was the wooden gate slam shut. She stood there and cursed whoever it was. When she looked down, she saw she had blood on her hands.

THREE

Avoiding the Queen's Arms, which everyone knew was the Eastvale CID local, Banks spirited Stott along Skinner's Yard, down to the Duck and Drake on one of the winding alleys off King Street. The cobbled streets were chock-a-block with antique shops, antiquarian booksellers and food specialists, all with mullioned windows and creaky wooden floors.

The Duck and Drake was a small, black-fronted Sam Smith's house with etched, smoked-glass windows and a couple of tatty hanging baskets over the door. Inside, the entrance to the snug was so low that Banks felt as if he were crawling under a particularly tight overhang in Ingleborough Cave.

The snug was also tiny, with dark wood beams and white-washed walls hung with hunting prints and brass ornaments. They were the only two people in the place. The bench creaked as Banks sat down opposite Stott with his pint of Old Brewery Bitter and his ham and cheese sandwich. Stott hadn't wanted anything at all, not even a glass of water.

'What is it, Barry?' Banks asked, chomping on his sandwich. 'Off your food? You look bloody awful.'

'Thanks.'

'Don't mention it.'

Stott was pale, with dark bags under his eyes and a two-day stubble around his chin and cheeks. His eyes themselves, behind the glasses, were dull, distant and haunted. Banks had never seen him like this before. Normally, you could depend on Barry Stott to look bright-eyed and alert at all times. Not to mention well groomed. But his suit was creased, as if he had slept in it, his tie was not properly fastened, and his hair was uncombed. He looked so miserable that even his ears seemed to droop.

'You ill?'

'As a matter of fact,' said Stott, 'I *haven't* been sleeping well. Not well at all.'

'Something on your mind?'

'Yes.'

Banks finished his sandwich, took a sip of beer and lit a cigarette. 'Out with it, then.'

Stott just pursed his lips and frowned in concentration.

'Barry, are you sure it's something you want to talk to me about?'

'I *have* to,' Stott replied. 'By all rights, I should go to the super, or even the CC. God knows, it's bound to get that far eventually, but I wanted to tell you first. I don't know why. Respect, perhaps. It's just so difficult. I've been up wrestling with it all night, and I can't see any other way out.'

Banks sat back. He had never seen Barry Stott so upset, so *consumed* by anything before, except that day when Pierce was found not guilty. Stott was a private person, and Banks wasn't sure how to handle him on a personal level, outside the job.

Was this a private, intimate matter, perhaps? Was Stott going to admit he was homosexual? Not that it mattered. Banks knew for a fact that two of the uniformed officers at Eastvale were gay. So did everyone else. They came in for a bit of baiting now and then from the more macho among their colleagues, who weren't entirely sure of their own sexuality, and for a certain amount of righteous moral disapproval from the one or two Christian funda-mentalists in uniform. But Barry Stott? Banks realized he didn't even know whether Stott was married, divorced or single.

'Is this off the record, Barry?' Banks asked. 'I mean, is it something personal?'

'Partly. But not really.' He shook his head. 'I can't understand it myself. I was so sure. So damn *certain*.' He banged the table. Banks's beer-glass jumped. 'Sorry.'

'I think you'd better just tell me.'

Stott paused. He took a handkerchief from his pocket and cleaned the lenses of his glasses. In the background Banks could hear the radio playing Jim Reeves singing 'Welcome to My World.'

Finally, Stott put his glasses back on, nodded and took a deep breath. 'All right,' he said. 'I suppose the most important thing is that Owen Pierce is innocent, at least of Ellen Gilchrist's murder. We have to let him go.'

Banks's jaw dropped. 'What are you talking about, Barry?'

'I was *there*,' Stott said. 'I *know*.'

Christ, what was this? A murder confession? Banks held his hand up. 'Hold on, Barry. Take it easy. Go slowly. And be very careful what you say.' He almost felt as if he were giving Stott a formal caution. 'Where were you? King Street? Skield?'

Stott shook his head and licked his lips. 'No. Not either of those places. I was outside Owen Pierce's house.'

'Doing what?'

'Watching him. I've been doing it ever since he got off.'

'So that's why you're looking so washed out?'

Stott rubbed his hand over his stubble. 'Haven't had any sleep in a week. Soon as I finish at the station, I grab a sandwich, then head for his street and park. If he goes out, I follow him.'

'All night?'

'Most of it. At least till it looks like he's settled. Sometimes as late as three or four in the morning. He doesn't go out much. Most nights he gets drunk and passes out in front of the telly.'

'And he hasn't spotted you?'

'I don't know. I haven't taken any great pains to hide myself, but he hasn't said anything.'

'But *why*, Barry?'

Stott smoothed down his hair with his hand, then shrugged. 'I don't know. I got obsessed, I suppose. I just couldn't stop myself. I was so *sure* of his guilt, so certain he'd beaten the system . . . And I knew he'd do it again. It was that kind of crime. I could feel it. I wanted to make sure he didn't kill another girl. I thought if I watched him, kept an eye on him, then either I'd catch him, stop him or, if he knew I was onto him, he wouldn't be able to do it again and the tension would get unbearable. Then maybe he'd confess or something. I wasn't thinking clearly.'

Banks stubbed out his cigarette. 'But why, Barry? You're a good copper. Brainy, diligent, logical. You passed all your exams. You've got a bloody university degree, for Christ's sake. You're on accelerated promotion. You ought to know better.'

Stott shrugged. 'I know. I know. I can't explain it. Something just . . . went in me. Like I said, I thought if I watched him long enough I'd catch him one way or another.'

Banks shook his head. 'Okay. Let's get this straight. You were parked outside Owen Pierce's house on Saturday night?'

'Yes.'

'What time?'

'From about five o'clock on.'

'Until?'

'About two-thirty in the morning, when he turned the lights off. He didn't go out at all except to buy a bottle of something at the off-licence around nine o'clock.'

'You're absolutely certain?'

'Positive. The curtains weren't quite closed. I could see him clearly whenever he got up. He was watching telly in the front room, but every now and then he'd get up to go to the toilet, or pour a drink, whatever.'

'And you're certain he was there all the time? He didn't sneak out the back and come back?'

Stott shook his head. 'He was there, sir. Between the crucial times. Definitely. I saw him get up and cross the room twice between eleven o'clock and midnight.'

'Are you sure it couldn't have been anyone else?'

'Certain. Besides, his car was parked in front of the house the whole time.'

That didn't mean much. Pierce could have stolen a car to commit the crime, and then returned it, rather than risk using his own and having his licence number taken down. When that thought had passed through his mind, Banks had experienced another irritating sense of *déjà vu*. He had felt the same thing the other day while going over the case files. It couldn't really be *déjà vu*, because it wasn't something he had already experienced, but it came with the same sort of frisson.

'What happened then?' he asked.

'He must have fallen asleep in front of the telly, as usual. I could see the light from the screen. It changed to snow at one-fifty-five, when the programmes ended, but Pierce didn't move again until two-thirty. Then he drew the curtains fully, turned out the lights and went upstairs to bed. That's all.'

'That's *all*. Jesus Christ, Barry, do you have any idea what you've done?'

'Of course I have. But I had to speak out. I've been struggling with my conscience all night. I could have spoken up yesterday and saved Pierce another night in jail, but I didn't. I didn't dare. That's my cross to bear. I was worried about the consequences to my career, partly, I'll admit that, but I was also trying to convince myself that I *could* have been wrong, that he *could* have done it. But there's no way. He's innocent, just like he says.'

Banks shook his head. 'I don't see how we can cover this up, Barry. I'm not sure what's going to happen.'

Stott sat bolt upright. 'I don't want you to cover it up. As I said, I grappled with my conscience all night, I prayed for an answer, an easy way out. There isn't one. I'll speak up for Pierce. I'm his alibi. I've abused my position.' He reached in his inside pocket and brought out a white, business-size envelope, which he placed on the table in front of Banks. 'This is my resignation.'

FOUR

Owen was confused. The Magistrates' Court had bound him over without bail, as he had expected, but instead of being en route to Armley Jail, he was back in the cell at Eastvale. And nobody would tell him anything. Wharton had received a message from one of the uniformed policemen just as they returned to the van after the court session, and he seemed to have been running around like a blue-arsed fly ever since. Something was going on, and as far as Owen was concerned, it could only be bad.

He ate a lunch of greasy fish and chips, ironically wrapped in Sunday's *News of the World*, washed it down with a mug of strong sweet tea, and paced his cell until, shortly after one o'clock, Wharton appeared in the doorway, waistcoat buttons straining over his belly, a scarlet crescent grin splitting his bluish jowls.

'You're free to go,' he announced, thumbs hooked in his waistcoat pockets.

Owen flopped on the bed. 'Don't joke,' he said. 'What do you want?'

'I told you.' Wharton came close to what looked like dancing a little jig like Scrooge on Christmas morning. 'You're free. Free. Free to go.'

Had he gone mad? Owen wondered. Had this new arrest been the straw that broke the camel's back? By all rights, it should be *Owen* going mad, not his solicitor, but there was no accounting for events these days. 'Please,' Owen said putting his fists to his temples in an attempt to stop the clamour rising inside his head. 'Please stop tormenting me.'

'He's right, Owen,' said a new voice from behind Wharton in the doorway.

Owen looked up through the tears in his eyes and saw Detective Chief Inspector Banks leaning against the jamb, tie loose, hands in his pockets. So it wasn't a dream; it wasn't a lie. Owen hardly dared believe. He didn't know how he felt now. Choked, certainly, his head spinning, a whooshing sound in his ears. Mostly, he was still confused. That and tearful. He felt very tearful. 'You *believe* me?' he asked Banks.

Banks nodded. 'Yes. I believe you.'

'Thank God.' Owen let his head fall in his hands and gave in to the tears. He cried loud and long, wet and shamelessly, and it wasn't until he had finished and started to wipe his nose and eyes with a tissue that he noticed the two men had left him alone, but that the cell door was still open.

Gingerly, he walked towards it and poked his head out, afraid that it would slam on him. Nothing happened. He walked along the tiled corridor towards the other locked door that led, he knew, upstairs, then out to the world beyond, worried that it wouldn't be opened for him. But it was.

Banks and Wharton stood outside, in the custody suite, and Owen now feared he would be rearrested for something else, still anxious that it was all some sort of ruse.

When Banks approached him, he backed away in apprehension.

'No,' said Banks, holding his hands out, palms open. 'I

meant it, Owen. No tricks. It's over. You're a free man. You're completely exonerated. But I'd really appreciate it if you would come to my office with me for a chat. You might be able to help us find out who really did commit these murders.'

'*Murders*? You believe I'm innocent of both?'

'They're too similar, Owen. Had to be the same person. And that person couldn't have been you. Please, come with me, will you? I'll explain.'

As Owen preceded Banks up the stairs, he felt as if he were walking in a dream and half-expected his feet to disappear right through the steps. On the open-plan ground floor, everyone fell silent as he passed, watching him, and he felt as if he were floating, weightless in space. His vision blurred and his head started to spin, as if he had had too much to drink, but before he stumbled and fell, he felt Banks's strong hand grasp his elbow and direct him towards the stairs.

'It's all right, Owen,' Banks said. 'We'll have some strong coffee and a chat. You've nothing to worry about now.'

Instead of taking him into a dim, smelly interview room, as Owen had been half-expecting, Banks led him into what must be his own office. It was hardly palatial, but it had a metal desk, some matching filing cabinets and two comfortable chairs.

On the wall was a *Dalesman* calendar set at June and showing a photograph of a couple of ramblers with heavy rucksacks on their backs approaching Gordale Scar, near Malham. Oddly, Owen found himself thinking he could have done a better job of the photograph himself. The venetian blinds were up, and before he sat down Owen glimpsed the cobbled market square, full of parked cars. Freedom. He sat down. God, he felt tired.

'What happened?' he asked.

'You were under surveillance,' said Banks.

'What? So there was . . . I mean, it was *you*?'

'Not me, exactly, but someone. Did you know there was someone watching you?'

'I had a funny feeling once or twice. But no, I can't honestly say I knew.' Owen started to laugh.

'What is it?' Banks asked.

Owen wiped his arm over his eyes. 'Oh, nothing. Just the irony of it, that's all. I was under surveillance because you thought I'd commit a crime, but as it turns out the surveillance gives me an alibi. Don't you think that's funny?'

Banks smiled. 'Ironic, yes. But a young girl did get killed, Owen. Horribly. Just like Deborah Harrison.'

'I know. I wasn't laughing at that. And I didn't have anything to do with it. I don't know how I can help you.'

'I think you do. I don't believe you haven't considered the problem over the past couple of days.'

'What problem?'

Banks sat forward and rested his palms on the blotter. 'You want me to spell it out? Okay. The reason we arrested you, Owen, was partly because you had been accused of a very similar crime before, and partly because we found strong physical evidence against you at the scene. It still looks very much as if the same person killed both of those girls, and we found evidence against you at both scenes.'

'The fingerprints and the hairs? Yes. And you're right: I *have* been thinking about how they could have got there.'

'Any ideas?'

Owen shook his head. 'I *did* go up Skield way, and I probably walked past the spot where . . . you know. I suppose I could have dropped such a film container, but

I don't think I had one with me. I told you about my camera. I didn't have it with me. As for the hairs, I suppose I must have shed a few during my walk, but I can't explain how they got on the victim's clothes. Unless . . .'

'Yes?'

The coffee arrived. Banks poured. Owen blew into his cup first, then took a sip. 'This is good. Thank you. Unless,' he went on, 'and I know this sounds crazy, paranoid even, but I can't see how any of it could have happened unless someone, the real killer, had decided to capitalize on my bad reputation, blame it on me, the way he knew everyone else would. It doesn't make sense unless someone tried to *frame* me for Ellen Gilchrist's murder.'

Bank started tapping a pencil against his blotter. 'Go on,' he said.

'Well, if you accept that premise, then whoever it was must have broken into my house while I was in jail and wrecked the place to cover up his true intentions. Or he could have walked in easily *after* the place had been done over. The front door was unlocked when I got back. The lock was broken, in fact. This person must have thought there was a good chance I'd get off, and he wanted some insurance in case that happened and suspicion turned back on him. He must have found the empty film container in the waste-paper bin and guessed it would have my fingerprints on it. I mean, if it were empty, and I'd opened it . . . Then he must have picked up some hairs from the pillow in the bedroom. That would have been easy enough to do.'

Banks nodded. 'Why not choose something more *obvious* to link you to the crime?'

'Failing my blood, which he couldn't get hold of, I can't

think of anything more obvious than my hair and finger-prints, can you?'

Banks smiled. 'I meant something with your name on, perhaps. So there could be no mistake. After all, the prints on the film container might have been blurred. He couldn't be *certain* they'd lead us to you.'

'But if you think about it,' Owen said, looking pointedly at Banks, 'he didn't need very much, did he? You all believed I'd murdered Deborah Harrison, so it was easy to convince you I'd also killed Ellen Gilchrist. There was no point risking anything more obvious, like something with my name or photograph on it, because that would only draw suspicion. No, all he needed were my prints and hair. He knew my reputation would do the rest. Even without the prints he could have been fairly certain you'd pick on me. I'll bet the minute you saw the film container you thought of me because you knew I was an amateur photographer.'

'That still leaves us one important question to answer,' Banks said. 'Who? Of course, it might be that the murderer was simply using you as a convenient scapegoat – that it was nothing personal – but it *could* have been someone who really wanted you to suffer. Have you any idea who would want to do that to you?'

'I've racked my brains about it. But no. The only person who hates me that much is Michelle. *Could* it have been a woman?'

'I don't think Michelle is tall enough,' Banks said. 'But, yes, it *could* have been a woman.'

Owen shook his head. 'I'm sorry. I wish I could help. Like you said, it was probaby nothing personal. I mean, whoever did it just wanted *someone else* to blame. It didn't matter who.'

'You're probably right. But if you think of anyone . . .'

'Of course. One of the neighbours might have seen someone, you know. They wouldn't speak out before because they all thought I was guilty and deserved having my house wrecked, but now . . .? I don't know. It's worth asking them, anyway. You might start with that prick Ivor and his wife, Siobhan, next door.'

'We'll do that,' said Banks, standing up to indicate the interview was at an end.

Owen finished his coffee, stood awkwardly and moved towards the door. He could still hardly believe that freedom was just a few steps away again.

'What now?' Banks asked him.

He shrugged. 'I don't know. I've got a lot to think about. Maybe I'll go away for a while, just get lost, like everyone suggested I should do in the first place.'

Banks shook his head. 'No need to run away,' he said. 'We know you didn't do it now. The press will fall all over themselves to support your cause, and they'll crucify us for getting the wrong man. Police incompetence.'

Owen forced a smile. 'Maybe. Eventually. And I can't say I'll be sorry. You deserve it. I remember what you've put me through. I remember all the terrible things you accused me of only yesterday. Perversion. Cowardice. Not to mention murder. But I can't see me getting my job or my friends back, can you? And I imagine there'll be a lot of people around these parts slow to change their minds, no matter what. Shit sticks, Chief Inspector. That's one thing I've learned from all this.'

Banks nodded. 'Perhaps. For a while.'

Owen paused at the door. 'Look,' he said, 'I don't expect an apology or anything, but could you just tell me again that you believe I'm innocent? Not just not guilty but *innocent*. Will you *say* it. I need to hear it.'

'You're innocent, Owen. It's true. You're free to go.'

'Thank you.' Owen turned and started to pull the door shut behind him.

'Owen?' Banks called after him.

Owen felt a little shiver of panic. He turned. 'Yes?'

'I *am* sorry. Good luck to you.'

Owen nodded, shut the door and left the building as fast as he could.

19

ONE

It wasn't until late Tuesday afternoon that a number of things clicked into place for Banks, and what had been eluding him, niggling him for days, suddenly became clear.

So far, there were no leads on the Ellen Gilchrist murder. Several cars had been spotted on King Street that night – big, small, light, dark, Japanese, French – but no-one had any reason to take down numbers or detailed descriptions. If the killer had used his own car, Banks reflected, then he may have parked out of sight, just around the corner on one of the sidestreets.

A couple of tourists unable to sleep on a lumpy mattress at a Gratly B&B said they heard a car pass shortly after eleven-thirty, which would have been about the right time, but they hadn't seen anything. So far, no-one in Skield had been disturbed by Saturday night's events, but that didn't surprise Banks. If the killer were clever, which he apparently was, then he would have parked off the road, well out of the hamlet itself.

Under Superintendent Gristhorpe's co-ordination, Susan Gay and Jim Hatchley were still out checking the victim's friends and acquaintances to see if she could have been killed by someone who knew her, or if anyone knew more than he or she was telling. The more he thought about it, though, the more Banks was convinced that the solution to Ellen Gilchrist's murder lay in Deborah Harrison's.

Also, when Banks arrived at the office that morning, he found a telephone message in his pigeon-hole from Rebecca Charters, dated the previous afternoon, asking him to phone her. When he rang Rebecca, she told him about surprising someone in St Mary's graveyard the previous afternoon. No, she hadn't seen who it was, couldn't even give a description. She laughed at her fears now, apologized for bothering him and said she'd been a bit jumpy lately. Yesterday, she hadn't hesitated to call, but now she had had time to think about it. Probably just a kid, she decided. Banks wasn't too sure, but he put it on the back burner for the moment.

Since Stott's revelation, after the inevitable bollocking from Jimmy Riddle and a reminder that he was close to the end of his allotted week, Banks and Superintendent Gristhorpe had also been engaged in damage control.

So far, they had managed to keep Stott's illegal surveillance from the press. And Owen Pierce certainly wasn't interested in blowing the whistle. As far as the media were concerned, Pierce had an unimpeachable alibi. All that had happened was that another innocent person had spent a night in the cells because of police incompetence. Nothing new about that. Eastvale CID came out of it looking only like prize berks, not like a combination of the Gestapo and the KGB.

As for Barry Stott, he hadn't resigned, but he had taken some of the leave due to him. God knew where he was. Wrestling with his conscience somewhere, Banks guessed. As far as Banks was concerned, though, Stott was over-reacting. So, he had let himself get a bit obsessed with

Pierce's guilt. So what? Things like that happened sometimes, and they rarely had dire consequences. After all,
Stott had only *watched* Pierce; he hadn't beat him up or
assassinated him.

Despite the hours of work a murder enquiry consumed,
routine work still went on at Eastvale Divisional HQ, and
routine papers still found their way to Banks's desk. On that
Tuesday afternoon, when he was distracted by thoughts of
Ellen Gilchrist, Deborah Harrison, Barry Stott and Owen
Pierce, a proposal requiring every patrol car be fitted with a
dashboard computer passed over his desk for perusal after
a report on the increase of car theft in North Yorkshire.

Because Banks wasn't thinking about it, because the
words simply floated into that chaotic, intuitive and
creative part of his mind rather than engaging his sense
of reason and logic, he was struck with that rare feeling
of epiphany as a missing piece fell into place. It felt like
the simultaneous telescoping and expansion of a chain
of unrelated words into one inevitable conclusion: each
element rolled firmly into place like the balls with the
winning lottery numbers: Car. Computer. Theft. *Spinks*.

It wasn't really intuition, but a perfectly logical process,
taking a number of facts and relating them in a way that
made sense. It only felt like a sudden revelation.

On Friday, when Banks had questioned John Spinks
about Michael Clayton and Sylvie Harrison, it had been
staring him in the face. But he hadn't seen it. On Saturday,
after his talk with Clayton, he had felt close to something.
But he hadn't known what. Now he did. He still had some
dates to check, but as he pushed the proposal aside, he
was certain that John Spinks had stolen Michael Clayton's
car and computer in August of last year. Whether that
actually meant anything remained to be seen.

Excited by the theory, Banks checked the dates and dashed into Gristhorpe's office, where he found the superintendent immersed in the statement of Ellen Gilchrist's best friend. Gristhorpe stretched and rubbed his bushy eyebrows with his fingertips when Banks entered. After he'd done, they looked like birds' nests.

'Alan. What can I do for you?'

Banks explained about his chain of reasoning. Gristhorpe nodded here and there, and when Banks had finished, put his forefinger to his lips and furrowed his brow.

'So Lady Sylvie Harrison and Michael Clayton found Spinks and Deborah drinking wine in the back garden on 17 August, right?' he said.

Banks nodded.

'And Clayton reported his car stolen on 20 August. I remember it because when he came to enquire about our progress, he thought he was so important he had to see the top man on the totem pole. About a bloody stolen car. I ask you.'

'I'm surprised he didn't go directly to Jimmy Riddle.'

'Oh, he did. First off. But Riddle's in Northallerton and that was too far for Clayton to go every day. So Riddle told him to keep checking with me. I put Barry and Susan on it. Clayton was like a cat on a hot tin roof. Not over the car, though.'

'The computer?'

'Got it in one.'

'Yes. That's what Susan said,' Banks mused. 'When Clayton recognized her that time we went to talk to the Harrisons. I should have realized at the time.'

Gristhorpe smiled indulgently. 'I think you can be forgiven that, Alan,' he said. 'Wasn't it about the same time the lead on Pierce came up?'

'Yes. But—'

'Anyway, let's assume that Spinks stole Clayton's car on 20 August,' Gristhorpe went on. 'He did some damage, but not much. It was the missing notebook computer that really had Clayton dancing on hot coals. We know it was a very expensive one, with all the bells and whistles, but Clayton's a rich man. He could afford a new one easily. It was what was *on* the computer that he was worried about. As I recollect, it turned up on the market a couple of weeks later, no worse for wear.'

'From what I've seen,' Banks went on, 'Spinks would have about as much chance of operating Clayton's computer as an orang-utan. But the point is that he was still seeing Deborah at that time. There's a chance she knew what he'd done. She wouldn't necessarily tell Clayton or her parents what happened, not when she was right in the middle of being rebellious, slumming it. And Deborah was bright, good at sciences. That computer would have probably been child's play to her.'

'So what if she found out something from it?' Gristhorpe suggested. 'Something important.'

'Maybe it wasn't that Clayton was having an affair with Lady Harrison, after all,' Banks said. 'That's what I thought earlier. But maybe they were involved in some scam. Perhaps Clayton had been cheating Sir Geoffrey or something.'

'You don't even need to go that far,' Gristhorpe said. 'Remember, HarClay Industries is big in the defence business. Big enough that Sir Geoffrey met in private with Oliver Jackson, of Special Branch, on the day his daughter was murdered.'

'And you think there's a connection?'

'I'm saying there *could* be. Micro-electronics, computers,

microchips, weapons circuits, that sort of thing. They're not only big money, but they have a strong political dimension, too. If Deborah came across something she shouldn't have seen . . . If Clayton was working for someone he shouldn't have been . . . selling weapons systems to enemy governments, for example . . .'

'Then either Clayton or his bosses could have had Deborah killed if she threatened to blow the whistle?'

'Yes.'

'And whoever killed Ellen Gilchrist simply chose a random victim to implicate Pierce?'

Gristhorpe shrugged. 'Nothing simpler. Not to people like that.'

'But they didn't bargain on Barry Stott's ego.'

'"The best laid plans . . ."'

'Why wait so long?' Banks asked. 'That's what I don't understand. Deborah cracked the computer around 20 August – if indeed that's what happened – and she wasn't killed until 6 November. That's nearly three months.'

Gristhorpe scratched his stubbly chin. 'You've got me there,' he said. 'But there could be an explanation. Maybe it took her that long to fathom out what she'd got. Or maybe it took Clayton that long to figure out someone had been tampering. You know how quickly things change, Alan. Maybe the information she got didn't actually *mean* anything until three months later, when other things happened.'

Banks nodded. 'It's possible. But I'm not sure even Deborah was bright enough to understand Clayton's electronic schematics. I know I'm not. I saw some of them the other day and they left me dizzy.'

'Well, you know what a Luddite I am when it comes to computers,' Gristhorpe said. 'But it could have been something obvious to her. She didn't have to understand it fully, just recognize a reference, a name or something. Perhaps someone else she knew was involved?'

'Okay,' said Banks. 'But we're letting our imaginations run away with us. Would Clayton even be likely to enter such important information in his notebook? Anyway, I've got a simple suggestion: why don't we bring Spinks in? See if we can't get the truth out of him?'

'Good idea,' said Gristhorpe.

'And this time,' Banks added, 'I think we might even have something to bargain with.'

TWO

Where was he? Swiss Cottage, that was it. London. The cash register rang and the swell of small-talk and laughter rolled up and down. He thought he could hear the distant rumble of thunder from outside, feel the tension before the storm, that electrical smell in the air, like burning dust in church.

After the police set him free he had gone back home, pushed through the throng of reporters, then got in his car and driven off, leaving everything behind. He hadn't known where he was heading, at least not consciously. Mostly, he was still in a daze over what had happened: not only his release, but the fact that someone must have deliberately set out to frame him.

And, as he told the police, the only person who hated him that much was Michelle.

They didn't seem to suspect her – they were sure it was a man, for a start – but Owen knew her better. He wouldn't put it past her. If she hadn't done it herself she might have enlisted someone, used her sex to manipulate some poor, sick bastard, the way she did so well.

So with these thoughts half-formed, one moment seeming utterly fantastic and absurd and the next feeling so real they had to be true, he had found himself heading for London, and now he was drinking in Swiss Cottage, trying to pluck up courage to go and challenge Michelle directly.

He was interested to find out what she would have to say if he turned up on her doorstep. Even if she hadn't engineered the murders to discredit him, she had slandered him in the newspapers. He knew that *for a fact*. Oh, yes. He was looking forward to hearing what she had to say for herself.

'Are you all right, mate?'

'Pardon?' It was the man next to him. He had turned his head in Owen's direction.

'I said are you all right?'

'Yes, yes . . . fine.' Owen realized he must have been muttering to himself. The man gave him a suspicious look and turned away.

Time to go. It was nine o'clock. What day of the week? Tuesday? Wednesday? Did it really matter? There was a good chance she'd be in. People who work nine-to-five usually stay in on weeknights, or at least get home early.

He found the telephone and the well-thumbed directory hanging beside it. Some of the pages had been torn out or defaced with felt-tipped pens, but not the one that counted. He slid his finger down until he came to her name: Chappel. No first name, just the initials, M. E. Michelle Elizabeth. There was her number.

Owen's chest tightened as he searched his pockets for a coin. He felt dizzy and had to lean against the wall a moment before dialling. Two men passed on their way out and gave him funny looks. When they had gone, he took four deep breaths to steady himself, picked up the phone, put the coin in and dialled. He let it ring once, twice, three times, four, and on the fifth ring a woman's voice said, rather testily, 'Yes, who is it?'

It was *her* voice. No doubt about it. Owen would recognize that reedy quality with its little-girlish hint of a lisp anywhere.

He held the phone away and heard her repeat the question more loudly – 'Look, who is it?'

After he still said nothing, she said, 'Pervert,' and hung up on him.

Owen looked at the receiver for a moment, then he smiled and walked out into the gathering storm.

THREE

John Spinks didn't seem particularly surprised to find himself back at Eastvale nick shortly after dark that evening. As predicted, he had been at the Swainsdale Centre bragging to his mates about how he spent the weekend in jail and had gone up before the magistrate. The arrival of two large uniformed officers only added more credibility to his tales, and he got quite a laugh, the officers told Banks, when he stuck out his hands for the cuffs, just like he'd seen people do on television.

He did look surprised, however, to find himself in Banks's office rather than a smelly interview room. And he looked even more surprised when Banks offered unlimited coffee, cigarettes and biscuits.

Gristhorpe and Banks had decided to tackle him

together, to attempt a good-cop bad-cop approach. Spinks already knew Banks, but the superintendent was an unknown quantity, and though his baby blue eyes had instilled fear into more villains than a set of thumbscrews, Gristhorpe could appear the very model of benevolence. He also out-ranked Banks, which was another card to play. They had Stafford Oakes waiting in Gristhorpe's own office, should their plan be successful.

'Right, John,' said Banks, 'I won't beat about the bush. You're in trouble, a lot of trouble.'

Spinks sniffed as if trouble were his business. 'Yeah, right.'

'Not only have we got you on taking and driving away,' Banks went on, 'but when our men searched your house, they found sufficient quantities of crack cocaine, Ecstasy and LSD for us to bring some serious drug-dealing charges against you.'

'I told you, that stuff wasn't mine.'

'Whose was it, then?'

'I don't know her name. Just some slag spent the night there. She must've forgotten it.'

'You expect me to believe that someone would leave a fortune in drugs behind? In *your* bedroom? Come off it, John, that stuff's yours until someone else claims it, and it'll be a cold day in hell before that happens.'

Spinks bit on his lower lip. He was starting to look less like a Hollywood dream-boy and more like a frightened teenager. A lock of hair slid over his eye; he started chewing his fingernails. Bravado could only take someone so far, Banks thought, but he knew it would be a mistake to act as if he were shooting fish in a barrel. Stupidity, along with stubbornness, can be valuable resources when all the big guns are turned on you. And they had served Spinks well for eighteen years.

'Got anything to say?' Banks asked.

Spinks shrugged. 'I told you. It's not mine. You can't prove it is.'

'We can prove whatever we want,' Banks said. 'A judge or a jury has only to take one look at you to throw away the key.'

'My brief says—'

'These legal-aid briefs are about as useful as a sieve in a flood, John. You ought to know that. Overworked and underpaid.'

'Yeah, well, my brief says you can't pin it on me. The drugs.'

Banks raised his eyebrows. 'She did? That's really bad news, John,' he said, shaking his head. 'I thought things were pretty bad, but I didn't realize that lawyers were setting up in practice before they even finished their degrees these days.'

'Ha fucking ha.'

The other chair creaked as Gristhorpe leaned forward. 'My chief inspector might be acting a little harshly towards you, son,' he said. 'See, it's personal with him. He lost a son to drugs.'

Spinks squinted at Banks. 'Tracy never said nothing about that.'

'She doesn't like to talk about it,' said Banks quickly. They had decided to improvise according to responses and circumstances, but Gristhorpe had thrown him a spinner here. He smiled to himself. Why not? Play the game. As far as he knew, Brian was alive and well and still studying architecture in Portsmouth, but there was no reason for Spinks to know that.

'Like everyone his age,' Banks went on, 'he thought he was immortal, indestructible. He thought it couldn't happen to him. Anyone else, sure. But not him.' He leaned forward and clasped his hands. 'Now, I don't give a tinker's whether you smoke so much crack your brains blow out of your arsehole, but I *do* care very much that you're selling to others, especially to a crowd that at one time included my daughter. Do we understand one another?'

Spinks shifted in his chair. 'What's this all about? What you after? A confession? I'm not saying anything. My brief—'

'Fuck your brief,' said Banks, thumping the rickety metal desk. 'And fuck *you*! Do you understand what I'm saying?'

Spinks looked rattled. Gristhorpe cut in again and said to Banks, 'I don't think it's really appropriate to talk that way to Mr Spinks, Chief Inspector,' he said. 'I'm sure he understands you perfectly well.'

'Sorry, sir,' said Banks, wiping his brow with the back of his hand. 'Got a bit carried away.' He fumbled for a cigarette and lit it.

'You his boss?' Spinks asked, turning, wide-eyed, to look at Gristhorpe. 'He called you "sir."'

'I thought I'd already made that clear,' Gristhorpe said, then he winked. 'Don't worry, son. I won't let him off his leash.'

He looked back at Banks, who had removed his jacket and was loosening his tie. 'He ought to be locked up, that one,' Spinks went on, emboldened. 'And his mate. The fat one. Hit me once, he did. Bounced my nose off a fucking table.'

'Aye, well, people get carried away sometimes,' said

Gristhorpe. 'Stress of the job. The thing is, though, that he's right in a way. You *are* in a lot of trouble. Right now, we're about the only friends you've got.'

'Friends?'

'Yes,' said Banks, catching his attention again. 'Believe it or not, John, I'm going to do you the biggest favour anyone's ever done you in your life.'

Spinks narrowed his eyes. 'Oh yeah? Why should I believe you?'

'You should. In years to come you might even thank me for it. You're eighteen now, John, there's no getting around that. With the kind of charges you're looking at, you'll go to jail, no doubt about it. Hard time. Now I know you're a big boy, a tough guy and all the rest, but think about it. *Think*. It's not only a matter of getting buggered morning, afternoon and evening, of giving blow-jobs at knife-point, maybe catching AIDS, but it's a life of total deprivation, John. The food's lousy, the plumbing stinks and there's no-one to complain to. And when you get out – if you get out – however many years later, you'll have lost a good part of your youth. All you'll know is prison life. And you know what, John? You'll be back in there like a flash. It's called *recidivism*. Look it up, John. Call it a sort of death wish, but someone like you gets institutionalized and he can't survive on the outside. He gets to need jail. And as for the blow-jobs and the buggery . . .' Banks shrugged. 'Well, I'm sure you'd even get to like that after a while.'

Banks's monologue produced no discernible effect on Spinks, as he had suspected it wouldn't. It was intended only to soften him to the point of accepting a deal. Banks knew that Spinks was already doomed to exactly the kind of existence he had just laid out for him, but that he couldn't, wouldn't, recognize the fact, and wasn't capable of making the changes necessary to avoid it.

No. What they were about to offer was simple, temporary relief, the chance for Spinks to walk free and keep on doing exactly what he was doing until the next time he got caught, if he didn't kill himself or someone else first. A sprat to catch a mackerel. Very sad, but very true.

'So what is this big favour you're going to do me?'

'First,' said Banks, 'you're going to tell us the truth about what happened last August. You're going to tell us how you stole Michael Clayton's car and his computer and *exactly* what happened after that.'

Spinks paled a little but stood his ground. 'Why would I want to do something like that?'

'To avoid jail.'

'You mean confess to one crime and get off on another one?'

'Something like that.'

'Christ, you're worse than the bloody criminals, you lot are.' He turned to Gristhorpe. 'Can he do that?' he asked. 'Has he got the authority?'

'I have,' said Gristhorpe softly. 'I'm a superintendent, remember?'

'Don't we need a lawyer or something?'

'What's wrong, John?' said Banks. 'Don't trust us?'

'I don't trust *you*. Anyway, why talk to the monkey when the organ grinder's here?'

Banks smiled. It was working. And he hadn't denied stealing Clayton's car yet.

'There's a Crown attorney in the building,' said Gristhorpe, 'and he can deal with the particulars about the charges and likely sentences, if you want to talk to him.'

Spinks squinted. 'Maybe I'll do that. What's the deal?'

'You tell us what we want to know,' said Gristhorpe, 'and we'll see you stay out of jail. Dealing becomes simple possession.'

'That's not enough. I want all charges dropped.'

Gristhorpe shook his head. 'Sorry, son. We can't do that. You see, the paperwork's already in the system.'

'You can lose it.'

'Maybe the odd sheet or two,' said Gristhorpe. 'But not all of it. The lawyer will explain it.'

Spinks sat silently, brow furrowed in thought.

Banks stood up. 'I've had enough of this,' he said to Gristhorpe. 'I told you it was no use. His brain's so addled he doesn't even recognize a piece of good fortune when he trips over it. Besides, it makes me puke sitting with a drug-dealing moron like him. Let him go to jail. He belongs there. Let him catch AIDS. See if I care.' And he headed towards the door.

'Wait, just a minute,' said Spinks, holding his hand up. 'Hold your horses. I haven't said anything yet.'

'That's the problem,' said Gristhorpe. 'You'd better make your mind up quickly, sonny. You don't get chances like this every day. We can probably get it down to probation, maybe a bit of community service, but you can't just walk away from it.'

Spinks glared at Banks, who stood scowling with his hand on the doorknob, then looked back at Gristhorpe, all benevolence and forgiveness. Then he put his feet on Banks's desk. 'All right,' he said. 'All right. You've got a deal. Get the brief in.'

•

FOUR

Large raindrops blotched the pavement when Owen left the pub. Lightning flickered in the north and the thunder grumbled like God's empty stomach. The drinkers out on the muggy street hurried inside before the deluge arrived.

Owen felt light-headed after all the drinks, and he knew he wasn't thinking clearly. Booze had made him just brave and foolhardy enough to face Michelle.

He walked along the main road past pubs and shops open late, head bowed, jacket collar turned up in a futile attempt to keep dry. Shop-lights and street-lights smeared the pavement and gutter. Hair that had been damp with sweat before was now plastered to his skull by rain.

He had forgotten exactly where he parked his car, but it didn't matter. Michelle's place couldn't be far.

He stopped a young couple coming out of a pub and asked them where her street was. They gave him directions as they fiddled with their umbrella. As he suspected, it was only a couple of hundred yards up the road, then left, short right and left again. He thanked them and walked on, aware of them standing watching him from behind.

Now he knew he was going to see her, his mind shot off in all directions. She wouldn't want to let him in, of course, not after what she had tried to do to him, not after what she had said about him.

Did he feel reckless enough to break in? Maybe. He didn't know. Given the address, her flat would probably be in one of those three- or four-storey London houses. Perhaps if he waited outside for her to go out, approached her in the street . . . She might have to go to the shop or go out to meet someone. But it was a bit late in the evening for that. Maybe if he waited until one of the other tenants went in, he could get to the door before it locked and at least gain entry to the building.

A white sports car honked as he crossed a sidestreet against a red light. He flicked the driver the V sign, then caught his foot on the kerb and stumbled, bumping into an elderly man walking his dog in the rain. The man gave him a dirty look, adjusted his spectacles and walked on.

He turned left where the couple had told him to and found himself the only pedestrian in quiet backstreets. The houses were all about three storeys high, divided into flats, with a buzzer and intercom by the front door. It wouldn't be easy.

Many rooms were lit, some without curtains, and as he walked he looked in the windows and saw fragments of blue wall, the top corner of a bookshelf, a framed Dali print, an ornate chandelier, flickering television pictures, two people talking, a cat sitting on the window-sill watching the rain – a panorama of life.

The walk had taken some of the steam out of Owen, but he still wanted to see Michelle face to face, if only to watch her squirm as he accused her of her crimes.

He climbed the steps and looked at the list by the door. M.E. Chappel, Flat 4. Would that be on the first or second floor? He didn't know. He crossed the street and looked up. Both second-floor windows were in darkness, as were those on the ground floor. On the first floor, bluish light filtered through the curtains of one, and the other was open to reveal a William Morris wallpaper design. That wasn't Michelle at all. The blue room was more like her.

He stood in the shadows wondering what to do. Rain drummed down, an oily sheen on the street. He didn't feel as brave now as he had on leaving the pub. The booze had worn off, and he had a headache. He needed another drink, but it was close to eleven; the pubs would be closing. Besides, Michelle would probably be going to bed soon. Now he was here, he couldn't wait until tomorrow.

A man and a woman huddled together under an umbrella approached the house, turned up the path and climbed the steps. The way they walked, Owen guessed they were a little tipsy. Probably unemployed and didn't have to go to work in the morning. He shrank back into the shadows. The man said something, and the woman laughed. She shook out her umbrella over the steps. It wasn't Michelle.

When she turned back to the door, Owen hurried across the street behind them. It was a hell of a long shot, but it might just work. They had their backs turned, the street wasn't well lit, and they couldn't hear him because of the rain and the rumbles of thunder. Adrenalin pumped him up and seemed to rekindle some of the earlier bravado. He was close now. It all depended on how slowly the door closed on its spring behind them.

As soon as they were both inside and the man let go of the door, Owen dashed on tiptoe up the steps and put his hand out. He stopped the door just before it had completely swung back and relatched.

He looked around at the houses across the street. As far as he could make out, nobody was watching him. He heard another door open and close inside the building, and the lights went on in one of the ground floor flats.

Softly, Owen pushed the front door open and slipped inside.

FIVE

Stafford Oakes quickly assured Spinks that the charges against him could be reduced to a manageable level – the drugs, especially. Add that he had no prior record, that he had been upset over a missed job opportunity and any number of other mitigating circumstances that affected his stress-level when he stole and crashed the car, and he'd probably get a few months' community service. Lucky community.

'So,' Banks asked him when Oakes had left. 'Why don't you tell us about it? Then we'll get the Crown to put the lesser charges in writing. More coffee? Cigarette.'

Spinks shrugged. 'Why not.'

Banks poured from the carafe he had had sent up. 'Off the record,' he asked, 'did you steal Michael Clayton's car on 20 August last year?'

Spinks snapped the filter off the cigarette and lit it. 'I don't remember the exact date, but it was around then. And I didn't *steal* it. Just borrowed it for a quick spin, that's all.'

'Why?'

'What do you mean, why? Because he treated me like shit, that's why. Fucking snob. Like I wasn't good enough to wipe his precious goddaughter's nose with.'

'This was just after he and Lady Harrison found you and Deborah drinking wine in the back garden?'

'Yeah. We weren't doing no harm. Just having a barbie and a drop or two of the old vino. He acted like it was too good for the likes of me. It was only a fucking bottle of wine, for Christ's sake. He'd no call to be so rude to me, calling me an idle lout and a thickie and all that. It's not my fault I can't get a job, is it?'

'And you did some damage to the car, for revenge?'

'No. It was an accident. I was still learning, wasn't I? That car's got a very sensitive accelerator.'

From what Banks had heard of Spinks's driving history so far, it might be a good idea if the court could somehow prevent him from ever getting a licence. Not that it seemed to have stopped him so far.

'Did you also take a notebook computer out of the car?'

'It was in the back seat under a coat.'

'Did you take it?'

Spinks looked at Gristhorpe. 'It's all right, sonny,' the superintendent said, 'you can answer any question Chief Inspector Banks asks you with complete impunity.'

'Uh? Come again.'

'No blame attached. It's all off the record. None of it is being recorded or written down. Remember what the solicitor told you. Relax. Feel free.'

Spinks drank some coffee. 'Yes,' he said. 'I thought it might be worth something.'

'And was it?'

He shrugged. 'Piss all. Bloke on the market offered me seventy-five measly quid.'

And the market vendor was reselling it for a hundred and fifty, Banks remembered. A hundred and fifty quid for a six-thousand-pound computer. 'So you sold it to him?'

'That's right.'

'Before you sold it, did you use it at all?'

'Me? No. Don't know how to work those things, do I?'

'What about Deborah?'

'What about her?'

'She was a bright girl. Studied computers at school. She'd know how to get it going.'

'Yeah, well . . .'

'You *were* still seeing Deborah at that time, weren't you?'

'Yeah.'

'And did she ever visit your house?'

'Yeah. Once or twice. Turned her nose up, though. Said it smelled and it was dirty.' He laughed. 'Wouldn't use the toilet, no matter how much she wanted to go.'

'Right,' said Banks. 'Now what I'd like to know, John, is did Deborah have a go with the computer?'

'Yeah, well, she did, as a matter of fact.' He turned to Gristhorpe, as if for confirmation that he could continue with impunity. Gristhorpe nodded like a priest. Spinks went on, 'Yeah. Deb, she was with me, like, when I . . . you know . . . went for a ride.'

'Deborah was with you when you stole Michael Clayton's car?'

'Yeah, that's what I said. Only don't use that word "stole." I don't like it. See, it was even more in the family with her being there wasn't it? Just like borrowing the family car, really.'

'Did you ever tell him it was the two of you who'd "borrowed" his car?'

'Course not. You think I'm stupid or something?'

'Go on.'

'Anyway, she didn't like the idea at first. No bottle, hadn't Deb. But soon as I got us inside, quiet as could be, like, and got that Swedish engine purring, she took to it like a duck to water, didn't she? It was Deb noticed the computer. Said she was surprised Clayton let it out of his sight given as how he was the kind of bloke couldn't even jot down a dental appointment without putting it on his computer. I said let's just leave it. But she said no, she wanted to have a go on it.'

'So what did you do?'

'After we'd finished with the car we went back to my house. My mum was out, as usual, and I was feeling a bit randy by then, after a nice fast drive. I fancied a bit of the other, but she went all funny, like she did sometimes, and after a while I didn't even want it any more. She had a way like that, you know. She could be really off-putting, really cold.'

'The computer, John?'

'Yeah, well once Deb got it going I couldn't drag her away from it.'

'What about the password?'

'Whatever it was, if there was one, it didn't take her very long. I will say this, though, she seemed a bit surprised at how easy it was.'

'The password?'

'Whatever it took to get the bloody thing going.'

'What did she say?'

'"Well, bugger me!" Not exactly those words, mind you, but that was the feeling. She didn't like to swear didn't Deb. More like gosh or golly or something.'

'And then?'

Spinks shrugged. 'Then she just played around with it for a while. I got bored and went upstairs for a lie-down.'

'Was she still playing with it when you went back down?'

'Just finishing. It looked like she was taking something out of it. One of those little square things, what do you call them?'

'A diskette?'

'That's right.'

'Where did she get it from?'

'I don't know. The computer was in a carrying case and

there were a whole bunch of them there, in little pockets, like. I suppose that's where she got it from.'

'What did she do with it?'

'Put it in her pocket.'

'Any idea what was on it?'

'No. I asked her what she was up to but she told me to mind my own business.'

'Did she do anything else with the computer?'

'Yeah. She tapped a few keys, watched the screen for a while, smiled to herself, funny like, then turned it off.'

'And then?'

'She told me I could sell it if I wanted and keep the money.' He looked towards Gristhorpe. 'I mean, she practically gave it to me, right? And it was in the family. Well, he was her godfather, anyway. That has to count, doesn't it.'

'It's all right,' Gristhorpe assured him. 'You're doing fine. Just keep on answering the questions as fully and as honestly as you can.'

Spinks nodded.

'Did she tell you at any time what she'd found on the computer?'

'No. I mean, I didn't pester her about it. I could tell she didn't want to say anything. If you ask me she found out he'd been fiddling the books or something.'

'What makes you say that?'

'Stands to reason, doesn't it?'

'Did she ever refer to the incident again?'

'No. Well, it wasn't much more than a week or so later when her mother caught us in bed. Then it was cards for me. On your bike, mate.'

'Do you know if Michael Clayton ever found out that you took it, or that Deborah used it?'

'I certainly didn't tell him. Maybe Deb did, but neither of them ever said anything to me about it.'

'And you got your seventy-five quid?'

'Right.'

'Is there anything else?'

'No, that's everything. I've told you everything.' He looked at Gristhorpe. 'Can I go now?'

'Alan?'

Banks nodded.

'Aye, lad,' said Gristhorpe. 'Off you go.'

'You won't forget our deal, will you?'

Gristhorpe shook his head. Spinks cast a triumphant grin at Banks and left.

'Christ,' said Banks. 'I need a drink to get the taste of shit out of my mouth after that.'

Gristhorpe laughed. 'Worth it, though, wasn't it. Come on, I'll buy. We've got a bit of thinking to do before we decide on our next move.'

But they hadn't got further than the stairs when Banks heard his telephone ring. He looked at his watch. Almost ten-thirty.

'I'd better take it,' he said. 'Why don't you go ahead. I'll meet you over there.'

'I'll wait,' said Gristhorpe. 'It might be important.' They went into the office and Banks picked up the phone.

'Chief Inspector Banks?'

'Yes.'

'Its Vjeko. Vjeko Batorac.' The voice sounded a little muffled and hoarse.

'Vjeko. What is it? Is something wrong?'

'I thought I should tell you that Ive Jelačić was just here. We fought. He hit me.'

'What happened, Vjeko? Start from the beginning.'

Vjeko took a deep breath. 'Ive came here about a half an hour ago and he was carrying a book of some kind. A notebook, I thought. It was a diary, bound in good leather, written in English. He said he thought it would make him rich. He couldn't read English so he brought it to me to tell him what it said. He said he would give me money.' Vjeko paused. 'That girl, the one who was killed, her name was Deborah Harrison, wasn't it?'

'Yes.' Banks felt his grip tighten on the receiver. 'Go on, Vjeko.'

'It was *her* diary. I asked him where he got it, but he wouldn't tell me. He wanted me to translate it for him.'

'Did you?'

'I looked at it. Then I told him it was nothing important, not worth anything, and he should leave it with me. I'd throw it away.'

'What happened then?'

'He became suspicious. He thought I'd found out something and wanted to cheat him out of his money. I think he was hoping to find someone he could blackmail. He said he'd take it to Mile. Mile can read some English, too. I said it was worthless and there was no point. He tried to snatch it from my hand. I held on and we struggled. He is stronger than me, Chief inspector. He hit me. Dragica was screaming and Little Jelena started crying. It was terrible.'

'What happened?'

'Ive ran away with the diary.'

'You said you read it?'

'Some of it.'

'What did it say?'

'If I am right, Chief Inspector, that girl was in terrible trouble. I think you should send someone to get it right away before Ive does something crazy with it.'

'Thanks, Vjeko,' Banks said, already reaching out to cut the call off. 'Stay where you are. I'm calling West Yorkshire CID right now. Jelačić was heading for Mile Paveliči's house, you said?'

SIX

Owen walked up the carpeted stairs in the dark to the first-floor landing. There, he found a timer-switch on the wall and turned the light on. He knocked on the door of Flat 4, noticing it didn't have a peep-hole, and held his breath. The odds were that, if she had friends in the building, especially friends who were in the habit of dropping by to borrow a carton of milk or to have a chat, she would open it. After all, nobody had buzzed her, and not just anyone could walk in from the street.

He heard the floor creak behind the door and saw the knob begin to turn. What if it was on a chain? What if she were living with someone? His heart beat fast. Slowly the door opened.

'Yes?' Michelle said.

No chain.

Owen pushed. Michelle fell back into the room and the door swung fully open. He shut it behind him and leaned back on it. Michelle had stumbled into her sofa. She was wearing a dark-blue robe, silky in texture, and it had come open at the front. Quickly, she wrapped it around herself and looked at him.

'You. What the hell do you want?' There was more anger than fear in her voice.

'That's a good question, that is, after what you've done to me.'

'You've been drinking. You're drunk.'

'So what?'

'I'm going to call the police.'

Michelle lunged for the telephone but Owen got there first and knocked it off its stand. This wasn't going the way he had hoped. He had just wanted to talk, find out why she had it in for him, but she was making it difficult.

They faced each other like hunter and prey for a few seconds, completely still, breathing hard, muscles tense, then she ran for the door. Owen got there first and pushed her away. This time she tipped backwards over the arm of the sofa. Owen walked towards her. Her robe had risen up high over her thighs and split open at her loins to show the triangle of curly golden hair. Owen stopped in his tracks. Michelle gave him a cool, scornful look, covered herself up and sat down.

'Well, then,' she said, pushing her hair back behind her ears. 'So you're here. I must admit I'm a bit surprised, but maybe I shouldn't be.' She reached for a cigarette and lit it with a heavy table-lighter, blowing the smoke out through her nose. He remembered the mingled taste of tobacco and toothpaste on her mouth in bed after lovemaking. 'Why don't you sit down?' she said.

'Aren't you frightened?'

Michelle laughed and put her little pink tongue between her teeth. 'Should I be?'

Her blue eyes looked cool, in control. Her long, smooth neck rose out of the gown, elegant and graceful. Even at twenty-four she still looked like a teenager. It was partly the flawless, marble complexion, the delicately chiselled nose and lips whose fine lines any sculptor would be proud of.

But it was mostly in her character, Owen realized, not

her looks. She *was* the cruel teenager who called others names, the leader of the gang who suggested new cruelties, new kicks, with not a care in the world for the feelings of the ones she bullied and taunted.

'If you really believe I murdered those women, then you should be scared,' he said. 'They looked like you, you know.'

'You were killing me by proxy. Is that what you're saying?'

'Can you give me one good reason why I shouldn't? You're not afraid because you know I didn't do it. Am I right?'

'Well,' Michelle said, 'I really found it hard to believe you had the guts, I'll admit. But then I was mistaken enough to think it takes guts to strangle a woman.'

'And you found out different?'

She frowned. 'What do you mean?'

'You did it, didn't you, Michelle? I'm not sure about the first one, about Deborah Harrison, but you did the second, didn't you? You killed her to frame me. Or you got some-one to do it.'

Michelle laughed and glanced towards the door again. 'You're mad,' she said. 'Paranoid. If you think I'd do something like that, go to all that trouble, you're insane.' She stood up and walked over to the cocktail cabinet. Her legs swished against the robe. Owen stayed close to her. 'I'd offer you a drink,' she said, 'but I think you've had too much already.'

'Why did you do it, Michelle? For God's sake why?'

She raised her eyebrows. 'Why did I do what?'

'You know what I mean. Kill that girl to implicate me. You broke into my house, stole the film container with my fingerprints on it and took hairs from my pillow. Then you

406

messed the place up to make it look like a hate-crime.'

Michelle shook her head. 'You're crazy.' She poured neat Scotch into a crystal glass. Owen could see her hand was shaking.

'And what you said to the police about us,' he pressed on. 'That stuff in the newspapers. Why did you tell those lies about me?'

'They paid well.' She laughed. 'Not the police, the newspapers. And I didn't kill anyone. Don't be an idiot, Owen. I couldn't do anything like that. Besides, I didn't tell any lies.'

'You *know* it didn't happen like that.'

'It's all versions, Owen. That's how it happened from my perspective. I'm willing to admit yours might be different. I'm sorry. I know I shouldn't sound so ungrateful. You did help me through college. You helped me financially, you gave me somewhere to live, and you certainly helped with my marks. It was fun for a while . . . But you'd no right to start spying on me, following me everywhere I went. You didn't own me. And you had no right to throw me out in the street like that. Nobody ever treats me like that.' Her eyes blazed like ice.

'Fun . . . for a while? Michelle, I was in love with you. We were going to . . . I can't believe you'd say that, make it all sound so meaningless. Why do you hate me so much?'

She shrugged. 'I don't hate you. I just don't give a damn about you one way or another.'

'You bitch.'

Owen stepped towards her. She stood her ground by the cabinet and sipped her drink. Then she jerked her head back to toss her hair over her shoulders again. It was a gesture he remembered. She looked at him down her nose, lips curled in a sneer of contempt.

'Oh, come on, Owen,' she said, twisting the belt of her robe around one finger. 'You can do better than that. Or can't you? Do you have to murder schoolgirls these days to get your rocks off?' The smile tormented him: a little crooked, icy in the eyes and wholly malevolent. 'I'm glad you've found something that turns you on at last. What are you going to do, Owen? Kill me, too? Do you know what? I don't think you can do it. That's why you have to do it to the schoolgirls and pretend it's me. Isn't that true, Owen?'

Owen snatched the tumbler from her hand and tossed it back in one.

'More Dutch courage? Is that what you need? I still don't believe—'

He didn't know how it happened. One moment he was looking at his own reflection in her pupils, and the next he had his hands around her throat. He shoved her back against the cabinet, knocking bottles and glasses over. She clawed at his eyes, but her arms weren't long enough. She scratched and pulled at his wrists, making gurgling sounds deep in her throat, back bent over the cabinet, feet off the ground, kicking him.

He was throttling her for everything she'd ever done to him: for being a faithless whore and spreading her legs for anyone who took her out for an expensive dinner; for telling the whole country he was a sick pervert who would be in jail if there were any real sting in the justice system; for framing him.

And he was strangling her for everything else, too: his arrest; the humiliation and indignity of jail; the loss of his friends, his job. The whole edifice that had been his life exploded in a red cloud and his veins swelled with rage. For all that, and for treating him like a fool, like someone she could keep on a string and order around. Someone she didn't even believe had the courage to kill her.

He pressed his fingers deep into her throat. One of her wild kicks found his groin. He flinched in pain but held on, shoving her hard up against the wall. She was sitting on the top of the cabinet among the broken crystal and spilled liquor, her legs wrapped around him in a parody of the sex act. He could smell gin and whisky. The robe under her thighs was sodden with blood and booze, as if she had wet herself.

Michelle continued to flail around, knocking over more bottles, making rasping sounds. Once she pushed forward far enough that her nails raked his cheek, just missing his eyes.

But just as suddenly as it had started, it was over. Owen loosened his grip on her throat and she slid off the cabinet onto the floor, leaning back against it, not moving.

Someone hammered on the door and yelled, 'Michelle! Are you all right?'

Owen stood for a moment trying to catch his breath and grasp the enormity of what he had done, then he opened the door and rushed past the puzzled neighbour back down to the street.

SEVEN

'I think Deborah Harrison lied to her mother about losing her diary,' Banks said to Gristhorpe as they waited for Ken Blackstone's call. It was well after closing-time. No hope of a pint now. 'I think she kept it hidden.'

'So it would seem,' Gristhorpe agreed. 'The question is, how did it get into Jelačić's hands? We already know he couldn't have been in Eastvale the evening she was killed. Even if the diary had been in her satchel, Jelačić couldn't have taken it.'

'I think I know the answer to that,' Banks said. 'Rebecca Charters surprised someone in the graveyard yesterday, in the wooded area behind the Inchcliffe Mausoleum. I thought nothing of it at the time – she didn't get a good look at whoever it was – but now it seems too much of a coincidence. I'll bet you a pound to a penny it was Jelačić.'

'It was hidden there?'

Banks nodded. 'And he knew where. He'd seen her hide it. When Pierce was released, and I went to question Jelačić again last week, he must have remembered it and thought there might be some profit in getting hold of it. It's ironic, really. That open satchel always bothered me. When I first saw it, I thought the killer might have taken something incriminating and most likely got rid of it. But Lady Harrison told me Deborah had lost her diary. I saw no reason why either of them would lie about that.'

'Unless there were secrets in it that Deborah didn't want anyone to stumble across?'

'Or Lady Harrison. If you think about it, either of them could have lied. Sir Geoffrey had already told me that Deborah *did have* a diary, so his wife could hardly deny its existence.'

'But she *could* say Deborah had told her she lost it, and we'd have no way of checking.'

'Yes. And we probably wouldn't even bother looking for it. Which we didn't.'

'Didn't the SOCOs search the graveyard the day after Deborah's murder?'

'They did a ground search. We weren't looking for a

murder weapon, just Deborah's knickers and anything the killer might have dropped in the graveyard. All we found were a few empty fag packets and some butts. Most of those were down to Jelačić, who we knew had worked in the graveyard anyway. We put the rest down to St Mary's girls sneaking out for a smoke. Besides, it's only in books that murderers stand around smoking in the fog while they wait for their victims. Especially since now everyone knows we've a good chance of getting DNA from saliva.'

'What about the Inchcliffe Mausoleum? Deborah could have gained access to that, couldn't she?'

'Yes. But we searched that, too, after we found the empty bottles. At least—'

The phone rang. Banks grabbed the receiver.

'Alan, it's Ken Blackstone. Sorry it took so long.'

'Any luck?'

'We've got him.'

'Great. Did he give you any trouble?'

'He picked up a bruise or two in the struggle. Turns out he'd just left Paveliči's house when our lads arrived. They followed him across the waste ground. He saw them coming and made a bolt for it, right across York Road and down into Richmond Hill. When they finally caught up with him he didn't have the diary.'

Banks's spirits dropped. 'Didn't have it? But, Ken—'

'Hold your horses, mate. Seems he dumped it when he realized he was being chased. Didn't want to be caught with any incriminating evidence on him. Anyway, our lads went back over the route he'd taken and we found it in a rubbish bin on York Road.'

Banks breathed a sigh of relief.

'What do you want us to do with him?' Blackstone

asked. 'It's midnight now. It'll be going on for two in the morning by the time we get him to Eastvale.'

'You can sit on him overnight,' Banks said. 'Nobody in this case is going anywhere in a hurry. Have him brought up in the morning. But, Ken—'

'Yes, it is Deborah Harrison's diary.'

'Have you read it?'

'Enough.'

'And?'

'If it means what I think it does, Alan, it's dynamite.'

'Tell me about it.'

And Blackstone told him.

20

ONE

At ten o'clock the next morning, with Jelačić cooling his heels in a cell downstairs, Banks sat at his desk, coffee in hand, lit a cigarette and opened Deborah Harrison's diary. Ken Blackstone had given him the gist of it over the phone the previous evening – and he had not slept well in consequence – but he wanted to read it for himself before making his next move.

Like the inside of the satchel flap, it was inscribed with her name and address in gradually broadening circles, from 'Deborah Catherine Harrison' to 'The Universe.'

First he checked the section for names, addresses and telephone numbers, but found nothing out of the ordinary, only family and school friends. Then he started to flip the pages.

He soon found that many of her entries were factual, with little attempt at analysis or poetic description. Some days she had left completely blank. And it wasn't until summer, when she had supposedly 'lost' it, that the diary got really interesting:

5 August
Yawn. This must be the most boring summer there has ever been in my entire existence. Went shopping today in the Swainsdale Centre, just for something to do.

What a grim place. Absolutely no decent shoes there at
all and full of local yokels and horrible scruffy women
dragging around even more horrible dirty children. I
must work hard on Mummy and persuade her to take
me shopping to Paris again soon or I swear I shall just
die from the boredom of this terrible provincial town.
In the shopping centre, I met that common little tart
Tiffy Huxtable from dressage. She was with some
friends and asked if I'd like to hang around with them.
They didn't look very interesting. They were all just
sitting around the fountain looking scruffy and stupid,
but there was one fit lad there so I said I might drop by
one day! Life is so (yawn) boring that I really might do.
Oh, how I do so need an adventure.

There were no entries for the next few days, then came
this:

9 August
Tiffy's crowd are a bunch of silly, common bores, just
as I thought. All they can talk about is television and
football and sex and pop music. I mean, really, darling,
who gives a damn? I'm sure not one of them has read a
book in years. Quite frankly, I'd rather stay at home and
watch videos. Tracy Banks seems quite intelligent, but
it turns out that she's a *policeman's* daughter, of all
things. One boy looks a bit like that really cool actor
from Neighbours and wears a great leather jacket. He
really does have very nice eyes, too, with long lashes.

After that, things started to move quickly:

12 August
John (Oh, such disappointment! What a terribly common, dull and ordinary name, like 'Tracy'!) stole a car

tonight and took me for a joy-ride. *Me!!* Little miss goody-two-shoes. It was brill! If Daddy knew about it he would have apoplexy. It wasn't much of a car, just a poky little Astra, but he drove it really fast out past Helmthorpe and parked in a field. It was so exciting even though I was a bit frightened we'd get caught by the police. When we parked he was like an octopus! I told him I'm not the kind of girl who does it the first time you go out, even if he did steal a car for me. Lads! I ask you. He asked me what he could do the first time, and I told him we could just kiss. I really didn't mind when he put his tongue in my mouth but I wouldn't let him touch my breasts. I didn't tell him I had never done it before. Though I came close with Pierre at Montclair last year, and if he hadn't been too much in a hurry and had that little accident first we might have done it.

Then, three days later, she wrote:

15 August
Tonight, in another 'borrowed' car, as John calls them, we actually did it for the first time! I made him take a van this time, because it's cramped in a little Astra, and we went in the back. I wasn't going to go all the way at first but things just got out of control. It didn't hurt, like they say it does. I don't know if I like it or not. I did feel excited and sinful and wicked but I don't think I had an orgasm. I don't really know, because I don't know what they feel like, but the earth didn't move or anything like that, and I didn't hear bells ringing, just a funny feeling between my legs and I felt a bit sore after. I wonder if I will ever have multiple orgasms? Charlene Gregory at school told me she can have orgasms just from the vibrations of the engine when she's on a bus, but I

don't believe her. And Kirsty McCracken says she can get them from rubbing against her bicycle saddle while she's riding. Maybe that's true. I sometimes feel a bit funny when I'm horse-riding. Anyway, when he finished, it was really disgusting the way he just tied a knot in the condom and threw it out of the window into the field, and then he didn't even seem to want to talk to me all the way back. Is this what happens when you give in to lads and let them have what they want? That's what Mummy would say, even though she is French and they're supposed to be so sexy and all.

17 August

John came to the house today. Mummy was out and he wanted us to go and do it upstairs but I was too frightened we'd get caught. Anyway, we barbecued some hot dogs on the back patio and I took a bottle of Father's special wine from the cellar and we drank that. Of course, Mother came home! She was very nice about it, really, but I could tell she didn't like John. Uncle Michael was there, too, and I could tell he really *hated* John on sight. John says nobody ever gives him a chance.

20 August

They all went to Leeds today – Mummy and Daddy and Uncle Michael – to some naff cocktail party or other, so I told John he could come over to the house again. This time I knew they'd be gone a long time so we did it in *my bed!* How sinful! How wickedly, deliciously sinful! I don't know if I had an orgasm or not, but I certainly tingled a bit, and I didn't feel at all sore. John wants me to do it without a condom, but I told him not to be stupid. I wouldn't even think of it. I don't want to get pregnant with his baby or get some sexual disease. That hurt him, that I thought he would have some disease to pass on to me. He can be so childish at times. Childish and boring.

But it wasn't until a later entry that Banks found out for himself what Ken Blackstone meant when he said the diary might be 'dynamite.'

21 August

I can hardly believe it, Uncle Michael is in love with me! He says he has loved me since I was twelve, and has even spied on me getting undressed at Montclair. He says I look like Botticelli's Venus! Which is stretching it a bit, if you ask me. I remember seeing it in the Uffizi when Mummy and I went to Florence last year, and I don't look a bit like her. My hair's not as long, for a start, and it's a different colour. I never thought Uncle Michael knew literature and art at all. Some of what he wrote sounds very poetic. And it's all about *me*!! I don't know what I shall do. For the moment, it will be my little secret. He's not really my uncle of course, just my dad's friend, so I suppose it is all right for him to be in love with me, it's not incest. It feels funny, though, because I've known him *forever*. Oops, I forgot to say how I know. Last night John and me stole Uncle Michael's car because he was so beastly to him last week at the barbecue (now I know why: Uncle Michael must have been jealous!!). Well, Uncle Michael had left his computer in the back seat. We took it to John's house (and thank the lord his horrible smelly mother was out – she really gives me the creeps) – and I couldn't get into all his technical stuff but it only took me about fifteen minutes to get the password to his word-processing directories: it's MONTCLAIR, of course. After that, it was easy. Uncle Michael puts everything on his computer, even his shopping-lists! When I'd finished, I reformatted his hard drive. That'll show him!

Banks put the diary aside and walked to the window. Mid-morning on a hot and humid June day, cobbled market square already full of cars and coaches. He wondered if this summer was going to be as hot as the last one. He hoped not. Naturally, there was no air-conditioning in Eastvale Divisional HQ, or in the whole of Eastvale, as far as he knew. You just had to make do with open windows and fans – not a lot of use when there's no breeze and the air is hot.

The diary wasn't evidence, of course. Deborah Harrison had read some of Michael Clayton's private files and discovered that he was sexually infatuated with her; it didn't mean that he had killed her. But as Banks sat down again and read on, it became increasingly clear that Clayton, in all likelihood, *had* killed Deborah.

The telephone rang. Banks picked it up and Sergeant Rowe told him there was a Detective Sergeant Leaside calling from Swiss Cottage.

Banks frowned; he didn't recognize the name. 'Better put him on.'

Leaside came on. 'It's about a woman called Michelle Chappel,' he said. 'I understand from the PNC that she was part of a case you've been involved in recently up there?'

Banks gripped the receiver tightly. 'Yes. Why? What's happened?'

'She's been assaulted, sir. Quite badly. Lacerations and bruises, attempted strangulation.'

'Rape?'

'No, sir. I was wondering . . . We got a description of the suspect from a neighbour . . .' He read the description.

'Yes,' Banks said when he'd finished. 'Dammit, yes. That sounds like Owen Pierce. All right, thanks Sergeant. We'll keep an eye open for him.'

TWO

Ive Jelačić was surly after his night in the cells. Banks had him brought up to an interview room and left him alone there for almost an hour before he and Superintendent Gristhorpe went in to ask their questions. They didn't turn the tape recorder on.

'Well, Ive,' said Banks, 'you're in a lot of trouble now, you know that?'

'What trouble? I do nothing.'

'Where did you get that diary?'

'What diary? I never see that before. You policeman put it on me.'

Banks sighed and rubbed his forehead. He could see it was going to be one of those days. 'Ive,' he said patiently, 'both Mile Paveliči and Vjeko Batorac have seen you with the diary. You asked them to read it for you. You even hit Vjeko when he tried to hang onto it.'

'I remember nothing of this. I do nothing wrong. Vjeko and I, we quarrel. Is not big deal.'

'Come on, lad,' said Gristhorpe, 'help us out here.'

'I know nothing.'

Gristhorpe gestured for Banks to follow him out of the room. He did so, and they stood silently in the corridor for a few minutes before going back inside. It seemed to work;

Jelačić was certainly more nervous than he had been before.

'Where you go?' he asked. 'What you do?'

'Listen to me, Ive,' said Banks. 'I'm only going to say this once, and I'll say it slowly so that you understand every word. If it hadn't been for you, an innocent man might not have spent over six months in jail, suffered the indignity of a trial and incurred the wrath of the populace. In other words, you put Owen Pierce through hell, and even though he's free now, a lot of people still think he really killed the girls.'

Jelačić shrugged. 'Maybe he did. Maybe court was wrong.'

'But more important even than Owen Pierce's suffering is Ellen Gilchrist's life. If it hadn't been for you, Ive Jelačić, that girl might not have had to die.'

'I tell you before. In my country, many people die. Nobody ca—'

Banks slammed his fist on the flimsy table. 'Shut up! I don't want to hear any more of your whining self-justification and self-pity, you snivelling little turd. Do you understand me?'

Jelačić's eyes were wide open now. He nodded and glanced over at Gristhorpe for reassurance he wasn't going to be left alone with this madman. Gristhorpe remained expressionless.

'Because of you, an innocent girl was brutally murdered. Now, I might not be able to charge you with murder, as I would like to do, but I'll certainly get something on you that'll put you away for a long, long time. Understand me?'

'I want lawyer.'

'Shut up. You'll get a lawyer when we're good and ready to let you. For the moment, listen. Now, I don't think we'll have much trouble getting Daniel and Rebecca Charters to testify that you tried to extort money from them in order to alter the story you told against Daniel Charters. That's extortion, for a start. And we'll also get you for tampering with evidence, wasting police time and charges too numerous to mention. And do you know what will happen, Ive? We'll get you sent back to Croatia is what.'

'No! You cannot do that. I am British citizen.'

Banks looked at Gristhorpe and the two of them laughed. 'Well, maybe that's true,' Banks said. 'But you do know who Deborah Harrison's father is, don't you? He's *Sir* Geoffrey Harrison. A very powerful and influential man when it comes to government affairs. Even you must know something of the way this country's run, Ive. What would you say for your chances now?'

Jelačić turned pale and started chewing his thumbnail.

'Are you going to co-operate?'

'I know nothing.'

Banks leaned forward and rested his elbows on the table. 'Ive. I'll say this once more and then it's bye-bye. If you don't tell us what you know and where you found the diary, then I'll personally see to it that you're parachuted right into the middle of the war zone. Clear?'

Jelačić sulked for a moment, then nodded.

'Good. I'm glad we understand one another. And just because you've behaved like a total pillock, there's one more condition.'

Jelačić's eyes narrowed.

'You drop all charges against Daniel Charters and make a public apology.'

Jelačić bristled at this, but after huffing and puffing for a minute or two, agreed that he had, in fact, misinterpreted the minister's gesture.

Banks stood up and took Jelačić's arm. 'Right, let's go.'

They drove him to St Mary's, and he led them along the tarmac path, onto the gravel one and into the thick woods behind the Inchcliffe Mausoleum. A good way in, he paused in front of a tree and said, 'Here.'

Banks looked at the tree but could see nothing out of the ordinary, no obvious hiding-place. Then Jelačić reached his hand up and seemed to insert it right into the solid wood itself. It was then that Banks noticed something very odd about the yew trees. Not very tall, but often quite wide in circumference, they were hard, strong and enduring. Some of the older ones must have been thirty feet around and had so many clustered columns they looked like a fluted pillar. The one they stood before had probably been around since the seventeenth century. The columns were actually shoots pushing out from the lower part of the bole, growing upwards and appearing to coalesce with the older wood, making the tree look as if it had several trunks all grafted together. It also, he realized, provided innumerable nooks and crannies to hide things. What Deborah had sought out for a hiding-place, and Jelačić had seen her use, was a knot-hole in this old yew, angled in such a way that it was invisible when you looked at it straight on.

Banks moved Jelačić aside and reached his hand inside the tree. All he felt was a bed of leaves and strips of bark that had blown in over the years. But then, when he started to dig down and sweep some of this detritus aside, he was sure his fingers brushed something smooth and hard. Quickly, he reached deeper, estimating that Deborah could have easily done the same with her long arms. At last, he grasped the package and drew it out. Gristhorpe and Jelačić stood beside him, watching.

'Looks like you missed the jackpot, Ive,' Banks said.

It was a small square object wrapped in black bin-liner, folded over several times for good insulation. When Banks unfolded it, he brought out what he had hoped for: a computer diskette.

THREE

Back at the station, Banks handed the floppy disk to Susan Gay and asked her if she could get a printout of its contents. He hoped it had survived winter in the knot-hole of the yew. It should have done; it had been wrapped in plastic and buried under old leaves, wood chips and scraps of bark, which would have helped preserve it, and the winter hadn't been very cold.

Ten minutes later, Susan knocked sharply on Banks's office door and marched in brandishing a sheaf of paper. Her hand was shaking, and she looked pale. 'I think you'd better have a look at this, sir.'

'Let's swop.' Banks pushed the diary towards her and picked up the printout.

De-bo-rah. De-bo-rah. How the syllables of your name trip off my tongue like poetry. When was it I first knew that I loved you? I ask myself, can I pinpoint the exact moment in time and space where that magical trans-formation took place and I no longer looked at a mere young girl but a shining girl-child upon whose every movement I fed hungrily. When, when did it happen?

Oh, Deborah, my sweet torturer, why did I ever, ever have to see you pass that moment from childhood to the flush of womanhood? Had you remained a mere child I could never have loved you this way. I could never have entertained such thoughts about your straight and hairless child's body as I do about your woman's body.

I seek you out; yet I fly from you. On the surface, all appears normal, but if people could see and hear inside me the moment you come into a room or sit beside me, they would see my heart pulling at the reins and hear my blood roaring through my veins. That day you won the dressage and walked towards me in your riding-gear, that moist film of sweat glistening on the exquisite curve of your upper lip . . . and you kissed me on the cheek and put your arm around me . . . I felt your small breast press softly against my side and it was all I could do to remain standing let alone furnish the required and conventional praise . . . well done . . . well done . . . wonderful . . . well done, my love, my Deborah.

The first time I saw you naked as a woman you were standing in the old bathtub at Montclair looking like Botticelli's *Birth of Venus*. Remember, my love, there were no locks on the doors at Montclair. One simply knew when private rooms were engaged and refrained from entering. Mistakes were made, of course, but honest mistakes. Besides, it was family. They aren't prudes about such things, the French, Sylvie's people. I hoped only for a brief glimpse of your nakedness as you bathed. I knew I couldn't linger, that I must apologize and dash out as if I had made a mistake before you even realized I had seen you. So fast, so fleeting a glimpse. And even now I wonder what would have happened had I not witnessed you in your full glory.

For you were standing up, reaching for the towel, and your loveliness was on display just for me. Steam hung in the air and the sunlight that slanted through the high window cast rainbows all about you. Droplets of moisture had beaded on your flushed skin; your wet hair clung to your neck and shoulders, long strands pasted over the swellings of your new breasts, where the nipples, pink as opening rosebuds stood erect. Even that early in womanhood your waist curved in and swelled out at the narrow hips. Between your legs a tiny triangle of hair like spun gold lay on the mound of Venus; the paradise I dream of; drops of water had caught among the fine, curled hairs, forming tiny prisms in the sunlight; some just seemed to glitter in clear light like diamonds . . .

I have other images locked away inside me: the thin black bra strap against your bare shoulder, the insides of your thighs when you cross your legs . . .

And so it went on. Again, it wasn't solid evidence, but it was all they had. Banks had no choice but to act on it.

FOUR

Owen gazed out of the train window into the darkness. Rain streaked the dirty glass and all he could see was reflections of the lights behind him in the carriage. He wished he could get another drink, but he was on the local train now, not the InterCity, and there was no bar service.

As the train rattled through a closed village station on the last leg of his journey, Owen thought again of how he had walked the London streets all night in the rain after killing Michelle, half-hoping the police would pick him up and get it over with, half-afraid of going back to prison, this time forever.

He had covered the whole urban landscape, or so it seemed; the West End, where the bright neons were reflected in the puddles and the nightclubs were open, occasional drunks and prostitutes shouting or laughing out loud; rainswept wastelands of demolished houses, where he had to pick his way carefully over the piles of bricks with weeds growing between them; clusters of tower blocks surrounded by burned-out cars, playgrounds with broken swings; and broad tree-lined streets, large houses set well back from the road. He had walked through areas he wouldn't have gone near if he had cared what happened to him, and if he hadn't been mugged or beaten up it wasn't for lack of carelessness.

But nothing had happened. He had seen plenty of dangerous-looking people, some hiding furtively in shop doorways or hanging around in groups smoking crack in the shadows of tower-block stairwells, but no-one had approached him. Police cars had passed him as he walked along Finchley Road or Whitechapel High Street, but none had stopped to ask him who he was. If he hadn't known different, he would have said he was leading a charmed life.

At one point, close to morning, he had stood on a bridge watching the rain pit the river's surface and felt the life of the city around him, restful perhaps, but never quite sleeping, that hum of energy always there, always running through it like the river did. He didn't think it was Westminster Bridge, but still Wordsworth's lines sprung into his mind, words he had read and memorized in prison:

> This City now doth, like a garment, wear
> The beauty of the morning; silent, bare,
> Ships, towers, domes, theatres, and temples lie
> Open unto the fields, and to the sky;
> All bright and glittering in the smokeless air.

Well, perhaps the air wasn't exactly 'smokeless,' Owen thought, but one has to make allowances for time.

Owen felt tired and empty. So tired and so empty.

Eastvale Station was in the north-eastern part of the town, on Kendal Road a couple of miles east of North Market Street. It was only a short taxi-ride to the town centre. But Owen didn't want to go to the centre, or, tired as he was, home.

He was surprised the police weren't waiting for him at the station, as they probably would be at his house. He didn't want to walk right into their arms, and however empty he felt, however *final* every second of continued freedom seemed, he still didn't want to give it up just yet. Perhaps, he thought, he was like the cancer patient who knows there's no hope but clings onto life through all the pain, hoping for a miracle, hoping that the disease will just go away, that it was all a bad dream. Besides, he wanted another drink.

Whatever his reasons, he found himself walking along Kendal Road. The day had been so hot and humid that the cooler evening air brought a mist that hung in the air like fog. At the bridge, he looked along the tree-lined banks towards town and saw the high three-quarter moon and the floodlit castle on its hill reflected in the water, all blurry in the haze of the summer mist.

Walking on, he came to the crossroads and saw the Nag's Head. Well, he thought, with a smile, it would do as well as anywhere. He had come full circle.

FIVE

By the time Banks and Gristhorpe got Chief Constable Riddle's permission to bring Michael Clayton in for questioning, which wasn't easy, it was already dark. One of the conditions was that Riddle himself be present at the interview.

Banks was pleased to see that Clayton, as expected, was at least mildly intimidated by the sparse and dreary interview room, with its faded institutional-green walls, flyblown window, table and chairs bolted to the floor, and that mingled smell of urine and old cigarette smoke.

Clayton made the expected fuss about being dragged away from his home, like a common criminal, to the police station, but his confidence had lost a bit of its edge. He was wearing sharp-creased grey trousers and a white short-sleeved shirt; his glasses hung on a chain around his neck.

'Are you charging me with something?' Clayton asked, folding his arms and crossing his legs.

'No,' said Gristhorpe. 'At least not yet. Chief Inspector Banks has a few questions he wants to ask you, that's all.'

Jimmy Riddle sat behind Clayton in the far corner by the window, so the suspect couldn't constantly look to him for comfort and reassurance. Riddle seemed folded in on himself, legs and arms tightly crossed. He had promised not to interfere, but Banks didn't believe it for a moment.

'About what?' Clayton asked.

'About the murder of your goddaughter, Deborah Harrison.'

'I thought you'd finished with all that?'

'Not quite.'

He looked at his watch. 'Well, you'd better tell him to get on with it, then. I've got important work to do.'

Banks turned on the tape recorders, made a note of the time and who was present, then gave Clayton the new caution, the same one he had given Owen Pierce eight months ago. Formalities done, he shuffled some papers on the desk in front of him and asked, 'Remember when we talked before, Mr Clayton, and I asked if you had been having an affair with Sylvie Harrison?'

Clayton looked from Gristhorpe to Banks. 'Yes,' he said to the latter. 'I told you it was absurd then, and it's still absurd now.'

'I know.'

Clayton swallowed. 'What?'

'I said I know it's absurd.'

He shook his head. 'So you're not still trying to accuse me of that? Then why . . .?'

'And remember I suggested that Deborah might have gained access to some sensitive business material, or some government secret?'

'Yes. Again, ridiculous.'

'You're absolutely right. You weren't having an affair with Sylvie Harrison,' Banks said slowly, 'and Deborah didn't gain access to any important government secrets. We know that now. I got it all wrong. You were in love with your goddaughter, with Deborah. That's why you killed her.'

Clayton paled. 'This . . . This is ludicrous.' He twisted around in his chair to look at Riddle. 'Look, Jerry, I don't know what they're talking about. You're their superior. Can't you do something?'

Riddle, who had read both the diary and the computer

journal, shook his head slowly. 'Best answer the questions truthfully, Michael. That's best for all of us.'

While Clayton was staring open-mouthed at Riddle's betrayal, Superintendent Gristhorpe dropped the printed computer journal on the table in front of him. Clayton first glanced at it, then put his glasses on, picked it up and read a few paragraphs. Then he pushed it aside.

'What on earth is that?' he asked Banks.

'The product of a sick mind, I'd say,' Banks answered.

'I hope you're not suggesting it has anything to do with me.'

Banks leaned forward suddenly, snatched back the pages and slapped them down on the table. 'Oh, stop mucking us about. It came from *your* computer. The one John Spinks stole that day he took your car. He's already told us all about that, about how he saw Deborah make a copy of the files onto a diskette. You didn't know about that, did you?'

'I . . . where . . .?'

'She kept it well hidden. Look, you know it's your journal. Don't deny it.'

Even in his shock, Clayton managed a thin smile and rallied his defences. 'Deny it? I most certainly do. And I'm afraid you'll have a hard job proving a wild accusation like that. Your suggestions are outrageous.' He glanced back at Riddle. 'And Jerry knows it, too. There's absolutely nothing to link that printout with me. It could have been written by anyone.'

'I don't think so,' said Banks. 'Oh, I know that Deborah reformatted your hard drive well beyond anything an "unerase" or "undelete" command could bring back to life, but you must admit the contents of the journal, the circumstances, all point to you. Very damning.'

'Fiction,' said Clayton. 'Pure fiction and fantasy. Just some poor lovestruck fool making things up. There's nothing illegal in that. There's no law against fantasies; at least not yet.'

'Maybe not,' said Banks. 'We never checked Deborah's clothing for *your* hairs, you know.'

'So?'

'You might not have left any blood or tissue, but I'm willing to bet that if we went over the hair samples again now, we'd find a positive match. That wouldn't be fantasy, would it?'

Clayton shrugged. 'So what? It wouldn't surprise me. Deborah was my goddaughter, after all. We spent a lot of time together – as a family. Besides, I was in court for the so-called expert's testimony. Hairs hardly prove a thing scientifically.'

'What about Ellen Gilchrist?'

'Never heard of – wait a minute, isn't that the other girl who was killed?'

'Yes. What if we found *your* hairs on her clothing, too, and hers on yours? Was she family, a friend?'

Clayton licked his lips. 'I never saw her in my life. Look, I don't know what grounds you've got for assuming this, but—'

Banks dropped a photocopy of Deborah's diary in front of him. 'Read this,' he said.

Clayton read.

His hands were shaking when he put the diary down. 'Fantasy,' he said, straining to keep his voice steady. 'That's not very much to go on, is it? It could be anyone.'

'Come on, Michael,' said Banks. 'It's all over. Admit it. You know what happened. You've just read her account. Deborah read your journal and found out you'd been secretly lusting after her since she was twelve. She was both shocked and excited by the idea. But only by the idea. She was flattered, but still too much of a kid to know how serious it all was to you. And she had a bit of a crush on you anyway. So she teased you, made up a bit of romance, flirted a little, the way young girls sometimes do to tease boys they know fancy them. Didn't she Michael?'

'This is absurd. You're not only insulting me you're also besmirching my goddaughter's memory.' He looked around at Riddle again. 'Sir Geoff—'

But Banks cut him off. 'Besmirching? That's a good word, Michael. I like that. *Besmirching*. Sounds naughty. Very public school. So let's talk about *besmirching*. Eventually, when it became clear you wouldn't leave her alone, Deborah threatened to tell her father. You knew that if Sir Geoffrey found out he would probably kill you. At the very least it would mean the end of your business relationship. That meant a lot to you, didn't it, Michael? The two old Oxford boys, still together after all these years. Sir Geoffrey's friendship meant a lot to you, too, but it didn't stop you lusting after his twelve-year-old daughter, a girl who wasn't even born when the two of you first met.'

Clayton glared, the colour drained from his face. 'You'll regret this,' he said, glancing at both Gristhorpe and Riddle. 'All of you will, if you don't stop this right now.' Banks could almost hear Clayton's teeth grinding together. Gristhorpe said nothing. Riddle polished his buttons with a virgin white handkerchief.

'You waited for Deborah in St Mary's graveyard,' Banks continued calmly, 'in the shrubbery that foggy Monday evening when you knew she would be walking home alone from the chess club. You were going to grab her and drag her into the bushes, but when you saw her take the gravel path, you followed her towards the Inchcliffe Mausoleum, where you snatched her satchel and strangled her with the strap. Maybe she knew it was you, and maybe she didn't. Maybe you talked first, tried to persuade her not to say anything, or maybe you didn't. But that's what happened, isn't it, Michael?'

'I'm saying nothing.'

'You didn't know she was going to pick up the diary she'd been keeping and hiding ever since summer, did you? Oh, Michael, but if you'd only been patient, given her a few more seconds, she would have led you straight to it and you probably wouldn't be here now. Isn't that how it happened?'

'I won't even dignify your accusation with a response.'

'When she told you she'd read your computer journal, Deborah didn't tell you that she'd copied the file about her onto a diskette, did she? But you knew she had a diary at one time. You bought it for her. That's another irony, isn't it, Michael? You knew she'd told Sylvie she lost it, but I wouldn't be at all surprised if you had a good look around her room after you killed her. After all, you had your own key to Sir Geoffrey's house, and he and Lady Harrison were out. Even if they came back and found you there, it wouldn't have surprised them. And you opened Deborah's school satchel, too, didn't you, to see if she kept anything incriminating in there. Just in case. The only place you couldn't really get access to was her school desk, but you reasoned she'd be unlikely to keep anything important or private there.'

Clayton put his hands over his ears. 'This is ridiculous,' he said. 'I don't have to listen to this. You'll never be able to prove anything. I want—'

'Now, I'm only guessing,' Banks went on, 'so stop me

if I'm wrong, but I also think, as you murdered Deborah, that you found out you liked it. It stimulated you. Maybe you even had an orgasm as you tightened the strap around her neck. I know you were far too clever to actually rape her because you know about DNA and all that, don't you? But you did mess around with her clothing after you killed her – partly for pure pleasure, I'd guess, and partly to make it look like a genuine sex murder.

'It was the same with Ellen Gilchrist, wasn't it? You'd been over and over it in your mind all week, planning how you'd kill again, anticipating the intimacy of it all, and when you did it, when you felt the strap tightening, pulling her back against you, feeling her soft flesh rubbing against you, that excited you, didn't it?'

'Really, Banks,' Chief Constable Riddle cut in from behind. 'Don't you think this is getting a little out of hand?'

Clayton turned and looked at Riddle, a cruel smile on his thin lips. 'Well, thank you, Jerry, for all your support. You're absolutely right. He's talking rubbish, of course. I'd never even met the girl.'

'That doesn't matter,' Banks went on, mentally kicking Riddle and trying to ignore his interruption. 'Unlike Deborah, Ellen Gilchrist was a random victim. Wrong place, wrong time. You got lucky when Owen Pierce was arrested for the murder of Deborah Harrison, didn't you? You thought he would get convicted, sentenced and that would be an end to it. But when the trial was nearing its close you started to worry that he might get off. The defence was good, the prosecution had only circumstantial evidence, and you'd heard rumours about evidence that would have convicted Pierce for certain had it been admissible. But you saw it all slipping away, and the focus perhaps shifting back towards you. So you went to Owen

Pierce's house while the jury was deliberating, and you either found the door open from a previous break-in, or you broke in yourself and made it look like vandals. It doesn't really matter which. You took some hairs from Owen's pillow, and you stole an open film container which you guessed would have his fingerprints on it. You set out to deliberately frame Owen Pierce for the murder of Ellen Gilchrist, knowing we'd also put Deborah's murder down to him, too, and close the file on both of them. But, you know what? I think you also *enjoyed* it. Just the way you did with Deborah. And I think there would have been more if we hadn't caught you, wouldn't there? You've developed a taste for it.'

'This is insane,' Clayton said. 'And you can't prove a thing.'

'Oh, I think we can,' Banks went on. 'Look what we proved against Owen Pierce, and he didn't even do anything.'

Clayton smiled. 'Ah, but he got off, didn't he?'

Banks paused. 'Yes. Yes, he did. But maybe you should talk to him about that. I'm sure he'd be very interested to meet you. Getting off isn't all it's cracked up to be in some cases. See, maybe you're right, Michael. Maybe we won't be able to convince a jury that a fine, upstanding citizen like yourself murdered two young girls. Perhaps even with the evidence of the journal and the diary and the hairs, if we find they match, we won't be able to prove it to them. But you know who *will* believe us, don't you, Michael? You know who knows quite well who "Uncle Michael" is, who knows what Montclair is and that there are no locks on the bathroom doors there. You know exactly who *will* know who is the writer and who's the subject. Sir Geoffrey will know. And you'll have gained nothing. In some ways,

I think I'd rather take my chances with a jury, or even go to jail, than incur the wrath of Sir Geoffrey over such a matter as the murder of his only daughter by the man he's trusted for more than twenty years, don't you?'

Clayton said nothing for a moment, then he croaked, 'I want my solicitor. Now. Get my solicitor, right now. I'm not saying another word.'

Bloody hell, thought Banks, here we go again. He called in the constable from outside the interview room. 'Take him down to the custody suite, will you, Wigmore. And make sure you let him call his lawyer.'

SIX

Owen sat in the Nag's Head nursing his second pint and Scotch chaser, trying to pluck up the courage to go over the road and see Rebecca and Daniel. The problem was, he felt ashamed to face them. They had believed in his innocence, and he had let them down badly. He knew that if there were to be any sort of salvation or reclamation in this business at all, he would have to tell them the whole truth, including what he had done to Michelle. And he didn't know if he could do that right now. He could hardly even admit to himself that he had become exactly what everyone thought he was: a murderer.

He looked around at the uninspiring decor of the pub and wondered what the hell he was doing here again. It had seemed a nice irony when he saw the sign over the bridge – full circle – but now it didn't seem like such a good idea.

The Nag's Head was boisterous, with the landlord entertaining a group of cronies with dirty jokes around the bar and tables full of couples laughing and groups of underage kids who'd had a bit too much.

He didn't know what he was going to do after he finished his drinks: either go home and meet the police, or have another and go face Rebecca and Daniel. More drink wouldn't help with that, though, he realized. He would feel less like facing them if he were drunk. Best drink up and turn himself in, then, return to the custody suite, where he should feel quite at home by now.

'What did you say?'

Owen looked up at the sound of the voice. There was a lull in the conversation and laughter. The landlord was collecting empty glasses. He stood over Owen's table. 'Sorry mate,' he said. 'I thought I heard you say something.'

Owen shook his head. He realized he must have been muttering to himself. He turned away from the landlord's scrutiny. He could still feel the man looking at him, though, recognition struggling to come to the surface. He had a couple of days' growth, a few more pounds around the waist from lack of exercise and a prison pallor, but other than that he didn't look too different from the person who had sat alone in that same pub one foggy night last November.

Best finish his drinks and leave, he decided, tossing back the Scotch in one and washing it down with beer.

Then, all of a sudden, the landlord said, 'Bloody hell, it *is* him! I don't bloody believe it. The nerve.'

The men at the bar turned as one to look at Owen.

'It's him,' the landlord repeated. 'The one who was in here that night. The one who murdered those two young lasses.'

Owen wiped his mouth with the back of his hand and stood up, edging towards the door.

'Nay, they let him off,' someone said.

'Aye, but just because they hadn't got enough evidence,' another said. 'Don't you read t'papers?'

'It was a bloody cover-up.'

'Bleeding shame, more like. Poor wee lasses.'

'A travesty of justice.'

By the time Owen actually got to the door, a journey that felt like a hundred miles, bar-stools were scraping against the stone floor and he was aware of a crowd surging towards him.

No time to sneak out surreptitiously now. He dashed through the door and ran across Kendal Road. Luckily, the traffic lights were in his favour. When he got to the other side of the road, he saw about five or six people standing outside the pub doors. For a moment, he thought they were going to give chase, but someone shouted something he didn't hear and they went back inside.

Owen still ran as if he were being chased. There was only one place he could go now. He dashed across North Market Street towards St Mary's church. When he was through the gate, running down the tarmac path, he could see, even in the mist, that the kitchen light was on in the vicarage.

SEVEN

Alone in his office at last, Banks went to close the blinds and looked out for a moment on the quiet cobbled market square and the welcoming lights of the Queen's Arms. Maybe he'd have a quick one there before going home. Still time. Finally, he closed the blinds, turned on the shaded table-lamp and lit a cigarette. Then he sifted through his tapes and decided on Britten's third string quartet.

For a long time he just sat there smoking, staring at the wall and letting Britten's meditative quartet wash over him. He thought about the Clayton interview, and especially about the new coldness in Chief Constable Riddle's manner towards his old lodge pal. Maybe Riddle wasn't so bad, after all; at least he had an open enough mind to change his opinions when the facts started to weigh heavily against them.

Then, when his cigarette was finished, Banks turned to Deborah's diary again, striving once more to understand what had happened between her and Clayton over the two months leading up to her death.

24 August

Disaster has struck! Mummy caught John and me in bed this afternoon. She was supposed to be at one of her charity meetings but she wasn't feeling well and came home early. It was a terrible scene with Mummy and John shouting at one another and I didn't like to see John at all behaving like that. I thought he was going to hit Mummy in the end but he broke a vase on the wall and a piece of pottery cut Mummy's face. Then when he'd gone Mummy said I absolutely must not see him again or she would tell Daddy. Then she cried and put her arms around me and I felt sorry for her. John said such terrible things, called her such horrible names and said he would do things to her I won't repeat even here in my private diary. I don't care if I never see him again. I hate him. He's gross. He even stole things from our house. He's just a common thief. A thief and a thickie. What could I ever have seen in him?

27 August

Michael came to the house today while Mummy and Daddy were out. He was absolutely livid about the other day with John. I didn't know Mummy had told him. He called me names and I thought at one point he was going to hit me. It was then I told him. I couldn't help it. I told him I'd read his journal about me and called him a dirty old man. He went so white I thought he was going to faint. Then he asked me what I was going to do. I said I didn't know. I'd just have to wait and see. Wait for what? he asked me. To see what happens, says I.

28 August

Michael really is rather handsome. And much more intelligent and sophisticated than John. Mary Taylor at school told me last term she had an affair with a married man, a friend of her father's, who was 38 years old! And she says he was wonderful and considerate at sex and bought her presents and all sorts of things. I think Uncle Michael might be even older than 38 but he's not fat and ugly or anything like most old people.

1 September

Michael came for dinner tonight. Mummy and Daddy were there, of course. I wore a tight black jumper and a short skirt. Out of the corner of my eye I could see him looking at my thighs and breasts when he thought I wasn't watching. It really is amazing how he can seem so normal and ordinary when we're all together, but when there's just him and me he's so passionate and can hardly control himself!

3 September

Michael came again today when everyone was out. He

told me he felt such powerful desire for me he didn't know if he could control himself. That was the word he used: *desire*. I don't think that anyone has ever *desired* me before. It feels rather exciting. Of course, he wanted to do it, and when I said no he got all upset and said if I let a no-good lout like John Spinks do it to me why wouldn't I let him? I must admit I don't know the answer to that. Except that he's Uncle Michael and I've known him all my life.

6 September

This is getting to be quite an adventure! Saw Michael again today and let him kiss me again. It made him happy for a while, then he said he wanted to kiss my breasts. I wouldn't let him do that but I let him touch them over my jumper. While he was doing it he took my hand and held it to the front of his trousers so I could feel he was really hard. I started to feel a bit scared because his grip was so strong and then I felt him go all wet and he gasped as if somebody had hit him just the way John used to do. *Gross*. I can't explain why I felt it then, but I started to panic a bit because I'd just been teasing really and this was UNCLE MICHAEL, and even if he isn't really my uncle I've still known him since I was a little girl. I just couldn't let him do it to me. It wouldn't be right. After he'd finished he went all quiet so I left.

8 September

School again. Sad, sad, sad. Saw Mucky Metcalfe in the corridor. Wonder if he knows I know he's been doing it with the vicar's wife?

There were no more entries until October, and Banks assumed that Deborah had been getting settled in at St

Mary's again in the interim. But even by late October, Michael Clayton still hadn't got the message.

24 October

Can't Uncle Michael understand that whatever it was we had is over now? I've told him I don't love him, but it doesn't do any good. He keeps coming to the house when he knows I'm here alone. Now he says he just wants to see me naked, that he won't even touch me if I just take my clothes off in front of him and stand there the way I did in the bath at Montclair. I suppose it's flattering in a way to have a sophisticated older man in love with you, but to be honest he doesn't seem very sophisticated when he keeps wanting me to touch that hard thing in his pants. I don't want to play any more. I suppose he must still be living in hope, but doesn't he understand that summer's over and I'm back at school now?

Obviously he didn't, thought Banks. It hadn't been just a summer romance for Michael Clayton; it had been a dark, powerful obsession. And beneath all the veneer of sophistication and experience, Deborah had simply been a naive teenager misreading the depth of an older man's passion; she was just a girl who thought she was a woman.

But even as Deborah grew worried by Clayton's persistence, she always kept her secret, always lived in hope that he would simply give up and stop pestering her. She clearly knew what dreadful consequences would occur if she told her parents, and she wanted to avoid that if she could. But Clayton wouldn't give up and go away. He couldn't; he was too far gone. Her final entry, dated the day before she died, read,

5 November (Bonfire Night)

Yesterday Uncle Michael grabbed me and held my arm until it hurt and told me I had stolen his soul and all sorts of other rubbish. I know it was cruel of me to tease him, and to let him kiss me and stuff, but it was just a game at first and he wouldn't let me stop it. I want him to stop it now because I'm getting frightened, the way he looks at me. You still wouldn't believe it if you saw him with other people around, but he really does change when he's only with me. It's like he has a split personality or something. I told him if he doesn't promise to leave me alone I'll tell Daddy when I get home from school tomorrow. I don't know if I will. I don't reallly want to tell Daddy because I know what he gets like and what trouble it will cause. The house won't be worth living in. Anyway, we'll see what happens tomorrow.

Banks pushed the diary aside and lit another cigarette. The gaslights around the market square glowed through the gaps in the blinds. The quartet was reaching the end of its final movement now, the moving, introspective passacaglia, written when Britten was approaching death.

Why do we feel compelled to record our thoughts and feelings in diaries and on tape, Banks wondered, and our acts on video and in photographs? Perhaps, he thought, we need to read about ourselves or watch ourselves to know we are truly alive. Time after time, it leads to nothing but trouble, but still the politicians keep their diaries, ticking away like time bombs, and the sexual deviants keep their visual records. And thank the Lord they do. Without such evidence, many a case might not even get to court.

When the music finished, Banks sat in silence for a while, then stubbed out his cigarette. Just as he was about to get up and go for that pint before last orders, the telephone rang. He cursed and contemplated leaving it, but his policeman's sense of duty and his even deeper-rooted curiosity wouldn't let him.

'Banks here.'

'Sergeant Rowe, sir. We've just had a report that Owen Pierce is at St Mary's vicarage.'

'Who called it in?'

'Rebecca Charters, sir. The vicar's wife. She says Pierce is ready to turn himself in for the murder of Michelle Chappel.'

'But she's not dead.'

'I suppose he doesn't know that.'

'All right,' said Banks. 'I'll be right there.'

He sighed, picked up his sports jacket and hurried out into the hazy darkness.